Empire's Ghost

Stephan Grundy

TLS

ISBN: 978-1-959350-53-8
Set in: Georgia 10pt, Brigstone 20pt, Victoriandeco Italic 30pt

©The Three Little Sisters LLC
USA/Canada

Chapter 1: Words and Shadows

"Forever Sea sunders our heart from our home,
Our forefathers' Fall left us exiles aye,
But the longing yet sings through our tongue and our
blood
For the land where our bones and our greatness still lie."
- "The West Remembered"; Tharandrostan song,
traditional.

Arudal looked down at the piece of blank parchment in front of him, as if the inspiration he needed might have suddenly appeared in neat black letters while he was looking at his other notes. The parchment remained stubbornly creamy-smooth, and the ink had dried on his quill. He sighed, wiping a thin glaze of sweat from his brow. Even with his window open and dressed only in a short tunic of thin blue silk, the heat of summer in landlocked Var Perenil was almost unbearable to him, just as he had thought he would freeze to death during the winter ice. The coastal city of Tharabruthnan, where he had been born and raised, was always cool and damp: it snowed no more than one year in three there, but seldom got hotter than a brisk spring day in Var Perenil...Arudal sighed again as the great clock of the Queen's Tower sounded its half-hourly chimes. At midday, he had an appointment to meet his academic supervisor, Dr. Grímhjálm, for lunch, and he had hoped to have more to show his professor for his last month's work.

Arudal swept his notes into a leather satchel and stripped off his tunic. Though Dr. Grímhjálm would not expect him to appear in full formal robes, he could not dress too casually for a meeting with his academic superior, nor could he bring himself to wear the short tunics with puffed sleeves and thin close-fitting hose that were the current fashion among the nobility of Var Perenil. Instead he pulled on breeches of nubbled black silk and a white linen undershirt, buttoning the silver clasps of a heavier coat-tunic of deep red velvet down the front of his body and fastening a silver-mounted girdle about his waist - old-fashioned, even archaic garb by Kantarean standards; but Tharandrostans were a conservative people. Carefully he combed his shoulder-length black hair straight and settled a plain silver circlet on his head to hold it back, then buckled on deep blue shoes with only a slight point to their toes.

Arudal blinked unhappily as he stepped out into the sunlight. The streets of Var Perenil were noisy and crowded, and the bright daylight fogged Arudal's vision so that he could see no better than most Men could on a dark night. He held himself carefully aloof from the throng of tall blurred shapes jostling about him, making his way along by hard-learned memory.

By the time Arudal reached Tiraneth's Crown, he was glad to step into the candlelit coolness of the inn. His sun-shadowed sight cleared a little in the dimness within; he wandered between the heavy oaken chairs and tables, trying not to peer too obviously at the faces of the others taking their midday meals there.

"Your pardon, young sir?" a server said, looking down at Arudal. Arudal's hackles bristled at the description - he was two years past his legal majority and just become a full adult, as his people counted it, but Kantareans would keep mistaking him for a schoolboy. "Is someone expecting you?"

"I am here to meet Dr. Grímhjálm Peregond," Arudal replied, drawing himself up to his full height and staring coldly up into the server's face. He was close enough to see the shiver of nervousness over the man's narrow features as he dropped his gaze.

"He is over there." The server gestured across the wide room, but Arudal could not make out the University's professor of Imperial philology at such a distance. "Allow me," the taller man said swiftly, guiding Arudal between the tables. For a moment, Arudal deeply wished that he were at home: there, everyone understood his daytime blindness, and he had his body-slave Cenlac to guide him when he must look for someone alone...

"Ah, Arudal," Dr. Grímhjálm rumbled as they drew nearer. "Punctual as always, I see. Do sit down."

Arudal seated himself, and the server asked respectfully what he would have to drink.

"A glass of Malefice '45," Arudal replied absently. The server bowed and disappeared in a rustle of blue velvet, and Arudal turned his attention back to Dr. Grímhjálm, but respectfully waited for his professor to speak first.

"How are you finding summer in the city?" Dr. Grímhjálm asked, his deep voice genial. The professor spoke Imperial with Arudal, as always. Though Arudal's command of Common was good enough for him to get along in Var Perenil, the Tharandrostan disliked the degraded form of his native language, while Dr. Grímhjálm's passion was for the Imperial tongue and its forebears.

"Very hot, sir."

Dr. Grímhjálm laughed. "Hardly surprising, since you're dressed for the chill and damp of your home. Have you ever considered wearing something lighter? You would be more comfortable, if your dignity could bear it - what do your people wear on the Southern trade routes?"

"Mariners go bare-chested in the heat, and I believe the Fel styles run to light silk robes. But that would hardly be suitable here."

"Whyever not?"

"I am not sure, sir," Arudal confessed.

The professor raised a bushy gray eyebrow. "Well, no matter. Tell me, how are you getting on with the problem of kâla- ?"

"With difficulty, sir." Arudal took his notes out of his satchel, spreading them out on the table. The server came back with the chilled white wine; he sipped carefully, letting the cold rich spiciness flow over his tongue as he pointed to his neat diagrams of sounds and mutations. "It seems as though there ought to be an irregular verb kaola- in Middle High Imperial, but I cannot see how that could have developed into the modern kala-."

Lunch was served as they talked: a light venison paté with flaky cakelets, followed by succulent slices of duck meat carefully arranged on a bed of Perenilean fennel, with a sweet chervil sorbet for afters. Dr. Grímhjálm nodded and frowned as Arudal explained his difficulties, and finally said, "Arudal, you have been working on this for two months now. Has it ever occured to you that you might do well to give it a rest and come back to the problem fresh?"

"No, sir. You wanted my paper two weeks from now, sir."

The professor shook his head. "Two more glasses of the Malefice, please," he murmured aside as the server whisked away the empty silver sorbet-cups, then, to Arudal, "I shall give you an extension on it if you promise to leave it alone for a while. In point of fact..." Dr. Grímhjálm looked directly into Arudal's face. Although the older man's blood was mixed, his slanted eyes were the true Imperial steel-and-amber, and it almost seemed to Arudal that he could see the deep golden flares that ringed the other's pupils glowing to a brighter yellow. "Have you thought about getting away from the city for a little while, perhaps seeing some new places before the State calls you back home?"

"No, sir."

"It chances that I have some friends who have a proposition that might interest you - and, indeed, could be very helpful to your work in the long term. They are in need of a translator who is skilled in Old High Imperial...I would go myself, but my old bones are no longer fit for much travelling."

"You are not so old, sir," Arudal said politely: he knew Dr. Grímhjálm was barely past an hundred.

The professor's lips twisted ruefully beneath his gray beard. "Not by your standards, perhaps."

Arudal blushed at his own inadvertent rudeness. At fifty years, Arudal himself had just come to manhood and, if war or sickness did not take him before his time, could expect to walk the green earth for another three centuries; whereas Dr. Grímhjálm would be lucky to live another fifty years. It had been grievously discourteous of Arudal to remind his professor of the difference between them, and he bowed his head in shame. "I crave your pardon, sir. I did not mean..."

"No, you sought to speak kindly to me, and in truth I should not have discomforted you, Arudal. Leave it be. At any rate, this is a young man's task, and you are rare in having both the strength of body and the knowledge to deal with it as needs be."

"What is the work, sir?" Arudal asked, trying to hide the tremble of curiosity in his voice. Already he was envisioning manuscripts that no one had seen before... monographs, translations, papers vastly more important and interesting than the painstaking work of ferreting out philological trails with the aid of dictionaries that would take a century of revisions yet before they were truly complete...and treasures to bring back to the Prince's Library, that we who truly preserve the Imperial heritage intact should have more than our outpost's records and what little we can glean from the lost realms of the South to keep in store...

"Something that should appeal to you," Dr. Grímhjálm said steadily, smiling down at Arudal. "My friends are searching for a certain genealogy - a search that will take them to the Western continent."

Arudal drew in his breath in shock. His heart fluttered a swift beat on his ribs, and the pale wine slapped against the chill-dewed crystal of the goblet in his hand like winter waves against a high breakwater. Not for seventeen hundred years, since the Empire's Fall, had any ship of the Middle Land sought the West and returned...

"Such a search is madness," he breathed, as if to convince himself.

"Not so," Dr. Grímhjálm said, the shadow of a smile still hidden in his beard. "I know that you pay little attention to Kantarean matters, but even you, young Arudal, should recognise the names of those who are going. Sir Shakhor; Sir Thoron; Sir Salarond; Dame Karsil; and Sir Eroth: you must have heard tales of them before."

The wine goblet in Arudal's hand was half-empty; he set it down with great care before he could drink more, or spill it. The names his professor had mentioned were known throughout Kantar and beyond: such a company, made up of five of the greatest knights living, might almost have given pause to the Lord of Martag himself. "What genealogy could..." Then, though, as Dr. Grímhjálm had said, Arudal gave little thought to the politics of Kantar, he realized what it must be. The Prince of Felatar had died a month ago without issue: now there were two rival claimants, Duke Garthin and Duke Helak, whose argument of precedence had not only split Felatar, but sent ripples throughout all the Kantarean provinces and principalities. It was whispered in some places, shouted in others, that an arbitrary decision by the King would touch off civil war - that only final and irrefutable proof of the precedence of one line over the other could resolve the matter in peace.

Or is this a tactic of sacrifice, to buy the King time to resolve the problem? Arudal wondered. He silenced the thought in his mind: a matter of such importance might overrule the usual laws against mind-reading the unconsenting, and his own talent would be of no aid in detecting such listening, though it shadowed his thoughts...In any case, could the King not be trusted by his subjects, the gods would not have given him rule: it was so in Tharandrost, and must be so equally in Kantar, where the last direct descendants of Avalar's line held the White Throne. Moreover, if Kantareans were going to seek out the remains of the Empire in its homeland after these long centuries, was it not Arudal's duty to the State to go and report back? And, finally: Dr. Grímhjálm was his teacher, bound by duty to do his best for a student. Dr. Grímhjálm would not send him on a hopeless mission, nor into his likely death.

"I will go," Arudal said; and though he knew he spoke softly, for he could hardly feel the hum of his voice in his throat, the words seemed to break like a shattering dome of marble in his ears.

Dr. Grímhjálm's smile spread more broadly. "That is well. I shall introduce you to your travelling-companions this evening at Sir Salarond's mansion." Then he sobered, his craggy face suddenly grim and stern as an ancient eagle's. "This one thing I charge you with, however: tell no-one. If it were known that one of your race were going on this mission, there could be...difficulties."

In spite of the spinning of his head, Arudal still thought to ask, "Why, then, have you chosen me?"

His professor laid a heavy hand briefly on the young Tharandrostan's shoulder. "Because I trust you, Arudal. And because I think that this may prove, in time, to be the best thing I can do for you. Finish your wine, and then I would suggest that you go home and sleep through the heat of the day, for you may be up late this night."

Chapter 2: Knights of the White Company

"Swords flash with sunrise light,
Washed red in blood of night,
Wound-rain stains armour bright -
The White Company rides still."
- "Ballad of the White Company", Master Verathal Andarien

Arudal spent a long time in dressing for the meeting as befitted his station and that of the knights with whom he would be travelling. He wore his most formal robes, heavy draperies of dark blue silk adorned with gray seed-pearl embroidery at the collar and bands of shimmering silver sealskin at hem and cuffs. Still unused to putting on the elaborate garments by himself, he had to struggle with his mirror to make sure that all the folds fell in the right places, wishing with all his heart that he could have brought Cenlac with him. On his head, Arudal wore the circlet of the Count-heir of his line, a band of adamant-dusted Valderian steel with a large black star sapphire on his forehead which matched the signet-ring on his finger. His girdle was silver, each of the linked plates marked with a six-rayed figure of black pearls, and a triple dagger of adamant-edged Valderian steel hung at his right side. For some time, Arudal wondered whether he ought to wear his falchion: Var Perenil was a peaceful city, and it was not the Kantarean custom to bear blades at formal events, but that was the way in Tharandrost, in memory of the nation's beginnings. *And these men are soldiers: surely they will not be offended by our customs.*

It was only a short walk from Arudal's rooms to the Lords' Quarter, for he had not stinted himself too much on accomodations. He felt less uneasy on Var Perenil's streets by night than by day: not only could he see more clearly, but there were fewer people about, no strangers jostling him and shouting.

Earl Sir Salarond's mansion was a tall, imposing building, its white marble gleaming with Moon-touched brightness in Arudal's sight - of course, the Earl was a healer-priest: he would have his home well-warded against magical enemies and creatures of Shadow. The facade was wrought in the elaborate stone lacework that graced many of the great buildings of Var Perenil, a style learned from the Bright Elves. In comparison with the high sharp angles of Tharandrost's Late Imperial architecture, it was too flowery and delicate for Arudal's taste, but impressive enough.

Carefully Arudal lifted his hand and knocked on the door. The sound of his tapping was almost lost in the thickness of the richly carved white wood, but the door swung open as though he were expected.

The man who stood before Arudal was rather tall, with Imperial features but the blue eyes and brown hair of mixed blood, dressed in the green and black livery of the Earl's House. He bowed gracefully to Arudal, stepping to the side.

"You will be Count Arudal Arumirun of the House of Arudal?" the servitor said smoothly. Arudal nodded - in Tharandrost, the heir to a title was always addressed by that title in courtesy. "Earl Sir Salarond bids me tell you enter, and be welcome."

Arudal took a deep breath, readying himself. He could feel the Earl's wards pressing against him as he lifted his foot to cross the threshold, then the warning shock of fire through his foot as it crossed the invisible line between the great marble door-pillars, and he bit his lip in anger and frustration. But there was nothing he could do, save ask, "Is Dr. Grímhjálm within?"

"Aye, your Excellency, he is. But will you not enter? You are expected."

Arudal was saved from having to answer by the approach of another man behind the servant. In the light of the row of candles blazing along the corridor in their gilded holders, Arudal could see him clearly, and recognised the brightness gleaming off the gold oak leaves of the Earl's coronet. The Imperial blood ran strong in Sir Salarond: he was no more than two inches above Arudal's own five foot six, and though his black hair was already streaked with gray, his cheeks broader and flatter than most Tharandrostans', head rounder and forehead lower, he could almost have passed for a purebred of the old line. Save for his coronet and the white belt and shortsword of a knight, the Earl wore no insignia of rank: he was dressed in a plain dark soldier's tunic and breeches, with knee-high boots of soft leather, as though he meant to ride out that night. He was very thin, almost frail in appearance, though his forearms were deeply corded with wiry muscle, and Arudal knew that he was a fell fighter as well as a great healer.

Sir Salarond waved his servant aside, nodding to Arudal. "Your Excellency."

"Your Grace," Arudal replied, bowing to the healer-knight. Sir Salarond reached out, taking Arudal's hand and leading him past the threshold.

"Dr. Grímhjálm warned me that you might have difficulty entering my home. I trust that no harm has come to you?"

"No, your Grace," Arudal managed to say through the cold of shock that numbed his tongue. How long had his mentor known? He had thought he had been so careful, not to show that he could see better by darkness than by sunlight, or that the Shadow-mist blurring his vision in daytime was anything more than the ordinary short sight that often afflicted scholars and mages...

"That is well. Come, the rest of us are waiting for you."

Still dazed, Arudal followed Sir Salarond quietly down the hall. The brightness of the candle-flames gleaming from the white marble facings of the walls was broken by paintings in heavy gilded frames. In other circumstances, Arudal would have liked to linger, but as it was, he saw only glimpses: portraits of former Earls and their wives, interspersed with scenes of a more historical nature.

Prince Avalar standing to denounce the Last Emperor with the flare of god-light burning gilded about his head and hands; King Etherdon riding out, sword uplifted, to call challenge on the Lord of Martag; Queen Celenthil of the Bright Elves, her golden hair shimmering down her back, speaking to the white falcon that had brought the beleagured King Galaroth the word that the host of the Elves was riding to break the siege of Var Ineth in what proved to be the last battle of the War of Ruin...the Elvish queen might have been painted from life, for she ruled yet in Tiragel...

At last they came to a door of shining black wood, inlaid with glimmering golden runes. Sir Salarond took Arudal's hand again to lead him through; even with that guidance, Arudal felt the wardings on the door tingling through his body as though he had stepped through a fall of prickling ice. The room was small and bare except for a little table on which stood crystal goblets and a dew-frosted decanter of pale wine, hung with white silken cloths that shimmered with a rainbow glow in the candlelight. Of the five who stood there, only Dr. Grímhjálm wore robes, and those were his usual professorial red. The others, like Sir Salarond, were dressed simply, and Arudal marked at once, with a shiver of relief and anticipation, that they were all armed. Not surprisingly, the Kantarean knights were all considerably taller than Arudal - big men, even for diluted Imperial blood - and more sturdily built, as though they had marched in plate and chain-mail all their lives.

Of all of them, however, it was Dame Karsil at whom Arudal found himself trying not to stare. The Elvish knight of Kantar was a legend in her own right: it was said that, when her beloved had been slaughtered by Dark Trolls some two hundred years past, she had vowed a vengeance upon Martag and all its creatures and works that, in its dreadfulness, had shocked Queen Celenthil so that she gave Karsil a choice between repudiating her madness-sworn oath or leaving her kingdom. And so Karsil had come to Kantar, and earned spurs and belt there - Kantarean women did not fight, but there was little difference between the sexes among Elves. Dame Karsil was over six feet tall, lithe and straight as a young birch; Arudal would not have known her on sight for a female. Even standing still as a rock, she seemed just on the verge of whipping into blinding motion. Her shoulder-length braid shone white-gold, and the green of her tilted eyes glowed like a cat's in Arudal's sight: neither night nor Shadow could hide the Elvish brightness. Her pale brows slanted straight up, and her ears - little larger than a human's, despite the jokes Men made about them - flared into points much sharper than the little peaks of Arudal's own, his personal legacy from the ancient trace of Elvish blood in the Imperial race.

Arudal had met Bright Elves before, for they would come to Tharandrost for the adamant trade and experiments in adamant-crafting, and there was even a Bright Elf teaching at the Prince's School - Dr. Gelethon, with whom Arudal had studied the High Elvish tongue and who also sometimes gave lectures in magic. But Dame Karsil's fine-boned face had nothing of the ageless serenity of the other Elves Arudal had seen. Instead, though no scowl of anger marred the delicately chiseled line of her lips, Arudal could see the leashed fury seething beneath the Elf's still face, like a cauldron of fire-stone veiled by a silk-thin layer of alabaster.

Sir Salarond murmured something beneath his breath as he closed the door behind them. The golden runes flared at once to life. Though they did not burn brightly, their light hurt Arudal's eyes.

"This is our translator?" the tallest of the Men - close to Dame Karsil's height, broad-shouldered and massive, with straggly dark hair and a keen eagle-nose - asked at once. "Before Utalkath, I think Magister Radthar was smoking dream-weed. He hardly looks old enough to read Common."

Arudal flushed in anger and embarassment; it was true that the long-lived noble houses of Tharandrost matured even more slowly than most of their race. Magister Radthar? he wondered. Is that not the name of the foremost among the King's Seers?

"Quiet, Thoron," Sir Salarond said. "I have the utmost confidence in Dr. Grímhjálm's advice. When he says a student of his is qualified for such work, there is no doubt of his judgement. Gentles, this is Count Arudal Arumirun who - the gods willing - shall make it possible to carry out our mission. Count Arudal - Sir Thoron, Dame Karsil, Sir Shakhor, Sir Eroth. You will forgive us if we seem to pry, but there are things we must know in order to determine for ourselves whether you are capable of enduring the...more physical dangers that may come with this mission."

"Of course," Arudal answered. "What manner of dangers do you expect? And... where are we going?"

"If you are to come with us, we shall explain everything in good time. If not - your pardon, but you may not leave this place with more knowledge than you had this morning. Be sure that no harm will come to you from this."

Sir Thoron grunted. "Do you know how to use that falchion?"

"I am taughten...was taught," Arudal corrected himself, "at Prince's School, and I have been studying privately with Lord Wetheren for the last year, though I am little a warrior by profession."

"Hah. If you were a Kantarean, I'd say you looked too small and frail for a fighter - but unless the State screwed up when they bred you, you're probably stronger than I am as well as faster. Shield, or left-hand weapon?"

"Shield, sir."

"That's good. It might keep you alive a little longer." Like a viper striking from hiding, Sir Thoron's longsword leapt from its sheath. Had Arudal not leapt half his body-length backward from the stroke, the tip would have just pricked his throat; he dodged sideways as he drew his falchion, parrying frantically against the knight's flurry of blows. Still, it was but a few moments before Sir Thoron's sword rested against Arudal's chest, and the tall Kantarean shook his head. "I suppose Wetheren's earned his fees. You're better than I expected, even given your natural advantages, but a long way from as good as I'd like. I suppose there's trollshit for a chance we'd find a translator who can actually fight well?"

"He's not so bad, Thoron," Sir Eroth said mildly. Of the knights, he was the most unremarkable in appearance: of medium height for a Kantarean Imperial, with a pleasant, open face, and short brown hair with blond streaks in it. Only the well-worn hilt of his falchion and the way he stood - relaxed but perfectly balanced, as though he could spring into action at any second - suggested that he might be as formidable a warrior as Sir Thoron. "As you say, he's very strong and quick - even by Tharandrostan standards, I think. With proper training and experience, he'd make as good a knight as any, for he's a better fighter than most squires when they begin service. And we're not bringing you along for your brains, you know. If you think the lad's in danger, it's your job to protect him."

"I suppose," Sir Thoron muttered, resheathing his blade as Arudal put his own away. "Can you do anything else in a fight?"

"I am not without skill at sorcery, sir," Arudal said. "More so than at blades, and given time and materials, I can also make rituals that will aid."

The eagle-nosed knight's mouth twitched in a grudging smile. "That'll be useful, anyway. I thought we were a little short in the realm of fighting magic - no offense, Salarond, you know how badly we need you to put us back together. And yes, I know, but we might need it before we get there. No more questions from me."

"Shakhor?" Sir Salarond asked.

Sir Shakhor ran a hand through his mass of blond hair. He was leaner than the other knights, with a narrow-planed face, almost as though there were a touch of Elven in his recent ancestry. "Have you ever spent much time outside a city - Arurak, was it?"

Arudal was on the verge of reminding the Kantarean knight of his title, but it was Earl Salarond, not he, who was both host and ranking noble: if the rough informality suited him, then Arudal had no right to object. "Arudal, sir. My summers were at my grandmother's estate in the mountains, and I am also much sailed."

Sir Shakhor raised a fair eyebrow, smiling widely. "Of course; all Tharandrostans learn to sail, don't they? And I'm told that between rocks and winds and currents, the Tharan cape is the nastiest piece of water on the western coast: you could be very useful if it comes to boats. Well, at your grandmother's estate, did you ever do more than fishing and hunting?"

Arudal paused. His grandmother Zinadir was the Mistress of the Hidden Estate; his summers with her had not been holidays, but training sessions in the gifts of his line - not only speaking with the Undead, but the other talents which he had been charged not to betray to Kantareans. "Some rock-climbing, sir."

"Foraging? Or long hunting trips where you had to rely upon your own skills in the woods? How well do you shoot?"

"I am very short-sighted, sir. I was not made to learn the bow at school, and I have not the keen eyes to look for small things."

"A nearsighted scholar, just what we need," Sir Thoron grumbled. "Morthugor's own help you'll be on watch."

Better than you think at night, Arudal thought angrily, but he held his tongue.

"Don't Tharandrostans know how to make spectacles? Or are you just too vain to wear them? Not that it would matter, since I guess you couldn't put them on under a helm."

"To each his own skill," sighed Sir Shakhor. "Eroth?"

The brown-haired knight looked into Arudal's eyes, and Arudal looked back. Sir Eroth's irises were a pale gray-blue, the ring about the pupil almost white... Sir Eroth shivered and turned his gaze away. "Which of the Tharandrostan mind-magics do you have?"

"Sir?" Arudal said, feigning not to understand him, though he knew quite well what Sir Eroth meant.

"I can tell that you have some talent - are you a Mindspeaker, by chance? Or a Mover, or a Diviner of some nature? Not a Firebringer, I think..."

"No."

"No," Sir Salarond broke in, "his gift is one that may be far more useful to us. Arudal is a medium, and quite a powerful one, if I am not vastly mistaken. Which also explains his short sight: no lens-grinder in the world could help him."

Dame Karsil shook herself, her green glare boring into Arudal. "Morthugast," she hissed under her breath. The Bright Elven word, "twisted sorceror", meant necromancer, but was freighted with a weight of loathing that the respectful Imperial agathusaftan, "Shadow-wise", did not bear. More loudly, the Elf said, "I was against bringing one of the Fallen in the first place. I do not wish to fight beside this creature."

Sir Salarond looked coldly up at Dame Karsil, then stalked over to the door and opened it. "I believe you know the way out, Karsil. You are as aware as I why Count Arudal is vital to the success of our mission - and he is not a Kantarean citizen; we can only ask his help, not command it. Further, I do not care to have my guests insulted in my own home. You know full well that Tharandrost has aided the White Throne since first Prince Avalar fled the ruins of the Western Empire, and your kin have been at peace with them since: it is not courteous to speak of them as the Fallen."

"We still remember the days when our kin were slain in the black temple of Morthugor in Tharabruthnan, and I am told that temple stands yet," replied the Elf. "If we truly have no choice than to bring this - Arudal with us, then I cannot disobey my orders. But can you, sir, look me in the eyes and tell me that I have spoken anything untrue?"

"A medium is not a morthugast. One is an inborn talent, the other is the choice of the magics and service of Shadow," Sir Salarond replied calmly.

"And there are no temples in Tharabruthnan save those of the gods," Arudal added. Now he spoke in Bright Elven, striving with all his will to keep his voice as level as that of the healer-priest and pronouncing each word carefully so that the Elf could not misunderstand him. "The worship of Morthugor was made punishable by death at the founding of our nation, nor, in Imperial days - though we kept our oaths to our Emperor and our commanders - did we ever do such things as you have spoken of. You have been grievously misinformed, Dame Karsil, which I regret, for your tales are told with admiration in my homeland, and it is our custom to give honour to the Elves always for the sake of the love that was between our folk in early days when you were our teachers, for the respect of your age and wisdom, and for your greater closeness to the gods." The words nearly stuck in Arudal's throat, but Dame Karsil seemed to be throttling down her own rage.

"It has never been the way of the Elves to fight beside any Men save Men of the Light," Dame Karsil declared, but with far less force than before.

"Then you shall not go against your customs to have me with you, for what else are Tharandrostans? If some of Imperial blood are Fallen - and the Fallen are our foes as surely as yours - I have heard it said also that the chief counsellor to the Lord of Martag was once a Bright Elf."

"Once, but no longer," Dame Karsil ground out, the Elvish music of her voice almost lost beneath her anger. "And what should I call the keepers of slaves?"

"Men whose customs are different from your own," Sir Salarond broke in. "Enough of this. Karsil, are you on this mission or not? I assure you, if it is necessary, I can and shall arrange your transfer to a different post."

Dame Karsil looked about at her companions, then back at Arudal. "You speak the True Tongue well enough," she admitted grudgingly in Bright Elven, then returned to High Common. "If I must, I will accept Arudal as a companion. But this on the one condition: that he must prove himself a worshipper of the gods and no servant of the Shadow that taints his nature."

Sir Thoron frowned thoughtfully, rubbing his jutting chin. "That isn't the worst idea I've heard. How?"

"Sir Salarond, ye are a healer-priest," Arudal said. "An ye willen, ye mayen seken the withins of my herte, for I am as yare to clearen this shameful thing that Dame Karsil hath of me yspoken - has spoken of me," he corrected himself, "as ye are to finden what manner of man I be."

"The full verbal endings dropped from Common five hundred years ago," Dr. Grímhjálm said softly to Arudal in Imperial, and Arudal blushed, realizing that his command of the tongue had slipped in his distress. He carefully repeated, "Sir Salarond, you may read what is in my heart, for I should like to be cleared of this... accusation?...as much as you wish to know that you can trust me."

"If you are willing, then I shall proceed," Sir Salarond agreed. "Stand still, Arudal, and do not be afraid."

The healer's lean hands touched Arudal's temples, and Sir Salarond murmured a few words beneath his breath in a soft lilting chant. Arudal felt suddenly dizzy: he could see nothing but the black gleam of the Earl's pupils, lit by single points of brightness within as if candles burned in the small dark room of his skull. Terathon of the Waters, Amanvon of the Stars, Aviyani of the Earth...Alar Fire-Shaper, Amandeth the Judge, Utalkath Warrior, Wind-Queen Avradir...It seemed to him that he scented the sweetness of incense such as was burned to the gods in the temples of Tharabruthnan, and heard the echo of a great bell rippling through the silence left by its ringing clang.

Then Sir Salarond's hands dropped, and slowly Arudal came back to himself. The healer-priest was smiling, his eyes warm. "There is no more need for doubt," the Earl assured his companions. "Now I think young Arudal is owed an apology, Karsil."

The two knights' eyes locked; at last the Elf gave way before the Man. "I misjudged you, Arudal, and misspoke," Dame Karsil admitted, her voice sweet as silver bells at dawn, then added in Bright Elvish, "Leikaker my kindred called me at home: heart of fire-stone, too easily kindled to anger and too slow to cool. I do not think that we shall ever be friends, but I am willing to have you as companion, if you are not too grievously offended to stand beside me."

"I would be discourteous indeed did I not accept words so fairly offered," Arudal replied in the same tongue. "I hope that you shall learn to think more kindly of my people through knowing me, as do those of your race who have dwelt in my home for longer than the life of a Man."

Dame Karsil nodded, turning back to Sir Salarond. "Since these matters are settled for now, shall we tell Arudal what it is we are truly doing?"

"I have one more question," said Sir Eroth. "Arudal, I mean you no discourtesy, but I have heard that mediums may draw the attention of Undead, as well as being able to see and speak with them. Is this true?"

Arudal frowned. Knowledge of mind-magic was not forbidden to tell outsiders, but it went against the grain to answer such detailed questions. Still, his life could depend on these men and what they knew of him, so much as he was able to tell. "Uncontrolled agathudalim - mediums - may summon Undead without knowing it, but I am not uncontrolled. Yet...as I may see beings of Shadow clearly, so they may see me, the more so if I am using my talent, and they will know me first for either a threat or one who may aid them in their troubles, depending on whether they are evil by nature or merely bound by some sorrow or shild or ill chance."

"I see," Sir Eroth murmured thoughtfully. "But those of evil nature may seek to attack you first - that might aid us in the knowing. And Sir Salarond speaks truly: as we seek into matters that may be kept only by the dead now, your talent of speaking with them could prove of inestimable value." He chewed at his lip a moment. "Well, I have no more to ask at the time. Salarond, I suppose we should explain matters to our guest now."

"Aye - but with this one constraint. Arudal, should you not wish to aid us, are you willing to forget this meeting and all that took place in it? Dr. Grímhjálm can avow that I can remove those memories without any harm to you, and without disturbing anything else in your mind."

"Yes," Arudal said firmly.

Arudal's stomach tightened with fear and excitement as Sir Salarond began to explain their mission. His guess had been correct: the knights of the White Company were undertaking this expedition to stave off civil war in Kantar - or, at the very least, to delay the crisis in hopes that it could be dealt with more peacefully. The very knowledge that the White Crown was acting upon the problem, even if King Edril did not reveal how, would calm matters for a little while...

"And there is no telling what resistance we may meet on the way," Sir Salarond added thoughtfully. "There is...reason to think that certain agents of Martag have been subtly encouraging this conflict, in hopes that it will break out into open war. There is nothing that would better serve the plans of the Lord of Martag than strife beneath the banner of the White Crown. Not knowing what we will find in the West, we chose speed and secrecy over naked force - but that necessarily leaves us the more vulnerable."

"When do we mean to leave?" Arudal asked.

"That, I think, depends on you," replied Sir Salarond. "How long will it take you to make ready?"

"Two days, perhaps...I must arrange for storage of my possessions, and..."

"Have no fear for that. My servants will look after everything for you; you need only pack what you must bring. There are two hours yet until midnight; can you be ready to ride before dawn?"

"Aye, easily enough, but I have no packhorse, only a steed for riding."

"That, too, we can supply. How good is your riding horse, and do you think he can travel by sea?"

"He is of one of the best lines in the State, of the pure Imperial blood, and will answer to little more than my thoughts," Arudal said proudly. "Else I shoulde not have taken the trouble to bringen him with me. Nor did he give any trouble on shipboard from Tharabruthnan to Agilath."

"Is he trained for battle?" asked Sir Thoron.

"I woulde not riden him into danger by choice!" Arudal replied. "He is gently raised, and I woulde not seen him comen to harm at the hands of Men, whom he should trust and love. Or of any other creature, for that matter."

Sir Thoron sighed gustily. "No wonder your lot haven't any cavalry worth speaking of except the Silent Guard. Amanvon help us if we're attacked on the road anywhere...Never mind, mayhap I know where we can find another war-horse. Well, your blade's good enough - Valderian steel with ground adamant?"

"Yes, sir."

"Stop calling me sir, you're a civilian. My name's Thoron, Sir Thoron if you have to get fancy, but the gods know I'm not going to waste breath calling you 'your Excellency'. Anyway, the sword will do. What kind of armour do you have?"

"Valderian steel chain - a knee-length hauberk with full sleeves and coif. And an adamantine helm, gorget, elbow- and knee-pieces, and gauntlets." Arudal spoke proudly: he had been given his grandfather's armour and sword on his forty-eighth birthday.

The big knight clicked his tongue. "Even Valderian chain's nothing but a set of holes to an arrow-point. Plate'll keep you alive longer. I'll get your measure before we go, and pick up some at the Palace armoury if I can, though you won't be an easy fit, small as you are. What sort of shield do you use?"

"A large escutcheon, sir...Sir Thoron."

"Standard for an infantry fighter, I suppose. I thought you didn't seem much used to blocking below the head with a sword. Is your shield anything special?"

"It has my family arms on it." A sword might last for generations; a shield, unless it were made of dragon-scale or other such material, would rarely survive more than a couple of battles, if that.

"Hah. I'll see what I can find for you. It wouldn't do to get all the way to the West and have to come back because our translator'd copped it."

"And it would be better," Dr. Grímhjálm broke in, "if you did not advertise your presence too clearly. If you must bring your own shield, Arudal, put a cover on it. It would go ill with us if you were found out and forbidden to go."

Sir Salarond frowned. "We may have another problem along those lines. I must report that Arudal has joined us - and there will be a great deal of difficulty with bringing a Tharandrostan on a covert mission of national security. Grímhjálm, are you sure that there are no Kantareans who can do what is needed?"

"None who are young and active enough to endure the hardships of the journey," the graybearded professor replied. "Imperial philology is not a favoured subject here."

"Ultar's going to have kittens about a Tharandrostan going with us," put in Sir Thoron. "Maybe we should send Arudal home now and start looking for someone else."

"O, no!" Arudal said, horror-struck. It seemed to him that he could see his hopes fading before him like the glittering trail of sunlight retreating over the waves before a boat. "Please, sir, I have already let you look into my heart. I will do almost anything to go along on this!"

Sir Thoron scowled, looking skeptically down at him. "If you're so eager for adventure, why didn't you join your own military in the first place? Did they reject you for being short-sighted, or something?"

Arudal gave him a cold stare. Though the Silent Guard was closed to him, Arudal could have gone where-ever else he pleased in Tharandrost's forces: a squire to a noble knight, or officer training and then a place on one of the State's greatships - or into the hidden unit where most of his family, living and dead, served.

But Dr. Grímhjálm spoke for him. "I think Arudal is not eager for the adventure itself, but for what lies at the end of it. It may surprise you to hear this, Sir Thoron, but some folk hunt knowledge as eagerly as you hunt Dark Trolls, and find a word in an old tongue to be worth more than a gold coin...Yet there is the problem of his citizenship. If he were squired to one of you, that would be a different matter, for a squire cannot be separated from his knight, nor the fealty-bond dissolved save by their own free choices: Sir Ultar could not order you to leave Arudal behind, nor could his own government forbid him to go."

If I had wanted to be a squire, Arudal thought, my father would have arranged service for me with one of our own...He thought of polishing armour and obeying orders, of being, in effect, a servant - and not to a trueblooded Tharandrostan knight, but to one of these strange Kantareans, foremost in their nation though they were. Yet is it not worth it, if that is the price of my passage to the West?

"That would solve a great many problems, if Arudal and one of us were willing," Sir Salarond said thoughtfully. "Elsewise...we would have to hope that we could get Arudal out of Kantar unnoticed by his own people, and try to convince Ultar to approve him for this mission as well. Which, I can promise you, would never happen, regardless of what our advisors have told us. Well, Arudal? You said that you would do almost anything to go with us. Does that extend to swearing your fealty in Kantar, at least for a time?"

Arudal gulped. But Prince Dolkhat, heir to Tharandrost's throne, had himself served his term as squire in the White Company. And who can reproach me for following his example? If I were squired to Sir Salarond, who shows me proper courtesy and respect...and who was our Prince's knight-father, yes! There would be nothing but honour in that.

"If necessary, yes," Arudal said, trying to keep his low voice from squeaking as he glanced over to his professor for support.

Dr. Grímhjálm nodded. "I believe it is. Trust me, Arudal: this will do you no harm, and perhaps much good. And without it, you shall have to forget all we have spoken of this night and return to your research, never knowing that men of the Middle Land have set foot once more upon the shores of the West."

"Uh...would I be your squire, Sir Salarond?"

"I don't think so," the healer-priest replied. "I will not have time to deal with you properly, and what you need most to know at the moment, you can better learn from a knight who is more a warrior than I."

To Arudal's horror, Sir Thoron was rubbing his chin again, looking at the Tharandrostan as though Arudal were a horse he might be thinking of buying. "Squire Arudal, eh?" he mused. "It might knock a little of the arrogance out of you, at least...Well, does anyone else want him?"

Sir Eroth's mouth quirked a little at the corner; Sir Shakhor was outright grinning. "A squire who's ten years older than I am?" the blond knight said. "Not a chance - and if you think I'm mad enough to try keeping him and Rhys together, you are very much mistaken. He's all yours, Thoron."

"Well?" Sir Thoron said to Arudal. "You swear fealty and obedience to me, I swear to protect you, feed you, train you, bail you out and give you a whack about the head when you get in trouble with the city guard, and make you carry my armour and wash the dishes."

Arudal opened his mouth and shut it again, looking helplessly at Dr. Grímhjálm. Why are you doing this to me? he wondered. The professor's gray-bearded face was perfectly straight, but Arudal thought he could see a crinkling of laughter at the corners of the older man's eyes. Still, he had been trained from infancy to obey his superiors, as he expected his inferiors to obey him; and Dr. Grímhjálm was his teacher, who had just given him an opportunity that anyone in his field of study would have traded his right arm and one testicle for. He would not tell me to do this without good reason.

"Go on," Dr. Grímhjálm said quietly. "You kneel and put your hands between his…"

As if half-stunned, Arudal knelt before Sir Thoron, lifting his hands and repeating the words of the oath Sir Salarond gave him. Though Sir Thoron smiled as he spoke his own vows, Arudal could hear the ring of sincerity in his voice. "May Amanvon and Amandeth hear and witness," the knight finished. He fished a heavy fealty-chain of plain silver out of his belt-pouch, draping it around Arudal's neck, and took the Tharandrostan's hands in his own again to lift his new squire effortlessly to his feet. "Now you call me sir," Sir Thoron said with considerable satisfaction. "And your first duty, squire, is - go get packed, and trade those damned silly robes for something you can ride all night in! Bring one packhorse's load and no more, unless you think you can explain to me why you have a need for more crap than your horse can carry. Go on, what are you waiting for? We'll be outside your guesthouse in two hours, and if you're not saddled up, armoured, and ready to go, you'll feel the back of my hand."

"Yes…sir," Arudal said, dazed. He bowed to the others; Sir Salarond took his hand and led him out.

Chapter 3: On the Road

"The fire's out, the door is locked,
The saddle on the horse.
Dawn's first light grays the eastern black,
So take the reins, lift up the pack,
No time to linger or look back:
Mount up now, set your course."
- "Journey Begun," Rander Laranost

Two hours later, Arudal was standing outside the guesthouse with Inmanat's reins in his hand and a pair of bulging saddlebags on the ground beside him, dressed in his grandfather's chain hauberk over a gambeson of soft padded leather and leather riding breeches. He still felt stunned; his world had changed more rapidly than the shifting landscape of a dream. This was not what I had in mind, he said to himself. Yet the warm night wind whispered wordlessly in his ears; the weight of Sir Thoron's fealty-chain was solid about his neck, and Inmanat's dark nose nudged softly at his hand in hopes of finding an apple there. "Greedy beast," Arudal said lovingly to the gelding, stroking the muscular curve of Inmanat's neck.

Arudal heard his companions before he saw them, the sound of their hooves clattering over the cobblestones. The knights were mounted on riding horses; behind them, squires on similar steeds led both heavy packhorses and big stallions whose steel barding gleamed through plain dark caparisons. One of the squires had an extra pair of horses, and without speaking, he dismounted and helped Arudal to load up the packhorse and get into the armour Sir Thoron had brought. Arudal had rather fancied himself in something like the "white harness" the others wore - all naked metal, gleaming fluted breastplates and shaped skirts of horizontally layered tassets.

The hinged steel leg- and arm-pieces Sir Thoron had brought for him were, indeed, almost the same as the knights', save that the inner bend of elbows, knees, and armpits were open rather than covered by delicately jointed lames, leaving only his chain-mail to protect him there. But his body armour was a simple shapeless coat of plates, slightly overlapping steel pieces riveted underneath a loose jerkin of heavy blue leather. True, it would protect Arudal nearly as well as the white harness, save that a sword would not glance from the flat plates as it would from the center-ribbed curves of the other fighters' breastpieces. And such harness as the others wore, especially the pieces with covered joints, took time and a skilled smith to fit properly if it were not to hinder its wearer, while the coat of plates would suit anyone of a general size - doubtless why Sir Thoron had chosen the armour he had for his new squire...But I shall look like a simple man-at-arms among high nobles, or a soldier in the ranks who was lucky in looting helm and gauntlets above his station.

The squire made to to hand over the reins of one of the warhorses - a great evil-looking black brute of a stallion, at least sixteen hands high; nearly a foot taller at the shoulder than Arudal's sturdy little Imperial steed. Arudal took the leathers nervously, thinking, I'll need a stepladder to get up on that son of a mammoth. But, to his relief, Sir Thoron shook his head, muttering, "Not until we get out of the city."Arudal mounted Inmanat, and the rest of the squires made room for him in their midst.

The ten riders rattled through the dark streets, occasionally separating for a moment as one of them guided his horse around a drunk making his way home from a tavern or passed out in the gutter. The black warhorse twitched at the reins whenever he saw a man down, and Arudal realized with a cold chill that the beast must be trained against its nature to trample fallen foes. A cruel use for a horse, he thought. What am I doing with these people? If I'd wanted to be in the military, I could have gotten a good billet at sea, among my own folk... but never sailing to the West: Prince Norombar still upheld his father's decision, that no more Tharandrostan lives be wasted in a search that had proven fruitless for so long.

They stopped briefly at the gates, where Sir Salarond spoke a few words to the guards. The great bar creaked aside; Arudal heard the clinking of steel deep within the polished black granite, and the city gate swung open.

The first pale blue of dawn was beginning to glimmer in the east when Sir Salarond commanded, "Off the road: there is a trail and a clearing a little way through the trees, and we shall make camp there, where we cannot easily be seen."

Arudal dismounted gratefully when they reached the clearing. He was soaked with sweat from the heat of the padded gambeson beneath his chainmail and the coat of plates Sir Thoron had brought for him, and his eyes were beginning to flutter closed: even a bedroll on the ground would be welcome. He turned to unload his packhorse, but Sir Thoron's gauntlet rang lightly from his helm.

"You see to my things first, then your own, squire! Your squire-brother Finvar there will show you what to do - pay attention to him: he's your senior in service by three years. The two of you can take first watch together."

Arudarat blinked as the squire who had been leading his horses trotted over and clapped him on the shoulder. "So you're my new squire-brother," the young man said cheerfully. Finvar was two or three inches taller than Arudal, heavily built, and what Arudal could see of his face through his helm-bars looked pleasant. The Artagelean burr to his light voice told Arudal that his fellow-squire was from the northern part of Kantar; he wore a rolled band of black and white fabric around his helm. "Do you know how to set up a tent?"

"No."

"Well, I'll let you see to the horses this time then. I think there's a stream about fifty yards down that way - don't take them for water by yourself! You never go anywhere alone if you can help it. Wait for the other squires to come with you."

It took Arudal some time to free all of their horses from saddles, packs, and bits: the Kantarean tack was different from the simple dropped noseband used in Tharandrost, and the warhorses, uneasy at a stranger's touch, stamped their platter-sized hooves and tried to bite Arudal when he eased the heavy bits from their mouths. "Sa, sa," he murmured to each stallion in turn. "Be good, beautiful horse, and thou'lst have apples and sweets of me when I can get them." The promise worked on Inmanat, who rolled his eyes forlornly when he heard his master speaking so lovingly to other horses, but the black stallion Sir Thoron had brought for Arudal snapped his big teeth a finger's breadth from Arudal's hand. By the time Arudal had managed to get headcollars and lead-ropes on the nine horses for which he was responsible, the other three squires were standing together with their own steeds and staring irritably at him through helm-bars and open visors.

"You couldn't have been any slower about that, could you?" one of them, a tall youth with a square of bright-chequered cloth flung over his shoulder, said irritably. "Ymwra's Blood, don't you know anything about horses?"

Arudal stiffened at the oath: Ymwra was one of the names that Plainsman slaves were forbidden to speak, one of the spirits of the southern tribes. Amanvon, surely a Kantarean knight would not take a Plainsman buck as a squire? But the lilt in the other's voice was unmistakable, as were the eyes glaring through his helm-bars - green-tinged blue, with the surprised roundness of Common Men's eyes - and Arudal drew himself up to his full height. "More than you, I dorste say, though I was not yborn to a servant's work."

"Peace and hush," another squire, whose helm glittered with a faint tracery of ornamental goldwork, said. "Words won't get the horses watered, and I don't want to explain to Sir Salarond why we let them founder in the heat. Come on."

Arudal followed, keeping a good distance from the Plainsman buck, who in turn stayed well away from him. The stream was wide and clear, rushing swiftly over dark brown rocks; Arudal would have liked to strip off his sweat-soaked armour and dive in, but the other squires did not so much as loosen their helm-straps, and he would not risk embarassing himself in front of a Plainsman.

"We may as well introduce ourselves," the squire with the gold-worked helm said. "I am Lostren, squire to Sir Salarond - Dr. Lord Lostren Telagon, fourth son of the Earl of Dan Iragal, though we don't use titles among ourselves." He spoke with the soft, almost drawling, accent of the Kantarean nobility; his voice was very deep, rolling up from the bottom of his broad chest, and he was only two inches or so taller than Arudal. "You are clearly a Tharandrostan of noble birth; you've been in Kantar long enough to speak Common properly when you're thinking about it, but chiefly in a quiet environment, since you start losing it the moment you're under any stress. I would wager at least ten crowns that you're a mage of some sort, and you didn't squire to Sir Thoron because the desire of your heart is to be a knight - you're probably a squire so that no one can order you to leave this mission, and you're really here because we needed a native Imperial-speaker as an interpreter, in case some form of the language is still spoken in the West. Well, am I right?"

Arudal thought about Lostren's words, and a faintness that had nothing to do with the heat and weight of his armour came over him. "Most likely," Arudal admitted. "Though my purpose is actually to read the older manuscripts, as I am a philologer specializing in Old High Imperial." But Sir Thoron mentioned Magister Radthar...there must be something more to that...

Lostren laughed. "It'll be interesting to see how you get along with Sir Thoron. He has got an education: it's a doctorate in disemboweling Dark Trolls." The other two laughed, as if at an old joke. "You and I have something in common: my own degree is in early Kantarean history, and I plan to go back to University life after I've won my spurs... Anyway, you've met Finvar; these others are Tirothar, squire to Sir Eroth, and Rhys, squire to Sir Shakhor. Dame Karsil doesn't have a squire, due to the fact that she's a flaming maniac who used to get her own killed off so often that no family in Kantar will let their son squire for her. What's your name?"

"Arudal Arumirun, Count-heir of the House of Arudal."

Lostren's dark eyebrows disappeared beneath the brim of his open visor, but he said only, "Well, that's enough. Let's get the horses out of the river before they make themselves sick."

To Arudal's relief, the warhorses followed a light tug at their lead-ropes, as did Inmanat, but the Kantarean riding- and pack-horses were more stubborn. In the end, Lostren had to hand his horses over to Tirothar and come to Arudal's aid. "You're used to a different style of horse-training," the young Kantarean noble said kindly. "My father says that, for a rider with a light touch, nothing can compare to Tharandrostan horses."

"Skitty beasts who'll dump you in the road as soon as look at you, and gods help you if you touch them with a spur," Tirothar murmured. "At least, if what I hear is true, you won't have any trouble with Black Rage there, though he's supposed to be the most high-strung horse in the White Company's stables."

Arudal looked dubiously at the warhorse Sir Thoron had chosen for him. The black stallion stood square with water dripping from his muzzle, flicking his ears nervously back and forth, and for a moment Arudal wished with all his heart that he had the talent of bespeaking animals.

"He should be the closest thing to what you're used to," Lostren assured him. "Come on, now, let's get these fellows to their grazing so we can have breakfast and go to sleep."

The sunlight was already bright enough to make it difficult for Arudal to see; he walked very slowly, nudging each foot ahead to be sure there were no unexpected traps in his way. "What's wrong with you?" Rhys snapped. "Haven't you ever set foot off a soft carpet before?"

"Hush, Rhys," said Lostren. "Arudal, do you need any help?"

"No," Arudal replied forbiddingly: he was not going to admit to being short-sighted where Rhys could hear.

By the time they got back, Finvar had raised Sir Thoron's tent and was busy rummaging food out of the packs. The other squires hastened to put up tents for their own knights; Arudal sat down next to Finvar, but his fellow waved him away. "Go ask Lostren to show you what he's doing: you'll need to know."

Arudal looked at the others, but the thickening Shadow-mist on his sight made it impossible to tell which of the three squires was which. Rather than ask, he chose one, only to find that he was peering up into the Plainsman buck's freckled face.

"Stop staring at me like that!" Rhys growled down at Arudal. "If you don't like me, you can leave me alone."

Arudal bit back the reply that came to his tongue and strode away. Now that he looked more closely at the others, he could see the faint glimmer of light about Lostren's gold-embossed helm: magicked, he guessed, to preserve the wearer from head injuries.

"Your help is much appreciated," Lostren told him. "Hold the pole for me...I'd say you're in the same state as I was when Sir Salarond took me on. In all my life, I'd never been on a hunting trip where we didn't have servants along to put up the pavilions, and I started out by trying to hang the ground-sheet on the center pole." He laughed. "And you're used to having slaves do it all for you. Now, for Amanvon's sake, don't say anything about that where Rhys can hear. It's not easy for him, being a Plainsman among high-born Kantareans. And having a Tharandrostan about isn't going to make matters any better for him, particularly if you keep staring at him as though you'd just scraped him off your boots. Try to remember that we're all squires together - Rhys has seniority over you by a couple of years, in fact - and do your best to treat him like a human being. It's not as though he has any more reason to like you than you do to like him."

"How did such a one as Rhys become a squire?" Arudal asked as Lostren knelt to stretch out a guy-rope. Plainsmen were considered citizens in Kantar - At least when they aren't rebelling or shooting Royal officials from ambush, Arudal added caustically to himself - but it was a long way from citizenship to the noble ranks of the chivalry.

"He was the only survivor of a village that was raided by Horse-tribes - his parents had left their own clan for some reason and were working there. Sir Shakhor was leading a patrol in the area, and they got there soon enough to wipe out the raiders, but not soon enough for the villagers. Rhys was lucky: he was knocked unconscious and the Horse-tribesmen thought he was dead, so they didn't bother sticking a spit through him...they saved that for the living. Anyway, Sir Shakhor felt just awful about the whole thing, so when Rhys was healed up, he took him on as a squire. And it wasn't a bad choice," Lostren mused. "Sir Shakhor is supposed to be the best woodsman in Kantar, and the Plainsmen have a knack for climbing and sneaking about in the trees. Rhys is a bit of a... whatever it is they call their mages...as well, he talks to land-spirits and such. It's not a huge amount of magic, but it's proved useful on occasion. And he's something of a diviner: he has flashes of what he calls the Sight - glimpses of the future or the past, or a sense of whether something is dangerous."

Arudal's back stiffened at Lostren's words. Magic, or mind-magic, were perhaps the most strictly forbidden things for Plainsman slaves in Tharandrost, those talents rigorously culled from their bloodlines by law. "Is he safe to have about?" Arudal asked, his voice very low. "Are you never worried that…"

Lostren's laugh was rich and full. "You don't know much about free Plainsmen, do you? Sir Shakhor is the only clan and father Rhys has now: Rhys would gladly die for him, or cut off his own right hand before doing anything that would shame him. If you must worry about someone, worry about Dame Karsil: she'd never betray us by choice, but she might land us in more trouble than if she did by being stiff-necked and fiery-tempered. If you want my opinion," the squire added softly, "she's a few crenellations short of a complete castle. There we go." Lostren hammered in the last stake and stood up, tassets clinking as he stretched. "At least we can sleep through the heat of the day. I don't know how anyone manages summer campaigns. Not that I like riding at night much, either; I prefer being able to see where I'm going - though that won't be a problem for you."

"What do you mean?" Arudal asked sharply.

Lostren spread his gloved hands out. "You didn't have any trouble walking down to the stream before sunrise, but you're more than half-blind in full daylight. You told me your House - and I told you I got my degree in early Kantarean history. You're a - an agathudal, Shadow-mind, you call it? A medium. I can see why you might not want to shout it around, but you can't hide it from anyone who's looking for it."

You're a little too clever, Arudal thought.

"Is it true that your House practices necromancy by mind-magic?"

"That gift existeth ne more," Arudal said, staring coldly at him. After a moment Lostren shuddered and looked away. "Well, maybe you'll tell me more when we get to know each other better. Dear gods, it's hot. I'll be glad when we get to the River where we can just laze about on a nice breezy boat - not that squires ever get to laze about. Breakfast."

Breakfast consisted of flat rounds of trail-bread, Perenilean dry cheese with fennel seeds, and garlic-pungent hard sausage, washed down with water from the stream. Except for the staleness of the bread, the food was not too dissimilar to what Arudal ate on days when he was working too hard to be bothered going to market or wasting time on a full meal in an inn.

"Eat well, squire," Sir Thoron said to him. "You're strong enough, but small as you are, you could use a good bit more weight on you. Any half-grown Dark Troll could knock you down with a shield-bash, let alone a normal-sized Man. Now, how long would it take you to make our camp invisible?"

Arudal looked up at his knight in surprise. "Longer than we are going to be here, surely, sir. True invisibility is difficult: I would have to cast the spell separately on each moving creature, because…"

"Forget it. Shakhor, can you tell Rhys to do his no-see-us charm before he goes to sleep?"

"Of course."

Indignant at his dismissal, Arudal was about to explain that he could do something to turn the casual attention aside quite easily, but Sir Thoron was already saying, "First watch, two candlemarks, then wake me. Since it's daytime, you may talk very, very quietly so long as you stay alert. If you see anyone coming - especially if they look important - wake me up at once. If you have to talk at all, let Finvar do it; I don't want Arudal to say so much as hello. You understand, squires?"

"Yes, sir."

After breakfast, Arudal and Finvar settled themselves down to watch with shields strapped on their arms, though, with the full Sun's light in his face, Arudal found it hard to see more than ten feet in front of himself: the world was a gray fog in his sight, his fellow squire's shape a dark blur.

"How long have you been in Kantar?" Finvar asked.

"Most of a year. I am come here at the beginning of Leaf-Turn, when the University term began."

"Hmm. I thought you were younger than that. I know your folk age slowly; are you full-grown?"

"Yes."

"How'd you get here? All Sir Thoron said was that he had a new squire from Tharandrost who needed to learn what to do, and I should thump you if you gave me any shit. My father is the Marquis dath Helludal, if it matters to you, by the way - Helludal is on the north border of Artagel, and yes, that is where Helludal black ale and amber spirit come from, and no, I don't have any." He laughed. "Just in case you should ask. Everyone does."

Arudal had no idea what Finvar was talking about, but smiled politely anyway. "How long have you been Sir Thoron's squire?" he said, just to have something to say.

"Three years. I'm hoping to be knighted when we come back from this. If I haven't managed to do anything notable by then, I might as well retire to a temple-cloister."

"Have you fought much?"

"A fair bit, here and there. I was at the Battle of Rathley Dale, but I didn't get to actually fight in it. The Shadowlanders fielded a full cohort of vampires against us unexpectedly, and there weren't enough charms against fear to go around, so most of the squires had to stay back at the camp. I was so angry, I was ready to eat my shield like a Northman berserk - but we couldn't have half our force panicking and getting in the way of the ones who were protected. And then, it's not easy to do something distinguished as a squire in the White Company. The knights are so good that when they go into battle, by the time we lesser mortals have a chance to draw sword, there's usually nothing left for us but chasing stragglers. Still," he said, more brightly, "everyone says the real chance to get noticed is on small-party missions like this. Is it true that landsmen always puke on boats on the ocean, anyway?"

Finvar's sudden change of subject caught Arudal by surprise. "What?"

"Tirothar's from the coast, and he was saying I'd probably be tossing my dinner all across the Western Ocean."

"Why?"

"He says the boats go up and down and it shakes the stomach until everything comes out."

Arudal shook his head disbelievingly. "I think Tirothar is having a...a play on you? It is healthy to be on the ocean. I have sailed all my life and never been sick from it, nor has anyone I know."

"That's reassuring. So, how did you get squired to Sir Thoron?"

Arudal told him the story as briefly as he could. Finvar let out a long soft whistle of breath. "You lucky son of a whore," he said. "All my friends were green as a Dark Troll's rotten dinner with envy when they found out I'd managed it. Half the men our age - my age, anyway - in Kantar would give their left nuts to be Sir Thoron's squire, and there you just walk in and...Squire-brother, there must be a god on your side."

Suddenly Arudal felt a familiar chill, as though the sweat trickling down the back of his neck had frozen to ice in an instant. He reached out with his mind, the world darkening around him until Finvar was barely a shadow against the blackness, and heard the threefold harmony of thoughts: There...smell them...there they are, the ones for whom we were sent...living...slay and eat...

"Sir Thoron!" he shouted, leaping up and drawing his falchion even as the horses started to rear and plunge against their ropes. "Waken! Finvar, wake them!"

"What's wrong?" Finvar asked, standing and drawing blade.

"Vampires! Three, that way - they comen swift!"

Finvar braced himself; then the falchion dropped from his shaking hand and he fled with a cry of terror. Arudal saw the burning light of a sword flashing red in the Shadow-night beside him as the vampires swooped into his sight. They were black-clad and pale-faced, an eerie corona of green-tinged light playing about them in the darkness; all three of them held rapiers like needles of blackness, and one turned its face towards him in a dreadful hiss of snake-long teeth. The vague shade of the man with the fiery sword leapt between Arudal and the vampires, and a streak of light arched over Arudal's head to sink shaft-deep into one of the Shadow-creatures. It wailed, high and forlorn, its white limbs beginning to curl away into mist as it sank down, but the other two closed on the swordsman.

Shield dropping to his side and the weapon in his hand forgotten, Arudal reached out again, dragging the gaze of one of the vampires to him by main force. Its eyes were like holes burnt in white parchment with twin red candleflames burning behind them; he stood firm. COME HERE! he thought, wrenching at it with all his will. For a moment it struggled; then its icy touch speared through his eyes, sinking into his brain. Something twisted within Arudal, wriggling like a cold worm in his head; he pushed again, and it was... not gone, but trapped, encysted in the quiet place inside him.

A second scream arose, rising and falling in an ear-shattering howl, and Arudal felt the last chill fading. The red sword lifted, its point swinging about like a torch-flame in a shifting wind. Arudal turned to look behind himself, and saw only Dame Karsil - as clear in the Shadow-Realm as elsewhere, for Elves were as real on the Other Side as on the green earth - lowering her bow and gently easing back from full draw to disengage a second white-glowing arrow.

Arudal drew a deep breath, trying to calm himself. The falchion in his trembling hand felt as heavy as if he had been fighting for half an hour, his left arm too shaky to lift his shield above shoulder-level. He had trained to do such things before, but in the heat of combat...Stupid, he told himself, you are stupid. You had its mind: you should have taken control of it and turned it against its fellows. If the Elf had not been ready, it would have been two to one on whoever that is...Or they could have had living reinforcements that you could not sense...

With a stern effort of will, Arudal closed his eyes, forcing the darkness away. When he opened them again, the sunlit world was no more than usually misty: now he could recognise Sir Thoron's tall figure, and only a slight red gleam shimmered about the longsword in his hand.

"Are there any more of them?" the knight asked Arudal gruffly.

"I thinke not, but leave me a small time." Arudal breathed out slowly, letting the Shadow come over him again. The dark spirit in his own soul, a shadow within the crystal of adamant set in black marble...farther out, the clear running water that ached against him like the slice of a silver knife...He stretched his senses away from the clearing as far as they would go, but found nothing. It was harder, this time, to push the Shadow-Realm back: at last he had to stare at Dame Karsil, at the colour of the Elf's green eyes shocking against the black and gray of the shade-world, and let her brightness pull him back like an anchor-chain tugging at a current-swung ship until the night faded into day-fog about him.

"No, there are no more." Arudal moved to sheathe his falchion, but Sir Thoron tapped it sharply with his own sword.

"Keep that out! There may be living beings coming behind them - and what, in Utalkath's name, happened to the third one? Did you see it go, or were you too frozen with fear?...Ah, the Abyss, where's Finvar? Did it take him?"

"He ran," Arudal admitted unhappily.

The others were tumbling out of their tents now, weapons drawn. Writing glowed blue-white on Sir Eroth's sword, and shimmers of gold flickered along Lostren's; Sir Shakhor's shone deep blue, and Sir Salarond's green-black blade seemed to draw in all the light around it. "Vampires!" Sir Thoron roared. "Two down, one missing, and Finvar's fled. Arudal says they're all gone - Salarond, your permission for my squire and I to find Finvar before something eats him?"

"You, Shakhor, and Rhys," Sir Salarond answered tightly. "Arudal stays here. Go."

Sir Shakhor glanced at the ground, then motioned to the other two, moving along in a light bouncy cat-trot. The rest of those who had been sleeping strapped on helms and shields quickly - Arudal noticed that they had been sleeping in chainmail. "Form into a circle - you in the middle, Arudal. Keep looking; the missing vampire can't be too far."

"It is ygone, sir," Arudal said. "I maye swearen that we shallen not of it more trouble getten, and there are no more Undead within a mile's half of here." Half a mile, he reminded himself in annoyance. Just because Common is a degenerate parody of what it once was is no reason to forget that it has its own grammatical rules now.

"And where did it go?" asked Sir Salarond.

"All is it ygone, sir, and ne shall it been back to stirren us, for it did not asterten. Ye mayen thereof full sikker been." In spite of his best efforts, Arudal could tell that his accent was getting thicker as he spoke, words from Middle Common slipping in to replace the modern ones, and he ground his teeth in frustration.

"For Amanvon's sake, Arudal, speak Imperial if you've forgotten Common," Sir Salarond said in Arudal's own tongue, which he spoke with only a little accent. "Now tell me what happened."

"I felt the three vampires coming in, sir, and I shouted. Squire Finvar drew his sword and tried to stand, but he was overcome by the Shadow-fear, and fled even as Sir Thoron ran out to protect us. Dame Karsil shot one, and Sir Thoron stabbed the other. The third one - I dealt with it."

The visor of Sir Salarond's coronet-ringed helm hid most of his expression, but Arudal could see his eyes widen through its slit. "I had thought that most magic was of little use against beings of Shadow."

"Some is, and some is not, sir," Arudal said diplomatically. "It is important for an agathudal to be able to protect himself."

Sir Salarond nodded, the gilded oak-leaves of his helm's coronet gleaming dully with his movement. "That is well-done, squire, and I believe we must owe Amandeth a gift of thanks for bringing you to us - not to mention a bottle of the best brandy to Dr. Grímhjálm. Were you able to tell how powerful they were, or whether or not there was another will controlling them?... though I do not believe for a moment that this happened by chance, or that vampires roam by day of their own choice."

"They were stronger than ordinary vampires, though by no means equal to, say, even the least of the Captains of Martag: I would guess them to be Ukuthrim of approximately the seventh rank. And they were sent for us."

"Well, well," Sir Salarond murmured, shaking his head. "I suppose your magic wouldn't extend to telling us by whom they were sent?"

Arudal thought a moment. He had the vampire he had captured; he could probe its mind at his leisure...but to do that without revealing all of what he was himself...

"Although I am no Seer," he said diffidently, "it may be that, given quiet and a little time, I could divine something without the risk of betraying us to anyone who might still be watching."

"Then you shall begin as soon as Finvar has been recovered...ah, there they are."

Arudal followed the direction of the commander's glance, and saw four figures approaching in the mist, the shortest of them held up by another. As they got closer, Arudal could see that Finvar was still gray-faced and shaking, a stain of what might have been vomit darkening his bright breastplate. Sir Salarond went to him at once, whispering something as he pushed up the senior squire's visor and touched his forehead, and Finvar straightened.

"There is no shame in failing before Shadow-terror like that," Sir Thoron said loudly, so that Arudal was sure the knight meant all the others to hear. "Before Utalkath, Finvar, I've fought such things for thirty years, and I was hard put to stand before three of them together. Even your black squire-brother was fear-frozen to the spot."

"Not frozen, Thoron," Sir Salarond said. "Arudal took out the third vampire himself with magic. Still it is true, Finvar, you have nothing to be ashamed of. Keep your shield on and sword by you, but sit down and eat something, and you may have one cup of wine to steady you. Come, now..."

"Huh!" Sir Thoron grunted, leaving Finvar to Sir Salarond's care and stalking over to Arudal. "Fastest spellcasting I've ever...but you smelled them coming, didn't you? Well-done, squire!" He clapped Arudal hard on the back, his gauntlet clashing loudly against the plates covering the Tharandrostan's torso, but Arudal hardly noticed the blow: he was wondering, not wholly easy in his mind, what Sir Thoron had meant by calling him "your black squire-brother".

"Now, Rhys," said Sir Shakhor to his own squire, "Arudal will see to the dead; can you ask your spirits if there are any living creatures of evil nature near to us?"

"Aye, I can do that thing, if someone will guard me down at the river.".

Sir Salarond sighed. "Sir Thoron and Sir Shakhor, I suppose."

Arudal was grateful that his helm hid his face, for he was struggling to control his annoyance at having the Plainsman compared to him, as if the buck were a true-born Seer of Imperial race - though he could not doubt that, if Rhys could be trusted, using his skills was the most sensible thing to do.

"Now, Eroth, Lostren," their commander continued as the two knights escorted the Plainsman away. "Do you think that this attack was meant to slay us, or as a warning, or a test of our strength?"

"That all depends on whether our foe knows about Arudal," Lostren answered at once, showing no hesitation in speaking up before the knight. "Those seconds of warning and Arudal's...spell, won the fight. Otherwise, Dame Karsil should not have had time to draw and aim before they were in among us, and though Sir Thoron can awake on the instant, he cannot snatch up his sword and run from his tent any faster than a man may. Either it was a real attack spoilt by our good chance that it happened on Arudal's watch, or else we are being watched at least hourly and it was meant to fail - perhaps in order to unnerve us or change our plans in some way. I think we are certainly being watched in some way, for anyone using vampires would order them to attack at night, if there were not so much more advantage to catching us sleeping by day: in the normal course of things, we should all be riding and armoured now. Though that does not, of course, rule out the possibility that whoever sent the vampires, even if he were watching, would have seen only a vulnerable moment with two squires on guard. And if that is the case, then the attack was probably meant to succeed, or at least to weaken us severely."

"I must concur," Sir Eroth nodded. "I should advise against changing our plans. That will do us little good if we are under such a close watch, and if we sleep by day and ride by night, we will be better able to meet any other creatures of Shadow that are sent against us."

Sir Salarond turned to Arudal again. "Wait, I almost forgot something of importance. Arudal, will waiting for half an hour or so make your scrying more difficult, as the event fades into the past?"

"No, sir." For time was not passing where the vampire lay trapped within him. "Sir, may I ask a question?" Arudal spoke in Imperial again, for he was not sure that he could phrase the question correctly in Common.

"Of course."

"Why is there no other mage on this mission? My skills are good for my age and training, but I can no more compare myself to the magicians of the White Company than to its fighters, and until last night, you did not know that even I would be with you."

"That is an extremely good question, Arudal. In fact, Sir Eroth also has some skill in magic, though he is best known as a fighter, and Rhys' abilities, though not highly trained, have proven very useful more than once. But the reason why none of the great White Company mages are with us is that, since the Wrath descended on the Western Land, to the best of our knowledge, magic no longer works there. You will remember that, according to Avalar's account, the spells of the Last Emperor's wizards could not touch him, and it was the undoing of the Imperial magics, as much as Avalar's Liberation and the destruction of the heaving land, that allowed the barbarian peoples to whelm the Empire."

As Arudal had learned it, Avalar, in his brief month as successor to the Last Emperor, had decreed the freeing of all the subject peoples and slaves, revoking the laws that held them bound by spells and swords, and their gratitude had been seen by the slaughter of the Imperial race, from which Avalar and a few of his fortunate supporters had escaped to the Middle Land. But since beginning his studies in Var Perenil, Arudal had looked at the Kantarean edition of Avalar's own History of the Fall, and he knew that Sir Salarond was telling the truth as he knew it.

"So I must rely on my sword and my sight when we reach the shores of the West?"

"Just so. Mind-magic is a blessing of birth, but true magic draws on the essence of the gods that they pour into the green earth - and from what little we know, that essence was withdrawn from the West when the Wrath fell, save only for that gift that was granted to Avalar himself. Hence a mage who is not a skilled fighter as well would be a burden upon us when we reach the Western continent, and helpless when it came to fighting, a danger to the rest if we had to protect him. I do not know if I will be granted the power of healing-prayers while we are there. One of the chief reasons I am coming along is that I am well-skilled in healing with knife and herb and stitch as well as through the grace of the gods."

Arudal swallowed. Here, Sir Salarond could heal the most frightful wounds - his companions could be gutted, blinded, and limb-lopped, but the healer-priest could make them whole again. There, with no recourse better than that of condemned mine-slaves to their veterinarian...even a scratch could kill with the fever...He shuddered, wishing heartily for a moment that he had not sworn himself as Sir Thoron's squire and could still back out of the expedition.

At last the two knights escorted Rhys back. The Plainsman had taken off his helm, his sweat-darkened red hair tumbling down his back in tangled curls, and his broad freckled face was pale under a sheen of sweat. "Report," Sir Salarond ordered.

"Sir, there are no living foes within three miles. But the land-gods here are distressed that we fare with a companion of Shadow, for they much mislike those who draw any part of that evil realm onto the green earth. So long as he holds the blood-drinker by him, they will not look with friendship upon us, though I have told them that the rest of us have no part in his necromancy." It seemed to Arudal that, although Rhys was trying hard to keep his face straight, his round startled eyes gave away everything the Plainsman felt, and Arudal could see the spoor of a smile etched on the buck's mobile lips. Arudal's heart knotted with anger.

"Explain yourself, squire!" Sir Shakhor told Rhys sharply. "We are still in a tactical situation, and this is no time for trouble among our own."

Rhys braced himself, his mouth tightening. "The land-spirits dislike Arudal because of the Shadow-taint on his soul. While he is with us, we shall have little luck from them, and there is nothing I may do about that, whatever my own thoughts may be. And Arudal did not destroy the vampire, but holds it trapped in his own power, and if he says otherwise, he is lying."

In the silence that followed, Arudal realized that everyone was staring at him. "Squire," said Sir Thoron, "I think it is your turn to explain yourself."

Arudal swallowed dry-throated. The world was darkening around him again, the swords of his companions - still unsheathed - shining more and more brightly before their shadowed shapes. The glowing traceries of gold on Lostren's helmet ached against Arudal's eyes; one of Dame Karsil's white-burning arrows rested in her bow, nocked and ready for drawing, and the Elf's green gaze seared from her pale face like a steady flame of copper-salts. Save for Sir Karsil's silent fury, Arudal could no longer see the expressions on the faces of the men around him; they had faded to dark shades against the blackness. A great enough fear, or anger, will make your talent flare, his grandmother Zinadir had told him. Be sure it never happens when you need to see where you're going - you're not a ghost yet, so you can't walk through walls!

"Please," he said softly to Sir Salarond in Imperial. "I am charged not to speak of this, but I give you my word that no ill to our mission shall come of it, and some good may."

"Agathurok," Lostren said to his knight, his accent impeccable: Shadow-fortress, the word used for those of Arudal's House who could catch the souls of the dead, or Undead, within themselves. "And...inmudalan agathusaftan." Mind-gifted necromancer. "Sir, I think it were better if we spoke to Arudal with but ourselves and perhaps Sir Eroth present."

"Such an amulet is a dangerous thing to have, though it may prove very useful," Sir Salarond said in Common. "Arudal, Eroth, come into our tent with us: I think we must examine it straight away. The rest of you, keep a good guard, and be ready to rush in if you are called for. Rhys..." The commander spoke in Plainsman for a few moments. Rhys replied unhappily, and Sir Shakhor said a few sharp words to him in the same tongue, whereupon his squire nodded and kissed the fair-haired knight full on the mouth - the salute of an obedient child to its father, or clansman to its chief, a noisy Plainsman custom that Arudal had always thought particularly unhygenic and disgusting.

"Arudal, put your sword away and come with us now," Sir Salarond ordered.

Arudal followed as best he could, trying not to shuffle too obviously until his foot caught in a guy-rope. He twisted in midair to keep his shield out from under him as he fell, bouncing off the palm of his right hand and back to his feet, but the motion yanked the rope too hard and Arudal heard the unmistakable sound of a canvas-wrapped pole sighing messily towards earth. Swords flared in his vision: the others were walking steadily towards him.

They think I was trying to escape...they're going to kill me now! he wailed to himself. Amandeth, how did this happen? To his own humiliated horror, a snuffle escaped Arudal's throat and he could feel the prickling wetness of tears spilling over his eyelids. Deliberately he put his hands behind his back, bracing himself against his shaking limbs: if he could not control his eyes, at least he could stand like a man while his comrades slew him.

To his surprise - the last thing he expected - he felt a strong, wiry arm going around his waist to hold him up, and heard Sir Salarond's faintly accented Imperial. "Arudal, is there something else coming?"

Arudal shook his head.

"Was this your first fight?"

"Yes, sir," Arudal choked.

"Can you see at all?"

Arudal shook his head. Sir Salarond guided him gently around something, nudging him to lower himself and crawl into a tent; the knight's deft fingers unstrapped his helmet, shield, and coat of plates.. "Lie down here. Lostren, mix a cup of cordial...twelve drops of lavender, twelve of chammomile, and three of sunwort. Arudal, breathe deeply and try to relax." The healer pulled what felt like a heavy blanket up over Arudal, but the squire could not stop shivering: he suddenly felt as though he had been struggling through the sea in Icemonth and pulled out into freezing air. "This is nothing to be ashamed of. After-battle shock happens to many men, especially after combat with the Undead, and it is worse for those who have fought with mind-magic. Eroth, do you know if he could have been harmed by taking the vampire into himself?"

"I do not know," the knight answered. "The soul-storing talent is so rare - I have only heard it rumoured once or twice, and never seen it."

Arudal tried to struggle up onto one elbow, but Sir Salarond pushed him back gently. One hand went behind his head to support it; the smooth metal rim of a cup touched his lips, and the powerful fumes of strong spirits scorched his nostrils. "Drink this now, Arudal," ordered the healer. Obediently Arudal drank, trying not to cough. Beneath the searing alcohol, the cordial tasted clean and faintly bitter; its heat ran down his throat, spreading slowly out from his belly, and he felt it gradually unlocking his shaking limbs.

When Arudal could speak, though his teeth were still chattering, he said, "I am in no danger from what I have done. I took it without harm, and it is...dormant inside me." He could not explain the stillness within him where no time passed, but his answer seemed to satisfy Sir Salarond.

"Well enough. And there is no risk of it breaking free?"

"None. I can cast it out to the Abyss or where-ever it should fare beyond both Shadow and the green earth, or force it to my commands."

"When you have recovered yourself, will you be able to make it answer questions?" Sir Eroth enquired. "And do you have to bring it out to do that?"

Still dazed and shivering a little, Arudal clung to his memory of what he had been told before he got on the boat for Kantar. "Please, sir, if you leave me alone, I can find out what we need to know of it."

"Arudal," Sir Salarond said gently, "we know now what you were commanded to keep secret, and it was not your fault that it was revealed. But you know that this is not the best thing to make clear to everyone in this party, let alone elsewhere, and we cannot help you to either hide or use your talents unless we know more of how they work...and someday that knowledge may save the lives of more than one of us, yourself included. I will swear an oath of secrecy, by Aviyani who guides my hands in healing, and so, I think, will both my squire and Sir Eroth."

Arudal was afraid that he would start crying again. He clenched his shaking hands tight and mumbled, "Swear."

Sir Salarond gave his oath, followed by Sir Eroth who swore by Avradi and Lostren who swore by Amanvon. "Now you are safe," the Kantarean commander said. "Tell me, Arudal, what exactly can you do, and what dangers does it put you in?"

"I can see the Ukuthrim, and sense them within half a mile, unless they are somehow concealed from me - and they can see and sense me, and touch me as if they were bodied. I can put out some of my own bodily substance for spirits to use, but I must be careful with that: too much, and I will pass out, and if I do not stop then, I could die. I have the full Mindspeaking complex, but not with the living, only with the Ukuthrim - speaking and reading thoughts, mind-probing and controlling: that is the gift of the inmudalan agathusaftan. And I can store souls - when they are just leaving the body, or if they are creatures of Shadow with little or no earthly substance. The only danger is that, if I take in too many or keep them too long, they will press against the walls of my mind and disorder my thoughts so that I cannot concentrate...it is like having a desperately full bladder. Because I am quiet-minded, it is more difficult for Mindspeakers to speak with me or hear me, and because I am an agathurok, it is uncomfortable as well as difficult for others to touch my mind in thought. And when I am using any of my talents, my sight is altogether of the Shadow-World, and I cannot...cannot see where I am going." The tears of fear and frustration and humiliation bit at Arudal's eyes again, and this time he could not keep them back. Sir Salarond held the Tharandrostan's head until he had finished, as if he were vomiting instead of weeping. There was one more thing Arudal knew about himself - but that he would not tell them: if they knew, they would order him to stay behind, and his secrets would have been spilled to no gain.

"How many is too many?" Sir Eroth asked. "And how long is too long?"

"I can take in up to ten spirits, but so many are uncomfortable. Undead, I can hold as long as I need, for their minds are silent. I have never taken a new-slain soul, but I am told that the length of time I can bear them depends on - how easily they fit."

The quiet knight breathed out slowly. "So you could hold this vampire, say, for three months - and then bring it out as a weapon under your command?"

"Yes. And..." The words shivered on Arudal's tongue, but he forced them out anyway. "I can call spirits from the Shadow-World. And if I desired to make an Undead, I could summon a spirit and force it into the form I wanted...or do the same with a soul in my storage."

"No wonder you are so reluctant to speak of your talents," Lostren breathed. "And that explains, as well...when you stare at me, I feel as though something is tugging at my soul, and it is very unnerving."

"That is because I am an agathurok," Arudal confessed. "It is...for one who knows, it is unmistakable."

Sir Salarond patted his shoulder. "We are beyond fortunate to have you with us," the healer said warmly. "There is a small matter we must deal with as quickly as possible for legality's sake - Lostren, I need the materials for a scroll."

"What is it?" Arudal asked in alarm.

"It is illegal in Kantar for anyone to keep Undead or practice any form of necromancy without a judge's warrant, and I cannot in conscience allow the breaking of the law in my command, so I am about to give you one." Pen scratched on parchment; Sir Salarond read aloud slowly as he wrote. "'I, Sir Salarond Bertilak, Earl dath Amerel, doctor of law and sitting judge of the Royal Commission of the White Throne, having been satisfied that due cause exists and the relevant security regulations satisfied, do hereby certify that Count Arudal Arumirun of the House of Arudal is warranted for the private possession of Undead and the practice of such activities relating thereto as are neither treasonous nor unreasonably dangerous to the innocent, within the borders of Kantar for peaceful and legal purposes. Given this fifteenth day of Sunmonth, Sixth Millennium 686; witnessed by Lord Lostren Telagon of Dan Iragal and Sir Eroth Ginfor of Bron Merathol.' There." Arudal heard the heavy dripping of sealing wax and the rustle of a ribbon. "Now, Lostren, I have a question for you. You are learning both healing and command. We have a patient here who is in a bad state, but who is capable, perhaps at great cost to himself, of gaining information which will aid in determining our strategy for both the long and the very immediate short term. Is he to be ordered to do that now, or do we let him sleep for a few hours - during which, for lack of that information, we and hence our mission may be in grave danger?"

Lostren made an unhappy noise. "For a healer, the patient comes first. But for a commander, it is the mission first and the soldiers second."

"Choose quickly, Lostren: there is no time to waste."

"Um. Arudal, are you able to question your captive now, and how much risk will that put you at, aside from general strain? And how much risk will there be to the rest of us?"

Arudal looked at the adamantine crystal within himself where the shadow lay silent. At last he said, "I am. There is little risk to me, and none to you."

"He should do it," Lostren answered at once, then paused. "Um, is that right, sir?"

"Are you willing to take the responsibility of giving that order?"

"Uh...Yes, sir."

"Lostren, you may take command. Relieve me."

"I relieve you, sir."

"I stand relieved," Sir Salarond answered. Metal clinked, as if the two were shaking hands.

There was a brief silence, and then Lostren said, "Arudal, interrogate your prisoner. Sir Salarond, will you relieve me?"

"You have command, Lostren."

"Is it your recommendation that you relieve me now, sir?"

"I should prefer to wait until Arudal's interrogation is finished."

"So be it. Arudal, what do you require?"

"Only quiet."

"As you wish. Sir Eroth, stand on guard; Sir Salarond, stand by for medical assistance at need, and maintain silence. Arudal, you may begin at will."

Arudal breathed deeply. He could see nothing now but the glittering adamant walls - then the vampire's thin face, mottled white like frost-patterns on crystal with the needle-tips of its teeth glinting beneath its ice-blue lips. Yet he could feel the kinship in its mind, a deep resonance beneath the core of his bones; and he reached within to its thoughts, peeling them back layer by layer as if they were his own. The Shadow-hate of the living, who saw sunlight golden upon the green earth, fueled by distant memories of the days when it - no, she, my name is Eluthia - was human, had suckled at her breast a babe that cried and coughed and grew cold and stiff; the wandering, drifting, in the frozen lands of black and gray, and the keen chill ache of hunger tearing her body like a silver wire tightening through her flesh, relieved only by the sweet-salt scent of the living and the blood and life-strength rushing into her like strong spirits, filling her with a heady power...a goddess for a few moments, until she, Eluthia, spilt it in a single great effort or hoarded it to dwindle slowly in the uncountable time of the Shadow-world where there was neither day nor night nor passing hours, but only a single stretched moment...A deep voice calling, not her name, Eluthia, but a summons that she, Eluthia, could not withstand, and she had gone, shackled by the magic that she, Eluthia, had no flesh to resist. The mage's face, living upon the green earth, was no more than an empty black hood in her sight, but he was taller than herself.

A silver sigil-ring set with a single black star sapphire burned purple on his finger and glacier-flames of blue and green writhed like snakes over his black robes. He named the names of those that she, Eluthia, was to slay: "Salarond and Lostren, Thoron and Finvar, Eroth and Tirothar, Shakhor and Rhys, Karsil the Elf, and anyone else who may travel with them" - and by some magic he showed her, not the faces that she could not see, but their shadow-shapes and scents. Then he sent her out into the blinding black day, over a great white wall that shone with painful brightness below her - yet not too long or far, Morthugor's shrieking mercy, for the sunlight had not drained her enough for hunger to paralyze her - sent with two strangers that she, Eluthia, hated as a wildcat hates the game-stealing eagle, but bound not to harm them, their voices scratching a glass-on-glass half-harmony with hers; and she scented the familiar spoor...and there was the broad shadow Finvar, his blood rushing sweet in his veins and sweeter still with the wave of terror. But beside him, though she smelled the thin living blood of an Imperial Man, it must be a ghost or wraith that she saw clear as any being of Shadow: short as a youth on the brink of adolescence, square-bodied in shapeless armour - small glittering gauntlet grasping a falchion-hilt, adamantine helm gleaming dully, and the brilliant gold-and-steel flare of slanted eyes that grew brighter and brighter, even as the strong deep voice rang all through her being, COME HERE. And though she struggled towards the rich salty flesh of the Man who had just cut down one of her comrade-foes, the summons wrenched her from the mage-shackles that bound her and drew her deep, deep, to stillness and peace, like the rest she, Eluthia, could not find in her Shadow-death...

Arudal blinked in the darkness, staring at the burning gold traceries of Lostren's helm. Quickly, before he could forget, he told them what he had learned: he described the sigil-ring, and how the mage had given the identities of all in the party save himself, adding in only, anyone else who may travel with them. "And he is not so far from here, or relatively not, as vampires of such power fly fast. The Ukuthrim have no sense of time, but I think they were not out much more than half an hour, since much longer would have drained her of all her hoarded life-strength, and...wait. Eluthia saw a white wall below her: that must have been the wall of one of the great cities, and magicked, or it would have been Shadow-lost to her sight."

"The Undead cannot cross into or out of Var Ineth," Sir Salarond mused. "So our foe is either in Var Perenil or Agilath - but I would guess Var Perenil. If he were watching us by simple means, he would have known we were up at night and left well before dawn, and must perforce stop to sleep."

"I think he must have gotten the information from one of the gate-guards," said Lostren. "A necromancer of that much power couldn't fail to have heard of the House of Arudal, and if he were watching all along, he would have had an image of you to give the vampires."

"Maybe," murmured Sir Eroth dubiously. "Not everyone pays as much attention to history as you do, Lostren. But you are right: he could have shown them Arudal. Unless you are warded against magical scrying, Arudal?"

"No."

"How long does it take to summon a vampire?" Sir Salarond asked Arudal.

"If I were to do it, it would depend on where the closest to me was - and not on the green earth, but in the Shadow-Realm. It is hard to explain, but space is different there: there could be a host of Ukuthrim here beside us, and yet they cannot touch the green earth until a way is opened, so that they cannot, for instance, drain our life-force...or disturb Rhys' little spirits," Arudal added, too tired to keep the edge of malice sheathed in his voice. "Or set terror on us; the Shadow-Fear comes from the warping of the two worlds when the Ukruthim manifest on the green earth. Close enough, and for me it would be a matter of but a few minutes; far enough away, and I could be searching for two or three nights. But he was using a ritual, and that calls for at least four hours for each one, nor can even the strongest mage do such a thing without resting between-times." As if to underscore his words, Arudal found his jaws cracking in a great yawn.

"My patient," Sir Salarond said pointedly, "also desperately needs to rest. If there are no more urgent questions, Lostren - and I have none - then it is my recommendation that we end this and that you be relieved."

"Relieve me, Sir Salarond."

"I relieve you, Lostren."

"I stand relieved." As the knight and his squire shook hands, the metal of their vambraces above Arudal's face swam slowly back into focus, the coal-glowing goldwork on Lostren's helm dimming.

"Sleep, Arudal," Sir Salarond commanded. "I believe we have a few hours of safety here, and you must rest now."

Arudal tried to lift his head, but found that his skull was as heavy as if he still wore helm and coif. Sir Salarond's forefinger touched his forehead, and he melted into boneless sleep.

Chapter 4: The Ducal Arms

(Garukhon) "Cousins we are, but brothers never,
Allies, but seldom friends.
We cannot forget what you tossed away,
Nor you forgive what we hold -
We cannot forgive your bastard might,
Nor you forget what we are."

(Almeth) "Truth and trust are not one word,
And, truth, they should not be.
Common folk fear; the wise are wary -
But I hold no grudges for the past:
I doubt what you are now."

- "Garukhon and Almeth", Act I, scene ii

"**A**rudal," a voice called softly in his ear. "Arudal, wake up." Arudal blinked, turning his face to his sweat-damp pillow. He had dreamed strangely in the heat...he had a luncheon appointment with Dr. Grímhjálm...A hand shook his shoulder. "Arudal, wake up!"

Arudal opened his eyes, looking up. At the sight of Lostren's sharp face within the open helm-visor, the memories flooded back with staggering clarity, roaring through his veins as though he had just drunk a thick cup of double black-roast tea. Arudal sat up at once - someone had taken his armour off as he lay unconscious, but his tunic was still sodden with sweat, the tail of his hair half-undone in a ragged mess. He wanted a cup of chilled mint tea, and a cinnamon pastry and a cool bath, he thought; it seemed as though he could still taste the garlic sausage from breakfast stale in his mouth.

"It's noon, and we must be going now," Lostren said. "Plans have changed a little. Come on, my fellow squire, we have packing to do and horses to saddle."

Arudal dragged himself out of bed, unwillingly buckling the stinking-wet gambeson around himself again and putting on the rest of his armour, though he left his helm off - it was too hot, and he hardly needed it in camp. But when he stepped out of the tent, something hard slapped him painfully on the side of the head. He cried out in shock, looking up to see that Sir Thoron had come up behind him.

"That wouldn't have hurt if you'd had your helm on," his knight said sharply. "If you need to protect your body, you need to protect your head: even Sir Salarond can't do anything for you if your brains are splattered. Get moving, squire!"

Arudal fumbled his helm on, biting his lip. His head would be bruised where Sir Thoron had hit it - had he not done enough to deserve better treatment? But the others in the party were all helmed, as though they expected an attack at any moment, and Arudal had to admit that they should know what was needed.

Finvar helped him take the tent down and saddle up the horses. It went quickly enough with two, though the senior squire hardly spoke as they worked, averting his eyes whenever Arudal looked at him - still ashamed that he had run from the vampires, Arudal guessed. He wanted to say something that would reassure Finvar, but could think of nothing that would not make things worse. Finally, though, the Artegalian blurted out, "Where did you get your amulet?"

"My...oh," Arudal said, remembering how Sir Salarond had covered up Rhys' accusation. "It is...a family inheritance."

"I might have guessed," Finvar muttered gloomily, tightening his packhorse's girth with a sharp tug.

Arudal cast about for a way to change the subject, and at last said, "Lostren said something about a changing of our plans. What is this?"

"One of the White Company mages contacted Sir Salarond about half an hour ago. We're supposed to go straight on to the Ducal Arms tonight. At least we'll be sleeping in decent beds, if no one tries to murder us in them."

Camp struck, their party mounted up. Arudal had one foot in Inmanat's stirrup and was about to swing himself up on the dark gelding's back when Sir Thoron's gauntlet rang off his helm. "Squire, I want you to ride Black Rage now," the knight ordered. "There might be trouble on the road, and I guess your pretty little palfrey will run like a scorch-tailed cat if any fighting starts."

Arudal disconsolately patted Inmanat's neck and crept up on the big warhorse. Black Rage snaked his neck around to glare at the squire. "Hsh, hsh," Arudal said, taking his reins without any great conviction. He had to raise his knee to chin-height in order to get one foot in the stirrup; gathering himself to spring, he misjudged the distance, and found himself scrabbling to climb up over the saddle as the warhorse sidestepped and whuffled his nostrils. Though Arudal was very long in the legs for his height, the stirrups seemed far too long for him. The cavalry saddle was much deeper than he was used to, cantle and pommel raised to brace the rider against the shock of a lance hitting, and, supple as he was, he found it hard to bend around his saddle to shorten the stirrups.

"Not like that," Finvar said, nudging his horse up to Arudal. "I measured while you were asleep: those are the right length for you. You're supposed to brace your feet straight-legged so you can keep your weight all the way down in the saddle and have something to push against when you strike - either lance or sword, the impact will still rock you."

Dubiously Arudal tried to do as the other squire had said. As his weight shifted, Black Rage reared, striking out with his hooves, and Finvar only just wheeled his own warhorse out of the way in time.

"Steady, boy, steady," Arudal crooned shakily, loosening the reins and shifting his weight again in the saddle. Black Rage dropped his front hooves, and Arudal settled deep and straight-backed, hoping that the horse had been trained to something like the Tharandrostan body-commands.

Setting out on the road, Arudal rode between the other squires. Sir Thoron had given him a shield of plain brown sand-drake hide, so his arms would not be recognisable, and, while he was asleep, Tirothar had managed to fashion a sort of light hood out of one of his own arming caps to cover up the glitter of the adamantine helm which marked Arudal's nationality and high birth unmistakably. As soon as the horses had walked themselves warm, Sir Salarond called for a trot - a brutally painful gait with the high cavalry saddles, in which Arudal could not rise with the horse's movement as Tharandrostan-style riding usually called for - then a canter. Black Rage's canter was wide, strong, and rather rough, a long way from Inmanat's smooth light-footed gait; the saddle had been made for a heavier man than Arudal, and slapped against his tailbone with every step. But nevertheless, the young squire found himself enjoying the power of the huge horse beneath him, like riding the autumn waves in a small boat. Lostren had advised him well: if Black Rage was high-strung for a Kantarean horse, Arudal found him superbly responsive, and far less easily frightened by leaves and shadows than Inmanat.

Arudal's sight was just beginning to clear in the darkening twilight as they came up to the Ducal Arms. He had stayed there on his way into Var Perenil the autumn before, and was looking forward to that night: a soft bed - his four hours of sleep had not been nearly enough - a bath, his sodden gambeson and horse-stinking leather breeches clean, and a good meal. To his relief, the innservants took the bags and reins of the horses from the squires' hands, leaving them to troop in through the common room after their knights.

As Arudal had remembered, the rooms in the Ducal Arms were spacious and well-furnished: large chairs and tables of polished oak, thick soft beds with carven headboards, and wide windows set with diamond-leaded glass. Their fireplace was huge; though only a small fire burned there in the summer heat, he remembered how warmly the inn's great logs had blazed in the coolness of Leafturn. A wooden bath was already filled by the foot of the bed, and Arudal cast a longing gaze at the clear water before he bent to help Finvar take Sir Thoron's armour off, glad that his helm hid the way his nose was wrinkling at the stench - not, the Tharandrostan reminded himself, that he smelled any better himself.

Sir Thoron sighed as he shed his gambeson, stretching out his heavy arms and twisting his body this way and that until the little bones of his back crackled. "Ah, better," he said, stripping off his sweat-darkened tunic and trousers and sinking down into the bath. Only a couple of scars marked his muscular torso: most of the knight's fighting had been with elite groups such as the Red Knights and the White Company, and such units had healers to match the dangers against which they were sent. Arudal and Finvar helped each other out of their armour, wiping each piece down neatly and setting them out along the floor. They had little more cleaning to do, for Valderian steel did not rust, but they had to check each of the straps on Sir Thoron's harness and their own, as well as the rivets holding Arudal's body-plates to their scuffed leather covering - always the weakest pieces: the dwarf-forged steel seldom gave way under any stress, but leather must twist and move, and, eventually, wear through. And the rivets were made of lesser steel so that they could easily be knocked out when the straps needed replacing; they, too, would give way in time.

A knock sounded on the door. Arudal, remembering that he was the junior squire, rose to answer, but Finvar motioned him down, shaking his head and laying a finger to his lips before going to the door. It was only the servant with their luggage, however. Finvar took the bags from him, and in turn handed over their filthy clothes and gambesons to be washed.

By the time it was Arudal's turn for the bath, the water was cool and not half so clean as it had been, but it was so much better than standing in his own stink that he could only be desperately grateful. He did not linger in the tub, for he could smell the savoury scents of food slowly filtering up from the kitchen. Finvar was already dressed, wearing heavy black hose beneath a doublet of gold and green brocade and a green surcoat with what Arudal assumed were the arms of Helludal - a Stone Troll's head proper, erased, within a wreath of barley, or. As well I brought one set of proper clothes, Arudal thought, but when he began to dress himself, Sir Thoron growled, "Don't you have any decent clothes that aren't so...so Tharandrostan?"

"Um...I do not think so, sir."

Sir Thoron looked down his arched nose at Arudal, then at Finvar. "I'm going on down for supper. Finvar, your clothes'll probably fit him like a tent, but try to find something. I do want you to wear your swords tonight," he added, belting his own on.

Finvar shrugged his thick shoulders as their knight left. "Let's see what we can do for you." He brought out a pair of peacock-blue hose - Arudal flinched at the brightness, but obediently tried them on. They were the right length of leg, but bagged on him like trousers, while Finvar's doublet fit him comfortably in the shoulders and belled out like a sail below his chest. Finally Finvar said in exasperation, "Come on, Lostren's closer to your size," and led Arudal over to Sir Salarond's suite.

Lostren, already tidily dressed in white hose and a white silken tabard marked with three black crescents in a triangle around a blue crescent, with a golden circlet on his dark brown hair, was just settling Sir Salarond's fur-edged cope evenly over the knight's shoulders. He took one look at Arudal and burst out laughing. Arudal drew himself up to his full height and glared until the commander's squire managed to calm himself.

"Sorry," Lostren said. "But if you could only see yourself - you look like a boy wearing his father's clothes for Yearturn Eve. I suppose you want to borrow something to wear to dinner?"

"Perhaps it would be better if I stayed in our rooms," Arudal answered stiffly, looking at Sir Salarond in hopes that the Kantarean commander would agree with him. But Sir Salarond shook his head, the oak-leaves of his coronet flashing.

"I would rather not have you seen, true enough. However, after this morning, I have no intention of leaving you alone longer than I can help. Especially not here, for there have been rumours of hauntings in this place since it burned down and was rebuilt a few years ago." He took the ivory comb from his squire's hand, sleeking a few gray-streaked strands of black hair back into place. "Go on and dress him, Lostren. I can manage well enough by myself from here."

Lostren rummaged through his packs, murmuring under his breath. At last he found a pair of deep crimson hose and a matching velvet doublet. The hose were a little short in the leg, and the doublet was worryingly tight across Arudal's back. He had hoped that, as he was shorter in the torso than Sir Salarond's squire, Lostren's doublet would fall low enough for decency, but the thickness of Arudal's shoulders and chest pulled it up so that the hem rode as it was made to, just above his crotch in front and the curve of his buttocks in back. "You're not nearly as skinny as I thought you were," Finvar commented idly. "You ought to wear fitted clothes more often."

Looking in the mirror the other squire held for him, Arudal found himself blushing at the immodest way his comrade's garb displayed him, the doublet cut to show off the taper from his muscular upper body to his trim hips and the hose clinging tightly to his rump and legs as if he were one of the young aristocrats lounging about the streets of Var Perenil - or one of their pretty-boys. Arudal's falchion, a heavy war-blade, looked out of place at his side, as did his triple-dagger: though their sheaths were black leather ornamented with silver and black-pearl mounts, clothes like this were meant to be worn with the slender rapier and main-gauche of the duellist. The red leather squire's belt Sir Thoron had given him fit with neither the weapons nor the clothes: it was scarred and scuffed, as though its last bearer had worn it hard.

"Damn," Lostren complained mildly, "you look better in my clothes than I do." Then he turned to Finvar and murmured something in his ear. Being short-sighted, Arudal was also keen of hearing, so that he heard every word clearly, "There goes any chance I had of getting laid tonight." The pointed tips of Arudal's ears burned painfully, and he had to control himself to keep from covering his crotch with his hands.

"Do you have a light cape that I might borrow?" Arudal asked.

"Not in this heat, surely? Besides, you do look very well. Comb your hair a bit, and then we'll go down to dinner."

Reluctantly, Arudal took the offered gold comb and tugged it through the soft black tangles about his shoulders. It seemed to him that there was little point in dressing as though he had just come from a fashionable tailor in Var Perenil when his looks betrayed his origins so clearly. As well as being shorter and lighter of bone than their blood-mixed cousins in Kantar, Tharandrostans were markedly finer-featured: the sharp arches of Arudal's black eyebrows and high cheekbones and the delicate line of his jaw were unmistakable. He combed his hair carefully over the small peaks of his ear-tips - the legacy of distant Elvish blood in the Imperial race, brought out in Arudal's line by generations of inbreeding, but sure to draw notice, for it was rare in these days for Elves to mate with Men. When Arudal gave Lostren's comb back, Salarond's squire grabbed his hand and turned his signet ring inwards to hide its sigil. "Much better, my friend. Come on."

The three squires made their way down the spiral staircase of polished oak to the common room. Arudal's stomach twisted with hunger and his mouth began to water; the savoury scents of meat and fruit pies almost made him forget how indecently he was dressed - and no one here will know who I am. The great doors were thrown open, a breath of evening air wafting in to cool the diners; outside, the last streaks of pale blue twilight still softened the glitter of Amanvon's Taper, the first star that kindled the others every night. Crystal and gold gleamed on the white tablecloths, warm in the flickering candlelight, and deep red and golden wines glowed like rubies and topazes in their pitchers and goblets. The squires took their places beside their knights, Finvar at Sir Thoron's right hand and Arudal at his left. Arudal was not pleased to see that he was seated next to Rhys, but the Plainsman buck - whose carroty hair clashed horribly with the tabard of Sir Shakhor's household, a gold stag's head on a red field - pointedly ignored him, turning his head to the side as if Arudal were simply not there.

Although Kantarean food was usually too highly spiced for Arudal's taste, the Ducal Arms set an excellent table: venison in a sweet blueberry sauce, roast suckling pig rubbed with thyme and sprinkled lightly with rose pepper, the last of the summer asparagus in a cream sauce sharpened with Ineth cheese and a touch of citron...Arudal ate with a good appetite, though he watered the heavy red Perenilian wine to half its strength. The cool summers of his homeland produced less powerful vintages, and in his first month in Var Perenil, he had found that he had neither the weight nor the head to drink like a Kantarean.

The dinner plates had been cleared away and stacks of blueberry and wild-strawberry tarts brought about, together with small glasses of very sweet dessert wine from Carthogan - "A Finist River vineyard, Sun-Runner grapes, and at least twenty years old, I should say," Lostren, across the table from Arudal, commented knowledgeably. "The slight citron-grass and rose-petal undertaste is unmistakable."

Arudal was about to reply when he saw that a stranger in a full suit of fluted Valderian plate was approaching their table, his helm tucked under his arm and a satchel in his hand. Sir Salarond turned his head, nodding. "Do join us, Sir Asdrek. Have you eaten?"

"Time is of the utmost urgency, alas," the knight replied. Deep lines graved either side of his mouth, and heavy thought-lines creased his broad forehead; his heavy-lidded eyes were dark in the candlelight, and his fine black hair was receding along the temples - more the face of a clerk than of a warrior, though he moved easily and swiftly in the heavy plate-armour. "Shall we go to your rooms?"

Sir Salarond rose, gesturing to the rest of the party. Arudal cast a longing glance backwards at the tarts in time to see Finvar swiping a couple of them, chewing hastily as he followed Sir Thoron towards the staircase; it was only with effort that he remembered his dignity enough not to follow the senior squire's example.

When they were all inside Sir Salarond's suite, Sir Asdrek brought a small crystal sphere out of his belt-pouch, rubbing his thumb over it and murmuring a few words. For a moment, the crystal glowed blue; then the brightness winked out again - a charm against scrying, Arudal guessed.

"What word do you bring from Sir Ultar?" Sir Salarond asked bluntly. "Has there been a change of plan?"

"Instead of going on to Agilath in the morning, you need to ride tonight. We have arranged a ship to meet you twenty miles upriver from the city and...convinced two Western traders to come along as your guides."

Arudal raised an eyebrow at that: he had always thought that the stories of Western traders coming sometimes to the Middle Land were no more than merchants' lies meant to make their goods sound exotic, but no one else so much as blinked. Sir Asdrek handed his satchel over to their commander. "Here are the papers you need to get you through at Agilath and Felatar. And - Sir Thoron, the Tharandrostan is your squire?"

"So he is."

"Please tell him to leave now."

Sir Thoron shrugged. "Arudal, go get all the gambesons and clothes back from the laundry and make sure all my things are packed and ready to go."

Hurt by the cold dismissal, Arudal found himself asking plaintively, "Am I, too, not on this mission y-going?"

"Not if you don't obey orders, squire!" Sir Thoron roared. "Get moving!"

Arudal left, not daring to look back: he could not bear to see Lostren or Finvar looking sympathetic - or Rhys looking triumphant.

It took him a little while to find the inn's laundry: several times, he saw a servant rounding the corner of the passage who scuttled away as soon as he or she got close enough to see Arudal's face. Finally he had to go to the kitchen and corner one of the serving-women, a Northman girl with a thick blond plait who overtopped him by half a handspan. Her blue eyes darted frantically from side to side, and her fingers flew to the silver shield-amulet resting on her generous bosom. "What do you want, sir?" she asked nervously.

"I am only for the laundries seeking," Arudal tried to reassure her. "Can'st thou tellen me where to finden them?"

Still clinging to her amulet, she pointed with her free hand. "Out into that hallway, fourth door down on the left, sir. I must go, I have a table to serve!"

"Thank you," Arudal said politely, but the blond girl was already fleeing. Arudal wondered what the Ducal Arms did to their servants to make them so terrified. And the Kantareans think ill of us for keeping slaves? he said to himself. No slave in one of our inns would behave as if it thought a customer were about to kill and eat it - they must treat their serving-maids frightfully here.

The laundry was a simple, clean room, with a middle-aged man in white robes lifting dirty clothes from their numbered wooden baskets, stacking them on one table, and intoning a cantrip to clean and dry them. Such minor wizards did much of the work in Kantar which, in Tharandrost, would be left to slaves: this man would be one who lacked either the gift, the training, or the ambition for greater magics, commanding the wages of a skilled craftsman for relatively light duties. His young female assistant - a plump, round-cheeked girl with her hair hidden beneath a white cap - folded the cleaned clothes carefully and replaced them in the baskets they had come from. Arudal politely waited until the launderer had finished one set of incantations before clearing his throat. A small magic was like a small amount of nitre; it might not knock down a stone wall if mishandled, but could still blow off the careless user's arm.

"Yes?" the laundry-wizard said, glancing back hastily.

"I require all the clothes from suites twenty-three, twenty-four, twenty-five, twenty-seven, and twenty-nine immediately," Arudal informed him.

The white-robed man shrugged. "Teri will carry them for you, sir."

The girl hastened over, stacking one basket on top of another - they had been cleverly made, Arudal saw, so that several could be stacked together in that manner - and heaving the two up in her arms with some difficulty. Weak as a Plainsman, Arudal thought scornfully: it was one of the ironies of life that most heavy labour in Tharandrost was done by a race with less than half the strength of its masters. "Put them all in suite twenty-three," he told her, lest she inadvertently walk in on the conference of the White Company knights.

"Aye," Teri panted, then looked sideways at him. "If you were a gentleman, lord squire, you'd help me carry these."

"Shut your mouth, girl!" the laundry-wizard snapped. "Can't you see he's...not used to such talk from the likes of you?" he added hastily, as though he had been about to say something else. Perversely, Arudal felt annoyed by the dismissal, respectful though it was. He went over and banged the remaining baskets into a stack, lifting it up. He could have carried the weight easily with one hand, though he needed the second to steady the boxes.

"Oo, you are strong," Teri said as soon as they were out of the laundry. "I'll wager you could pick me up like a kitten." Although her plump face was already pink with effort, she managed to flutter her eyelashes at Arudal.

"You do not look so weighty," Arudal said absently: she might have been a little heavier than he, no real test of his strength if he had chosen to carry the laundry girl and her load together.

Once they were in Sir Thoron's suite, Teri set her baskets down and arching her back in a stretch that thrust her plump breasts up. "Are you expecting your knight back soon, sir?" she asked Arudal hopefully.

"I do not know."

She moved closer to him with a little wiggle of her hips. "There's a nice room just down the hall for gentlemen who want - special entertainment, sir. If you haven't any other duties tonight, I'd be ever so pleased to see to it that you enjoy your stay here."

At last Arudal realized what she was trying to tell him, and a prickling flush of embarassment crept over his face. "I'm sorry," he stammered. "We're leaving soon...I have things to do, I have to pack, and..."

Teri sighed. "Ah, well. But you'll remember me when you come back, won't you? Come, a kiss for memory, and because you were nice enough to help me." With another little wriggle, she was pressing her breasts against Arudal, tilting her face down to meet his lips. Her kiss was surprisingly soft, her breath fragrant with strawberries, and Arudal cursed the short-cut doublet and tight hose that made the swelling at his groin all too evident. Teri did not pull away at once, but her fingers caressed him, just there... "Are you sure you won't come with me?"

Arudal shook his head violently, not trusting his voice.

"I know you'll come back, anyway. And…good luck, where-ever you're going." She turned and left the room, her hips swaying, leaving Arudal badly confused and with the straining between his legs fading into a faint soreness. In all his life, he had never been approached thus by a female, nor imagined that he could be.

He settled down to repack their belongings, but the task only reminded him that he had been thrown out of the Kantareans' conference, even though Rhys had been allowed to stay. They should trust me by now, Arudal thought bitterly. Had he not let Sir Salarond read his heart, and aided greatly in the vampire attack - and even told them what he had not been meant to reveal to any Kantareans, though in truth Rhys and Lostren were more responsible for that than he? The packing done, Arudal thought about it a moment and then put his armour on, including the helmet: Sir Thoron was less likely to hit him for being too eager than for being unready.

Still the others had not come back, and Arudal sat disconsolately in one of the large padded chairs, staring at the embers of the little fire. There was a strange noise at the back of his hearing - he had been listening to it a little while, it seemed, before he noticed it. A soft moaning, a sound of distant sorrow or rage…There have been rumours of hauntings, Sir Salarond had said. At the thought, the noise seemed to grow louder, and even in his warm gambeson, Arudal felt a faint chill.

Murder, the voice whispered. Murder and betrayal. Only the guilty escaped alive…no burial rites, but a pond in the wood, a stone sewn into my belly to make me sink with the others…someday they shall come back, and then I will have my vengeance…

Who are you? Arudal whispered silently, casting out with his inner senses. Now he could feel the cold ethereal touch, the ache of the Shadow-world and the hunger for life denied - a shade, rather than a ghost; too weak to be dangerous, but bound in bitterness and hate. Something at the corner of his eye caught his attention: dark glistening liquid pooling under the door, the last glow of the fire gleaming deep red from its spreading surface…the door opening.

"Arudal!" Finvar said. "Wake up - oh, good, you're armoured already. Help me into this, will you?"

Arudal shook his head as he stood, wrenching his sight out of Shadow. He could still feel the shade at the edges of his awareness as he knelt down to quickly buckle the straps on Finvar's leg armour. Though he was not looking forward to another night's riding, he was glad that he would not have to sleep in that room.

"You didn't miss much," Arudal's fellow squire told him cheerfully. "Cursed Intelligence men - I've heard Sir Ultar has his privy charmed so no one can tell whether he's gone in to piss or to take a dump. There you go - give me a tug on the chin strap, will you? I just got this helm repadded, and it's still sort of squishy if I don't pull it really tight." As soon as Finvar was armoured, he swept up a pair of saddlebags. "Are you all right with the others?…Morthugor's turds, Sir Thoron should have gotten a Tharandrostan squire to do the heavy lifting a long time ago. I'd heard your race was strong, but you're so small…no offense meant. Come on, he wants the horses saddled and loaded now. I hope he doesn't make us ride the warhorses all the way to the river, my tailbone's just about broken as it is and I can't imagine what yours feels like."

"Just a moment," Arudal said as they came down into the common room. He darted into the kitchen. The Northman girl who had told him where the laundry was jumped and screeched as she caught sight of him, grasping for her shield-amulet again. "A second of your time only," he said, standing in front of her so she could not escape. "I want some apples or carrots and sugar-crystals for horsen."

"Yes, sir...right away, of course..." she babbled, hastily rooting through jars. A few seconds later she thrust a cloth bag into his hands. "Take those, I hope they're all right, sir. Please, if they're not, it's not that I meant...I only..."

"Thank you," Arudal said, cutting her off and turning to leave in bemusement. The serving maid did not look as though she had been ill-used. Her limbs were well-fleshed, and her skin and hair had the same healthy shine as those of his own parents' house-slaves, a sign of good feeding and good treatment, but she acted like the most miserable Plainsman doe in a Dockside tavern.

The Ducal Arms tended its patrons' horses as well as the customers themselves; Inmanat had the smug look of a horse with a bellyful of warm oat mash, though he still stretched his neck out hopefully as soon as he saw Arudal. "Greedy beast," Arudal said affectionately, holding a brown lump of crystallized sugar for the horse to lip from his palm. "Thou'lst get fat." Black Rage eyed his own sugar lump suspiciously, as if no one had ever offered the warhorse a treat before, but at last condescended to take it; Sir Thoron's roan destrier drew back his head in surprise, snorting and stamping, then snapped his teeth at Arudal's hand. Arudal stayed where he was, crooning to the horse; finally the large soft lips flapped over his palm.

"What do you think you're doing, squire?" Sir Thoron asked roughly. "Your palfrey may be a pet; these are fighting animals."

"I thought they would take to me more readily if I gave them treats, sir," answered Arudal. "They are slow to let me bit them yet, and we may need them to answer quickly someday."

"Hmph," Sir Thoron snorted. "We'll ride the warhorses down to the river." Finvar groaned softly, but his knight ignored him. "Get a move on, there's no more time to waste."

A thin sliver of Moon gleamed above, the stars bright and clear through the cool summer night. Sir Thoron ordered Arudal to ride at the head of the party. "Have you ever fought from horseback?"

"No, sir."

"Well, Black Rage knows what he's doing. Try not to cut his ears off - thrusts or back-swings only, if you can. In Artegal they won't use anything but a thrust if they can help it, and Prince Merkon's all for cuts once the lances are down, but I say any way you can kill the foe is good. Pity you didn't train for the Silent Guard."

"I am not a Mindspeaker, sir," Arudal said stiffly.

"Stay alert. Shout at once and rein back if you sense anything coming," Sir Thoron ordered him. "And if, Utalkath forbid, your horse goes down, jump and pray, and try not to get trampled by anyone else. Don't drop your shield to protect your leg, either. Salarond can fix a limb even if you get it chopped off, but even he can't do much for an arrow or lance-tip through your eye-slits."

The road was clear in Arudal's sight, brighter than in full day. Even though the saddle slammed painfully against his rump and crotch when Sir Salarond ordered them to pick up the speed, it was pleasant riding at night. An owl swooped over the road, the barring of its great silent wings pale in the moonlight; farther off in the woods, Arudal heard the sharp bark of a fox. It reminded him of night-time hunts with his cousins at his grandmother's estate, Uridar, Muraseph, and himself riding ahead with boar-spears, and Arothir bringing up the rear with her crossbow.

The first streaks of gray were just brightening the eastern sky when they came to the shore of the Karasindi. A flock of geese rose from the reeds, yammering like a pack of hounds in full cry. Out in the middle of the water, the black shadow of a boat broke the slow-moving starlit ripples; its nose swung against the current, the heavy oars stretching down from the sides like the legs of a giant water-bug to push it towards the shore. The knights and their squires dismounted, Arudal stifling his groan of pain. He hoped Sir Salarond wouldn't disdain healing small injuries, for he knew his buttocks and inner thighs would be bitterly bruised.

The boat moored close in, and the party led their horses through the waist-high reeds, the mud sucking at their feet and calves with every step - more work for the squires before they could sleep, Arudal thought wearily. Valderian steel might not rust, but they shouldn't leave mud on it, and the greave-straps would have to be carefully cleaned and oiled to keep them from weakening with the damp. A broad plank stretched out from the ship's side, and one by one they led the horses carefully up it: then the plank drew back, and the boat slipped out into the river again - silently outstripping the current, Arudal marked with approval. It was a very fine craft, a sleek, narrow-built raider dromon; similar to his own Greywing, which his father had given him at his coming-of-age. When the horses were settled, Arudal praised and stroked them, giving them a little more sugar to soothe their nervousness at being on the water before he cleaned the mud from their hocks and hooves.

Their cabins were tiny: there was barely enough room for Finvar and himself to spread out their bedrolls beside Sir Thoron's narrow cot. Arudal's eyelids were drooping, and the muddy boots and pieces of leg-armour were leaden-heavy in his hands when he and Finvar squatted down to clean them, but they doggedly stuck with the job until the silver metal gleamed with a rainbow sheen and the leather straps ran smooth and soft through their fingers. Sir Thoron was still up on deck by the time Finvar sighed and said, "Well, we can't do any better than that. Pity you don't know any cleaning-spells - or can you do anything about dirty armour with magic?"

"It would take twice as long and three times as much effort by ritual," Arudal replied. "Although if I had any idea that I was going to be doing this sort of thing, I might have tried to learn such cantrips. But they are not so common in Tharandrost as here."

Finvar looked faintly embarassed, as most Kantareans did when reminded that slavery was practiced in the State, but said only, "Well, I'm for bed, and you had best be too."

Even as Arudal slipped into unconsciousness, he felt the dromon tugging to a stop, but he was too sleepy to worry about it.

Chapter 5: On the Karasindi

"Dark vein, threaded silver with fish,
Cold vein, teeming rich with life,
Snow-blood from the mountains' peaks,
Earth-blood flowing swift to the sea.
Great river, thou life of our land..."

"Karasindi", Alagron Rathol

It was early afternoon when Sir Thoron finally rose, shouting at his squires, "Wake up! Get breakfast and put your armour on: I'll see you on deck and ready for a little training in an hour, or know the reason why!" Though small, the ship's galley was well equipped; a thin nervous-looking man was expertly stirring up omelets, and there was a stack of griddle-cakes beside the stove. Arudal and Finvar carried their food up to the deck, joining the other squires. Sir Salarond was nowhere to be seen, but Sir Eroth and Sir Shakhor were already training, falchion and shield against longsword and dagger, and Dame Karsil was doing some sort of complex sword-work by herself, a series of movements that reminded Arudal of the unarmed fighting-dances practiced by Tharandrostan women - fertile women were not encouraged to learn blade-work, but they had their own means of staying fit and defending themselves at need. The Elf's sword wove a blurring net of light through the mist: Arudal watched in awe. *And she is only a little over three hundred - young for an Elf; what are the old ones like?* The Karasindi's banks slipped along smoothly; through the dark day-mist, Arudal could see the gentle curves of hills rolling away to either side, with black patches here and there that must be stands of trees.

"We've just passed over the border into Ithel," said Tirothar. "Karameth - my family's lands - isn't far from here. The trees are cherries - see how they're netted against the birds? The vines on those terraces are mostly Black Riverfoot, with a little bit of White Everlife. In a while we'll come up to Avalar's Seat, which is the stump of an old volcano: it's the ash still in the soil that gives our wines their fire and flint. We brew some amber ales as well, but ale's not fit for the better classes - eh, Finvar?" he added slyly.

Finvar punched him hard on the shoulder. "Weak Southern blossom," the Artegalian said. "You haven't the belly to drink like a man, and there's the truth of it."

Tirothar stepped nimbly back to avoid another blow. "We'll ask your black friend, then," he countered. "I'll wager half a crown you wouldn't drink ale if you could have wine, would you, Arudal? In your homeland, ale's only fit for ...sailors and such, am I right?"

Arudal had not missed Tirothar's slight hesitation, nor the way his blue-gray eyes flickered towards Rhys. But he answered truthfully, "We do not have so much grain that we can afford to brew from it. At home we drink wine or sometimes brandy-cordials, with cider for those who have not the coin for wine."

"And you've never tasted ale?" Finvar asked, amazed. Arudal shook his head. "You poor creature! I'll have to do something about that as soon as I can. As for you, Tirothar, this afternoon you'll see what kind of blows an ale-drinker can land."

As Sir Thoron had promised, they spent the afternoon training on deck. Arudal was still stiff from riding the warhorse, and the knight was an impatient taskmaster, but, to the Tharandrostan's surprise, Finvar made up for his roughness. "The classical Imperial style suits you well - I suppose it was designed for men just like you. But it's meant for shield-lines, not one-on-one: it's too static, too easy to predict, and too easy to throw off-balance in single combat. You have the advantage of speed, but I've still got the reach of you, and I'm...let's see, you're pretty solid through the shoulders and chest. So you weigh...twelve stone, maybe?"

"Ten stone," Arudal corrected; his small bones made him lighter than a Kantarean his size and build would be.

"All right. I'm a good five stone heavier, half your size again. You're stronger than I am, but if it comes to brute force between us, I only have to move two-thirds of my weight and you have to move half again yours. So you have to fight close enough for your reach, but not so close that I can just knock you over with my shield - or pin you, maybe, if we're fighting by a wall. Come at me again, and I'll show you what I mean."

Finvar side-stepped Arudal's rush neatly, throwing his shield against the Tharandrostan's sword-side. For a moment, Arudal was stuck between the shield and the boat's rail, unable to free his arm, and Finvar reached over his shield to tap him ringingly on the helm. "I'll bet they never showed you that at school. But if you're expecting it, you can avoid it: dodge if you have the room, or drop low with your shield high - from there you can kneecap me, or if you're lucky, get in with a thrust to gut me. You need to think more fluidly; I can tell you're used to fighting against the same style all the time, but there's always someone who learned differently out there. And you need to remember that weight is also power. You're frighteningly strong for your size, but when a lighter object meets a heavier one, it's the lighter one that's going to move. The Imperial style is actually designed for dealing with that, but I bet you've never really practiced it with anyone who had more than a couple of inches or much weight on you. Now, come on again..."

By the time they broke for dinner, Arudal had gone several rounds with each of the White Company knights and their squires. Their skills were daunting: even Rhys was better than Arudal could have guessed, making up for his lack of speed and strength with a tremendously precise sense of timing, range, and control, and Arudal's own timing and accuracy suffered from his instinctive shock and rage at seeing a blade in a Plainsman's hand, as well as the constant surprise of the lanky redhead's range - a longsword at the end of Rhys' arm had the same reach as a bastard sword or short glaive wielded by a Tharandrostan. At the end of the session, Arudal was so exhausted that he found it difficult to unstrap his armour, and his abused muscles, beginning to stiffen, groaned with every movement. He was painfully hanging his gambeson up to dry when Lostren walked in. "Come on, Arudal, Sir Salarond wants you."

"I didn't know Sir Salarond was that sort," Finvar grinned, shaking his sweaty hair back. Lostren clicked his tongue at him, but made no other reply, and Arudal limped after the other squire - one of Sir Thoron's blows with the blunted practice sword had left a swelling red welt across his left hamstring when he'd lifted his shield to block a feint to his head.

Sir Salarond was down in the hold, holding up a lantern and checking the labels on the barrels against a list in his hand. "Arudal, something is wrong here, and I want your advice on this," he said without preamble. "How long do you think this fresh water will last us?"

Arudal looked at the barrels, then the list, and estimated the crew that a dromon this size would carry, reckoning the figures in his head as every high-born Tharandrostan youth learned to do - he had learned his multiplication and division on crews and barrels of water and hardtack and salt beef. "Barely six weeks, sir, and that only if the weather is fair. But the Western continent cannot be so close: it must be at least three months away."

"How do you know that?"

Arudal paused. He knew because the best Tharandrostan Mindspeakers, if they were linked by blood, could send messages back and forth to Fel: his cousin Arothir sometimes complained about being gotten out of bed to get urgent news to her older brother Binakron, commanding the Blood-Rage in the State's southern fleet. But the Empire had needed both Mindspeakers and magic to communicate with Tharandrost. And besides... "If it were so close, our ships would already be trading there. Sir Asdrek said we had Western traders as our guides: what manner of vessels do they come in?"

"No one has ever seen them," Sir Salarond said gloomily. "They anchor well off-shore at night and send smaller boats in with their goods; then the smaller boats sail out at night."

"I would guess, sir, that if our guides told you that this was all the water we needed, that they are not sailors themselves, or were hoping we would either be cast away at sea or die of thirst," Arudal told him. "Are the other provisions the same?"

"As nearly as I can tell, yes. But perhaps you would like to inspect?"

Arudal shook his head as he ran down the list. It looked like one of his own mathematics papers from the age of thirty - perishables badly misbalanced with the foods that would keep forever, too little water and too much brandy, and no allowance made for calms or foul weather. "I hope, sir," he said severely, "that you had planned to discuss this with someone else before you set out on the Western Ocean."

"Aye, but I thought I might as well make use of you since you were here. What's wrong with your leg?" the commander added as Arudal limped along beside him.

"Bruised, sir."

Sir Salarond smiled. "Thoron has a heavy hand. And no doubt you're sore from riding so long. Well, I can do something about that - stand still." He put his hands on Arudal's aching shoulders, murmuring something, and the warmth of his touch swept through Arudal like a wave washing away all his pain and stiffness. "You're not to expect minor healings most of the time, since if we get into a fight I'll need all my power to patch everyone up, but there's no harm to it now - Aviyani being merciful," he muttered under his breath. "I was suspicious already, but this tears it: we will have to stop in Felatar." He paused. "Arudal, if things go badly wrong - would you be able to command and helm this ship?"

"Without difficulty, sir, so long as there were enough crew left to man her. I have one of my own very like her, and my father is one of the best helmsmen in the Prince's fleet."

"Truly the gods sent you to us," Sir Salarond said, but that did nothing to assuage Arudal's unease. It was becoming clearer and clearer to him that this mission was not well-planned: so much secrecy and haste did not bode well for success. Are the Kantareans so arrogant, that they think a handful of legendary knights are enough to deal with anything, without making any effort at preparation? But he had heard too much of Sir Salarond's skill as a leader to believe that, and nothing he had seen gave him reason to doubt that the tales were true. As well, in the darkness of the hold, he could see the shadows of the worry-lines gathering at the commander's eyes like ghosts to a blood-offering, and guessed that the Kantarean noble was at least as distressed at this latest difficulty as Arudal was himself.

"Sir, may I speak to our guides? It may be that I can find out why they gave such bad advice."

Sir Salarond's face grew more mournful, as though he were wrestling with something inside him. At last he said, "I do not even know for sure that it was they who advised the provisioning of this ship."

"What of the captain? Surely he..."

Sir Salarond cut him off with a wave of his hand. "He does not know where we are going, nor will he, until we are well out of sight of land. Nor do any of the crew. This is a Secret Service vessel, and they are used to following orders without explanation. In any case, what I want you to do is calculate our needs for the journey tonight: we will reach Felatar tomorrow, and I must have a list of requirements before then."

"Yes, sir."

"And you said you know some ritual magic. I assume you brought your own tools - yes? Well, then, make a list of the components you will need for protective wards, for charms of friendship and translation, if you are able - hmm, and for passing unseen. Dr. Melkoth has a theory that ritual magic may work where other magics will not, and though we could hardly bring a mage just to test that theory, since you are with us, it is worth trying." The commander paused, frowning. "What do you know of magical necromancy?"

"It is not in Tharandrost oft ytaughten," Arudal answered carefully.

Sir Salarond raised an eyebrow, staring closely at Arudal. "Should I ask why that question unnerves you so, then? Let me put it another way: have you any means of influencing Undead other than your mind-gifts?"

"No, sir," Arudal answered, relieved. "I cannot even put up a ward against them, for..."

"For the obvious reason, yes. Well, never mind. As a useful exercise, try to think of the magics that might be needed on our journey, if ritual magic does work where we are going, and write out the material requirements, keeping them as light as possible. You are dismissed, squire."

Chapter 6: An Unexpected Meeting

"Delicate the knowledge-dance
Drinks mixed of truth and lies,
Courtship where love is lacking,
Spying where truth is vowed."

- "The Diplomat's Duty", Sir Ermendil Keravan

Their ship reached Felatar at mid-morning. The city was built on a large island in the broad mouth of the Karasindi where it poured into the ocean; the long rows of docks and the sounds of men shouting back and forth from the decks of the vessels maneuvering along the river - everything from full-sized warships to rowboats - sent a pang of homesickness through Arudal: thickly fogged as his vision was in the bright daylight, he could almost pretend for a moment that he was home in Tharabruthnan, with the morning mist hanging in a thick curtain over the water. The smells of salt water and fish and tar, the cries of fishmongers along the wharves...But the only language to be heard was the quick chopped Common tongue, harsh or drawling with various accents, and there was no deep comforting foghorn-note shivering beneath the calls, only occasional shrill whistle-blasts when one boat came too near to another. The helmsman deftly steered their dromon towards the north side of the island, where a huge chain of rusty iron links blocked the narrow passage of water, and a small boat rowed out to meet them.

"Halt!" a black-haired man in finely embroidered robes called out from the little boat. "Permission to come aboard?"

"Permission granted," Sir Salarond replied. A pair of crewmen hauled on ropes, lowering a chair and lifting their challenger carefully back up.

"Lieutenant-Commander Sir Miratek, sir," he introduced himself, saluting Sir Salarond. The officer's Imperial blood was clear in his features and colouring, though he was tall and heavily built: Arudal guessed that he must be of noble lineage. "We were not expecting you, General, sir."

Sir Salarond raised a slanted eyebrow. "Our papers are in order, Lieutenant-Commander," he said carefully, proffering a sheaf of parchments. Sir Miratek looked them over slowly and carefully, soft breaths hissing out through his teeth as if in disappointment, then he signalled to the men guarding the chain. One unhooked his end; the other turned a crank-wheel, reeling it in.

"You may pass, sir," Sir Miratek declared when the passage was free. "I shall show you where to dock."

The docks around the north side were almost deserted: only a couple of vessels - sleek dark narrow-hulled craft like their own dromon - were moored there, but a troop of guardsmen whose steel helms were crested with blue, green, and white plumes stood watching attentively. Arudal noticed that they were all armed with repeating crossbows as well as swords and halberds, and several of them were staring hard at him as their ship pulled in.

"Tharandrostan?" the lieutenant-commander asked, jerking his head towards Arudal. Sir Salarond nodded. "He stays on board, sir."

"By no means," Sir Salarond replied. "If General Thindozan has a problem with Sir Thoron's squires, he can discuss the matter with us himself."

"No aliens are allowed in these precincts, sir," Sir Miratek stated doggedly.

"Arudal has sworn fealty to Sir Thoron, and through him to the Crown of Kantar, and hence is to be legally considered as a citizen for the duration of his time as a squire. Do not haggle points of law with me, Lieutenant-Commander!"

Sir Miratek's pointed chin jutted out angrily, but whatever he might have been about to say, he clearly thought better of it, restraining himself to, "This way, sir."

The Intelligence building - for so Arudal assumed it must be - was a solid, massive structure of red granite, built in the clean-lined Classical Imperial style with heavy pillars and barrel-shaped vaulting. The guards stepped aside and saluted sharply as Sir Miratek led their party through, and Sir Salarond returned their salutes. Arudal wondered when, and if, he would be required to salute as well, and if he was supposed to use the Kantarean gesture of flat-palmed hand to chest at a horizontal right angle, or the Tharandrostan salute with fingertips straight up and palm out beside the right shoulder.

General Thindozan's office was a stark room with a massive desk and one chair. The general himself hardly looked military: scrawny, his blue uniform hanging off him in folds, with wisps of white hair sticking out all over his head and a severe tic in the muscles of his right cheek, he started violently when Sir Miratek brought them in.

"G-gods!" he stuttered. "S-sir Salarond, wha-what are you d-d-doing here?"

Sir Salarond stepped forward. "General, we require supplies for a long away mission."

"Wha-what are you d-doing?" Thindozan repeated. "T-tell me about it."

"Classified," Sir Salarond replied sharply, but the general's pale eyes were already rolling at Arudal.

"W-why is that squire st-staring at me?" he yelped. "Make him st-stop it."

Arudal looked hastily away, wondering how such a man could ever have achieved his rank - if the general were going senile and should be relieved soon, or if the incipient hysteria was all a pretense.

"I trust we have your permission to requisition what we require?" Sir Salarond continued.

"Y-yes, you have. S-sir Miratek will s-see to your qu-qu-quartering now - g-go on, g-gentlemen, I have w-work to d-d-do." Thindozan saluted them, and they all saluted back, though Arudal had some difficulty with the unfamiliar Kantarean gesture.

"Either salute is acceptable, squire," Sir Thoron told him quietly as they marched out and back through the halls. "But for Utalkath's sake, try to actually do one or the other, rather than flopping around like a dying fish!"

"Here are your rooms," Sir Miratek said finally. "Have you a list prepared for our quartermaster?"

"Of course." Sir Salarond handed the lieutenant-commander two sheets of parchment - Arudal recognised his own handwriting on one of them.

"I presume you will wish to leave with the tide early tomorrow morning, sir? Then make yourselves comfortable, gentlemen. If you wish to go back to your ship or out into the city, you need only ask one of the guards to guide you. Do not wander around here by yourselves, as that may be dangerous. I would also remind you that the unauthorized use of magic - or mind-magic," he added, looking pointedly at Arudal, "is strictly forbidden here, and any attempts to do so will be detected and dealt with immediately."

"Afternoon off, sir?" Tirothar said brightly as soon as the door had closed behind Sir Miratek. The knights looked at each other: if Arudal had not known better, he would almost have sworn that they were Mindspeaking, but perhaps they had merely known each other long enough to guess the others' thoughts.

Sir Eroth shrugged. "You might as well."

"Go buy presents for your girlfriends back home," added Sir Thoron. "But all of you stick together, stay out of trouble and don't drink too much. Finvar, you're responsible for Arudal, you understand? Wear your swords, but I'd best not hear of you using them without a good reason."

"Yes, sir!" Finvar answered enthusiastically.

Sir Salarond considered the squires for a moment. "Lostren, you are in charge for the afternoon. I trust you to keep good order among your fellows, and I know that all of you will bear yourselves as befits squires to the foremost knights of Kantar."

Over Arudal's protests, Lostren insisted that Arudal should wear the same clothes he had borrowed at the Ducal Arms the night before. The other squires were similarly dressed in doublets and bright hose, even Rhys - whom Arudal privately thought looked like a Southern dancing ape in the Perenilean fashions, all gangly legs and dangly arms, with a tuft of red chest-hair sticking out of the doublet's laced neck.

"Where to?" Tirothar asked when the guard had led the five of them out to the street.

"We're not far from the market square, and I promised Perethi I'd send her a present," answered Lostren. "We can start there, and see what happens next."

Arudal stayed close to Lostren and Finvar to keep from being jostled by the crowd. He felt as though people were staring at him, and not being able to see whether it was true made the sensation even more unpleasant. The market square in Felatar was huge, bigger than those in Tharabruthnan or Var Perenil: this was, after all, Kantar's chief center of ship-trade, with everything from mammoth-ivory from the Far North to exotic reptile-skins and bright-coloured live birds from the South - some of which had undoubtedly been brought up by Tharandrostan traders. After a little while, Arudal scented the unmistakable rich burnt odour of black-roast beans, and pulled the others aside to the stall he had found. The trader was a Terashi, a tall, slim man with swarthy skin and a hooked nose, dressed in a swathe of red and yellow silks with a scimitar hanging at his side, and as soon as he saw Arudal, he burst into a torrent of broken Imperial. He wanted three times as much for the black-roast tea as Arudal would have paid in Tharabruthnan, and it took a long time for Arudal to beat him down even to half the price, the Terashi complaining all the time that Arudal was ruining him.

"What is that stuff?" Finvar asked when Arudal had paid a quarter-crown and received two pounds of black-roast beans in return, along with a little mortar and pestle for crushing them.

"It is a sort of tea from Fel," Arudal explained. "It is very good when one must make early arisings in the morning or stay up late at night, and nice also after meals."

A few minutes later, Rhys saw a stall hung with little dolls and strings of roots and bones, and hurried over without saying a word. Arudal's nostrils tightened. Even from here, he could smell the musty stink, and the old Plainsman doe sitting in the stall was a particularly disgusting specimen, toothless and wrinkled, with a large hairy wart under her chin and nameless stains all over the brilliantly chequered cloth of her shawls and skirts. Rhys jabbered with her for a little while; at one point she looked up at Arudal, glaring and making some sort of gesture with her crooked fingers.

"What is he doing?" Arudal murmured to Lostren.

"Buying spell-components, I should imagine," the young nobleman replied. "And he seldom gets a chance to speak with a Wise One of his own people."

Arudal would have turned his back and walked away, if the squires had not been so strictly charged to stay together. Rhys' voice was getting louder, his hands flying rapidly in that annoying way Plainsmen had, as if they were too stupid to use or understand spoken language without miming everything they said, and the hag was responding in kind. At last she nodded sharply, reaching beneath her counter and doing something before she brought out a small embroidered bag, which Rhys promptly hung around his neck as soon as he had paid her. Arudal greatly disliked the smile on the buck's freckled face as he stepped back to join his comrades, but he would not give Rhys the satisfaction of asking what he had bought. Tirothar, however, was not so restrained.

"What's that?"

"A protection against creatures of evil," Rhys replied smugly, and Arudal gritted his teeth, knowing full well that Sir Shakhor's squire meant him.

Creature, indeed! he thought. Neither you nor that old witch would have been allowed to live to adulthood at home, buck; we know better than to let mages breed among our slaves.

Next they went to one of the larger jewelry shops on the edge of the square, where Lostren dithered over pearl-set brooches, finally, at Arudal's recommendation, picking out a pretty piece of filigreed goldwork in the shape of a crescent set with half-round rainbow pearls from the South. He would have paid the price the goldsmith asked without question had Arudal not stepped in to speak for him: Tharandrost lived by trade, and even the highest-born knew how to value such goods. "My thanks, Arudal," Lostren said, satisfied, as they walked away. "Perethi should be delighted with this."

"Are you betrothed, then?" Arudal asked politely.

Lostren laughed. "Off and on - Perethi has a bit of a temper. I'm hoping this will keep me in her mind until we get back. What about yourself, then? Do you have a girl to buy things for?"

"I have not been assigned a wife yet, though it may be that I will be mated to my cousin Arothir when I have finished my doctorate and returned to the State."

Lostren only nodded, but Tirothar's thick eyebrows flew up. "Your cousin? But that's..." he began, even as Finvar said, "Assigned a wife? You don't get to choose one?"

"We are bred with thought and care for the bettering of our children," Arudal said, as he had been taught from childhood. "And the House of Procreation can far better tell who is suited for matings than we coulden of our own devices."

As he spoke, Arudal became aware that Finvar and Lostren were looking at him with expressions that might have been pity, and Tirothar looked horrified. Rhys was ignoring him altogether, making an ostentatious show of watching the passers-by.

"You poor creature," Tirothar muttered. "How can you bear to be...mated, like a prize stallion? And to your own cousin!"

"The gifts of our line are strong and of worth to the State," replied Arudal proudly. "My father's own parents were full brother and sister, and my parents are also cousins."

Tirothar drew back from him, blue eyes almost as round as a Common man's with shock and fingers forming involuntarily into the Circle of Aviyani, as if Arudal had just told him that his family sacrificed an Elf to Morthugor at every moon-dark. "Aviyani preserve us!" Sir Eroth's squire exclaimed. "That is..." He paused, his cheek hollowing as if he were biting the inside to keep from completing his sentence.

"The custom in Tharandrost," Lostren finished smoothly for him. "And you cannot argue that it has not served their race well - though I myself would not care to live so."

"The gods forfend!" Tirothar agreed. "No wonder the Tharandrostans have fallow seed. Arudal, you are lucky that there is nothing worse wrong with you than short sight."

Finvar cuffed his fellow squire hard on the shoulder. "Shut up," he ordered. "You haven't known Arudal long enough to be that rude to him - he hasn't said anything about your big nose yet, has he?"

"My nose is not big!" Tirothar insisted with the sudden indignant flare of a man forcibly denying the truth - the offending feature was, in fact, rather long and prominent. "Nothing like as big as your ale-belly, anyway."

Lostren got between the two of them before Finvar could swing his fist in earnest. "We could go back to our knights now," Sir Salarond's squire said ominously. "I'd hate to have to pull rank and spoil our last free afternoon for a while - but if you don't let this discussion die a swift and quiet death now, I shall do, understand?"

Tirothar hung his dark head; Finvar grinned sheepishly. "Yeah. Fine. Hey, we can settle yesterday's question now. Arudal, do you feel like trying a pint of ale? I'll wager that somewhere in this city we can find the real Helludal black. Which is actually a stout, but never mind; it's all ale."

Glad enough to have the conversation shifted away from his place in the State's breeding programme, Arudal said, "I would like to try it."

After a little walking, Finvar spotted an inn-sign showing a cask dripping drops in colours from pale gold to solid black. "There!" he said with great satisfaction. "That should serve what we're after, or I'm a dwarf."

"That you certainly are not," replied Rhys, a smile twitching the corner of his wide mouth for the first time that day. "Else, look you, you would not be offering to buy us all a pint, would you now?"

Finvar shook his head in disgust, then smiled back. "First round, then. Come on!"

The Dripping Cask was quite crowded, the air hazed faintly blue with pipe-smoke. With some effort and a few apologies, the five squires managed to squeeze in at the end of one of the long pine tables, and Finvar whistled and waved his hand to catch the eye of the tall, dark-haired barmaid making her round with a trayful of large clay mugs. The girl glanced briefly at them - appraising the quality of their clothes, Arudal guessed, though she was too far away for his misted vision to make out her expression - then hastened over to them. "What will you have, sirs?" she enquired.

"Five pints of Helludal black," Finvar ordered, and the girl smiled brightly at him.

"Ah, you're from the North - I can tell by your voice. Five bronze pennies, if you please."

Finvar dug in his belt pouch and dropped some coins into her hand. She glanced at them and favoured him with another smile, flouncing her hips a little as she walked away.

"What do you think of her?" Finvar asked Arudal.

Arudal shrugged. "What should I think?"

"Sir Thoron said I should take care of you, and you probably haven't ever made an arrangement with a friendly wench in your life, so..."

It took Arudal a moment to realize what Finvar was proposing, and when he did, he jerked away in shock. "How could you...how could I...?" he sputtered, then realized he was speaking Imperial. He swallowed hard, collecting himself, and tried again. "It is not seemly for such as I to lien with..." Don't call them lesser races while you're in Kantar, his father had warned him. "She is not of my kyth, nor maye I risken a child to engendren, for that it is most starke forbidden."

Finvar blinked as if he were trying to make sense of what Arudal had said, and finally settled on, "Well, if she's not to your taste, that's all right. I just thought you might like the chance to get laid while the State isn't looking over your shoulder, and she's a fine-looking wench. If you don't want her..."

Lostren cleared his throat meaningfully. "What does 'stay out of trouble' mean to you, Finvar?"

"It's all right, I can't get pregnant," Finvar answered cheerfully. Tirothar muffled his snicker, but Rhys laughed loudly.

Lostren sighed. "Let me put it this way. Our knights told us to stick together, and I don't want to spend half the afternoon watching your arse go up and down - or to hear you trying to convince Sir Salarond tomorrow that you caught crabs in the privy."

"Stand well back - crabs can pole-vault," Tirothar pronounced with dire solemnity, which cracked at once into a giggle.

Arudal listened to this discussion in horrified fascination. Perhaps I do not entirely understand the Kantarean sense of humour, he thought as the barmaid put their mugs down. She bent particularly low in front of Finvar, who sighed exaggeratedly as she walked away. "Probably the last chance any of us will get for the next year," he muttered. "Ah, well." He inhaled the scent of his drink, then raised the clay mug high. "May the grain grow high over our foes' corpses!"

The others echoed the toast, and they all drank. Finvar tossed off half his mug in a single deep draught, but Arudal sipped very carefully, rolling the dark ale over his tongue beneath its cuff of solid yellow-white froth. The taste was strange, but not unpleasant - almost like a thick black-roast tea, though with a rich creamy texture, and only a faint clean hint of bitterness. Though the ale was not as strong as wine, he could still feel a faint warming glow from it.

"What do you think?" Finvar asked, wiping the foam from his lips.

"It is good," Arudal said, rather surprised. "Better than I expected."

"Told you so," Finvar said in satisfaction, drinking again.

"Excuse me, gentlemen," a deep voice said behind Arudal. "May I join you?"

Arudal looked back. The man who stood there was a middle-aged Tharandrostan in sober robes of deep blue velvet, about Arudal's own height, but more solidly built. His shoulder-length gray hair was held back with a silver fillet; he bore no obvious insignia of rank, but he wore a knight's white belt and fealty-chain of adamant-dusted Valderian steel.

"Be welcome," Lostren said, and the newcomer pulled up a chair, settling himself next to Arudal. For a man of his apparent age, he moved with surprising informality; Arudal wondered if his own shortsightedness and the stranger's gray hair were deceiving him.

"Allow me to introduce myself. I am Sir Daurar Agranonun, a diplomat in the service of the State. You will forgive me for this intrusion, I trust, but I could not fail to notice the presence of one of our own."

Arudal's stomach clenched into a hard knot, and the faint bitter aftertaste of the Helluval ale stung acid in the back of his throat. He wondered if he were in trouble - if he were about to be ordered not to go on the mission, or if he had done something grievously wrong in becoming squire to a Kantarean knight without the permission of the State. Still, he inclined his head politely to Sir Daurar. "Sir," he said. "I am Count Arudal Arumirun, heir to the House of Arudal." As he spoke, Arudal wondered about the diplomat's own patronymic; Agranon, "Intrepid", was not a man's name, but the name of a ship, and he had given no House...

"Well-met, your Excellency," Sir Daurar said, and Arudal relaxed fractionally. "And these your friends..?"

Arudal quickly introduced his companions, although he could not keep his voice from tightening when he got to Rhys. To his surprise, the diplomat acknowledged the young Plainsman with the same grave nod of his head that he gave to the others.

"And all of you are squires, I see. Are your knights here?"

"They are elsewhere occupied, sir," Lostren answered respectfully before Arudal could speak.

"I see," Sir Daurar murmured thoughtfully. "May I ask after their names?"

Lostren swallowed hard. Though the minds of the living were closed to him, Arudal would have wagered a full crown that Sir Salarond's squire was thinking something along the lines of, Can I tell him? Is this supposed to be a secret? But finally he said, "I have the honour to be squired to Dr. Sir Salarond; Tirothar is squired to Sir Eroth, Rhys to Sir Shakhor, and Finvar and Arudal to Sir Thoron."

The diplomat raised a winged gray eyebrow at the last name, and Arudal was surprised to see a faint quirk of his lip, as though Sir Daurar were struggling hard to repress a smile. There was something oddly familiar about the expression, though Arudal would have sworn that he had never seen the man before. One of my father's associates? But surely he would have mentioned...

"I had occasion to work with the White Company once," Sir Daurar said. "It was a fascinating experience...How long have you been Sir Thoron's squire?"

"Only a few days," Arudal admitted.

"If you don't mind my asking, how did this come to pass? I had...gathered the impression that Sir Thoron was not necessarily enthusiastic about our people. And not only would I have expected you to be squired to one of our own, but Sir Ephlaganilan - our ambassador in Var Perenil; you will probably have met him when you arrived in the city - mentioned to me several months ago that you were studying at the university there."

Arudal was saved from having to answer at once by the barmaid coming to enquire what Sir Daurar would have to drink. The diplomat casually ordered a mug of amber ale before turning back to Arudal.

"A matter of good chance, sir," Arudal said, hoping that would turn Sir Daurar's attention away.

Instead, the older man looked intently at him. "Go on - or would you prefer to speak with me in private?"

"Sir," Arudal said, trying to keep the fear from his voice, "My knight ordered me to stay with the other squires."

"Perhaps I should enquire no more, then." The barmaid set Sir Daurar's mug down, and he drank with every sign of enjoyment, gracefully dabbing the foam from his lips with a silken handkerchief. "Do you expect to be in Felatar long?"

"I cannot say, sir. That depends on our knights."

"Do you go to Var Perenil often, sir?" Lostren broke in.

Sir Daurar smiled rather wistfully. "Occasionally. Loswe, my wife, is from the city."

Lostren drew in his breath. "Not Loswe Matherol?"

"You know her?" Although the diplomat's face was very calm, it seemed to Arudal that he could see something moving deep beneath it, like a powerful current below a still sea.

"I knew her slightly when she was at the university," Lostren replied. "I lost touch with her after her boyfriend Minludal was murdered and she dropped out - four or five years ago, that would be now."

Arudal breathed in deeply, staring hard at Sir Daurar. The knight looked flatly back into his eyes, and Arudal felt a faint tingling chill, the familiar brush of the Shadow-World. A powerful necromancer, he thought vaguely, or else...Sir Daurar could not be an inmudalan agathusaftan; he might be a strong medium...no: he had seen them too easily; he could not suffer Shadow-blindness. Arudal was glad that the deep reading of thoughts was forbidden outside certain circumstances, and casual reading impolite save among friends and family. But Mindspeech was not: he heard the diplomat's voice in his head, though it sounded faint and far away, as though Daurar were deliberately trying to pull back even as he spoke. *Your Excellency, I gather from your reluctance to speak aloud that you have been recruited for some covert purpose. Given your talents and your heritage, I must establish that this is with the permission of the State.*

I cannot say anything about it, Arudal replied silently - though he could not bespeak the living with his thoughts, anyone could answer a Mindspeaker while the mental contact was held.

I see. The fleeting touch faded, and Sir Daurar turned his gaze away. The others at the table were looking at them with that peculiar worried fascination Kantareans often seemed to have when they saw Tharandrostans Mindspeaking. "My apologies," the diplomat said smoothly, and turned to talk of Var Perenil and the university - which he seemed to know quite well; Arudal wondered if he had studied there in his youth. When their mugs were emptied, Sir Daurar bought them another round of ale, joining them in the Helludal black, and after a time rose. "You must excuse me now, but I have an appointment to keep. Good winds and smooth sailing until we meet again."

"Fair winds and a straight course," Arudal replied.

Finvar gestured to the barmaid again, but Arudal caught his hand.

"Huh?"

Arudal shook his head, waiting to speak until Sir Daurar was outside. "We need to go back now," he murmured urgently. "Come on."

"But..."

Lostren nodded. "Aye. No argument, Finvar. Hurry."

The five of them made their way quickly back to the Intelligence building, passing through the guards' scrutiny and back to their quarters. Sir Thoron, Sir Eroth, and Sir Shakhor were dicing in Sir Thoron's rooms, but Lostren took the rest of them to Sir Salarond's suite. The commander was busy grinding a green paste in a mortar; Arudal's nostrils twitched at the pungent herbal scent that filled the room.

"Sir," Lostren said, "we may have a problem."

Sir Salarond raised an enquiring eyebrow, and Lostren told him briefly and succinctly about their encounter in the inn. At the mention of Sir Daurar, Sir Salarond frowned, but said nothing until Lostren was done.

"That was an unfortunate chance, but there is little Tharandrost can do now, with Arudal's squire-oath sworn. Still, none of you shall leave this building again until we are ready to depart. You did well to come straight back."

Uncomfortable as he was, Arudal could not help asking, "Sir, what do you know of Sir Daurar? He said he had worked with the White Company before."

"That is true enough. He was with us as a consultant for a time - ostensibly a diplomatic consultant, although..." Sir Salarond's lips pressed into a thin line, and he looked past Arudal, as though he were considering his next words with great care. At last he said, "Sir Daurar's official duties are diplomatic, but he is a necromancer of great skill."

Given your talents and your heritage, Sir Daurar had said. But magical necromancers were even rarer in Tharandrost than inmudalim agnusaftim. Only Arudal's line had kept that skill alive after the Western Empire fell, and guarded it largely for their own.

"There was something very strange about him," Lostren said thoughtfully. "The only Tharandrostans I have ever seen drink ale by choice were students at our University." He grinned. "They always think it's exotic. And I would have thought Sir Daurar far too old for Loswe - she and Minludal were both in my year at school. Still, I suppose her taste is consistent." He sighed.

"What do you mean?"

"Minludal, as you might guess from his name, was a Tharandrostan, and he was studying diplomacy as well as, of all things, necromancy - there was a joke going about that he wanted to be Tharandrost's first ambassador to Martag. Still," he added, "it seems a worrying coincidence that we were attacked by vampires on the road, and that we should chance to meet a necromancer with an interest in our mission here. Could Sir Daurar have managed three vampires as strong as the ones that attacked us?"

"Sir Daurar," the healer said heavily, "if my information concerning him is accurate, would be very nearly a match for any one of the Captains of Martag. He is said to have mastered...well, never mind. Yet I cannot imagine him endangering Arudal for any reason."

"If he knew that Arudal were with us," Lostren countered. "He did recognise you, Arudal. I was watching him from the moment he came in the door, and I saw how he looked at you. But our...assailant...didn't seem to know who you were, only that there was, or might be, at least one other member of our party."

Arudal had no idea of how to answer. He could not imagine any Tharandrostan diplomat making such an attack on Kantareans...at least not without good reason. But if the State knew about this mission, and had some reason to want it not to succeed - then I should not be here; I should ask for freedom from my oath. Then he remembered what he had seen in Eluthia's thoughts, and sighed with relief. "It was not Sir Daurar," he said firmly. For the mage who summoned the vampires had been taller than Eluthia, perhaps close to six feet, and Sir Daurar was Arudal's own height - it was very seldom indeed that any Tharandrostan stood taller than five foot eight or so.

Sir Salarond raised an eyebrow. "How...of course. You may tell me the details later. Quill and parchment, Lostren." The healer waited for his squire to bring his writing materials, scratching hastily. "Now take this to Sir Miratek. Arudal, come along to Sir Thoron's rooms. Assuming that I get the permissions I need, you will not be leaving them until I come to take you out - because I am expecting some trouble. Hopefully, Sir Daurar will not see fit to make a major diplomatic incident out of this."

Greatly troubled, Arudal followed him obediently back. By the time they reached Sir Thoron's suite, Sir Miratek was already standing braced by the door.

"Sir, our security arrangements, as you should be aware, are more than adequate for such difficulties. I see no need for additional wardings."

"In this case, I do," Sir Salarond told him firmly. "While the full details are classified, it should suffice that I am more than convinced that this is necessary. If you so desire, you may either watch my work yourself or send a mage of appropriate competence."

"Please do not begin until he arrives, sir," Sir Miratek said, turning on his heel and walking away.

The mage sent to watch Sir Salarond was a tall, thin man in deep green robes. He bore no visible insignia of rank, and did not salute, only nodded and said, "Pray proceed, your Grace."

Sir Salarond's eyes half-closed; his hands began to move in slow passes as a soft murmur issued from his throat. Arudal found himself trembling as the shimmering power rose like sunlit mist around the room, coiling about the walls and solidifying at the door. As Sir Salarond worked, the waves of shivering ran more violently through Arudal's body, cold sweat springing out on his forehead, until the healer-priest spoke his final word and the might he had raised suddenly settled firmly into place. The green-robed mage jerked his head sharply and walked off without saying a word.

"I trust that did not discomfort you unduly?" Sir Salarond asked Arudal. Arudal managed to shake his head, although he felt wrung out, as though a bitter fever had just broken in his body. "Well, then. Stay here and rest; if you sense anything untowards, send Lostren to me at once. Finvar, you stay with him as well."

Arudal lay down on one of the beds without complaint. He closed his eyes, but the spinning of his head made him feel sick, so he opened them again to see Lostren staring down at him.

"Do such magics always take you this way?" Lostren asked.

Arudal swallowed hard, trying to choke down his nausea. He had not recognised what Sir Salarond was doing - the wardings at the Hidden Estate were looser, and set by magicians' wills rather than priestly callings. Gummy saliva filled his mouth and he gulped again, then abruptly lost the battle, leaning over the edge of the bed to spew. Before the second wave of retching hit him, Lostren had an empty chamberpot in place to catch the dark flood of ale and half-digested bread.

"Surely two pints weren't too much for you?" Finvar asked. Lostren shook his head, his mouth pressed into a tight line.

"I'm going to get Sir Salarond," Lostren said. "You make sure he doesn't choke if he keeps throwing up."

His empty stomach still heaving, Arudal lay curled on his side, miserable and ashamed of himself. I've done nothing but be ill and get into trouble, he thought. I should not have come...

Sir Salarond crouched down beside him, taking Arudal's head in his hands and looking into his eyes. Despite himself, Arudal found himself blinking and trying to look away from the healer-priest's bright gaze. Arudal could not make out what Sir Salarond said then, the words blurring and sliding away from his ears; but his nausea eased almost at once, and the shaking faded from his limbs.

Salarond sighed. "Finvar, out. You stay, Lostren."

Finvar left, though not without casting a reluctant glance back over his shoulder, and Lostren moved in closer as the healer sighed again. "Well, well, Arudal. What are we going to do with you?" He was speaking Imperial, which worried Arudal a little.

"Sir?"

"It seems that active wardings against Shadow do nearly as much harm to you as to any creature from which I might protect you. Were you aware of this?"

"Uh, no, sir," Arudal mumbled.

"How could you not be?"

"Such things are not needed in Tharandrost, sir," Arudal answered, though with little confidence in his voice.

The corner of Sir Salarond's mouth twisted; Arudal could not tell whether it was amusement he saw on the commander's face, or distaste, or a little of both. Finally Salarond shook his head. "To my mind," he murmured, "you seem to be cursed, rather than gifted."

Lying down, Arudal could not brace himself as he wished, but he lifted his head to meet the healer-priest's eyes. "The gifts of Amandeth are not the easiest to bear, sir, but they are nevertheless his gifts to his chosen ones."

Strangely, it seemed to Arudal that a look of sorrow drew Sir Salarond's face in at that. The healer touched his forehead. "Manon filkaeth nol morthugor parethri," he murmured - Bright Elvish: The High One may shape even what is twisted to his ends.

"Sir?" Arudal asked, but Sir Salarond did not seem to hear him. "Mint tea with anise for Arudal, to settle his stomach," the healer advised his squire. "And keep him in bed - play chess with him, or cards, or something. I fear that I may have given a worse shock to his system than I thought at first - that was meant," he added grimly, "to be a warding fatal to beings of Shadow. Had you lingered too long in fetching me, I fear it might have proven likewise to Arudal."

Arudal was about to protest that he did not feel so ill, but abruptly his sight darkened and he felt his limbs stiffening with cold. It seemed to him that he could see the Shadow-shapes crowding about him, hear their soft whispers icy against his ears...then the world brightened again, and his cheeks stung as though someone had slapped him sharply.

"By the oath you gave me, squire!" Sir Thoron's deep voice rasped. "Stay here - don't go slipping away again! Amanvon, the fright you gave us!"

Arudal blinked, looking up into his knight's craggy face. "I have not anywhere ygone, sir," he stammered. "I am here all of the time been..."

"Salarond thought we might lose you," Sir Thoron told him roughly. "But we're sailing out tomorrow at dawn, with or without you, so you'd best be in health enough to walk onto the ship by then. And no more fainting fits either - eh, squire?"

"No, sir," Arudal answered.

Amazingly, Sir Thoron smiled. "That's more like it. Sit up and eat your dinner, and then you can go through the crap Requisitions sent up and see how badly they misread your handwriting. Which is nearly illegible, by the way. Don't you know how to print a plain hand?"

"I write as I was taughten, sir."

"Well, you can damned well learn how to write so the rest of us can read it. Not that Finvar isn't worse. Your handwriting is just atavistic; his is downright sloppy. Isn't it, Finvar?"

"Sir!" Finvar said, a clear note of amusement in his voice. "My shieldwork's much better than it was. You said there wasn't time for everything, sir."

"I probably did, at that. Bring that table over here so Arudal can eat something without spilling it all over himself. And think carefully about whether there's anything you can't live without for the next year, because the gods only know what we'll find in the West, and this will be your last chance to stock up at the Crown's expense for a while."

Finvar opened his mouth, but Sir Thoron reached over to thump him lightly on the head before he could speak. "And there'd better not be a request for women on the list either, whether you think you can live without for a year or not. You'll just have to resign yourself to strengthening your sword grip."

"Aw," Finvar muttered, ducking his head in a flush of embarassment.

Sir Thoron looked at Arudal. "I suppose I don't have to worry about that with you. I...hmm." The big knight dropped his gaze, almost as if he, too, were embarassed by something that he would not talk about. "I guess we'll deal with things as and when they come up. Finvar, that table; see that he eats well."

Thoron rose and left the room as Finvar dragged the table over to Arudal's bedside, swinging a chair for himself about. There was a covered dish and two plates on the table; when Finvar lifted the cover, Arudal smelled the delicious scent of roast fish. Though he had not been hungry before, the sight of the two sea-trout lying on a frondy bed of dill brought the water to his mouth.

"What was wrong with you?" Finvar asked as the two of them began to eat. "Lostren wouldn't tell me anything, but he looked scared to death, and Sir Salarond was acting like he was afraid to do anything to heal you. Did that Sir Daurar do something to you with mind-magic?"

"O, no," Arudal answered. "I...reacted badly to Sir Salarond's spell. Such things can happen."

Finvar frowned. "I've heard of that, yes. Are you going to be all right?"

"Yes." Arudal picked up a large bite of trout, chewing it slowly and carefully to forestall any more questions while he had his mouth full.

Before they had finished eating, Lostren came in, carefully holding a steaming bowl in gloved hands. He grinned broadly when he saw Arudal sitting up. "Praised be Amanvon!" he said. "Sir Salarond was almost ready to take you to your own embassy. If you hadn't come round...well, never mind. He sent this for you, anyway. You're to drink it when you finish going through your requisitions."

"What is it?" Arudal asked as Lostren set the bowl down in front of him.

"Something that's good for you. I hope," Lostren muttered. "You can take normal healings?"

"I...yes."

In spite of Sir Thoron's complaints about his handwriting, Arudal found that Requisitions had followed his list accurately enough. They had sent up several small lumps of lapis rather than powder, but the little stones had already been sensitized to magic; Arudal could see their faint bluish glow in the candlelight. Lostren hovered over him until he had finished sorting the spell-components, then pressed the bowl into his hands. "Drink this and go to bed. You'll feel better in the morning."

The darkish liquid in the bowl had a slightly bitter taste, and numbed Arudal's tongue as he drank. He could feel it taking effect almost at once, blurring the candlelight softly in his eyes. He was barely able to get his clothes off and crawl into bed before he fell asleep.

Chapter 7: The Voyage Begun

"Glittering wind-flung spray in sun,
What matter where we turn the prow?
If the sailing's well-begun,
The leaping waves are joy enow."

- Felatar, traditional

Arudal woke a little before dawn when the servants came in with fresh candles and hot porridge. He felt rested and light, as though he had never been ill. Mindful of their forthcoming journey, he dressed for shipboard, pulling on his sea-boots of silver seal-fur soled with sharkskin and a hooded sealskin cape. Finvar kept stealing nervous glances at him, as if he might collapse at any moment, but Arudal ignored that, eating with a good appetite.

When his fellow squire started to armour up, Arudal raised an eyebrow. "On shipboard?"

"Sir Thoron always wants..." Finvar started. The door from Thoron's own chamber swung open.

"Arudal has the right of it," Sir Thoron boomed. "No armour on shipboard unless we're training. Or...how well do you swim, Finvar?"

"Uh. Not that well, sir."

"Thought not. Both packed and ready to go? You'd better be, we're leaving now. Arudal, get my armour bag."

The weight of two sets of armour and his own bag of clothes and ritual components was not too much for Arudal to carry, but the bulk of the bags made them awkward. He had to twist and turn to get through doorways, trotting to keep up with his tall knight and less-burdened squire-brother.

Sir Shakhor, Sir Eroth, and Dame Karsil were already waiting at the dock with their squires. The starlight gleamed softly from the Elf's pale hair, casting glints of silvered emerald from her eyes; even the Men stood out clearly to Arudal's sight. Glancing behind, he saw Sir Salarond and Lostren following at a more leisurely pace. In spite of his burden, Arudal shivered a little with excitement - or maybe a faint tingle of fear: once their boat cast off, there would be no turning back to the Middle Land until they had done what they were setting out to do.

One by one, the company walked up the gangplank. Finvar helped Arudal, heavy-laden as he was, down into the ship.

"When you've put those away, get a lantern and come with me," ordered Sir Salarond. "I would have you look at our supplies again before we cast off."

The hold was full-laden with food, water-casks stacked one atop the other. Arudal went through the list thoroughly. At last he was satisfied that the ship held enough to feed and water its crew, as well as the horses, for at least four months. "All is well, sir."

"Good." The healer contemplated Arudal thoughtfully for a moment. "And with you? Your colour is back, at least."

"I am all right, sir."

Sir Salarond's broad brow furrowed. "You frightened us all badly last night. I thought..."

"Lostren told me, sir," Arudal said swiftly. "Truly, I am well now. I did not mean to be a burden."

"No burden, only...I should never have forgiven myself if I had harmed you. Yet what am I to do, if on the way we have need of magics that you cannot bear?"

Had their mission been for Tharandrost, Arudal would have known plainly how to answer: the State's need was of more worth than any one man's life. But this was a matter for Kantar, and though he was Sir Thoron's squire, there was yet a loyalty that stood above the oath he had chosen.

After a few moments, Salarond shook his head. "Pray that such a choice does not come about, then," he said, and Arudal could not tell whether the commander was giving an order or answering his own question.

The ropes were loosed, the anchor pulled up; the great iron chain that barred the way was cranked aside, and the dromon glided swiftly along the channel towards the sea. She eased out into the harbor, slipping easily between the fat-bellied merchant cogs and past the little fishing boats, out towards the open ocean. The first swell lifted Arudal's heart with the prow, the smooth wave-rhythm of homecoming that beat through the veins of every Tharandrostan. For we are men of the sea, made by the gods to sail and seek afar, he thought, the old words echoing in his head with the crashing of spray against the ship's bow. Arudal glanced almost enviously at the helmsman, steady at the wheel. He would have loved to steer this craft himself, to feel her leaping smoothly beneath his touch like a spirited steed. The first mist of dawn was beginning to touch his sight - but Tharandrostans learned young how to steer ships through the thickest fog, for their coast was often locked in mist even on the brightest mornings. Smiling, Arudal leaned against the rail, and for a little time it seemed to him that he was home again, with the wind behind him and the bow's spray shedding from the slick silver fur of his sealskin cape.

The sound of retching beside him broke his reverie. Finvar was bending over the rail, casting up loudly. A sharp pang of worry went through Arudal: had his squire-brother been poisoned? Surely Sir Daurar would not have...

"Ack," Finvar muttered, pulling a handkerchief from his belt-pouch to wipe his mouth. There was an odd greenish cast to his skin, and he looked quite miserable. "Arudal. You lied. It goes up and down..." He groaned and bent over again, heaving.

"Perhaps you ate something bad?" Arudal suggested. "Should I ask Sir Salarond to see to you?"

"Bugger off," Finvar grunted between retches.

Arudal hurried light-footed in search of their commander, only to find him standing with a palm to Tirothar's forehead and murmuring. Sir Eroth's squire looked as bad as Finvar, though the colour was coming quickly back to his face.

"Sir," Arudal said when Sir Salarond turned away. "Please come at once! Finvar is very ill."

The healer raised a shaggy eyebrow. "Him, too? Well, I can deal with that."

Arudal followed along as Sir Salarond went to Finvar, treating him much as he had Tirothar. "Light food and light duties only today," Sir Salarond told the pale-faced squire. "By tomorrow, you won't know that you were ever seasick. Go on down to the galley: Lostren is making a tea to soothe abused stomachs."

"Is this truly from being on the sea?" enquired Arudal.

Finvar glared, but Sir Salarond laughed. "Not everyone grows up on shipboard, Arudal," he said kindly. "Finvar has never been on water wilder than the Karasindi in his life: it is not to be wondered that he finds the sea strange."

"But I thought that Men of Imperial blood were all born to the sea, whether raised to it or not."

Their commander shook his head, graystreaked hair feathering back around his face. "Consider our history, Arudal. The strongest strain in us from the elder days comes from the forebears of the Horse-Tribes. Though it is true that all those who returned to the Middle Land were mariners, yet blood may mix and run in odd eddies - as you should surely know."

Arudal nodded. From childhood, he had been taught how to track hidden and open traits of descent, starting with the simple colours of flowers and cats and going on to the intricacies of his own interwoven pedigree. He did not know whether a stomach for the sea was a hidden or an open trait, for there was no reason to trace it in Tharandrost, and so he asked Finvar, "What of your parents? Does either of them get sick on the ocean?"

Finvar spat the last taste of vomit out of his mouth and snarled, "My parents have better sense than to go on the ocean." He turned and stomped heavily towards the galley, lurching from side to side on the rolling deck like a drunk in a high gale.

Sir Salarond sighed. "Arudal, Arudal. How long have you lived in Kantar?"

"The most of a year, sir."

"Did you ever talk to anyone other than Dr. Grímhjálm?"

"I had to arrange my studies with the University, sir, and also to explain to the Library when I needed extendings of a book's time."

"You had no friends at University?"

"I was there to study, sir," Arudal said reproachfully. He left out that it had been strongly suggested to him that he not become too familiar with the Kantarean students.

"No wonder...well, never mind. Finvar will doubtless forgive you when he is feeling more himself, so long as you leave the subject of seasickness alone. Incidentally," Salarond added, "I know how hard you have been trying to behave yourself with Rhys, but not everyone understands your feelings. Do try a little harder, and remember that the two of you may end up warding each other's backs when we reach our destinations - yes?"

"Yes, sir," Arudal said dutifully. An order was an order, whatever he thought himself.

"Good lad." Sir Salarond patted him on the shoulder and moved off. After a little time, Arudal wandered down to the galley where Lostren was passing out his herb tea to the other squires. Lostren looked quite cheerful, black hair tousled and cheeks pink from the brisk sea-wind, but Rhys seemed as unhappy as Tirothar and Finvar, and was staring darkly into his steaming mug.

"That smells very nice," Arudal said to Lostren. "What is it?"

"Mint and anise and chammomile, chiefly, with a touch of vargwe added just at the end. You can't have the vargwe if you don't need it - and you obviously don't - but I'll give you some of the tea."

Arudal stirred a little honey into his mug to sweeten it and sipped. It really was very good, and the mug was nicely warm against his chilled fingers.

"Aren't you afraid to wear sealskin on the waters?" Rhys said suddenly.

Arudal looked up into the buck's freckled face, blinking. "Why should I be?" he asked in turn, startled enough to reply as if Rhys were a human being.

"We have a saying: 'Never wear a bear's skin to the wood, nor a seal's on the sea.' There are, look you, both bears and seals that can take off their hides and walk like men, and if they see that you adorn yourself with the skins of their family, they will hunt you for revenge through three generations - as who would not," the Plainsman added, "upon seeing their kin murdered and their bodies stripped for pride?"

Arudal shrugged. "There are few who do not wear sealskin on the ocean, for that it does not get spray-soaked and freeze like wool: nothing is better against cold and wet. I have never heard such tales."

Rhys touched the little embroidered bag at his neck, and it seemed to Arudal that he saw a faint light shimmer about it through his misted eyes. "I suppose you would not have." Then, as if reminding himself of something, the Plainsman said rather stiffly, "What of the rest of you? I have never seen a Kantarean wearing sealskin."

"Nor I," Finvar replied thoughtfully. "I wonder why? In Helludal, we wear boots lined with fleece in the winter, but they still get soaked and cold - sealskin might be better in snow and icy water."

Lostren shook his head. "It is from piety and gratefulness," he told them. "When our ancestors defied the Empire, and the ships of the True began to set sail from the West to the Middle Land, the seals and dolphins guided them safely to harbour, but aided to turn about the ships of the Fallen. Since then it has been counted ill in Kantar to slay those messengers of Terathon Water-Lord, our allies in time of need. Only the..." He looked at Arudal and coughed, his face reddening.

"I have never that hearden," Arudal said, drawing himself up to his full height. "I am sure it must be myth, and no true history."

"But it is documented in..." Lostren began. Even with his day-misted sight, Arudal did not miss Finvar's foot kicking the other squire hard in the ankle. Lostren shut his mouth tightly, and turned back to stirring his tea.

"I think Arudal's cape and boots look quite well, and are obviously very practical for shipboard," Tirothar said with rather forced cheerfulness. "What are the boots soled with, anyway? I noticed you weren't slipping about the way the rest of us are."

Arudal answered, and the conversation turned to other things, but he could not help thinking of Sir Salarond ordering him to behave with Rhys, and wondering what the other knights had told their squires about him - it was clear that, among themselves, Kantareans still spoke of Tharandrostans as among the Fallen. Yet the truth will show itself as they come to know me, Arudal thought hopefully.

Still, though the other squires tried to include him in their talk, Arudal felt lonely and out of sorts. As soon as he could, he finished his tea and went above-decks again. Through the morning mist over his sight, he could just see the glimmering shapes of a shoal of little jellyfish floating in the swells, their clear caps glistening with tiny rainbows in the sunlit water. The ship was still heading due South - Arudal guessed that they would sail that way for a day or more, until they were well out of sight of other vessels. He wondered when, or if, he would be allowed to speak with their guides.

"Arudal," Lostren said, coming up beside him.

"Yes?"

"Look, I...I'm sorry if I offended you. I know you've been having a hard time of it so far, and truly, I didn't mean to suggest anything about you or your people. Uh, I know you're not really used to Kantarean company, so...well, I do like you, and I hope you're still willing to be friends with me." Lostren's voice was soft, his tilted gray eyes open wide. Arudal wondered if he was speaking for himself, or if Sir Salarond had told him to come and apologize.

"What were you going to say?"

Lostren blinked, looking curiously at him.

"When Finvar kicked you," Arudal elaborated. "'Only the...' something."

"Oh. Er." Lostren shifted from foot to foot. "In the Histories of Verethen, it says that only the Fallen still kill seals and dolphins. But Verethen was from eastern Artegal, and had no reason to be familiar with Tharandrostan custom. It is likeliest that he wrote that just for literary emphasis."

"I see." And I would believe you, if I could.

"I didn't even think about Tharandrost; I was just repeating what I had memorized from the Histories."

There was an old saying in Tharandrost, that must go back to the days before proper healing became common: Don't scratch at a scabbed wound. Arudal heeded that now, despite his urge to press Lostren on the point. "I see. I am not offended."

Lostren nodded decisively. "Good. Shall we go below and see how the horses are?"

Arudal followed him down to the stabling-hold, into the warm smells of hay and straw and horses. Inmanat neighed in greeting, stretching his neck over the wooden gate and mouthing at Arudal's hands and belt-pouch hopefully, and Arudal stroked his soft nose and rubbed him about the cheeks and ears. "There's a good horse," Arudal crooned to him. "Good, brave horse, to make such a faring as your ancestors did....No, I've nothing for you now, but I shall bring you treats next time."

The warhorses were less happy, tossing their heads and neighing and stamping their hooves on the heaving planks as if they could pound the ship into stillness as they would a downed foe. Arudal wondered if it had been wise to bring them, after all: three months was a long voyage even for the sea-accustomed Imperial steeds, and he had always heard that the heavy Kantarean cavalry-horses were not so enduring. A flash of black along the floor caught his eye, and he heard a muffled squeak; in the shadows, he could see the shape of a large cat with a rat dangling limply from her mouth.

"Puss, puss," Arudal murmured, crouching down and rustling his fingers along the planking. The cat stared greenly at him for a few moments, then trotted over to drop the rat at his feet and receive her due caresses. She was not all black, but a dark tortoiseshell, with little golden tufts glinting through her long fur like gold-wire braiding in a noblewoman's sable hair. Her ears were high-tufted, her back legs long and powerful. Arudal thought that she must have Western Tree-cat blood in her, as many ship and harbour-cats did wherever Tharandrostan vessels put into port. Inmanat leaned down over his gate to lip softly at Arudal's hair, and for a few moments he felt utterly content.

Lostren was watching him with an odd expression on his face - Arudal could not tell what the other youth was thinking. But after a little while, Lostren said softly, in his barely-accented Imperial, "You have been very homesick, haven't you?"

Arudal nodded: there was no sense in denying it. He thought of the hearth-fire in his parents' mansion, the warm flames that were called the heart of the home always burning in the middle of the large room hung with richly coloured tapestries, the soft rugs underfoot with his mother's cats curled on them, and his father's great wolfhound lying by the fire in a heap of gray fur, rain pattering softly against the small glass windows, and his eyes prickled with tears.

"Remember," the other squire went on, "you can always talk to me if you want to."

The cat stood up on her hind legs with her paws on Arudal's chest, purring and rubbing her whiskered face along his jaw. Arudal petted her in place of the words that would not come to him.

They sailed south for three more days. Then, towards sunset, a fresh wind sprang up, blowing strongly towards the reddening glow of the Western sky. Sir Salarond stood on the deck with his eyes closed, breathing the briny air deeply into his lungs. It seemed to Arudal that he could feel something stirring about the healer-priest, and he kept his distance, waiting for Salarond to speak.

"Time to put about," Sir Salarond said at last. "Arudal, you may take the helm."

"Thank you, sir!" Arudal exclaimed, hurrying over to relieve the steersman. The ship moved lightly to his steering, like the finest horse answering to a moth-wing brush of rein and heel; he felt the wind catching in her sails, lifting her swiftly over the dark water.

Though he had to lid his eyes against the red-gold mist of the setting Sun before him lest all his sight be darkened, his heart seemed to swell with a feeling he could not name - longing, perhaps, or a joy that ached in his chest like an old wound even as his blood sang in his veins. The Westward course seemed well-known to him, as though he were turning homeward after long away, and yet his heart beat with all the excitement of steering a ship towards an harbour still unseen.

Then he heard Dame Karsil's high pure voice lifting in song, and though the Elf sang alone, with no harp nor flute weaving among her words, it seemed to Arudal that he could hear the echoes of music chiming through Karsil's throat.

"Evening Star over sun-red Sea,
Faring in air's wandering,
Gleaming light through the blue aloft,
Shining clear, sign of gods' hope,
Bear us out through the sunset's door,
Guide us beyond all shadows,
Through star-bright night, through the sun-bright day,
To sorrows' end, the fair lands..."

Arudal's eyes stung with tears, though he did not know why. It felt as though each note of the Elf's song swept painfully across the strings of his heart, like a fleeting glimmer of something he had longed for so deeply that he had not known his desire until the moment of seeing it just beyond his reach. Now he understood why Men said that there was peril in the voices of Elves: even had Prince Norombar spoken himself to command it at that moment, Arudal thought that he could not have turned the ship's helm from the West.

Chapter 8: Warnings of the West

"If you seek without surcease
Nor pause, but drive unflinching on,
Fear, lest you find your heart's desire
Changed beyond reckoning, once won."

- "Imitations", tr. from the Bright Elven by Lord Hethrin dath Balaron

The next day, Sir Salarond called all of their company to the ship's little briefing room. There were two strange Men there already: both tall and lanky, with light brown hair hanging down in braids about their long brown faces, and alike enough to be brothers. They were dressed strangely, in breeches and tunics made of little bands of blue and green cloth woven tightly together, with beaded fringes at the tunics' hems; their bright cloaks were also woven from thin bands, fringed and beaded. Their blue eyes rolled like those of nervous horses as they looked at the Kantarean knights, and Arudal saw a thin sheen of sweat glazing their narrow foreheads. He knew that these must be their guides from the West - and though he had not known what to expect, he found himself sadly disappointed.

"Gentlemen," Sir Salarond said to his companions. "These are Atharath and Gormok, who have kindly consented to show us the way to their homeland and advise us as to how we may best proceed. They will tell us what to expect, and then you may ask questions of them. Atharath, would you begin?"

"It is of three months asailing til reach the Westes shore," the taller of the guides began. Arudal found his thick accent almost impossible to understand - yet here and there, bits of strange familiarity crept through: he wondered what the guides' native tongue was like. Arudal could tell by the bemused looks on the others' faces that they were having almost as much trouble as he; even Sir Salarond sometimes had to ask Atharath to repeat himself. But gradually what they needed to know came clear: the course they would have to sail, and the perils on the way, wind and rock and maelstrom, the great graysharks of the deepest ocean that men called ship-eaters - some longer than the dromon itself - and sea-drakes large enough to sink a two hundred-foot greatship, let alone their smaller craft...Little wonder, Arudal thought, that no ships have come back to tell of the West! At least this vessel should be warded against the notice of sea-beasts, though magic is chancy at best against old drakes; thanks be to Utalkath that the Great Dragons never dwelt but on land.

"The Ferth of Hatin ren far inland," Atharath went on. "There finn'st Hatin's City where sea-ships gather, and much cheaping is betraded - many goods for gold," he added at the Kantareans' bewildered looks. "There getten hengst for wains, if you've brought none."

A sudden brightness shone in Arudal's mind at the half-familiar word, and he said carefully in Imperial, "What is your native tongue?"

Both Western men jerked back, staring at him, and Gormok made a complex sign with his fingers. "That is sorceror-speech!" he said - not in Imperial, but in a tongue that might have been a thick and far-removed dialect, almost easier for Arudal to understand than the Westerners' mangled Common. "You are of the Mordhagoernim."

Arudal shook his head violently: in Imperial, the last word must be Morthugorunim, the children of Morthugor. "I am a...a studier of languages," he said. But their guides shrank back from him, and Atharath was shivering.

"Arudal!" Sir Salarond snapped. "What did you just say to them?"

"I only asked after their native language, which seems to be a form of Imperial," Arudal answered, bewildered. "Truly, I did not mean to upset them."

"You seem to have done a damned fine job of it," Sir Thoron rumbled. "Get back by the door, squire, and don't say anything else unless you're asked to."

Arudal backed away from their guides, wondering what he had done wrong as Atharath and Gormok burst into a babbling argument, speaking so fast that Arudal could only catch a few phrases. "Look at them...kin to the Dark Ones..." Gormok was saying, and Atharath replied with something like, "But no Elf would ever..." "No gold's worth it," Gormok insisted. "...living, and burnt in a wooden cage."

Atharath slapped his companion hard. "What care we of them? Free men, and rich...we knew the Eastern sailing was risky, and had nothing to lose...get what we can of it, and Shadow take the goodfolk." Then he glanced fearfully at Arudal, and fell silent.

For a little time there was no sound in the room save breath. Then Sir Salarond said, "Arudal, were you able to make anything of that?"

Arudal repeated what he had heard.

"This will not be as easy as we hoped," Sir Salarond sighed. "In truth, I had wondered what memories of the Empire lingered in the West - and now I fear I know." He looked searchingly at his companions, and Arudal felt his stomach squirm. "Eroth, Shakhor, Rhys, and Karsil - you four are the best for talking to our guides, I think. You stay here; the rest of us will go outside and consider this."

Arudal glanced at the four their commander had chosen - the Elf, the Plainsman, and the two knights who showed the least of pure Imperial blood - and suddenly understood. .

"This will be more difficult than I had hoped," Sir Salarond said as soon as they were outside the door. "I wonder just how keen their memories are, after seventeen hundred years?"

"He said that Imperial was sorceror-speech," Arudal contributed.

"And what else? You went white as the dead at something."

"He asked me," Arudal said reluctantly, "if I was one of the children of Morthugor."

"I see. So, we know that the Empire's evils have not been forgotten - and that some sort of magic, or at least that old worship of the Shadow, still lives in the West. I wonder who the Dark Ones are? Did some of the Fallen survive, or is the Imperial race remembered by ancient pictures and tales?...In any case, that will make it harder for us to travel easily there."

Arudal considered the others. Sir Salarond and Lostren, both of the nearly pure bloodlines of Kantar's high nobles...Tirothar was tall and thin for Imperial stock, and blue-eyed; if his dark hair were lightened, he might pass for Common easily enough. But for all Sir Thoron's size, his eyes were unmistakably slanted, and any keen gaze could see the true steel-and-amber in their gray-black irises with the golden-brown ring about the pupil. Finvar's heavy bones might suggest a mingling of Northman blood to one looking for purity, but his features were clearly Imperial, and Arudal himself...He had seen his own face, near enough, in the oldest paintings his family had brought from the West: he might have been the brother or son of that first Arudal Agathusaftan who founded their Tharandrostan House, rather than his grandson through the generations of seventeen hundred years.

"Some magic of disguise?" Tirothar suggested hopefully.

"Perhaps. We still do not know if, or how, magic works there - if we are lucky, we may be able to find out more before we reach our destination. And what magic may cloak, magic may pierce as well."

Arudal thought longingly of the gift of Mind-Reading. Regardless of the language of their thoughts, a skilled Mind-Reader could find out all they needed to know from their guides in less than a day. He had that gift strongly - but only for the dead: the thoughts of the living were as silent to him as the footsteps of ghosts to others. Yet... "Sir, do you not know magics that would open our guides' minds to you, and be sure that they have not decided to deceive us? Atharath and Gormok are not, I think, the most honourable of men."

"If they were," Sir Salarond said heavily, "they should not have agreed to guide us to their shores for any reward. They are adventurers at best...but you, of all people, should know that it is wrong to open another's mind without consent."

Though such laws seldom applied to the Undead, Arudal remembered vividly the scathing lectures his parents had delivered to his younger brother, whose gifts were attuned to the living. He felt the pointed tips of his ears reddening; but Sir Thoron snorted.

"They aren't Kantarean citizens, and you're the only law out here, Salarond. What's more important: rights that hardly apply to them, even if they weren't scum who'd sell their own people out, or getting this damned pedigree - if it even exists - and staving off a civil war?"

Sir Salarond's broad brow furrowed, his lips tightening.

"Shadow take it," Thoron added, "you can issue yourself a warrant, on the grounds of the security of the White Throne or some such. Ultar wouldn't hesitate for a moment, and all the gods know he won't complain when he sees it in your report. The White Company gets things done: that's why King Edril called on us for this, instead a bunch of King's Own with ramrods up their arses."

"Sir Ultar is not in command of this mission. Yet...I take your point," Sir Salarond said reluctantly. "Lostren, attend me. The rest of you stay here."

Thoron grinned fearsomely at his commander's back. "Well, squires," he said softly. "You're on a real White Company mission now - half-planned, half-legal, mostly half-arsed, and undoubtedly altogether successful, if it doesn't turn out to be another wild goose chase. Are you enjoying it?"

"Yes, sir!" Finvar and Tirothar chorused. His grin echoing his knight's, the Artegalian added, "But it won't be a real White Company mission until we get to use some nitre. We've been out several days and not blown anything up yet, sir."

"Oh, we will." Sir Thoron patted Arudal's head. "When Salarond's done here, squire, you ask him for a laxative. You look as though you haven't had a good shit for a week."

"Sir?"

Thoron only laughed. "It must be something in the Tharandrostan diet. I've never seen one of you who didn't look constipated most of the time."

Now I know I don't understand the Kantarean sense of humour, Arudal thought. I hope they were joking about the nitre.

Sir Salarond and Lostren came back before the others had left the briefing room. Lostren was holding a broad-bottomed ship's decanter close to his chest - it looked full of deep red wine, but Arudal could see the glimmer of power reflecting from the diamond-cut crystal. "Be ready to rush in if you hear trouble," Salarond said quietly to Thoron, who nodded.

They waited for perhaps a quarter of an hour before Karsil, Shakhor, Eroth, and Rhys filed out. "All is well," the Elf's high voice chimed. "They drank without trouble, and Sir Salarond assures us that they will remember nothing of this. But stay here on watch."

The Sun was halfway down the western sky by the time Sir Salarond and Lostren left the briefing room. The commander's face was pale, his graying hair disheveled as though he had been running his hands through it over and over. Though he walked steadily enough, his pupils were huge, as if swollen by the weight of knowledge he had drawn from the Westerners' minds. "To my quarters," he ordered. Lostren had a sheaf of parchments in his hands - Arudal could see a rough map drawn on the top one.

"It was well that we chose to do this," Sir Salarond said when they had all seated themselves in his little chamber. There was hardly room for the whole of their company there; the knights took the chairs and bed, leaving the squires to settle themselves cross-legged on the floor. "Listen carefully. Lostren took notes, but I do not know how much longer my mind will hold all that I have learned..."

Arudal watched closely as Sir Salarond pointed to the first map, explaining the hazards of their sea-faring in much greater detail than Atharath and Gormok had given - not sailors themselves, as Arudal had guessed before, the two Westerners had not been able to tell the route accurately until Salarond had dragged the memories from the depths of their minds.

"And that is the easy part. The Men of the West remember Imperials as a race of demons, and will strangle a black-haired child in its cradle, lest any taint come upon them. Lostren, the demon-picture."

Lostren ruffled through his parchments, coming up with a grotesque sketch. It showed a dwarflike creature with huge slanted eyes in an inhumanly-angled face, thin arms and legs dangling from a wedgelike body. Arudal looked at it in repelled fascination: distorted through near seventeen hundred years of fearful memory as it might be, he could still see the roots of the classical Imperial features in it - of his own features.

"The site we seek - the libraries of the Imperial Seat - lies some five hundred miles inland. But they believe it to be cursed and inhabited by beings about which no one will speak: it is perhaps fifty miles from the nearest settlement. Our guides' minds could tell us no more than that there was great terror on that place, and that none who had sought to loot the remnants of the Imperial Seat had ever returned living from there, though sometimes revenants..." In the dim light from the porthole, Arudal could see the grayish cast under Sir Salarond's skin, as though the Westerners' fear had sunk into his mind with their memories.

"The land map, Lostren," the healer-priest said gruffly. "Here, you see, is our best route there - at least, the best our guides could think of."

Arudal looked at the map closely. He had seen copies of old maps of the West; there was even an original preserved carefully under glass in the public section of the Prince's Library. The face of the land itself had changed greatly in the Fall, but a few points were still recognisable: Hatin's City, for instance, had once been the harbour Murumban, the chief point for voyages between the West and the Middle Land, though then it had been in a deep bay, rather than at the end of a long firth.

"We may be able to pass through Hatin's City without too much trouble, for the people there are used to strangers from ships, but once we are out in the open countryside, things may be very different. We pass through farmland or hills for most of our journey, then another two weeks or so through thick and dangerous forest, before we come to what they call the Cursed Lands. There our maps end."

"What of magic?" Arudal asked. "Will spells work in the West?"

"Some seem to, and some may not. Our guides are fearful of sorcerors and witches, but I could not tell quite what they meant: they are not learned men. They know of at least lesser charms of healing, so the grace of the gods has not withdrawn altogether from the West. As to the darker magics they feared - whether those are true magics of the sort we know, or the curses of Morthugor's priests, I am not sure."

"Is Morthugor still worshipped there?" enquired Eroth.

"By some, apparently. They seem to know the true gods, though often by different names, and a host of godlets and spirits. But here and there, like pockets of infection in a half-healed wound, are places where the darkest ways are still followed - and thicker, as might be expected, nearer to the ruins of the Imperial Seat. You, Arudal," he added, "managed to frighten them near-witless by speaking in the Imperial tongue."

"It is cause to weep," Karsil said softly, "that those who came once to free the West of Morthugor's Avatar are remembered now only as the embodiments of that same Shadow. Truly the hearts of Men turn as swiftly as their generations! At least the Westerners have not forgotten that the Elves are their friends."

"Aye," Sir Salarond agreed. "We may all find ourselves glad of that. Indeed, Karsil, you may have to speak as our ambassador to the Elves along the way, for there are several settlements of your fair folk in the forests, where they hid from the Empire's might in the dark years. They have little to do with Men, and there is no knowing how they will look upon our quest."

"I can tell you that now," Karsil replied, her wide green eyes narrowing. "Amanvon made us for many purposes: for the joy of our singing beneath the night sky, and for the beauty of our works - but also, to guard the green earth against its foes, for the gateways to Shadow had already been broken long before Queen Celenthil first lifted her eyes to the stars. If the evils left by Men sleep where the Imperial Seat stood, the Elves will not gladly suffer Men to awaken them again, not even for the sake of Avalar's descendants. If we wish to achieve our mission, it were best to avoid my kin."

"But I thought that Avalar cleansed the Imperial Seat," Tirothar broke in.

Lostren shook his head. "The Seat itself, yes. He did not write of more in his History of the Fall, but his private letters speak of...let me see if I can remember..." His brow furrowed; though there was enough daylight through the porthole that Arudal could not see his face too clearly, it seemed to him that the other squire's thoughtful expression made him look older, almost professorial. Lostren spoke slowly, as though translating in his head, "When the fires of the Wrath died, nothing was left aboveground of the temple of Shadow, save smoke and blackened stones. I pray that the gods destroyed what lay below as well! My men had not the strength to shift the fallen rocks that had been raised by magic. There were many other steads in the city that the Wrath dropped most heavily upon, though before they had been no different than others to look upon, and it seemed to me that I felt a great foreboding when I neared what remained. It will be long years, I fear, before those pockets of darkness can be unsealed and made wholesome, let alone rebuilt. The Imperial Library is more than half-destroyed, for many books burst into flame, and whole wings were cut off when their roofs and walls caved in. I had set a division of men to clear it, but that labour was no more than half-started when the uprisings began. We fled with the work still undone: maybe, if the gods will, what seemed to destroy the lore then will save it from the torches of those my predecessors had enslaved. Alas, that the gift of freedom should bring such a repayment! But better, yet, than that men labour in collars and chains for the sake of their birth: had I known what should come after, I would still have freed the Empire's slaves, for in mastering other races came the first root of our corruption..." Salarond's squire stopped abruptly. "That is the only time he wrote specifically of what the Wrath had done to the Imperial Seat. His other letters only mention the fires and earthquakes, and the lightnings that struck down the chief worshippers of Morthugor. Sir?" he added, turning to Salarond. "Were you able to tell what the Western histories of the Fall say?"

"Atharath and Gormok are not learned men," Sir Salarond replied. "As well ask any tiller of the ground what he can recite of Avalar's writings...It may be that we can find out more when we come to Hatin's City. Meanwhile, we must decide who shall spend these next months in learning the language from our guides."

"Surely I am the best suited to that, sir?" Arudal said. "I can already speak with them after a fashion."

"Most decidedly not you," Salarond answered sternly. "Karsil, you will have to do as much of the talking as possible when we get there, while the rest of us will do better to stay silent, playing the part of servants, or bodyguards, perhaps."

Are we to return to our ancestors' homeland like thieves skulking in the night? Arudal thought bitterly. That greatness of which all the lore and might of the Middle Land is but a shadow - must we return now only to find it degraded far below those shards of memory we kept alive? That is a bitter end to a dream that began so fair!

"Now listen before I lose any more of what I learned from their minds," Sir Salarond went on. "We can only pass as travellers from afar..."

Chapter 9: A Confrontation

"War between clans,
Rivalry over a woman,
Hatred between two:
Truth must end it, or swords."

- Plainsman proverb

Arudal slept ill that night, turning uncomfortably in his hammock to the deep sound of Sir Thoron's snoring and Finvar's softer snuffles. At last he could not bear to lie still anymore, and got up, pulling on tunic and breeches and cloak and creeping barefoot along the narrow corridor between the rooms of the lower deck. The utter darkness was brighter than day to him; even the starlight above was too faint to blur his vision. Arudal moved soundlessly, so that the night helmsman did not even lift his head to look as the Tharandrostan passed him - it seemed to Arudal almost as if he had slipped into Shadow without knowing it. Yet the planks of the deck were hard beneath his cold bare feet, and he could still feel the warmth of his sealskin cape about his shoulders, the salt taste of the air in his mouth: the Undead were forever past such things, in the empty aching chill of the Other Side.

Walking down the length of the deck, he saw the faint glimmer in the shadow of one of the masts before he could tell who was there. Rhys stood with his back braced against the mast-pole, his eyes closed as he murmured something. Arudal's hand dropped without thought to his side; but he had not put on his belt, and did not have so much as a knife.

The Plainman's eyes opened, and he started back, his hand flying to the embroidered pouch at his neck as he hissed something in his own tongue. Arudal crouched, ready to defend himself as best he could unarmed, but Rhys shook his head.

"You startled me, Arudal," he said. "I saw the shimmer of your cloak in the starlight, and thought...well, best not to mind what I thought. What are you doing up so late?"

The first words to Arudal's mind were, Who do you think you are, to ask me such a question? He bit them back, and said instead, "I could not sleep. And thou?"

"I could not, either...It seems to me, look you, that there is something that does not wish us to make landfall in the West. I thought that I might spy it out, but however I try, I can see naught but fading mist. But what of you? You are a, a ghost-seer - are there spirits of Shadow about us?"

"Not to my knowledge," Arudal answered stiffly.

"Would you tell me if there were?"

Arudal paused, his mouth open.

"It seems to me that it would be better if we were truthful with each other, as is the way among my own folk when there are such troubles between two," the Plainsman went on. "It is easy to tell how little you like me. And you are everything I would expect a high-born Tharandrostan to be: arrogant beyond belief, ever looking down your nose at those whose blood is less pure than your own - as proud of the darkness you inherited from your ancestors as the Kantareans are of the light Avalar followed, and touchy as a cat in a thunderstorm with it, so that the rest of our fellows hardly dare to say more than good day to you lest you take offense. I expect that you are as cruel and bloodthirsty as any of your race as well, save that you have had no chance to show it; but if you could have your way, you would have stabbed me just now and tossed my body over for the sharks - would you not?"

The flush warmed Arudal's cheeks against the cold sea-wind: he knew what his first response to the sight of a Plainsman practising magic had been. "Yet had I helden a blade in hand," he said slowly, "I woulde not have used it on a companion, for all..."

"Go on. I spoke harsh words to you: it is your turn to give them back."

Arudal stood flat-footed as though he had been caught ringingly on the helm with the full weight of a practice blade. All the things that had been in his mind since first meeting Rhys seemed to vanish as he tried to shape them, like clay dribbling out of his hands as soft mud. He could not truthfully say that the buck was unworthy of being Sir Shakhor's squire, for he had seen that the woods-skilled knight valued Rhys as highly as Sir Thoron valued Finvar; Rhys' magic, that Arudal had thought a dangerous abomination, seemed to be used for no other purposes than those Arudal himself would have. Dirty as a Plainsman, lazy as a Plainsman... Rhys bathed as often as any of them, and served his knight as eagerly; Arudal could not even criticize his table manners. "It goeth against the grain," he said at last, "to seen one of your race not only free-walking, but honoured as highly in this company as I. That is not as it should be."

"At least you will tell the truth," Rhys answered. "I had begun to wonder if you would claim that there was nothing amiss between us, or that it was all on my own side."

"I woulde not speaken untruth thus in return for honesty - no, not even to a Plainsman."

"And yet you think ill of me for no reason other than my birth?"

"Thou showed'st me thy hate quickly enow," Arudal answered, the roll of the ship's deck beneath his feet steadying him. "Thou wert glad enough to betray what I woulde not have spoken, after the vampires were comen upon us."

"Aye, I was. Ask yourself, then, what reason I had to trust you, when the land-spirits spoke to me in anger of what you had done and not told? And who would not be uplifted on seeing, as I thought, a foe prove his evil so swiftly?"

"There was naught of evil in what I did, and our commanders were well-pleased!" Arudal said. But he knew how satisfied he would have been, had he caught Rhys trying to betray their company.

"As may be. But have you anything more to say to me? Or is it all out between us now? Have I said aught that is untrue about you?"

"I have ne darkness from my ancestors, and I wot not by what right thou say'st that, save that it is ever easy for a slave to speaken ill of his masters when he knoweth that no punishment shall follow."

"Is that how you see it?" Rhys murmured, his voice crackling like drops of water steaming from hot ash. "But who among the children of the gods would pride himself on bearing such a curse as you suffer, with eyes blinded by the Sun's clean light and the chill of Shadow already on your soul? I would not take that on myself for all the riches and power the Western Empire could have offered."

"The gift of my line is ne curse! And I was happy enow, until…" Arudal stopped, shocked at what he had almost said to the Plainsman.

"Until you came with Sir Thoron?" Rhys asked. "And there, maybe, is why I am trying to talk with you now. Look you, we have something in common, you and I. We are both exiles from our peoples, even among these our friends - my friends, anyway: I do not know if you can name any of our company so. And is it, perhaps, that you hate me not least because I am not so lonely here as you?"

"I see no need to further with you speaken," Arudal said, turning away and walking back down to Sir Thoron's chamber. The knight and Finvar were still sleeping soundly, but even when Arudal was warmly wrapped in his blankets again, his hammock gently rocking with the swaying of the ship, the cold would not leave his limbs. Rhys is only a Plainsman, and they are deceitful and cunning with words, Arudal said to himself. But that thought gave him no comfort, and it was a long time before he slept.

Chapter 10: Storm at Sea

"The hungry sea knows not good nor ill,
Her own ancient hunger is all.
So when waves are breaking high over the mast,
And each breath through torrent seems like your last,
Then pray that Amandeth take your soul fast,
For the sea will not heed your call."

- "The Hungry Sea", Kantarean traditional

Though he had been wakeful the night before, Arudal rose early, going down to the galley in the brightening dawn. The delicious scent of frying fish already filled the little chamber; the cook nodded to Arudal as he came in.

"Don't suppose you'd like to lend a hand, would you?" he asked, flipping the sizzling fillets in their pan on the fire-box as expertly as any Tharandrostan cooking at sea. "The day crew's going to be coming by for their breakfasts in just a few minutes, and I'm running behind."

"What would you have me do?" Arudal said.

"Cook 'em or clean 'em, whichever you prefer."

Arudal looked down at the big basket of shining mackerel, a few still flopping weakly - the net must have just been drawn up. He was not dressed for being elbow-deep in fish entrails, so he moved to take the cook's place by the stove, and the thin man squatted before the basket, his sharp little knife flashing. The cook watched him carefully for the first few panfuls, but Arudal, highborn as he was, had been helping his father in galleys most of his life - even Count Arumir did not scorn to turn his hand to cooking a good catch when they were out on the sea, any more than he would have refused to gralloch his own deer.

"Good lad," the cook said, satisfied. "I'd swear you'd been doing that for twenty years...sorry, expect you have. It's easy to forget how slow your folk age. So how long have you been in the White Company?"

"Not long," Arudal temporized - he did not know how much Sir Salarond wanted the crew to know now. "And you?"

The other man laughed, separating another mackerel from its bowels and head in a single neat flicker of his blade. "I'm Secret Service, not White Company. Secret Service only in name, though, like a lot of the crew. I'm just Verhin the ship's cook - don't fight, no one tells me anything, and I don't want to know neither."

The dark tortoiseshell cat came padding in, sniffing the air and purring loudly. To Arudal's surprise, instead of giving her a few fish-heads, Verhin selected the most lively of the fish still twitching in the basket, tossing it into a corner. She sprang after it, slinking out with the mackerel flopping weakly in her jaws.

"Is she yours?" Arudal asked.

"Who?"

"The cat. She is a very fine creature."

Arudal saw the smile flickering across Verhin's thin face. "Aye, I guess you could say that, after a fashion. Keeps the rats down lovely, and doesn't cost much to feed - and I expect she's glad to have someone besides me who pays a little attention to her. Good luck to have aboard, as well. They say the ship won't sink while she's on it. That's why I picked up my little ghost-sight ring, so I know when to drop her a treat."

Arudal thought of how strangely Lostren had looked at him when he was talking to the cat on the stable-deck, and the pointed tips of his ears warmed. "You have been very homesick, haven't you?"... Had Lostren, unable to see the ghostly cat, thought Arudal was speaking to an imaginary creature as a child might?

The first of the day crew began to file in, and Arudal and Verhin were too busy to talk for a while. Several of the sailors stared oddly at Arudal as he served their food - in surprise and, Arudal suspected, a little gloating, as if they thought he had been ordered to help the cook as a punishment. Still, they seemed wary of him. Only Miraran the daytime helmsman greeted him by name.

"Morning, Arudal," the stocky, weathered man said cheerfully. "Can I get you to take over for a while during the day? I think we'll be in for a blow by late afternoon, and heavy work ahead by evening: Jannis is good, all right, but it may take both of us to keep the ship on course this night, and I'd as soon leave him to his rest in the day."

Weather-sense, Arudal thought; for the sky and sea were calm now, with no sign of hard weather in sight. "An Sir Thoron will allow it, certainly."

"Much appreciated. I'll have to take it back when things get rough - my orders, you know - but if you'd like, you can stay by me as long as you're able."

Arudal agreed gladly, for he had little experience in sailing through bad storms on the open sea: his father had been careful to seek out reports from those with weather-sense before setting sail with his family aboard. But thinking of the helmsman's weather-sense reminded him of something else. Casually he glanced at the silver ring on Verhin's hand - not so much as the faintest glimmer of magic shone about it. A weaker agathudal, whose earthly sight was not so heavily overcast by the Shadow-Realm, would not have noticed; but Arudal knew that Verhin had lied to him. And now he knows my mind-gift as well, or at least something of it.

"Do all the crew members on this ship have mind-magics?" Arudal asked quite casually when the day crew had all been fed and he and Verhin were beginning to wash up.

The cook started, his dark eyes widening, then gave a rueful little laugh. "Only a few," he answered. "No more than what you're used to, I dare say."

"I see." Just Verhin the ship's cook, indeed! Arudal thought. After seeing Verhin clean the fish, he was quite sure that he would not want to face the man with knives in an alleyway; and Verhin must be an agathudal himself, or at least gifted with some manner of sight beyond the ordinary. But everyone on this ship is on our side...or should be. Yet Arudal could not help thinking of the woeful state of the dromon's provisions at first: could the ship's cook have had anything to do with that? After a few days of short rations and thirst, even the strongest fighters would be easy prey...

Sir Salarond was happy enough to let Arudal take the helm for Miraran through most of the day, though Sir Thoron grumbled, "You'll make up every missed hour of practice when the weather clears, and don't think I'll forget it." By midday, the wind was already freshening, and when Arudal asked about the clouds - for his eyes could not make out the thin white trails of the upper airs in a sunlit sky - Finvar said, "Yes, the first mares' tails are blowing over."

"How fast?"

"As fast as any winter storm from the mountains," Arudal's squire-brother answered. "Is that bad?"

"It is not good, anyway. I think you might ask Lostren to brew up some more of his tea for you before Verhin has to put the fire-box out."

"Thanks," Finvar said dryly - but he went off to find Lostren.

It was mid-afternoon when the first heavy scattering of rain showered down to darken the sails. Arudal was almost relieved when Miraran showed up to take the helm, gliding gracefully across the lurching deck.

"Well-done, Arudal!" the steersman said. "And thank you." He frowned, bushy dark eyebrows drawing together over his crooked nose. "It's going to be quite a bit worse than I thought this morning - not sure how I missed it. If we weren't so far out, I'd advise turning back now. As is...you can stay with me a while, like I promised, but don't argue when I tell you to get safely below. You aren't essential crew, and damned if I'm going to explain to Sir Thoron how I was responsible for his squire getting swept overboard! He'd have my liver to pad his helm with."

"Yes, sir," Arudal said reluctantly. He thought he heard Miraran mutter, "...don't like this storm at all," but he could not be sure of what he had heard beneath the crashing of waves and the rising wind beginning to moan through the rigging.

As the weather grew rougher, Arudal found himself admiring the Kantarean helmsman's skill more and more: at least some of the men of Kantar had not forgotten that the Western Empire had once been the master of the oceans. Lightning cracked sharply through the seething purple-black clouds overhead; the ship heeled to port, slowly righting herself. "Below decks, now - and keep hold of a line!" Miraran snapped at Arudal, his wet face white with strain as he struggled with the wheel. Arudal struggled over the deck, gasping for breath through the heavy rain and gouts of spray and blinking the water from his eyes. He glanced up for a second to see the cat clinging to the mast, sparks flying from her bristling dark fur as her mouth opened in a warning yowl that he heard even through the shrieking of the storm. Her eyes glowed ice-green, and Arudal wondered how he had mistaken her for a living animal - but the ghosts of beasts often seemed more a part of the green earth than the Shadow-realm, unless they were bound by curse or magic...

The ship lurched hard to starboard as Arudal started down the stairs, and he barely saved himself from a headlong tumble. It seemed to him that he could feel all the little hairs on his skin prickling up, as though lightning were about to strike. It was dark below, but he was easily able to see his way to Sir Thoron's cabin, and the shapes of his knight and Finvar were pale ghosts in the darkness. Finvar clung to the bed, looking altogether miserable with terror and illness; Sir Thoron's big hands were locked tightly about the arms of his chair, bracing himself against the ship's tossing.

"Who is that?" Thoron called out.

"Arudal, sir. Miraran said it was too dangerous for me to be above."

"It damned well is!" Sir Thoron agreed. "Squire, can you tell if this is anything but a natural storm?"

Arudal paused, bracing himself lightly against the door-jamb and letting his body sway with the ship's motion. It seemed to him that a faint chill brushed over the edges of his nerves, a tantalizing glimmer like a movement just at the corner of his eye; but when he tried to focus on it, there was nothing there. "Sir...I am not sure. I cannot sense anything clear."

"Go to Salarond's cabin and see what he thinks. Then get your arse back here as soon as you can - and for Amanvon's sake, be careful!"

Arudal made his way back down the black corridor, to Sir Salarond's cabin. To his surprise, a flash of light blinked through the air as he stepped into the room, a faint shock jerking through his body, and he saw the glimmer of Lostren's white blade and the sinking green-black darkness of Sir Salarond's sword.

"Hold, it is only I," Arudal said, trying to keep the tremor from his voice, even as Dame Karsil said, "You need not fear, it is Arudal."

"That is well," Sir Salarond answered, audibly relieved. "Arudal, go and bring the rest of our companions here - tell them to bring both bows and swords. My mislikings are growing quickly, and I would not have us separated at this time."

Arudal had to lead the other knights and squires one by one through the darkness below the deck. Even Lostren's tea had done little to settle Finvar's stomach - his hand was clammy in Arudal's, and he staggered like an ancient drunk, so that Arudal had all he could do to keep his fellow squire from hurting himself in the passageway. Rhys was the last of them, and Arudal bit his lip when he realized that he would have to take the buck's hand.

"What are you waiting for, Tharandrostan?" Rhys' lilting voice said angrily. "I can no more see in the dark than any other man - or are you hoping for me to fall and break my head?"

Arudal grabbed Rhys' thick wrist, pulling him along as he would a recalcitrant slave...but when the ship plunged suddenly, he found that he was bracing himself against the Plainsman's greater weight to keep the buck from being flung forwards on his face, as he would have with any of his companions, and holding him up as he got his footing again.

"Uh. Thanks," Rhys husked. Arudal could see the naked fear on the Plainsman's face, white beneath the dark spattering of freckles across his cheeks.

"Come on," he said roughly, guiding Rhys as he had the others. He could tell from the ship's wild diving and pitching that the storm was growing worse. The waves would be sweeping across the deck above, and all the gods help any man who was not lashed firmly to wood against the water's blows!

Terathon Water-Lord, spare us your wrath, Arudal prayed silently; but the words going through his head were less kind, the Hymn of the Dead at Sea. *...and no wave but marks our dead; Though the Sea feed for ten thousand years, she calls yet to be fed...* The ship's wood shrieked in protest, plank grinding against plank; Arudal heard the constant rumble of thunder from above - and it seemed to him that he could hear something else, a far-off yammering wail.

Rhys' hand tightened on Arudal's arm, as if they were dear comrades clasping wrists in greeting. "Do ye hear that?" the Plainsman asked softly, his voice barely audible through the ship's moans and the battering din of the storm.

"Yes. Come on!" Arudal said again, dragging Rhys the few steps along to Sir Salarond's door. The light flared again as they stepped in, and Arudal could see that all the company - even Finvar, though spasms of nausea still racked his body - had their weapons drawn.

"Brace yourselves and draw swords," Sir Salarond shouted. "There is a great darkness at the heart of this storm, and it shall be on us soon."

If it were not for me, Arudal thought bitterly, he could have set a proper warding on this chamber. But, clinging to the door-jamb with one hand, he unsheathed his falchion. It was well for him that there was no light in the room, for with his Shadow-sight fully on him, he could see in the darkness as well as any man by day - better, for the swords of the White Company knights and their squires burned in coloured flames; Lostren's gold-traced helmet gleamed, and the bag of muck about Rhys' neck seared Arudal's eyes, so that he had to look away from it.

Sir Salarond lifted his hand, murmuring something, and Arudal's sight went blind-black, with only the glimmering of the weapons and Dame Karsil's cat-green eyes to mark where his companions were. The light was uncomfortably hot, the skin of Arudal's face beginning to scorch tender as though he stood too near to a fire; he had to look away from the healer-priest, and could not bite back his soft moan.

"Do you sense anything, Arudal?" Sir Salarond asked.

"I...I am not sure," Arudal replied. He reached outwards...and it was as though he were looking through another pair of eyes, halfway up the mast, clinging with all the strength of his claws as he yowled a warning against the intruders who sought to harm his ship. "There are dark things out there, many of them - not Ukuthrim, for I cannot feel them, and they move too swiftly for me to see them clearly."

Sir Thoron cursed. "And no armour in this," he muttered. "What do you say, Salarond?"

"Arudal, can you tell what they are doing?"

Arudal paused and breathed deeply, closing his eyes against the painful brightness, and reached again, looking out through the ghostly mind of the cat. "Trying to cut the ropes...tear the sails..."

"All those who can shoot, take your bows," Sir Salarond commanded. "And ropes to lash ourselves to the ship with. Arudal, you will stay here below, unless you feel any Undead coming in."

The White Company fighters sheathed their weapons and made their way to the door. Arudal could see the glow over the short bows and arrows when his companions uncased them; Dame Karsil's Elven longbow glimmered like a white birch against the night, and stars shone at the tips of her arrowheads. I would fight too, Arudal thought unhappily.

The ship jerked and shuddered: Arudal could feel her slewing around as the bow rose, tilting upwards as though she were swiftly climbing a mountainous wave. His companions staggered, grabbing for whatever they could brace themselves against. Arudal thought miserably of his poor Inmanat, sealed in the dreadful thick-aired dark of the lower hold, with no way of knowing what was happening to him, or why. The ship rose until she was standing nearly on end, then pitched suddenly down, slamming them all to the floor. The keen copper taste of terror flooded Arudal's mouth, and he wished with all his heart that he was above with Miraran, where at least he could see what was happening.

The company picked themselves up, clutching at walls and bulkheads to keep from being flung about. When the door banged shut behind Sir Salarond, shielding Arudal's eyes from the healer-priest's light, Arudal could see again, but it was little comfort. He sat down, locking his arms and legs about the deck-bolted chair, and sought the ghost-cat's mind once more, to watch the fight through her gaze.

A great black wave crashed down over the deck; for a moment, the screaming wind was silent, and then the ship broke free into the air once more. Dame Karsil, pale in the darkness with a rope lashed firmly about her waist, was the first back to her feet: a streak of white flame flew from her bow, and Arudal heard the unearthly scream of one of the black things that fluttered about the ship like flakes of soot from a windswept bonfire. The others followed her in shooting, but the wildly pitching deck was throwing their aim off. Above, one of the sails hung half-rent from the foremast - not cut free, still catching the wind, but no longer under the control of those few frantic sailors still struggling to keep the mastery of their ship. Great hills of dark water rose and crested: if Miraran and the crew failed for a moment, one would strike the dromon broadside...and they would go down, down to all their deaths.

Arudal clenched his fists. It was worse than anything to wait helpless here below, the air growing stuffy and thick in his lungs. Yet the dark things hovered well out of sword-range; he did not know how to shoot a bow, and his mind-gift was useless against daemons, who had once been kin to the gods and were real beyond the Shadow-Realm as well as in it...Wait.

He breathed deeply, though it seemed that his straining lungs were hardly pulling in any air. Eluthia waited inside him, untroubled in her clear adamant prison: now Arudal gathered his strength, opening the gateway within himself even as he reached into her cold mind. Go and slay me those daemons who hover above, he ordered. Do no harm to any other - and when they are gone, knot those ropes they tore asunder. Though he thought in words, it was something more than words that sank deep into the Ukuthri's thoughts: the images of the dark things flying above, the knowledge of ropes spliced as they had been severed. Eluthia's red eyes flamed from her frosty face, and she leapt upwards, passing through the wood as though it were no more than the faint mist in her sight.

The White Company knights and their squires were shooting steadily, their arrows hissing through the storm's blackness like a shower of stars. Eluthia's rapier was a sliver of night in the darkness; her foes left their work to press about her, backing her into the mast. Even through the vampire's sight, their shapes seemed to coil and shift, but she dropped one after another, their bodies writhing away into black mist beneath her needle-thin blade.

Then Arudal saw the streak of light flickering through the air, the white Elf-arrow sinking deep into the Ukuthri's breast. For a fleeting second, Eluthia looked down at it, and though her smile stretched painfully over snakelike fangs, Arudal felt the human warmth of relief washing out through her insubstantial Shadow-flesh.

Released! Eluthia thought gladly - and she was there no longer: Arudal sat gasping for breath, alone in the cabin. Had Dame Karsil missed a shot at the daemons - or had she taken the chance to slay the vampire, without thought for how Eluthia was aiding them?

The ship plunged violently sideways, and Arudal heard the shriek of rending wood. Amandeth, he prayed. I think my time upon the green earth may be at an end. I shall stay in Shadow, or go on, at your will - though for myself, I would choose to return home first, and bear back what knowledge of the West I have gained, that my death not be wholly wasted. Yet my soul is in your hands...

Arudal could feel the dromon wallowing deeper, and it came to him that, if he could not fight, at least he could bail. He stripped off cloak and boots - they would only hinder him if he were waist-deep in water. Little more steady on his feet than a landsman, he made his way carefully down the pitching corridor, to the faint sound of shouts above the storm.

Lanterns bobbed and swung in the lower hold, their flames hardly more than embers. Arudal staggered from the stairs, falling knee-deep in cold water; the horses were screaming and struggling. Someone thrust a full bucket into his hands, and another man grabbed it from him, passing it along.

Arudal worked frantically with the crew, trying to shut the horses' cries of terror from his ears. His clothes were soaked through in moments; his choking breath came harder and harder, but he did not pause for a single second in the endless work of stooping and swinging the heavy buckets along, though the first men were beginning to drop from exhaustion about him.

Panting hard in the thick air, his arms and back aching, Arudal hardly noticed that the seas were easing until the water that had been above his knees was no more than halfway down his calves - the leak must have been patched, and though the ship still wallowed, she was no longer pitching uncontrolled over the heavy waves. At last the doors to the hold sprang open again, a breath of fresh air wafting in to flare the lanterns, and Arudal sagged exhausted against the wall.

"Keep bailing as long as you can," the first mate's sharp voice ordered. "We have weathered the worst of the storm."

Arudal looked around him, the Shadow-Realm clearing from his sight. He could see several horses' bodies half-floating in their stalls, the low waves lapping over their manes - not Inmanat, praised be Aviyani; the sturdy little Imperial horse's eyes were rolling wildly, his head hanging low and froth on his muzzle as though he had been ridden to the end of his strength, but he was still up. Arudal broke from his place in the line, stumbling through the water to stroke his horse's wet neck for a moment and let Inmanat rub against him. "Shh, it is all right, my darling," he murmured. "The storm is over, and all is well."

By the time Arudal staggered up the stairs in search of dry cloths to rub the horses down before they could take chill, he was so tired that he could hardly walk. But one of the crewmen who leaned against a bulkhead pushed himself forward to give Arudal a pat on the shoulder. "Well-done, lad," he murmured, straining his trembling lips into a smile. "Is your little pony all right?"

"He will be," Arudal said, trying to smile back. Dry the horses...no, first to the galley, to ask Verhin to make up some warm mash for them...down to get some grain, so...dear gods, would the fodder all be ruined by salt water?

The sailor pulled a small clay flask from his belt-pouch, uncorking it with his teeth and taking a deep swig. "Have a nip of this before you lie down - keep you from catching cold."

Arudal took the flask and drank. The harsh spirits seemed to burst into flame in his throat, and he wheezed, his eyes watering.

"Do you good," the seaman said in satisfaction. "On you go, now."

The White Company riders had stowed their tack in their rooms. The small felted horse-towels, meant for wiping sweat from hard-ridden beasts, looked pitifully inadequate; it did not take Arudal more than a moment to snatch up the men's bath-towels as well before he made his way back down to the stabling-hold. He did not need to bother with a lantern - he could see well enough how the horses - those that still lived - leaned shuddering against the close wooden walls. Sir Eroth's golden stallion, poor creature, had been next to the breech: the warhorse lay still with its skull half-caved in beside the hastily-cobbled mess of sail-canvas and planking that plugged the hole in the ship for the time being. The other dead ones, Arudal guessed, had died of fright: Tirothar's dun palfrey, two of the pack-horses, and the white-maned gray and roan warhorses that had belonged to Sir Salarond and Rhys. All the gods be praised, none of the steeds were down screaming with broken bones - Arudal had grievously feared that the battering of the storm casting them about in the stalls would snap their legs.

Arudal suspected that he should begin with Sir Thoron's warhorse, the most valuable of his knight's beasts. But he could not forsake Inmanat, who trusted him: he rubbed the little dark gelding until his shivering slowed and his thick coat was beginning to dry properly, speaking kindly to him all the while. When he neared the stall where Sir Thoron's tall destrier stood, the horse turned, letting fly at the wooden barrier with his back hooves.

Scared horse'll kick if he can't run, Arudal remembered his family's Horsetribe groom Boraitiz saying, not glancing up from the hoof he held firmly on his knee as he carefully trimmed the frog of Count Arumir's black stallion. Don't bother him without you've got a real good reason to.

Arudal thought his knees might be trembling from more than tiredness when he unlatched the gate to Black Rage's stall. But, to his surprise, the ill-tempered warhorse nuzzled up and rested his head over Arudal's shoulder, in that way horses seemed to have of saying, Oh, I am glad to see you! Black Rage let Arudal rub him down, even belly and tail, and butted his brow-ridges hard against Arudal's chest as though the Tharandrostan had raised him from a foal.

Arudal dried off all the warhorses that would let him touch them first, then the palfreys, then went back to Sir Thoron's destrier, who had calmed at last. He was just starting on the first of his knight's packhorses when he saw the golden lantern-light over the stairs, shadowing the lanky figure with a yoke of gently steaming buckets over his shoulders.

"Huh!" Rhys grunted in surprise. "You're the last one I thought to see doing such work."

"The horsen have…" Arudal struggled for words; he was too tired to think of how to speak Common. "Most sore a fright. No one else camen."

"The cook told me one of us had asked for warm mash for them, so I waited for the first batch," Rhys said - apologetically, swinging his yoke off with a soft grunt. "Here, I'll help you with that, if you like."

Arudal handed him one of the last dry cloths. Rhys looked at it, raising a ruddy eyebrow. "Ymwra's Blood, our knights may not be too pleased with you for stealing their towels."

"Horsen need them," Arudal answered.

The Plainsman smiled. "Aye." He lifted his lantern higher, peering about the stable-hold. Do I look that bewildered and wide-eyed in full daylight? Arudal wondered. Then Rhys went to his knees in the water beside the body of his warhorse, letting out a soft moan. "Ah, my bright one, my fair one," he cried. "My brave one, never flinching from battle, son and grandson of the green earth's noblest steeds, born of Ymwra's blood upon the fields!"

Arudal flicked the dry cloths out of his hand just in time before Rhys clasped his arms about the neck of his fallen horse, rocking over it and keening. The Tharandrostan could not keep his lip from curling slightly at the Plainsman's unseemly grief - his own folk learned to rein in their tears in the face of death, even when a beloved lay cold before them - but at the same time, he could not help feeling some sympathy for Rhys' loss: he himself would have mourned Inmanat as deeply as if the little dark gelding were a man. Without another word, Arudal went back to rubbing down the packhorses himself, leaving Rhys to voice his grief in peace.

Coming back from the kitchen with the last buckets of warm mash, Arudal almost bumped into Sir Salarond in the corridor. Thankfully, the light that had glowed about the healer-priest was gone; he held a lantern as any man might. "At least we still have some horses," Sir Salarond said. "Squire, report."

Arudal told him quickly which of the steeds they had lost. Salarond winced, almost groaning. "Whitemane was dear to me: I grieve him. And more, this will weaken us sorely if we must fight from horseback. Three good warhorses will not be easy to replace for any gold, and there is no telling how the steeds of the West are bred and trained now. But you did well to see to them as soon as you could. I should have come earlier myself, but there were more than a few men who needed my healing." Now Arudal could see how worn their commander looked, gray beneath his fair skin and with deep bruised circles under his eyes.

"How goes it with our folk? I saw nothing of the battle after Dame Karsil shot Eluthia."

Though Arudal had tried to keep the reproach from his voice, Sir Salarond shook his head. "You need not blame the Elf for that. She had no way of knowing that the creature belonged to you rather than our foes - and all wights of Shadow are alike in her mind. Still, it was a great help that you sent the vampire. It killed several of them, I believe, and drew the rest in from their work of wrecking the sails. Thus we had clear shots at them, and when they knew their numbers dwindled, they swept down to the deck to attack, so that we were able to slay them all with no more damage done to the ship. Finvar fell and was struck on the head: he managed to breathe a good draught of seawater as well, but he will live. When the daemons gave up on their wrecking and closed on us, Eroth took a bad wound to the shoulder, and Sir Thoron to the leg. Both of them will be abed for a day, but they, too, shall recover without difficulty. None of the White Company were slain, but we lost five of the crew." Sir Salarond took a deep breath, looking closely at Arudal. "Have you much more to do below?"

"I must give out the last of the feed, sir. And we must get the bodies of the dead horses out and do something about the water still standing, for it will chill the horses and damage their feet if they are left in it overnight."

"Hmm. I think I can see to that. You are clearly about to fall over where you stand: finish feeding them, and then go on to bed." Sir Salarond walked on a little distance, then turned. "And for Amanvon's sake - not to mention Thoron's and Finvar's - take those clothes off and try to wash the horseshit out of your hair before you go back to your cabin."

Chapter 11: Suspicions

"Avalar had a vision,
To purge the Empire's ill,
Atoning in a new land
Of pure hearts and clean will.

"Avalar had a vision,
No secrets of the State,
No sacrifice of the lesser,
To policies of the great.

"Avalar had a vision,
Of kings who kept his vow
Of rule held untainted,
Where is his vision now?"

- "Avalar's Vision", anonymous, Var Perenil

Arudal was shaking worse than any of the horses had been by the time he made it back to the cabin with a sailor's rough tunic and breeches belted about his waist, but he was cleaner than he had been. Sir Thoron snored loudly in his bed already; Finvar was sitting up in a chair, a bandage wrapped about his head.

"There you are," Finvar said with a tired grin. He wrinkled his nose. "Amanvon, Arudal, what were you doing, rolling on the stable floor? You look like a drowned cat."

Arudal knew he had been too tired and cold to do a proper job of washing: his tangled hair was still full of wet straw and other things, and he was glad enough that he could not smell himself.

"Half-drowned, perhaps," he said, smiling wanly back at the other squire. "I helped with the bailing, and then to tending horsen."

Finvar raised his eyebrows, then winced as if the movement had pulled painfully at his head injury. "Dear Amanvon, the horses! I did not dare to let myself think of them...You missed a good fight, above. I got two of the daemons myself, but then I lost my footing, and woke up with Sir Salarond telling me I'd cracked my skull. If I'd landed much harder, I would have spilt my brains and not be here now - but no real harm done. Salarond patched me up; he said I'm to stay awake through the night to be sure the healing holds, and should be fine by tomorrow. Tell me, how is my Windfoot?"

"He is fine, but Sir Salarond, Sir Eroth, and Rhys all lost their warhorses."

Finvar drew in his breath in a deep hiss between his teeth. "Oh, dear. Whitemane was the best destrier in our company - easily worth a baron's estate, more dangerous than a knight in battle, and Salarond loved him like a son. And... does Rhys know? He always said that he could talk with his horse."

"Rhys was mourning him below when I last saw," Arudal answered. Then, reluctantly, "I had not known that Plainsmen cared so for their steeds. At home, we usually hire Imperials of lower birth or men of the Horsetribes as grooms, rather than trusting them to slaves."

"Aye, the Plainsmen's goddess Ymwra - Rhys swears by her - is a horse-spirit," Finvar said. He frowned. "Two of the knights' warhorses dead...Arudal, I may as well warn you now. You'll probably have to give up Black Rage to Sir Salarond."

Arudal sighed, half relieved, half sad. The Kantarean destrier trusted him now, and he in turn had begun to feel the first warm stirrings of love when Black Rage rested his great head on his shoulder, but... "It is as well. I knowe nothing of fighting from horseback, and Sir Salarond can usen him better than I."

"You don't mind being mounted on a palfrey when the rest of us have warhorses?" Finvar said.

"Inmanat cometh of the most noble line of steeds in the Middle Land."

"Hah, you are a surprise. A Kantarean of your breeding and...bearing would likely be stamping and throwing things at the idea that he had to ride like a maiden in a battle-company. But then," Finvar went on thoughtfully, "a Kantarean like that probably wouldn't have soiled his hands - and his hair," he added, grinning, "taking care of the horses."

"What do you mean?" Arudal asked, suddenly wary.

"Shit. Sorry, Arudal. I open my mouth and all my guts fall out. I only meant that you give the impression of being very noble, and maybe above volunteering to do grotty work with your hands. I didn't mean anything by it, really."

Finvar looked down at the table-top as he spoke, and Arudal remembered what Rhys had said - only last night? - about the others in their party being afraid to speak with him lest they give offense. If he had not been so tired, he might not have said what he did then, but his exhaustion dropped the defenses of his heart as surely as a worn arm would let a shield droop.

"Do I seem arrogant and touchy to you?"

"Where did that come from?" Finvar asked.

"Rhys told me...last night..." Arudal's voice trailed off. He felt suddenly idiotic, and shamed to have made so much of a Plainsman's words.

"Ah," Finvar said, his light burred voice gentle with understanding. "That is a custom of his people when they are angered: they will say what they think to each other until the matter is either resolved, or it is clear that only swords will end it. It's not a bad custom, altogether... Anyway, I think you are just very shy, and far too sensitive for your own good, so that you take the smallest things to heart. A bit proud, maybe, but that is as you were raised, and I've known worse sons of nobles from Kantar. And all that's nothing when the forces of Martag are on our trail. You know," he went on brightly, "our enemies had a vampire as well as the daemons, but they lost control of it. Instead of attacking us, it went up the mast and turned on the other creatures in its host. Karsil shot it before they could get hold of it again."

Arudal felt a sudden powerful urge to tell Finvar that the vampire had been his, that, even kept below by Sir Salarond's order, he had played a great part in the fighting above. Instead he said, "So you think the daemons and the storm were sent by Martag?"

"Who else? They must have been tracking us at least since the vampire attack outside Var Perenil. I didn't know that Undead could fly over water, though. At home, we always said the best way to get away from a ghost or wight was to cross a stream. Is the sea different?"

"The sea puts not such fear in the Undead as fresh water - think on it: the sea itself is a great graveyard. But those who are not drowned themselves or starkly compelled by another's will must cross the sea dryshod in ship, or else one must summon them from the Shadow-Realm where water is not," Arudal answered. "Yet the Lord of Martag was once a prince of the Empire, and fled to the Middle Land only after his death."

"Summoned by magic..." Finvar mused. "Arudal, do you think there might be a traitor on this ship? Secret Service vessels are all supposed to have the strongest protections against scrying; how else could our foes have found us? Do you want to go and talk to Sir Salarond about this now, before anything else happens? We're all tired, and some of us are wounded; a traitor could murder us in our beds tonight."

I want to go to sleep, Arudal thought. He was swaying where he stood, and not from the slow rise and fall of the deck beneath him; and even Finvar's soft Artegalian accent was growing more difficult for him to understand.

"The vampire was ours, not theirs," he said vaguely. "And a daemon could have followed us over the waves and called its kindred. Daemons are not halted by any waters, unless they be greatly blessed."

"I don't understand Imperial very well, Arudal," Finvar said patiently, and Arudal realized that he had slipped back into his own tongue. He repeated himself in Common as best he could.

"Oh. But how did it find us in the first place?"

Arudal had no answer for that: he knew only so much of the lore of daemons as was relevant to the study of the Undead. Finvar started to rise, and Arudal put out a hand to stop him. "No, you are wounded and you need to rest. I shall go to Sir Salarond, if you think I should - but is it worth telling him now? Should we not speak to our knight when he wakes, and let him decide?"

"We should tell Salarond," Finvar answered firmly. "The White Company isn't like other units. Squires are supposed to pay attention and think for themselves, because we'll all be leading units of our own someday."

Arudal thought of how Sir Salarond had made Lostren take command and order him to interrogate Eluthia: of course, the general's squire might well be a general himself in time. He rose to his feet, stumbling off.

Lostren was brewing something over a fire-box in Sir Salarond's chambers, murmuring to himself as he sprinkled a pinch of powder over his little cauldron. The commander's squire looked tired, his wet dark hair sticking up in spikes over his head, but his gray-ringed amber eyes were still bright and alert.

"Amanvon, Arudal, you look..."

Arudal cut him off with a weary hand-gesture. "I know. Where is Sir Salarond?" At least Lostren spoke perfect Imperial; he would not have to struggle to force his thoughts into Common.

"Making the rounds of his patients one last time. Are you all right?"

"Yes, but there is a matter about which Finvar wanted me to speak with him."

"Ah. Sit down there and wait, you're in no condition to be traipsing all over the ship. And put your cloak and boots back on before you freeze to death!"

Arudal obeyed Lostren's order unquestionably, gratefully accepting a steaming mug of the stuff the other squire was brewing.

"You'll want honey for that. It's bitter," Lostren warned him. Still, Arudal drank it unsweetened. As Lostren had said, the tea was bitter, but with a clean astringent aftertaste that seemed to clear the thick glue of exhaustion from his mouth and throat. He was already feeling better when the healer-priest came in at last.

"Arudal, what are you doing here?" he said wearily. "You ought to be in bed."

"Sir. Finvar thought I ought to speak to you...he would have come himself, if he were not hurt..."

"Well, what is it?" Salarond sighed.

"Finvar wondered if there was any chance that someone on this vessel might have marked us out for our foes to follow, since this ship should have been well-protected against scrying."

Sir Salarond nodded slowly. "The Horsetribes have a saying, I believe, about not teaching your grandmother how to milk a mare. I have been wondering the same since this storm began. No daemon should have been able to follow us undetected, which means that they must have had some means of finding us beyond those usually available: if there is not a traitor on the ship now, then some item must have been placed upon it before we left the Middle Land - a little seeing-stone hidden in a crack between two planks, perhaps..."

"Has the Secret Service any specific reason to thwart this mission?" Lostren asked.

The healer-priest's brow furrowed, even as Arudal raised his eyebrows in shock - it seemed unthinkable to him, that a branch of Kantar's military should think to go against the will of the White Throne.

"Not to the best of my knowledge," Sir Salarond said. "Yet...General Thindozan is...shall we say, a difficult man to work with. The White Company has had run-ins with him before, and he is very protective of his Service's secrets and autonomy." Arudal tried to keep the disbelief from his face, remembering how the general had stammered and babbled. Sir Salarond raised an eyebrow. "I see you were taken in by his manner...In any case, that was why I was reluctant to tell him anything of our mission. But I think other foes are more likely: Lostren, kindly give Arudal your analysis."

"In order of likelihood, Martag is far the highest," Lostren said at once. "In the long run, they stand to gain the most by a civil war in Kantar, and so far the methods used are consistent with their skills. The Lord of Martag launched the War of Ruin during a period of internal destabilization for Kantar, and it is generally accepted that, if the same sort of circumstances arose, he would do the same again. If there is one thing that has saved Kantar over the millennia of his rule, it is that he is impatient in his aggression - the surviving texts from the period just prior to the War of Ruin suggest that, had he waited another five years, he might have triumphed then. And we would be foolish to assume that even the best-watched of our services is free of his agents: it is sadly reasonable that a Secret Service man working for Martag could be the source of the latest incident. Secondly, either Duke Garthin or Duke Helak could see more advantage to himself in an open conflict than in waiting on the chance that we may prove him the rightful claimant to the throne of Felatar. When I last spoke to my eldest brother, he mentioned that he and the King are both greatly concerned about the build-up of military allies: either of them could be planning a quick strike. Again, Secret Service agents are immune neither to political loyalties nor to the promise of preferment, and a claimant to the Principality throne who seemed to have a sound plan could have subverted one. Thirdly, it is not impossible that the Secret Service itself may see advantage to conflict within Kantar. They were set up to deal with internal strife, and surely stand to benefit in gold and power when such strife occurs."

Arudal's mouth dropped open. How could that be? he thought. Surely men in such a trusted service must serve their King first...and if they wavered, would it not be clear at once?

Salarond smiled sadly at Arudal, almost as if he had read the Tharandrostan's thoughts. "Kantar is not like your home, Arudal. It is...what might be called the price of our freedom, that even the highest - or most hidden - servants of the State may keep their minds to themselves. Avalar felt that even disloyalty, freely chosen, were better than loyalty assured under compulsion. As for the Secret Service: it is answerable only to the Crown, and I have suspected for some time that there are a few among its commanders who feel that they know more of what is good for the country than King Edril himself does. It is certain that they have, in the past, committed actions which would be considered rogue by most others."

"As has the White Company," Lostren muttered softly. "Recently."

Salarond shot his squire a rueful glare. "True enough. But our...difficult choices... are generally matters of military necessity, whereas the Secret Service is a political entity, and one with a specific interest in maintaining and increasing its own power, as well as that of the King. The gods know, I have advised King Edril, as often as I can, to keep the Secret Service on a short leash. But they serve a needed function, and finding real evidence of misdoing on their part can be surprisingly hard."

Arudal tried to suppress his next thought, then remembered what Finvar had said about White Company squires being encouraged to pay attention and think for themselves. "Sir," he said, "if you mistrust the Secret Service so greatly, why are we dependent on their vessel and men to take us to the West."

Sir Salarond heaved a deep sigh. "The short answer is, we had no choice. The White Company is chiefly a heavy cavalry company. We have some mages and men with other skills, but not ships or many professional sailors. Also, the Secret Service was the only group that could get hold of our guides and make the necessary arrangements with the speed the King desired - and it was he who called them in, even as he selected us from the White Company. Finally, such rot as there may be in the Secret Service is only here and there...it may be spreading, but I would be remiss if I forgot that most of its men are true servants of the Crown. Even the worst probably think of themselves as serving Kantar, though such service..." He shook his head. "Very well, Lostren: are Martag, one of the claimants, and the Secret Service itself, your only suspects?"

"There is also Tharandrost," Lostren said reluctantly. "They would stand to make huge gains if trade through Felatar were disrupted. But that seems the most unlikely of all my thoughts, since Tharandrost is currently thriving and has always maintained a policy of non-involvement in Kantarean affairs: their position..." Lostren glanced at Arudal and closed his mouth.

Exhausted as he was, Arudal's hackles prickled up: he thought he could guess what Salarond's squire had been about to say. If Kantar ever decided that Tharandrost was a threat...There were perhaps a quarter of a million true-born Imperials in the State, as many immigrants of diluted or Common blood - and twice that number of slaves. But Kantar stretched from Felatar on the southern coast to the northern border of Artegal where the Ice-Folk dwelt, from the western coast to two hundred miles past the Karasindi. Moreover, all the peoples of Kantar could easily breed their numbers several times over in a Common Man's short lifetime; with all the help magic and mind-magic could give, Arudal would be lucky to sire three children in the three hundred years of life left to him. It might cost Kantar dear to destroy Tharandrost; but the White Throne could replace its losses of life in twenty years - the Adamantine Throne, not in a millennium. Arudal knew that Kantar looked upon his nation as a Northman might look upon a dog with wolf-blood in its veins: tolerated for its usefulness, but never trusted, and risky - but possible, at need - to put down.

"I mean no ill to you by that, Arudal," Lostren added quickly. "It is only that a full analysis must consider all possibilities. And Sir Daurar had the chance to set a psychic trace upon you when we met in Felatar - would you have known if he did?"

"Not if he were skilled enough," Arudal admitted reluctantly. But it would have been easier for Sir Daurar to compel him to summon Undead and order them to attack his comrades: a swift probe into his mind, setting the compulsion to do the deed and forget it afterwards. A trace strong enough for a man or daemon to follow over such distance would be much harder to hide. Reluctantly, he said so, not looking directly at either Sir Salarond or Lostren.

"It would have been easier for Sir Daurar to touch one of us who has no powers of mind, if he had meant to do so," Arudal added. "But I would not be surprised if there were someone on this ship who could detect such a trail, were it activated."

The corner of Sir Salarond's mouth twisted ruefully. "I wondered if the various... skills of the crew would escape your notice. I had not thought that you would speak with them as much as you do, though."

"Do you know what talents each man has?" Arudal asked.

"In most cases, only what is officially listed," the healer-priest answered, his lips tightening as though he had bitten into a sour piece of fruit. "But I have worked with some of these men before, and do not doubt that Sir Ultar knew what he was doing when he requested this ship. Yet I also notice that the three likeliest of Lostren's scenarios come through one or more Secret Service personnel - whether corrupt or following corrupt superiors' orders - which inclines me to be cautious."

"If there is a seeing-stone or something similar on board, have we any way of finding it?" Lostren broke in.

Stones, Arudal thought. His brain felt numb and sodden from the cold and exhaustion, but the thought teased at the edge of it like the rubbing of a hangnail. Seeing stones...clear and dark crystal, amethyst, obsidian, blue topaz...clear stones, easily hidden in water. Truth-stones...tiger's eye, chalcedony, lapis...Then he remembered the lumps of lapis that had been sent up to him in Felatar, when he had asked for powder. "Sir," he said, "I have something that may be worth looking at."

Sir Salarond and Lostren followed Arudal to Thoron's cabin. The knight still snored on his bed; Finvar was playing cards against himself, laying them out in patterns of lines and crosses, with a small pile of coppers on either side of the table.

"Who's winning?" Lostren asked with a grin.

"I think he is; I'm not on best form tonight," Finvar answered.

Arudal dug through his pack until he found the little leather bag with the pieces of lapis in it. They clattered softly on the table beside Finvar's card game. Sir Salarond looked at the deep blue stones for a moment, then moved his palm across them, murmuring something. The flecks of gold seemed to gleam more brightly in the candlelight; the faint glow Arudal had noticed before grew stronger over one, deepening to a swirl of purple-black.

"That one," Arudal said, pointing.

Sir Salarond reached for it, then drew his hand back, his eyes widening. "Aye," he said grimly. "There is something there - I think it is well for you, and all of us, that you did not seek to crush it in your mortar before this. You know nothing of the lore of daemons?"

"Very little, sir."

Salarond took the leather pouch from Arudal's hand, carefully capturing all the small stones without letting his flesh touch them. "Now we have a dire quandary indeed. Do we risk freeing the being within this stone, and take the greater risk of trying to deal with it, to find out more of what we should know - or do we toss it overboard, where it can do us no more harm, and leave ourselves no wiser than before? Lostren?"

"If we can learn from it, we should," Lostren said at once.

"Finvar?"

"What is it? Surely if there is a risk in letting it loose, there are enough of us to kill it before it can do any harm?"

"Arudal?"

Arudal thought a moment. Had the imprisoned wight been an Ukuthran, he would have answered as swiftly as the other squires. But dealing with daemons, even for the best of purposes, tainted the soul as surely as any deed of darkness might... "Sir, I should ask the counsel of Dame Karsil and Sir Eroth in this matter, for the Elf is greatly staunch against evil and Sir Eroth, I think, is wise. Even if we had the skill to force truth of a daemon, that can be no fair working."

Salarond's shaggy eyebrows flew up. "I would least have looked for such words from you," he murmured in Imperial, before switching back to Common. "That is wisely spoken, and what I had meant to do myself. Lostren, in your hunger for knowledge, you must not forget that some knowledge is tainted: thus many of the Wise of the Empire fell. As for you, Finvar, you should have learned by now that not all danger strikes at the body, or may be quelled by sword and bow. What risk of soul is it worth, to know whether we may trust the crew of this ship?"

"If we cannot make this crossing, or know that a ship shall be waiting for us on our return," Lostren answered sturdily, "then it does not matter whether our souls are that little more vulnerable to the Shadow when we reach the remains of the Imperial Seat. The best position in the world is useless if the troops cannot get to it."

"I know what Sir Thoron would say if you woke him up," added Finvar.

"And none of it repeatable in polite company," Lostren muttered under his breath.

Sir Salarond spared his squire a quelling glare. "You, go fetch Eroth and Tirothar - I hate to rouse Eroth from his healing sleep, but Arudal has the right of it. Arudal, get Karsil, Shakhor, and Rhys."

Arudal knocked gingerly on the door of the Elf's cabin. "Come in, Arudal," Dame Karsil's melodious voice lilted - easy enough, Arudal thought, for an Elf's keen hearing to recognise his tread in the passageway.

The glow of a single candle gilded Karsil's pale hair, gleaming from her clear green eyes like a streak of gold through emeralds. Her long fingers held a thick white swan's quill, and Arudal could see the graceful characters of the Bright Elvish script curling in silver ink over the parchment on the table before her. Dame Karsil wore a long robe of shimmering white silk, and though she had fought as hard as any of those on deck, she alone showed no sign of dirt or weariness, so that the Tharandrostan suddenly felt very small and grubby beside her. The Elf's nose did not wrinkle at the stable-stink still hanging about Arudal, but it seemed to Arudal that he could see a hint of contempt on Karsil's finely-molded features.

"What is it you want?" Dame Karsil asked.

"Sir Salarond has sent me to bring you to Sir Thoron's cabin, for there is a matter concerning which he would speak to you," Arudal answered - in Bright Elven, though Karsil had addressed him in Common.

"Indeed." Dame Karsil rose to her feet and strung her tall white bow in a single movement, swirling her swordbelt about her waist and a quiver of arrows over her back as though she were dancing. "Well, let us go, unless you have another errand to run."

Arudal bit back angry words: a squire, he reminded himself, should learn humility in his service - even though it was not really a service he had chosen. "I have only to awaken Sir Shakhor and his squire. But go on, if you will."

At Sir Shakhor's door, Arudal paused a moment. He could hear faint snoring inside, and a softer melancholy chant, a tune that reminded him of the songs field slaves sang in the dark of their bunkhouses after sunset. Rhys would still be mourning his dead horse, Arudal guessed; and he found himself loath to disturb that grief. Yet he had his orders: he knocked on the door.

"Who is it?" Rhys' choked voice answered.

"It is I. Sir Salarond wants all of us in Sir Thoron's cabin."

Rhys opened the door. His mass of red curls was wildly matted, full of straw and bits of muck, and he smelled - little worse than Arudal himself, Arudal had to admit. Around his neck was a thick braid of ruddy hair with little beads woven into it: hair from the mane or tail of his dead horse, most likely, Arudal thought. The Plainsman's face was smudged and swollen from crying. Behind him, Sir Shakhor was already sitting on the edge of his bed, pulling on his boots.

"Well, what is it now, Arudal?" Shakhor asked. He shook out his mane of blond hair, then tied it back with a leather thong and rose to his feet.

"Sir Salarond will explain everything, sir. You may want to bring your weapons."

"And armour?"

"He did not say, sir."

Chapter 12: Daemon's Rede

"Let the study of daemon-lore be forbidden, save as knowledge is needed to combat them, and let that knowledge be restricted to only the wisest and most trustworthy. For it is sure that no one has ever gotten good of dealing with a daemon, nor been the better afterwards for it, and such may in no wise be turned to the service of the gods."
- The Code of Avalar, Book III, Sec. 15: Forbidden and Restricted Magics, ii., 12

"**A**manvon blast it!" Sir Thoron roared when the White Company knights had been arguing for almost a full candle-mark. "It's a few moral scruples or this mission - let's just do it and get it over with."

"I shall not deal with a daemon," Dame Karsil replied, drawing herself up to her full height. "It may be different for Men; but my kin would see the taint upon me in a moment if I assented to such a thing."

"Then take your pointy ears out of here and let us do what you think you're too good for," replied Thoron. "There's no telling what else that thing could be calling down while we sit here working our jaws."

Sir Eroth grimaced. "I like this little better than Karsil does, but you have a point, Thoron. We should either face the daemon or cast it overboard as swiftly as we may."

"And a little harm to us now," Shakhor put in, "may save us from much greater harm later. After all, we do not know that this was the only such trap laid here: I would not leave such a thing to the chance that a mage might requisition the appropriate ritual components. With any luck, the daemon can tell us if any more of its kin, or magics pertaining to them, are present. I think we would be hard put to survive another such attack on the ship."

A silence fell as they all looked at Sir Salarond. At last the healer-priest nodded. "Dame Karsil, you may leave. The rest of you, armour up. Eroth, Thoron, Finvar, I do not want you to join the fighting unless there is no other choice, but put your armour on anyway. Arudal..." Salarond looked at Arudal for an excruciatingly long time.

"Daemons are different in kind and nature from the Ukuthrim, sir," Arudal said.

"Aye, but they are chiefly beings of the Shadow-Realm...Still, you shall be outside the wards, and with three of us wounded and Karsil unable to aid..."

"I shall wait outside the door," Dame Karsil interrupted. "If fighting is needed, be sure that I am the most eager here to aid in slaying creatures of Shadow!" She glanced sideways at Arudal, and Arudal was suddenly certain that the Elf had known that Eluthia was his, and shot her in spite of that.

"So be it, then," said Salarond. "Lostren, fetch my pack."

The circle of powdered Valderian steel glittered on the floor like a ring of adamant, the black triangle within it sucking up the candlelight. A ring of carefully-dribbled water from the Well of the Hallows darkened the caulked planks around the powdered steel; within, the names of the gods and their holy symbols shone silver where Salarond's forefinger had carefully traced them. In the middle lay the piece of lapis, a solid dark nugget in the middle of its writhing purple-black aura. Arudal had known how to set the magical wardings, for there was always a slight risk that a daemon might be able to follow an Undead from the Shadow-Realm; he knew, as well, how such a creature could be sent back. Eroth, to Arudal's surprise, knew the spells of compulsion, though he had murmured something about having hoped that he would never need to use that lore; Sir Salarond would be able to bind it from harming them, or to cast it out from the green earth if there was need. Save for Thoron and Finvar, whom Sir Salarond had ordered to sit on the bed, the rest of the knights and their squires stood about fully armoured, the points of their shields resting on their thighs and their drawn swords in their hands.

"Amanvon, Watchful Lord," Sir Salarond prayed - speaking in Bright Elven, the tongue given by the Elves' Maker. "Hold your hand over us, who must dare a lesser evil in hopes of a greater good. Let our darkness not be unbrightened by your stars, nor our souls clouded by what we must do - not in hopes of power for ourselves, nor willing harm to others, but to defend ourselves and stave off suffering for those who have not earned it, and for the sake of the White Throne, which bears and protects your blessings upon the green earth. Shadows of evil fade in starlight uncorrupted; as our forebears held true to your stars even through all dark, be with us now, and guard our souls from the peril we undertake. So be it."

"So be it," Arudal sighed with the rest, though the Kantarean form of the prayer made him a little uncomfortable and he found himself shifting his feet nervously.

Eroth lifted his falchion, pointing its white-glowing tip at the stone. When he spoke, it was in Old High Imperial; he pronounced each word carefully, as though he had learned them by rote. "Shadow-born, rise to the green earth! Where you hide, there is no light; I call you forth in the names of Darkness and Death and Shadow, and you cannot escape me. For my will is a chain of steel; my will is a shackle of adamant, and you are bound by my power. Come forth to me, child of Morthugor! Speak naught but the truth, in the Common tongue, and answer in full all I ask of you. Your Master's will holds you, and my words are your bonds."

Arudal's darkening Shadow-sight dimmed the light of the single candle in the cabin; the deep purple-black glow of the lapis nugget strengthened and rose, writhing and coiling into solidness. Slowly it took form - the shape of a man of the purest Imperial blood, wearing a spiked circlet of black-shining vorgath. The jagged points of the sable metal gleamed adamant-tipped, matched by the gleam of the daemon's teeth as it spoke.

"Who are you, to compel me thus? My Master's will does not constrain me to obey you: you are neither evil enough to hold me by our likeness, nor good enough to rule me by the force of that which I hate."

"Your words have no power over us!" Eroth said, his voice thin and strained against the daemon's sonorous purr. "You are held within our circle, and cannot escape; you are bound to answer what we ask. Now tell us truthfully: who bound you into that stone, and what commands did that being or beings give you?"

The daemon bared its glittering teeth. "I came willingly, and my task is to call my lesser kin to feast. I see that they have marked you already - you will find those wounds hard to mend. But you shall not escape those who seek you now, for they know where you sail."

"Who seeks us?" Eroth insisted. "Who sent you with us?"

"Your foes seek you and sent me." A true answer, Arudal thought, but useless - will this daemon keep outwitting us thus?

"What are their names? From what lands do they hail?"

"Rathaka called me, and Arut and Varile and Nantafar and Sirias brought me to you, and Arudal carried me on shipboard. Rathaka was born in the green lands of the Great Plain, and Arut is from the lands of the Horse-Tribes and Varile is Perenilian and Nantafar was born in Artegal. Sirias hails from Felatar, and Arudal is Tharandrostan, a true son of the Empire's Fall."

Arudal clenched his hand tightly on his falchion hilt. Was the daemon trying to convince Eroth that he was one of their foes? Or was it only to taunt them with the uselessness of its information? - Sirias might as easily be an unwitting supply clerk in Felatar as a deliberate enemy; were the others spies or couriers of Martag?

"Are there any more creatures of the Shadow on this ship?"

"Aye, there are two."

"Where?"

"One is hidden in the stables, and one is in this chamber."

"Are there any other magics that would do us harm, or bring harm upon us, or reveal us to those who might seek us, upon this ship?"

"Aye. Every third water-barrel holds a stone that may be scried, for all the wardings here."

"And no others?"

"No."

Eroth turned his head to Sir Salarond. "Anything else?" he whispered tightly. Sir Salarond murmured back to him, and he said, "Are there any upon this ship who would betray us?"

"Your guides will sell you, if they can," the daemon answered without hesitation. "The others are loyal to their service."

"Enough," Salarond said. Arudal realized that the air in the cabin had grown chill, and he could smell something upon it, like a faint distant hint of rot upon an icy breeze; a shiver brushed over his body like a rustle of cold silk. We almost spoke too long, he thought. Praised be Amanvon, that Sir Salarond was watchful! The healer-priest stepped forward, lifting his blade. "Depart, child of Morthugor, back to the darkness beyond the World's Gate. Flee now the light, and do not return, lest the gods' brightness over the green world char you to ashes and dust. Take all that is of you with you, leaving no taint upon this place; go without harm, and without word to any, nor tidings of your departure. Be gone!"

Salarond's light flared so brightly and suddenly that Arudal had to cry out, dropping his sword and clapping his hand to his seared eyes. Trying to blink his sight clear, he found that he had fallen to his knees; his palm was wet with tears - but the room was warm again, its air smelling of nothing worse than the stable-stink that still hung about himself and Rhys, and the daemon was gone. Salarond took Arudal's hands, raising him gently to his feet.

"We might have done that better," the commander muttered, then, "No, Eroth, I am not blaming you. It takes a special skill to gain useful answers from a daemon, and I am glad enough that none of us are practiced in it. And we have learned what we most need to know - I shall see that the crew is detailed to remove the stones from the water barrels."

"Can we trust them for that?" Lostren asked. "The daemon said only that they were loyal to their service - not to the White Crown. It could have meant the Secret Service, or even a hidden agent's service to Martag."

Salarond paused, open-mouthed. "That is so. Those of us who are still able, then...I heard Rathaka's name, and thought that to be the end of matters. Martag sells such things for the sake of sowing deception and destruction in Kantar, as well as using them to their own advantage: a safe enough chance for them, since no one of good will would utilize such means. And some of their enchanted items pass through the Horse-Tribes - the daemon itself might have arranged its sale to the unknowing; we cannot tell how much power it had to act from within the stone. That, too, has happened before, that Martag will slip such a thing into trade goods and give it leave to wait until it sees a chance to do harm. Yet if there were a traitor on the ship, or among those who loaded our supplies...It is possible that the seeing-stones were set by the Secret Service, or at least one of its factions, perhaps with no direct harm meant, but it is also possible that they were put here by an agent of Martag, or some other with the intention of doing us ill. We cannot risk that chance."

"Who is Rathaka?" Arudal asked.

"She is the commander of the Vampire Fifteenth, a mage and warrior of Dark Troll blood mingled with Elf. Best not to think on how that came to pass," Salarond added grimly.

"She?" Arudal said in surprise. Women fought as equals among the Elves; a Tharandrostan maiden who was divined early as infertile might train in weaponry and go into combat like a man, but Arudal had thought that no other nation allowed females to fight.

"Aye, Martag does not keep its women from risking their lives in the field, if they are strong enough to wield a sword well or skilled in battle-magics. They are pleased enough to turn the chivalry of Kantar's knights against us, for many men cannot bring themselves to lift sword against a woman, though she be a deadly foe. But there is no time to talk on such things now if, as I fear, we are being followed closely. Now, Arudal, the daemon said that there were two creatures of Shadow on this ship. I would guess that it meant you and another..."

Arudal thought that he had hidden his feelings from his face, but Salarond stopped at once, laying his hand on Arudal's arm. Arudal flinched away, but the healer-priest held him. "I did not say that any of us thought so," Sir Salarond murmured to him. "It is the way of daemons to speak as will give most hurt, and to sow strife where they can. What I meant to ask is: if there is an Undead being on this ship, can you seek it out?"

"There is only the ghost of a cat," muttered Arudal unhappily. "She brings luck, and does no harm."

"Ah. So that is its information about the Shadow-Realm accounted for. In that case, let us go straight on to the hold, those of us who are still hale."

"Why so many seeing-stones, sir?" Tirothar asked. "Would one not have been enough?"

"That, too, makes me think that they were laid by the Secret Service. Belt and shoulder-straps - and the sort of people who wouldn't use a falchion to kill a fly when they could use a pound of nitre. Most likely, they meant no worse than keeping a watch on us...Nevertheless, we shall remove the stones, though it may be a troublesome process."

Sir Salarond had understated the matter, Arudal thought as he and Tirothar heaved up the last of the water barrels. There was no easier way to find the traitor stones than to drain each barrel slowly, going through it cup by cup to look for the tiny clear gem hidden within and pouring the water back into an empty vessel. By the time they were done, it was almost noon, and Arudal was swaying where he stood, too tired to keep his eyes properly open.

"Arudal," said Salarond gently, "I know you are worn out, but there is something I must ask of you before we lie down. Are you skilled enough in ritual to deceive one of these stones into sending false information? I can give you strength for a little time..."

"Why bother?" Sir Shakhor asked before Arudal could marshal his thoughts. "They cannot have been meant to send images from inside a water barrel. If they were set by enemies, and are all cast into the sea at the same time, with luck any who would pursue us will think that we were so grievously damaged in the storm that our ship could not keep afloat for a full day afterwards."

Sir Salarond gave him an exhausted smile. "That is well-said. Would you like to do the honours? Be careful," he added, "that no one from the crew sees you doing it."

"You may trust me," the fair-haired knight replied, gathering up the stones from the cloak on which they lay with a sweep of his palm, like wiping up a spattering of bright water-droplets. Rhys followed him up the stairs to the upper decks, leaving Sir Salarond and Dame Karsil with the three remaining squires.

"Now," Salarond sighed, running a damp hand through his gray-streaked mane, "do any of you have any more dire warnings that must be dealt with before we go to sleep?"

"Uh, sir," Tirothar said, raising his hand. "Sir, I am in grave danger of falling flat on my face from exhaustion."

Salarond barely spared him a moment's glare. "Arudal, can you tell if there are any more Shadow-wights following this ship?"

"I cannot sense daemons, sir. But I will try." Arudal closed his eyes, letting the darkness well up about him. Planking and decks fogged away from his inner sight; the sea dimmed into a heaving mist...In the stables below, the ghost-cat curled up in Inmanat's damp straw, purring over the life-drained body of a rat; but beyond the ship's shadowy edge, all was quiet, above and below, as far as Arudal's mind could reach. For a moment, free of the aching tiredness in his bones, he wanted to keep going beyond his own boundaries, slipping from his sore and weary flesh into the numbing Shadow-cold...Arudal dug his nails into his palms, letting the sharp little pain bring him back. He blinked hard until the lantern-light shed only a misty golden glow over the barrels of water and salt pork, and his comrades' faces were no more blurred than usual in his sight. "Nothing of the Ukuthrim, at least, sir."

"That is well. Consider yourselves relieved until this evening: you have all done mighty work."

Chapter 13: Disguises

"Flower and seed and fruit are one,
'Neath Aviyani's hand.
She sows and brushes pollen's gold,
To nurture treasures in her hold,
The pure blood of our land -
Flower and seed and fruit are one."
- "Flower and Seed and Fruit", hymn of the House of Procreation

The next few days passed without incident. Finvar spent most of his time down with the horses, calming them until they no longer neighed and battered their stall-doors at every shift of the wind; he had a way with them that almost made Arudal think of the Mind-gift of bespeaking animals, though he claimed it was no more than familiarity and affection. The four Sir Salarond had chosen to speak with their guides - Karsil, Eroth, Shakhor, and Rhys - were most often closeted with Atharath and Gormok, learning the language of the West, while Arudal sat outside the cabin door, listening carefully and making notes. He had been right in thinking that the tongue of their guides was closer to Imperial than to Common: but though it was unpolluted by the leavenings of Plainsman and Northman languages, over fifteen hundred years of sound-shifts had left it with similarities that stood out only to the ear of a philologer. *I will have enough material for several theses when I come back to Dr. Grimhjalm,* Arudal thought happily. Although it was frustrating not to be able to interrogate their guides himself, he sent the others in with long lists of questions, and wrote out a structure for the Western grammar to make the process of teaching the rest easier.

It was at such an evening session that Sir Salarond at last brought up the point of altering the appearance of those who showed the Imperial blood most clearly. "We dare not trust illusion," he mused. "Even if we could count on such spells working in the West, any skilled mage may see through it. I have herbs that may lighten dark hair slightly, but no strong dyes...Can we do more with ritual?"

Arudal thought about that for a little time. *Shape-changing...A man might become a beast, with the proper spells and use of an enchanted hide;* he rather liked the image of himself as a great Artegalian lynx or Perenilian lion such as a nobleman might hunt with, padding along beside his comrades. But he somehow doubted that anyone in their party had such skins with them, and the less attention they called to themselves, even in a bustling harbour-city, the better. Tharandrostans did not alter their hair colour - why would they, when it was one of the marks of their bloodline, either raven black or the rare rich gold that, like his own point-tipped ears, showed the trace of a distant Elven forebear?

Yet...there were magical ways to bring out hidden traits. Most often it was done upon conception, when powerful spells could be used to aid the right trait in linking to its match - his own conception had been thus enchanted - or while the child was growing in the womb and still malleable. It was harder after birth, and more difficult the deeper the change went; both magical talents and mind-magic were almost completely resistant. But little things such as colouring...

"Perhaps," Arudal said softly, giving his comrades an appraising look. It would take little work to gray Sir Salarond's hair completely; that was only a matter of pushing it in the direction it was already going. Finvar...Arudal would have wagered gold that there was Northman blood in his ancestry. For himself, Arudal knew that he carried the hidden trait for golden hair - Arothir was fair, and half of their children would be blond as well if they were mated. Lostren would be more difficult, for the Elven coloration was almost lost in the Kantarean Imperials, among whom marriages as close as first cousins were strictly forbidden. Yet if he had to, Arudal suspected that Lostren could trace his pedigree back to the earliest days of the Imperial race, and then...it was the part of a ritual mage to be artist as well as magician: Arudal would see what he could do.

"And will it last if we go where magic no longer works?"

"It will be a true change, drawn from what is already in the blood," Arudal answered.

"Then make yourself ready to do it as soon as you may - for there is no telling how long we have."

For Finvar, the spell was a surprisingly simple one; only a slight twist, like reaching out to turn over a die. The Artegalian said that his younger brother Dakar was fair-haired, and readily admitted that their grandmother had been the daughter of the Jarl of Fenviðr, the wide region of marshes and woods that had once bordered on Helludal and was now part of it. With his thick hair gone ash-blond and braided into a plait down his back, Finvar might have been any clean-shaven, stocky young Northman thane - though his blood was not diluted enough for him to raise a beard; the animal-like hair that marred the faces and bodies of the lesser races seemed to be a trait that was quickly lost forever in breeding with the Imperial race.

Lostren, as Arudal had guessed, was the hardest to change. They sat for more than a candlemark within the circle Arudal had traced while Lostren recited his pedigree on both sides, following its tree-branching out and out. Arudal let the other squire's voice wash over him, his awareness searching deeper into the drop of blood Lostren had let fall into his silver goblet... He had begged dried rosemary from Verhin the cook, sprinkling it over Lostren's hair with a small charm of memory. If the blood of House Telagon were touched by that of a lesser race, it would not be something that they spoke of often - Lostren might not even know it in his mind; it would be his blood that remembered... "And she was wedded to Corocan, son of the High King over the tribes of the lands that would become Var Perenil, who was said to be foresighted and had hence taken service with the Imperial army as was allowed to barbarians in those days and reached the rank of Commander..."

There! Arudal thought: given the name, for an instant, he saw the image of a tall man with red-gold hair held back by a silver fillet, wearing the red tunic and black breastplate of the old Imperial forces, his hand lifted as though he were giving an order. Corocan's blood would be long-lost in his distant kinsman, only the faintest trace remaining - yet it was enough for Arudal to draw up that image in Lostren's blood, superimposing it over the other youth's face and pulling, twisting... not bringing out a trait that had survived in hiding, but rather, using the linkage between Lostren and his far-off ancestor to make the one liker to the other...

Lostren made a surprised noise and slumped over. His heart pounding with fear, Arudal ended the spell as quickly as he could, breaking the circle. As the power drained from it, he took a step towards Lostren, but his legs collapsed under him; arms shaking, he crawled strengthlessly to the other squire's side, praying that Lostren had not been harmed - how could his rite have dropped them both so? At least Lostren was breathing deeply and regularly, and the rite had worked well enough, for his black hair was a bright red-gold now; there was actually a sprinkling of freckles across his narrow-arched nose and cheeks. After a moment he opened his eyes - still Imperially slanted, but cat-green, almost as green as Karsil's, with a pale gold rim about the pupils.

"Whew! I thought you said this was a minor spell, Arudal. That hit me like Utalkath's falchions... Did it work?"

Arudal silently handed him a mirror. Lostren stared, surprised, at his altered image. "Tell me," he said after a moment, his voice flatly controlled, "that you can change me back before we can go home. I don't believe Perethi would fancy me as a Plainsman."

Arudal stared stupidly at him, the words Lostren had spoken coming back to him. Corocan, son of the High King over the tribes...In his tranced state, it had meant nothing to him; now his mouth dropped open with shock, and he found himself babbling. "Of course, Amandeth forgive me, I'm sorry, Lostren, I'll do it now if you..."

Lostren shook his head, dried rosemary scattering down from his red-gold hair. "No. This mission is worth more than our pride, and no one to whom it will matter - I hope," he added with a sharp glare at Arudal - "will see me like this. In any case, a strong bleach and a dose of henna might have done as much, save for the eye-colour."

"I'm sorry, I didn't know..."

"I had forgotten myself," Lostren sighed. "Corocan was mentioned in one genealogy, which, as you can imagine, I had assumed to be spurious. If it had not been for your memory charm, I doubt I should have come up with it at all."

"I'm sorry," Arudal repeated numbly.

"Better this," Lostren answered, "than being burnt as demon-spawn, or failing in our mission." Arudal could not tell which of them he was trying to convince, but he nodded. "Still, I think I shall watch to see how you turn out."

Arudal could not argue. Silently he cleaned up the circle he had drawn for Lostren, retracing it about himself. The tip of his wand drew amethyst-glowing letters: the names of Amanvon, creator of Elves and guide of the Imperial race, Amandeth, who had shaped and gifted his own line, Aviyani, Lady of Healing, who shaped the fruit in the bud and the child in the womb…Within himself, he did not have to look far: the Elvish fairness was only shadowed by his black hair, not lost…only a little difference at his conception, a touch to what magic had already guided…Arudal shuddered in the sudden wave of dizziness that came over him. He tied up the last knots of the spell, and reached for the mirror.

Although his features had not changed, Arudal could hardly believe that he was looking at himself. The little peaks of his ears stood out more sharply against his silky golden hair; the delicate wings of his fair eyebrows drew the gaze more intensely to the fineness of his high cheekbones and slant of his amber-ringed gray eyes…

"If you were taller," Lostren said softly, mirroring Arudal's own thoughts, "and not so wide in the shoulders, you could almost pass for an Elf now…You must be very careful, else, if we meet any of Karsil's kinsfolk, we shall have more trouble than you can imagine. They will not love one of their own who walks in Shadow."

Arudal glanced suddenly at Lostren. Lostren's eyes were wide, the gold-rimmed pupils swollen in their green irises - as though he were in a trance of foresight. An icy shiver of suspicion ran down Arudal's spine, even as his knees began to buckle beneath him again with the aftermath of his night's magics. He breathed deeply, forcing himself to stay upright.

"Lostren?"

Lostren blinked. "Odd, how such little changes can make so much difference," he said in a normal tone of voice. "I suppose we had best go report your success to Sir Salarond."

Sir Salarond - his hair and brows fully silver now - waited in his cabin with the others. He had used herbs to lighten the hair of Sir Thoron and Tirothar to a rusty deep brown; their bodies were farthest from the Imperial type, and Salarond thought that the less magic needed, the better. Arudal could feel Lostren bracing as if against expected mockery, but his knight only nodded soberly. "Well done, Arudal. We should be able to pass unsuspected now."

"Save among my kin!" Dame Karsil snapped. "How dared you take so close to an Elvish shape?"

"I made no change save my colouring," Arudal replied to her. "It is no fault of my own that your forebears found mine fit to wed."

"Before your ancestors gave themselves to the Shadow, yes," Karsil said. "But if you think thus to claim Elvish blood and rights…"

"Soft, Karsil," Sir Salarond broke in. "I am sure no such thing was in Arudal's mind. Arudal only did with himself as with Finvar and Lostren - neither of whom, I would guess, chose among the races of their ancestors."

Lostren's blush flared red, and brighter still when Rhys bowed to him. "For myself, Lostren, I find you better-born than before," the Plainsman squire said. "It is only the god-born line of the old High Kings that bore hair like gold in a flame, and I rejoice to learn that you are royal as well as noble. Were I not sworn to Sir Shakhor, who is my father and all my clan, I should offer you my service, even though I know that the sign of your blood must be hidden again when this mission is over. It is in my mind, though, to wonder what else this magic has brought forth in you, for there is a brightness about you that I did not see before."

"There will be time for that later, Rhys," Salarond told him soothingly. "Karsil, is Arudal really more likely to bring trouble among your kin than before? There have always been a few golden-haired Imperials, and I have seen Tharandrostans as blond and fine-featured before..."

"Look at him!" Karsil said. "I had not seen it earlier, for that his black hair and arrogant manner made him so clearly a Tharandrostan - but Arudal might be a half-breed of the first generation, rather than millennia removed from the days when the Unfallen Imperial race were our closest friends among Men. Is this, then, what your State's magics seek to create: a race long-lived and fair as Elves, but blinded by the clean lights of Stars and Sun? That would be an abomination as foul as anything ever wrought by the Fallen Empire."

Arudal thought uncomfortably on certain treatises of inheritance he had read theorizing a possible link between the visible "Elvish throwback" traits and further extension of the Tharandrostan lifespan, but said nothing.

"Yet Arudal's gift is not obvious to your eyes, is it?" enquired Sir Salarond.

Karsil bit her lip. "Not to mine. But I am young yet in years, and little in power compared to even one who has seen a single millennium pass. If Arudal stood before Queen Celenthil, her gaze would strip away every secret of his mind and heart, did she so will it, and there are those of our race who are greater seers even than our Queen." Her ice-green eyes met Arudal's, gazing carefully at every line of his face. "Yet I can see now that there is nothing to be done, unless Arudal can change his features as well as his colouring. I expected a Tharandrostan, alien to my race for many swift-changing generations of Men, and that was what I saw. If my kin look straight at him, then, dark or fair, they will see his bloodlines clearly enough, small and ungracefully-made though he is."

Arudal glared up at her, but from the corner of his eye he could see Sir Eroth nodding. "Aye, the resemblance is remarkable," the brown-haired knight murmured. "And more so when you are both angry...But did we not say earlier that it would do us little good to go to the Elves, who are more likely to hinder us in our search for the Imperial Seat than to aid us?"

"That is so," admitted Karsil. "Among Men," she added, her mouth twisting in distaste, "I suppose Arudal could be explained easily enough as a half-breed, though I will not claim his mixed blood as kin to my own line."

Sir Shakhor laughed suddenly. "The two of you have more in common than fine features and pointed ears, I think. I never knew till now that Elves were as finicky about their pedigrees as Tharandrostans."

Karsil's hand went to the hilt of her longsword as she whirled on him. "How dare you compare the Children of Amanvon to...to...?"

"We have held this discussion once already, Karsil," Sir Salarond growled, a warning snap of command in his voice. "You have been a knight of Kantar long enough, I think, to begin to understand military discipline as it is practiced here - and you had your chance to leave this mission in Var Perenil. Now remember your oaths, Lieutenant-Commander, and hold your tongue!"

Dame Karsil dropped her hand from her swordhilt, but drew herself up to her full height, looking down on the Kantareans. "You will excuse me," she gritted. "It may be best if I go to meditate before I say - or do - something we shall all regret."

"You are excused, Lieutenant-Commander," Salarond told her.

Arudal was angry enough himself at the insults Karsil had given him; he was more than half-tempted to set the circle about himself again and purge every sign of his distant Elvish forebears from his face, if he could. Small wonder, he thought as the Elf stalked from the room, that the old Imperials turned against the Elves, if this is how they think of us when not veiling their feelings from politeness!

"My apologies, Arudal," Sir Salarond said as soon as the door had banged shut behind Karsil. "But you know as well as I how necessary this is. As will Karsil, when she has had a few hours to cool off and think about it."

"I am not troubled, sir," Arudal said, somewhat untruthfully. "In any case, Lostren has a harder burden to bear than I."

Rhys' upper lip pulled back in a snarl, but Sir Shakhor laid a quelling hand on his squire's arm. Lostren had gone very pale, his face white beneath the thick waves of red-gold hair.

"Thoron," Salarond said quietly, "I believe your squire is very tired from his magics. I suggest you take him to your cabin and put him to bed now."

Arudal flushed as his knight took him by the arm and led him out, Finvar trailing quietly behind. What did I say? he wondered.

"You might as well sleep now, since you'll be up running the decks at dawn," Sir Thoron informed Arudal as he slipped into his night-robe. "You're falling behind in your training with all this Western language crap, anyway: a hard day's exercise will do you good. You too, Finvar." He waited until Arudal had climbed into his bunk, then turned and left, growling to himself.

"What did I say?" Arudal asked Finvar.

"I think it's technically known as 'making it worse'. Amanvon's sake, Arudal, isn't it bad enough for Lostren to find out there was a Plainsman in the woodpile without you, of all people, rubbing it in?"

"But I was only trying to..." Arudal protested. Finvar turned his back and blew out the lantern, leaving Arudal to contemplate the injustice of it all. He had meant nothing but sympathy for Lostren; the Plainsman taint in the Telagon bloodline was so far back - more than three millennia - that even the strictest mages of the House of Procreation would consider it negligible. And after he had poured out all his strength doing something that a bit more foresight and simple hair-dyes could have managed, if they had thought of it beforehand...

Ritual magic was like that, huge efforts and complex theory to get even relatively minor physical results; Arudal could still feel the deep trembling in his bones from the spell he had done on Lostren, and knew that he would feel like a wrung-out swab-rag in the morning. Everyone is angry with me, and I don't deserve it. The taunt of "Elvish throwback" had stung him often enough at school for Arudal to feel flicked on the raw now, and Karsil's arrogance made it all the worse. Small and ungracefully made, indeed! He was the height a nobleman of his race ought to be; the physician at Prince's School had always spoken well of his proportions, and even Sir Thoron praised his quickness.

Yet... "Finvar," Arudal said plaintively, sitting up in bed and looking over at Thoron's other squire, "Is there any way I can apologize to Lostren?"

"Keeping your mouth shut would be a good start," Finvar said without opening his eyes. "Not using this as a way to get at Rhys would be another."

"But I wasn't..."

Finvar grunted and turned over. "Doesn't matter, if everyone thinks you were. Shit, Arudal, how would you feel if it were you?"

"My ancestors would never have..!"

"See? I bet if you'd asked Lostren this morning, he would have said the same thing - but what's he going to say now, with Rhys thinking he's a High King reborn and hanging on every word? Leave it be: everyone gets over everything in time. Except the Elves, I guess, but Karsil's a madwoman...why do you think she's only a lieutenant-commander after all these years in our military? Now go to sleep, we've got a hard day ahead of us tomorrow."

True to his word, Thoron had both his squires up and running before dawn. Finvar was excused from climbing the rigging, but Arudal had to go up and down until his shaking hands could no longer grasp the ropes - and then Thoron ordered him to armour up for falchion-practice.

"Don't look at me like that, squire, I'm doing you a favour!" Sir Thoron snapped at Arudal. "Someday you may have to turn and fight when you can't run any longer; and do you think a band of Dark Trolls will let you have a drink of water and a rest before you pick up your sword?"

I'd like that better if I didn't think I were being punished for something I hadn't done, Arudal thought, but he heaved up his shield nevertheless, shifting his weight to the balls of his feet and watching for Thoron's first move.

Sir Thoron battered his squire mercilessly; Arudal was too tired to skip backwards or sideways from his blows...but, to his surprise, he found himself turning strokes where he would have tried to dodge before, and instead of retreating when the big knight made as if to walk over him, he thrust straight to Thoron's face with a blow that could have been fatal, had it been a sharp tip instead of the padded end of the practice sword that struck the helmet's eyeslot.

"Now that was well-done!" Thoron said in amazement. "I'm beginning to think that you might make a real fighter after all. Come on, get your shield up; one good stroke won't end a battle."

Arudal wearily lifted his shield again. Sir Thoron closed on him in a flurry of battering strokes; strengthened a little by his knight's praise, Arudal fought back as best he could until his empty stomach twisted and he dropped to his knees. He was panting too hard to keep from choking on the bitter drops of bile, wheezing desperately to catch his breath through his strangling throat.

At once Sir Thoron was unfastening Arudal's helm and gorget, staring closely at his squire as he gradually got his breath back under control. "Enough for now, I suppose," the knight said. "Still, you didn't hold up too badly, considering how soft you've had it these last weeks. Armour down, have a wash, and get some food into you. Finvar! Get over here! You've had a good rest; I'd better see you fighting twice as long."

Arudal picked up helm, shield, and sword, and limped on down to their cabin to take his armour off. His trembling fingers could barely manage the buckles; the padding and leather of his gambeson were sodden through so thoroughly that he had to wipe the sweat from his chainmail and the inner pieces of his coat of plates. Another spasm of nausea caught him halfway through, and he sat with his head between his knees until it was over.

A knock sounded on the door. "Come in," he said dully.

Lostren entered, carrying a tray with a steaming pitcher, a mug, and a round loaf of bread filled with cheese. Out of the corner of his eye, Arudal might have seen only the neat braid of bright red hair and the tray, and thought himself at home for a second; but his misted eyesight had taught him to recognise movement and stance, and Lostren's graceful pride could no more be mistaken for the subservient glide of a Plainsman than could Karsil's elegantly flowing motions.

"I thought you might need this," Lostren said. "I've seen men in better shape after real battles."

Arudal hung his head, deeply ashamed at the thought that had crossed his mind for a heartbeat and by the other squire's kindness to him. "Lostren," he said timidly. "Last night...well, I didn't mean..."

"I know," Lostren replied. "And Karsil was a great deal nastier to you, and meant to be. Even the best knights of Kantar, I think, are not entirely without prejudice in some matters. Drink first, then eat; it looks as though you've sweated half your weight away."

Arudal poured the mug full, sipping carefully at it. It had a strange taste: a slight scouring bitterness, yet not unpleasant, underscored by honey and...salt? Surely not; but he found himself draining the mug eagerly and refilling it. He could almost feel the draught draining out into his body, like rain into dry earth, soaking away the aches of his bruises and stiffening muscles.

"Thank you," he murmured with all the gratitude that was in him, drinking again. "I do not know why you are so kind to me, when I..."

"Because you have already saved my life," Lostren said. Arudal looked sharply up at him, and saw his pupils swollen as if he were staring into Shadow, only a narrow rim of greenish-gold about the black like water ringing the edge of a maelstrom. "In the house of the Lord of Hatin's City, the other stable-boys would have torn the hoods from our hair, and then there would have been no escaping: we would have been bound and gagged at once, and burned on the spot, our mission destroyed before it had begun. But none will look askance at a red-haired foreigner, or see the old darkness in a fair youth of Elf-blood, and so we shall pass out safely..."

Arudal's heart tightened cold in his chest, like a fist clenching on an icicle. He knew the gift of Seeing when it was before him; yet mind-magic was the most difficult of all abilities to grant by magic...unless it had passed hidden through all the generations from Lostren's red-haired forebear; and even then...

"Arudal?" Lostren asked. "Are you all right?"

Arudal nodded. "Do you know what you just...did?"

Lostren's eyes narrowed. "I think...I am not sure," he confessed. "I saw something, and spoke, but I can hardly remember. Only that some ill fate has been turned aside, and that by your doing."

"And you have never shown any sign of the mind-gifts of Seeing?"

Lostren shook his bright head slowly. "It does not run in the Telagon line, though sometimes one of us will be born a Mindspeaker, and my eldest brother has the gift of reading Truth - not so uncommon in the high lines of Kantar."

Arudal nodded. Foresight, Mindspeech, Truth-reading, and Healing: those were the chief gifts of the nobly born of the Imperial race. Perhaps one in twenty among the nobles of Kantar showed those talents...and yet...

"But Rhys said something of this to me," Lostren went on. "He said...that though most of his folk with red hair are not gifted, all those who are gifted have red hair and green eyes. I wonder if...in striving to..." His voice failed him.

A marker trait, Arudal thought. If a relatively trivial physical trait were linked strongly enough with something deeper - it was possible, yes; and it came to him that he had never seen a green-eyed Plainsman in Tharandrost. And Lostren had mentioned his ancestor's foresight in the middle of the ritual. "It is possible," he admitted aloud.

The corner of Lostren's mouth twisted up wryly. "And when you restore me to my proper appearance, the Plainsman's foresight will be lost along with his hair and eyes."

"Almost certainly, if the traits are so closely bound."

"A difficult choice, indeed," Lostren sighed. "I shall take it as Amanvon's will for this mission, and not worry any further until our work is at end. Nor should you, Arudal. Now eat something before you fall over again, and then wash and wrap up warmly so you don't take a chill. Sir Salarond says that already he is beginning to feel a certain change in the flows of power, and we should be prepared not to rely on the gods' healing through him."

Wonderful, Arudal thought.

Lostren patted him on the shoulder and rose to go, then suddenly turned. "Arudal, do you know anything about training Foresight? It must be possible, the King's Seers call visions on command."

"I can show you how to go into a trance, and how to concentrate on something you are seeking," Arudal said, relieved to be on more familiar ground. "Beyond that - my talents are those of speaking and hearing, not of knowing."

"And with...well, never mind. But any help you can give me will be welcome."

"Of course," answered Arudal, feeling his heart somewhat eased.

Chapter 14: Karsil's Squire

"Take care of your weapons, and honour your knight,
And never complain of the burdens you bear,
Though a young squire's duties seem heavy and hard,
You'll soon learn the worth of the chain that you wear.

"Take care of your weapons, and honour your knight,
A squire's first lesson is how to obey,
Be you willing and ready, whatever's to hand:
You'll cherish in time what you learn from this day."
- "Exhortation", Sir Athathor Karbamirun

The next morning, when the White Company knights and their squires sat on the sunlit deck eating their breakfasts - save for Dame Karsil, who lounged against the side-railing with alert grace as she watched the others - Sir Salarond began to outline their plan more thoroughly. "As traders in the marketplace, we should draw no more notice than any caravan or shipload from afar would in Felatar; Hatin's City, our informants assure me, is accustomed to foreign merchants. That will give us a good share of local coins as well, and the less we must use weigh-rings of precious metal or coinage with the marks hammered off, the better it shall be. But we must be able to play the part of merchants and guards well enough to be believable..." The lean healer-priest looked about at his companions.

"Count me out of the merchanting," Sir Thoron growled. "I'll just stand there with my hand on my sword and look violent."

"And you're so good at that," Sir Eroth murmured, quirking a brown eyebrow upward. "Sadly, I haven't had to drive a bargain anywhere but Geraid's armoury in a very long time. I don't think I can get much of a price for our wares."

Sir Shakhor also shook his head when Salarond's glance met his. "I care less for trade than I do for cities. But when we go into town, I always let Rhys do my bargaining for me."

At their commander's enquiring gaze, Rhys said, "Sir, I have a bit of a way with such things. My father was a horse-trader as well as a groom, and used to the worth of town-folks' money as well as bargaining goods for goods."

"That's one, then. Lostren? Do you know much about your family's trade?"

Lostren sighed, pushing back his bright hair. "Sir, I could be very helpful if we meant to bargain for wine by the tun and wain-load. I couldn't tell you the price of silk in Dan Iragal, let alone what we might get for it in a strange place."

"I can deal for a knife or a shield," Finvar added. "That's about it."

"Tirothar?" Sir Salarond asked.

"Much the same as Lostren, sir," the lanky squire said regretfully. "But Arudal knows how to bargain. At least, he got Lostren a good price on a brooch for his girlfriend."

"Hmm." Sir Salarond squinted down into his mug of small beer, swirling the thin scum of foam on the top as if he might read an answer in its patterns. "Arudal, you speak the Western tongue better than any of us. Can you drive a bargain among common folk in the market?"

"Even the best-born among us learn the skills of trading at school, sir," Arudal replied. It was, after all, the nobles of Tharandrost that had to negotiate with the princes of Afalach for the grain shipments that fed their nation and the timber that kept their fleet on the waves. Much of that was done by women, but the southern trade that brought back the exotic goods through which Tharandrost prospered was in the hands of the great ships' captains.

"Well enough. You and Rhys shall oversee our selling, then, while the rest of us guard the wares or go out to learn what we can - assuming," their commander added, looking up at Karsil, "that trade is not too far beneath the dignity of one of Elvish blood."

"The Elves do not deal in goods as Men do," Karsil told him coldly. "Yet I suppose that one of mixed blood might have learned such skills."

The Elven knight was looking down her sharp nose at Arudal again, and he could not help asking, "If trade is beneath the dignity of the Elves, how do folk get their daily bread in Tiragel?"

Karsil's green eyes narrowed in a glare, her delicate lips tightening. Arudal wanted to smile sweetly at her, but he knew he should not provoke the Elven knight while they must be wary - as they would have to be until they were safely back in the Middle Land with their information delivered to King Edril.

To Arudal's surprise, however, Dame Karsil's anger softened into a more thoughtful look. "If you must claim to be of Elvish blood - and I suppose there is no other choice - then perhaps you should know something of Elvish ways. It is little surprise that you would not have been taught of them in Tharandrost."

Despite her clear contempt, now that Arudal thought of it, it did seem strange that the economy of Elf-Home had never been taught as were those of the other lands with which Tharandrost traded - only their exports and imports, with no time given to the other factors that shaped a nation's prosperity. But he said nothing, and Karsil continued.

"It is not the way of the Elves for any to do labour in which they do not delight, save in the very gravest need. The Gray Elves are a younger race than we, and take little joy from great craftings in stone; their hearts are with the sprouting seed and ripening grain, the lowing of cattle and the soft wool of sheep and the heavy-laden fruit trees. They dwell outside our cities and tend the earth, and gladly bring food for those whose hands are turned to the shaping of gems and metal and stone, and we in turn give them such craftings as they desire for the easing of their work and the beauty of their homes and lands. There is no need for such keeping of accounts as humans use, save when we deal with you. If one Elf wishes something, another is always glad to give it: the builder of houses finds joy in his task, and in knowing that his work of art is brought to life by lives within; the maker of jewelry is fulfilled to see his ring glittering on a fair hand; and the farmer's heart is warmed to see another take pleasure in the sweetness of an apple. Only the crafters of weapons must sometimes weep to see their art used in full earnest, when there is no way of defending against misguided children of the gods save by cutting them down - yet even swords are made with love for their many ripples of folded iron and steel, for their sweetness in balance and their song when they cleave the air." For a moment, it seemed to Arudal that the hidden anger that always tightened Karsil's face like a bow never loosed from the string eased a moment as she spoke of the home from which she had exiled herself. Then her mouth snapped taut again. "But I suppose that you, who must bind men with iron fetters and rule them with whips, cannot imagine a realm where all work and give to others freely and from their hearts, or greet the dawn with pleasure in the day to come instead of burdened tears. Nor will you ever understand us."

"I do the work that pleaseth me best," Arudal answered, stung by the Elf's sharp tone. "It delighteth me more than anything to find knowledge of our tongue and share it with those who care about it. I know that there are Bright Elves who feel no differently about their lore, for there are a few such even in Tharandrost - one teaches at the Prince's School, and several are comen thence for the sake of their studies in adamant-crafting."

"Your leisure is bought with the tears and suffering of others, whom you rob of even their short lives," Dame Karsil countered.

Sir Salarond coughed. "This is not the time to argue the laws of your countries," he said quietly. "Karsil, how do Bright Elves manage when they do not dwell side-by-side with their cousins who tend the earth?"

"There are always some who love the woodlands and the plains as much as the fairest pillars of stone. They hunt and fish and gather, even as the Green Elves do; our forest cousins wander far and wide, and also trade with those who live in smaller holdings, though they seldom come to the great cities, or even deep into farmed lands. Remember, too, that Elves are not as driven by their bellies as Men: even a fighter or smith or stonemason, or anyone at a task that calls for food to fuel strength, can go three days as easily as three hours without eating or drinking, and what food we do prepare has more virtue in it than the meals of Men."

Oddly, it came to Arudal at that point that in all the time he had known Dame Karsil, he had never seen her excuse herself to use the latrine - an enviable trait in an armoured fighter, he thought, especially a female. He had wondered how she would manage if she had need to.

"If your folk dislike fighting so much, how do you get such fine warriors?" Finvar asked cautiously.

"Did I say that we dislike fighting?" Karsil answered cooly. "It was long, even as we reckon it, before Men first walked in the light of the Sun, and longer before they showed that the Shadow had twined a small root into the hearts even of the best of them. Before that, we guarded the gateways of the green earth, and slew the Children of Morthugor and his foul and twisted mockeries of life as was meet for us to do. Amanvon knew that sword and bow would be needed as surely as chisel and athanor, and thus, as some of us are born to strike the harpstrings and weave words, others were born to strike with blade and weave strategies: war had arisen between the worlds long before Celenthil opened her eyes to the starlight. And there is as much beauty in the dance of the sword - at least, as the Elves perform it - as in any other; it is the dancer and the blade that are the truth of its wielding, though its proof is the foe's death. But our sorrow comes in that there are times when the sword must be raised against other children of the gods, when they turn to - or are taught in - evil ways."

Arudal thought of how he had seen Karsil practising by herself on the boat as they sailed down the Karasindi, and how it had reminded him of the mithalapar-dances, the unarmed fighting-forms of Tharandrostan women. I wonder if I could learn to fight like that? he thought longingly. The Imperial style, even in its most developed classical form, was straightforward and efficient, a style for small men who must close quickly and win in a well-placed blow or two against foes with greater reach and weight: it was effective, but hardly beautiful. But if the Elves did not have such long lifetimes to practice their own style in, would they be so skilled against others? Or have they studied the sword so long that they have stripped away everything that is not useful, and left not only perfection in killing, but perfection in beauty as well? Arudal was not enough of a fighter to guess from the little he had seen of Karsil's practice, but sometime, he thought, he would ask Sir Thoron's opinion on it.

"Dame Karsil," Sir Salarond said, almost as if he had heard the thoughts in Arudal's mind, "is the Elven style of fighting like to have changed much between the Middle Land and those of your kindred who dwell in the West?"

"Unless the Bright Elves themselves have changed there - and I think that most unlikely - not so. Our art of the sword was honed to perfection before Morthugor's Avatar rose to darken the Western lands. Our older warriors, who know their craft as they know how to walk or sing, may each have gone far beyond what the younger ones are still learning, so that a Man's eyes might not be able to see that the style is the same; yet to us, it is unmistakable."

"Then - with Sir Thoron's permission - I would have you teach Arudal what you can while we are on this voyage."

Karsil's lips tightened as she looked down at Arudal. "Even were it right to do so, his body is not suited to it. You can see for yourself: his reach is too short, and he is clumsily built, topheavy and over-muscled about the chest and shoulders. He will be too slow as well."

"I think that your prejudices are blinding your eyes, Karsil," their commander told her softly. "Arudal, stretch out your arm - yes, thus. You see, his limbs are long for his height, and if you had bothered to watch him practicing with Thoron, you would see that he is as quick as any Elf, swift even for his own breed." Arudal could feel the tips of his ears reddening at being discussed as if he were a Plainsman being sold in the marketplace, but he said nothing. "In any case," Salarond added, "Pererad White-Hilt once said to me that if he could not teach the art of the sword even to a Dwarf, then he could not truly say that he knew it. Perhaps it is not fair to compare you to the leader of the Queen's Blades, but then, Arudal is not so great a challenge."

"So now you seek to move me by my pride?" Karsil asked, a small ironic smile twitching up the corner of her mouth. "Well, I see the cleverness of your choice, if you wish to pass Arudal off as kin to my kindred, though I doubt its wisdom very greatly. Still, I shall teach your Tharandrostan as he is able to learn, if Thoron is willing to give up his squire to me until we make landfall."

Salarond looked at the big knight, raising a shaggy gray eyebrow. "Well, Thoron?"

"If you insist," Sir Thoron growled. "Though I don't see why you want to try to make fine silver out of a perfectly good length of steel. Likely you'll just have long enough to confuse my squire altogether and give me twice as long to set him straight."

The healer-priest smiled. "I think you underestimate Arudal's quickness of learning. He has the wit to think about what he is taught, and will, I would guess, be a better fighter for it in the end."

"O, very well," grumbled Thoron. "Karsil, you will remember that Men have to rest and sleep and eat; I won't have you making my squire ill before we reach the West. If we have to fight, he follows my orders, not yours, and if you think you need to beat him, ask me first."

"Elves do not beat their students," Karsil replied coldly.

"No, they just slice a bit off at a time with their tongues. And I'm not lending you my squire so you can make him a whipping boy for everything Tharandrost has done since the days of the Eighteenth Emperor, either. If I hear you mistreating him, I will have him back, you understand?"

"I will bespeak Arudal as fairly as I may and still teach him," answered Karsil.

Sir Thoron looked down at Arudal, his dark eyes narrowed. "Arudal, do you want to do this? You've kept your oath, and been a good squire to me thus far: I shall not lend your services to Karsil against your will."

"If our commander thinks it is needful, sir, I am willing."

Sir Salarond nodded.

"Done, then." Thoron reached out to clasp wrists with the Elf, her narrow fingers gleaming white against the sun-darkened skin of his burly forearm.

"Arudal, you may move your gear and bedding into my cabin," Karsil said. "Do not disturb any of my things, and expect to stay very quiet when I am not working with you. When you are done moving, you may fetch my second sword and your own shield out here, but you are not to put on any armour, and you shall take your boots off."

Arudal hastened to do as the Elf had told him, stowing his bedroll, packs, and armour neatly in a corner. Karsil's second sword, like the one that hung at the Elf's belt, was a slim longsword; it was sheathed in plain white leather over thin springy wood, and three small green gems glittered brightly from its filigree-wrought silver pommel. The hilt was decorated with intertwining leaves and flowers of filigree as well - as useful as braided wire in keeping the grip from growing slippery with blood or sweat, but only an Elf would think to adorn a sword thus.

For the rest of the day, Arudal tried as well as he could to follow the intricate footwork-patterns that Karsil was showing him. The longsword felt odd in his hand, as though he were holding a willow-wand; it would be some days, Karsil said, before she showed him what to do with it, but she wished him to grow used to its balance and feeling as he moved. As she had promised Sir Thoron, Karsil always addressed Arudal more politely than she had before, but it seemed to him that he could feel the contempt in her green gaze whenever he trod a finger's-breadth wrong, and she never spoke any word of praise to him.

"You shall eat in my cabin this night, and I shall begin to teach you manners," Dame Karsil said when she allowed Arudal to sheathe the Elvish sword at last. "Wash yourself first and put on clean clothes: you smell like a Man who has toiled hard." By her tone of voice, she might have been saying, you stink like a Plainsman. Arudal gritted his teeth and did not answer.

 Still, he was pleased enough to strip off his sweat-soaked tunic and breeches and dive into the Sea, the icy water a blessed shock about his heated body. The strain of controlling his muscles so completely had tired Arudal worse than if he had been fighting; the Imperial race was stronger to endure than common Men, but no match for Elves. The other squires joined him in a few moments. Lostren's dive was almost as graceful as Arudal's own, but Finvar clutched his knees to his chest with a great yell and splashed into the water like a boulder. Tirothar and Rhys jumped in more cautiously; Tirothar's strong strokes suggested that he was used to swimming in the current of the Karasindi, but Rhys paddled about like a dog, and stayed in only long enough to wash the sweat of the day's training from his body before he called for a line to haul him back up. Finvar's swimming was little better, his limbs thrashing wildly and splashing whoever was near him, but he seemed to be enjoying himself. "Nice swimming in water this warm," the Artegalian gasped when Arudal surfaced beside him. "Winter at home, we have to break the ice for our baths."

Having nothing to say, Arudal swam downwards again with a swift flick of his feet. There was a game noble Tharandrostan children often played at naming-day parties: a handful of silver coins, sometimes with a few gold quarter-crowns mixed in, would be scattered widely in a clear deep pool, and the children would dive to gather them up. Arudal had always been good at that, and would have been the winner more times than not if his eyesight were better. He twisted in the water, looking up at Finvar's thick-muscled pale legs kicking hard above him. For a moment he thought of playing Shark as he would with his friends at home, grabbing the other squire's ankle and pulling him down to wrestle beneath the surface, but regretfully decided that he did not know whether Finvar would take that as an offense.

Arudal's head broke the surface again just in time to hear Sir Thoron booming, "...enough, squires, you don't know what might be in the water with you, and all of you together wouldn't be a full mouthful for a deep-ocean grayshark." Arudal could not help glancing quickly down, looking for the pale blue-gray of a long back gliding beneath him, but saw nothing save water darkening from green to black.

More lines were tossed over, and Arudal climbed quickly up to the deck, vaulting one-handed over the side to rub the salt-stickiness from his body with a damp cloth. He pulled his breeches on for decency's sake; the sea wind shivered a rash of goosebumps across his bare arms and back, but he could not bring himself to put his sweat-sodden tunic on again.

Karsil had already put a white robe on by the time Arudal got to the cabin, and was sitting quietly at the table. She looked as clean and unruffled as ever, staring cooly at him, and she spoke in Bright Elvish. "Dress yourself properly, and then you may pour a glass of wine for each of us. You will find goblets and a flask in my travelling chest."

Arudal dithered a moment: she could not mean that he was to change clothes there, in front of her..? *Well, if she mislikes my body, it was she who gave the order, not I.* Still, he turned his back, dropping his clean silk tunic over his head first so that its hem would hide his buttocks as he changed smallclothes and breeches. He was just reaching for his sealskin boots when Karsil said, "You shall not wear those in my cabin. I would prefer to see you going barefoot."

"As you wish..." Arudal faltered. He did not know what Elvish military titles might be, nor how a squire should address a knight in that language. But Karsil gave no sign of noticing that he had omitted anything, and so he fetched out the goblets and flask she had ordered, setting them on the table and pouring as he had learned to do in his fostering-years as a page in the house of Duke Azarlokan.

"Stop," Dame Karsil said coldly.

Arudal tilted the small crystal bottle back with a careful quarter-twist so that no stray drop would trickle from its neck. "Finavi?" *The word, wise lady, was appropriate for a teacher;* Arudal hesitated to use it, lest he should misspeak, but Karsil acknowledged with a flicker of one delicate golden eyebrow.

"The pouring of wine is a thing fair in itself: joyful labour went into crafting that draught, and the life-strength of the fruit from which it was brewed. You pour as if to absent yourself from table, and to set the goblet at the elbow of one who will drink it without a thought for vintner or cup-bearer."

And that took me nearly a year to learn, Arudal thought indignantly. Though naturally soft-footed, his eyesight had made it difficult for him to tell when a cup needed refilling, and to manage it with the quietly unobtrusive grace that the Duke expected of his pages; he had not been allowed to serve at table when there were guests present until two years into his five years' fostering.

"I fear there is little hope of teaching you in such time as we have, but I will show you what I can. Watch carefully."

Dame Karsil took the flask from Arudal's hands, holding it up so that the candlelight caught the smooth swirling rainbow-glimmers of the subtly patterned glass and glowed like pale gold amber from the wine within. Her leaf-green eyes shone as she tilted it again, the wine flowing in a glittering stream from the thick rim around the small bottle's neck to the shallow silver bowl of the goblet. Simple as her gesture was, Arudal found himself gazing as if at a master dancer's performance - though there was hardly the least thing that he could fix upon to distinguish the Elf's pouring from his own.

"Do you try again," Karsil ordered.

Arudal held the flask up for a moment as she had. Its curves were sleek beneath his fingers, cool and heavy as polished gemstone - was it glass indeed, or carved from Elvish crystal? He had only the vaguest idea of how wine was made, and it was hard for him to imagine Elves in simple farm clothes picking grapes, but he could see the candlelight shining in the pale wine like a drop of gold poured into the heart of a smooth-wrought adamant, its stream tinting the polished silver bowl of the second goblet to pale electrum, and the scent that rose up from it, though delicately sweet as the faintest breeze of spring stirring through an open window, almost dizzied him.

"Better,"Karsil allowed grudgingly. "Sit down." As Arudal sat, she lifted one of the silver goblets, turning the fine-patterned stem in her long fingers. "May what is twisted be made straight once more, and the shattered be made whole." She sipped from the rim - hardly more than a breath of the wine's scent, and a few drops upon her lips. Arudal did not know what to say, but he copied her gesture.

For a time the Elf looked at Arudal thoughtfully, her face like a mask of translucent alabaster in the candlelight. "If you are to learn anything from me," she said at last, "you must forget the haste of Men. There are some of my kindred who might spend a thousand Sun-turnings in contemplation of a well-wrought cup before ever a drop of wine touched it."

Three years or so? Arudal thought. But 'Sun-turning' in Bright Elvish could mean a year as well as a day...A thousand years?

Karsil was still speaking, "Your bones would be long dust by then: your race had more than thrice the span of other Men, and yet could not forget that they were hastening towards Death with every heartbeat. The fear that will hinder everything I teach you is the same as that which turned the Empire towards darkness: Morthugor promised the Twentieth Emperor power over Death, and gave him only the knowledge of Shadow. But the seeds were set long before that, when you desired more than was rightfully given you, and became masters instead of teachers...Yet the blood of the Elves was mingled with that of your ancestors in the earliest days when the West was freed. It has come to me now to see whether that which is twisted can truly be made straight...or must be cast into the fire for the gods to melt and remake utterly."

A cold chill ran through Arudal's bowels. Is she speaking of our mission? he wondered. Karsil had been knighted by Kantar, aye, and followed its orders for the most part, but he was sure it was only for the sake of her own quest of vengeance that she did so; he could believe that she had her own mission in mind for the West. Or...Arudal had scarcely believed it when she agreed to teach him, after all the things she had said. Was she judging him now, and would she slay him as she had shot down his vampire if she found him not changed to her liking? He could not ask; there was none aboard to whom he could voice such thoughts. He could only listen, and wait, until Karsil touched her goblet to her lips again and began to speak of how the wine was made.

"Arudal," the Elvish knight said thoughtfully after a time, turning his name in her mouth as though she misliked its taste.

"Finavi?"

"No one born of Elven blood, however mixed, should bear a name in the tongue of the Fallen - and what does it mean?"

"It means 'of princely mind', Finavi."

Karsil shook her head, her long fair hair shimmering like a waterfall in the candlelight. "That will not do." She looked at him, considering. "Yet you will not answer to anything too strange at need, I would suspect. A name must be chosen carefully, lest it turn in the hand like an unfamiliar weapon to cut its bearer...You stare at me like a cat, and keep to yourself and walk in the night like one; and you have a cat's arrogance as well. Ari, 'little cat' - that will suit you well enough for now, I think. And all little cats are much the same, until they grow up and prove their nature. You may be a hunting lion in time, or a black-coated rathra that preys on the children of the gods."

Arudal said nothing, but inclined his head slightly. She could, he supposed, have chosen worse names for him.

"At least you are courteous enough," Dame Karsil mused. "I suppose that was well-beaten into you."

"Finavi," Arudal protested quietly. "Tharandrostans would no sooner beat a child than a horse."

Karsil raised a delicate eyebrow. "Would you truly tell me that the lash never falls upon a child's back in your lands, when you have looked at young Rhys with the whipping-post in your eyes? Though I would not doubt that you treat your horses better than your slaves."

Arudal had been trained not to squirm when he was uncomfortable, but he knew what Karsil would say to anything he could reply to that. He held his silence, hoping for her to change the subject.

"If you have not come to abhor slavery, as all the children of the gods do by the inmost urgings of their hearts, before this mission is over, then I shall have failed with you," the Elf said quietly.

"Each thing has its own nature, Finavi," Arudal replied. "Do you seek to turn me from mine because it is not yours?"

Karsil leaned forward across the table, the green anger glimmering like the glow of copper-veined coals in her eyes. "Morthugor corrupted or miscreated much: what cannot be healed must be destroyed before it wreaks further harm. You are tainted by your birth and rearing, so much so that I would have no hope for you, save that Sir Salarond found a spark of goodness lingering yet in your black soul - and the gods have sent you to me, for reasons they alone know. But do not presume too far, Ari, nor offend thus against the gods in your speech again. Are you able to sing?"

"Finavi?" Arudal said, utterly bewildered by her sudden change of subject. "Yes, I can sing, and play the harp as well."

"I would hear you sing of something that is dear to your heart."

The first thought that came to Arudal's mind was the 'Hymn to the Prince', the Tharandrostan dedication to their ruler, but he was sure that would only provoke Karsil's wrath. Nor did he dare sing the hymns to Amandeth that he had learned in his own House as a child, for those spoke of the gift that the god had given to their line, of gazing into Shadow and walking in the dark realm under Amandeth's hidden star. Instead he drew a deep breath and sang,

"White sails bloom out in the western wind,
My ship skims Terathon's foam-flowering land,
Leaping the waves like a colt in the spring,
In joy she answers the helmsman's warm hand.
Salt spray strokes my face as beloved's caress,
The wind in the sails is the glad steersman's song,
Seals swim 'round us as hounds to the hunt,
Riding the Water-Lord's meadow along.
Fair ship, brave ship, fly over waves!
Fair ship, sweet ship, sail-banners bright,
Let faring not end over waters I love,
Though day's blue give way to the star-gems of night..."

Karsil sat thoughtfully for a time after Arudal had finished. "Not altogether ill," she said at last. "Your voice is deep and harsh, like all the voices of Men, but there is even beauty in the croaking of dwarves when they sing of their anvils and steel, as they were made to do. And I can hear that you love the music, and what you sing of. I had feared that you would be so ill-sounding that I must forbid you song in my hearing, and silencing even the worst of voices is a sorrowful thing."

Arudal's feelings ruffled a bit at her words: Dr. Durakhon, who taught music at the Prince's School, had told him that, were he not too high-born to perform on the stage, he might have considered a career as a singer; while Arudal's own single regret about his singing voice was that his range was bass-baritone, rather than the full deep bass for which the best operatic roles were written in Tharandrost. Yet, having heard Karsil sing, he could not deny that the finest human voice was rough beside the voices of Elves. He supposed that he should be greatly complimented that she was able to bear his own singing at all.

"You may go to sleep now, Ari," Karsil went on. "I would not have Thoron saying that I am mistreating you. And I have heard it said that Men think more deeply in their dreams than in their waking minds. Perhaps you will think more on what we have spoken of, and learn."

After a week of training, Karsil finally declared that Arudal might begin to work with the sword she had lent him. "Your footwork is as light and subtle as a charging wild boar in rut," she told him. "Still, you are at least beginning to learn a little of the principles of movement, and, much as it pains me, there is no time to teach you properly. If I had you for fifty years and you were not hindered by a Man's need for sleep and rest, I might make a true swordsman of you: though both the means and ends of your race are twisted, those who planned the shaping of your body did not work entirely without skill. Now go to my cabin and look in the large chest where I keep my armour. There you will find a light buckler with a pattern of greenwork and silver which matches the wire-work on the hilt of the sword you are using: put it on."

Arudal did as she had ordered. He had seen the buckler before when he armoured Dame Karsil for training, but had thought that it must be for show: its surface was all covered in delicate leaves and flowers done in enamel and filigree, that he was sure would crack beneath the lightest blow of a wooden practice sword. But perhaps she only wants me to grow used to its weight and movement, and will give me another when we begin to spar, he thought.

The buckler was so light on his arm and its strapping so well-made that Arudal could scarcely tell he had it on. But it was well that he was small-boned, for even Lostren's wrist would have been too wide for the Elf-built leather straps snugging the little shield tight to its holder's forearm. Walking back to the deck, Arudal felt unnervingly exposed under the buckler; the small round shield was three handspans' diameter, perhaps half the overall size of his own escutcheon, which covered him from nose to knee in ready position. Experimentally he moved it up and down a little as he walked.

"Not like that!" Karsil said sharply. "A wheel moves most swiftly when it is rolling; a round shield rolls likewise. Stand there." She stepped behind Arudal, pulling his arms into position, then guiding his left hand with her own. "The shield's own weight and shape move it, while you merely guide it where it is needed. Nor should you hold it so straight and close: you are not hiding behind the wall of your large board now. Just as the sword is used both to strike and guard, so you may both strike and guard with this shield: they are equal partners in the battle-dance, and both grow living from your body."

To Arudal's surprise, after only a few hours, he was beginning to grow comfortable with the buckler. Karsil had shown him that, if he remembered to use his full swiftness and turn his body to slip incoming blows, he could ward himself as well as with the large pointed escutcheon to which he was accustomed; and further, he could block or press a foe's swordarm to open his guard far more easily than with the big shield. "Yes, in the thick of a heavy press, where your movement may be hampered by others and many blows coming in at once, the larger shield will be more help to you. But so long as you can move freely and have no more than two foes to face - while it is enough to guard low with shield and high with sword - this will serve you better. I wonder that the Imperial race did not always make more of buckler fighting, for that it is so well suited to the light and swift."

"I can tell you why that is," Sir Thoron broke in. The big Kantarean grunted as he forced his helm off, shaking out his dark mane of sweat-soaked hair. "The Imperial style is meant for doing battle in disciplined formation, often few against many and often with shields locked tight. Do that with a buckler, and you'll have a wooden leg to match it pretty soon, if you don't get gutted right off. I wouldn't let you train Finvar like that, but no one's ever going to send Ari into a full-scale battle, so I guess you can't hurt him too badly."

"Sir?" Arudal said, bewildered. He had never expected to be a front-rank soldier, but it hurt his pride to be so casually dismissed.

"Ah, come now, Ari. You're a good squire and you'll make a good fighter someday, but you can't see well enough to command anything farther away than the end of your sword, and it would be sheer murder to set you in the front line. Besides, I know the way Tharandrostans work: the State wouldn't risk your precious bloodline in pitched battle, any more than Duke Sindabron would ride his best racing filly into a war. No: if you ever have to fight, it'll be when you run into something by accident, and Karsil's doing right to train you for that."

"Thank you, sir," Arudal said.

Thoron nodded; Arudal was not close enough to make out his expression, but he said, "Now run Ari through that again so I can have a better look at it, and then you'll have to let him rest for the day. I can tell he's getting too tired to learn anything right, and Salarond has some questions he wants translated for our guides."

Arudal breathed deeply, letting his shoulders relax as Karsil said. "Take your guard up again, Ari..."

By the time he had run through the exercise at full speed once more, ending in a salute with sword-point uplifted and shield fully extended, Arudal could feel the buckler trembling on his arm, and even the palms of his leather gloves were soaked through with sweat. Still, shaky as he was, Karsil had not given him the command to ease his stance, and he held the position, although now even the light Elven armament felt heavier than any double-weighted practice weapon he had ever lifted.

"That's good!" Thoron said in surprise. "If you can manage to do those moves as well when someone's swinging sharp pointies at you, you've got a fair chance of staying alive. I think the buckler's better-suited to you - it forces you to use all your speed, and you don't go to sleep behind your shield. Now armour down and wash quickly, Ari. Salarond wants to see you in his cabin as soon as you're ready."

As Arudal took his armour off, it struck him that all the Kantareans had picked up Karsil's name for him. It was, he realized, actually a false diminutive for his own name, for in Common, the diminutive was formed by adding the suffix -i to the first syllable. He was unsure how he felt about that - it was a little unnerving, since in Imperial the -i suffix indicated a feminine. The proper diminutive for Arudal, which his grandmother still, to his annoyance, used, was "Miru", while "Miri" was his cousin Arothir. But he supposed it was best that his comrades get used to calling him by the Elven name, however they thought about it, lest one of them should slip while they were in the West.

After two weeks, though she complained bitterly about the haste, Karsil allowed Arudal to begin sparring again - first with herself, then with the other members of the White Company. The Tharandrostan was shocked when the delicate buckler took one of Sir Thoron's blows at full-strength: the stroke almost knocked Arudal off his feet, but the shield's enamel was not even chipped. He was more surprised at how much of a difference fighting in the Elvish style made to him. Where before, he had been lucky to score one killing touch in four on Finvar, now he was beating the other squire as often as three times of five once in a while, using the light buckler to deflect the weight of the Artegalian's blows instead of meeting them full-on and to press and tangle the other's sword-arm while he worked around Finvar's larger shield.

Nor was he as vulnerable to the heavy shield-presses the bigger men used against him, for, unhindered by the large pointed rectangle of his old escutcheon, he found it easy to slip away from them. Even Karsil admitted that Arudal was doing surprisingly well under her tutelage, though she was as cold and strange as ever in the evenings, so that Arudal missed the cameraderie of Thoron's cabin - as much as he had time to, between working on the Western language and, whenever they got a chance, teaching Lostren what he could in regards to using the gift of the Kantarean's dubious heritage. It was not so bad by day; but at night, half-awakening to the soft pale glow of the Elf's single candle, Arudal found himself listening to the silence as though he could hear Sir Thoron's raspy snores and Finvar's softer snuffling breathing, and longing for their human sounds and warmth.

Chapter 15: Landfall

"Seabirds cry my birth-shore's name,
Circling white o'er cliff and sound,
And though my surging deck is home,
My feet are aching for firm ground.

"Seabirds cry my birth-shore's name,
Fair my sailing - fair its end.
My anchor splashes dark through foam,
I raise thanks to the faithful wind,

That bore me swift to unknown strand,
That bears me back to tread my land."
- Twelfth Emperor Ramuraph, called the Navigator

The sailing grew worse as they neared the West; Arudal found himself more and more impressed by the Kantareans' skills as they eased the ship through treacherous rocks and shoals. He guessed that Lostren and Rhys were not the only ones on board with some measure of foresight, for more than once, their vessel changed course suddenly, skirting a wide berth about a portion of ocean that looked no different than any other even to Arudal's Shadow-sight. But at last, as evening neared, they heard the faint cry, "Land ho!" from the foredeck, and scrambled up to see.

The setting Sun cast a rose-gold brightness over the West, and the craggy cliffs stood out high and dark against her light. The sea-mews shrieked above, gliding in circles over the mast - just so, Arudal thought breathlessly, his seafaring ancestors had been welcomed home. And whatever the folk who dwell here now have made of it, he thought, this is our home.

Sir Salarond looked at the rough maps in his hand, and talked with the helmsman for a little time. "We should be half a day's sailing from the mouth of Hatin's Ferth," he mused. "Our guides say that there is a small cove where we may put in without risking a harbourmaster's enquiries...Ari, you see well in the dark. You and Karsil will watch for that cove, or for any place that seems safe enough to land and unload our horses."

"Yes, sir!" Arudal said gladly - for this would be his last night under Dame Karsil: he felt as though he had dived too deep, and, though his lungs were straining to burst in his chest, he had just sighted the light above the water's surface.

It was close to midnight when Arudal saw the break in the cliffs with a glimmer of moonlit sand beyond; he and Karsil called out, "Drop anchor!" together. The dromon swung to a gently rocking stop, and Arudal went down below decks to tell the others. Sir Salarond came up, and, after a brief conference with the helmsman, the ship nosed slowly into the tiny bay.

"Best to disembark tonight. By the time we get to Hatin's City, this ship should be long gone. Karsil, call up a few archers and keep us covered as we unload - Arudal, you're in charge of getting the horses saddled and safely off."

The horses nickered and whinnied, tossing their heads and whisking their tails as Arudal led them up from the lower decks. The warhorses, well-trained as they were, gave no trouble going down the wide gangplank - Arudal supposed that they were used to charging across narrow bridges. But the riding horses and packhorses tended to balk, so that he had to walk Inmanat up and down several times to convince the lesser steeds that it was safe to follow. There was a cold bite in the air here; Arudal counted the weeks in his thoughts, and realized that they must be halfway into Holymonth already - the harvests long since in, the last of the apples just being plucked - and within two weeks of the Feast of Amandeth and the Day of Mourning...

"Come, come, little horsie," he murmured to the last packhorse, which was standing frozen six feet from the shore. "Come, come, see, all your friends are over here, there's nothing to be afraid of." I hope, he thought. But at least if there were any threats ashore, none of them sprang from the Shadow-Realm. "Good horse... come on, dry land, nice grass, come along, come along..." Eventually the horse answered to Arudal's gentle tugging on its bridle, and he led it over to where the other squires were taking turns holding horses and getting their knights armoured.

"Are we in such a hurry to reach Hatin's City, then?" Arudal asked, rather bewildered. "Why not stay here for the night?"

Finvar straightened up from strapping on Sir Thoron's greaves and looked him in the eye, then shook his head and muffled his laugh. "In a smugglers' cove, Ari?" he whispered. "Didn't you guess why we put ashore here, instead of at the main port?"

"I thought it was to keep out of sight and avoid trouble?"

"Just so - and what sort of person needs to keep out of sight and avoid trouble close to a big trading city?"

"You can educate Ari later," Thoron told Finvar. "Now pay attention to where those straps are going, or I'll warm your arse with a few of them." The knight was hardly bothering to keep his voice down - and why should he, Arudal realized, when between horses and armour they could be heard by anyone in the area who cared to listen? If there were smugglers or other ruffians about, better not to seem afraid.

"Karsil, Thoron, you ride in front," Salarond ordered. "Shakhor and Rhys, you take the rear with Ari and Eroth in front of you - keep a lookout behind and call out if you see anyone. Tirothar and Finvar, behind Karsil and Thoron; Lostren, beside me. Mount warhorses..." He sighed, and though his helmet hid his face, Arudal could hear the sorrow hissing through his breath like a cold wind through the pines. "You've no experience fighting from horseback, Ari, so you take your palfrey, and leave Black Rage to Eroth. We'll keep an easy pace, let the beasts get their land legs back."

As they rode, Arudal found himself more and more thankful for the warmth of his gambeson and helm-padding beneath his chilling armour. The scents of pine and frosty earth bit clean through the icy air. He wished now that he had thought to pack his heavy winter clothing - they had sailed north as well as west, and it would be a long cold journey inland at this time of year. The horses, fresh and nervous after the voyage, tugged at their reins and pranced sideways; it was well, Arudal thought, that they had no need for haste.

They still had not reached the edge of Hatin's Ferth by dawn, but Salarond took a brief glance at the horses - heads hanging, one or two beginning to blow a little from the weight of packs or armoured riders, an unaccustomed strain after their months of confinement - and declared that they would have to make camp. "Shakhor, I want you and Rhys to quickly scout the area and make sure that no one's been watching us. And you, Ari...when you're through with the horses and putting Thoron's tent up, see me."

Arudal thought about suggesting that he might be more helpful before full sun-up, but did not argue, going quickly to his tasks and then coming back to their commander. "Sir."

"I want you to perform a small magic - anything by use of a spell. That pebble there, for instance. You said you know sorcery; could you make it crumble to dust if we were at home?"

"Certainly."

"Do so now, please."

Arudal pointed at the pebble, whispering the words that brought the sorceror's fire up from inside himself - that should have sparked from his fingertip to the little jagged rock, bursting asunder the tiny measure of power that held it to a single piece. He could feel the sparking as he spoke his spell, and the might behind it, but nothing happened; it was as though he had tried to light a lamp, only to find that it had plenty of oil, but no wick. Arudal shook his head.

"My turn. You are at least a little stiff from riding, after being at sea so long?"

"Yes, sir."

Sir Salarond laid his hands gently on Arudal's shoulders, murmuring softly. Arudal felt a faint inner tingle, a slight easing of the stiffening muscles in his inner thighs - but he was still sore, feeling none of the immediate relief that Salarond's healing had given him before. Dutifully he reported everything he felt.

"I see," the healer-priest said thoughtfully. "Go lie down, Ari. You'll be woken for third watch."

It was midday when their company struck camp and mounted up again. From where the Sun hung in the south, halfway across the chill blue sky, Arudal guessed that they were farther north than Var Perenil. Once or twice he started at the strange chuckling sound of an unfamiliar bird; but Shakhor reported that the nearest tracks of men or horses were at least three days old.

"This is almost like home," Finvar said cheerfully as they rode - Salarond had rearranged their order during the daytime so that Arudal was in the middle of the party. "We'd be hunting elk and deer at this time of the year, or bears while they're in full autumn fat. Summer's for small beasts, we say, fall for big game, and winter for dark things - trolls and dire wolves and such, and sometimes brave men go looking for barrow-ghosts."

"And spring?" Arudal asked.

"In spring we leave animals to give birth unmolested, so we'll have game for another year. What sort of hunting are you used to? - I'm sorry. You probably don't hunt much, being short-sighted and all."

"We have wild boar, and those are better speared than shot." Arudal thought painfully of riding out on hawking parties, listening to the cries of the other young nobles as their birds plummeted upon ducks or herons far beyond his vision. "I do not need keen eyes for boar-hunting."

"Ah, that's sport enough for anyone, and you can hunt them year-round. If you ever get a chance, though, come up to Helludal in the autumn and I'll show you boars the size of your palfrey and bears you'd swear had mated with Stone-Trolls."

"Mangy-skinned?" Tirothar asked, glancing over at Finvar. "Not a bite of meat worth eating on them?"

"I'm not talking about your grandmother," Finvar retorted.

Tirothar put out his tongue at the other squire. "Anyway, real hunting is what we do with Perenilian lions, and don't they make your puppy-dogs look pathetic? Our lions can outpace a wolfhound twice over, and not make a single sound until they've brought the prey down - not scaring it all through the woods by barking at it until it's too tired to run and the meat isn't fit to eat."

"You've never seen an Artegalian wolfhound on the hunt," countered Finvar. "I'd match one against your little kitties any time, so I would."

"Enough of that," Sir Salarond told them sharply. "It's not too early to start thinking about who you're supposed to be, nor is it too early to practice keeping your tongues in your mouths. I won't wager our lives that nothing of the Middle Land is known over here."

Arudal had liked the discussion on hunting better, but he obediently settled himself. Their cover story, such as it was, was that they were merchant-adventurers from the South, lately hired on as Karsil's bodyguard - for an Elf in Hatin's City would draw notice, but not suspicion. Salarond had brought a certain quantity of precious stones and fine silks, as well as some lesser goods, to sell: that would give them local coinage without bringing attention to foreign mint-marks. They had a few coins that the minting had been beaten out of as well, and small bar-ingots of copper and silver, but it would be better to have recognisable money.

Arudal had taught the others what he could about bargaining and selling in a strange market, for he himself had been strictly enjoined to keep his head down and try to pass unnoticed: Atharath and Gormok had sworn that Elves never mated with Men, and whether that was true or not - many common folk in the Middle Land likely held the same - the knights were all of the opinion that it was easier to hide Arudal than explain him. Although this was not the history I meant to seek when I agreed to come to the West, Arudal thought bitterly. He was still less than sure that the decision was not based on Karsil's delicate sensibilities, since she was likely to be speaking for the party in most things, and an Elf could get away with far more strangeness than any of the Men could.

By sundown, they had reached the fork of a well-kept road, and Salarond nodded in satisfaction. "There should be an inn not more than a candlemark's ride from here, if I have not led us completely astray."

"What did our guide say of it?" asked Sir Eroth.

"The food is plentiful and cheap, and the customers not overly inclined to be either light-fingered or snoopy," Salarond summarized bluntly. "I doubt that we should expect too much, but it should be safer and warmer than sleeping by the side of the road. And if we have failed greatly in any respect, I would rather find out now, when we have a fair chance of escape, than in a city which may be well-guarded."

As promised, it was little more than a candlemark's time when they saw the lights burning up ahead, two torches wavering in the wind before a large, squat building with a peaked roof. They rode up before the front door, and Salarond and Karsil dismounted. "Stay here until I come for you," Salarond ordered in the Western tongue - which, to Arudal's pride, most of them had learned to speak reasonably well on the way.

After a little time, Salarond came out again. "Ari, you'll stay with the horses tonight. Innkeeper says there's plenty of straw for bedding in the stable, and I'll see there's food and drink sent out to you. Unload them, lads."

In the darkness, Arudal clenched his fists until the edges of his gauntlets bit painfully into his palms. He had been looking forward to a warm fire and a hot bath, not sleeping under his cloak in lumpy chainmail with his head pillowed unrestfully on the plate pieces of his armour. But he could see why Sir Salarond was unwilling to leave the horses with no one to watch over them - and it would be cruel to set Rhys as guard on our steeds, when he is still so clearly mourning his dead mount.

Arudal brought the horses into the stables and set to rubbing them down and cleaning their tack. He took his helm off for that task, but left his coif and arming-cap on to cover his hair and the pointed tips of his ears, and give him more the look of a guard than a servant boy. The stables were lit by lanterns; though the wicks burned clear, the oil had a strong fishy smell - Whale-oil, he thought, lifting Inmanat's front right hoof up and beginning to clean it. The little horse's new steel shoes still glittered brightly: Sir Salarond had insisted that the horses be reshod on shipboard just before they disembarked.

"I'll do that for ye, m'lord," a stableboy said hopefully. The lad was a couple of inches taller than Arudal himself, but skinny, with knobbly wrists hanging out the sleeves of his grimy woolen garment. His dirty hair hung about his face like a tangle of brown moss; Arudal found his own nose wrinkling at the smell, and the wheedling tone of the servant's voice put the Tharandrostan's back up - he had learned early in life not to trust a slave which seemed to be cozening work.

"I'll do it myself, thank you," Arudal replied, hoping that the stableboy would hear the dismissal in his voice and go away.

"That's surely not work for a lord like you, with your fine armour and sword and all," the servant lad whined. "I've a knack with horses, you'll be proud of them when you ride them out in the morning..."

And if that's true, Arudal thought, could you guess how long they'd been at sea?

"This is my duty, and no other's," he said sternly. "If you wish to aid, you may fetch them an oat-mash."

"Aye, m'lord," the boy said, backing away.

Before Arudal had finished with the horses, three other boys had gathered at a respectful distance, watching him and whispering as they scratched themselves - fleas and lice; do their owners never wash them? Arudal thought. None of the youths had any weapons besides a small belt-knife; they all looked as dirty and miserable as the first one. If they aged at the same rate as Plainsmen, Arudal guessed that they were all somewhere between fourteen and seventeen; the oldest showed a wispy smear of brown beard-hairs across his cheeks.

"M'lord?" the boy who had brought the mash said. "Can I ask...are you one of the Elf-lord's guards?"

Arudal was startled by the question, but not too surprised; it was only dress and titles that distinguished male and female Elves in the eyes of Men, and they had assumed that Karsil would be considered male until she said otherwise.

"I am," he admitted consideringly.

"Have you seen Elf-Hall yourself, m'lord?"

Arudal shook his head.

"And those big horses - are they true Elvensteeds? I never seen their like, m'lord."

Arudal paused. "They come from far away. Don't go into their stalls: they don't know you, and they will do their best to kill strangers." Which, he reflected, was even almost true, and might help keep curious fingers away from the tack that hung neatly by each box. Arudal looked surreptitiously at the other guests' beasts. They were mostly draught oxen, but there were two horses there as well - large animals, around fifteen hands tall, but with none of the smaller Inmanat's grace or power; he would not have given either of them a second glance at a horse fair. But we shall probably see better in the city.

"Ooh."

After a little while, much to Arudal's relief, the stableboys withdrew without asking him any more questions, and Finvar came in with a large bowl of stew, a loaf of bread, and a pitcher of ale. Like Arudal, he was still wearing most of his armour but had taken his gauntlets and helm off, his ash-blond hair hanging in a thick tangle about his face. He sat down on a bale of straw, balancing the bowl next to him, and Arudal came to join him.

"Stew's not bad, even if it does taste kind of funny," Finvar said after his first bite. "The ale's good, though." Arudal broke off a piece of bread and dipped it in delicately, sopping up the broth. It was spiced with some herb he didn't recognise - hot, like some of the spices from Fel, but with a mintily pungent tang underneath. The ale was lighter than the Helludal black Finvar had pressed on him in Felatar, amber and robust, with a thick creamy foam on top. "Gods above, Ari, you should see the fuss they're making over Karsil in there. Well, no, maybe not; it'd put you right off your dinner. You'd think they'd never seen an Elf before."

"Maybe they haven't," Arudal said absently, still trying to decide whether he liked the peculiar spice or not. "This inn doesn't strike me as the sort of place Elves would tarry often."

"Well, I'm glad enough we stopped. My arse is telling me it thinks I fell down a mountain on it."

"I myself wouldn't listen to anything your arse says," Arudal answered. "It's likely to be nothing but wind."

Finvar stared at him in astonishment a moment, then laughed. "Amanvon, Ari, you do have a sense of humour after all. Where were you hiding it?"

Arudal shrugged. In truth, he was finding himself glad of the other squire's company. Here in this strange place, there was something comforting about Finvar's blunt solidity, as if they had known each other far longer than the three months they had travelled together; and after Karsil's chilly presence, the Artegalian's rough friendship seemed oddly warming to his heart.

Arudal slept on the straw in Inmanat's stall that night, resting comfortably in spite of his bruises in the familiar smells of horse and hay. It almost reminded him of his childhood, when he had crept away to the stables whenever he felt lonely and miserable, to sit talking with the horses and barn-cats and Boraitiz - the Horsetribe-groom had listened patiently to the young Tharandrostan, his flat copper face seldom showing any sign of impatience or annoyance. Sometimes he would give a few words of blunt advice, or tell Arudal stories about heroes who had ridden the North Wind and duelled with the Sun, such tales as Arudal's most distant ancestors might have listened to in the days when they rode over the plains, before they followed the Elves to the West at the behest of the gods.

Now, looking back on those days, it seemed to Arudal that Boraitiz had viewed Tharandrost and everyone in it with a sort of bemused respect, as a mighty nation of sorcerors who, nevertheless, were ignorant of the strangest things. The Horsetribesman was not a slave, of course; he had left his tribe as a young man of fifteen, when Arudal was a small child at the same age - and now, some thirty years later, Boraitiz's coarse black mane was silvering fast and he moved with a creaky limp in the wintertime damp. Arudal wondered if the groom would still be alive when he came home; they aged so fast...

A cold salt wind blew from the sea when they mounted up in the yard the next day, the Sun shining brilliantly through the ice-bright sky. The frost in the inn's courtyard had already been trampled into dark wetness on the cobblestones by the crisscrossing tracks of boots and hooves, but ice-crystals sparkled from the needles of the dark pines that lined the road, crunching under the horses' steel shoes. The party rode quietly, for the most part, though Salarond got Arudal to give him a brief summary of his night in the stables.

"That fits well enough with what we heard in the inn," Salarond remarked. "You did well to keep to yourself, Ari: let us hope you can continue to do so." He paused. "It is...unfortunate to know that the like of our warhorses is not to be found here, but you gave a good enough answer. A pity that we have no Elvensteeds..."

"Not so," Dame Karsil broke in. "Each thing to its own nature: Elvensteeds were never born to carry armoured Men into battle, nor to withstand the shock of lance breaking on shield - I did not learn such skills of fighting until I came to Kantar. Be glad of what is made to be yours, and do not seek to wish it other than it is, for Morthugor hears all vain longings - and may aid them." She turned her head to look back at Sir Salarond as she spoke, but for a moment her cat-green eyes met Arudal's, flaring through the Shadow-mist on his sight.

Chapter 16: Hatin's City

"The ruins of our pride we leave
To those we harmed: let all we owned
Be our small payment on that debt
For which no mortal good atones.

"And, sated with their just revenge,
May they gain wisdom with the years,
And raise walls better from downed stones
Than once they mortared with slaves' tears."
- "The West Relinquished", Sir Vararel, formerly Lord Abarkan

The road wound along the edge of the high cliffs of Hatin's Ferth, deep-grooved sandstone plunging far down to the tiny sprays of foam rising like whalebreath from the heavy waves crashing against the jagged rocks below. Seabirds screamed and wheeled white below the cliff-edges, their calls hauntingly familiar to Arudal, as though in sailing here he had come home again. The travellers paused briefly at midday for a lunch of hardtack and dried meat, washed down with icy-clear water from a stream, changed horses - save for Arudal; Inmanat had grown soft in his three months at sea, but was well able to keep going for the day - and rode on again.

"We should reach Hatin's City by nightfall," Sir Salarond said. "There we may find lodgings for the night, and tomorrow we shall hire a booth in the marketplace. Easily enough done, if our informants told the truth..." He frowned.

Hatin's City nestled at the end of the long inland tongue of the sea like a broken eggshell in a gull's nest of cliffs, towers rising jaggedly about the uneven edge of the white walls. By the time the party was riding down the winding path amid the rocks, the city was already shadowed by the crags that rose behind it, the water dark before. Arudal guessed that it was close to the size of Tharabruthnan, perhaps a little larger. Ships jostled at the docks, little fishing boats weaving in and out among bigger crafts: Arudal saw nothing nearing the size of the great warships of Tharandrost and Kantar, but there were plenty of pot-bellied cogs and long sleek dromons. Lanterns glimmered from the smaller ships slipping out into the ferth, like glow-worms against blue twilight: Arudal guessed that they would be fishing for octopus or other fish best caught in the darkness.

The landside gates of Hatin's City were still open, guarded by a pair of tall sentries with great two-handed swords slung over their backs. The flames of the fresh-lit torches flanking the gates glittered off the gold patterns inlaid in their bronze kettle-helms and breastplates; their wide trousers billowed out beneath like wind-filled sails of blue satin, and their puffy blue sleeves were slashed to show gold cloth below. Arudal thought that they looked both silly and barbaric, and when he glanced sideways, he saw that Finvar was biting his lip as though to keep from laughing. But other sentries, less richly clad and armed with longbows, stood at the top of the wall, and Arudal could see the brightness of gilded metal moving behind the barred arrow-slits of the two round towers that flanked the great gates. However its soldiers might be dressed, he thought that Hatin's City was well-guarded.

At the head of the party, Dame Karsil had taken off her helm. Her long hair spilled down over her shoulders, shimmering pale in the shadows as though it caught the first light of Amanvon's Taper gleaming above, and the sentries bowed to her in unison.

"Hail and welcome to Hatin's City, Fair One!" the man on the right said. "Our lord did not tell us to expect you, or we should have had better greetings ready."

"That is little wonder, for I doubt that he knew of my coming," Karsil answered.

"Then, if you have no pressing business elsewhere this night, will you allow us to send news of your coming to Lord Hatneth, that he may guest you and your companions as is fitting?"

"Aye, you may do that," Karsil replied.

"If you will, please enter. I am known as Shakarah. I fear we can offer you only the hospitality of our guardhouse while you wait, but you are more than welcome to such as we have."

"The offer graces him who makes it," the Elf said, swinging gracefully down from her horse. The rest of the party did likewise, leading their steeds in between the high bronze wings of the gates. At a few sharp words from the one who had greeted them, other sentries came out to take the reins.

Their guide gestured at the bronze-bound door of the tower on the left. "In here, if you will, Fair One."

The bottom floor of the guard tower was surprisingly comfortable, with thick rugs on the floor and braziers casting a glow of warmth through the round room. A low table of dark wood stood in the middle; Shakarah seated Karsil in the single chair while a junior guard - a younger man in plain blue with no gold adornments on his bronze breastplate and helmet - hurried to bring wine and goblets and another collected stools for the rest of them.

When they were all settled, the guard who had brought them in said, "Fair One, will you tell me what brings you to Hatin's City? It is seldom that we see your folk here."

"I fare to visit kinfolk of mine," Karsil told him - a safe enough thing for her to say. "And these my guards wished to stop here for a few days to sell the goods they carry, and perhaps trade for more."

The sentry - captain of the guards? Arudal wondered. Or was it only that Lord Hatneth gave the finest uniforms to those men who would be seen first? - looked carefully at the rest of the party, dark eyes narrowing. Arudal felt a faint chill under the big man's gaze: Shakarah might be dressed as a high court's jester, but the hard lines about his eyes and mouth were not the marks of a fool's grin.

"Is this young one also of your kindred, Fair One?" he asked.

"Of mixed blood...but yes," Karsil answered. If Arudal had not shared her cabin for nearly two months, he might not have heard the reluctance dimming the ring of her clear voice like a speck of grit on a shining bell; but the guardsman inclined his head respectfully towards Arudal.

"And your guards...merchants, you say?"

"Yes. We have come far and through places where even two of our kind could not travel safely. These Men were willing to bring their trade past their usual routes to accompany us."

Shakarah raised a grizzled eyebrow, his gaze passing swiftly over them again. "You are indeed generous, Fair One, to have allowed your guardsmen to use such equipment of the Old Metal."

"How not, when we depended on them?" Karsil replied.

"Indeed," murmured Shakarah. He glanced at Sir Thoron. "I enquire not for myself, for I cannot afford such things, but for our ruler's sake: is there any hope that you would part with any piece of your guardsmen's harness, or that you have brought more of the Old Metal with you for sale?"

Karsil shook her head, and Thoron rumbled, "Too far to go to get home. As well ask to buy horses."

Shakarah sighed. "I thought it unlikely...but tell me, where is your home? I do not recognise the sound of your speech."

Clever, Arudal thought, to ask Thoron what he could not ask Karsil without seeming rude - and a good thing he chose the one of us who speaks the Western tongue worst.

"Far off...westest and southest herefrom," said Thoron. "Not good in your language."

"So I hear," Shakarah remarked dryly. "Ah, well...Your names, gentlemen?"

They introduced themselves, and thereafter Shakarah made simple conversation until a pair of trumpets sounded an harmonious note outside. "Ah," the guardsman said. "Lord Hatneth's bearers have arrived."

Two trumpeters in wide-sleeved tunics and puffy breeches like those Shakarah wore stood before a large litter enclosed with hangings of blue silk patterned with gold; a pair of sturdy men in similar garb stood between the front traces, and another pair behind, and six torch-bearers around it. Shakarah assisted Karsil and Arudal into the litter, pulling the dark blue hangings closed around them. The lantern hanging from the roof swung as the litter slowly rose on the shoulders of its bearers, casting a wavering orange light around the little compartment. The seats were comfortable enough, padded with thick velvet cushions, but the heavy scent inside made Arudal feel as though he were smothering in flowers and honey, and Karsil's delicate nostrils tightened as the litter began to move.

Are these slaves bearing us, or servants? Arudal wondered. His stomach knotted at the thought of how Karsil might speak to the lord of the city if she found that she had been brought to his presence by slaves - a host could turn more easily to a captor than an open foe, for they could hardly refuse to put their horses in his stables, no more than they could set a watch at night in his house; and he had no faith in Karsil's ability to hold her tongue if she saw what offended her. Amanvon, he prayed with little hope, please let her, if just this once, be more wise than righteous!

The trumpets sounded again and again as the litter passed through the streets, drowning out the mutter of voices with their clear brass harmony. Between the trumpeters and the thick covering of the litter, Arudal could not make out any of the shouting clearly - perhaps, he thought, if he had spent more time on the Western language and less time at swordwork with Karsil, he could have done better.

Perhaps half a candlemark had passed between the time they left the gates and the time the litter settled slowly down and another of Lord Hatneth's men pulled the thick silken blankets aside. Like the others they had seen, this one wore the hugely bloused sleeves and breeches, both slashed to let gold cloth shine through the blue satin, but his tunic was decorated with a mane of long gold ribbons fluttering down around the collar, and his pale brown hair was twisted up into a myriad of gold-ribboned braids woven together about his head. He bore no sword, but Arudal could see the blue shimmer playing about the polished black stave in his hand. Dangerous, whatever it is, Arudal thought, and then, So some magic does work here!

"Greetings, Fair Ones, and welcome to the hall of the Hatnethim," the stave-bearer said in a soft, musical voice. "Lord Hatneth rejoices that you have seen fit to brighten his city with the light of your eyes, and bids you to guest with him as long as it pleases you to stay: you are to think of all within these walls as your own."

His accent was markedly different from those of Atharath and Gormok; Arudal noticed that several of the grammatical features of his speech seemed to differ as well, though not quite enough to be incomprehensible, and his voice rose and fell in a way that suggested a tonal component - high and low forms of the same tongue, on their way to becoming different languages altogether? If only we had learned the language from a better sort of people! The possibility of class-separated dialects had never occured to him: everyone in Tharandrost, from Dockside fishermen to Prince Norombar, spoke the same clear, grammatical Imperial, for nothing less would be tolerated by the State's schools. But the Common tongue differs from nobles to peasants; I should have thought that the same might be true here. Still, if Lord Hatneth is so eager to greet Elves in his city, perhaps he will speak Bright Elvish. And if I have time to study the speech here for a little while, this will make a fascinating chapter for my book on the Western language. The "high Western" actually seemed further removed from its Imperial roots than the "low Western" they had learned from the two smugglers...

"...and Ari, who travels with me to learn more of his mother's kindred," Karsil was saying, the high singing lilt of her voice transfiguring the harsher sounds of the language to something more like the stave-bearer's dialect.

The beribboned man's pale eyes widened a little, and Arudal remembered what their informants had said about Elves never mating with Men; but he said only, "Come with me, if you please, Fair Ones. Chambers have been prepared for you, that you may refresh yourselves after your travel if you wish. Lord Hatneth has not sat down to table yet, and he would not seek to hasten such valued guests. Be assured, your guards and horses will be seen to."

"I thank you for that," Karsil replied, and the two of them followed the...herald? Seneschal? Arudal was not certain whether to curse or bless the fate that had brought them so quickly to Lord Hatneth, when they knew so little about the West and nothing of what the arrangements or etiquette of a great lord's house might be. As a young page, he had often heard the proverb, 'Better to be disemboweled than embarassed', and he felt more awkward and out of place here than he had on his first day in Duke Azarlokan's household. But he moved as Karsil had taught him to, trying to show the grace and dignity of one who could afford to wait unhurried for a thousand years between the asking and answering of a question, and hoped that he was showing something of the certain ease with which Karsil bore herself.

The stave-bearer led Karsil and Arudal along torch-lined paths of smooth patterned marble between whispering fountains and close-clipped trees; late in the year as it was, a few white petals still shone dimly from their dark beds. Lord Hatneth's palace was low and sprawling - a pleasure mansion, rather than a fortress, Arudal thought: it must have been long since Hatin's City was threatened by a serious foe.

A few clear flute-notes rose from behind a clump of shadowed trees, breaking suddenly into long trilling arpeggios that slipped into a haunting melody. At first Arudal thought little of it, save that it was beautiful; it was no strange thing for a great lord to have musicians hidden in his garden. But Karsil lifted a high-swept eyebrow and said softly to him in Bright Elvish, "That, unless I am mistaken, is a dethil."

Arudal drew in his breath, suddenly shaken and awed. The little night-singing bird had been rare in the West even before the Fall; he had read of it in poetry and old writings, but never imagined that he might hear one. Star-voiced singer, silver flute of the Moon...your voice echoes in stillness, across the sundering Sea; yet your song is lost to Men forever, when the last memory's bearer dies... "Not lost," he whispered to himself, barely moving his lips. "I hear it now." The ache tightened in his chest as he kept walking behind Lord Hatneth's man, farther from the high liquid singing: he wanted nothing more than to let himself be lost in the wonder of it, and yet...For all he knew, adethil could be common as sparrows here and now; at least, their guide seemed to take no notice of the bird's voice, his satin breeches rustling ahead of them at the same steady pace.

The chambers to which Lord Hatneth's man led them were warm, with thick rugs on the floor and bright-embroidered tapestries hanging over the white marble walls. Their bags already sat by the door. A sweet fresh scent rose in wisps of steam from the huge black-mottled stone bathtub, and a crystal decanter of deep red wine stood on the lapis-inlaid table beside it; fresh linen towels hung on a rack close by.

"I shall leave you to refresh yourselves, Fair Ones. When you are ready, pull on the cord by the door: it will summon me." Their guide bowed and departed, closing the door behind him.

Karsil stretched herself, bending and twisting gracefully to let Arudal reach the laces of her armour as she had taught him to before she slipped quickly out of her tunic and breeches. Folding the Elf's clothing, Arudal noticed enviously that - unlike his own - there was no trace of sweat on Karsil's garb, only the marks of her armour. He turned his head modestly as she stepped into the bathtub, sinking down into the water.

"Do you not mean to bathe, Ari?" Karsil's high voice fluted. "I think you need it more than I."

"I meant to wait until you were finished, finavi," Arudal stuttered.

"There is no need for that. The bath is easily big enough for two."

Karsil had told him several times that Elves did not fear the sight of others' bodies as Men did, but it was one thing to undress before her with his back turned, and another to share a bath with a female, of whatever race. Yet he did not know if they were being watched, or how much Lord Hatneth might know of Elvish customs...He could feel the tips of his ears burning with his blush as he disarmoured and took his clothes off, and he could not bring himself to look directly at Karsil. At least the candlelight shimmering on the water hid their privates beneath it, and even unclothed, it was hardly possible to tell a female Elf from a male above the waist. Karsil's nipples were as small and pale as his, and her chest, lacking the sturdy rounding of the Tharandrostan's pectorals, actually flatter. Her shoulders and long wiry arms were likewise slim in contrast to Arudal's solid muscles, but deeply corded from three hundred years of sword-work; with a little effort, Arudal could imagine that he shared the tub with another youth.

Despite his uncomfortable awareness of Karsil's presence, Arudal could not help sighing as the warmth began to sink into his aching body, soaking away the sweat and grime of two days' riding and a night in the stables. He hoped the rest of their party was being half so well-treated: this was the sort of hospitality he would have expected at home. Still, he could not help recalling the strange words of Lostren's vision, The other stable boys would have torn the hoods from our hair...We would have been bound and gagged at once, and burned on the spot.

Bathed and clean, Karsil dressed herself in a robe of shimmering white silk bound with a girdle of overlapping gold leaves set with gleaming green stones that matched her eyes. She cast through Arudal's baggage for a moment, then drew out his blue-black silk robe, holding it up and looking critically at the cut and the white seed-pearl embroidery upon the breast - he had not brought his best clothing, but he had thought that there might be need to dress well at least once along their path. "At least there is no sealskin on this one," she murmured. "Very well, Ari: it will do." She frowned when she saw the dark leather shoes that matched it, however, looking contemptuously at the heavy silver ornaments stitched onto the smooth hide and the toe-points of silver-filigreed Valderian steel. Arudal braced himself for a lecture, but Karsil, too, must have been considering the risk that they might be overheard. Instead she held the shoe to her own foot to measure the length and width, then nodded and brought out a pair of white velvet slippers with silver embroidery. "These may be too long, but I think you can wear them. Brush your hair, Ari, and then you may brush out mine as well."

Arudal still felt strange when he looked in the mirror and saw the fall of golden hair framing his face, his pale eyebrows arching over his darkly slanted gray eyes. But he could not deny that he looked very well: a little thinner in the face than he had been, perhaps, his neck and shoulders more sharply muscled from the months of sword-practice on-board and his waist a bit narrower within his belt of silver plates set with black pearls. Karsil shook her head vigorously when she saw his circlet of Valderian steel with its black star sapphire. "No. You are young enough by several hundred years to leave your hair unbound. Now come and brush mine." She seated herself on a stool, and Arudal stood behind her, stroking the length of her pale hair with the soft-bristled brush. It passed through his hands like the long silky plume-tail of a Western Tree-Cat, warm and alive. His slim fingers suddenly felt rough and clumsy with the callouses of sword-work and sailing, and he was almost ashamed to touch the Elf's hair with them. Although he had been Karsil's loaned squire for two months, she had never asked this of him before: Arudal wondered if she had finally decided to accept him, or if she were only putting on a show for any unseen watchers.

When Arudal had brushed her hair to her satisfaction, Karsil tied it back with a simple twist of fine gold wire and strode over to the bell-cord. Their guide appeared so quickly that Arudal was certain that he had been waiting close by - perhaps where he could overhear them, or watch through a hidden peephole?

"If you will follow me, Fair Ones..?"

The guide led Arudal and Karsil swiftly through a maze of passageways gleaming with gold and precious stones set into carved marble - barbarian brightness, Arudal thought, like the grotesquely showy uniforms of Lord Hatneth's guards. The marble gave way to elaborate mosaics, chips of ruby and sapphire, emerald and amethyst and pale chalcedony glowing in the light of candles in gold holders. They were walking too quickly for Arudal to make much sense of the pictures; but once he caught sight of an onyx-haired demon-figure with huge black star sapphires set at a tilt for its slanted eyes, ruby-gleaming drops of blood spurting from the wound in its breast, and his heart fluttered chill beneath his ribs when their guide made a brief sign of warding as he passed it. For all their short lives, their memories live more strongly than our own, Arudal thought. It was well to remember that, despite the courtesy Lord Hatneth was showing his false identity, these Western men would hold themselves as his deadliest foes if they knew...

Lord Hatneth's great hall was a single dazzle of ruddy gold and candlelight to Arudal, as though he were walking straight into the setting Sun. He swallowed hard and blinked quickly several times, trying to keep the stinging water in his eyes from welling up and flowing down his face. If Karsil had not taken his hand to guide him, he would have stumbled blindly as a mole in the sunlight.

A clear horn rang out thrice. In the echoes of its notes, a man's voice called, "Welcome the Fair Ones to Lord Hatneth's hall! Lord Karsil and Lord Ari bear the greetings of the Elves to Lord Hatneth!"

And there is a neat bit of political show if I ever heard one, Arudal thought. As Duke Azarlokan's page, he had learned how a guest of distinction should be announced in order to cast favour upon the lord who received him, without ever going so far that anyone could take issue with the honours assumed. The dazzling brightness in the hall, reflections of gold and fire shimmering with every step he took, kept him from seeing Karsil's face, but her narrow hard fingers tightened on his hand, and he could guess that she was less than pleased.

They mounted stairs of gold-crusted marble to the raised dais on which Lord Hatneth's table stood; Karsil was seated upon the city-ruler's right side, and Arudal to his left. For honour? Arudal wondered. Or so that we may not speak privily between us?

Lord Hatneth's table was made from great slabs of lapis inlaid with gold; the tableware was gold cast into fantastically elaborate shapes. It took Arudal a few moments to guess which pieces were meant to be spoons and which eating-tines - a more difficult distinction since the Western eating-tines were single-spiked, unlike the double-pronged forks common in Tharandrost, or the triple-pronged ones used by most Kantareans. The goblet-bowls were thick uncut crystal bowls, with stems of gem-set gold; Arudal wondered if that was merely for ostentation, or because the West had never regained the art of cutting crystal.

Lord Hatneth himself was a tall man; even when they were seated, the top of Arudal's head did not come much above his shoulder. At first glance, Arudal thought him to be fat as well, for his clothing was a massive array of gold flounces and streamers glittering with little blue gems, but a closer look showed that the body inside the wide froth of garb was lean. The city-lord was dark-skinned, darker than a Terashi, though not quite as black as Men of the Far South. His hair was hidden by layers of blue-jeweled gold lace cascading down from his glittering cap, but there was something in the cool assessment of Lord Hatneth's pale blue eyes that made Arudal think of a merchant-captain totting up the likely worth of a new cargo in his head. *This is a city of traders,* the Tharandrostan reminded himself. *Best to be worth something to him, should we need his aid...but not too much, lest he be loath to let us go!*

"It is an honour and a delight that you have come to guest with me, Fair Ones," Lord Hatneth said, bowing from his seat first to Karsil, then to Arudal. He spoke the Bright Elvish tongue fairly well, but with an odd flatness. *As though he had learned it from books, and seldom heard how the Elves sing their words,* Arudal thought - *perhaps never. If the high tongue here is tonal, he should have picked up the Elvish tonalities without difficulty if he had ever heard it spoken.*

"You have received us well," Karsil answered. Arudal could recognise the faint stiffness in her voice, but he guessed that Lord Hatneth would hear only its beauty, and be charmed: he reminded himself to speak as little as he could.

"It is more than my pleasure," the city's ruler said. "You must surely have come from afar, and from mighty lands indeed. I am told that you even equipped your guardsmen in the Old Metal to withstand the perils of the way."

"It is not so rare in our lands as it seems to be in yours," Karsil told him; and Arudal could not help thinking, *If only our wretched guides had told us how valuable iron and steel are here! We could easily have replaced our lost warhorses, if such beasts exist here at all, provisioned ourselves for the journey, bought all the native guides we needed...and the long-term chances for trade!* The House of Arudal had never been overly wealthy; Arudal had a brief image of ships bearing the banner of his line, the six-pointed star above a warship, argent stark against the vorgath field, beneath Tharandrost's single vorgath tower on light azure field - ships unloading a cargo of iron ingots, to sail home again filled with gold and rare gems. *If,* he reminded himself with a faint cold chill, *we could conceal our race from them! Now I can guess why none of our ships ever came back from the West...*

"...far to go yet, and a much further road back," Karsil was saying. "Dead guardsmen are little help on the road, nor can wealth protect us against bandits."

"Is that all? You could nearly hire a small army for the worth of a single suit of the Old Metal. Even if you lost half your men in every engagement, you would have no trouble finding more at the nearest village, eager to risk their lives for what you could offer."

"My kin would not thank me for bringing a host of strange Men to their homes," Karsil said, her voice colder now. "Nor will I betray those who have come so far with me."

"But they are only merchants, Fair One!" Lord Hatneth protested gracefully. "Is it a matter of a condition in their contract? I am sure that I can help you to deal with the problem, if so."

The words were innocent enough, but there was something in the tone of Lord Hatneth's voice that made Arudal's back tighten, as though he could feel arrows aimed at it. If one suit of steel armour is worth so much - what would he do for ten?

"Perhaps, Lord Hatneth," Arudal broke in, "we might speak not so much of trade for a few items now, as of trade for many later. Karsil is of the pure blood, and has no concern for wealth, save as a little is needed to fare through the lands of Men. But in the realms about our home, it is not only Elves who hold the secrets of the Old Metal, and our guards are not the only merchants willing to risk far travel for worthy profit."

"Ah," Lord Hatneth said. The candlelight glinted off the yellow ivory of his teeth. "I beg your pardon, Lord Karsil, for troubling you with matters of little moment to your fair kindred. Will you allow me to speak of them to your young kinsman instead, perhaps at some later time where we may sit with tablet and pen to deal with more precision?"

"If Ari wishes to speak to you of trade on behalf of his father's house, that is a matter for him to decide," Karsil answered. "Though he may not seem so to you, he is of age as we count it for the mixed blood, and has been brought up to such things as I have not."

Lord Hatneth raised an eyebrow. "Indeed! Forgive me, Lord Ari. We see your kind so seldom that I would have taken you for a youth of no more than fourteen or fifteen, as the years pass for us. I did not mean to slight you. But if you will think this night on the length and difficulties of the way you had come, and on what manner of loads might be brought and how long it would take, we shall hold more converse on this matter in the morning. If you will forgive me asking, how far have you come and how far are you going?"

"We have travelled six months already," Karsil said before Arudal could speak. "And we have perhaps another three months before us: we go to visit distant kin, that Ari may learn more of his mother's people. More than that I may not speak of: where we fare, and what we shall do there, are matters for the Elves."

Lord Hatneth waved his hand in a glittering flash; Arudal saw that the rings on his fingers were linked to an openwork pattern of gold tendrils that covered the back of his hand as well. If these barbarians had steel, I would call them greatly rich, Arudal thought.

"Of course, of course...But you have never come this way before, and know little of Hatin's City?"

"That is so."

"Then, if it please you, I shall tell you some of our history. I am told you shall be a few days here, while your guards sell their goods and replenish your stocks for the road onwards?"

"Indeed."

"Well, I shall tell you of the city, and mayhap you will find some places here of interest or delight while you wait for your guards to be through with the things of Men. This harbour was first founded by the Mordhagoernim, the accursed Imperial race - though that was in the days when they still showed a fair face to the world, before they came with slaughter and branding bars and whips."

To hide his thoughts, Arudal sipped quietly from his goblet. The pale drink was not wine, though similar, he guessed, in strength. He thought that it might have been brewed out of elderflowers or something of like taste, and wondered if the arts of cultivating grapes had also been lost here in the Empire's Fall.

"From here, the Children of Morthugor sailed the Forbidden Road eastward to lands of monsters and giants, where dwelt men with the heads of dogs, and others whose heads grew below their shoulder-blades, and such monstrosities. They grew crueller year by year, and set us to build and toil as their slaves: many of the walls that were built before the Empire's Fall were mortared with our blood. But at last the Wrath of the gods fell upon them: the Imperial Seat was destroyed, though the place where it stood is blighted forever with evil, and none has stepped within those bounds and come out to tell of it. When fire plunged from the sky and the earth shook, many of our walls fell; the Imperial governor's palace, that had been on a cliff hanging over the sea, plunged into the water and was lost - so far down that none of its treasures ever washed up on shore, nor can any man hold his breath long enough to dive for them. The great waves destroyed the ships and changed the harbour's shape, and the earth lifted to either side of the bay, forming the ferth: since then, we have never built below the clifftops again. The hands of the gods shattered our chains and wiped the brands from our brows; we slew all of the demon-race, as we still do whenever one with any trace of that taint is found, and no man nor woman has ever been held to slavery again. But the city was in chaos. And it was then that my First Ancestor Hatin, who had fought in chains for the amusement of the Mordhagoernim, took up his sword again and gathered his companions from the arena. They brought order to the streets, and he was hailed as lord; he oversaw the rebuilding of city and harbour, and from then it has been Hatin's City, ruled by the Hatnethim."

As the first course, a thick clear jelly-like soup with little pink shellfish suspended through it, was served, Lord Hatneth went on to talk about the city's history since the Downfall while Arudal listened carefully. Except for the Lords Hatneth, titles were bought rather than inherited; blood, it seemed, counted for nothing, money for all. As in Kantar, education and healing had to be purchased, rather than being supplied by the State. There was nothing, so far as Arudal could tell, that he could liken to knighthood: fighters here served for pay alone, though the best could contract for a pension in case of grievous wounds in combat, and Lord Hatneth made it clear that he was willing to allow them to take over the contracts of several of his top guardsmen - eager, in fact. Arudal was glad that he had mentioned the possibility of trade in iron, for he could tell that the city's ruler was looking on them as an investment now.

"But no man is less than any other in our city, save as his abilities and wealth make him so," Lord Hatneth went on proudly. "Though my line were the first lords by strength and the gratefulness of the people, now we uphold our place by being first and wisest in trade and administration." He had to use the Western word for the last, as Bright Elvish had no such term. "The evils of mastery and slavery have not tainted us since the Empire's fall, nor does any man swear oaths which make him another's slave in deed if not in name, and the ties between - myself and my guards, say - are the honest ties of contract. Our people pay no taxes…"

"How, then, do you keep your streets in such good order?" Arudal asked politely. Though he had not seen the road inside the city, he knew a smooth ride from a bumpy one.

"The Builders' Guild charges a toll for their use, and with that they make repairs. Likewise, those who wish protection from thieves and footpads pay their share to the Warders' Guild and fix a badge to themselves and their homes and businesses: those who want a service should pay for it. You need not worry about such things while you are here, of course," Lord Hatneth added quickly. "As your host, and knowing how differently such things are done among the Fair Ones, I shall see to all such matters for you; I shall be well enough repaid if you bring good word of my welcome to your kindred, and my hopes - to those in your land who concern themselves with such things - of long and profitable trade between us." He lifted his glass, and Arudal returned the toast politely as the servants, their huge-puffed sleeves and skirts rustling like a stand of gaudy Southern flowers in the wind, cleared away the remains of the soup and bore in large platters carrying little roast deer stuffed with plums and bread. The spices in the dark sauce were strange to Arudal, sharp and sweet at once, but pleasant enough; the deep red wine poured with this course seemed to be a mixture of plums and honey, a little sweet for a game dish, though it complemented the sauce nicely. Lord Hatneth spoke to one of the servants, his voice rising and falling softly so that Arudal could not quite make out the unfamiliar words until the city's ruler turned back to him.

"Lord Ari. Although you are older than I guessed at first, I should like to offer my heir to companion you while you are in our city. He is sixteen years - two from full manhood by our reckoning. I hope that the difference between you is not so great that you will find his company tiresome rather than enjoyable."

"I am sure I shall be delighted," Arudal answered. Lord Hatneth's heir would serve as a spy for his father, of course; but Arudal suspected that the city ruler's purpose was more to strengthen the long-term bonds of trade, for even an Elf of mixed blood could still be dealing with Hatin's City when Lord Hatneth's grandson was long in his tomb. "Does he speak the Bright Elvish tongue as well as you do yourself?"

"Alas, no. But I hope that he shall learn from you, and perhaps, if it pleases you, he may teach you more of our language, though I am told that you have a passable knowledge of it already."

Lord Hatneth's son, so far as Arudal could tell beneath the gaudy flounces of gold cloth, was a shorter, paler-skinned, and more heavily-built version of his father. He bowed to the guests, greeting them in clumsy Bright Elvish, "Stars and Moon shined on your path. It pleased you, I am Berek Hatneth."

"Berek," Lord Hatneth said in the Western tongue, "these are Lord Karsil and Lord Ari. You shall be Lord Ari's companion while they are here. Though you should not forget that he is of a man's full age, I think nevertheless that you will be able to entertain him when we are not speaking of business, and perhaps he will help you better yourself in the speech of the Fair Ones."

Berek nodded and seated himself next to Arudal, looking down curiously. Arudal guessed the boy to be close to six feet tall, heavy-boned and grossly well-fed, his plump face pallid beneath its natural darkness. I wonder if he has ever so much as saddled his own horse, Arudal thought. Unless he was greatly mistaken, Berek had not had even as much training in weapons as a boy destined to be a mage would get in Tharandrost.

"Speak our tongue at all?" Berek asked hopefully in Elvish.

"Not yet as well as I might," Arudal replied. "I would learn more of it from you, even as your father would have you learn from me."

"Ah, good!" He slipped into Western again. "What manner of entertainments would you like tomorrow? I do not know what pleases the Fair Ones, but there is much to see and do in this city. There are plays, and houses of delight, and then the fighting-matches..." Berek stopped suddenly; Arudal guessed that his father, knowing rather more of the ways of Elves, had kicked his ankle at that.

"It would be best, perhaps," Lord Hatneth broke in smoothly, "to let Lord Ari tell you what he delights in doing, so that you may show him about as he pleases."

"Of course, Father," Berek said, chastened.

The evening seemed to wear on a very long time. Although Arudal had long since learned the art of eating lightly from each course in a formal meal, after three months at sea, the rich red meat seemed weightier than usual in his belly, and he was still stiff and sore from two days of riding after their long voyage. Karsil, as ever, showed no sign of tiredness, but Arudal found himself having to stifle yawns more and more often. To distract himself, he asked himself where Lord Hatneth might have put the other members of their company. As he did, he felt a peculiar prickle of foreboding - a sense almost like an untrained Mindspeaker trying to press through the Shadow-walls of his thoughts. I must go to them, he thought.

"Lord Hatneth," Arudal said. "Could you tell me where our guardsmen have been quartered? I have just remembered that they still have one of my bags, which has writings of mine in it that I will need to look over tonight."

"If you wish, I shall send someone to fetch it for you. The hour is growing late, and I believe that the inn where they are staying is some way from my palace. You do not need to trouble yourself with the journey there."

"I should prefer to go myself, if that does not offend you," Arudal replied. "Though it might be best if you would send a guide with me."

"At least consent to ride in a litter befitting your consequence! This is a well-ordered city, but not without some quarters in which it is not best for a stranger to be alone at night. If you must go, I would have you carried in comfort and well-guarded."

"That is kind of you," Arudal said.

"I shall come with you also, Ari," added Karsil. "I wish to find out for myself how it is with them, and how long they think their trading will take before they are ready to travel on again."

Chapter 17: The Free City

"They know not they should thank us,
These lawless folk we guide,
Both savages and children,
With wildness their pride.

They'd crouch in smoky hovels,
Their bellies void and cold,
To pick lice with their nails,
To die, not yet grown old.

We feed them, clothe them, warm them,
And teach them seemly ways.
To lead, our care and toil -
Ingratitude, our praise."
- "The Imperial Duty", Sir Athathor Karbamirun

"Now," Karsil whispered to Arudal as soon as their litter began to move, "what is it that you are so eager to do tonight? Or do you fear some plot of Men that escaped my thoughts altogether?"

"I felt...I do not know what. I would have named it a moment of Foresight, but I know that I have no hint of that gift. Perhaps it was truly only nervousness, or perhaps..." Sometimes a buried gift of the mind would reach out in desperation; Tharandrostans were closely examined to find such latent talents, but not Kantareans. If it had been one of their comrades... Arudal clenched his jaw in frustration. If only he had the Mindspeaker's gift with the living as well as the dead, as his cousin Arothir did, he could have found out what was wrong at once. And if Lord Hatneth could arrange the death of even one of their party members so as not to rouse suspicion, there would be a full suit of steel armour for him to buy. Arudal thought of poison in the inn's soup, or an assassin waiting inside the door to the privy, and cursed the chance that had put Dame Karsil, the knight least fit to deal with the subtleties of strange rulers of Men, into Lord Hatneth's palace and separated them from the counsel of Sir Salarond and Lostren. *But perhaps I am not least fit of the squires for this,* Arudal told himself. *Rhys, and maybe even Finvar, would have been far worse off than I, for our folk have long had to deal with rulers like Lord Hatneth in the South.*

"I wonder," Karsil murmured, her breath stirring softly in Arudal's ear, "what it is that Lord Hatneth would not have us see about his streets at night? For all he speaks of the fairness of his city, it seems to me that there is something less than fair about it. Elves do not shun the great cities of Kantar, nor even, though there is far better reason, do all of us keep away from Tharabruthnan. The sooner we may bid our host farewell and be on our way, the better it will be, I think. There is something about this place that I mislike, though I cannot name it."

Arudal let the slight on his home go, for his own thoughts had passed along the same lines earlier. The heavy silken hangings of the litter muffled the sounds from outside: snatches of raucous singing, or the occasional noise of a shout, came faintly to him, but he could not make out the words. Still, it seemed a noiser city than Var Perenil at night.

In the darkness, Karsil's pale face was clearer to Arudal's sight than in broad daylight, the emerald gems of her eyes gleaming darkly. Her narrow jaw was set firm, and it seemed to him that he could see the look of cold anger on her features, like a delicate sculpture wrought of iced steel. The Elven hearing was keener than his own; Arudal whispered, "Can you understand what they are saying outside?"

The Elven knight turned her gaze on him, and Arudal saw her lips whiten. "I wish that I could not, and I shall not repeat it. The Men of this city are worse than beasts; beasts do not mishandle their females so."

Arudal sat bolt upright. "If a woman is being harmed, we must stop to aid her!" He was about to shout to the litter-bearers, but Karsil grasped his shoulder, her mouth twisted with loathing.

"I think there is nothing we can do, Ari - unless you would offend Lord Hatneth by bringing back an unwashed child-whore to his hall."She grimaced bitterly. "If that is your desire, no doubt he will be glad to find you a better one than you could by yourself."

"Finavi!" Arudal gasped, deeply shocked. He could feel Karsil's hand shaking on his shoulder - she is as distressed as I, he told himself.

"But I forget; you are not allowed to mix your precious bloodlines with the lesser races, are you? No doubt female slaves in Tharandrost are perfectly safe from the lusts of their masters."

Arudal only looked at Karsil, torn between a desire to strike her across the face and an inexplicable counter-urge to collapse weeping on her shoulder. After a moment, Karsil let go of him, passing her hand across her forehead as if to wipe off sweat - though Elves never sweated.

"No, I am sorry, little cat. I spoke only from the distress of my soul, that there is nothing we can do here. And even if you were raised to protect women only because they are valuable brood-stock, it is no small thing that your heart leapt at once to saving an unknown maid of Common blood in a strange city, without thought of the dangers to yourself....Be silent, little cat. I must meditate now, lest I be overwhelmed."

Karsil's eyelids dropped halfway, and Arudal thought that he could see a faint milky film dulling their bright greenness, her face stilling to marble serenity. He had heard that the Elves could relive times past as though they happened yet; he wondered if she were walking among the frail glimmering towers of Elf-Home now, her betrothed beside her - or perhaps in battle, her sword weaving a blood-spattering net of flashing silver. He had seen enough of Karsil in the past months to know that the anger of Elves demanded release as surely as that of humans. For himself, Arudal could only feel shock that such vileness as she had heard outside could exist. Though Karsil had spoken of his folk in bitterness, she had inadvertently told the truth.

And Dockside, where sailors and fishermen drink, is rough enough at night - but even there, no man dares lay violent hands on a prostitute: the State protects those who sell their personal services as surely as it licenses them as sterile and examines them twice-weekly for disease, and there is no tavern or alley in Tharandrost where our laws do not rule.

But if there were a part of Hatin's City where those lived who could not afford to pay the Warders' fees? What law would run there, beyond the sense not to risk offending the wealthy? Even wild Plainsmen picking lice in their hovels, Arudal had heard, had a rough sense of clan justice and custom which kept them from all slaughtering each other in drunken rages: what recourse did the wretched of Hatin's City have?

At last the litter lowered smoothly to the ground. A guard pulled the hangings aside; Karsil's eyes opened, and she rose and got out in a single smooth motion, Arudal trailing behind her. The inn's battered sign showed a writhing shark with two harpoons through it, exaggerated rows of teeth snapping at the air.

Two guards went in before them, two following behind. The hairs at the back of Arudal's neck prickled, and he wished that he had been allowed to wear his falchion in Lord Hatneth's hall, or thought to arm himself before leaving; he had only his belt-knife to defend himself with. If only men were taught to fight without weapons as women are! he thought. I should not feel so vulnerable then...

The air inside the inn was thick and smoky: Arudal recognised the scents of ordinary pipeweed, dreamweed, and burnt poppy, but there were other smells he could not put a name to, and they mingled with the sharp reek of the Western berry-wines spilled and staling, ale, and raw spirits, as well as the close fug of unwashed bodies like a taint of mold upon the more pleasant scents of baked bread and roasting meat. The torches and the roaring fire in the hearth did not cast enough light to keep Arudal from recognising the figures of the White Company knights and their squires half-ringed about a table in the corner with their backs to the wall. They had all covered their armour with dark cloaks, helms kept close beside them on the benches, but now and again, a silvery flash of steel showed through.

"You will stand to guard us from behind," Arudal said to Lord Hatneth's men, and walked forward to take a seat facing the others as Karsil did likewise.

"How is it with you?" he asked as he sat down - speaking Common, trusting that there was no chance that the guardsmen would recognise the speech of the Middle Land.

"Praised be all the gods and spirits that you have come, Ari!" Rhys said before any of the others could speak. He reached out to clasp Arudal's hand in both of his; Arudal caught himself just in time to keep from flinching back from the Plainsman's touch. "I take back any sharp words I may have spoken about your Shadow-gifts, for where the cleansing magic given by the gods does not flow, such skills seem needful, and I did not know if I had gotten through to you. There is a darkness in the room we were given, a sucker of life-strength. I felt it, and Lostren, though the others did not."

Arudal raised an eyebrow, and Lostren nodded. "I felt a touch of cold, and almost fainted: I still feel weak in the legs from it," the red-haired noble said quietly. "I think it is not by chance that we were sent here, or put there - though it was the only room in the inn that wasn't full."

Sir Salarond brushed back a helm-matted wisp of gray hair. "My guess is that the chamber is haunted by some manner of ghost. In the Middle Land, I could have cleansed it easily, but..." He shrugged, and Arudal thought uncomfortably of how it had felt to try his sorcery here - the spark, the sense of fuel ready, but no wick to link the two into flame.

"Do what you can, squire," Sir Thoron ordered briskly.

The others led Arudal and Karsil to their chamber, the guards trailing behind. "Stay outside," Arudal said to them. Like well-trained hunting-hounds, the four bronze-armoured men separated, one standing on either side of the door and the other two on the side of the corridor opposite.

Arudal drew a deep breath and stepped into the room, letting his sight slip into Shadow as the others followed behind him. At first he saw only dark mist, felt only chill. Then, in the corner of the room, he saw the two bedraggled figures, the larger one holding the smaller in its lap. They were of the mixed types and colourations that marked the folk of Hatin's City: the bigger one had straight brown hair and Terashi-swarthy skin; the smaller, beneath its dirt, was dark-skinned as the folk of the Far South, but pale-haired. By its much-mended dress and long brown hair, he guessed that the bigger one was a girl, though her figure was hardly more than skin stretched tight over a bundle of bones. The little one wore a tattered tunic that could not hide its swollen belly above bare stick-thin legs; several of its toes were missing, and its feet were blackened and swollen, as if by frostbite or charring.

Poor ghosts, he thought, swallowing hard. They must have crept in here, perhaps fallen asleep in the corner where they sat, and died there, never noticing when their bodies were tossed out on the rubbish-heap...

"I will not hurt you, nor will any of my companions," Arudal said gently as the girl looked up at him, then tried to scrabble away, protecting the boy with her little withered shape as though she expected a kick or a whip-blow to fall at any moment. "Don't be afraid."

"Who are you?" the girl quavered. "Are you...oh, please, are you a customer? I'll do anything you ask, we haven't eaten in days." She started to tell him in lurid detail what she would do for a few coppers or a bowl of stew. Many of the words were strange to Arudal, but the sense was far too clear.

"No!" Arudal said, sickened. "No, please. I only want to help you...what are you doing here? How did you get here?"

"Please, we're so hungry. There was a young man here with beautiful red hair, he gave us some food, but that was a long time ago..."

Lostren had mentioned a chill and feeling faint - it often happened with ghosts who thought they were still living, that they would remember taking life-force as being given food, or healing if they had died of wounds. These two could have killed many times, draining unwary sleepers dry in this room, and never known it. Still, Arudal crouched down on his haunches, holding out a hand to each of the children. Deliberately he lowered his shields slightly, letting a little of his own strength flow into them.

"Thank you, sir," the girl said, and the boy smiled at him, a pitifully radiant smile beneath his dark sunken cheeks and huge gray eyes. Arudal knew that he should send them on now, but he could not help being curious.

"What are your names? How did you come here? Where are your parents?"

"I'm Halta and my brother is Barasith," the girl said. Despite their differences in colouring, Arudal was not surprised that they were siblings; he knew that mixing breeds could lead to wide variations in families over the years. "I'm eleven years old, and he's eight. Our father was a city guardsman. He was good, too; he was going to be promoted to be one of Lord Hatneth's guards. But when I was ten, Mother got sick. She couldn't work, and we had to pay for the healers, so Father had to get a second job. He wasn't very good at anything but fighting," she added miserably. "So we couldn't afford much food, and he got thin and tired and couldn't fight well enough for the city guard, so they kicked him out. He kept the other job, but he gave us all his food, and then he got sick, and we couldn't pay for the healers, and he died." Arudal frowned. Tharandrostan healers were employed by the State, their services free to all citizens; Kantarean healers charged for their work when they could, true, but their oaths forbade them to hold back their aid from anyone in need.

"None of our uncles could afford to keep us, so I went on the streets, and Barasith tried to run errands, but I was already too skinny to be worth much, and the other boys beat Barasith up. The lady who runs this inn was really nice, though. She took us in as servants, and we got to eat some of the scraps from the kettle, and she let me turn my trade here for half what I got, although I didn't make very much. But after a few days here, Barasith fell asleep too close to the hearth and the cloths on his feet caught fire, and I couldn't do anything for him. He kept screaming until the inn-lady brought him some broth with sleepy stuff in it. We both ate it - I couldn't help it, I was so hungry, though I only took a few spoonfuls - and he went to sleep all quiet in my lap, and his feet haven't hurt him as much since, except when he gets really hungry."

I think I would like to take a torch to this place, Arudal thought, rage and tears clotting together to a choking lump in his throat. He did not bother asking Halta how long it had been; even ghosts who knew they were dead and worked regularly with humans had trouble with measuring time. Instead he coughed and stood up, saying as calmly as he could, "Halta, there is a place where you shall both be fed and healed, and I will take you to it. Come with me."

Arudal lifted Berasith's chill weightless form from his sister's arms. He met the boy's eyes, drawing him into the stillness of his own mind. For a moment Arudal hesitated. Even such weak ghosts could be useful, controlled and sent out...But these two had suffered too much in life already. His body perfectly still, Arudal pushed within, casting the little spirit out - out beyond Shadow, beyond the worlds' rings, where-ever it was the souls of Men might go.

"Now you," he murmured.

Halta rose to her feet, her back straight and proud, and Arudal saw the sorrowful recognition blooming on her face. "We're dead, aren't we?"

Arudal nodded.

"You're so pretty, so bright...Are you the Toll-Lord's messenger?"

"In a way."

She took a step forward, hesitated, her bony chin quivering. She was nearly as tall as Arudal, and the little sharp knives of her cheekbones and dainty line of her jaw showed that she had been an attractive child once, for a Common girl. Eleven years old - Amandeth help us!

"How long were we dead?"

"It doesn't matter. Your time of waiting is over. Come to me, Halta."

The girl stepped forward as if to embrace Arudal. He put his arms gently about her - deep in Shadow as he was, he could feel the sharp edges of her bones through her worn gown, feel her shivering in fear and hope. Then Arudal opened his mind. She came into him willingly, but hesitated at the other threshold.

I have no way to pay you, except...

No! It is not needed. Go to your kin, and may you find more joy on the Other Side than on the green earth.

Thank you...

She went through, and was gone. Arudal sank to his knees in a paroxysm of silent sorrow and relief, clasping his arms about his chest and trying not to weep. Only his anger at Lord Hatneth's plot held his aching sobs back. One or two of their company would have seemed to die of sickness, leaving their armour to be bought; the rest might have been moved to the palace then, but it would be too late for the dead. We must get out of here as soon as we can - especially since the innkeeper is a poisoner.

"Ari! Ari, is it over?" Sir Salarond was saying. Even through his mail gloves, the healer-priest's hands were warm against Arudal's chilled flesh. Slowly Arudal pulled himself out of Shadow, until Salarond's lean gray-bearded face showed foggily to his sight.

"It is over," he said heavily. "They weren but children..." But they would have killed you, all unknowing.

"Yes," Sir Salarond murmured, a world of sorrowful understanding in his voice.

Arudal coughed back tears, let their commander help him to his feet. "Sir," he said, "who is it that owneth this inn?"

"A man by the name of Galorit."

"Not a woman? He is not married?"

"No," Sir Salarond answered, clearly puzzled. "He said something about the joys of bachelor life when he showed us to the room. Why?"

For a moment Arudal deeply wished that he were among his own people: he could simply open his mind to let his thoughts be read, rather than having to batter his heart into words. But he said, forcing the effort of shaping the Common words correctly to restrain his bitter fury, "The woman who used to own this inn had poisoned them. Clearly the current innkeeper has a better way to get rid of the unwanted, but I should be careful of the food here anyway."

Sir Salarond drew in a deep hiss of breath. "Oh. I see. Now sit down by the fire, Ari, and Lostren will brew something to warm you up - with the water from our own waterskins," he added sardonically. "You look far too close to the verge of death yourself."

Arudal sat down and let himself be wrapped in a thick cloak, though it did little to still his shivering. Knowing how to do something, and actually doing it, he thought, were very different things. He had been told often enough in his training that he would probably have to persuade unknowing ghosts through to the Other Side at some point in his career, for that was one of the duties of an agathudal, but he had never guessed what it would really be like. At least the children had gone willingly, without trying to flee or fight: it would have been horrible beyond description if he had needed to force them.

And would their lives not have been better as slaves in Tharabruthnan - fed, kept safe, and healed as necessary, instead of having to claw for survival like rats in a city's wastepipes? The lowest Dockside tavern would not starve a Plainsman whelp until his belly bloated with hunger, or put him down because it was cheaper than calling a healer; even a condemned mine-slave would be tended by a vet. As for allowing - forcing! - a girl as young as Halta to whore... Arudal clenched his fists tight to stop their trembling: he did not know whether he was angrier about the children's deaths, or their lives - or that he himself had been able to do no more for them than end their torments.

The tea Lostren made for Arudal was astringent in spite of the honey-sweetness, the warm tingle of vargwe prickling life back into his chilled hands and feet. As he sat sipping at it, Karsil reported on all that had taken place within Lord Hatneth's hall, though she said nothing of the incident on the way to the inn.

"I think we should get out of here tonight," Sir Thoron said. "This place is a scum-pit. It would be too easy to make us disappear, and I don't trust any promises of future trade to keep us alive. If the city's run by the sharpest merchant in it, that's just likely to mean he's looking for the best chance to screw us over."

Arudal thought of Lord Hatneth's offer of his son as a companion. Was the youth meant to be spy, or hostage? These people were too foreign for him to guess.

"I would be out of the city as soon as we may, as well," Shakhor put in, and Rhys nodded vigorous agreement.

"Still," Eroth mused, "we need to sell what we have. If other places in the West run as Hatin's City does, we cannot wander about penniless. Perhaps if we were to offer our goods to Lord Hatneth, with a steel knife or camp-hatchet thrown in to sweeten the deal..."

In the end, Arudal had the guards see to transferring their trade-goods to the palace, but took charge of the knife and small wood-axe himself. He and Karsil left the other White Company knights setting up the watch in their rooms, though he suspected there would be little disturbance that night.

Arudal's discussions with Lord Hatneth began early and dragged on into the afternoon. Struggling to repress his revulsion for the man with whom he was dealing, Arudal felt woefully out of his depth most of the time, and clung to his insistence that he could make no binding contracts for his House. Nevertheless, a series of tentative agreements were written up that he, supposedly, would carry back for signature. With steel prices roughly agreed on, however, it took less time for Arudal to bargain a decent repayment for their trade goods - helped in no little measure by Lord Hatneth's eagerness to get his hands on any bit of the Old Metal he could: Arudal guessed that the show of wealth was at least as important in this city as the possession of wealth.

"But lastly," Lord Hatneth said, "there is one thing to which you must agree. Berek is of an age to begin earning a man's place: I would have him journey back with you as my emissary."

"That is not possible," Arudal said flatly.

"Why?"

Arudal's thoughts flew wildly about. Of course they could not give Lord Hatneth's son the least chance to discover who they were and where they came from - but what excuse could he give? At last he said, "We are going to visit my mother's kin. The caravan will leave us before then; but I cannot take a strange Man with none of our blood into the Elf-Home."

"Then let him go with the caravan, and meet you on the road back," Lord Hatneth replied calmly. "I will even pay an apprentice's fee, scaled to his station in life. You will find it more than adequate, I assure you. And you, in turn, shall have his service as an apprentice merchant: seeing this day's work, I think he can learn much from you."

"I cannot make such a decision on my own," Arudal temporized. "If you will allow me the chance to consult with Karsil and with the caravaneers as well...for it is their duty to see to our safety..."

"Of course." Lord Hatneth snapped his long fingers, and twenty guards, fully armoured in bronze and armed with wicked-looking bronze crossbows as well as swords, filed in. "Guards, please escort Lord Ari and Lord Karsil in safety to the inn where their bodyguards are staying. They have a matter of great importance to all of us to discuss." His tone was pleasant, but Arudal could sense its undertone, like a cold swift current sucking at his feet below the sea's quiet surface. His only question was how far Lord Hatneth would go - would he have them killed if they refused to take his son with them, or not?

Once more in the thick air of the perfumed litter, Karsil and Arudal rode a little time in silence before Karsil suddenly murmured, "Tell me the truth, Ari: having seen what Men do to one another when they have the power to, can you see now why slavery is evil?" Her eyes met his, their clear green drowning-deep as sunlit seawater, and he could not look away, though his heart beat faster and he could feel the fear-sweat chilling on his sides.

"No," Arudal answered.

"You say that still? At least you are no coward...But words are one thing, and deeds another. What of the ghosts you dealt with last night? Did you set them free, or keep them to serve you?"

"I sent them onward. Yet," he added, "if they had lived, they would gladly have accepted collar and brand in exchange for food and safety." Arudal thought of what Halta had tried to offer him instead, and the tips of his ears flamed hot. He could not speak of that to Karsil, but she raised a pale eyebrow.

"One of us knows less about the nature of Men than he thinks. Still, you set the ghosts free: why, when you might have found use for them along the way?"

"They were children, and had suffered enough in life. It was heart-rending enough to look at them: how, then, could I have borne to keep them with me?"

"You found it easy enough with the vampire."

"That was a different matter - and you slew her."

"Yes, to save her from you."

"The proper task of the Undead," Arudal said stiffly, "is to aid the living from Shadow." After a moment, for it was clear that Karsil knew his full nature, he added, "Two weak and frightened children, ghosts or not, could hardly have proven much aid. And I cannot hold an endless number of spirits: some of our group may yet need my help before this mission is done."

"Help!" Karsil spat. "Ari, I want your word on this: that if Amanvon wills my passing, you shall not seek to hold me in Shadow; and that you shall consult with each of our companions to find their will in the matter before we go much farther. I hope they shall all deny you; but if they would choose that evil, let it be their own choice at least, and not yours." Karsil's glare softened a little. "Still, you freed those you might have kept enslaved, as much as you may try to justify it with all that is worst in you. I saw your face last night, and I do not think you paused to weigh the strategies of gain and cost before you sent those children on. And if you, tainted in blood and thought-warped by the unrepentant Fallen for fifty years, may change for the better, how much more hope might there be for Lord Hatneth's son?"

Arudal said nothing: he had grown used to Karsil's slights on his race and person, so that they were no more than the dull ache of an old bruise on his heart. But there was some truth in her last words, at least, for Berek might rule Hatin's City someday, and if he learned better ways from them, there might be no more girls like Halta forced to sell their bodies on the streets then. If they could manage it without jeopardizing their mission...And if they refused to take Berek, Lord Hatin might bring their mission to an abrupt end.

When they reached the inn, the guards did not wait for Arudal's command, but formed themselves into a body about Arudal and Karsil, marching them in and down the corridor to the White Company's chamber without paying any heed to the stares of the customers in the busy common room. The foremost guardsman banged roughly on the door, shouting, "Open, in the name of Lord Hatneth!"

Arudal thought of how the White Company would answer this demand, and hastily called, "It is ourselves, Karsil and Ari: you need not fear." Yet, he added to himself. I hope.

Finvar opened the door. At least the White Company knights had kept their swords sheathed, but their helms were on. Arudal wished he could see well enough in daylight to know how the guards were responding - whether their fingers were near the crossbow-triggers, or their bodies tensed for their commander's orders to attack.

Karsil's high voice fell soothingly across the nerve-jangling tension in the chamber. "Take off your helms; we have a business proposition to discuss. I do not know why we are so guarded..."

"For your esteem and protection, Fair One," the foremost guardsman broke in, his voice harsh and creaky as branches rubbing in the wind after the Elf's smooth song. "Lord Hatneth wishes all to know your worth and the value in which he holds you, else two of us would have sufficed."

Do I believe that? Arudal wondered. It made a certain odd sense, from what he knew of Hatin's City. But still, when a ruler sent so many guardsmen to a conference where a matter in which he had a strong stake was being decided, it was difficult to believe that he would abide it peacefully if the answer were "No". Deliberately, he changed the language to Common, wishing he could see the guard-commander's face better. "Lord Hatneth wishes us to take his son with us as an apprentice on our journey."

"Absolutely not!" Thoron burst out. "Who does he think we are?"

"A pair of Elves with a bodyguard of merchants," Sir Salarond answered dryly. "Ari, was he willing to buy our stock?"

"Yes, at a good enough price. We could replace our horses and leave this evening - if we can leave."

They were all silent a moment, thinking about that, until Eroth said, "Lord Hatneth's son will not speak our tongue, so there is little danger that he will overhear something he should not. And he could prove useful as a guide."

"Until we get where we're going," Thoron growled. "I don't think the story will hold up to wandering into the old Imperial Seat."

"We could leave him in an inn before that," suggested Arudal. "I told Lord Hatneth that his son would not be allowed into the Elf-Home, and he was happy enough at the thought that the boy would wait further back along the road until we came out again."

Shakhor shook his head. "And if our guest gets killed along the way?"

Thoron showed his teeth in answer. "We have no reason to come back here. If he comes, the risk had better be all his. I'm not having any of ours killed to protect some spoiled noble cub - can he fight?"

Arudal shrugged. Berek had looked unpromisingly soft, but he could have been mistaken.

The squires had been quiet; now Lostren spoke up. "Ari, do you think we can get out of here alive without Lord Hatneth's son? Is Lord Hatneth the sort to trade off what must be unimaginable wealth in his hand for the prospect of long-term purchases?"

Arudal thought about it. The value of their armour, even at the rates of their tentative agreement, which he was sure was far lower than actual worth here... compared to what Lord Hatneth would have to pay for one such suit...He seeks, Arudal thought suddenly, to establish his son's position unquestionably; else he would not send him off with us. There must be something wrong with Berek: but I think that he must be our only hope of escape... How was it that we failed to learn the worth of steel from our guides? But the answer to that question was so obvious as to deserve scorn.

"I think that we cannot refuse this offer and live to escape," Arudal said at last, and Lostren said, "My thoughts are just the same."

Thoron only nodded, and Shakhor muttered grudging agreement, while Eroth murmured, "I don't think we can take the risk of turning Lord Hatneth down. Even if we made it out of the city, which is unlikely, we have enough dangers to face on the road without being hunted by an army - though at least we would not have to fear magic."

"We cannot be so certain," Arudal said. "Lord Hatneth's steward carries a staff enchanted by some method: they may have learned other means of magic than those we know."

"Or ritual may work, as Dr. Melkoth theorizes," said their commander. "In any case, I have decided. Go back to Lord Hatneth, and tell him that we shall take his son, but he must supply his fighting gear, provisions, and horses, and we accept no responsibility in case of Berek's accidental death. Ask if there are warhorses for sale here, and see about replacing our pack-horses as well. We leave at dawn."

Chapter 18: New Companions

*"You may map the road down to every pebble underfoot, you may ready yourself
for wind or rain, snow or scorching heat, and plan your halts inn by inn.
But this no man may always guess: whom you shall meet on your journey, and
how it is they shall deal with you, or you with them. Do not seek to hold yourself
apart too much, but take those gifts of good or ill that the gods send you: in
them, as truly as in whatever you seek, you shall find your adventure."
-Lady Geliwe dath Uthaglar, The Adventures of Sir Paramel, Book I, p. 17.*

A light frost misted the brown grasses as the White Company party set
out from Hatin's City the next day; the red-gold streaks of dawn were
already paling swiftly in the sky behind them. Arudal, riding in the
middle of the party next to their new companion, breathed in deep
breaths of the clean frosty air as though he could wash the taint of the city from his
lungs and tried to keep the resentment from his face when Berek spoke up.

"Do you always get up so early?" the plump youth asked. "I hardly got any sleep
last night. How far do you mean to ride today?"

Fat and spoiled as a horse on grass all summer, Arudal thought unkindly: he had
not slept much either, staying up to arrange the purchase of provisions and horses
- such as they could buy in Hatin's City; Lord Hatneth had looked at him blankly
when he mentioned horses trained for fighting. The best Hatin's City had were the
riding horses of Lord Hatneth's messenger service, undistinguished beasts trained
to a two-handed use of the reins. Arudal had also directed the choice and packing
of Berek's gear while the larger boy sat about looking vague - though, remembering
his own struggles with Sir Thoron's tent, Arudal was not altogether without
sympathy for him. But at least I am worth the trouble the others have had to take
with me, Arudal thought. What can this creature possibly do that will make up for
having to nursemaid him?

"We usually start earlier, and we shall ride as far as we can, I imagine." Arudal
squinted against the day-fog: there was something about the set of Berek's body on
the horse that seemed strange, but he couldn't see well enough to tell what, aside
from the Hatneth scion using both hands on the reins - as the Western horses were
trained for - and having a seat like a sack of turnips. "If you sat up straight and tried
to keep your balance, you might ride more comfortably."

Berek made an effort, but even through the mist on his sight, it looked to Arudal
as though he was leaning to the side. At least Berek was no longer wearing the
gaudy plumage of Lord Hatneth's court: his trousers and tunic were woven of many
bright strips of cloth, some with threading of gold and silver, but they were of a
decent cut rather than ballooned, slashed, and festooned with streamers.

"Is your saddle slipping? Stop a moment." Arudal straightened his own back slightly; obedient to the shift of his rider's weight, Inmanat halted and stood still, letting Arudal lean down to check the other's girth. It was tight enough, but Berek had let the stirrups fall away from his feet - for his height, the Western noble was short-legged in comparison to the Imperials. Sighing, Arudal took in Berek's stirrup-leathers, then rode around him to do the other side.

"Keep your feet in the stirrups, and it will be easier for you to balance," Arudal ordered. He remembered how, as a child, Boraitiz had taken his stirrups away after he had mastered the rudiments of riding, getting him first to trot, then to canter, and finally gallop with only the grip of his knees and his own sense of balance to hold him. It would be a long time before Berek managed so much. If he ever did: Arudal had been a lithe child even for his people, easily able to land rolling and come unhurt to his feet when his horse threw him, but Berek would crash down like a load of glass ingots. "Before the gods, do your folk not ride at all?"

"Only messengers and such," Berek answered, seemingly unashamed by his lack of skill. "Why do your peddlers not drive wains like sensible folk?"

"We came by high and dangerous mountain passes. Wagons could not have made it through," Arudal said easily: they had prepared their story to stand up to such questions. Even as he spoke, he was trying to judge the tones of Berek's speech: did that particular rise and fall indicate a degree of contempt, and if so, was it inherent to the language, or an idiosyncracy of the speaker? He longed to ask outright, but did not dare - perhaps when he had known Berek longer, or while he was teaching the boy Bright Elvish, he could find out more directly.

"You...do not ride?" Finvar asked haltingly from Berek's other side, where he had been trying to follow the conversation. "Why?"

"Why should I?" Berek said. "We pay people to ride when we have need of swiftness. And true men stand on their feet, not beholden to other creatures. It is said that the Mordhagoernim are riders, but a staunch man with his feet planted on the earth can defeat them. That is but an old women's tale, yet there may be some truth in it: all the oldest pictures and statues of the demon-race show them horsed."

Finvar looked bewildered, lost in the swift rise and fall of the high Western tongue, and Arudal translated quickly for him, trying to force his interest in the language to over-ride his anger. The Empire's former slaves had destroyed the treasures of the West, ground them in the dirt - if what Berek said held true for the rest of the continent, Inmanat and his kin were the last of the true-bred Imperial steeds, the most priceless bloodlines of the Imperial Seat lost forever, and that was a destruction to make the gods weep.

Berek did not wait until Arudal had finished, but spoke loudly over him. "Is that a traders' tongue? You will teach it to me."

Arudal temporized, "It is the tongue of Men in our land. You will learn the Elvish language first, as your father asked."

"I won't have you talking in a language I don't know!" Berek insisted, his face growing red. He jerked on the reins, and his horse side-danced, forcing him to scrabble desperately to keep his seat. Finvar groaned silently and rolled his eyes, and Arudal needed no mind-gift to know what his fellow squire was thinking.

"Berek," Arudal said severely, "your father paid an apprentice's fee to us, not the price of servants, tutors, or bodyguards. You will learn what you are here for, and you will not try to give us orders, or Lord Karsil will send you back home with your prentice-price around your neck."

To his surprise, Berek was silent at once, his lower lip quivering as he stared wide-eyed at Arudal. The Western boy looked as though he were about to burst into tears, but Arudal fixed his gaze on him until Berek shuddered and dropped his eyes.

"Before Amanvon, Ari, what did you just say to that miserable creature?" Finvar asked.

Arudal kept his voice low as he answered without looking directly at Berek. "I threatened to send him home. I wonder if his father threatened him with something more dire, should he fail on this journey? If we only knew more of these folk…"

"We wouldn't be lumbered with this quivering lump of lard," muttered Finvar. Arudal was surprised at his squire-brother's vehemence, so at odds with the friendly greeting he had gotten from the Artegalian himself; but then, Finvar had no more reason to think well of the Hatneth clan than the rest of them did, and there was nothing about Berek to engender either friendship or respect.

The trees thinned as they rode further along. By the time the company stopped for their mid-day meal, as well as Arudal could tell in the thick day-mist, they had come to some manner of open land. Berek slid off his horse painfully, half-falling, half-staggering to the ground. "There is a village with an inn not far from here," he said hopefully. "We could stop there for the afternoon."

Though Berek's remark had been addressed to Arudal, Sir Salarond turned around and regarded the large youth dispassionately for a moment before he rummaged in his pouch for a sealed clay pot. "Take this and rub it on your legs," the healer-knight said carefully - his command of the Western tongue was not too clumsy, if not as good as Arudal's. "It will help with the aching, and you will not stiffen up as badly while we eat. Are there inns farther along the road?"

"There is another village some…" The tip of Berek's tongue poked out of his mouth, as though he were trying to think on a very deep matter. "Maybe a day's walk from here, maybe longer. It is too far to reach today," he added hopefully.

"If that is so, then we shall plan to camp by the road this night," Sir Salarond declared. "Now go and put the salve on."

Berek straightened his back, looking down at Salarond with a sudden renewed arrogance. "You are only Lord Karsil's bodyguard. Who are you to say where we shall stop?"

Arudal held his breath, waiting for their commander's reply. But Salarond only said calmly, "The safety of this group is mine to order. As you travel with us, you shall follow my orders. Either Karsil or Ari will tell you the same. Now go!" Although the healer-priest had not raised his voice, the note of command in his last two words seemed to catch Berek across the face like a whip, and he stumbled away into the fog, out of Arudal's sight.

Once he had begun to eat and Sir Salarond's medicine had worked on his legs for a little time, however, Berek became almost pleasant, detailing the lands and villages on their route with what sounded to Arudal like the accuracy of a youth who had had trade routes beaten into him despite his most indifferent attempts to learn. This area of good earth produced mostly rye, fruit, and an assortment of fruit wines and spirits; two days' walk farther inland would lead them to rough hills populated by shepherds and goatherds, where they would be able to buy clothes of thick wool and sheep-hides against the snows that were surely coming soon. Few people went deeper into the Barren Hills: if they followed their planned route, they would be in danger from bears, wolves, outlaws, and perhaps the rare ice-cats - which, as Berek described them, sounded something like a white form of the rathra, or at least shared its abilities to conceal itself and fascinate its prey.

But arathra are magical beasts, Arudal thought. How could their cousins work the same enchantments in these lands? Unless they stem from mind-magic rather than true magic...

Reluctantly, when they had finished eating, Arudal boosted his clumsy charge into the saddle, ignoring Berek's grunt of pain. He would be hurting worse by the end of the day, for Sir Salarond had told them that they would ride a little faster in order to reach the second inn Berek had mentioned.

After less than half a minute of trotting, Arudal had to reach over and take the reins of Berek's horse: the boy clearly had no control over the animal even at that gentle pace. The Tharandrostan could not stifle his own contempt. Thus far, the people of the West had proven to him only what he might have expected from a race of slaves suddenly given freedom, wholly lacking in morals, honour, or skill. If Avalar had known what would rise here in the Empire's stead, surely he would never have acted as he did, Arudal thought. My forebears were right to keep the old ways in their own land, even at the risk of Kantar's wrath.

The crimson sunset in their eyes was fading to low embers beneath the darkening blue sky by the time the party reached the village, its wooden palisade of sharpened logs a black crown against the last light in the West. Karsil nudged her horse forward to stand before the gate, answering the sentries' hail in a voice clear as the first glimmer of starlight from Amanvon's Taper above, and the heavy wooden lattice swung open to admit them. A couple of pigs rooted in the muddy streets, and Arudal could smell the sharp urine-stink of tanners' vats when the wind shifted, but the town was tolerably clean otherwise, the houses whitewashed and brightly painted, with candles burning warmly in the windows. He marked that the roofs were more sharply slanted than he was used to - perhaps to let snow slide off? Berek had said that it would snow heavily later in the winter.

The inn was easy to recognise: its fresh-painted signboard showed a sheaf of wheat leaning against a mug of frothing ale. "Tirothar, it's your turn to see to the horses," Sir Eroth ordered his squire. "You'll stay and guard them tonight; watch the packs until we have our rooms."

As Tirothar was collecting the reins, Arudal said to Berek, "You, go with him and see if you can learn how tack and saddles go off and on."

Berek stared at him in shock. "You pay your guardsmen to tend horses for you! Why should I..?"

"Because sometime on this journey you may have to," Arudal told him coldly. "Get going!" He bit his tongue before the next words, Or I shall order you whipped, came out.

As Berek limped off behind Tirothar and the rest of them walked into the inn, Salarond said softly to Arudal, "Ari, are you not being rather rough with that boy? He is still a child, and despite his upbringing, he is trying hard."

"Is that what you call trying hard, sir?"

"Has he complained of the pain of riding once this afternoon, even though he is clearly half-crippled with it?"

Arudal thought about that for a few moments. He was about to allow Sir Salarond that point when the commander spoke again, "It would be well for you to remember that the Empire ended at the will of the gods."

Although Salarond's tone was mild, Arudal felt that he had been rebuked more sharply than he had ever been by Karsil's keen tongue. He could say only, "Yes, sir," but he found himself gritting his teeth as they made their way to a candlelit table - and wondering if, perhaps, Sir Salarond had some trace of the Mind-Reader's gift, to guess the tracks his thoughts had followed that afternoon and what he had almost, from habit, said to Berek. Perhaps some of his remarks to Berek during the day had been a little harsher than necessary, but he had not so much as cuffed the boy's head, as Sir Thoron would do to Arudal himself.

Anxious to turn the subject to something else, as soon as they had sat down, Arudal told their commander of how Berek had responded to the threat to send him home. "And I would have guessed that nothing would have made him happier."

Salarond rubbed his chin. "It would not surprise me if Berek's place did not depend on his proving of himself in some way. If we send him back..." He shrugged. "Who knows? I would not have chosen to take him with us if there had been any way to get out of it, but now that he is here, we may as well make the best of it. And he is proving useful to some degree."

Sir Thoron made a noise halfway between a grunt and a snort. "If we have to fight or run on horseback, that boy's dead meat unless he can learn to ride. Seems to me that Ari's being too easy on him for his own good. Squire, find out what they have for food here, order whatever everyone wants to drink, and see about rooms for the night."

After a certain amount of negotiation around the table, Arudal got up and went over to the wide counter of polished stone before the row of barrels, wondering briefly at how closely it resembled the bars he was used to at home. As in inns in Tharabruthnan, this bar-counter even had the deep hollows filled with small food for drinkers to nibble at - little salt fish, stacks of dry flatbread, olives floating in brine with a long bronze spike to stab them out, and similar things. Finvar came over to help Arudal carry the trays of drinks back to their table.

As Arudal distributed the mugs of ale and berry-wine, he saw that Berek was back, and staring distraught at him again. "What is it now?" he asked, more than a little irritated.

"How is it that you - an Elf-lord - are doing servant's work for these Men?"

Thoron must have caught enough of the Westerner's words to make sense of them, for he glanced around at the other customers in the common room - their faces pale blurred ovals in Arudal's sight - and muttered, "Ah, shit," beneath his breath. Arudal realized that his knight had forgotten the roles that they were meant to be playing.

"I speak your tongue better than the others do," Arudal explained quickly. "It is no more than...courtesy - " he had to use the Elven word, for there was no Western equivalent - "for me to aid them."

"Courtesy?" Berek frowned. "What is that?"

Arudal struggled to think of words in the Western language that might explain what he meant. "It is...to consider the needs and desires of others before your own," he said at last.

"But they are your servants, are they not?"

"It is the mark of nobility to show courtesy even to those lesser than oneself, when that is fitting," Arudal replied, hoping most sincerely that Sir Thoron was not following the conversation, though he could see the twitch of Sir Salarond's mouth, and Dame Karsil raised an approving eyebrow.

Berek chewed unhappily on his fat lower lip. "But you pay them. What more do they need?"

"Courtesy, loyalty, honour, and trust," Arudal replied in Bright Elvish, to which Sir Thoron said, "Ari, take the stick out of your arse and save the moral philosophy, if that's what you're on about, for another time. Did you order food?"

"Yes, sir." *And the gods be thanked that Berek can't understand Common! I doubt that our deception will last much longer in any case, but by the time he realizes what is truly going on, we will be too far away for him to get any messages to his father.*

The White Company's usual practice in a strange inn was to sleep in a single room, setting guards through the night, but the chambers at the Sheaf and Cup were small enough that no more than four of them could squeeze into one room. Sir Thoron took his two squires and - reluctantly, Arudal thought - Berek, who was limping badly and seemed to have serious trouble carrying his pack up the stairs. Finvar moved to help him, but Arudal shook his head. "Let him carry his own gear."

"It hurts just to watch," Finvar protested. "Surely, until he's toughened up a little..."

"If you do him a favour once, he'll think you owe it to him forever," Arudal replied.

Finvar opened his mouth as though he were about to speak, then shut it again and sighed. "Something always goes funny on small-party missions," he said gloomily. "Still, maybe this is the last of our strange luck out of the way."

The inn had no proper bath, but it did have a heated room where travellers could sweat the day's dirt from their bodies before pouring buckets of cold water over themselves, an arrangement which seemed to delight Finvar when he and Arudal took their turn to clean themselves. "Now this is more like it," the Artegalian said, stretching out luxuriously to toss a dipper of water to hiss into steam on the hot stones on top of the low stove. "The stone-bath is how we bathe at home in the winter. It's healthier than climbing in and out of a tub in the cold, and better for easing out the aches from riding - I don't mind saying that I'm still a little sore after going soft at sea."

Arudal said nothing, but when Finvar took up a whisk of leafy twigs bound together with a single peeled wand and began lashing his sweaty body, he could not help asking, "What are you doing?"

"This keeps the blood flowing and gets all the poisons out of your body. It doesn't hurt. Go on, try it."

Dubiously Arudal took the whisk from Finvar's hand and began beating his own limbs lightly with it. He had to admit that the rough tingling felt pleasant enough, sending the drops of sweat flying from his body like pale jewels in the candlelight.

"I'll do your back, if you like," Finvar offered, and Arudal gave the bundle of leaves back to him.

The door of the sweat-bath opened to let Tirothar and Lostren in. It was dark enough for Arudal to see the amusement on Tirothar's face as the lanky squire said, "So it's true what they say about Tharandrostans, then? I hadn't guessed you for that type, Finvar."

"Take that shite and stick it where it belongs," Finvar replied amiably before Arudal could ask Tirothar what he meant, not ceasing to whisk Arudal's back. "And make yourself useful by closing the door and pouring some water on the stones, you're letting the steam out. What are you doing in here, instead of watching the horses, anyway?"

"Sir Eroth thought his riding horse might be developing a limp, so he said I could come wash up while he poulticed it. Speaking of horses, do you know what that fat ninny did this evening?"

"What? Ari, your turn to whisk." Finvar turned around on the bench so that Arudal could lash him with the leaf-bundle.

"He let me show him how to take the tack and saddles off, but first he put the saddles flat down as if he wanted to break their trees, and then, when I started seeing to the horses' feet and asked him to help brush them, he said something along the lines that he wasn't a hired man and looking after animals wasn't in his prentice's contract - I think that's what he said, though he mushes up the language something awful."

"The high form of the Western tongue is tonal," Arudal corrected him.

"That explains everything - thanks so much. Anyway, not only can I not understand our new companion, I don't even think I want to."

Lostren stretched out on one of the upper benches, leaning his head against his crooked arm. "Their culture seems to be entirely based on contract and pay, with no intangible aspects other than a great emphasis on face. Berek probably thinks that tending animals, even horses, is a very low-status job - rather as you would feel if you were asked to muck out a pigpen, I should imagine. Myself, I should recommend a little more tolerance for him, as we shall need his friendship further along the road - even if he does not yet know what friendship is."

Arudal looked sharply up at Lostren, even as Finvar said, "Ow! Not so hard, Ari! Whisk, don't flog."

"I'm sorry," Arudal replied absently. He wondered if Lostren had been struck by one of his moments of ancestral foresight, but didn't like to ask in front of the other squires. In any case, before he had a chance to speak further, Finvar enquired, "What do you mean by that?"

"The inhabitants of Hatin's City seem to work entirely from the profit-motive. I had thought that we had missed the words lacking from their language because our teachers were adventurers, but - did you not hear Ari trying to explain some of them this evening?"

"You mean when he was talking in Elvish? That's enough, Ari."

"Exactly. Until and unless he learns differently, we may expect Berek to flee when we are in danger, or betray us if he sees a benefit to himself - because I doubt that he has ever had a chance to see anyone acting differently."

Finvar sat quietly, sweat dripping from his thick body for a few moments. "Poor bastard," he said at last. "I wonder why his father insisted we take him, and why he so fears to be sent back."

"If we knew that, I suspect we would be a good deal better off," Lostren murmured grimly. "Or aware of potential dangers, at least...I cannot even guess at how far parental love might be expected to go in Hatin's City."

Arudal thought of Halta's story: Father had to get a second job...he gave us all his food... At least the common folk there had as much care for their children as any Tharandrostan might - but even in the household of the Prince of Tharandrost, the heir had the right at any time to challenge his father to the death for rule, and that had happened twice in the State's history. So there was no single generalization that might cover both Halta's father and Lord Hatneth.

"What does Sir Salarond think?" Tirothar enquired.

"My knight is keeping his own counsel," replied Lostren, even as Rhys came in, closing the door quickly as though he had been in such heat-baths before. Arudal could not help noticing how hairy the Plainsman's body was, his chest covered with a sparse ginger pelt that ran in a trail down his belly. A reddish stubble was beginning to disfigure the line of Rhys's jaw and chin as well.

"And what is it that has you all so silent?" the young Plainsman asked after a moment. "Surely it was not of me you were speaking, was it?"

"No, we were talking about our new companion," Tirothar answered.

Rhys lifted his shoulders and palms in an expressive shrug - Arudal was surprised at how little the Plainsman gesture irritated him now. "If we come to another inn when a week is past, I'll wager any of you a pint of ale that the big gowk will have run back to his daddy's house by then."

"I'll take that wager," said Finvar at once.

Rhys smiled ruefully. "Now, why do I think you might have some inside knowledge there? But I made the bet, and I'll stick by it."

A light snow was falling by dawn, dusting the dark brown shingles of the pointed roofs; the horses' hooves cracked through the thin layer of ice on the road to squish in the cold mud below. Arudal shivered as they rode, grateful for Inmanat's warmth beneath him, but wishing more than ever that he had thought to bring his winter clothes - the sweltering summer weather of Var Perenil seemed very far away now. At least he was able to wear his sealskin boots now that he was out from under Karsil's direct tutelage, and no longer forced to play the role of an Elf before critical eyes; and Berek promised that there would be wools and sheepskins for sale within two days at the very most.

Cold is a little thing, Arudal told himself, forcing himself to sit up straight in rebuke to the figure slouched beside him. And it will seem warmer when the horses are warmed properly and we ride faster. Now he understood why the folk here used heat-baths as the Northmen did, rather than tubs: he would have welcomed sweating under the hissing steam again.

"Fair hunting weather, indeed!" Finvar called merrily. The Artegalian was wearing a peaked brown fur cap with a thick rim of red fox-tail over his helm: it looked silly to Arudal, but with the chill of his own helmet's metal seeping even through the thick padding, he was willing to concede that Finvar might be the more sensible of them. "Sir Thoron, may I get out my bow?"

"We're not stopping just because you saw a rabbit," Thoron growled. "Before Amanvon, there's no difference between you and one of your wolfhounds, is there?"

"Wolfhounds can't ride horses, sir," Finvar answered, utterly undaunted.

Thoron laughed. "All right, but I meant what I said. If you get a good shot at something small and close, take it; otherwise, no wasting your arrows."

"Thank you, sir." Finvar expertly strung his small bow, whisking an arrow out of the quiver under his cloak. Even in daylight, Arudal could see its bluish glimmer - the virtue of their armour and weapons had not been lost when they set foot in the West, though he wondered if the enchantments on their gear would work as well here. But with or without magic, Arudal thought that Finvar's bow would not fail its owner: he had seen it close up on the long crossing, and it was a beautiful piece of work, a long piece of springy white bone laminated between strips of red yew and pale ash, polished to a fine gloss.

"Do you know how to shoot?" Arudal asked Berek, though he had little hope of it.

"Why should I? We can..."

"You can buy game, I know," Arudal said wearily. "Perhaps you will learn more on this journey. What about fighting?"

Berek drew himself up as well as he could. "Do I look like a guard to you?"

If Arudal had not been trying so hard to conceal his own shivering, he might not have spoken as sharply as he did then. "Are you of any use whatsoever?"

The Western boy looked away, his lips quivering, and Arudal quietly cursed himself. He almost missed the soft mutter, "...was learning magic."

Icy air hissed in past Arudal's teeth, biting into his lungs. Here was the answer to a question that had waited unanswered in the Middle Land for more than a millennium and a half, and he had nearly spoiled it by his crude handling. As gently as he could, he asked, "Can you tell me more of that?"

Berek glanced sideways, and Arudal was sure he read terror in the youth's pale blue eyes. "Of what?" he whispered. "I didn't say...I'm not supposed...Wait, Elves don't fear the Art as Men do - do you?"

"No."

Arudal might have learned more then, but Sir Salarond called to Karsil, at the head of the party, to speed up into a trot, and he had to take Berek's reins again, trying his best not to look at the unlovely sight of the fat boy bouncing and floundering painfully in the saddle. Cantering, Arudal could tell at once, would be out of the question for some time. He sighed, and tried to advise Berek on keeping his seat as well as he could, but his charge's thighs were obviously too battered and sore to get a decent grip on the horse. A better steed might have helped - but even were Arudal willing to let the oaf sit Inmanat, the little Imperial horse would have tossed him off the first time a dead leaf skittered across the road or a gust of wind scattered snowflakes in his face.

The snow fell more heavily as they rode. Rather than stopping by the wayside to eat - for that would have meant halting to look for wood and build a fire - the company chewed jerky and hardtack while the horses grazed their way along. Arudal alternated his hands on the reins, keeping his free hand inside his tunic for warmth and promising himself that he would be dressed more warmly tomorrow if he had to put on every piece of clothing he owned.

The next village they came to, about mid-afternoon, was smaller, but its palisade was higher and thicker. "Wolves come out of the hills here and try to get into the villages in Ice-Month," Berek said, shivering into his strip-woven cloak and glancing fearfully about, while Arudal wondered briefly at how well the Imperial names for the months had survived the Fall. "Sometimes earlier, when the winter has been bad; and if there has been long hunger, sometimes men will take the shape of wolves and prey on their fellows."

"What is he saying about wolves?" Finvar asked hopefully. Arudal told him.

"Ah. There are Northmen who will put on the skin of a dire wolf to bring on battle-rage, and some of those who serve Martag can become dire wolves altogether in the wintertime, what we call wargs - half-man, half-beast, and wholly outlawed. The wood-dwellers and those who live near the border never go out in the snow without at least a silver-tipped arrow or silver-shod staff. Still, I think we have little to fear."

That, Arudal thought, was true enough: Valderian steel would cleave Shadow-flesh as well as that of any creature of the green earth, and the White Company was used to fighting worse than werewolves.

The village inn was already crowded, thick with the smells of wet wool and goat-hair cloaks dripping on the floor. A huge fire blazed in the hearth; bent brown-faced country-men crowded around it, rubbing their gnarled hands in the warmth and talking in a dialect that Arudal could barely make out. Still, when Karsil lifted off her helm, the crowd parted around her, so that the Elf seemed to move through the soft lilting babble in a ring of silence. Shawled women scooted off the benches when Karsil sat down, leaving plenty of room for the Elf and her company, and the short wide woman who had been tending the bar wriggled out around its carved wooden edge to elbow her way through to them.

"Fair One, may I serve you?" she said, bowing deeply. Her accent was a little clearer than those of the folk around, and Karsil inclined her head graciously.

"Warm food and drink for my companions," the Elf replied. "For myself, a little wine will be enough. And we should like to stop here for the night, if we may."

"Of course, Fair One!" The woman bowed again, bustling back to her place and shouting to the two boys who had been carrying trays of clay mugs through the room.

Once, Arudal thought bitterly, such folk would have felt just as honoured to serve my own ancestors. But he was too grateful for the warmth in the tavern to hold such thoughts for long, his mood improving swiftly as the chill faded from his armour and his occasional sputters of shivering finally eased. Remembering how the folk of the last inn had stared at him when he followed Sir Thoron's orders, Arudal kept his arming-cap on his head and sat a little way from Karsil, so that the villagers would be less likely to mark the similarity in their features.

One boy came about a tray of with steaming mugs. Arudal sniffed his carefully before he sipped, and was glad to find that it was hot cider spiced with something that tasted rather like cinnamon or cloves, and sweetened with honey. Fresh bread with pots of soft white cheese followed swiftly, and then a thick stew which Arudal guessed to be goat seethed in some sort of strong dark berry-wine - elderberry, or something very like it, but with a hint of juniper as well. Though the cold had kept him from thinking about food, now his legs felt hollow from hunger. He ate with great appetite, and was still a little hungry when the servants brought around fresh pies, so that it was an effort to wait until the hot mixture of sweet berries and chopped nuts in the flaky pastries had cooled enough to bite into safely. Finvar had not been so cautious, and was waving his hands before his mouth to cool his burnt tongue, while the other squires laughed at him.

"If you don't dare, you'll never do anything," Finvar said to them, but Tirothar and Lostren only laughed harder - it had been Rhys' turn to see to the horses that night. Thinking of that reminded Arudal of how he had had to wait for his food the first night on the road, and he said, "Berek, go take Rhys his dinner."

The Western boy shot him a sullen glance, but was slowly rising to his feet when Sir Salarond broke in, "That was a noble thought, Ari, and you should not be deprived of the pleasure of Rhys' thanks. Berek, sit down and let Ari do it."

Arudal bit his tongue against a sharp reply, but collected up a full platter, and stopped by the bar on the way to get Rhys a fresh mug of hot cider. *At least there are none of my own kind here to see me serving a Plainsman,* he thought.

Even without a fire, the stables were warm: as well as their horses, there was a pair of big draught oxen there, their dark eyes rolling as they placidly chewed their hay, and several stalls filled with the milling backs of long-haired goats and sheep. For a place where goats were stabled, the smell was not too bad, and Arudal could see that both hay and straw were as fresh as he could have asked for his own precious horse. Rhys was sitting at his ease on a haybale, helm and gauntlets beside him, and talking to a stable-hand in much-mended woolen trousers and tunic.

At first Arudal thought that the stable-hand was a young man, several inches taller than himself and as broad in the shoulders; but when she turned to look at him, he saw the low swell of her breasts and the clean beardless face framed by the sandy short-cropped curls. Rhys followed her gaze, and his jaw dropped in surprise.

"Ari!" he exclaimed. "Who would have thought that it would be you bringing my dinner, now?"

Arudal's hands tightened on the platter - but there had been no gloating in the Plainsman's voice, only the same friendly tone of banter Rhys used with the other squires. So he replied as lightly as he could, "Does not someone have to feed the animals?"

Rhys laughed. "Well, I thank you anyway. Malni," he said, speaking in slow, careful Western, "this is my travel-companion Ari, of whom I told you."

The stable-girl looked down at Arudal, her broad round-eyed face open and interested, but showing none of the awe of the other Western Men in the presence of an Elf - or supposed Elf. "You are very young for such a journey, are you not?"

"Not as my folk reckon it," Arudal said shortly. "And I think that I have thrice your count of years."

"Sorry if I offended you! I didn't mean to be ill-mannered, but we are maybe more plain-spoken here than you are used to. Where is it you are going?"

Arudal repeated the story they had given Lord Hatneth, and Malni's eyes did widen a little then. "That is a great journey," she said wistfully. "I don't suppose you have need in your caravan for another?"

"No!" Arudal told her sharply. "It will be a dangerous trip, and no place for a woman."

The stable-girl snorted, drawing herself up to her full height. "I can take care of myself as well as any man in this village, and I'll prove it to you now if you like." She crouched slightly, opening her hands as if she meant to grapple with him.

Rhys was grinning widely, and Arudal had to suppress the impulse to kick him in the ribs. The Tharandrostan knew better than to take on a woman in unarmed fighting - her stance was worryingly like those women took at mithlapar tourneys, and if that art had survived in the West, it would be more than embarassing for a peasant girl to send him flying head over heels in front of Rhys. But women's weaponless combat was only for self-defense in extremity: it would not help Malni on the road if there were real fighting, even if they had any reason to risk bringing another native with them.

"What good is skill with your hands, if you are attacked by wild animals or bandits with weapons?" Arudal said reasonably. "Do you have any idea how to use a sword?"

Malni lowered her hands, but her jaw still jutted fiercely. "I killed three wolves with my pike last winter, and I won the Sunheight-feast's archery contest the last two years running."

"Indeed, she would be better than our other new companion," Rhys put in.

"Can you ride?" Arudal asked, certain of the answer.

"I know how to drive a wagon. And think about it, if you keep on into the hills and beyond them this winter, you'll need one. What will you do if one of your men breaks a leg or catches lung-fever, fling him over your horse like a sack?"

"It is not my choice to make, anyway," Arudal told her, for he could think of no answer to that argument. A wagon would slow them - but so would the snow, if it got heavier; and the best rider could break a leg if his steed slipped on bad footing.

"Then you will recommend me to Lord Karsil?" Malni asked eagerly.

"Rhys, this is your problem," Arudal growled. "You recommend her."

Rhys shrugged. "I shall be out here with the horses all night. Go on, Ari: would it not brighten up our company to have a fair and cheerful fighting-may with us? Indeed, I am getting tired of seeing nothing but ugly male faces."

"Rhys wants us to do what?" Sir Thoron burst out when Arudal had explained the situation. "A girl? First we have to take a half-blind scholar - no offense, Ari, you've turned out to be a good squire and you'll make a fine fighter with a little more seasoning - then a useless political lump of lard, and now Rhys wants us to bring his stable-wench along? Is this a mission, or a travelling minstrels' show?"

"If she really can fight, we might want to think about it, sir," Finvar put in. "My own grandmother was a shield-maid before she married my grandfather."

"There would be some advantage to having a local who knows the area along," Sir Shakhor mused. "Though I'd much prefer a hunter or tracker, someone who's used to living rough. And you say she can't ride?"

Flushing, Arudal repeated Malni's suggestion about the wagon.

"Hmm." Sir Salarond swirled the dregs of his cider about thoughtfully. "That isn't the worst idea I've heard, especially..." He looked at Berek, and Arudal could almost hear his calculations. The Hatneth had slowed them badly that day, but if he could be packed into a wagon, with Malni's bow and pike - if her skill lived up to her boasts - as protection if an enemy came that close, then he would be less of a drag on the party, and less of a danger if trouble came. "Eroth, Karsil, what do you think?"

"I think we should find out if the girl really can fight or shoot," Eroth said. "A village champion in a place like this - might mean no more than hitting a target one time of ten, or it might mean that she can shoot the eye out of a flittering sparrow: you never know with country folk. But killing wolves with a pike at least calls for courage, if she is telling the truth."

"I shall see for myself," Karsil said, slipping gracefully from her seat on the bench. She dropped her gauntlets into her helm, picking up the longbow that leaned unstrung on the wall beside her. "Finvar, bring your little bow as well."

By the time they had found practice staves and set up a makeshift target on a straw bale outside the end, quite a crowd had collected around them. Arudal watched with interest, although he was beginning to shiver from the night cold again.

"Here, boy," an older man said, tapping him on the shoulder. "Put this on, you look like you're freezing." He handed Arudal a thick cloak of wool lined with goatskin; Arudal wrapped it gratefully about himself, in spite of the smell.

The stable-girl had dressed in a sleeveless jerkin of sheepskin with the fleece turned in over her woolen tunic, leaving her arms free; her short curls were covered by a cap of boiled leather with sheepskin ear-flaps. Sir Eroth picked up one practice-stave, handing the other to her, and they moved to opposite sides of the circle drawn in the snow.

Sir Eroth's attack was sudden enough to catch Arudal by surprise; Malni barely got her stave up in time to keep from catching the blunt tip in her solar plexus. Instead it skidded along her ribs, but she recovered well, swinging and thrusting with furious enthusiasm. Her footwork was nonexistent, her control clumsy compared to the knight's: still, she managed to get in a lucky thrust to his right thigh, the villagers cheering her on. As Sir Eroth went down on one knee, he rapped her wrist lightly - Arudal could tell that he had pulled the blow, but the stave flew from her hands, and before she could recover, the tip of Sir Eroth's staff was resting on her chest.

Malni bowed to him, a crestfallen look on her face, and reached out to help the knight to his feet. Sir Eroth's back was to Arudal, and he could not hear what was said then, but the stable-girl nodded. Someone came out of the crowd with a longbow and a quiver of arrows, and they moved over to the archery targets.

"Do you mean to shoot against her?" Arudal asked Dame Karsil quietly.

"No. Our purpose is to find out how good she may be, not to show how good we are - or to humiliate her."

It proved, however, that the stable-girl had not been boasting about her skill with a bow. At twenty-five paces, she split a willow-wand cleanly; at thirty-five, even with the blowing snow, she was able to put four arrows into a handspan's space on the straw bale in less than half a minute. Arudal listened enviously as Finvar described the shots to him through the villagers' cheering - even the flames of the torchlight obscured his vision so that he could not quite make out what was happening.

"Rhys found himself a good one there," Finvar said, grinning. "If he changes his mind, though, I wouldn't give you a copper half-penny for the future of his goolies."

Arudal looked at him in bewilderment.

"Ah, I'm sorry. I'd almost forgotten...never mind. Don't worry about it."

"Enough," Karsil was saying to the girl.

Malni turned, grinning against the snow blowing into her face, and said, "Will you take me?"

Sir Salarond coughed loudly, but Dame Karsil ignored him. "Come with me: I would speak with you alone."

As the two females walked off and the crowd began to clear, Arudal looked around for the man who had lent him the cloak. He had caught only a glimpse of a heavy, weathered brown face under a fleece-lined cap - even were his eyesight better, the village folk all looked much the same to him, not differing as widely in colouring as the people of Hatin's City. He stood in the snow waiting, but no one came up to him. At last he went back inside and said to the innkeeper, "Please, someone lent me this outside, and I can't find him to give it back."

The stout little woman glanced at the cloak and smiled. "That's old Mikit's. He's a kind one, right enough. That's him over there, just to the right of the hearth." She ladled a mugful of steaming cider from her great kettle. "Take this to him with it, will you?"

Arudal carried the mug and the cloak over, trying not to look too confused. There were several villagers there, all with their cloaks stripped off to show thick baggy-sleeved tunics and sleeveless jerkins like the one Malni had worn.

"Mikit?" he said.

"Aye, that's me, lad. Ah, the cloak, thank you. From foreign parts, are you? You should get yourself something warmer to wear than all those metal pots, they'll chill in the cold weather something wicked."

Arudal held out the mug. "This is for you as well, sir."

"Thanks again, lad!" Mikit took the mug, draining half of it in a single swallow. "Now there's manners for you, boys," he said to his companions, and then to Arudal, "I'll tell you what, lad. Are you staying a little while? No? Well, come round to my house in the morning. My sister makes the warmest cloaks and hats for three villages around, and we'll get you fitted out so's I don't have to worry about you freezing out there in the snow, hey?"

Arudal thanked him and went back to his companions, more than a little taken aback. After Hatin's City, this friendliness was the last thing he would have expected. But after all, the people of Var Perenil are not like those in the countryside - even Finvar is as different from Lostren as apples from black-roast beans.

"So what in the Abyss is Karsil playing at?" Thoron was asking. "Not that I'll complain too much about having another good longbow with us. The more so since that's what they seem to use around here - if it comes to an ambush with archers, they'll have the range over most of us."

Sir Salarond's lips curved slightly. "Indeed. I would guess that she means to take Malni as a squire. That is, of course, only a guess: she may have something else altogether in mind."

"A girl!" Tirothar squeaked. "As a squire?"

Lostren laughed. "Why not? It might work out better than with the male squires Karsil's had - she might not drag a peasant girl into the worst part of the heaviest battles on her first fight. And Karsil's a woman herself, isn't she?"

"As far as anyone can tell with Elves," Tirothar muttered. "But a human girl, and a peasant at that - it's not right. How could she ever be knighted? And besides that, it's just not right."

"I suggest you tell that to Dame Karsil," Sir Eroth said, smiling himself.

"What's all the fuss about?" Berek asked Arudal crossly.

Arudal tried to tell him, but got only the expected blank look and, "If she can shoot well enough to hire her, what's it matter?"

"Being a squire is a place of honour, even though it means serving a knight and obeying his orders," Arudal explained patiently. As he went on, he used the Bright Elvish words where Western was lacking - though several of those, in turn, were loan-words from Imperial: fealty and chivalry were concepts of Men, not of Elves. "A squire is in a bond of fealty to his knight, just as a knight swears fealty to the Crown - that means freely offering loyalty and service, in war and in peace, whatever is needed. Although squires usually receive some pay, that is a token: the important thing is that the knight is as a father to his squire, teaching him both the arts of war and the proper conduct of a knight - the ways of honour, chivalry, and courtesy. Squires of gentle birth, or those taken on because they have great promise, are usually expected to become knights when they have proven themselves in both valour and honour." Arudal left out the fact that, particularly in more rural lands, knights would often take on older men of lower birth who would do a squire's service for pay and bear the title, but would never themselves be knighted: that, he thought, was too complex for the moment, and he thought it unlikely that Karsil had such an arrangement planned for Malni. Even as he simplified matters for the Western boy, though, it seemed to Arudal that he was trying to explain music to one deaf from birth: the words that had been woven through all his life were no more than simple sounds to Berek.

"What do you mean by honour?"

Arudal stalled. He knew exactly what he meant; but it was a different thing to explain in words - in Bright Elvish, as in Imperial or Common, it was self-explanatory, and in the Western tongue, there was no equivalent. "It is...upholding your oaths, keeping faith with those to whom you owe it. Never acting deceitfully nor unfairly, and striving for what is right rather than for personal advantage. As for chivalry..." The loan-word in Elvish was almost the same as its Imperial source, and went back to the pre-Imperial language that his forebears had shared with the Horse-Tribes, the tongue of the Wheel-Folk. Once it had meant the virtues of the mounted tribes, as contrasted to those of land-grubbers - the Horse-Tribes still used a word of the same derivation with the original sense. In the Imperial days, the chivalry-word had come to mean the best qualities of the Imperial race: still mounted rulers, but taking on the sense of protecting the weak and dealing on fair and equal terms with the strong; and from there, it had come to indicate all that went with knighthood. No wonder the concept is alien to a race that knows little of horses! "When you have seen enough of honour to know it, maybe chivalry will make sense to you as well."

"And what exactly is a knight? Is that the title of your best guardsmen?"

"A knight is usually a fighter, yes, but not always...Men, and sometimes women in my land, have been knighted for skill in magic or scholarship. The knights uphold the realm: it is a title showing their honour and their service to the Crown."

"What are they paid for this service?" Berek asked.

Arudal sighed deeply. This was not, he thought, the time to explain the difference between a knight's salary and that of a skilled man-at-arms in war: it would only settle the Hatneth's ideas of worth as something to be expressed in money.

"Knights are respected by all for the virtue they have proven and the service they give freely to their lords. They are not paid for their oaths, but enter into their service willingly and gladly, promising their lives, if need be, with their fealty."

"So knighthood is a form of vow-slavery, then?"

Arudal's first impulse was to slap the boy's fat face - was Berek deliberately trying to be insulting and obtuse? But then he thought on some of the conversations he and Karsil had held on the nature of freedom. Karsil had never ceased to insist that Arudal was as unfree as any Plainsman in shackles, for the nature of the duties he owed the State, even to wedding by the choice of the House of Procreation, just as a slave might be bred. And Arudal had to grant that the squire's service he did for Thoron could be seen as differing in no external particulars from most of the services his body-slave Cenlac did for him at home. The true difference in the latter lay in Arudal's oath and its ultimate end, his release by being accepted for the greater service of knighthood or by Sir Thoron's consent to let him go; as for the former - Arudal could not quite define it, but he knew that a difference existed. Thinking further, he said slowly, "Quite the opposite: one is service demanded by honour, the other is service forced by necessity."

Berek set his jaw, and Arudal thought irrelevantly of how much like his father it made him look, even with the strong bones smoothed by his plumpness. "A slave by choice is still a slave. In Hatin's City, we are all free, for we saw long ago how oaths lead to slavery."

Arudal thought of eleven-year-old Halta trying to sell her half-starved body on the street, and how her father had been forced to labour himself to sickness and death. It seemed to him that they had known less of freedom than any slave in his family's house, but Berek was still speaking proudly. "My father's guardsmen have their contracts, which set out clearly what they will and will not do and at what price, but my father doesn't own them: they can terminate at any time if they get a better offer. Can your knights do that?"

"Certainly not! They pledge their loyalty - " another Elvish word - "with their oaths."

"Slavery," Berek said triumphantly, folding his arms and leaning back. "A free man can go where he will and do what he likes, so long as he can pay his own way."

"Do you owe no loyalty to friends and family, then?" Arudal asked. The word he knew for "friend" in Western seemed to be something like "business partner" in derivation; he wondered if Malni would be able to improve his vocabulary in such matters.

"Families take care of their own. As for friends, if they can't keep up, it's their look-out," Berek answered casually.

Arudal sighed once more. "That is not a wise attitude for you to take now. Where would you be if I had left you to ride by yourself?"

"You signed my apprenticeship contract, which sets out that you will keep me with you except when you go into the Elven-Home. And I know how much you were paid for it, so I don't think you have any reason to complain about the conditions."

If this keeps up, I shall hit him, Arudal thought, and said, "Excuse me. I must... go visit my horse."

"Why? Didn't Rhys take its tack off right?"

The Western Men, Arudal remembered, were rather straightforward about bodily needs. Caught between anger and a surprising laughter, he said, "Never mind. Excuse me," and made his way hastily out to the privy.

Arudal sat for a little while relieving himself, suppressing the urge to bang his head gently against the wooden wall. If Lostren had indeed had a vision of Berek's friendship being needed to save them - "As Finvar says," he murmured to himself, "we're screwed." He finished his task and cleaned himself, but sat there for a few moments more, thinking longingly of his quiet student's chambers in Var Perenil, far, far away from obnoxious Hatneths, peasant-girl squires, and every other insanity he had suffered since agreeing to come on this mission. Or a nice berth on shipboard as a proper Tharandrostan officer's squire, he thought again, as he had so many times before - I could at least be doing my military service with my own kind, even if the Silent Guard would not take me. But then, Arudal reminded himself, he would never have met Finvar and Lostren. Nor ever seen the Western Land with his own eyes - mixed and disillusioning blessing though that had turned out to be.

In his haste to get away from Berek, Arudal had hardly noticed that the privy door had no latch, though the row of holes along the wooden bench suggested that privacy for one's functions was of little importance here. Now the door opened; he looked up to see Malni's tall figure in the doorway, and bolted to his feet, hastily scrabbling his breeches up.

"What on earth is wrong with you?" the stable-girl asked. "Caught short?" She was grinning widely, and though the light of her lantern blurred her shape a little, Arudal could see the red squire's belt about her waist.

"I, I...don't women have a different privy? Don't you knock?"

"Why?" She strolled in casually, dropping her own breeches, and Arudal fled in undignified panic. Avradi and Aviyani! he thought. Karsil will have to tell her...she can't do that sort of thing around men!

Arudal slowed down as he entered the inn again, trying to calm his breath, though he could still feel the furious heat of his blush like a sunburn on his cheeks and ears. Treading in as dignified a manner as he could, he went back to their table, where the knights were, to his relief, discussing the sensible matters of buying a wagon and getting more blankets and warm clothes.

"Ari," Sir Salarond said finally, "you will go with Rhys and Malni tomorrow in order to buy a wagon and some cold-weather gear. We shall need heavier tents, if they are available..." Arudal took the list in at a single hearing. As a page, he had been taught to remember without needing repetition, and though his tricks of memory had been learned in regards to the furnishing and provisions of a ducal household, the White Company's needs were simple enough. When Salarond had finished, he paused thoughtfully. "You are not used to hard winter travel, are you?"

"No, sir." Arudal thought longingly for a moment of the times he had been taken to the Hidden Estate for the Sundark festivities. Even in the lower part of Tharandrost's mountains, the snow was seldom deeper than his ankles at the end of the year, but he had always been wrapped up warmly in fur blankets, listening to the jingling of bridle-bells as the sturdy draught horses drew their wagons over the thin white blanket on the ground and looking up at the falling flakes, pale glimmers against the darkness...

"And Rhys is from the southern plains...Finvar, you shall go with them as well: I think of all of us, you know best what will be needed."

"Yes, sir," Finvar agreed cheerfully. "Sir, if we shall have a wagon, then I think if we can, it would be well to provision ourselves differently. If the weather gets harder as we go inland, we shall want plenty of honeyed foods, and also fatty sausages and such, for the cold burns the strength from the body more quickly than anything. And this is the best time of year to buy meat of the sort we need. They should have slaughtered just as the weather turned freezing..."

The little spikes of helmet-matted gray hair sticking up from Sir Salarond's head waved as he nodded impatiently. "Yes, yes. I shall leave that to your judgement. If this inn has a bath-house, we were best to use it now. It may be some time before we see much warm water again."

The knights cleaned themselves first, then left the stone-bath to their squires. In the dim light of the candles, Arudal could see Berek's blubbery rolls of fat more clearly than he liked, and was disgusted again: no one in Tharandrost - and certainly not a youth in reasonable health - would be allowed to come into such a condition. The Westerner's degenerate shape was the more shocking next to the bodies of the squires. Heavy-set as Finvar was, his extra weight was no more than a healthy layer of padding over thick muscle and bone; though Tirothar looked lanky when clothed, naked, the wiry muscles stood out sharply under his skin. Lostren was neatly made without an ounce of spare fat, close to the classical Imperial build, though taller and narrower in the shoulders and chest than Arudal. Despite the discrepancy between himself and the others, Berek lounged in a state of sublime ease, his flabby thighs and gross belly quivering as he slapped the sweat from them with one of the leafy whisks, and Arudal looked away quickly, shuddering. It took a few moments for him to drive the sight from his mind and settle down, half-closing his eyes and breathing in the welcome heat.

The door opened: Arudal heard Tirothar's squawk of surprise, then yelped himself, his hands going hastily to cover his privates as Malni strolled in, unconcernedly naked. She looked at the cowering youths, shaking her head.

"What is the matter with you?" she asked, seating herself on one of the upper benches. "First Ari runs from me in the privy, and now you all grab yourselves as if I were a werewolf come to bite off your stones. Bright Ones with us, has none of you ever seen a woman before?"

"You can't come in here!" Tirothar squeaked. "It's not - not decent! Get out!"

"I don't speak your tongue." She paused, then said, "Do men and women never bathe together where you come from?"

"No!" Arudal answered firmly, keeping his head turned away from her. "It's not..." He fumbled for the Western translation of decent, but the word escaped him. "Not fitting. Not seemly."

"Finavi told me that the squires were bathing now, and I should go clean the stables off myself," Malni said. "If I understand, I am to follow her orders, yes?"

Arudal paused, trying to arrange his flustered thoughts into the Western language. "Such things are different among Elves," he said at last. "Among Men in our land, women are...they should hide their bodies from men, save the man to whom they are wedded."

"But you are of Elf-blood yourself, are you not, Ari? Why do I affright you so?"

Arudal was scrambling for an answer when he heard a strange high-pitched sound: for the first time since they had met, Berek was laughing. A hot red tide of rage mingled with embarassment rose behind his eyes: he would have slapped the fat youth then, if he had dared take his hands away from his private parts. As it was, he said savagely, "Shut up, Berek!" and then fought down his temper enough to answer, "I was not raised in the Elf-Home, but among Men."

"Huh! Well, I shall obey finavi's command, whatever the rest of you think."

Tirothar got up and sidled crabwise to the door, hands still over his genitals and trying to keep from showing her his buttocks. If the other squire had not looked so ridiculous, Arudal would have followed his example at once. But he had already lost too much dignity in front of the peasant girl that night - and he could not deny that she was in the right to follow Karsil's orders. Even in his confusion, Arudal had noticed, as well, that she used the title by which he himself had addressed Karsil in his time as the Elf's loaned squire - Karsil must have told her new squire to call her that, for Arudal was quite sure that Malni did not speak Bright Elvish; and that, he thought, was something of a compliment to himself.

"What is she saying, Ari?" Finvar asked. Arudal looked at his squire-brother. Finvar had let the whisk in his hand droop to shadow his privates, but otherwise seemed undistressed by the female intrusion on their bath. Arudal explained.

"Ah. Well, there's no harm in it. Usually at home we take the stone-bath separately, but the women can hardly help seeing us when we go out to roll in the snow - and the other way, as well." He grinned. "You're sure she doesn't speak our language? You'll get a crick in your neck with it turned around that way, and she's a pretty one to look at. Much nicer than me, if your tastes don't run against the stream."

Arudal thought that Finvar was about to say something more, but Lostren coughed. The Artegalian closed his mouth abruptly, giving Arudal a peculiar look, then quickly turned away and began to whisk himself vigorously.

Has everyone around me gone mad? Arudal wondered. He noticed that Berek had made no effort to cover himself. Malni's shamelessness was not her own, then, but truly ordinary here; and he thought of slaves he had seen at heavy labour, the women, like the men, stripped to a bare loincloth with their udders dangling like animals'. Without meaning to, he found himself comparing that memory to the brief glimpse he had inadvertently gotten of Malni's body: shoulders as broad as his own, arms muscled as one might expect of an archer, breasts smaller and hips wider than a Tharandrostan woman's, but firm and sturdily made...At least he would grant that the peasant girl had nothing to be ashamed of in her nakedness; but he heartily wished that she had waited until the men were through.

"What...strength bow you pull?" Finvar was asking Malni clumsily.

"An hundredweight and a fifth," she replied, pride in her voice.

Finvar's brow creased with the effort of translating the weight. Their informants had taught them the measuring system used in the West, but it was confusing to most of the Kantareans: the ounce was the same, and most of the weight-words were largely unchanged; but a Western pound was only ten ounces rather than sixteen, and a Western stone was ten Western pounds, rather than fourteen Imperial - thus six pounds and four ounces lighter altogether than the Imperial stone. Arudal, who had learned most of his mathematics in the form of currency and weight conversions between Tharandrost, the Terashim, and the folk of the Far South, said quickly, "Seventy-five pounds."

"That is a strong bow," Finvar agreed. Arudal thought that it was rather a light pull, even for a woman - most Tharandrostan bows went up to an hundred and fifty, and a strong trained man could easily draw well over two hundred - but he supposed that for someone of Common blood, it would be very heavy, especially since longbows were supposed to be harder to draw than the short recurve of the Imperial archers.

"Do you shoot?" Malni asked him.

"I shoot...short bow. From horse. Show you tomorrow. Pulls...shit, Ari, what's an hundred and twenty pounds in Western?"

"Two hundredweight less one stone and two," Arudal translated.

"Yeah. That. But...short bow is easier, you understand. Not as tight."

"Ah," Malni said, clearly satisfied. "May I try it tomorrow?"

"Sure."

By this time, Arudal was beginning to feel desperate for a bucket of cold water, but he couldn't hear Malni so much as shifting on her bench. At last he said, "Malni, I need to go out. Will you please at least turn your head?"

"Why? You've nothing to be ashamed of - you're very pretty, you know."

Arudal cringed inwardly in embarassment, but drew a deep breath to calm himself and said, "I would ask you to respect our customs as well as you can while you're with us. Please!"

"Oh, very well."

Arudal hastened towards the door that led into the antechamber, but Finvar said, "Ari, there's no buckets out there. They roll in the snow, the same way we do at home. Go on, it's dark, no one will see you."

Reluctantly Arudal went out the other door - to protect his modesty, he would have foregone the enjoyment of the sharp chill after the stone-bath's heat, but he knew that he had to clean the sweat from his body somehow. Finvar had been right, though: the snow was still falling, and only one sputtering torch, shielded beneath the inn's overhanging eaves, lit a little patch of churned snow outside the stone-bath's door. He ran past it, out into the darkness where he could see clearly, and flung himself down to roll, gasping in pleasure as the icy chill bit into his overheated skin. The only thing he could liken it to was diving off the edge of a ship after sweating at the sail-ropes on a hot day, but this was so much more intense that there was no describing it: the blood seemed to rush to his head, almost dizzying, but leaving him with a vast sense of purified contentment. Even the realization that he would have to come back in through the stone-bath or walk around and through the inn naked could hardly shake the pure feeling of total physical ease - though he hesitated at the door all the same.

She is a Common woman, after all, Arudal reminded himself. Why should I be more concerned about her than about a bath-house slave? With an effort of will, he opened the door and went in. Though he could not keep himself from covering his privates with his hands, at least he was able to walk proudly rather than scuttling as Tirothar had.

"Good, isn't it?" Finvar said as Arudal took his place on the bench again. "I tell you, it almost makes winter worthwhile. At home the drifts pile up past the eaves of the houses, and you can step out of the bath straight into snow above your head. Northman women even give birth in the stone-bath when they can."

Arudal nodded, but he was already thinking of something else. He would have to get Berek alone somehow to ask him about magic in the West: it was clear from the boy's reaction that he would not speak of it when the party members he thought of as Men were within hearing.

Thus he waited until Berek had gone out to the snow, then left the stone-bath to get dressed. Arudal went out again for his second roll, then clothed himself hastily and followed the Western boy through.

Sir Thoron was already snoring sonorously in their little chamber; Berek was clumsily taking his boots off. Arudal tapped him on the shoulder. The fat youth started, looking at the Tharandrostan with sudden terror.

"Come with me," Arudal whispered. "I would speak with you alone." He gestured for Berek to buckle up his shoes and put his cloak on.

Cringing like a slave that expected a whipping, Berek followed Arudal down the stairs and outside into the snowy darkness. The stone-bath's heat still glowing within him, Arudal found the cold easy to bear, though an icy wind had sprung up to whip the snow about them.

"Earlier today," Arudal said softly, "you said something of learning magic. I would know more."

Berek glanced around fearfully, his pupils wide in the darkness.

"There is no one within earshot, and you have nothing to fear from me. Come, tell me what you know of magic and how it works here," Arudal coaxed.

"Is it not the same everywhere?"

"It is different in our lands," Arudal answered. He debated with himself for a moment as to how much he should tell Berek, but finally said, "Many of our spells do not work here as they do at home: the Wrath changed this part of the world."

Berek nodded. "There are tales of how the Mordhagoernim can cast fireballs from their fingertips, or point at a stone and say, 'Fall', and the stone will fall to dust. But I had always thought those to be children's tales, like stories of the lands where men's heads grow beneath their shoulders." He paused, and Arudal saw a look of brightness shivering slowly into his face, like the little white petals of a sun-greeter beginning to tentatively unfold in a ray of light. "Magic is the slow process by which the world works, which, if a wise man can grasp, he can turn it to his will. A spell cannot shake a stone to dust in an instant - but if a castle is built on rock, and there be any weakness or crack in its foundations, a spell can seek them out: the mage may learn that a war will come to pass in ten years' time, and set his enchantment, so that when the arrows begin to fly, the castle's walls are found to be crumbling underfoot. And therefore foolish and ignorant men fear magic, but for those who are able to grasp it, it is the highest of studies."

Do I look like that when I speak of philology? Arudal wondered - for Berek's plump dark features transformed as he spoke, so that there was almost a look of beauty on his face. Perhaps I have, after all, misjudged him.

"How does the mage bring his will to pass?" Arudal asked carefully.

"First he must learn how the world is made, the lore of stones and plants and weather: a rock cannot be made to shatter unless it is already flawed, even if only in the slightest. Things cannot be made to turn against their nature, but they can be made to strengthen or lessen some part of it. And all things are bound together, some more loosely and some more closely. A sapphire shares some part of the nature of the sky, as silver does of water and gold of fire; and if two things have once touched, then they shall always be touching. The mage must know this, and how all things are bound: then he may make rites that use these likenesses to shape his will."

Arudal nodded: this was the root of ritual magic, the laws of sympathy and contagion.

"And then he must study the skies, for if the stars are set wrongly, then there will be no power behind his spells: the strength of all magic comes from the stars."

Arudal drew in a deep breath. The Wrath had blasted all the might of the gods from the earth in a single instant: of course the mages of the West had learned to draw upon the power of the untouched heavens! And that would be harder to reach and thinner in strength than the world-might used in the Middle Land...

"I see," Arudal murmured. "How much do you know of these things?"

"Some little bit," Berek answered, not without pride. "My father let me start studying magic when I was ten, on the condition that I never speak of it: he knew how useful it could be if worked in utter secret. But I brought my books with me - I can read my ephemeris and cast the stars for almost anything. My teacher warned me that I was not wise enough to lay spells, lest I make a choice now that should destroy me in some years' time, but if I were ordered to under the terms of my 'prentice-contract...." He trailed off hopefully. Arudal could not help smiling: he remembered when he had learned his own first spell of sorcery, the same he had tried to work on the pebble when they landed. There would be no counting the number of innocent little rocks he had blasted to dust that week...

"We shall see. For now, would you be willing to speak of these things to the other members of our party? Several of them are skilled in magic as it is practiced in our lands, and would greatly like to know whether those skills may work at all here."

Berek chewed his lower lip a little, his eyes dropping; but at last he said, "I will speak to them, if you are sure it is safe and they will keep my secret. Magic is not against the law, but if it were known in the City that I am learning magic, there would be none willing to trade with me for fear of enchantment, fear that I might beguile them or enslave their souls. If enough folk were made afraid or angry, they might bring me to the burning-cage in spite of my father's strength, as if I were a black-haired babe."

"We shall not speak of it," Arudal reassured him, though the boy's words set his back up: he had no doubt that those very things were what Berek, or at least his father, intended. Kantar and Tharandrost had strict laws against personal assault with magic or mind-magic; here, such things would be beyond enforcing, and the only control would be the burning-cage for those foolish enough to be found out. But, out of fairness and because Berek had taken a risk in telling him what he needed to know, he said, "And if you please, accept my apologies for saying you were useless. The knowledge you can give us is..." Arudal was about to say "beyond price", but thought in time of how a man of Hatin's City might take that, and said instead, "quite sufficient to make up for your other lacks."

"Does that mean you will get a carriage, or a wain, or something else so that I don't have to ride?" Berek asked hopefully.

Arudal gritted his teeth. He recognised the trained merchant's reflex of re-negotiation whenever value was admitted, but that hardly meant he had to like it. "As it happens, we had already decided to buy a wagon here. Not for your sake," he added quickly to keep Berek from getting inflated ideas of his worth to the party, "but because our healing magics do not work here as they would at home, and there is always the chance of an injury or illness that could keep one of us from sitting a horse."

"I think the horses themselves are doing me that injury," Berek muttered.

"It is also true," Arudal told him severely, "that you are slowing us down so that it will hardly make a difference if we bring a wagon. Still, I shall continue trying to teach you to ride." Even though I think the effort is hopeless, he added to himself. "Now let us go to sleep, for we must rise early if we are to get the things we need and leave this village tomorrow."

In actuality, it took the White Company party two more days to get themselves
and their wain fully fitted out for the journey. Rhys' command of at least Low
Western was improving with amazing speed: he seemed to spend every spare
moment talking with Malni, and had shown her the rudiments of horse-riding.
Unlike Berek, the peasant girl seemed to be a natural rider, graceful and sensitive
to the movements of her steed. Once or twice Finvar, watching, nudged Arudal and
made some remark which completely passed the Tharandrostan by, though Arudal
gathered it was meant to be rather rude.

Sir Salarond and Sir Eroth had time to interrogate Berek on the subject of
magic in the West, and after some coaxing, Berek was convinced to show them
his books. Much of the lore in them was familiar to Arudal and the Kantareans
as ritual magic, but the key elements - the need to draw power from the stars and
the slowness of magical effect - were new and, in some cases, disconcerting. The
Westerners also knew the stars and constellations, not only by different names,
but in a different way. Where the Kantareans held that the gods ruled the moving
stars that ringed the Earth, the Westerners thought that all stars were themselves
gods or spirits, and thought of the constellations as actual families of beings that
would aid or strive against the moving stars. And through all that, Arudal could
not help remembering how it had felt to try sorcery here, the irresistible sense that
the power he was used to was still there, but somehow impossible to reach - as if it
needed only some slight change in the way he was working for the spark of his spell
to leap to its fuel.

Still more importantly, at least to Arudal, was the fact that he had gotten a
chance to update his growing dictionary of the Western language and correct some
of his guesses about its grammar, as well as clarifying the tonal component in High
Western - only semi-tonal, as it happened, or it would have been far more difficult
for him to understand Lord Hatneth and Berek. He had more than enough material
for a full thesis now; for a series of books, in fact. And it's mine, all mine! Arudal
gloated. Not only the language itself, but the information it provided on Imperial:
among the questions it answered, High Western had an irregular verb kula-, which
had to derive from the hypothetical Middle Imperial kaola- that had so vexed
Arudal back in Var Perenil, but the semantic shift suggested that the original kâla-
had provided both kaola- and kala-, with a separation of meaning occuring in the
century when Old Imperial gave way to Middle Imperial, and kaola- being relegated
largely to the dialect of the lesser races within the Empire, even as most Plainsman
slaves spoke their own haphazard dialect of Imperial. Dr. Grímhjálm would, Arudal
thought, be amply repaid for having sent him on this mission.

The snow kept falling steadily. By the time they were ready to leave, it was knee-deep in places, so that Malni had to block the wheels of the wain and fit on the wide wooden runners that would allow the draught horses to draw it as if it were a sledge. Tirothar claimed that she had remarked on what magnificent draught-animals their warhorses would make, being so much larger and more heavily muscled than the Western steeds, but Arudal was not sure whether he believed that or not. In any case, she certainly seemed to know how to handle the wagon. She was driving it when they set off, with Berek sitting beside her, looking disconsolate as she tried to explain to him how to handle the reins and the little popping-whip - not used to strike the horses, as Arudal had thought in horror that it might be, but cracked above their heads with a sharp noise to get their attention.

Although the weather had grown even colder, Arudal himself was far more comfortable than he had been on the way to the village, with a thick shirt of woven wool strips under his gambeson, warm sheepskin gloves lined inside with a second layer of the silky-soft wool yielded by the long-haired Western goats, as well as a sort of tabard of goat-wool over his armour beneath a long cape of sheepskin with the fleece turned inwards and a rather battered sheepskin cap - a present urged on him by old Mikit - on his helmet. The war-horses had blankets over and under their barding to keep the worst chill off the metal; the others were more lightly blanketed, and their lower legs were all wrapped against the snow. Rather to Arudal's surprise, their clothes and bedding were remarkably free of the vermin he would have expected after three days in a village inn with no magic to charm insects away: it was the local custom to hang garments and blankets up in the smoke of the stone-bath to dry while it was being heated, which drove out fleas and lice.

Chapter 19: Amandeth's Eve

"The Sun dies into darkness,
And fiery leaves to mould,
The candle's light must gutter,
The beating heart grow cold.

"Shadow-Lord, Soul-Claimer,
Guide our ghosts through night,
To dead and living offer
Your blessing as our light..."
- Amandeth's Eve hymn (House of Arudal variation)

For two days, they rode on into the hills without trouble, seeing only the occasional shepherd or goatherd with his flock. Finvar had gotten an ointment to keep their lips from cracking in the cold, and Arudal soon realized that the Artegalian's advice about bringing sweet food and fatty meats was sound as well, for when they stopped to eat, he found himself craving those things. He only regretted that there was seldom a chance for him to make his black-roast tea in the mornings, for its warming strength would have been welcome against the shock of leaving the thick-felted tent for the icy air outside. They still forced Berek to ride for a couple of hours daily, but, freed from the brutal effort of eight to ten hours in the saddle every day, even he was gradually hardening to the rigours of travel. Sir Eroth and Arudal often took turns riding in the wain with him, asking him questions about the Western magic, and as the Hatneth began to feel more at ease in that regard, he also became cheerier and less sulky about turning his hand to camp chores.

The hills grew higher and rougher as they travelled, their whiteness marred in the daylight by blotchy gray blurs which, as night fell, resolved themselves in Arudal's sight into great rocky crags and small gnarled trees. The horses found less and less grazing beneath the snow, and had to be fed grain from their stores - Arudal thought they would have had to bring a wain in any case in order to feed their steeds on the way through here. Because Malni told campfire-tales of dead men walking in the Barren Hills, though Berek scoffed at most of her stories, Sir Salarond ordered Arudal to take a double watch each night and sleep in the wagon during part of the day. She had also, perhaps more worryingly, pointed out that few people ever tried to cross through the Barren Hills, and almost never in winter, with which Berek agreed: he said that trade from the other side usually came to Hatin's City by river down past the hills and to the sea, then up by ship.

Their third day out was Amandeth's Eve. Sir Salarond spoke the first prayers for the dead before they mounted up, and they rode in a silence broken only by the crunching of the horses' hooves through the snow and the occasional creak from the wain's wooden runners or jingle of armour. Arudal was beginning to feel miserably homesick, as he had not been since his first months in Var Perenil. Even surrounded by Kantareans, he had felt at home on the ship, but this bleak cold land seemed to go on forever. At home, the wind would just be biting with the first breath of winter, the trees in full flame; there would be baskets of apples everywhere for the Feast of Amandeth, the air in his home sweet with a trace of myrrh and nightspice in memory of the dead, and the vases in front of the funeral statues in the drawing room filled with flowers and bright autumn leaves.

Or maybe the family would have gone up to the Hidden Estate, singing in the sharp frost of the mountain air: there, the living and the dead would feast and worship together in the little black marble chapel, the ghosts giving their blessings to their kin on the green earth and the live family members doing honour to those who stood beside them in Shadow. Although Arudal did not have the heart to sing, the memory-songs for the dead and the hymns to Amandeth that were sung on these days every year ran through his head in mournful counterpoint to the sound of Inmanat's hooves beneath him.

If he died on this mission and Amandeth did not give his soul leave to linger in Shadow - unlikely; but as a ghost, if the other party members were slain as well and the ship never came back, he would have to find a way dryshod across the Western Ocean - it might be that his family would never know what had happened to him. Arudal thought of his mother Minlulin weeping quietly as she brushed the long fur of her cats, his father riding alone and sorrowful in the woods of their little estate outside Tharabruthnan, and his younger brother Arukhat sitting red-eyed from crying in the mews where he always went to be alone, and almost snuffled a little himself.

Towards dusk, Inmanat began to shy and balk, as though there were something in the snow before him that only he could see. Arudal stroked his neck, murmuring, "Good horse, brave horse," until Inmanat stood steady, then breathed deeply, letting his sight fall into Shadow and casting about with his mind as far as he could. He had no sense of any Ukuthrim as far as he could reach. Forcing his awareness back to the green earth, Arudal tried again to urge Inmanat forward, but the horse shied again and crow-jumped suddenly sideways, even as Finvar frowned and reached for his bow with one hand, steadying his own steed back with the other.

"What is it, Ari, Finvar?" Sir Salarond called, turning his horse to ride back. "Is something there?"

"Not Ukuthrim, at any rate, sir," Arudal said. "It may be that he smells wolves or other wild animals, or only that he is tired and balky."

"Windfoot is uneasy as well, sir," Finvar added.

"Hmm." The healer-knight raised his voice. "Bows out, all! Look carefully; there may be trouble."

With Salarond's horse only a few lengths ahead of him, Inmanat followed along again, though he shook his head and neighed loudly. Arudal reached down to slide his arm into his shield-straps. He was carrying the large escutcheon on horseback, for there was no hope of managing a buckler and reins at the same time.

The mournful howl of a wolf rose and fell through the gathering gloom, its cold eerie sound prickling down Arudal's spine. Inmanat whinnied, backing up and tossing his head violently. With uneasy thoughts of the rocks and broken ground hidden by the snow, Arudal did his best to soothe his mount. Sure-footed as Imperial horses might be, wolves would be less of a danger to the two of them than a panicked dash over uneven footing. *At least if there are wolves nearby, there is unlikely to be an ice-cat here: if ice-cats are so like to arathra, they will kill other predators or chase them from their range.*

The first arrow struck Arudal's shield with a shock that went through his arm, banging it against Inmanat's side. The little Imperial horse reared, shrieking, and broke into a wild gallop; there was nothing Arudal could do save keep his seat and try to steer Inmanat away from what looked like the worst patches of rocky ground - the gods be thanked, he could see well enough in the dimness to tell! Behind him, he could hear shouting and a deep angry snarl; from what, there was no guessing, for it sounded louder than any earthly creature should be able to make. Another arrow sang past his ear, and with a great effort, Arudal managed to guide Inmanat into a wide circle: better to have his shield than his unprotected back towards the unknown archer.

Now Arudal could see the lightning-flashes of his comrades' swords, and the dark shapes of men jabbing at them with pikes from the ground. A huge gray dog or wolf leapt up at Sir Thoron, its weight tearing him from his saddle. As the scent of blood reached Inmanat's nostrils, the horse screamed again, bucked fiercely, and tried to wheel. All Arudal's strength and skill could not keep him moving towards the combat, but the Tharandrostan managed to get his horse to circle instead of fleeing straight away.

Thoron was on his feet again, his red-flaming sword blurring out in fierce stabs as he tried to hold the giant wolf from his throat. Finvar wheeled his steed behind the animal, hacking down, but then had to turn to defend himself from two of the pikemen; from the wagon-bench, Malni was holding off another one...Then Inmanat began to buck again in earnest, and Arudal had all he could do to stay on and barely in control of his horse, though he was almost crying with frustration and shame.

At last Inmanat stood blowing and trembling in the snow, his blanket soaked and dripping with sweat. The battle was over, the White Company members dismounted and looking at the bodies of their attackers - it was dark enough now for Arudal to see them clearly. He rode Inmanat back at a slow walk, reluctant to look his comrades in the face when - as it must seem to them - he had fled from the fight.

Sir Thoron grunted as Arudal slipped from his horse's back. "Told you your palfrey'd run," the knight said. "Damn shame we lost the warhorses on shipboard." He thumped Arudal on the shoulder. "Now don't take on about it, my squire. You've nothing to be ashamed of - it wasn't any cowardice in you that took you out of the fight. You don't know how to fight from horseback anyway; you'd have been little help." The knight's woolen tabard was blotched with blood, but from the ease of Thoron's movements, Arudal thought that it must all have come from their attackers. None of the dead bore any more armour than a few mismatched bits of hardened leather - a cap on one, another's breastplate, arm-bracers on a third - and padded woolen jerkins, now mostly sodden with blood. The clothing over the travellers' plate-armour must have deceived the outlaws into thinking it was safe to attack, for though there were more than twenty slain on the ground, they had had no chance against the heavily armoured Kantareans.

Behind him, someone gasped, and Arudal turned to look. The corpse of the giant wolf was shifting, its hide spreading out as the body drew inward upon itself, until what lay there was clearly a man beneath a huge wolf-pelt, its paws splayed over his arms and empty mask drawn down over his brown-bearded face.

"Don't touch that!" Salarond snapped as Finvar bent closer in curiosity. The Artegalian squire leapt backward as if he had been struck with a whip.

Sir Eroth and Tirothar were going among the bodies, their blades stabbing sharply downward to make sure that none of the attackers still lived. One cried out at the last blow - and suddenly a wave of dizziness swept over Arudal, his sight blackening, and he fought for breath. Something was pressing hard against his mind; it felt as though the walls of his skull were beginning to bend inwards beneath its force. He fought back as best he could, envisioning his mind as a fortress walled with adamant, his strength surging out to push the unseen assailant away.

Then, as swiftly as the attack had come, it was gone. Arudal realized that he was sitting down in the snow, hands pressed against the sides of his helm, with his companions staring at him.

"First battle takes some like that," Thoron said roughly. "You'll get used to it."

Arudal's knight was turning away when Sir Salarond took him by the arm. "No, Thoron. This is more than first-blood sickness. Get your squire up and come into the wain with me."

Thoron lifted Arudal to his feet as though he were weightless. "Take your helm off before you puke in it. Can you walk?"

Arudal lifted his helmet off and took a couple of steps. His legs were shaky, but he was able to hold himself up.

Malni was still standing on the wagon-board with a bloody pike in her hands, staring down at the ragged body of the man she had spitted. Like the rest of them, he wore a wolfskin sewn to his cloak, though there had been no sign of any but their leader changing shape, and no Shadow-glimmer hovered over the animal pelt. Malni's thick sheepskin jerkin was slashed in two places, but there was no sign of blood on it: she had been lucky.

"Go on," Salarond said to her. "You did very well, and there's no shame in being shocked at your first kill."

Malni gulped as though she were trying not to throw up, nodded, put down her pike carefully, and swung down from the wagon. Berek was huddled in the back, and Salarond ordered him out unceremoniously.

"What's so important about a new squire getting sick the first time he sees men killed, then?" Thoron asked.

Instead of replying directly, Sir Salarond turned to Arudal. "Ari, can you tell us what happened there?"

"I think...I have never felten it before, but I thinke when that last man was killed, his spirit tried...tried to get in."

"What in Amanvon's name do you mean by that?" Thoron demanded.

Arudal looked down at the floorboards. When he said nothing, Sir Salarond told the other knight, "Arudal has the gift of keeping spirits. I had hoped, when he said nothing about it, that he would not be at risk in battle - but I see now that I was wrong. Arudal, do you have his soul inside you, or did you turn it away?"

"I turned it away," Arudal answered. "I didn't think - I coulde have taken and kept him if I had thoughten to be ywarned, but it was so sudden..."

"Will this happen whenever you are present at a death?"

"I knowe not, sir. Those with my talent...agathurokim usually have other duties than battle. I oughte to be able to shielden better against spirits if I am awaiting..."

Sir Thoron made a strangled noise. "Salarond, are you telling me that my squire can't be allowed to fight?"

"You saw what happened to Ari there. Imagine that in the thick of battle, if his shielding were to fail or be overcome by a stronger will. It was the gods' blessing this time, that his horse kept him far from the fighting until the bodily danger was over."

Thoron struck himself on the forehead, his gauntlet ringing off his helm. "Aaugh. Salarond. This is turning into one of the screwiest gods-cursed mission I've ever been on! What do you think I'm going to do with a squire who has to be - how far does this thing work, Ari?"

"Approximately some fifty paces, sir. At least, I was tolden that a spirit muste to be within that range for me, for me to..."

"Right. Fifty paces from anyone actually getting killed."

"We didn't bring Ari along as a fighter, Thoron," Sir Salarond pointed out patiently. "We didn't even bring him so he could be your squire. But it's your responsibility to keep him out of danger, and you needed to know this."

"If that's the problem, all we have to do is leave him on that nervous wreck of a palfrey, and I can guarantee he won't come near any danger other than getting his neck broken." Sir Thoron threw up his hands. "I don't know. Maybe we should just go make sure the wolf-man isn't getting up again now that it's dark, hmm?"

"Are you fit, Ari?" Sir Salarond asked.

"Yes, sir."

"Can you tell if a spirit is still in a body?"

"Yes, sir, if the body is dead."

"Come along."

Arudal looked at the man in the wolf-fell for a little while. He had been a large man even for the Western Common race, heavy-boned; his bare arms and chest were covered with thick hair, so that it was hard to see where man and wolf separated, save that the man's arms bore thick rings of burnished bronze. Arudal could feel no spirit lingering within him - but both the man and his pelt glimmered bluish-black in Shadow. Dutifully Arudal reported that; Sir Salarond picked up a pike to lift the wolf-hide away from the body, then nodded to Sir Thoron. Thoron's sword flashed down in a streak of red fire; the bearded head rolled free, a little blood dribbling dark from the neck, and the gleam died about the headless corpse, though it still shimmered over the wolf-hide.

"It would probably be best to burn it," Sir Shakhor suggested. "But we ought to track these men back to their lair. If we didn't kill them all, a fire here would make us easy meat for any archers they might have left."

"True enough," Salarond agreed. "But I don't like leaving it, even for a little time. Karsil, can you touch such a thing without taking hurt from it?"

"I can. It is seldom indeed that tainted magics of this sort can harm an Elf, and this is not a thing of such power that I need fear it." The Elven knight stripped off her gauntlets and knelt down, rolling up the pelt fur-side in with fastidious flicks of her long fingers; Lostren brought a sack out of the wain, and Karsil dropped it in and tied the sack up tightly. Sir Salarond held his hands palm-down over it, praying for a few moments, and then carried it into the wagon.

"Now you are right: we should go in search of them. Shakhor, Karsil, Thoron - you three, and your squires, should be sufficient to manage it, for I have never heard of bandits leaving their main strength back when they attacked a group on the road."

As Rhys lit two covered lanterns, Arudal went back to Inmanat. To both his relief - for he had feared that the horse would be grievously chilled - and his shame that he had not been able to see to it himself, he saw that Malni had already rubbed the dripping sweat from the little gelding's hide and changed his sodden blanket for a dry one. "Thank you," he said gratefully.

"You're welcome," she replied. "He's such a sweet little thing, I wouldn't want him catching a chill. I've never seen anyone ride like you, either! I thought sure you were going to be killed when he started running, and then when he bucked..."

"I was well-taught," Arudal answered, awkward at her praise. He was a good rider by Tharandrostan standards, but by no means a great one: there had almost always been a few in his own age-group at school who could outdo him on horseback. "And you fought well. We were right to bring you with us."

"So you were," Malni answered unabashed. "You deserve a reward for speaking up for me."

Before Arudal could say anything, she had grabbed him, bending down to kiss him soundly on the lips. He was too surprised to break free, standing still in her embrace and waiting for her to let go of him.

Arudal heard a deep grunt beside him, as though someone had just been punched in the stomach. He turned his head to see Rhys, staring at the two of them in - dismay? Anguish: even he could recognise the look of pain on the Plainsman's scruffy-bearded face. Dear Amandeth, he doesn't think that I mean to breed with her, does he?

Rhys turned and stamped off, lanterns in his hands, and Arudal stammered, "I must, must go now. Excuse me!" He put his helm back on hastily before Malni could try to kiss him again and hurried back to Sir Thoron, who was talking in low tones with Shakhor and Karsil.

The bandits' tracks were easy to follow up the hill in the snow. They found the two archers lying behind a ridge of rocks, their sprawled limbs already stiffening. The long shaft of one of Karsil's arrows stood out of the eye of one; the other had a shorter arrow through his throat, and a couple of broken shafts showed where the Kantarean shots had struck the stony natural barricade. Karsil paused a moment to retrieve all the arrows - she, Shakhor, and Finvar could shape their own shafts and fletchings, but there would be no replacing the Valderian steel heads here in the West - and they went on.

The tracks led back further to a cave in the rocks. They smelled the fire-smoke before they saw the first glimmer of light, drawing swords and spreading out into a formation. After a few moments, Karsil murmured, "If anyone is in there, they neither move nor breathe."

Sir Shakhor looked at Arudal. The Tharandrostan closed his eyes, reaching outwards, but sensed nothing. "No, sir," he whispered.

Cautiously the party approached the cave. Its mouth was very narrow, and protected by another high ridge: one man with a pike could hold off a whole band of attackers there. Thoron moved forward, going in first, with Karsil and Shakhor behind him and the squires following after.

The bandits' lair proved to be several linked caves, filled with a scattered mess of filthy blankets, clothes, and a mixed jumble of things, mostly broken. As they entered the last one, Arudal heard a muffled gasp followed by Rhys crying out in the Plainsman tongue. He looked up, and bit back a retch. This had been the outlaws' storehouse; but what hung from the ceiling was two human corpses, gutted, smoked and roughly haggled at with knives, as though the bandits had just sawed off hunks of meat whenever they got hungry. The heads were still on, though eyeless and earless - the smaller still had its long sand-brown hair falling almost to the floor; it might have been a woman. Both throats gaped bloodlessly, slit vertically from the breastbone down to the chin like the throats of bled pigs.

"May the gods be with us," Sir Shakhor murmured. "I had thought we might sleep here tonight, but - no. Not for all the gold in the old Imperial treasuries."

Finvar gulped agreement; the rest of them could say nothing.

"I think," Karsil said, "that it were best if we carried the bodies up. Let fire cleanse both the murderers and their victims."

When they had returned to tell Sir Salarond what they had found, he agreed that Karsil's plan was the best. Rhys did not even look at Arudal when he agreed to help Malni guard Berek and the wain, but Arudal needed no gift of reading feelings to sense the chill coming off him. The rest of them loaded the bodies of their attackers onto the pack-horses, leading the animals carefully up the path to the cave. Being the smallest and lightest, Arudal stood on Finvar's shoulders to get the two bodies off the bronze hooks from which they hung, though he shuddered at the touch of the butchered human flesh even through his gloves.

Sir Salarond did his best to straighten the half-stripped limbs of the bandits' victims, covering the ravages of their devourers with the least filthy of the blankets before laying them beside the fire-pit with the assorted human bones that had been scattered about the caves. The bandits themselves, the company put behind those they had killed, arranging everything that would burn beneath and around the bodies - though Arudal knew that there was nowhere near enough fuel there to char even one corpse to ash. His cousin Uridar was a priest in the temple of Amandeth, and had told him many things about the care of the dead; Arudal had learned some of that lore from his relatives at the Hidden Estate as well, for many of those with his gift became Amandeth's priests, and often-times there were corpses left over from Grandmother Zinadir's necromantic work that had to be disposed of, usually by burning. But if the White Company knights could not burn the corpses altogether, at least they were making an effort, and in this weather, there was no hope of digging a pit deep enough to keep even one body from the wolves. Arudal also noticed that Sir Salarond had not ordered the werewolf's hide placed on the fire: their commander must have suspected that there was not enough fuel to burn it completely.

One of the outlaws' chests held a reasonable store of silver and copper, with a few pieces of gold and some jewelry. Although none of them could detect any taint on it, still, no one was willing to take it. Sir Salarond spread the treasure out over the bodies of the two victims: some of it might have belonged to them once.

The fire was already beginning to chew outward from its pit before they had finished, the cave beginning to fill with smoke and the horses growing restive with the smell. Still, Sir Salarond stopped at the doorway. "It is the Eve of Amandeth. Here at this bale-fire, we honour you who receive and judge the dead. Though I am a healer, sometimes by your will my hands must fail: I honour you, for all Men must die, as the gods decreed in the first of days. Star shining through night's blackness, the year turns towards darkness: we honour you."

"We honour you," the others whispered - Arudal as well, though this was not the ritual he knew.

"Lord of Judgement, before whom all Men must stand, look upon our deeds in life: we honour you."

"We honour you."

"We remember the dead who have passed beneath your cloak. None may know your will, or know when you will call us; but let us answer without fear, and go forth, trusting you to receive us and guide us into those lands of which none returns to tell. In doubting you, the Empire fell to evil and put its hopes in Shadow; by trusting you, our forebears were spared. We remember: we shall not fall."

"We shall not fall," the Kantareans whispered, while Arudal squirmed a little inside.

"For those who have died in this last year, we pray to you. For these two whom the bandits murdered, and all their other victims, though we do not know their names, we pray to you. For Sir Cordon, Sir Erekhazor, Sir Soromir, Sir Aramound..." Salarond's list was long, little to Arudal's surprise: a knight in the White Company would see many friends slain in the course of a year. "Gatharost, Gathrudeth, Azrahar, Mulkhumanon, Zorgudal..."

Arudal listened with his head bowed in respect as each of the White Company members spoke the names of their dead. Though he had no one to remember thus, when his turn came, he spoke in his own tongue, reciting the invocatory part of the rite as his family had always known it, though the roast-meat smoke from the cave was stinging tears from his eyes and burned sore in his throat with each breath.

"Lord of Darkness, come to us as the year darkens: in the Sun's night, we hail you. Lord of Shadow, silent between the stars: in the year's night, we hail you. Friend of Men, Keeper of Souls: in the blood of the slain, in your own god-fire, we hail you. For your sake, we fear not darkness nor death; Light of Shadow who guides us beyond the green earth, pursuer inescapable and refuge at last, bearing us beyond the Doom of Men. We remember the dead who have passed beneath your cloak, and those who stand yet to guard the walls of the world in the Cold Realm, our kin and our friends: may their memories guide us yet, and their hands rest upon ours to strengthen us. Let us not flee the dark in fear, but stand strong to greet and welcome you, as those did who have gone into starless night before us. Lord of Shadow, Friend of Men: as the summer falls to death, as the world falls to darkness, we hail you here, Claimer of Souls, and all those you have brought to your realm this year."

No one else spoke when Arudal was finished; but Finvar and Tirothar, who stood closest to the cave's mouth, were muffling their smoke-coughs. Sir Salarond gestured them away, and without speaking, the company led their unburdened horses slowly along the difficult path down the rocky hillside, lanterns bobbing like a string of fireflies over the snow.

Malni, Rhys, and Berek had set up the camp while they were gone, hacking up one of the little twisted trees for firewood and lighting a good blaze - safe enough, since it was unlikely that another robber band shared this territory. Rhys and Malni were sitting on opposite sides of the campfire, Rhys glaring sullenly, Malni looking steadfastly down at the piece of wood on which she was whittling. Berek, unsurprisingly, had seated himself furthest from the smoke and was chewing on a sausage.

"Watch rota?" Sir Thoron asked Salarond while the squires unharnessed, tethered, and fed the packhorses.

"As for last night, I think...Hmm." Sir Salarond's brow creased, and he looked unhappily at Arudal for a very long time, long enough for the Tharandrostan to start shifting uneasily from foot to foot. Then Arudal realized what he must be thinking. Amandeth's Eve, like Sundark, was one of the nights that was sometimes said to call the Ukuthrim forth from the Shadow-Realm; slaying the wolf-bandits hardly meant that they would be safe if the Undead also walked here. He still had some black-roast tea, and if he were on all three watches, there would be time to grind the beans and brew a large pot.

"Sir, I am able to stay up all night if I may sleep in the wain tomorrow," Arudal said.

"I know that, Arudal. I wish...Well, I suppose there is little choice. Karsil, you are able to take all three watches as well?"

"Certainly."

"Let it be so, then."

The company ate in near-silence. Every so often, Arudal would look up and see that one of them was staring at him, although Rhys was steadily avoiding his gaze. What is it now? he wondered. Are they angry at me because, alone of the White Company, I had no names of my dead to speak? Twice Malni moved over to sit nearer to him, and both times Arudal managed to shift away from her, even though the last time left him in the worst of the smoke-trail from the fire, so that his eyes watered burningly and his lungs ached with every gust of wind.

As the squires were scrubbing the pans and plates with snow, Rhys came over to Arudal. Even through the bars of their helms, Arudal could see the Plainsman's face clearly in the darkness: Rhys' bones stood out more clearly after the days of travel in the cold, lending him the gaunt intensity of a prophet, and the scraggly beginnings of a red beard spreading across his jaw and chin made him look as wild and desperate as any of the bandits they had slain that night.

"Malni's not for you, see?" Rhys hissed at him. "I want you to keep away from her, Tharandrostan." He spoke the last word as if it were a curse.

"I don't want her," Arudal murmured back. "What would I do with her?"

"I begin to think that you really don't know. Nevertheless. I want you to leave her alone."

"Tell her to leave me alone. I certainly didn't ask her to, to..."

"To kiss you? If she knew what you were, she never would have."

"For the gods' sakes, Rhys! I don't care what she thinks of me. Tell her what you like, so long as it doesn't put the rest of us in danger."

Rhys paused, his set look of anger fading into confusion. "Mayhap I shall - you will swear to me that you mean nothing dishonourable towards her?"

"Gladly."

"Well, then. I had thought that you might intend to...but never mind. You likely don't, at that." He walked away, leaving Arudal distressed, but clearer in his thoughts. Obviously Rhys had feared that Arudal would take Malni's maidenhood and abandon her, as a man of the lesser races - or even a Kantarean - might do. Even if the Plainsman spoke from jealousy, Arudal thought, it was well that he had been concerned for the girl's safety: it was clearly not true that all Plainsmen were no more than rutting beasts where their does were concerned. He wondered who else had seen Malni kissing him, and if that was the reason why the other members of the party had been staring at him so oddly over dinner. But they must know that my seed belongs to our unsullied race, that I would not waste it in lying with her even if she were such a maid as to stir my desires. Briefly Arudal thought of his cousin Arothir - almost twin to himself now, golden-haired and fine-featured, and his likeliest mate; he shifted a little at the unaccustomed warmth in his breeches, but the strange feeling died down quickly.

In spite of Sir Salarond's concerns, the night passed without incident. Arudal spent most of his long watch in a half-trance, waiting to see if any trace of the Ukuthrim would come to his awareness; but - surprisingly, since the state of the bandits' lair suggested that they had been there for quite some time, so that he might have expected unquiet ghosts - there was not the least hint of any Undead as far as Arudal's senses could reach. Still, in spite of the black-roast tea, he was grateful when the dawn began to blur his sight and he could curl up under his blankets in the back of the wagon-sledge, oblivious to the hard boards under him and the creaking of the wood as Malni urged the draught horses into a walk.

Chapter 20: Shadows of the Fallen

"The taint in the blood stains dark on the bone,
A stain no bright waters can clean
(Springs up from roots, however deep-sunk),
Nor time wear away what has been.

The taint in the blood stains dark on the bone,
As memory shadows new sun
(Rises from depths, poison black in the well),
As old tree shades sprouts new-begun."

- "The Taint in the Blood", Perelan Haregift

Arudal awoke some time later, lying drowsy under his warm blankets. The wain's creaking sounded very like the boards of a boat; with his eyes closed, the scents of salt meat and grain in his nose, he could almost imagine that he was in the hold of a ship being rowed across calm waters...He must be half-dreaming, for he heard Sir Salarond and Sir Eroth talking, as clearly as if they had taken the places of Malni and Berek at the front of the wagon.

"But do you think he knew?" Sir Eroth was saying.

"The problem is that I am not sure," Salarond answered heavily. "I had believed it impossible...yet I find it hard to believe that anyone could have spoken like that without knowing. Even those of us who don't speak the language recognised some of the words - the most relevant ones."

"Uhm. But you know what they're like."

"Every so often, I begin to think I do, and then they do something else unexpected. I know I told you about that one time when..."

"Yes. The Northmen have a saying about expecting wolves to change their pelts. Of course," Eroth added, "many of their dogs are half-wolf: they aren't a folk best-known for their logic."

"No. I'm beginning to wonder if it wasn't a mistake, though, in spite of the prediction."

Did Berek say something awful again? Arudal wondered. Then it occurred to him that the knights could well have overheard it when the Westerner called knighthood a form of slavery.

"Well, we can't do anything about it now. I suppose we could leave him at the next village we come to, but I think that would cause more trouble than it solved."

"Ironically enough." Sir Salarond sighed. "If we were really wrong to bring him, leaving him could be a real disaster. And if we weren't, it would be cruel and unjust. He'd never get home by himself."

"Karsil thinks there's a solution to the practical side of that problem."

"I've heard quite enough of what Karsil thinks on the subject all morning, thank you. The White Company has been many things, but - in spite of what some people, including Karsil's relatives, say - we've never been child-murderers, and we aren't going to start now. Especially not since we really may need him."

Salarond had said something about a prediction, too; Lostren must have mentioned his moment of foresight to his knight - though the thought of having to rely on Berek's nonexistent sense of friendship made Arudal shudder.

"I wasn't recommending it," Eroth said mildly. "You could Truth-Read...No, you couldn't, could you? And even if magic worked properly here, if he had been blocked heavily enough, you would still know no more than you did before."

"That is what worries me. Especially since some magic does work here. If I had been wrong, he could damage us quite badly."

Fully awake now, Arudal crawled out of his blankets. He had slept in his cap to keep his head warm; shivering in the icy air, he pulled on a strip-woven shirt of thick wool and his cloak over it. Arudal was sure that he knew as much about the magic of the West by now as either Sir Salarond or Sir Eroth: if they were worried about Berek doing them harm by magical means, he should be in on the discussion.

One of the knights turned at the sound, his head a fuzzy dark silhouette against the day-mist over Arudal's eyes. Blurred as the Tharandrostan's sight was, he knew that the sun must have come out at last; there was not so much as a cloud to protect his eyes. "Good afternoon, Arudal," Sir Salarond said, his voice rather chilly - it was he who sat in the passenger's seat, while Sir Eroth was driving. "Have you been awake long?"

Arudal hesitated, caught between his sense of truthfulness and the embarassment of admitting to eavesdropping. Finally he said. "No, sir. I heard you talking about Berek and magic."

"Ah." Sir Salarond sounded relieved; Arudal guessed that their commander must have wanted the party's third mage in on the discussion, but been unwilling to wake him after ordering him to keep watch all night. "Yes. How much do you think he can actually do?"

"It is hard to tell, sir. He is in the habit of keeping secrets about it, but now that he has started talking, I do not think that he would conceal any of his abilities. He is too proud of being a magician, and too enthusiastic about magic, to do that very well, I think. Sir."

"Hmm."

"Still, he has admitted to enough skill that I think he could cause us a great deal of trouble if he wanted to. From what I understand, he might be able to...oh, make bones that had broken once likely to break again, or bring us to the particular notice of ice-cats, if they are as much like arathra as they sound. If he guessed that we were going to the Imperial Seat, there is no telling how much damage he could do - inadvertently, possibly far in excess of his actual power."

"That seems like a reasonable analysis," Eroth put in. "I would have said much the same."

"Yes," Sir Salarond agreed. "Well, we can only arrange things so that he understands that his survival depends on ours. You don't need to armour up yet, Arudal. We shall be stopping for the night in an hour or so, and I think perhaps I shall let you keep the full night-watch at least until we are out of these hills. It is possible that I am only unnerved by what we saw last night, but there is something about the land here that seems unclean to me."

"Yes, sir."

Arudal's bladder was quite full. He lifted up the rear flap of the wain, and - after looking quickly around to make as sure as his dim vision could that Malni was out of sight - let fly over the edge with a considerable sense of relief. When he turned back, it looked to his day-fogged eyes as though Sir Eroth and Sir Salarond had their heads bent together as if whispering to each other, but they moved apart as he came back.

Looking about, Arudal could tell at once what Sir Salarond meant. Although the gray-blotched blur of the hills was the same as it had been, it seemed to Arudal as if the snow were slightly dingier. He saw no outright glimmers of magic, nor did he sense the nearness of any Ukuthrim, but he felt, for no clear reason, a general sense of foreboding.

"Has Lostren said anything about this, sir?"

"About Berek?"

"No, sir. About travelling here."

"Not to me, at any rate." Sir Salarond's lean face creased in thought. "Rhys!"

The Plainsman wheeled his riding horse and trotted back to the wagon. "Sir?"

"Are you able to speak to the spirits of the land here?"

"I don't know, sir. This is far from home, and my folk never dwelt on this continent."

"I think we shall halt and let you try as soon as we come to a good place to stop."

Rhys tilted his head, looking up at the hills. Although Arudal could not see his expression, the tone of his voice - half-disgusted, half-fearful, as though he were looking at a rotted corpse that had just twitched - made his thoughts clearer than his words did, and his Plainsman accent was stronger than Arudal had yet heard it. "Look you, sir, I'm after thinking that there will be no good place in any near travel here, nor am I wishing to speak to anything that might be dwelling here, unless you should order it of me."

"If it is so clear to your senses, I see no need to order it. Back to your place."

Rhys trotted off into the fog: he was riding paired with someone, though Arudal could only see the two of them as vague dark outlines.

"Well, Arudal. Can you detect anything untoward?"

Even as Sir Salarond spoke, Arudal's sight was darkening until the gold tracery on Lostren's helm and the gleam of Finvar's bow flared bright against the blackness. Now he could see the unhealthy gray-greenish tinge to the hills. He still had no sense that there might be Ukuthrim near upon the green earth, but it seemed to him that he could feel them pressing about in the Shadow-Realm. This would be, perhaps, one of the places where the walls between the worlds were thinner: Arudal could tell that, if he wished, he could easily summon an Ukuthran, or several of them, forth to do his bidding. He hesitated, but then told himself that Sir Salarond should at least know the resources available to him.

"Sir, all of this land is slightly tainted in some manner, though I can see no source or unliving thing. But if you wish me to, I could call an Ukuthran to seek further or aid in guarding us: here, it would take but a little time."

"No!" Salarond snapped. "Amanvon and Aviyani, Arudal, I shall deal with you myself if you try such a thing!"

"Sir?" Arudal said, hurt and bewildered. Sir Salarond had shown no such signs of anger and revulsion before, when the Tharandrostan had told his commander what he could do. "Sir, I meant no ill by it, only that you shoulde knowen what weapons were ready to your hand, should you choose to usen them. How have I offended against you?"

"Never mind, Arudal. You are not to summon anything. Is that clear enough?"

"Yes, sir."

Arudal subsided into silence as Sir Salarond picked up the small black telescope that lay on the seat beside him, turning his head to scan the hills with practiced smoothness. It came to Arudal that, oddly, Sir Salarond had been addressing him by his full name since yesterday evening, rather than by the - from the Kantareans, at any rate, affectionate - false diminutive that Karsil had given him. It was not only strange, but worrying, for Berek still believed Arudal to be half-Elven, and there was no telling when they might have to take up the masquerade for others again; while Arudal's own name was far too obviously Imperial. So was Shakhor's, for that matter, but while the tracker-knight might be able to pass unnoticed among Westerners, Arudal, even with golden hair, would still be dangerously Imperial-looking if he were not thought to be of Elven blood.

Arudal had been brought up never to question his superiors, but being in the White Company, with other squires that were encouraged to speak their minds, had affected him somewhat. So now he said, "Sir, if I may ask a question..."

"Yes?"

"Why are you calling me by my full name again, sir?"

Sir Salarond looked at Arudal for a little while without answering. Finally he said, "Because it seems appropriate. Be quiet and do whatever you do, if you can do it without drawing unwanted attention."

Arudal let his awareness slip back into Shadow. Even the chill that came from looking into the Cold Realm was almost welcome, for it numbed him against the hurt of his commander's harshness. It seemed to him that he must have done something grievously wrong in offering to summon Undead for Sir Salarond, but since the healer-priest already knew he had that talent - had given him a legal warrant to keep Undead! - he could not see why mentioning it had angered Salarond so deeply. *I wish I were home,* Arudal thought. At home, he had always been petted and praised for his talent, as the most talented full inmudalan agathusaftan and agathurok in several generations.

The Kantareans' coldness towards Arudal continued while they set up camp and ate: even Finvar avoided his gaze and mumbled when he tried to start a conversation. Malni only made matters worse, for she was trying to sit next to him and no one else seemed to want to. Finally, when the squires took the utensils to scour them, Arudal decided to follow Rhys' example of plain speaking, and came over to his squire-brother.

"Finvar," Arudal said, "I knowe thou art wroth with me for that I wasn't in the battle. But surely thou mustest have hearden Sir Thoron: thou knowest Inmanat was never ytaughten for fighting, and he panicked - I coulde not him halten!" He thought of mentioning how Finvar had been overcome by Shadow-Fear when the vampires attacked, but that, he was sure, would only make matters worse.

Finvar looked away. "Yes. I know. That isn't it. And speak Common properly, for the gods' sakes, will you?"

"What is the matter?" Arudal said, as carefully as he could.

"I don't want to talk about it. Especially not here." Finvar turned his back and walked away.

Arudal stood like a deep-rooted tree, shocked into absolute numbness. Finvar had been his friend since his first day as Sir Thoron's squire. What could have changed that? If the Artegalian thought he had fled out of cowardice - but Finvar had said that was not the problem, and had seen him stand firm when the vampires attacked their camp. *But I wasn't in the battle on ship-board...but he wasn't angry with me after that...but he heard Sir Salarond order me to stay below then...*

"Is something the matter, Ari?" Malni asked him, walking up close.

"No. Go away."

The Western girl's mouth dropped open, the blood draining from her face as though he had struck her hard in the belly. She raised her fist as if to strike him, then shook her head angrily, the ear-pieces of her sheepskin cap flapping like a scent-hound's floppy ears. "Talk to me that way if you like. See if I care!" She stamped off, leaving Arudal with the feeling that he had gotten off lightly. Still, he had barely taken another breath before the shock of Finvar's rejection bit down again, great jaws clamping on his heart.

Lostren was crouching with his scrubbing rag a little distance away. Arudal stood still, torn between the desire to ask him what was wrong with everybody and the fear that Lostren, too, would turn away from him as his squire-brother had.

But surely he can hurt me no more deeply, Arudal told himself. *And if the choice is between being an outcast for the rest of this mission and turning back to the last village, I think I should mount Inmanat and ride away this night.*

"Lostren?" Arudal said tentatively.

"Yes?" The other squire's face showed no sign of his thoughts, and though he was quailing within, Arudal pressed on. He spoke Imperial, for he could no longer trust his command of Common.

"What have I done, that everyone seems so angry with me?"

Lostren stared at him for a long time, still with the same closed expression. "If you truly do not know," he said at last, "then you do not deserve what has been thought of you."

"I don't know! I thought it was because I, alone, had not lost anyone to death in the last year, or because my horse ran when the wolf-bandits attacked, so that I could not aid in the fighting. But Finvar said the second was not so, and this anger seems too great for the first. Such treatment must have clear blame to justify it, whatever the heart behind it feels."

Lostren set his plates down in the snow and straightened up. "That is true. And, although I was as shocked as anyone, I have been thinking on the matter all day, and I cannot see any reason why you should have called to Morthugor before us. Even if you worshipped him, or meant to work us ill..."

"Called to Morthugor!" Arudal interrupted, horrified. "Before Amandeth and Terathon, what delusion is this? When should I have done such a thing?"

"The invocation you spoke last night, when the rest of us spoke the names of our dead - Arudal, did you truly not know that the names 'Lord of Shadow', 'Lord of Darkness', and 'Friend of Men', were never used for any other than the Twisted One? Or guess how the rest of your prayer might sound to Kantarean ears - or Elvish, when Morthugor was once worshipped by the blood of slain Elves and the fires kindled in his temples by their bodies?"

Arudal could only stare at him, his heartbeat thumping loudly against the sides of his skull.

"And surely," Lostren continued, his voice gentler, "you must be aware that to Kantareans, your race is half-judged as guilty already, not only from the lessons of history, but from the customs you insist on keeping. You, in particular, with your Shadow-gifts - is it surprising that we thought ill of you hailing the Lord of Shadow as a beloved friend?"

"My family's gifts were given to us by Amandeth in early days, that we might stand between the green earth and those wights of the Cold Realm who would prey on its children, instead of abiding to aid as Amandeth intended for those he would choose to share his burden," Arudal answered shakily. "Before the gods, have I ever done aught else?"

"No. And the longer I speak with you, the more I suspect that we have misjudged you. If your forebears chose to see in Amandeth some of what the Empire once worshipped in Morthugor, and call him by the name 'Lord of Shadow', still, you can hardly be blamed for praying as you were taught. For you did pray with heart and soul. And that, I think, disturbed us most of all."

Arudal thought back to the conversation he had overheard in the wagon. His heart gripped tightly in his chest; the blood rushed from his face, and his legs swayed weakly beneath him. We've never been child-murderers...Had the knights seriously been talking about killing him? Or abandoning him until they came back, if they came back for him at all? To live out his life in a sheep-herding village, without hope of rescue, his book on the Western language of no interest to the shepherds and goatherds around him and all his research left to rot like fallow seed in a forgotten bag, sprouting a little in dark and damp and then dying...after he had trusted himself wholly to them in aid of a mission that had nothing to do with himself or his country, coming at their behest to answer their need?

"Excuse me," Arudal said with the forced calm he had learned as Duke Azarlokan's page. "I need to step out for a moment. I shall be back shortly."

He walked away from Lostren and the camp, until though he could see the others more clearly than in daylight, he was sure they could not see him. Only then did Arudal let himself collapse, sinking to his knees in the snow and wrapping his arms tightly about himself, rocking back and forth as he silently sobbed out his heartbreak. They had been his friends, he had been sure of it...even Karsil had let him brush her hair, shining and silken beneath his hands...He had only wanted to do what was right, to honour Amandeth and bless the dead as he had been taught to all his life...

Eyes squeezed tightly shut as the hot tears chilled on his face, the blood roaring in his ears from the effort of stifling his sobs so that no one would hear them, Arudal did not know he was no longer alone until Sir Salarond coughed loudly. Arudal looked up to see Finvar and Karsil lowering their bows - Finvar with a miserably sheepish expression, Karsil's Elven face set fiercely. The others, save Malni and Berek, were gathered about with drawn swords, their blades flaring like the rainbow corona of the Northern night against the darkness.

Sir Thoron slammed his red-glowing sword back into its sheath with a noise of disgust. "Is this the way knights of Kantar behave?" he asked. "We came out ready to do battle with an evil magician because some people were all spooked, and here we are pointing the weapons that have slain champions of Martag at a young squire crying in the snow...Shit on that. Shit all over that. Come on, Ari." Thoron reached down to help his squire up. Arudal held gratefully to his knight's strong arm, letting Sir Thoron walk him back to the camp and set him down by the fire. "Paranoid pack of dickheads," Thoron muttered. "Don't worry, Ari. You're still my squire, and if anyone has any more shit to give you, they'll have to go through me first."

"Thank you, sir."

"No need to thank me, squire. You've kept your oath well, and I've never been the first to break my end of a vow. Now get some food into you - I saw you, you hardly ate tonight - and brew up another pot of that nasty stuff you drink. We need you to take all three watches again, and...You don't really have an amulet against fear of the Undead, do you?"

Arudal shook his head.

"Shit again. I was hoping you could lend it to Finvar and trust your, your talents to protect you. Is there anything you can do to help him?"

Arudal thought about it. "Maybe. I can try, at least, if he's willing to…trust me."

"He damned well will be," Thoron said grimly. He took a dried sausage out of the bag and thrust it into Arudal's hand. "Here. Eat."

Arudal was still chewing on the last bite of sausage when Finvar came over and sat down beside him, thick shoulders hunched. "Uh, Ari?"

"Yes?"

"I think I, uh, owe you an apology. I didn't really mean to…uh, I just…anyway, this place makes me as nervous as a cat in a dire wolves' den. Uh, Sir Thoron says I'm to talk to you about standing up to the Undead."

"Yes." Can I really help him? Arudal wondered. He himself had been born on the Hidden Estate, and spoken to the family dead, literally, from his cradle; Grandmother Zinadir told him that they knew how strongly he had inherited the House's line-gift when they saw him gurgling happily and reaching out to the ghost that had come to test him for Shadow-sight instead of crying in terror. But Arudal thought back to what his grandmother had told him when he was a small child of twenty, asking why so many people were afraid of the Undead. "Do you know what Shadow-Fear is?"

"Uh. Not really. Just that it's something that happens when living Men see the Undead, and that it's stronger with the more powerful ones."

"Indeed. The cause of Shadow-Fear is that, when the Undead manifest on the green earth, they bring a little of their realm with them, more or less according to their own power. Because you are sensing something that you know should not exist, your mind revolts against it. Animals are sensitive to the presence of the Shadowed Ones even when hidden, because they depend less on their eyes and more on their other senses than Men do. The Elves do not feel Shadow-Fear at all because they have a different sort of being beyond the green earth than Men do - I can see Dame Karsil clearly even when my sight is all in Shadow. The first step to overcoming Shadow-Fear is knowing what it is, and why you fear. It is not because you are afraid of the Undead themselves, nor that they are evil by nature, but because their being is something that Men were not meant to bear. Just as pain is a warning of wounds, so Shadow-Fear is a warning of the dangers of being close to the Undead; yet a brave man can learn to accept that warning without letting it whelm him and go on nevertheless, even as he can fight and march with the pain of a bodily injury if there is need."

"I see. Do you know that you speak Common better when you're explaining something?"

Trying to get off the subject because he's afraid, Arudal thought sympathetically. But I shouldn't let him. "Yes. And then, as with anything, experience makes the touch of the Shadow-Realm less frightening. The man who is used to facing a certain danger comes to stand up blithely where one unaccustomed to it, however strong of heart, may find himself quailing. Were you not afraid the first time you dived off a high rock into the sea?"

"I have never dived off a high rock into the sea," Finvar said with considerable feeling. "But I think I know what you mean. The first time I went after a wild boar with a spear…"

"Exactly."

"But how can I get used to it? I can't very well start with smaller Undead and work my way up to the Lord of Martag, can I?"

At the Hidden Estate - barring the presence of the actual Lord of Martag - Finvar might have done just that, but Arudal forebore to mention it. Instead, after considering a moment, the Tharandrostan said, "Look into my eyes."

All the time they had been together, Finvar, like the rest of the party, had avoided Arudal's gaze so instinctively that Arudal suspected he had never thought about it; while Arudal, in turn, had grown up with the knowledge that he must not stare at anyone whom he did not wish to frighten.

But now I will learn if he really does trust me. The only way to train a horse or hound to bear the presence of the Undead was to expose the animal in the presence of a human whom it loved and trusted, and who also felt no Shadow-fear; it seemed to Arudal that Sir Thoron had been right to compare Finvar to a wolfhound, and that the same techniques should work on the Artegalian as on the beasts to whom he was close.

Arudal fixed his eyes on Finvar's, letting his sight slide into Shadow as he did, until all he could see was the other squire's vague outline within the faint glow of his armour and the brighter glimmer of his short bow leaning by his knee.

It was only a few breaths before Finvar turned away, shuddering. "Dear Amanvon," he breathed shakily. "What are you doing?"

"Nothing," Arudal answered. "Again."

Finvar's gauntlets grated metallicly as he clenched his fists, forcing himself to stare into Arudal's eyes. It seemed to Arudal that he could almost feel his squire-brother's soul, firmly anchored in flesh as it was, straining to answer the call of the silence within his own mind. This time, however, Finvar held himself by sheer force of will, until at last Arudal said, "Enough," and wrenched his own sight painfully back to the green earth.

Finvar was shivering; Arudal could hear the muffled sound of the hooped tassets of his plate-armour clashing softly beneath his wool over-tunic and cloak. But he still had not dropped his gaze; and now he reached out to lay his gauntleted hand on Arudal's armoured thigh, his warmth faint through the layers of metal and leather.

"If I didn't know you..." he whispered. "But I do, and I'm glad Lostren explained things to me. It was breaking my heart, thinking that you, then that I had...Forgive me, Ari?"

"I already have."

"Will this help?"

"I hope so."

"Thank you." They sat close together, touching but not speaking further, until Sir Salarond said, "First watch, ready yourselves - everyone else, get some sleep." Arudal got out his fast-dwindling stock of black-roast beans and began to crush them hurriedly as their commander went on. "Keep a close eye on the horses. I've double-tethered them; they may be our first warning. If they start acting strange or restless, wake the rest of us fast. Malni, take a few of Karsil's arrows - save them for shooting at anything that looks unnatural. If you've shot them all, stay in the wain: your pike won't touch creatures of Shadow. Arudal, give the alert if you see any changes in the, the whatever it is out there. And don't forget to keep a watch on the sky as well. Rhys, Lostren, the same goes for you two.

Sing out if you sense anything changing, or feel any danger: I'd rather wake up to a false alarm than sleep through a real one." He went over to Dame Karsil, gesturing her to bend down to that he could speak softly in her ear. Even the Elf's grimace of anger was beautiful, but no less frightening for that, and Arudal resolved firmly not to turn his back on her, and to keep his shield towards her lest a shot from her bow should go astray...at least she had not yet thought to ask for her buckler back. Or has she realized that I might be more vulnerable to arrows with a smaller shield?..No, enough of that.

The first watch was kept by Arudal, Karsil, Sir Eroth, Tirothar, and Berek. Arudal and Karsil settled themselves at opposite sides of the camp, Arudal looking west and Karsil east; Sir Eroth took the north, Tirothar and Berek the south. With his sight sunk in Shadow, Arudal did not see the clouds scudding across the stars, but he felt the strengthening wind even through gambeson, plate-coat, and heavy wool, and the strong bitter heat of his blackroast tea grew more welcome as the night chilled. It seemed to Arudal that the faint greenish glow across the Barren Hills had brightened slightly, but he still saw no signs of any danger, and the change was not great enough for him to speak.

Sir Thoron, Finvar, Sir Salarond, and Lostren replaced Sir Eroth, Tirothar, and Berek at second watch. Even through Shadow, Arudal could tell by Sir Salarond's watchful stance that their commander was expecting trouble; he could feel the tension himself, vibrating through the tainted earth as though the hills about them were the rim of a great crystal bowl humming to the touch of an unseen finger. Arudal wished that he had paid more attention to the old geography of the West in his history classes: if he had, he might have been able to guess what had been here before the Fall - although, as they had seen, the Barren Hills had evil enough of their own in these new days.

Arudal was not sure when he noticed that the horses, who had been sleeping or snuffling about for grass under the snow in a rather desultory fashion, were all standing still, facing westward. Before he could speak, Sir Salarond called softly, "Beware! Lostren, wake everyone."

The horses were beginning to stamp and shuffle; Arudal heard Inmanat's low whinny, as familiar to him as a friend's voice, and then saw the faint purple-black glow of the cloud moving swiftly over the farthest hill. The others were hastening out, the chain-mail in which they had slept clinking muffled beneath their cloaks as they jammed their helmets down over their heads; Arudal shouted, "Sir, it's coming this way. I can't see what..." His voice failed him for a moment, but he was able to swallow hard and go on. "A troop of men on horseback, sir, in old-fashioned black armour. No weapons out - the foremost is gesturing towards us."

"Form a square," Sir Salarond ordered. "Arudal, Berek, and Malni inside: keep down!"

As the riders neared, Arudal saw that the leader had pushed his pointed visor back, his face snow-pale against the black metal. He was dressed in full plate, though his followers wore only light chain and helms. Arudal had seen the same armour and helms in paintings from the Western Empire: long pointed tassets guarding the outer thighs over chain-mail skirts, conical helms with beaklike visors, sharp-ribbed breastplates...Behind the leader rode a standard-bearer. Arudal drew in his breath. The faint glow of magic about the battle-flag shimmered over its deep gules field, picking out the vorgath sun of the Fallen Empire, when the worship of Morthugor had darkened the red field and blackened the golden sun of earlier Imperial days.

"Hail to thee, nobly born!" the leader called out to Arudal. His face was as familiar as any of the purest Imperial blood, his slanted eyes glowing ice-gray against his white skin, with an inner ring of coruscating amber about the black holes of his pupils. Agathan, Arudal thought - Undead, but not Ukuthran; a person to be respected, rather than a monster to be used or slain. He spoke in High Imperial, the same form of the tongue that was still used for formal speech in Tharandrost; his voice was deep, cold, and stern. "What brings thee and thy companions here on this hallowed night, when the sons of slaves creep into their holes like worms? And why stands one of the accursed Elven-kind with you, and is not bound, but weaponed?"

Sir Salarond stepped forward. "We would pass in peace, on an errand of our own of which we may not speak, but for which the Elf is needed. Will you let us go freely?" He spoke the High Imperial tongue well - not to Arudal's surprise: Prince Dolkhat, after all, would not have been squire to

a knight for whom the rulers of Tharandrost had little respect. The Agathim must have been in full manifestation, as clear to the sight of the others as to Arudal, for Salarond was looking the black-armoured leader straight in the eye as he spoke.

"Cousin, it is our duty to guard these ways as we may. Our blood we shall not hinder unless we must; but we must ask a toll, for we have long ridden these midnight roads, and grievous pain and hunger are upon us. I can see that you have slaves with you, as well as the Elf." His black-gauntleted hand pointed gracefully at Berek, Malni, and Rhys in turn. "Give us one of them, and we shall let you go your way unhindered."

Salarond shook his head, pale moon-rainbows shimmering over the sheen of his helmet in the darkness. "None of our party are slaves. All are freely born, and free still. Nor would I give any over to you, even if I could."

"Then, cousin, I fear that we must do battle with you - until all of one side are slain, or yield, or the dawn takes us."

The Agathan dismounted in a single graceful motion and clicked down his visor. He is so small, Arudal thought irrelevantly. Is that what I look like to Kantareans and Westerners? His followers dismounted behind him, spreading out in a practiced flanking motion that would take advantage of their numbers. Arudal felt the rush of Shadow over him, and readied himself to reach out to the leader's mind. Then, to his right, someone screamed, and he heard the sound of armour clanking and running feet over the snow - Shadow-Fear; he hoped with all his heart that it was not Finvar who had fled. But the black-clad dead were charging as the White Company fighters shifted, trying to cover the breach in their line, and Arudal could do nothing but step out to close the gap and meet them. He did not dare to try touching the Agathan now, for if he stood locked in thought with the leader, the rest of the spectral band could cut him down like autumn fruit.

The bows sang as the Shadow-host closed: Karsil's arrow streaking like a white comet, followed by a firework-trail of blue and a dimmer-glowing white streamer - Finvar and Malni's shafts, Arudal guessed. Karsil's arrow struck the leader's black shield in a shower of sparks; Arudal did not have time to see if the other two had slain their targets, for the black-armoured warriors were on them.

Arudal's buckler flicked up, blocking a blow to his head without thought as he swung cross-body beneath his foe's arm. Ripples of white light shimmered along the blue-steel length of the Elven blade in the darkness, and the chill of the Agathan's armour bit through the sword's metal into his hand. The Imperial Agathim were slower than he had expected, not much swifter of movement than well-born Kantareans - Tharandrost's centuries of breeding had served its children well. Still, he barely ducked a dark sword's thrust, its shadow-edge skittering soundlessly over the top of his helmet; and the edge of his shield caught just enough of the back-stroke to take the strength from the blow. Two of them were facing him at once; he blocked low with his buckler, high with his blade, twisting his hips and turning his hand to drive the block into a counter-thrust through his foe's shadowed eye-slit - Karsil had drilled him mercilessly on point control. A shock of icy cold ran up the bone of Arudal's arm, so that he could barely hold the sword as the black-armoured figure wailed into nothingness; for a moment he had only the buckler and his own agility to guard him.

The Agathim fought in dead silence, their swords striking without sound and no blows ringing from their shields. Only when they were slain did they cry out, a high keening shriek of despair fading into nothingness. Arudal's own hoarse breathing inside his helm almost deafened him to the noises of the living men's armour clanking, their soft grunts as they struck or struggled to block the powerful blows of the Undead, the terrified screams of the horses... Arudal's first kill had been a lucky stroke; now he was hard-pressed to stay alive, seldom daring to open his guard by hitting out.

Arudal's sword struck hard against an Agathan's black blade, and for a heartbeat, he thought he had an opening. But faster than he expected, the Shadow-sword was gone from his foe's hand. With perfect timing, the black-mailed man ducked under Arudal's forehand stroke, grasping his wrist and twisting it hard to the right. Over-committed, Arudal felt his feet leave the ground, sky and earth whirling about him until he struck the ground with a bone-rattling thump. His arm was still twisted almost to the point of breaking; the weight of the Agathan kneeling on his chest seemed that of a living man - easy enough to heave off, save that he could not struggle against the other without the bone of his arm giving way.

The deep cold voice of the Undead leader called out, "We have your lord! Will you yield to us?"

"No!" Sir Salarond shouted back.

Gasping from the shooting pains in his arm, Arudal opened his mind. Come to me...

You are...of the House of Aglarek...the Agathan thought. Even in pain and frightened as Arudal was, he could not help feeling a faint glow of pride. His forebear Arudal Agathusaftan, fourth son of that House, had founded his own line after the Fall, when no one knew if all his elder brothers had lived or died - but the blood ran strong and true.

I am. Come to me.

My lord, I cannot leave my duty...Arudal saw the twin lights brightening, ice ringing fire, inside the other's eyeslits; he was resisting with all his strength, but Arudal was stronger.

As suddenly as if an anchor-rope had snapped, the weight was off Arudal's chest, his twisted arm straightening with a pang that made him gasp aloud. His sword lay on the ground a few feet away; if he were lucky, he could wriggle over and grab it before any of the other Agathim looked back.

Arudal's fingers were almost on the hilt when he heard the human cry - a deep grunt of agony cut off quickly, the sound of an armoured body falling into the snow. All his senses still tingling with Shadow-cold, it seemed to Arudal that Finvar came to his awareness as if his squire-brother had just stepped into view from behind a curtain, holding out a hand towards him.

Arudal...

Without thought of anything else, Arudal reached out towards Finvar before the Artegalian's misty shape could fade.

Come here. He already knew the shape of Finvar's soul, how it would fit within him, and Finvar came eagerly, without even a second of fear - as if they had practiced for this just that evening, touching and looking into each other's eyes. A moment of cold pressure, as if Arudal's snow-chilled helmet were tightening around his temples: then it was done.

Arudal shook his head to ease the tightness, breathing deeply to steady himself, and closed his hand on his sword-hilt. But the moment's delay, or what he had done, had drawn the attention of the Agathim. He was just rising from his knees when he saw that one of the black-mailed Undead had turned, the flat of his dark falchion-blade coming down on Arudal's helm with the force of a Dwarven hammer.

Chapter 21: Aftermath

(General Vargoth): "How to calculate our victory? Soldiers don't need fancy maths; just subtract our own dead from the enemy's; add the value of our plunder and position; there's what we've won."

(Lieutenant Melior): "But what of the loss of my friends?"

(General Vargoth): "Lad, if you subtracted that, no one's gains would ever add up to victory."

- The Iron-Shield March, Act III, scene i.

The brightness bit into Arudal's head when he opened his eyes, so that he almost cried out from the pain; he could see nothing but a foggy dazzle. When he tried to shift to ease the pain a little, his stomach convulsed; agony exploded through his skull as he turned his head to keep from throwing up on himself.

"He's awake!" Lostren called out. Even the other squire's soft voice reverberated painfully around the inside of Arudal's head. Hands lifted something damp off his face, laid something cooler on - almost soothing, except for the shattering drumbeat of his pulse inside his skull.

"Good," Sir Salarond answered. "Don't let him fall asleep again. I thought we were going to lose him, and he's far from out of danger yet."

"Did we...did we win?" Arudal croaked. He knew he should speak Common, but his mind could not form the words.

"We won," Lostren assured him.

"Finvar," Arudal mumbled. "Finvar, we won. I stood and fought..."

Arudal heard Lostren catch his breath, a single soft gasp. "Ari - Finvar is dead."

"I know." In spite of the blinding burst of pain in his skull, Arudal pushed himself halfway up. "Tell them...you must tell them! Don't burn his body! We have to keep it...the better-preserved it is, the easier..."

"Ari, lie down." Lostren pressed him gently back. "You were hit on the head, and you've got a bad concussion. You need to stay awake, but don't try to talk."

"No. I have to tell you. Finvar's body...where is it?"

"The other squires are gathering wood for a pyre now. Calm down, Ari. We can't dig a proper grave in frozen ground, and you wouldn't have him left for the wolves, would you?"

"No! Lostren, listen. If his body is burned, I won't be able to put him back when we get home - there has to be something to heal, for his soul to go to, it's much harder with a stranger's body. Even a piece of bone, a tooth...but the whole body is easier, he's used to the shape it is now..."

"What are you...?" Lostren started. Then he drew a deep breath. When he spoke again, his voice was ragged - with hope? "Ari, are you saying that you caught Finvar's soul when he died?"

"Yes! I have him here, with me - if magic worked, if we could heal his body now, I could restore..."

"Amandeth's blessing," Lostren breathed. He raised his voice again. "Sir Salarond! Sir! Come here, please, sir!"

Each of their commander's light steps against the wagon-boards felt as though he were treading over Arudal's head with spiked boots, but in his relief, he barely noticed. Lostren quickly explained the situation to his knight, Sir Salarond making occasional thoughtful noises.

"If we pack him tightly in snow..." the healer-priest said after a few moments of consideration. "The freezing will damage him further, but it's easier to heal frozen flesh than replace rotten. Arudal is correct in saying that a piece of bone would be enough under the best circumstances, but it would call for a far greater healer than I to regrow the whole body. And, with luck, we'll be back where magic works before the last of the snow melts. Go see to it, Lostren. I want to examine Ari now."

Sir Salarond's gentle fingers pulled back each of Arudal's eyelids in turn. Arudal whimpered at the light bursting through his head, but tried not to pull away. Carefully the healer probed at his skull, while Arudal gritted his teeth against the scream struggling to break from his throat.

"Well, you are very lucky," Salarond told him at last. "I don't even think your skull is cracked. All the same, I shall want you to stay awake for at least twenty-four hours. Otherwise, there is too much risk of losing you - and, I suppose, Finvar as well. Are you able to tell me what happened to you?"

"The Agathan I was fighting - he grabbed my arm and threw me down," Arudal said. The pain was subsiding a little now, though all of his bones seemed to be echoing the throbbing ache in his skull. "That was when their leader asked you to yield again. Then I took the one that was holding me, and I was going for my sword when Finvar was killed. I thought I could get up and attack them from behind without being noticed, but one of them saw me and hit me while I was getting to my feet."

"He grabbed you?" Sir Salarond said. "Ah, of course; you mentioned that you could touch, or be touched by, creatures of Shadow. What do you mean by Agathan?"

"It is...a word of respect. Not like Ukuthran - Agathan means a person who is in Shadow, rather than a monster. Was Finvar our only, our only..."

"The only one killed? Yes. Tirothar was disordered in his mind from Shadow-Fear for several hours, but he has come back to himself. Eroth has lost the use of his shield-arm for the moment, though - if my herbs have not lost all their virtue - he should regain it within a few days. And we have all, if I do not miss my guess, lost a fair amount of life-strength from being so close to the...Agathim, you call them? An interesting distinction. Drink this. I am afraid I can give you nothing stronger for the pain, lest it put you to sleep, and you must not sleep now."

Salarond helped Arudal to lift his head and put a cup of lukewarm liquid to his lips. Arudal swallowed gratefully, the sweet wetness washing the taste of stale vomitus from his mouth and soothing his racked throat. The agonizing dazzle of brightness in his eyes had faded; now he could see the knight's silhouette against his fogged sight. "In any case, we shall be here for a few days. You are not fit to be moved, and Rhys and Lostren inform me that it is safe enough here now. Do you need a bed-pan?"

"Uh...yes. Sir."

Salarond lifted Arudal's blankets, gently sliding something underneath him. Somebody had undressed Arudal when they put him to bed; although his bladder was throbbing, it took him a very long time to release it. Sir Salarond sponged him off expertly afterwards, as Arudal turned his aching head away in embarassment. "I'm sorry, sir. I..."

"Still have one foot far too close to the edge of your grave," Salarond interrupted briskly. "Now...can you speak with Finvar? Or is he able to hear me, or to speak through you..?"

"I can...open my mind so that he is aware of everything just as I am, sir. And I can tell you what he says, though it would not be recommended for me to let a captive spirit speak through me."

"Can you do that without hurting yourself now, or would it be better to wait until you are healed?"

"I can do it now, if you like, sir."

"Very well."

Arudal let himself drop into the silent crystalline place within his mind. There the Agathan waited, in time unpassing; and near, yet sealed away as if by walls of unbreachable adamant and gleaming black vorgath, was Finvar. Even in the stillness within himself, Arudal could feel the life in Finvar's soul, for though he had been slain, he was not a creature of Shadow, only caught in the moment between departing his body and faring forth on the long journey of Men. But Finvar was dead; and so Arudal could open his mind to him, letting his squire-brother see through his eyes and hear through his ears.

"Can you hear me, Finvar?" Sir Salarond asked distantly.

Sir! Finvar exclaimed. Sir, what has happened?

Arudal passed the question on, and Salarond answered, "You fought very well, and we won the battle. We are keeping your body safe; if Ari lives, then when we return home, the gods willing, we should be able to restore you to life and health."

Ari, you'd better take good care of yourself, Finvar said. After all, you'll be fighting for two now. As the jarl said to the shield-maiden. Arudal felt his laughter like a little bubble of warmth within. Does Sir Thoron know that I'm...going to be all right?

Arudal repeated his squire-brother's last words. Sir Salarond nodded. "If he hasn't been told yet, he shall be soon."

Uh, what are you doing with my body?

Arudal told him, and it seemed to him that he could feel Finvar's shudder. Do me a favour, Ari? Don't make me look at it, all right?

As you wish.

And Ari...thank you. If it hadn't been for your help, I would have fled the field in terror again when they came at us.

I am not sure you should thank me, Arudal thought reluctantly. If you had fled...

I might be alive. Or our rank breaking in two places at once might have let them in, and given them the victory. And then they could have chased the stragglers at their leisure - no one ever knows what the gods might have willed. But I fought without flinching, and died honourably: what man can ask for more? You don't have to feel guilty about it, Ari! Finvar added suddenly, and Arudal knew that he had unwittingly opened his thoughts a little too wide. I'm sorry to miss the rest of this mission, but it's the tradition in Kantar that when a squire dies fighting for the kingdom, he is always knighted posthumously - and not many of them get to come back to enjoy it.

"One more thing," Salarond said reluctantly. "Finvar, is there anything we should know about...packing meat in snow to keep?"

Ech. Arudal felt his squire-brother's shudder; but his own mind was open enough that he could see Finvar's thoughts, the Artegalian forcing the image of his own cold body to shift to that of a gutted elk beneath dark pines, great furry gray dogs sitting about with their tongues hanging out and staring hopefully at the entrails. For a large animal, you'd take the bowels out of the body cavity. Rinse all the crud you can out with cold water, then pack the body tightly with snow. If the stomach is still usable...well, if you can, open up stomach and bowels, wash them out, and pack them separately. Otherwise they'll heat and rot, maybe even burst, if they don't freeze through fast enough, and I don't think it's cold enough to freeze an undressed carcass in time.

Arudal could hear his own voice shaking as he told Sir Salarond what Finvar had said, though he tried to hold Finvar's images - fur-cloaked hunters breaking the ice on a stream and carrying wooden buckets of water to slosh through the elk's body-cavity, the memory of a heavily Northman-accented voice saying, "If no one else wants the paunch, I'll take it home for Gytha to make a pudding in" - firmly in his mind to keep his own thoughts from distressing his squire-brother.

"Thank you," Salarond said. "Rest well." He nodded to Arudal.

Arudal slowly separated his awareness from Finvar's, leaving his squire-brother to the timeless stillness within him - if he did not speak to Finvar again, it would seem to the Artegalian as though not a moment had passed before he was awakening, please Amandeth, in his own restored body. He explained this to Sir Salarond. The commander's brow creased. "I cannot promise that we shall not need Finvar's advice again as we press on into winter. Most of us have campaigned in heavy snow, but he grew up in the north of Artegal. Still, I shall try to trouble him as little as may be."

Arudal winced as a set of heavier footsteps jarred through the wain. Sir Thoron's rough voice seemed to boom through his head, "Ari! What is this that Lostren is trying to tell me about Finvar?"

"Sir," Arudal whispered. The Common tongue was coming back to him easily now, as though speaking to Finvar inside his mind had opened a pathway to it. "Sir, I have his soul kept safe. If we preserve his body..."

"Careful, there!" Salarond told the other knight sharply as Thoron descended on Arudal's pallet with his arms outstretched. Thoron halted just in time: Arudal thought that his knight had meant to sweep him up in a bruising bear-hug, but instead, Thoron squeezed his shoulders lightly.

"Well done, squire," Thoron murmured. It seemed to Arudal that he could see a gleam of water standing in the big knight's dark eyes, Thoron's deep voice catching roughly in his throat. "Stepping in to fill the gap was the right thing to do, though I think we could have closed to hold them off anyway. And...did you get any of them?"

"Two," Arudal said - with no little pride, now that he thought about it.

"Very well done. Salarond, how long before Ari is back on his feet?"

"Three to five days, at least."

"Hmmph. Take good care of him." Thoron patted Arudal awkwardly on the shoulder again and lumbered out, the floorboards shaking beneath his tread.

Arudal tried to push himself up on his elbow, but Sir Salarond laid a hand on his chest. "No, Ari. Don't move. I want to show you something." The healer held a small mirror in front of Arudal's face.

The first thing Arudal saw in his reflection was his eyes - one pupil swollen so that it almost filled the iris, one shrunk to near a pinpoint. He was as pale as any of the Agathim, his skin actually whiter than the damp cloth on his forehead and translucent, like eggshell-thin alabaster. The lump on his skull showed poison-dark through his golden hair. *Dear Amandeth, am I going to die anyway now?* Arudal wondered, with a chill little shiver of nausea.

"Will you stay flat in bed and ask for the pan when you need it?" Salarond pressed him. "Even if Malni is the one watching over you?"

"Uh...yes, as long as she is not the one who, who..."

"We can arrange that, Ari," the healer soothed. "You may not be hurt as badly as I thought you were, but you are not out of danger yet. There may still be some bleeding inside your skull, though I would expect you to be more disoriented if you were in a worse state." Salarond had changed to Bright Elvish, and Arudal answered in the same tongue.

"I had almost lost Common for a few minutes, at least to speak, but it came back when I touched Finvar."

"Do you speak any of the tongues of the Horse-Tribes?" Salarond asked. Now he was speaking in the Sky-Tail dialect, the language of the largest tribe and the one most often used by the different tribes for trade among themselves.

"I know Sky-Tail from...word-lore, but not well to speak." He switched over to the dialect he had learned from Boraitiz. "White Wolf is the only dialect that I speak well. Our chief family groom is from that tribe, and he taught me when I was a child, so that I became interested in the likenesses of words."

"I see. Very good, Ari." The commander went back to Imperial. "Now, do you have any idea why the...Agathim?...thought that you were our leader?"

"I think it must have been because they could see me more clearly than the rest of us, sir. The Empire used necromancy quite freely in the latter reigns, and they certainly knew that they were dead - they could even have been in Shadow before the Fall." Arudal knew that some of the duties of his own kinsmen in the State's service involved overseeing Agathim used for covert work or as messengers when greater than human speed was called for, but that was not his own secret to share. Most Tharandrostans would be shocked, even appalled, to know that the Spectral Service existed; it was certainly not something to speak of to Kantareans.

Salarond gave Arudal a long, thoughtful look. "Hmm. I have been, I think, adequately rebuked for mistrusting you once already. And Aviyani forbid that I should distress a patient in your condition by pressing into sensitive matters when there is no need to - but if you have any more thoughts on this subject, now or later, I would appreciate you sharing them with me." The healer's voice was gentle, but Arudal could hear the steel of the order beneath the softness, like a blade wrapped in velvet.

"I shall, sir. Uh...I mean no offense by it, but it may be that I am the most clearly of pure blood in our party, and golden hair was seldom seen in Imperial days except among the highest families - it is more common in Tharandrost now because of the closeness of our breeding, just as more of us have gifts of the mind than in earlier days."

"Indeed," Salarond murmured, as if speaking to himself. "Well, Ari, you are best off resting for now. We shall speak more of this when you are better recovered."

Arudal tried to nod, but could only move his head a little. Suddenly his jaws stretched in an uncontrollable yawn that ended in a moan of pain.

"Have you any black-roast beans left?"

"Yes, sir. In my pack."

"Good."

Sir Salarond moved quietly away; Arudal heard him rustling about a little, then going out. The next set of footsteps was heavy, slow, and clumsy: Arudal knew it was Berek even before he heard the voice.

"You're not an Elf," Berek said. His voice was high-pitched, almost shaky, as though he were terrified by Arudal - or by his own bravery in speaking up.

"Not of full blood. You knew that."

"Not even half-blooded. You...nearly all of you...are Mordhagoernim."

"No."

"Do you think I'm stupid?" Berek challenged, a shivering whine in his voice. "I already suspected before last night. When I saw...them...I knew. With the golden hair, you look so much like Lord Karsil that I didn't guess when it was just the two of you together, but the rest of you...you could dye your hair, but you couldn't change your eyes, could you?"

"What are you going to do about it?" Arudal asked, his thudding heartbeat pounding through his skull. Right now, even Berek could stick a knife in him where he lay, and he didn't think he had the strength to stop the boy.

"I don't...All of you, you were fighting to defend me, weren't you? It pointed at me, and I could tell it wanted me."

"Yes. Yes, he did, and yes, we were."

"Malni said so, but she would believe any good of you."

Arudal would have raised his eyebrows if he could have. Surely Malni could not speak High Imperial...no: Rhys must have told her proudly how he had fought to keep her safe.

"Had we given one of you over to them, we could have passed without fighting." And had I known that Finvar would be killed, I would have traded your life for his gladly, Arudal thought. But, though he would far rather have seen Berek fall in the battle than his squire-brother, he could not even make himself believe that he would have surrendered a companion - even an unwelcome one of lesser blood, even one like Berek who could not so much as imagine loyalty or honour - to his death without a fight.

"Why didn't you?" Berek burst out quietly. "Finvar was killed, you were nearly killed, Tirothar was raving and witless with fear for most of the night...We could all have been killed. Why didn't you just give them the peasant girl and go on?"

"When Shakhor and Karsil took their squires on, they swore to care for them as best they could. As for you - Whether you understand it or not, you are one of our own now. Even though it meant risking all our lives, we could not knowingly give your life for our safety."

"Then," Berek said, his light voice suddenly bleak, "I owe you more of a debt than our contract covers. I have nothing with which to pay you now, but when we have returned to Hatin's City, I can pledge my share of my father's trade that you will be paid in gold and goods as befits the cost of my life."

Arudal's mouth seemed to fill with something nasty and bitter. If he had been sitting up, he would have spat. "In our land, it is considered an insult to speak of honour as though it may be purchased." Although great deeds - such as saving the life of a king's son, for instance - might be rewarded with titles and lands of nobility...but mentioning that would only confuse the issue for Berek. "Rather, remember this if you are ever asked to show a like loyalty to us."

"Would you make a slave of me, then?" Berek asked. Arudal could not tell what feelings were behind the words: the boy's voice was tightly controlled, blank as an empty mirror.

"Not a slave, but a man of honour. If you were a slave, there would have been no reason not to give you to the Agathim." In truth, Arudal would have fought just as hard to protect his body-slave Cenlac, or old Finna the cook who was always ready to slip the master's children sweet biscuits when they had been sent to bed without dessert, or...any of his family's household slaves, really: the Imperial line had been created to care for the lesser races as well as to rule them.

"I will think on that." Arudal heard Berek's breath coming more harshly, as though it had taken a physical effort for the fat youth to speak as he had. "Anyway, you need not think that I will betray your secret to others. If I did, I would burn in the cage with you, for fear that your magics had tainted me."

Arudal was not sure how far he believed that, but he said nothing. The wagon creaked, and suddenly the rich scent of black-roast tea filled his nostrils, his mouth watering a little even as his stomach twisted.

"Ari, I've brought you your brew," Malni said. "Berek, get away from there and let me give it to him. Lord Salarond says he's not to try to sit up if it can be helped."

Berek grunted, but Arudal heard his weight shifting away. It hurt too much for him to flinch from Malni's hand sliding beneath his neck; helpless, he had to let her raise his head and hold the cup to his lips as he sipped carefully.

Salarond, or whoever had brewed the black-roast tea, had known what he was doing. The familiar rich-bitter taste was comforting, and even seemed to make the pain in his head recede a little, like the first waves of an ebb-tide slipping just below the high-water line. "Poor thing," Malni crooned. "And you fought so bravely - Sir Thoron says you killed two of them. Finavi is starting to teach me how to use sword and shield as you do, but it's harder than it looks."

Waste of time, Arudal thought. He had begun to learn how to fight at the age of twenty, with a little wooden sword and shield made for a child's hands, and he knew how far he had to go to approach the skill of any of the White Company knights, even with his inborn advantages of speed and strength. A full-grown woman of Common blood, just beginning to learn... impossible: she should keep to her archery. Though Rhys is very good, considering, he admitted grudgingly to himself. And it was also true that Arudal had not really been trained with the intention that he should serve the State in combat; he had only learned what all boys in Tharandrost, even those destined to be mages or artisans or fishermen, had to know, so that his skills, even with Karsil's tutoring, were just up to those of the other squires.

He wished that Malni would be quiet, but she kept talking. "Rhys says that the Mordhagoernim demanded our lives, and that you fought to save us. Ari, I want to thank you...however I can."

"You're welcome," Arudal muttered. He wanted to say, Let me drink my tea in silence and then go away, but he could not bring himself to speak so roughly to a woman.

"No, I mean it. If there is anything I can do for you...anything at all..." Malni's voice had dropped to a low purr, and Arudal could just feel the tips of her fingers lightly stroking the blankets over his chest. He thought of the kiss she had given him, and of the girl at the Ducal Arms.

"I am betrothed at home," he said bluntly. It was not quite true; but he and Arothir had always assumed that they would be mated.

Malni's hand stilled. "Oh," she said. Then, "That's all right," and she began to pet him again, lifting his head for another sip of tea. "Do you need your compress changed? Sir Salarond mentioned that the bandage should be freshly moistened as often as possible."

It was three days before Sir Salarond pronounced it safe for Arudal to move on again. Sir Eroth had regained some of the feeling in his shield-arm, though the harm done by the Shadow-blade was healing only very slowly. Arudal's legs were still rather shaky under him, and he was beset by frequent pounding headaches, but his pupils had largely returned to normal, and the black-bruised lump on his head had subsided enough that he was able to wear his helmet again. As was his duty, he had told Sir Salarond about his conversation with Berek; their commander said little, but Arudal could tell that he was thinking deeply on the matter. The worst annoyance of Arudal's convalescence, however, was that it was almost impossible to get rid of Malni: she was constantly making possets and changing the herb-soaked cloths on his head, and fussing over him until he felt like the last kitten left from a sickly litter. She ignored his crossness blithely, or gave him soothing answers, saying that she knew he was in great pain and could hardly be held responsible for ill temper. Even having told her that he was betrothed at home did not seem to change her attitude: either such things made little difference to the folk of the West, or Malni simply did not care.

In desperation, Arudal finally said, "Can you not see that Rhys would make a much better mate for you than I?"

Malni put her hand on his forehead, smoothing out a few wrinkles in the damp compress. Arudal's muscles twitched with the effort of not grabbing her wrist and pulling it away: for two days he had done nothing but lie there, and he was beginning to feel restive, like a horse that had not been ridden for too long jumping and kicking at every touch of a fly against its skin. "Rhys is a nice boy, but he is only a boy. He may be a year older than I - but at this age, a girl is already a woman, while a boy is not yet a man."

"I think that is not so. Rhys has seen far more of battle than I. And, I believe, acquited himself nobly," Arudal added. It seemed to him as though he were speaking through glass, unreal: he could not believe that he was saying such things of a Plainsman. Yet it was true, and Malni would surely be looking for the talents of a warrior in a potential breeding partner.

"So I have heard," she said. "And he did hold his place in the square against the Mordhagoernim."

"He has been Sir Shakhor's squire for nearly two years now, and is likely to be a knight before I am." Arudal bit back the thoughts that followed those words, that Kantar had truly become degenerate. The White Crown might be slower to knight a Plainsman than if Rhys were of Imperial blood, but so far as Arudal could tell, Sir Shakhor was grooming his squire for knighthood's estate as surely as Sir Salarond was teaching Lostren to command. And it was true enough that if Rhys could be made a knight at all, he probably would receive belt and spurs before Arudal, who had yet to finish his doctorate before he even began military service in Tharandrost.

Malni nodded thoughtfully. Her round eyes were very blue, with faint threads of yellow radiating out from the pupil as though she bore a slight drop of Imperial blood. Even in the wagon's dimness, Arudal could see the look on her broad-cheeked face: she might have been staring far over the sea at the first distant cloud-rim of an unknown land. "Lostren has been telling me of knighthood, as best he can. He speaks our tongue well, though not quite as well as you do."

Then it's his turn to deal with the next innkeeper, Arudal thought as Malni went on. "It sounds a wondrous thing, that folk may live their lives so wholly by trust and faith, with each other and with their lords. I had never known but that the great and powerful were all like the folk of Hatin's City, a tangle of spiders with the greater eating the lesser - when I swore my oath to finavi, I did not know what an, an honour she was offering me." Malni used the Bright Elvish word for honour, and Arudal made a mental note of that: not only the Imperial word, but the concept, had truly been lost in the West. But would Kantar really knight a female Man? - Karsil, if the stories about her were true, had received belt and spurs before she had ever made mention of her sex, and human distinctions of gender hardly applied to Elves.

"She would not have done it if she did not think that you were worthy. Or could become so." Arudal kept his voice even, very careful not to let any of his hurt creep into it. For that little while in Hatin's City, he had felt as close to Dame Karsil as, he guessed, anyone had ever been since she had come to Kantar. And now, does she look on me as her failure?

"It grieves me that she likes you so little. I asked her why, and she said only that it was not a thing to be told me yet, but that I should beware of you. But Lostren and Rhys say that she judges you unfairly. Is it because you are half of human blood, and she expects you to be fully an Elf?"

"Something like that, yes."

"That is sad. Has it often been so for you before?"

"Marriages of different kinds seldom go well." So take the message and leave me alone!

Before Malni could commiserate any further on his supposed trials of birth, Arudal said, "Rhys has done well teaching you to ride. You may have noticed that he is quite skilled with horses?"

"Not so skilled as you," Malni answered airily.

"That is only time, and long training. For one of his race, he is exceptional." In truth, Arudal had no idea how well Plainsmen in the wild rode; but slaves were seldom allowed to mount horses at all.

"His race...Rhys and Lostren are of a different kindred from the others, are they not? And Lostren is higher-born than Rhys?"

"What makes you think that?"

"I am not sure," Malni confessed. "Their colouring, maybe. And Rhys speaks differently, and when we are all together, if he is not with his knight, I have noticed that he will stand a little closer to Lostren, and look at him as if he expects something."

"Lostren is very high-born, but not of the same race as Rhys: there are redheads in many kindreds." Although never in the Imperial lineages unless those had been mixed with Plainsman or Northman. But if I can make her start thinking about Rhys, maybe she will turn her attention to him and leave me alone. Arudal scrambled desperately for something to say about the Plainsmen that might make Rhys more interesting to Malni, and came up with, "Rhys' folk are..." undisciplined, brawling, insolent savages. "A free people: they speak their minds easily, and chieftains must have the approval of their warriors when they would do battle. They love their horses as their children; you may have seen the tears in Rhys' eyes when he grooms his riding-steed and thinks of his warhorse who died on the way here." Malni nodded slowly. And if the truth of all else I say is veiled for her sake, Arudal thought, that much I must truly grant Rhys, and accept that there is more humanity than I thought in his race as well as himself. "They are..." liars and braggarts, who care far more for the sound of their own words than for any thread of truth that might be hidden in them, and illiterate primitives as well. "They put great value on speaking well, so that some of the most honoured among them are not warriors or leaders, but poets. And they do not write their histories as we do, but remember them in lengthy works of epic, so that the singers of a tribe are revered for bearing all the lore of their heroes and deeds." Arudal wondered if Malni herself could read and write. It seemed unlikely.

"Rhys does not speak particularly well," Malni observed.

Arudal tried to shrug, wincing as the movement sent a stab of pain through his head. "He was not raised among the tribes. The village where his family lived was raided..." He told her the story as Lostren had told it to him, watching Malni's pale brows draw together. Yes, go on, he urged silently. Maybe sympathy will do what praise will not. "And Sir Shakhor has found him to be a worthy squire," Arudal finished.

The girl thought about that a moment. "I hope I may do as well," she said at last. "But tell me: how was it that you came to be Sir Thoron's squire, rather than finavi's?"

At his wits' end, Arudal rolled his head a little and moaned. "Please, it hurts to talk."

"Are you feeling worse? Should I fetch Sir Salarond?"

"No...no, just leave me be quiet for a little time. Please."

Malni set about changing the compress on his forehead again, but at least she was silent, for which Arudal was deeply grateful. In all his life, he had never thought that he would have to praise a Plainsman for anything besides the skills and temperament of a slave. And at home, even had Rhys not been put down early, as he assuredly would have been the moment his talents were recognised, there would have been no thinking of matching him with a doe as spirited as Malni: such a combination could only produce unruly and troublesome whelps. They make worse matings in the wild, Arudal soothed his conscience.

Children's histories of Tharandrost's earlier days often showed pictures of bare-breasted does with lime-spiked hair beating their chests with the flats of swords as they screamed encouragement at the whooping hosts of their bucks. Those histories referred vaguely to atrocities, but left out the specific details of what the Plainsman females had done with captured Imperials - but Arudal knew what could still happen when civilized folk fighting Plainsmen were caught by their savage enemies, and in comparison to the wild does with their skinning knives and jagged testicle-bodkins, Malni seemed as docile as a Kantarean noblewoman at her needlepoint.

Over the days of his convalescence, Arudal learned more of what had happened in the battle with the Agathim. Karsil still was not speaking to him, but the Kantareans had all been shaken - or shamed - out of whatever delusions they were suffering concerning him. It was, indeed, Tirothar that had run as the fight began, overcome by Shadow-Fear and witless; even hampered by terror, Lostren and Rhys had managed to hold their ground all through the battle. Berek had fallen to the earth and cowered there; Malni, secure in her blind trust for Dame Karsil and the other knights, had acquitted herself well, shooting where she got a chance until she had run out of Elven arrows, though after that she could do no more: she had tried to stab from the second rank or block the blades of their foes from her comrades, but her bronze-headed pike had simply passed through the Agathim and their weapons without doing them any harm. Finvar had been killed when the point of a Shadow-blade had driven up beneath the hooped plate-skirt of his armour, entering his belly just above the groin and sliding up through him.

Though Shadow-swords did not tear the flesh of living Men - save agathudalim - they killed it where they passed. It had been a mercy that the rotted wall of a major artery had burst almost at once: otherwise, without magic, Salarond could not have healed the wide track of dead flesh through Finvar's bowels, and it would have been a long and agonizing dying for him. Eroth's injury was no more than a deep bone-bruise from a mace-blow that had dented the pauldron of his shield-arm; had he been armoured in ordinary steel, the Shadow-weapon would have passed straight through it, and the arm been lost altogether.

Even though Arudal knew that Finvar's soul was safe and well within his own, that they would not have to consign his friend's cold body to flame or worm, he found himself on the verge of tears when he actually saw Finvar's rounded face gray-white against the snow heaped tightly about him, a sweat-iced wave of ash-blond hair over his brow and snow filling his open mouth. Thank Amandeth, the rest of Finvar's body was covered with snow and burlap wrappings, so that Arudal did not have to look at the open cavity. It was bad enough to know that the snow-packed barrel beside the corpse held Finvar's entrails...Arudal thought again of the names of the dead that the Kantareans had spoken before the Lord of Shadow. How could soldiers bear it, to see their friends die again and again, and still go on?

Arudal had not feared so greatly for himself, even in the battle, as he sorrowed to see Finvar lying dead before him; and he thanked Amandeth that, when he would do his own required term in the military, he would not be a front-line fighter, but serving the State in the quiet of Shadow, where he would never have to look at a dear companion's bowels spread bloody and dirty on the earth. It was not that Arudal was unfamiliar with the sight of dead bodies - hardly so: would a smith's child would be unfamiliar with hammers and tongs? - but the corpses used for training at his grandmother's fortress were tidy ones, usually unmarked, or at worst, with their throats neatly cut and sewn back together. And, more importantly, none of them had been friends of his, or even slaves he had known in life: the Hidden Estate often received those slaves who were condemned to death in any case, that the State might get some use of them in payment for their crimes.

Chapter 22: Knowledge and Choice

"Knowledge is power, power forces truth, though it be between evil and wrong. A simple man may keep his heart clean; a ruler must hold the harder to what good he can, for it is the worst part for him to sacrifice his people to his conscience's ease.

"And yet, if the ruler is not guided by his conscience, he is no better than a tyrant.

Therefore, seek no power willingly, for it brings only sorrow; but happy is the man who may be free of such a burden, and follow the dictates of his soul pure-hearted without harm to others."

- Twentieth Emperor Indizer, Meditations, p. 93.

As the squires untethered the horses for departure - though Arudal was still excused duties - Arudal heard Rhys cry out, "Someone, come and have a look at what it is I have found!"

Arudal swung himself slowly and carefully down from the wagon, walking over to the others gathering around the Plainsman. Rhys was pointing down by his feet, into the scuffed and trampled snow.

"Karsil, what do you make of this?" Sir Salarond was asking.

"It is not magical, if that is what you mean," the Elf replied. "Yet there is something about it I mislike - and I do not think that it was one of us who dropped it."

"Is it safe to touch?"

Karsil paused before she answered. "I can say only that I believe there is no enchantment directly upon it." She paused again, repeated, "Yet there is something about it...Thoron, was this not where you were standing when you slew the leader of those accursed ghosts?"

Sir Thoron looked about, shuffling in the ravaged crusts of trodden snow and dead grass as if to retrace his movements. "It might have been. Yes, we were close in to the horses at that point. And there - " he gestured to a freshly ice-dusted patch of bare earth where the snow had been shoveled away - "is where Finvar went down. I'd say I was about here, yes."

"Arudal," Sir Salarond called. "I want you to have a look at this."

Arudal moved a little faster, though his head pounded softly with the exertion. He crouched down so that he could see whatever it was they were talking about.

The item that Rhys had turned up was a thick silver ring with a large flat stone, lying face-down. As Karsil had said, there was no glimmer of magic about it; but there was something attractive about the smoothly moulded curve of band and bezel, the solid artistic perfection of heavy simplicity in silver that often characterized Imperial jewelry. He picked it up, turning it over. The stone was black - a black sapphire, Arudal thought - inlaid with the tiny shape of a horse beneath a six-pointed star, both in silver; the wide, heavy band was just the perfect size to slip on over his own right forefinger. Lest that be taken ill, he held it out instead for the others to look at.

"I know what that is," Lostren said suddenly. "It was the signet given to Imperial messengers on a mission. And in perfect condition: a collector would pay a considerable price for it."

"Imperial messengers," murmured Sir Salarond. He took the ring from Arudal's hand, murmuring something. Still there was no sign of any magic about it: if the Agathan had borne it since the Empire's Fall, it was only from habit, as was often the case with the Undead. "I suppose it is worth keeping for its historical value, if nothing else. Ari, keep this with you. Do not put it on; but if you detect anything magical or unusual about it, tell me."

Dame Karsil muttered something in Bright Elvish that sounded very much to Arudal like "giving a hawk charge of a songbird's nest", but she quieted when Sir Salarond looked hard at her.

"There must be something of magic in the metal, at least," Arudal said thoughtfully. "Otherwise it would not have stayed upon an Agathan's hand...but it could simply be an alchemical alloy such as Valderian steel or steel-glass, rather than enchanted itself." He turned it over in his fingers again, looking closely, but still saw nothing save the smooth beauty of the ring itself.

I should tell Sir Salarond about my prisoner, Arudal thought. I could ask him...Salarond had wanted him to interrogate Eluthia, but the memory of the commander's anger when Arudal had suggested summoning one of the Ukuthrim as a scout was still raw and fresh. Still, he had been taught all his life never to hide information from a superior...and he won't kill me or abandon me here, not with Finvar in my keeping.

Arudal cleared his throat. "Sir, may I speak with you in private a moment?"

Sir Salarond raised a shaggy gray eyebrow, but nodded, walking away from the others with Arudal. When they were past the clearing of trodden snow, Salarond said, "What is it now?"

"The Agathan that threw me down - I captured him in turn. If you wish me to interrogate him, I shall."

"Why did you say nothing of this before?" Salarond's voice was mild, but Arudal could see the spark of anger glowing in his gray-rimmed eyes, like coals heating beneath a smith's bellows. Arudal thought he had mentioned taking the Agathan, but Sir Salarond must not have understood him, and it was true that he should have made himself very clear to the Kantarean.

"Hurt as I was, I did not think I had the strength to draw information from his mind, if he would not tell me freely."

"Arudal. You should know better than to second-guess your commander on such matters - or your healer, for that matter."

"Yes, sir. I won't do it again, sir. I'm sorry."

"Consider yourself reprimanded. Now. I think you still are not fit for a psychic battle, but we shall see what your prisoner is willing to tell us. Can you bring it into full manifestation in daylight?"

"Not easily, sir, and it would cause him great pain. If you order me to, I shall, but only under protest. Sir." Arudal was trembling slightly when he had finished speaking, but he was quite certain that he was within his rights to object to - what could only be called torture. Arudal was not even sure he could bring himself to force the Agathan out into the scorching agony of full daylight, for an Undead that was not fed full on the strength of the living could not bear the rays of the Sun without the greatest suffering. "I could ask him questions without harming him."

"I think for this purpose I shall ask the questions myself. Nevertheless, we shall wait until evening, if that is your recommendation."

"Very much so, sir."

"Good."

Arudal looked up at Sir Salarond in surprise, but the knight was already walking away, his plate tassets clinking softly under his cloak. What did you expect? Arudal thought. He looked down at the Imperial messenger's signet in his hand, turning it over and over. It would fit so neatly on his own finger - but he knew better than to put on strange rings, even though he could see no gleam of magic about it. Instead he slipped it into his belt pouch and went back to the others.

Arudal still was not allowed to ride Inmanat. Instead he sat in the wain with Berek and Malni, asking them questions and making notes until his head began to ache from focusing his eyes on the parchment, then teaching them Bright Elven and - for there was little point in trying to keep it from them now - Common, and trying not to look at the burlap cocoon hiding Finvar's frozen body in its snow packing, or the barrel beside it.

"How much longer do we have before we reach another town?" Arudal finally asked, repeating the sentence in Elven and Common.

Berek and Malni looked at each other; Malni shrugged. "Now you know why folk seldom travel through the Barren Hills," she said. "I can't even guess."

Berek's brow furrowed, as though he were trying to visualize a map. "Three more days, maybe. There is a good-sized trading town called Cirrod on the river about...a day or so upstream, at the rate we're going. Do you think we'll stop there?"

Arudal thought about it. The halt had cost them dearly in terms of fodder for the horses. Their steeds would be lucky to make it out of the Barren Hills without going on quarter-rations, but he guessed that Sir Salarond would try to avoid larger settlements if they could - especially since Berek had betrayed his knowledge of their origins.

"I don't know. What do they trade?" he asked reflexively.

"Grain, fruit, and wine from the plains around; furs and herbs from the Wood-Folk to the north; amber, bronze ingots, and precious stones from the west, silks and other fine fabrics, and wrought bronze, silver, and gold-work via the sea routes to our city," Berek recited in a familiar rote sing-song - Arudal knew he himself would have sounded the same if asked about the exports of, for instance, Fel. "Some exotic herbs and spices from the sea-routes through our city, but there is little market for them outside Cirrod. If my father had not given you such a good price for your load, you might have gotten better money for some of your goods there, but probably not have been able to sell all of them."

"I see." And I think we will certainly avoid it, travelling as we are with Lord Hatneth's son.

After dinner that night, Sir Salarond ordered Lostren, Eroth, Thoron, and Shakhor to accompany himself and Arudal into the wain, while the rest of the party stayed on watch outside.

"Do you need any ritual preparation?" Salarond asked.

Arudal shook his head, relieved at how little it ached. "No, sir. For a conjuring, we would want to draw a circle, but it is not necessary for this. I shall not bring him out unless I am sure of my hold."

"Very well."

The knights and Lostren drew their swords, exchanging quiet looks: Sir Salarond must have explained matters to them as they rode. Arudal took a deep breath, sinking into Shadow. The swords flared brightly against the dark mist, an aurora of shimmering colours: the still crystal place waited within him, where it always was - Finvar in his stillness, waiting to be summoned to life again, and the Agathan near by him in the cold silence of Shadow trapped in clear adamant.

Arudal reached into the Imperial soldier's mind. There was something familiar to its icy shape, like a well-known crystal goblet between his fingers: the Agathan might almost have been one of Arudal's own kinsmen in Shadow, with whose help the young agathudal had learned to use his gifts. Ostarak... Arudal knew the Agathan's name, and with that, he tightened his grip, opening the gateway within himself and guiding the other out, pushing him through the Shadow-door into full being on the green earth, but somehow - Arudal could not say quite how he did it, only that he knew he was doing it, as naturally as keeping his heart beating - holding the Agathan wrapped in his own mind, so that he could not draw the life-strength from the breathing Men about him.

Arudal heard a soft gasp from one of his companions. He knew what they would see: a faint misty shape, coalescing and sharpening until, save for his paleness and the cloak of Shadow-Fear about him, Ostarak might almost have been a living man. The Agathan was close to Arudal's own height, perhaps a little shorter, but his light chainmail clung to a sturdy figure with broad shoulders and massively muscled chest, some twenty or thirty pounds heavier in life than Arudal. The sight of the Imperial soldier's shape clear against the flickering glimmers of magic and darkness of Shadow struck Arudal with a sharp pang of homesickness, but he thrust it from him: this was no time for such feelings.

The Imperial messenger bowed to Arudal. "My lord of Aglarek," he said formally. "It seems that I am your prisoner."

"You are. Ostarak, I regret to inform you that the rest of your troop are slain."

Ostarak sighed, a faint sound like wind rustling through dry leaves. "We rode together so long...I beg leave to give you their names, that you may do them honour."

"I shall."

"Sir Darthumazad Ertarikun was our commander, who offered you passage and a chance to yield..." Arudal listened solemnly, committing the Imperial names to memory. It hurt to hear them: each could have been a Tharandrostan, a member of his own scarce and precious race - a friend or a kinsman, even. It seemed wrong that he had been among their killers, and he regretted his pride in the battle.

"Thank you, Ostarak," Arudal said when the Agathan was done. "I shall remember; I shall do honour. But now, I fear, my commander has questions which I must require you to answer."

Ostarak stared into Arudal's face, the rim of amber fire about his pupils glowing bright enough to cast radiating shadows through the gray crystal of his irises. "Will it suffice if I give you my word to truthfully answer any questions which do not betray my post?"

Arudal wanted to say yes, but Sir Salarond was staring intently, not at Ostarak, but at Arudal himself. And there was no way in which a squire could justify usurping a commander's prerogative in such a matter.

"That is up to my commander to decide. Sir?"

The set of Salarond's wiry shoulders eased just slightly as he said, "We trust your honour, for you and yours have dealt honourably with us. But what we ask, we must know the answers to. Arudal."

"Sir."

"See that it is so."

"Yes, sir." Although Arudal did not move, it seemed to him that he was closer to the Agathan, almost as though he stood doubled: Ostarak's Shadow-cold thrilled icy and silent through him, but at the same time, he could feel the warmth of his own skin wrapped about his body like a cloak and the hot blood pulsing through his veins to the pounding beat of his heart.

If the Aglarek gift survived, then the Empire cannot be altogether dead, Ostarak was thinking. *Even if Lord Arudal strips my mind, it is worth it to know that we did not lose everything when the earth burst into flame and the mountains fell...I have not ridden in the cold and dark this long in vain.*

"Ostarak," Salarond said. "Why do you address Arudal as you do?"

"Sir, only one House that I have ever heard of has the gift of Mind-Speaking those who dwell in Shadow, and Lord Arudal told me himself that he was of that line."

Salarond's face was no more than a gray shadow in the darkness, but it seemed to Arudal that he could see his commander's questioning look.

"The founder of the House of Arudal was the fourth son of Duke Aglarek, sir. After the Fall, there was no way of knowing if his brothers had lived or died."

"Most of the Houses of Tharandrost were founded for the same reason, at the same time," Lostren added. "It was always a post for younger sons."

Arudal flashed a grateful look at the other squire. Lostren's eyes glimmered slightly greenish from the eyeslots of his gold-ornamented helmet - had he a small measure of otherworldly sight, as well as Foresight, from his Plainsman ancestor? But there was no time to think about that; Sir Salarond was already speaking again. "Why did your troop linger in Shadow?"

"We were messengers, sir, and it was laid upon us that we must carry out our duties in life or death. We were riding for the Imperial Seat when fire sprang from the earth..." The image in the Agathan's mind struck Arudal with full force. It seemed to him that he was galloping swiftly over a smooth road through the green fields, certain in the knowledge that Commander Sir Darthumazad bore the signet ring that would ward off all mishaps, protect them from any hindrance of foe or mischance unless the Lord of Night himself barred their way...At first Ostarak thought his steed had bucked, but it was the ground itself tossing and crumpling; the screaming of horses and men tore through his ears as he fell. A searing burst of pain up his leg, the jagged end of his shinbone sticking out white through a gush of blood...a deep booming beneath him, and the ground humping up and cracking into trickles of flame, the grass catching fire, the smell of scorched hair and flesh on the burning wind in the second before the fire crawled over him, ate into his lungs as he drew breath to scream...and then the cold hunger in the dark, but even the ice-cutting pain of Shadow was better than that stark second of burning agony before he slipped into the darkness...

Arudal was panting hard, his arms clasped tight about his chest. His grandmother had warned him about slipping too far in when he Mind-Read, and he had found control easy enough before, but he had never done this with a stranger, never when it meant more than proving his talent and pleasing his family and teachers.

"I'm all right," he gasped. "Keep on."

"What message were you carrying?" Salarond asked firmly.

"We went to bear word to the Imperial Seat that the False Prince had been seen in Murumban, but escaped before he could be captured. Had we been sent sooner..." The Agathan's voice trailed off into a hiss of cold wind. Though he had narrowed the gateway between them to keep from being altogether whelmed by Ostarak's feelings, Arudal's heart clenched miserably with the other's knowledge that a grievous error had been made by his commanders; that fear of the Emperor's wrath had delayed the governor's report long enough to allow Avalar to reach the Imperial Seat, and bring the Empire to its end. Almost seventeen hundred years to think on it...Time meant little to the Undead: the knowledge was still bitterly fresh, yet weighted with a sense of countless years as well - a torment endless and unchanging, unmeasured, without the healing that time brought to the living.

"And since then?"

"We rode, and waited...until you slew my comrades."

"Do you know the way to the Imperial Seat through this changed land?"

"Only as the road lies in Shadow. Not the ways that living men may take - save my lord of Aglarek, if he would ride with me."

A shiver ran up Arudal's back, and he did not know whether it was fear or excitement. He had seen the Shadow-horses, as fine as the best steeds in the Prince's stables. Though they were no more than memories in the minds of ghosts, part of him could not help longing to mount up: the Shadow-steed would be as real to his touch as Ostarak's steely grip on his wrist, or the ghostly sword that had nearly split his head.

"Were you bound to the Barren Hills where we met you?" Sir Eroth asked softly. "Or can you ride freely?"

"We rode from Murumban to the Imperial Seat and back. But only there - where the earth lifted beneath our hooves and the fire took us - could we touch the green earth and take, if we were lucky, the life-strength to ease our pain for a little while."

Now Arudal understood what he had seen and felt in the land the night of the attack. A shared anguish strong enough to shift some twenty-five men into Shadow at once, a unified act of desperate will fueled by the power of their deaths...that had weakened the walls of the worlds and left its mark upon the earth, even through the fires of the Wrath.

There was silence for a little time, until Salarond said hoarsely, "Tell us what you can of the Imperial Seat as it is now and whoever - or whatever - still dwells there."

"Not by my will," Ostarak whispered. But Arudal was already deep within his mind, and the walls of the Agathan's resistance crumbled like the crenellations of a sand-fortress beneath the rising tide.

"Our ruler is still there, with those who serve under him. The treasures of Empire are buried beneath fallen stone, but that is nothing to the Shadow-Realm. Yet the city is at war, for there was a second claimant. Our Emperor was closest to the Ruby Throne when the False Prince fled from his own slaves: he took the rule, as his blood entitled him to, and those who were faithful to him have guarded him and fought for him. But the Imperial Seat is garrisoned in two parts now - we seldom do open battle: the Emperor and the Pretender watch each other, and wait, and gather their strength."

"One gods-cursed thing after another," Sir Thoron muttered under his breath. No one else spoke.

"Show me the Imperial Seat as it is now," breathed Arudal, his words barely whispered to give shape to his will. He did not need to try to fix the images in his mind: they sprang full-blown and set, so that he knew he could sit down and draw a map to scale. He had seen the drawings made by one of Prince Avalar's artisans, showing the remains of the Wrath - the great fallen towers of stone, corridors blocked off by heaps of earth and broken archways, roofs long shattered and open to the sky - and also maps of the Imperial Seat as it was before the Fall, both in school and on the ship journeying here: the main areas of the City were already familiar to him, his knowledge of where the Emperor's palace and other great buildings such as the Imperial Library and the Hallows of Healing had been now overlaid upon Ostarak's memory of the City.

The Agathan did not remember its destruction, but two images vied in his
mind: the living streets where he had once marched, and the walls and buildings
that glimmered whole in his Shadow-sight now, phantoms of light in the empty
darkness.

And what Avalar, or the gods working through him, had sealed off, time...and,
perhaps, the wills of the two rulers who struggled now in the Fallen Seat...had
freed again. There were no longer hidden pockets of darkness such as Avalar had
written of; but through Ostarak's sight, Arudal saw the white-faced dead in their
black armour and uniforms marching in sentry rounds through the streets, beneath
the Shadow-memory of gleaming stone and soaring archways, as if the ghosts
still guarded what once had been there. Or is still? Surely the Undead could not
rebuild...

Ostarak must have caught some flicker of what was in Arudal's mind, for the soft
wind-sigh of his voice went on. "I cannot speak for the Emperor, but this much I
can guess: if you will offer him aid against the Pretender, it may well be that he will
grant you whatever you desire if it is within his power. I think it will gladden him to
know that some of his kin still live, when we had thought that all were dead, out to
the Empire's utmost bounds."

Now Arudal could feel his strength beginning to wane, his head aching more
and more severely. He coughed and said, "Sir, I cannot hold too much longer."

"Take him back in," Salarond ordered. "If we think of more questions, we can
ask later - and we may yet need him to guide us."

Arudal breathed deeply, settling himself. Having claimed Ostarak once, it
was easier to do it again; and the Agathan came almost willingly, as if he found
Arudal's mind a place of refuge. The flaring coronas of the swords - the blue-white
writing on Eroth's blade, the greenish-black glow about Salarond's, Thoron's
red and Lostren's gold and Shakhor's blue - dimmed in his sight, the shapes of
the armoured men bulking solidly from the darkness, and Arudal found himself
breathing hard, as if he had just broken the surface after a long dive. He swallowed
hard and said, "It is done, sir."

"Leaving us with more questions than we had before," Salarond said drily. "But
that is not your fault: you did well. Did he answer you well enough for you to sketch
a map?"

"Yes, sir."

"Lostren, get Arudal his pen and parchment. The rest of you may go back to
sleep or the regular watch schedule. Ari, you're still in no condition to keep watch.
Draw your map and then go to bed."

Arudal had learned the skill of map-making in school - vital training for a nation
of sailors and explorers. Although his hands trembled slightly, he was able to trace
the straight cross-hatching that would give the map its scale, lightly sketching in
the main streets and buildings. A single shimmering thread still linked his mind
with Ostarak's; he drew upon the Agathan's thoughts as though they were his own,
marking out the lines between the Emperor's territory and that of the Pretender.

It was not until he had finished that Arudal drew his breath in dismay. The Imperial Library, or its remains, was precisely in the middle of the no-man's-land, the deserted zone that twisted like a broken-backed snake through the city's streets. Daunting as the thought of negotiating with one of the two great Agathim had been, this was worse. They would, as Ostarak had suggested, have to ally with one against the other: and Arudal thought that there was little chance that they would not end up paying the price for their treasure in blood.

"Are you done?" Sir Salarond asked. Wordlessly Arudal handed him the map. Salarond turned it this way and that in the flickering lamp-light, frowning. "Does Ostarak know how many troops each side has?"

Arudal concentrated, drawing the knowledge from the Agathan's mind into his own as if he were reeling in a fishing-line. "The Emperor has...something like five hundred, the Pretender somewhat less, perhaps three to four hundred. But many of the Emperor's men are like Ostarak and his troop, bound to guard certain places or ride certain routes, so that they cannot be of full aid: all those upon whom it was laid to serve the Imperial Crown beyond death must follow him, yet can only do so in such wise as the spells that hold them to Shadow bind them to. So there are sentries who cannot leave their posts, messengers who cannot depart from the track of their rounds, Far-Seers who can gaze only at the places given for their watch, and so forth. The Pretender's men - and women," Arudal added in surprise, distressed at the image that burned into his mind, of long black hair spilling shining from beneath a steel cap-helm, delicate white hands grasping the recurved stave of a short bow...he had known that women had served in the Imperial army once, when their race was more fruitful...

"Go on, Ari," Salarond ordered patiently.

"The Pretender's troops are all free of movement, for they would not have been able to follow him if they were bound."

"An interesting tactical problem. The advantage is the defender's: he can hold, perhaps forever, but never reach out to take and hold more...And thus, seventeen hundred years of stalemate?"

"Just so, sir. Ostarak says that the borders have not changed at all in a long time, though how long is impossible to tell from the awareness of an Agathan. Still, I think we may take it that the real struggle is a magical one, between the Emperor and the Pretender themselves."

"Indeed." Salarond's gray eyebrows drew inward, the line between them deepening in the lamplight. "A long and subtle war, as magic works here now. And a balance...delicate enough, perhaps, to shift under the weight of our company? Or so it may be hoped by whichever one we approach."

Arudal wanted to ask his commander which of the two great Agathim the White Company would fight for, though he knew it was too early for Sir Salarond to have made his decision. Something in his heart drew him to wish that Salarond would offer their services to the Emperor, but he did not know why. It could be only that, having touched Ostarak's mind so closely, some trace of the ghost's loyalty lingered in his own soul like the faint scent of Arothir's perfume lingering in her shed cloaks.

Or perhaps it was an echo of the old songs he had grown up with, the songs from Tharandrost's first days as a military garrison, when the soldiers sang of the homeland they had left, and their troth to the Emperor beyond the Sea. But the White Company's choice would not be made by feelings, least of all by his. The Kantareans, after all, were descended from those nobles who had rebelled against the Emperor, and held Prince Avalar to be their highest hero: if anything, their hearts would incline them to the Pretender.

As Salarond stared at the map, Arudal, almost without thought, drew out Sir Darthumazad's messenger-signet, running his fingers over the smooth cold silver and inlaid stone. Had its magic been destroyed in the Fall? It must have, or the White Company party could not have slain its bearer and his troop...Or would it still protect those who stopped to make a challenge outside of their destined round? A spell strong and subtle enough to give such a general protection might not show up in the ring: the jewel itself might be only a catalyst for a spell sourced, say, through the Ruby Throne, not in itself magical, but a centring point for a great, yet diffuse magic. Or the Imperial Crown? But Avalar wrote that he had ordered it destroyed, for he would not wear the emblem of those rulers who had worshipped Morthugor. Yet Ostarak mentioned the Crown - but no: surely that was only as we refer to the rulership of Tharandrost as the Adamantine Crown, or Kantar as the White Crown, or...

Arudal breathed deeply, letting the image of the silver horse beneath the star flicker through his mind as he widened the thread that linked his thoughts with those of the Agathan. Ostarak, however, knew only that the signet gave protection: he was a soldier, not a mage, and his memories and trust in the emblem were only those set in the days when he had lived.

"Sir, this ring..."

"Yes?"

Quickly Arudal told Sir Salarond the thought that had come to him. Salarond frowned deeply; then his face cleared, his fine-boned jaw setting firm in decision. "Put it on. At worst, it may...provide us with an introduction."

As Arudal had thought, the ring fit perfectly upon his right forefinger, slipping on like a caress of polished silk. Save for its weight, he would hardly have known he was wearing it.

"Do you feel anything?"

"No, sir."

"Well enough. Speak up at once if you do. We will be watching you for signs of anything amiss, but that is for your protection, not because we mistrust you."

Sir Salarond had not apologized for his earlier mistrust, Arudal noticed, but he could not hold that against the Kantarean. Salarond had been doing his duty as best he could, after all, and Arudal had been told often enough that in war, it was usually better to stick firmly by a wrong decision than waver around a right one.

"Thank you, sir."

"If you feel anything strange from it, lay down your weapons and shield immediately, and be ready to take it from your finger on my command."

"Yes, sir."

Although Arudal had expected more discussion of the matter as they rode, Salarond remained silent - keeping his own counsel, as Lostren had said before. They passed through the Barren Hills without further incident, replenishing their stores of food and fodder at the first town they came to, upon the eastern bank of the Cirrith. Despite the cold and the snow heaped along its banks, the wide river still rushed fresh and clear, the ice only now beginning to thicken in a glaze between the dead reeds where its waters eddied more slowly into shallows. There was no sign of any ford or bridge. Lostren looked enquiringly at Arudal as they reined their horses back at the water's edge, and it seemed to Arudal that he knew what the other squire was wondering.

"The binding of a death-doom in Shadow is stronger than the fear of running water," Arudal told Lostren softly. "The ghosts of the drowned will haunt the rivers where they died; Sir Darthumazad's troop were bound to ride their route from the Imperial Seat to the coast and back again, so that this river would not have hindered them. The will or spells of a necromancer, if powerful enough, may force the Undead over water or fire that they could not otherwise cross. And a few Agathim are strong enough in their power or simple will to go over running water of their own accord, else the Lord of Martag could never have threatened Kantar west of the Karasindi."

Lostren nodded thoughtfully, the gold tracery on his helm glittering in the cold winter sunlight. "That is worth knowing. Are there any wards that cannot be passed at all?"

"In theory, not save they be set by the gods. But it takes more strength to defy a ward than to set it: the advantage is with those who use the nature of the green earth."

"Unless they stand in Shadow themselves," Karsil broke in. It was the first time the Elf had spoken to Arudal since Amandeth's Eve, and her green eyes gleamed from the shadow of her steel helm like emeralds shining beneath clear ice. "Would you be able to cross this river if you were not dryshod?"

"Finavi," Arudal said, half-bowing to her from the back of his horse, "I am an excellent swimmer. As is Inmanat: were we all mounted on horses of his breed, if we did not have the wain to bring across, the lack of ford or bridge here would not hinder our journey in the least." At least not if it were summer, he added silently to himself. The first thickening of ice along the bank suddenly looked a great deal colder as Arudal realized belatedly that it would not be unlike Dame Karsil to demand he prove himself by stripping down and jumping into the river. But to his relief, she only turned away from him, nudging her horse back to the other side of the party.

"Have you ever considered a career in diplomacy?" Lostren murmured. "That was one of the more polished refusals of an insult I've seen."

Arudal smiled. "Elves do generally find some worth in politeness. Even when they might rather not."

This town was larger than the ones they had passed through on the eastern side of the Barren Hills, and some of the bigger houses were built of stone rather than wood. The cobblestoned streets were clear of snow and ice; even through the day-fog, Arudal saw passers-by looking up curiously at the ring of their horses' steel-shod hooves over the stones. We are lucky that the roads are not so paved, Arudal thought. At least when our steeds lose their shoes, we will be able to keep riding them without harm, if we are careful. If we had to ride on stone for long, we should be in a sore plight in this land without iron!

The town actually had two inns, the Golden Feather and the Trout and Hook. They went to the larger of the two, the Golden Feather, where the innkeeper was glad enough to rent them a room big enough for the eleven of them to share, though she had to bring in beds from other chambers to make up the number. As soon as Arudal had finished carrying Sir Thoron's bags and his own in, and seen to cleaning his knight's armour and gear, then his own kit, he made for the stone-bath. He had never gone so long without washing in his life, and though he had managed to push the awareness of his matted hair and stinking garments away while they were on the road, the moment he stepped inside a dwelling place, he could hardly bear the feel of his own skin. As for his hair - Tharandrostan military personnel usually kept their hair shoulder-length and loose, but they seldom had lengthy inland duty. Now Arudal knew why his companions braided their hair back and many Kantarean soldiers cropped their heads: he was certain that there were things crawling inside the thick tangles rucked over his skull, and he wanted to wash his arming cap for a week before he put it back on.

As he stepped into the heat of the stone-bath, though, Arudal stood as if stunned, his state of filth forgotten. The image of Finvar's body packed in snow - frozen through, left out in the cold of the wain, while he was here alone in the candlelit warmth by the glowing stones of the stove - struck him like a physical blow, and if he had not known how unseemly it was to weep for the dead in a public place, he might have broken down in tears.

Finvar is not really dead, Arudal consoled himself. He had grown used to the faint sensation of the other squire's soul in his mind, like the accustomed pressure of a shoe that was slightly too tight in one spot: now he had to think to be aware of it. Yet he had seen the snow in Finvar's mouth, the ice glazing his eyes... For a horrifying moment, Arudal suddenly thought he understood why it was that mediums had so often gone mad in the old days before Princess Sir Murnitir had pioneered her science of the mind. He breathed deeply until his breaths no longer came ragged and shaky, reciting to himself her part in the Litany of Heroes: Princess Sir Murnitir, youngest daughter of Prince Manorak, sought out both the known and the unknown workings of the mind, that we might cure madness and that no hidden faults might hamper the use of our race's gifts.

She was the first woman of Tharandrost to bear the belt and spurs of knighthood; the title of Dame was created afterwards, but we remember her by the honour she bore in life. Because of Murnitir's work, and that of those who had come after her, Arudal was able to tell himself that he was suffering from no worse than the shock of the discrepancy between what he had seen and what he knew - a shock kin to Shadow-Fear, when the mind suffered from trying to grasp the presence of something that went against the knowledge of instinct - and from the natural strain of grief disallowed expression by his conscious knowledge that there was no good cause for it.

Naming the shuddering pain in his chest calmed it, and Arudal wondered if he should wake Finvar to enjoy the stone-bath...No: it was kinder to let him sleep where no time passed, until he could be restored to life.

Arudal took the whisk from the wall where it hung and sat down, relaxing as the first beads of sweat began to spring out on his body. He knew it would not be long before the others began to join him, but this was the first time he had been alone for months. Almost alone: he could still feel the two souls within himself, and he wondered how those whose minds could sense the living, Empaths or Mind-Speakers, managed long terms of duty. With difficulty, he suspected; Arudal knew that the development and application of Murnitir's science of the mind had revolutionized the Tharandrostan military, making it possible not only to ease the personal strains from which every soldier, Mind-Gifted or not, suffered at some time, but also to keep such gifts as Empathy from shutting down from stress or shock or when there had simply been too much of others' thoughts and feelings for too long to bear. The need for mind-healing among soldiers was even great enough that occasionally fertile women were allowed to go on military vessels if there was little chance they would see combat: since Murnitir's day, the science of the mind had been largely a female profession.

Arudal was less than pleased to see that the next member of their company into the stone-bath was Rhys. Briefly he wondered what was keeping the knights - who normally bathed before their squires; but Sir Thoron had only given Arudal a distracted pat on his shoulder and told him to go on.

Rhys came over to sit down beside Arudal. Arudal could not help wrinkling his nose a little at the smell, though he knew that he himself must stink just as badly, and trusted that Rhys would not take it as a sign of his old distaste resurging. Arudal braced himself, wondering if the Plainsman was going to warn him away from Malni again.

Rhys ducked his head, smearing the first trickle of sweat from his face as if he were embarassed. Arudal said nothing, waiting for him to speak.

"Ari," the Plainsman said without preamble, "I want to thank you."

Arudal raised his brows in surprise. "For what?"

"For speaking so well of me to Malni."

"Ah. Is..." Arudal was not sure what one said to people who had to arrange their own marriages. "Does she like you now?"

Rhys sighed. "As a friend, she said. Is that not a curse under the name of a blessing?"

"I have heard that it is best if you can be friends with the one you marry, as well as breeding together," Arudal offered. "Arothir and I are friends."

The Plainsman shook his head sadly. Unbraided at last, his red hair stood out in a greasy cloud about his lean face, waving as he moved. "I do not know whether I should pity or envy you, for the customs of your people. Elsewhere, look you, when a woman says she wants to be friends, it means that the man has no hope at all: he might as well be her brother." Rhys held up a dirty-nailed hand. "Yes, I remember you saying that your grandparents were siblings. Believe me, that does not happen elsewhere."

Arudal thought about it as he dipped up a ladlefull of water, pouring it onto the hot stones in a hissing cloud of steam. Then the situation came clear, as though he had turned the end of a spyglass half a twist to bring a blur into sudden shapes. Kantarean affections between men and women were, after all, more like those Tharandrostans formed with beloved friends of their own gender. Although Arudal himself had never been in love, he remembered very well how his more precocious friends would try to pair off, quarrel, and come to pour out their troubles to him. Khatiraz, a year ahead of Arudal in school and now squired to Sir Mizukhon, had been particularly desperate, always falling in love with boys who were attached to someone else or simply not interested in him. The familiarity was oddly reassuring, and now Arudal had some idea of what counsel to give.

"Perhaps if you seemed a little colder to her, she would not take you so much for granted," he suggested. "There are always some who want most what they cannot have, and if Malni had not been one to reach out for what was beyond her grasp, she would not be with us now."

Rhys nodded slowly. "Aye. And you are the strangest of our party to her, and the most remote - no offense meant."

"None taken. She thinks me to be something other than I am, in any case."

Rhys' mouth twisted halfway into a smile. "Yes, I have heard a great deal about Elves and half-Elves from her. Mayhap when this mission is over and she is on her way back to Kantar with us, we can tell her the truth. Hmm...I fear to suggest it, but do you think that if you seemed to pursue her, she would be less eager towards you?"

"She would end up hanging about my neck like an amulet," Arudal said: he had seen how much less well that ploy worked than the converse. "No."

"Well, we shall see." Rhys looked as though he would speak more, but the door opened and Berek, Tirothar and Lostren came in. Tirothar flopped down on one of the benches with a noisy sigh; Lostren seated himself more quietly, and something about the set of his mouth and the remote light graying the green of his transformed eyes made Arudal think that his thoughts were troubled.

He knows something we don't, Arudal thought, and Sir Salarond has told him to keep quiet about it. But Lostren greeted them cheerfully enough, saying how glad he was to be getting clean at last, and the talk turned to other campaigns where the White Company had travelled without the benefit of any civilized amenities. Arudal had nothing to say; nor did Berek, but the Hatneth was listening to the conversation in a way that made Arudal wonder just how much of the Common speech he had managed to pick up. I will have to remind everyone to watch their tongues around him, he thought. Berek may be fat and unpleasant, but he is far too bright for - our good, quite possibly.

When they were done, Lostren said that he would go and relieve Malni in the stables so that she could wash. Although Arudal was beginning to feel a little faint from hunger, he offered to go along as well, hoping that Salarond's squire would talk to him alone.

Malni was sitting on the straw in a long-limbed sprawl, stroking Inmanat's muzzle as he investigated her hair. "No, lad, it's not hay, even if it's the right colour for it," she was saying to the horse, and Arudal smiled involuntarily. She looked up, and her own smile spread into an open grin as she saw him. "You look the better for your bath," she said.

Arudal had no idea how to reply to that, but Lostren said, "No doubt you will too. And the gods know we smell better...Go on, we look after the horses while you're in there." His command of Western had, indeed, improved considerably; he had probably spent a good deal of time talking to Berek and Malni.

"That's kind of you. Thank you." She rose easily and strode out, keeping her distance - probably, Arudal reflected, to keep him from smelling her until she was clean. Inmanat whuffled softly, and Arudal went over to pet him, running his hands along the little horse's dark sides to see how much condition he had lost on their trek.

"You were fat and soft from lazing about on shipboard, you know you were," he said affectionately to the gelding. "You're an easy keeper, you are. Those warhorses may be all big and fierce, but they're losing flesh faster than I like to see, while you're just now starting to look like a horse and not a barrel again." It was true: the muscles of the sturdy little Imperial steed's shoulders and haunches were rippling under his thick winter coat, his saddle-girth down to the notch it had been in before Arudal went to University, when he had been able to ride every day. Arudal had worried about the strain of the long daily riding after their sea-trip, but Inmanat was positively thriving on the hard work. In contrast, the ribs were beginning to show a little on the warhorses' barrels, and their haunches had lost some of the heavy power that had driven Kantar's cavalry to victory on hundreds of battlefields over the last thousand years. Arudal reflected that, thus far, the big horses had wasted vastly more time and fodder than they were worth; but one might as well ask a Kantarean knight to give up his sword - or his manhood, Arudal thought with a touch of malice - as his battle-stallion.

"Maybe we shouldn't have brought them," Lostren said gloomily. Arudal looked over in startlement; but if the other squire had read his thoughts, he was hiding it well. "It's not as though we expected to be charging down armies...well, one never knows: we may yet need them. At least they won't run from Undead in battle."

"I suppose not," Arudal agreed. He had never thought of Kantarean warhorses being trained to face the Ukuthrim in a fight; but of course, the Kantarean cavalry would never have been able to stand against the hosts of Martag if their horses ran from the scent of the Undead. Briefly Arudal wondered how such training was managed...he knew that it took long, careful, and patient work to make a living horse willing to bear the presence of the Agathim, but perhaps if stallions were simply guided according to their own inclinations to respond to a threat with aggression rather than fear... "Are we likely to be fighting the Undead on horseback, then?"

Lostren cocked his head to one side, looking carefully at Arudal. He had braided up his red-gold hair again, the water-darkened plait hanging over his shoulder. "That depends on what we run into along the way, and what we find when we get there. Many of the streets of the Imperial Seat, if they're not destroyed or filled with too much rubble, should be easily wide enough for us to ride along. But as for how we'll be fighting - or even," he added pointedly, "for whom we might be fighting, that has yet to be decided."

"Um." Then Arudal realized what had been bothering him ever since he saw the vision of the Fallen Seat in Ostarak's mind. "Sir Salarond does realize that we'll have to have some sort of protection against Shadow-Fear and having our life-strength drained by the Agathim, doesn't he?" Except for Arudal himself, of course, and even he was uncertain how well his natural resistance to being drained would protect him against so many of the Undead at once. "With that many in one place, a Man would hardly last more than a few heartbeats."

Lostren laughed. "Teach your grandmother to milk a mare, as the Horse-Tribes say. Sir Salarond has been fighting the Undead since before you spoke your first word of Imperial."

That was probably true, Arudal reflected: Sir Salarond's noble blood was relatively pure, so that their commander was probably in his second century. Still, Arudal had gotten used to thinking of himself as the party's expert on the Shadow-Realm, and the reminder stung a little.

"What about Dame Karsil, then?" he asked. "Even as an ally, I don't think we'll be able to get an Elf into the Imperial Seat. The Agathim...seldom change their thoughts from what they were in life." Make that, are lucky to remember what millennium it is, Arudal thought to himself. His great-great-great-granduncle Aruhar, who had overseen some of his later training, would often answer news of current events with, "Amandeth curse it, why does Prince Manorak allow that? He never let them get away with that sort of thing before." To which the nearest family member would reply by saying, "It's Prince Norombar now, sir, and this is sixteen eighty-three" (or whatever year it was) - which Aruhar would have forgotten five minutes later.

Magic had been the old lich's passion, and there he had learned and grown until he knew more than any living man; but Arudal had always believed that, if his own name had not been passed to the eldest son in every other generation, Aruhar would never have called him anything other than, "Boy". A few of the greatest Agathim, such as the Lord of Martag, were able to keep adapting to the changes of time...but the Fallen Imperials had held Elves to be their greatest foes. Even if the leader of one side were somehow able to bring himself to accept her, Karsil would never be able to pass among their allies in safety.

Lostren's face moved as though he were chewing at the inside of his cheek. "We shall see," he said at last. "If you want to be useful, you might start thinking about a way to arm Malni against the Undead."

"Could she not use Finvar's bow?" Arudal asked.

Lostren gave him an annoyingly superior look. "Of course, you don't shoot, do you? Have you ever heard of anyone using someone else's bow?"

"No, but I thought...I mean, if we had to, I don't think he'd grudge it...I could ask him."

"I'm sorry, I didn't mean to talk down to you. With use, a bow grows to its user. Even if Malni could pull it, the wood and bone have bent and stretched to Finvar's reach and grasp. Her arms are longer than his...are, and she'd hold it differently; everyone does. It would weaken the stave a little for her to shoot it even once; for her to practice enough to be worthwhile with it..." Lostren shook his head. "Forget it. She could take his sword and shield, but she'd never learn to use them in the time we have. Not his bow, though. Aviyani and Amandeth willing, he may want it again."

Eventually Malni came back with a platter of food. Rhys walked beside her: Arudal had doubted that the Plainsman really would be able to take his advice. But maybe it will go better as she gets to know him, he thought.

"The knights are still closeted in the room," Malni told them. "They said we should go ahead and eat, as they may be a while. Would you like to stay out with us? There's plenty of food here."

The horses were already reaching their heads hopefully over the stall-gates, and Inmanat nickered at Arudal. Dinner seemed to be some sort of roast in a thick sweet sauce, but there was a bowl of stewed carrots on the side. Arudal scooped a bit out, letting his horse lip it off his palm. "I think we shall go in, but thank you."

As they left the stable, Arudal told himself that the twisting of his stomach was only the smell of the food tugging at his hunger. But he knew better: he was afraid that they might be talking about him, renewing the discussion of leaving him... killing him.

No, Sir Thoron won't let that happen, he reassured himself. The others might be able to deceive me into thinking they meant me no ill, but not Sir Thoron. And they must know that they need me to complete the mission.

"Come now, Ari," Lostren said cheerfully. "They're not holding a Court of Chivalry in there, only - I would guess - deciding on our strategy for the next stage of the mission." He lowered his voice. "We all do feel bad about what happened back there, you know. We were unjust to you, and it was wrong. But you can't keep thinking about it, or there will come a point somewhere along the way - maybe in a fight, maybe in our negotiations - where you hesitate a second because of it, and then something bad will happen."

Arudal looked into Lostren's green-gold eyes. His pupils were no larger than usual - with the Foresighted, they always seemed to swell under the force of a vision, Avradi alone knew why - but Lostren spoke with the certainty of knowledge. The other squire's lean shoulders twitched as though he were bracing himself against Arudal's gaze, but Lostren did not look away as he usually did. "Trust me on this, Ari. You have to let it go."

Arudal knew that forgetting what he had heard would not be so easy, but he nodded all the same: Lostren was right. On a Tharandrostan military mission, Arudal would have gone to the party's Mind-healer to talk about his lingering fears, but here, he would simply have to manage it himself.

Tirothar and Berek were sitting down and eating already. There were two large trays with platters and mugs on them on the end of the table, and as Arudal and Lostren came nearer, Tirothar said, "They want you two to take those in."

Arudal gulped, his heart suddenly hammering against his ribs again. No: Lostren is right, I have to trust them.

The two squires, their hands full, stopped at the door of the room. As he had been trained as a page, Arudal did not put the food on the floor or even raise his voice, but spoke clearly, projecting through the door, "Sir, we are here."

He heard the sound of the bolts sliding, and Sir Thoron opened the door. "Took you long enough," he said gruffly. "Come in."

The knights were sitting around the room's one table, looking at the map Arudal had drawn. Salarond gestured for the squires to put their trays down and sit. "Count Arudal Arumirun. Am I correct in thinking that you may be considered a trained expert in regards to the Undead?"

"Ah…" Grandmother Zinadir would have rapped Arudal's knuckles if she had heard him make such a claim. But Sir Salarond had called him by his full name, and the healer-priest's voice had taken on the same peculiar cadence as when he had given Arudal his warrant for holding the Undead - a judge's cadence: he must have something legal in mind. "I have had fifteen years of training in that regard, your Grace."

Salarond's chin dipped just slightly - acknowledging, Arudal thought, that he had read the situation correctly. "Sufficient. In your expert opinion, your Excellency, is there any chance of Imperial Undead from the time of the Fall tolerating the presence of an Elf among them, under any circumstances?"

Where does he want me to go with this? Arudal wondered. Why couldn't he just ask? "In my opinion, your Grace, there is, at best, a vanishingly minute chance of the very most powerful and capable late Imperial Undead - that is to say, of the ninth rank or above - if given an overwhelming incentive to do so and reminded of it constantly, to be able to tolerate the presence of an Elf." Arudal spoke as firmly as he could: it was true, though he hoped that he was not destroying his commander's plans. But Sir Salarond's chin dipped slightly again, just the faintest signal of approval, and, emboldened, Arudal went on. "There is no chance of any Fallen Imperial Undead beneath the ninth rank, unless completely under the control of a more powerful will or spell, being able to exhibit such tolerance."

"Based on what we know of the circumstances in which this mission must be carried out, your Excellency, in your opinion, would the presence of an Elf among our party inhibit our ability to fulfill it?" He is leading me, Arudal thought. But in any case, there was only one answer he could give.

"Most certainly, your Grace. I can say with all confidence that Dame Karsil's presence in the area of the Fallen Seat would not only present an extreme danger to herself and the rest of us, but would make it significantly more difficult, if not completely impossible, for us to achieve our stated goal. I had meant to address your Grace on this very problem, as I could see no way around it, and..."

"That will do, your Excellency. Thank you. Dame Karsil, as recently given evidence has strongly indicated that your presence on the crucial portion of this mission would severely compromise the party's chances of carrying it out, I order you to separate from the rest of us before we reach the Undead-controlled area around the Fallen Seat and to remain behind at an appropriate place until our return."

"Thank you, sir," Karsil said coldly. Her perfect face was blank, but her eyes blazed the startling green of copper-salt flames in Arudal's sight. He let out a long breath, unaware that he had been holding it, even as he wondered what exactly had just happened.

"Lostren, you and Ari bring your dinners in here," Sir Salarond ordered, his voice warming to normal as he spoke to his squire. "I want the two of you to listen in for a little while."

"Yes, sir."

As the bolts clicked closed behind them, Lostren let out his breath in a long silent whistle. "Ari, I think you just helped save Karsil from a court-martial."

Arudal felt his eyes widening with shock. "You're joking."

"No. She must have refused to ally with one of the Agathim under any circumstances. I think I can even guess..." He stopped, his lips tightening into a thin white line. "Well, never mind what I guess. We should hurry up."

Arudal followed the other squire's rapid footsteps, his mind whirling. If the Agathim of the Fallen Seat had been locked in struggle for almost seventeen hundred years - what would happen if one of them gained the victory over the other? Between them, even in a state of war, they controlled the land for fifty miles around...

Was Karsil right to refuse to have anything to do with this? Arudal wondered. If we save Kantar, but loose the shadow of the Fallen Empire on the West - how can we answer to the gods for that? By the laws of Men, Kantarean or Tharandrostan, it was the White Company's only to follow their commander's lead, and the squires' only to follow their knights', but...Arudal had been taught all his life how, though Tharandrost had kept its troth and served the Empire, the soldiers of the colony had silently refused to accept the state worship of Morthugor and the cruelties that followed it, resisting the demands on their souls that lay beyond the bounds of their oaths. And their staunchness had been justified: when then-Governor Khatirost had declared the State to be an independent principality, he had officially acknowledged that Avalar had been right to obey the gods and his conscience above all human law. It was that line - a thin thread to the Kantareans, perhaps, but a wall of adamant to Tharandrost - that separated Tharandrostans from their Fallen kin. And Arudal wondered now whether he had it in him to cross it...Or to keep from crossing it.

By the time they got back to the room, Dame Karsil was no longer there. She must have gone off to meditate; and Arudal wished with all his heart that he could do likewise. But he took his seat and began to quietly nibble at his dinner while Sir Salarond talked.

"To sum up: I think that we should approach the so-called Emperor first. Strategically, the addition of an effective mobile group to a largely static defense will make more of a difference than adding it to a mobile, but insufficient, attacker's force. Further, we have the opportunity for presentation to the Emperor's side, and if any virtue lingers in the messenger's signet, it may help to protect us from unnecessary encounters with the opposition on the way in." He looked at Arudal. "And chance, or the will of the gods, seems to have provided us with an appropriately credentialed and talented ambassador. Regarding your prisoner, Ari, how long can you keep him under control while he is, ah, externalized?"

"If I am given a night to work with him first, sir, indefinitely, with a result similar to a spell of mastery. Otherwise, only while I am conscious and not distracted by any other psychic challenges."

"I see. If you tell me your requirements later, we shall arrange time for you to work with him. You and he will be primarily responsible for getting us safely through the Undead-controlled area around the Fallen Seat. Berek seems to feel confident that, given the correct materials, he and we together should be able to work spells which will give ourselves and our horses the necessary protection against Shadow-Fear and life-draining, but when we are finished here, you, Eroth, and I shall consult further with him. Unless there is absolutely no way to avoid it, you are under no circumstances to engage in further combat until we have made direct contact with the Emperor and, if possible, retrieved the materials we were sent for. If that means taking precipitous evasive action - that is to say, running away as fast as you can or hiding while the rest of us fight - you shall do so. Is that clear?"

"Yes, sir," Arudal said unhappily. At least Finvar won't see me running from combat, he thought - Well, he would understand a direct order to keep back, anyway; he said he had been told to stay behind at least once.

Salarond's voice softened a little. "I'm not asking you to like it, Ari, I'm telling you to do it. I'm sure you are intelligent enough to understand why."

"Yes, sir."

"You are capable of reading the minds of the Undead, are you not?"

"Yes, sir."

"When we encounter Imperial Undead, either within the target zone or, if it happens, on the way, you will first mentally establish which side they are on. If they belong to the Emperor, you will address them and explain that we are on our way to seek an audience with him. Otherwise, you will at once do your best to take control of their leader and halt them. If fighting is necessary, you will have him order your preservation. Until we have the texts we require, you are the least dispensable member of this party, and shall conduct yourself accordingly, even if that means suppressing your native inclinations towards bravery and chivalry. You may be certain that none of us will think the less of you for having the self-discipline to do so for the sake of achieving our goal." Sir Salarond looked about at the other knights. "The rest of you are, equally, under orders to protect Arudal. Magister Radthar's Foresight is now proven true. He predicted that we would need the help of the one Dr. Grímhjálm should choose for us, and now I believe I know what lay beyond the obvious in his vision."

The healer-knight touched the map lightly with his forefinger. "Until we have consulted with the Emperor, we cannot form more than the most basic tactical plans. Hopefully, he will be able to inform us where in the Imperial Library the genealogies are kept and in what condition the relevant part of the Library is currently. Ari, it is possible that you will be going in alone or accompanied only by Agathim while the rest of us fight, though if we can arrange it, Lostren will probably be with you to protect you and aid in your search. I believe we can come to no further conclusions tonight, unless one of you has anything to add to this. Lostren?"

"No, sir."

"Ari?"

Arudal knew that he should simply reply in the negative, but his curiosity was pressing too hard against the bounds of his will to be silent. "Uh, sir...Sir, I mean no disrespect by it, but... I know there were some problems with bringing me, and you couldn't have known the, the extent of my mind-gifts. What would you have done if I hadn't come?"

Salarond's lean face sagged a little, and though he was barely into middle age as the high-blooded of Kantar counted it, it seemed to Arudal that he could see the full weight of several decades of battle in the healer's amber-ringed gray eyes. "The best we could, Ari. Foresight is often a chancy thing to rely on; but in such cases, it comes into its own: Magister Radthar advised us to trust your professor, and that proved well-founded. Salarond, Shakhor, you may go now. Lostren, tell Berek his presence is requested."

Chapter 23: Gems and Stars

"Gleams of fire in dark night,
Captured in stone's crystal core,
Dreams of mage's word-sown light
Smoke in candle-flame the door -
Herb and stone and flame the ore,
Words the hammers of our might,
Our forge, the circle on the floor,
Smithing spells in dark of night."
- "Mage's Glory", Imperial, traditional

The spells of protection, Berek insisted, would require a number of things that they did not have and could not buy where they were. In any case, Cirrod was the nearest crossing: otherwise, the party would have to go at least two weeks' travel out of their way in order to ford the river.

"The Mayor of Cirrod is a friend of my father's," Berek said hopefully. "We could stay with him."

"I think that would be unwise," Salarond responded, his voice iron-stern. "You know by now that we are not travelling for trade, and additional...complications might be unfortunate. While we are in Cirrod, you are no more than Lord Ari's apprentice, do you understand?"

Berek pouted, his plump dark face sagging like a lump of rye dough. Arudal glared at him. "Yes, sir," the Westerner said, subdued.

"Watch him closely, Ari," Sir Salarond said when Berek had left the room. "If he means to betray us, Cirrod will be his best chance. Before Amanvon - though I would be slow to order it - I could almost wish that you were able to read the thoughts of the living!"

Berek had described Cirrod as a "good-sized trading town". Arudal would have called it a small city; he asked Berek about the difference, and found that the city-word had come to mean specifically either a city-state such as Hatin's City, or the capital of a major country, as with a couple of the largest ports on the southeastern coast of the continent.

Cirrod was built around a raised fortress on a hill, its whitewashed walls gleaming above the town like a castle of ice. The stonework was simple and blocky, with none of the solid elegance of the early Imperial period, or the high decoration of the later Empire; but the fortress looked impressively thick-walled and forbidding. Most of the rest of the city was built in the style that was coming to be familiar to Arudal: high-peaked roofs with ice-glazed wooden shingles, cobbled roads with wide snow-filled gutters, and the occasional stone mansion enclosed by low walls.

The wooden eaves of the houses were carved, sometimes elaborately, with sprays of flowers and curling leaves. Looking at them, Arudal felt a strange sense of double vision: it seemed to him that the patterns shifted before his eyes into intertwining snakes and beasts twisting about themselves, round-eyed horse's heads staring from gable-ends through the fog, and an inexplicable wave of homesickness swept over him. Arudal blinked hard. Tharandrost was nothing like this...

Not Tharandrost, Helludal. For a moment, it almost seemed to Arudal as though he were looking out at the winter city through Finvar's eyes, rather than the other way around; even the day-fog on his sight was very like the heavy mists of Helludal... He pushed the feeling back; but his heart was pounding, and his palms sweating inside his leather gloves. He had been told that living souls were harder to hold than the Undead - especially the soul of a close friend or beloved: the unconscious temptation to open to them was always there, and sometimes could lead to madness in truth, when the borders of awareness blurred too far between the agathurok and the in-dweller. Still...

Finvar, does this really look so much like your home?

Except that the carvings are different, very much so. We build just like that, with the roofs sloped so that the snow will slide off when it becomes too heavy - low roofs can break under the weight towards the end of the winter. And sometimes we thatch rather than shingling; but it is very much like.

The strange doubled feeling faded as Arudal spoke to Finvar, as though, by addressing him, the Tharandrostan had managed to separate their minds again. Still, Arudal could feel the warmth of his squire-brother's presence within him, and could not bring himself to wall Finvar completely into silence.

The streets were easily wide enough for the wain. Sometimes they had to stop and wait for an ox-cart to pass, but most goods seemed to be carried in smaller carts pulled by donkeys, or even with their traces laid over the shoulders of a husky man. Many of the cart-drawers were crying their wares: their accents were harsher than those of Hatin's City, but easy enough to understand. Where the larger streets crossed, there were a number of little wooden stalls selling hot food and steaming mugs of berry-wine or cider, the scents wafting tantalizing through the icy air. Malni was trying very hard not to gawk open-mouthed, but her rounded blue eyes were very wide as she looked around. Arudal guessed that she had never been more than a day's travel from her village before. Still, she sat straight-backed on her horse, bearing up proudly under the stares of the townsfolk - who had likely never seen a troop of armoured riders, nor anything to match the Kantarean warhorses. Dear Amandeth, please don't let the Mayor invite the "Elves" together to his fortress. I do not think Karsil and I could manage so well together now!

It was no trouble to find a decent inn with room for themselves and even their mounts, although, when Arudal looked at the stables - for it was his turn to tend the steeds again that night - he could see that they were meant more for oxen or donkeys than for horses. But the straw was clean, the hay sweet-smelling and good and the water fresh, and their mounts did not care if their stalls were a little wide, or the stall-gates rather low. Since all the songs he knew were in the Imperial tongue, Arudal did not dare to sing aloud, but he hummed to the horses as he cleaned their hooves and combed them. Their shoes were standing up to the rigors of travel rather better than he had feared, at least so far: whoever had shod them on shipboard had known his business.

Eventually the strain of long riding and the natural growth of the hooves would have the shoes off anyway, but they were holding well thus far. Arudal did notice the faint glimmer around the steel shoes of the warhorses. If they were not Valderian steel, at least they were some sort of magical alloy that would be able to strike the Undead. Wise, Arudal thought. He remembered a conversation he had overheard while pouring wine for Duke Azarlokan and Sea Marshal Aglaraman late one night at the Duke's castle; the two men had been talking about hunting, and the Sea Marshal had pulled back the lip of the gray wolfhound that always followed at his heels to show the Valderian steel caps over the dog's huge fangs. "He's taken more than twenty Undead for me," Sir Aglaraman had said proudly. "If you can get a good hound over his fear of Shadow-creatures, he's better against them than any Man." Arudal wondered if the same were true for Kantarean warhorses.

While Arudal brushed Inmanat and the destriers, Berek was currying the packhorses - clumsily, true, but without any of the fear or distaste he had shown earlier, and from the corner of his eye, Arudal thought he actually saw the boy pat one on the nose. *Perhaps there is hope for him yet.*

"Will you take me with you when you shop for what we need?" Berek asked. His command of the Common tongue was improving with frightening speed.

Arudal thought about it. Berek would be very useful in bargaining for precious stones and scarce herbs, since he should know what their prices ought to be. And technically, Arudal had signed his apprentice-contract. On the other hand... "Is there any chance that you will be recognised here?"

Berek gestured vaguely over the swell of his belly beneath his thick strip-woven tunic of plain wool. "Not in this," he said. Even speaking Common, his voice rose and fell with the contemptuous tonalities of High Western. "If I come here...I go in a litter to the Mayor's house, in silk and cloth of gold and a good hat. Street people don't even see me. In this, when I go to the Mayor's door, I am kicked away like a beggar before I say my name."

"If I were to go," Arudal corrected absently, "I would be kicked away."

"Even as apprentice of an Elf-lord, I would dressed fitting to my place of birth and respect of Shining Ones."

"Would dress fittingly, or would be dressed fittingly. I see." *And believe you; but what if Lord Hatneth has already managed to send word to watch for you? In that case, though, they would already have been marked out, and could do nothing but trust Berek to keep silence.* "Yes, you may come."

In a short while, Lostren came to tell Arudal that he should clean himself up and dress well: Sir Salarond wanted him to start looking for the things they needed now, since there was every chance some of them would not be readily available or easily found. Arudal spared a longing thought to the mages' supply shops in Tharabruthnan and Var Perenil, which could be trusted to have everything from sparrows' feathers to dragons' teeth, with walls full of glass jars of herbs and trays of stones laid out under glass in a neat range from flint and beach-pebbles to adamants, sapphires, rubies, and emeralds. Here, even if they could find all the components needed for the rites, they would have to disguise what they wanted in a range of other purchases to be sure that no one guessed what they were about.

The shopping party consisted of Arudal, Berek, and Sir Eroth. Mindful of what Berek had said about noticing the similarities of their race when they were all together, Sir Salarond was unwilling to send out a larger group. He also instructed Arudal to start by buying a good hat and to keep it pulled down to hide the peaked tips of his ears and as much of his face as he could without looking furtive or silly. If questioned, Arudal was to fall back on the story they had used in Hatin's City, but hopefully he would be able to play down the Elven traits of his appearance sufficiently to avoid excessive attention.

"You should get yourself a nice cloak as well," Berek said as they stepped out into the frosty air. "Jewelers and dealers in rare herbs talk not to people who look like sheepers."

Sir Eroth's cheek twitched as though he were suppressing a smile. "Shepherds. But he's right, Ari."

Berek knew where the best furrier in the city was. A guard in bronze armour stood by the door inside, stepping forward with a scowl when he saw the trio in their wool and sheepskin cloaks, but Berek spoke up at once. "Master Ari has just concluded one leg of a long journey, and he wishes to purchase wraps more fitting to his station before he returns to his homeland."

Clever, Berek, Arudal thought. Purveyors of the best personal goods in a city like this would probably do a lot of their business with merchants who had just made successful trips and found the unaccustomed solidity of ready money in their purses to be, as his mother said, dragging their belts to the ground. As if to prove Arudal's point, the guard bowed, his scowl easing into a faint smile. He spoke to Sir Eroth - understandably; he must think that the older man was the master merchant, and the two younger ones his apprentices. "Please come in and be welcome, good Master Ari. Master Alacan shall be with you very shortly."

When Arudal and his companions left the furrier's, Arudal was swathed in a thick coat of what Master Alacan called blue fox, but Arudal would have called white - ice-white, with just the faintest scatterings of gray-black hairs giving the heavy soft pelts a bluish cast. His head was covered warmly by a matching fur hat, ear-flaps coming down on either side of his face and a great puff of the thick tail-fur in front. It was seldom cold enough in Tharandrost to wear such heavy clothing, save in the mountains, and Arudal had to admit he was enjoying it: he felt almost as though he really were a cat, warm and sleek inside his own luxurious pelt.

Sir Eroth was dressed similarly, except that instead of the blue fox, his coat and hat were what the furrier called silver fox, black brindled with shining gray-white, while Berek, whom they did not dare dress too well, had a simpler coat and hat of heavy leather lined with rabbit fur - they would have given him their castoffs, but, weighing near as much as Eroth and Arudal together, the fat youth would never have been able to fit into anything of theirs. The knight had taken over the role of "Master Ari" smoothly enough, passing Arudal off as his nephew "Little Ari" and saying, "Berek, let us see how well you can deal for furs," then watching with cool appraisal as Berek carried out the negotiations.

There had been a difficult moment when Master Alacan asked Berek about his household - they had stuck to the truth to some degree, saying simply that they had picked him up as an apprentice in Hatin's City - but Berek had lied so smoothly and neatly that Arudal almost found himself believing the Hatneth's account, though realizing what a talent for deception the fat youth had did nothing to set Arudal's mind at ease.

Things went equally smoothly at the jeweler's. Sir Eroth actually seemed to know more about precious stones than Arudal did, making a careful selection among the black star sapphires and a stone Arudal had never seen before, that Berek called black opals - black, indeed, but glimmering with flecks of intense coloured fire that shifted as the stone was moved, glimmering blue and purple, green and red and gold. Mindful of Berek's advice, perhaps, the knight also chose a few balas rubies, clear stones of a deep rich red colour. He regretfully shook his head over the emeralds, and remarked that he was more likely to sell pearls in Cirrod on another journey than to buy them there on this one, but selected several lumps of raw amber half the size of his fist.

Arudal did not have to pretend to smile when Sir Eroth turned to him and said in a convincingly avuncular tone, "Now, Little Ari, you may choose one stone for yourself and one for your girlfriend. We won't be here long enough to have them set here, but there may be time in Hatin's City on the way back. This is a particularly good place for balas rubies, and one would look well against Rothe's pretty golden hair..."

That was certainly true: Arudal could easily imagine the stone's deep red glow setting off the rich gold colour of his cousin's long hair, or nestled against the whiteness of her throat. But Arothir's father was a Duke. Even had the colours of his House not been dark gules and argent, so that much of Arothir's jewelry was Valderian steel or white gold set with rubies or balas rubies, she could have had as many as she liked; while Arudal was quite certain that she would be as surprised by the unfamiliar beauty of the black opals as he was. And besides, if black opals were as soft as the ordinary sort, they might need the spares: it was far from unknown for even the hardest precious stones to crack under the stress of magic. He shook his head. "These are prettier," he said firmly, pointing to the rainbow-shimmering gems.

The trio had to go to several herbalists before they had all the plants and oils they needed, and then came the lengthier process of finding the miscellaneous items. It would be easy enough to shoot a raven for its blood and feathers when they were on the road again, but black-dyed candles were another matter: the Westerners used purple as a funerary colour, and seemed to prefer bright shades in everything. Keeping up their guise as merchants, they had to buy a quarter-hundredweight load of myrrh, as that was only used in temples, not sold for scenting homes; nightspice was unknown here, but Berek thought that a tiny pinch of asafoedita would suffice magically. Saltpetre baffled all three of them, for Arudal and Eroth knew it only as a spell component, and Berek knew that it was imported in quantity, but not why. At last, in desperation, Arudal asked Finvar if he had any ideas, and found that saltpetre was commonly used for - of all things - curing ham and bacon, and that any butcher could tell them where to buy it.

The White Company party stayed in Cirrod another five days. Sir Eroth's shield-arm still had not fully recovered, and Sir Salarond wanted the warhorses to be in the best condition possible before they set out again. The first evening, Arudal felt a peculiar tingle from the Imperial messenger's ring. As Sir Salarond had directed, he disarmed himself at once, but nothing happened: no sudden compulsion to attack his comrades, no irresistible summons to go elsewhere, no feeling of illness or pain. Arudal did wonder if the ring's protection - if any strength still lingered about it - had something to do with them being overlooked by the Mayor, for he was certain that the people of Cirrod were no less enthusiastic about Elves than those of Hatin's City.

Is it protecting us because we are following the appointed track towards the Imperial Seat, or as closely as we can? But why, then, did it not keep us from the notice of Sir Darthumazad's troop for their sake? Because of the Agathim's hunger, perhaps: a spell to speed messengers on their way would do no good if the messengers, or their horses, died of starvation on the road. Maybe if I get a chance, I can ask the Emperor. The thought sent a guilty thrill through Arudal. Even in its Fall, the Empire had been great in many arts now diminished; but it seemed to him that there was something to be feared in seeking knowledge from those whose evil had brought down the Wrath.

The White Company's path led them west-northwest from Cirrod now. The weather was growing colder yet: they had renewed their supplies of the ointment Finvar had recommended, but it was not enough to keep their lips from cracking or the skin on their noses from beginning to peel. Arudal almost envied Rhys his beard, which had come in thickly by now: the other members of the party had to wrap scarves around the lower halves of their faces beneath their visors.

When they stopped two nights out of Cirrod, Sir Salarond decided that they were far enough from civilization to work magic safely. Even heated by braziers, the wain was cold enough that Arudal shuddered at the thought of taking his gloves off to work a ritual, but to his surprise, Berek showed no sign of being daunted.

"My teacher told me that a true mage could cast his spells even with the flames gnawing his flesh," the Westerner said when Arudal asked him if he would be able to manage the delicate work of painting sigils with cold hands. "When I undergo initiation into mastery, I shall have to face worse than this." He looked steadfastly at Arudal as he spoke, his plump face set in a calm resolution that Arudal had never seen in him before. So he only whinges when he has no desire to bear hardship, Arudal thought. Or perhaps his love of magic is, at least, enough to overcome his bodily discomfort. Who would have thought it? Then Arudal had to bite his lip to keep from laughing: had he himself not undertaken this entire journey and even accepted the humbling burden of being Sir Thoron's squire from a similar quirk of personality, if not from the same specific motive?

The party's mages had chosen Tirothar as the object of the first spell: if they could successfully ward him from Shadow-Fear, then they would know that their rituals would work as they needed to. Eroth's lanky squire sat nervously upon a folded piece of canvas beside Arudal, his sweaty palm clasping the Tharandrostan's around a black opal as Sir Eroth painted a circle about them in the sticky mess that Berek had painstakingly mixed from saltpetre, ground amber, oils of mistletoe and yew and blackpetal, and raven's blood. Berek had to trace the symbols and speak the words that would call down the power of Amandeth's Fortress, the hidden planet beyond the last of the world's rings. Arudal sat quietly, breathing slow and deep from his centre. He could see the faint glow above the circle and sigils that enclosed them, but it was far weaker than such a thing would have been in the Middle Land.

Berek drew a deep breath, releasing it slowly as he lifted his hands. In Arudal's deeply Shadowed sight, the Westerner no longer looked like a lumpy sack of lard. Instead, his figure bulked huge and solid as a great rock rising from the sea, each slow movement a dance of dignity and awe, and the bright fire of the black opal glimmered like coloured sea-light from the darkness between his fingers. Each to what he was made for, a small part of Arudal's mind muttered, but he paid no attention to the thought: he had learned to let the jabber of his surface thoughts fade unnoticed when he was concentrating on a ritual.

"Toll-Lord, I call thee," Berek intoned, half-singing the rise and fall of the High Western tonalities. "Thou who keep'st the gate, who wards us from the Maker of Slaves and all his evil works - from Mordhagoernim and ghosts, from all sorcery and necromancy and all manner of ill that threatens from beyond the walls of the Dark Realm - Toll-Lord, I call thy aid. Though thy light is hidden, let it stream down upon us; let it glow in our souls as the fire glows from the black stones. We have paid thy wages in the mouths of the dead, we have set thy wages in the tombs of the dead, that thou may'st take thy toll and guide them past the realm of Shadow. Now, with thy fair-bought might, I set this warding, that the hungry debtors who wander impoverished in the blackness between the green earth and the glowing homes of the gods may cast no fear upon this man Tirothar dath Karameth. The touch of one who fears no Shadow is upon him: once touching, always together, within the sight of all gods and spirits." Berek bent forward, setting the black opal first upon Tirothar's forehead, then over his heart, and lastly above his navel. Holding it there, he chanted, "This I bind, with word and will: no ghost nor wraith, no wight nor evil sucker of blood, no spectre nor shade nor ghoul, nor any shell of forsaken soul, may set fear in the mind or the heart or the bowels or the marrow of Tirothar dath Karameth. My word is as strong as the unshaken stars; my word is the might beyond the green earth's ring. So it is spoken: so it shall be."

With Berek's last words, Arudal felt a slight tingle in his palm where he touched Tirothar, and the faintest corona of light seemed to glimmer around their joined hands and the black opal where Berek held it to Tirothar's belly. If they had been in the Middle Land, Arudal would have thought that Berek's spell, though beautifully performed and as solid as the four of them had been able to make it, was simply lacking in power: but he had no idea how magic drawing on the stars should look to his sight.

"It is done," Berek said, straightening. Tirothar let go of Arudal's hand. With some relief, Arudal surreptitiously wiped his palm on his cloak as the lanky squire stood.

Berek's rapt look slowly dissolved into a wide grin. "I did it," he said softly. "I really did it - I could feel it flowing through me."

"Indeed," Sir Salarond replied. "Will we need to wait for the spell to take full hold, or can we test it now?"

"It should be in full force." Berek's voice was still shaky with wonder, but his hands were steady as he put the black opal down, and he showed no sign of tiredness. Perhaps it was only because the Western youth was still too excited to feel the strain of the spell - but from his own experiences, Arudal would have expected Berek to be completely wrung out.

"The two of you, step out of the circle," ordered Salarond. "Arudal, bring out your Agathan."

Arudal let himself sink into the crystal stillness within his mind, forcing himself to turn from Finvar's warmth to Ostarak's chill. He opened himself, pushing gently even as he tightened his hold on the Imperial soldier. *Frighten Tirothar, if you can, but do not harm him.*

As you will, my lord.

Ostarak's pure Imperial features framed by jet-black hair were heartbreakingly familiar after months of seeing no one but Kantareans and Westerners: the Imperial messenger could easily have been one of the guardsmen who taught Duke Azarlokan's pages to fight with blunted swords, or one of the soldiers standing watch before the Prince's palace that Arudal had passed on his way to school. His pale face was perfectly clear to Arudal's eyes and did not change as the Agathan moved into full manifestation, but Arudal heard Tirothar suck in his breath. Ostarak took one step towards Sir Eroth's squire, then another.

It worked! Arudal thought for a second. Then Tirothar sobbed out, "No!", and Arudal heard the clatter as the other squire stumbled frantically back, saw the shadowy figures of Sir Eroth and Sir Salarond grabbing him.

"Enough," Salarond said firmly. Arudal drew a deep breath, pulling Ostarak back to his clear timeless prison, and forced his sight out of Shadow again, blinking in the red glow of the braziers. Tirothar's breath was coming in deep hitching gulps, as though he were struggling to keep from breaking down in tears, and Berek's lips were quivering.

"What did I do wrong?" Berek asked miserably. "I felt it, I know I did. There was as much magic there as in anything my teacher ever did."

Sir Eroth laid a hand on his arm. "You did nothing wrong. I think you simply were not able to raise enough power to make the spell as effective as it needs to be. Tirothar, calm yourself. You stood longer than you did before, and there is no man in the White Company who has not fled in Shadow-Fear at least once in his life - save, I suppose, for Arudal, who was bred to withstand it. It took bravery enough to be the first to try a new spell of this nature."

Tirothar gulped hard, straightening his back. "Yes, sir. Thank you."

"But how shall we raise more power than that?" Berek asked. "My teacher would often repeat a spell over thirteen nights, but with so many of us to cast two spells each on, not to mention the warhorses, we could be at the other side of the continent before we were done. The conjunctions of the stars will not aid us unless we wait for some time, for the Toll-Lord has just come into square to the Lady of Life in the family of the Trout, so that his power is dimmed, and they are both slow-moving."

No one spoke. It seemed to Arudal that the same answer must have occurred to all of them at the same time, but no one was willing to say it until, in a very small voice, Berek muttered, "I know what you are, yet...I do not think you are truly evil. Still...my teacher forbade me to even think of such things, but there might be another way..."

"Blood magic." Sir Eroth's voice was utterly neutral, his face blank.

Salarond sighed. "It is not against the law."

Arudal said nothing. On the Hidden Estate, he had learned in theory how to use the life-force of animals to strengthen a spell, but he had never done it nor seen it done. Briefly he wondered: if Ostarak drew in enough life-force, would Arudal himself be able to use some of it for a working as if he himself were an Agathan? But Sir Salarond was still speaking.

"And I do not think that any of us is likely to be tempted to go from slitting a sheep's throat to the greater power of slitting a man's. That is the danger in blood magic, and why our ancestors forsook it when they learned more of both magic and ethics than the simpler peoples know. But though we have long held it best not done if there are other ways, it is not illegal, nor - so long as it is done without cruelty and for good purpose - is it hateful to the gods."

"I should think not!" Arudal found himself saying. "At the beginning of Slaughter-Month, my father sacrifices a bull every year before the Northmen in our lands so that Gefn - that is what they call Aviyani - will give good harvest in the year to come, and there is both prayer and magic in that."

Shocked at the unfamiliar words that had come out of him, Arudal shut his mouth hastily. The others were all staring at him, their eyes wide in the braziers' dim light.

"Ari?" Sir Salarond said tentatively, then, "...Finvar?"

Dizzy, Arudal closed his eyes. In releasing Ostarak, he had failed to close the shields within himself - not deliberately; but his longing to have Finvar beside him and the sense of his squire-brother's nearness had betrayed him. He bit his lip, the slight pain forcing him to focus his mind, and pressed Finvar's awareness down from behind his eyes.

"It is I," he said at last. "Arudal, I mean. I'm sorry."

"What happened?"

"I just...My shields were open a little. I'm sorry. It won't happen again." I hope.

"Ari," Salarond said gently, "are you putting yourself at risk by keeping Finvar within you?"

"No, sir!" Arudal answered. He did not know if Sir Salarond would order him to cast Finvar out, if it came to that; but he was certain that he must not even hint at the danger of madness that might arise if he could not keep their minds more thoroughly separated.

"Are you sure?"

"Yes, sir."

"If I were to ask a Tharandrostan Mind-healer, would she tell me the same thing?" Sir Salarond pressed.

"Yes, sir," Arudal insisted, although he could feel his heart beating faster, and knew that he was lying.

Salarond cleared his throat. "I can only take your word for it now. But if, when we get back, I find out that you are concealing the truth on a matter that could endanger this mission, it shall go hard with you." There was no softness in the commander's cultivated voice, and a faint chill dew of sweat broke out on Arudal's brow. As a member of the Kantarean military, however nominal, he could be brought to court-martial, even executed if necessary: and although the State's regard would probably save him from the ultimate penalty, he could still be in more trouble than he could even imagine. At the very least, it would kill his chances of being allowed to serve in the Tharandrostan military in any other than the most basic capacity - ten years of shuffling requisitions for ships' paint and replacement uniforms, say - and, probably, of doing anything significant for the State for at least fifty years. He would certainly be called back from Kantar in disgrace...

"Sir, if I have any difficulties which might present a danger to the integrity of my mind, I shall let you know about it at once."

"Hmm." Salarond stared at Arudal for a while longer. The commander's dispassionate regard was far more intimidating than any of Sir Thoron's shouting, but Arudal stood his ground without blinking, and at last Sir Salarond looked back to the others. "Returning to the original subject. Can any of you think of any other methods of making our spells of protection as strong as they must be to stand up to...how would you describe the Emperor and his rival, Arudal?"

"Liches, sir, and likely arch-liches. I have no doubt that they are of the ninth rank or above; certainly powerful enough to achieve solid manifestation upon the green earth and probably powerful enough to create a form with all of the abilities of a physical body, yet with none of its weaknesses."

"To Fallen Imperial arch-liches, then, not to mention the effects of massed Undead in one place."

Berek looked at his shoes. Sir Eroth half-closed his eyes, his brow furrowing in thought, but he did not speak; Tirothar only shuffled uncomfortably, his gaze darting about as if he very much wished to be elsewhere.

"Has anyone any substantial practical or moral objections to using the lives of animals for this purpose?"

Tirothar muttered something that even Arudal's keen hearing could not pick up.

"Speak up or be silent, squire," Sir Eroth ordered.

"Sir...can it be morally right to kill animals for magical purposes?"

Eroth looked at the lanky youth for a moment. "Squire, what is your cloak made out of?"

"Uh, sheepskin, sir."

"And the rather nice coats we bought in Cirrod?"

"Fox skins, sir."

"Do you eat meat, squire?"

"Frequently, sir. Uh, you're saying that it really isn't any different to kill animals for magic than for clothing and food?"

"What do you think?"

Tirothar's light brows drew together as he shifted from foot to foot. "I suppose not. If we're killing them to take what we need from them in any case, and don't hurt them more than we have to for slaughter..."

"And I daresay you won't object to eating fresh mutton and pork while we're travelling."

"No, sir," Tirothar said, more enthusiastically. "But, uh...Dame Karsil may have something to say about this."

Salarond smiled. "You may be surprised. When Elves hunt, they always dedicate the lives of their prey as an offering to the gods, nor do they scorn to work in leather and bone. They know that the children of the gods were made to eat flesh as well as bread; and though they have no need of blood-magic, they are not wary of it in the way that we are, for, as a people, they suffer far less than we from the temptation to go beyond what is lawful or right in the search for power. So we are decided, then. Eroth, you and Tirothar may armour up and relieve Thoron. Berek, you may clean up here and go to sleep until your turn on watch. And Ari...I think you will spend tonight working on your shielding. While I am not an expert on psychic maladies, I am still the medical officer here. And if I see a repeat of tonight's performance, there will have to be something done about it."

"Ah...yes, sir. Thank you, sir."

Salarond raised a gray eyebrow. "Why?" He looked at Arudal a moment. "Never mind. Just make very sure that you take care of the problem. Do you understand?"

"Yes, sir."

The two knights and Tirothar left the wagon. Berek stood staring at the painted canvas - probably, Arudal thought, trying to think of a way to fold or roll it without smudging the sigils. Arudal watched him for a little while, then sat down and closed his eyes, shivering even inside his foxskin coat. If he understood correctly, Sir Salarond was willing to condemn Finvar to the certainty of death for the sake of completing their mission.

And for preserving my sanity, Arudal admitted to himself. If he went mad, he would be at best a burden to the party, at worst...He, like all agathudalim, had been required to speak to a Mind-healer at least once every two weeks at home, and to visit one at the Tharandrostan embassy in Var Perenil no less than once a month. To be sure of his full cooperation, it had been made very clear to him what could happen when someone of his talents lost his grip on reality: Princess Sir Murnitir's work had vastly lessened the incidence of madness among mediums, but not eradicated it altogether. Sir Salarond had been willing to risk a battle rather than deliver any of the party's members to the Agathim; but if it came to a choice between Arudal's sanity, maybe his life, and Arudal and Finvar being lost together, there was only one decision their commander could make.

Amandeth, may I never be a commander who has to make such a choice! Arudal thought. In military training classes in school, he had always hated the essays on ethics that forced him to put himself in the place of the commander who must send one company to its death in order to save several others, or make the decision to abandon - maybe even mercifully kill - the wounded who could not be brought along if a troop were to have any hope of survival. He liked the reality even less as its object. And Sir Salarond is a healer by nature. What must it be costing him to face this possibility - the worst of battlefield triage in cold blood, without even the urgency of gaping wounds?

But there was one thing Arudal could do to save Finvar and spare Sir Salarond the cruel choice between them. I want Finvar with me; but I want more for him to live. Arudal forced his breathing to deepen, his heart gradually to slow, and began the difficult task of blocking his awareness from that of his friend, walling Finvar more and more deeply into the silence of his mind.

At each village where the White Company party stopped, they bought lambs or young pigs, enough to slaughter one every night until they reached the next village. That sufficed to work their spells, at least well enough to protect them from Ostarak - whom Arudal judged as being of the fifth rank among Agathim, strong enough for a ghost, but by no means nearing the power of the great Undead. And if anyone doubted that it would be enough for what lay at the end of their journey, no one spoke of it. At any rate, they were doing the best that they could. Sir Shakhor was an excellent campfire cook: he and Rhys gathered what herbs they could recognise within sight of the camp every night, and the company ate hot roasts for breakfast and cold meat throughout the day, until Arudal began to think that he would do almost anything for a decent meal of fish.

The Kantareans seemed well-pleased with their menu, though, and even Berek did not complain about having to feed, water, and clean up after the animals bound in the back of the wain. It was not long before the Western boy had gained back the little weight he had lost on the first leg of their travelling, and perhaps a bit more, while Malni, who had seldom gotten fresh meat except at slaughtering-season in her life, was positively ecstatic.

Their journey through the plains to the edge of the woods was remarkably peaceful. Once the tingling of the Imperial messenger's ring woke Arudal from a sound sleep, but nothing more came of it than it had the first time. They made camp just outside the trees, settling around the fire at sunset to discuss the next step.

"The chief hindrance from here to the edge of the Fallen Seat's territory, I regret to say, is likely to be the Elves who dwell in these woods," Sir Salarond stated. "They will not look with favour upon our mission…"

"Indeed not!" Dame Karsil broke in. The Elf was sitting a little apart from the others, and though her long hands rested quietly in her lap, it seemed to Arudal that he could feel her anger as surely as if she were clenching her fists. Salarond spared her only a glance before he went on.

"And I believe that there is none of us who would be capable of dissembling well enough to deceive them. All we can do, therefore, is evade their notice, and that we can only do with foreknowledge of where they are. We cannot take our wain beyond the last village of the Wood-Folk, where this road ends: Berek, we shall part company with you there until we return. Malni, Karsil and I have discussed this, and we believe that you should stay with him, as we have neither spare arms nor armour that can protect you against the Undead."

"Finavi, may I not at least go as far as you are going?" Malni asked. "Surely you did not take me as your squire only in order to leave me behind when the way became dangerous?"

Karsil's face softened a little, the delicate muscles of her jaw unclenching as she looked at her squire. "No, I did not. But I have not decided yet when I shall leave the party, or where I shall go when I do. And even if I wished to see you fighting for one of the Fallen, as I do not, your bravery alone would not be enough to withstand the weapons of Shadow."

"Finvar's chain-mail and helm fit me well enough, even if his plate does not, and you have taught me to use sword and shield," Malni protested.

Karsil rose silently and put a hand on Malni's shoulder. "Come with me, squire," she said. The two of them walked off beyond the circle of firelight, into the woods, until Arudal could no longer see Karsil's tall glimmering shape and Malni's shorter, stockier one among the trees.

"Sir," Berek said diffidently, "will you not need my help in magic where you are going? There is still time for me to work the spells of protection on myself."

Arudal stared at him: he would have been no less surprised if the fat, timid Westerner had sprouted a third arm. He had assumed that Berek would be grateful to avoid the worst dangers of their mission, not to mention the hardship of weeks of travel through the forest. In fact, he had expected Berek to whine about his contract in hopes of getting out of the most dangerous and difficult part of the journey.

A faint smile touched Sir Salarond's lips, as though he had just seen a favourite theory proved. "Ritual magic is too slow to be of much aid where we are going. But it is noble of you to offer."

"Then, while I wait, will you leave me with something that is yours, so that I may do my best to work spells of protection and success for you?"

Arudal thought of the fear trembling in Berek's voice when he had spoken of the burning-cage. The youth could well be risking his life by doing magic in the confines of a little village. Karsil and Malni could ride swiftly enough to escape most natural threats, and the locals probably would not be able to pursue on horseback, but Berek had only cantered once or twice over very short distances, and been starkly terrified each time: if he had to ride for his life, it would be even money as to whether he died of being caught or of breaking his neck. He is brave in his own way, after all, Arudal thought. And - can I hope that he has even learned something of loyalty? It struck him that Berek's virtues, though largely expressed in the negative, had become more real over the course of the journey: he had stopped complaining about helping with chores and sitting on watch, he had not breathed so much as a whisper that might have betrayed his companions...though the makings of a fighting knight were not in him, he had, in short, slowly become all that they could expect of a pure mage on such a mission. And, had Berek meant to betray them, he could have done so in Cirrod simply by being clumsy in speaking to the locals at the wrong time; he could always have been lying about the fate that would await him if he were found traveling with the Mordhagoernim.

Sir Salarond's thoughts must have run along the same lines, for he said, "Again, it is both brave and noble of you to offer. But you can best serve us by seeing that the wain and its contents are safe while we go on."

"No. Let him do it." Lostren's voice rang with command, and Sir Salarond's amber-gray eyes glinted angrily as he turned on his squire: even in the White Company, there were forms that had to be observed. The commander opened his mouth - perhaps to slap Lostren down - but closed it again as he looked into the young noble's eyes.

"Aye, sir, I believe he should," Rhys added softly. "Sir, it is in my heart, look you, that we shall need Berek's aid before this is over, though we may never see how it has helped, and I can see that the Foresight of the High King's line is upon Lostren."

Sir Salarond gazed thoughtfully at the two red-haired squires for a little time, then nodded. "I shall take your suggestion," he said at last. "Now. As I was saying, we must know where the Elves are likely to be in order to avoid them, and there is one among us who has ridden through this forest a great many times. Arudal, you said that you could work a long-lasting mastery upon your prisoner?"

"Yes, sir."

"You shall do that this night, and, when we have passed the Wood-Folk's village in two days' time, Ostarak shall ride with us as our guide." Salarond's lean face was set hard and grim, as though he misliked the command he gave, but there was no waver of doubt in his voice. "Meanwhile, each of you think upon what you can leave behind. Only two of our pack-horses are protected, and we would find it hard to lead more through the wood in any case. We must travel as light and swift as we can."

Chapter 24: Shadow's Reach

"The shark circles in widening darkness,
Rot spreads, hid in oak's sickened heart.
Who names that which stands in the shadows? -
Still shadows under stairs, waiting,
Shadows rustling under the trees?"
- "Candlelit Nights", Perelan Haragift

When they left the little village of the Wood-Folk behind, Arudal saw at last why Sir Shakhor, rather than one of the more famed fighters of the White Company, had been chosen for this mission. From horseback, the ranger-knight was able to find trails that would have been invisible to Arudal even were he on his knees with his nose in the leaf-mould; he led the horses around treacherous patches of ground that looked like any other to Arudal; and he seemed to understand even the songs of the foreign birds as if he bore an amulet that gave him the skill to speak with animals, though his ability came from nothing but long years of training. Once only Arudal saw him stop, dumbfounded: just as the Moon was about to set on their night-watch, the silver trail of a dethil's liquid song arose from one of the snow-whitened treetops, clear and pure as the glimmer of the stars through the icy night.

Shakhor froze in place, his head tilted back and his hands on his helm, as though he would have removed it to listen unhindered, but did not dare to move lest the little bird be startled into silence or flight. Rhys, who had been turning to put a large stick on the low-burning fire, stopped half-crouched, the heavy piece of wood in his hand drooping slowly to the snow. Barely daring to breathe, Arudal's eyes flickered over to Ostarak. Even the Agathan stood in awed stillness, his open mouth and wide eyes black against the whiteness of his face, and Arudal caught the trail of his thought like a leaf rustling through his skull: The Friend of Men be with me, I have not heard a night-singer raise her voice thus since I lived. Perhaps it is a sign...A single spark of hope flared painfully beneath the ghost's insubstantial breastplate, burning sharp and brief as a glowing bit of leaf wind-whirled from the fire, and was gone just as quickly. But still the dethil's shimmering song poured over them, until tears prickled at Arudal's eyes from the beauty of it.

When at last the little bird fell silent again, Arudal felt somehow cleansed, light-limbed beneath his armour, as though its voice had washed away all the fears and worries of their mission for a few moments. He could feel Finvar's warm pressure within him - without thought, he had opened his mind to his friend so that the Artegalian could share in the dethil's heart-stopping song - and even the harshest thoughts of the consequences that might come were barely enough to force Arudal to strengthen his inner shielding again, for such matters seemed to shrink to remote pinpricks in the shining brightness of the stars over the night-shadowed snow.

Ostarak was a better guide than Arudal had expected. The Tharandrostan had feared that the Agathan's Shadow-blindness and his death-binding would have kept him from knowing what lay on the road he had ridden for near seventeen hundred years. But even from Shadow, Ostarak knew where the Elves dwelt and where their main patrol-routes ran - though Arudal thought that the power of the messenger's signet, if it still bore any, must be aiding them yet, for the Agathan said that there were always a few small groups of Elvish warriors roaming the forest freely in order to turn back or slay whatever would enter or leave the lands around the Imperial Seat. A ring fifty miles across was a long way to patrol, and, skilled and tireless as the Elves were, they could not be everywhere; but though the White Company took what precautions they could, they had to light campfires against the bitter cold, and there was no way to muffle the sounds of their going so as to hide them even from the ears of Men.

Arudal usually rode as close to Ostarak as he could manage - though horses could be protected against Shadow-Fear itself, breaking them of their instinctive fear of the Undead was another matter, and not only was Inmanat uneasy, but the high-spirited steed of the ghost's memory was a little fractious even beneath Ostarak's skilled hands.

Ostarak himself was a surprisingly enjoyable travelling companion. In his night of probing into the Agathan's mind to bind him, Arudal had done his best to dim the tormenting knowledge of the final irrevocable failure that had kept their message from reaching the Imperial Seat in time. That memory was too deeply ingrained to wipe out without destroying part of Ostarak's mind, but Arudal wrapped it around with the easing of time that came to living men, like wrapping a brick in thick cloths so that, though it might press aching against flesh still, its sharp edges no longer gnawed. Obedience came easily, for Ostarak had been as accustomed as any Tharandrostan to obey his superiors by both rank and birth. Arudal also found, somewhat to his sorrow, that Ostarak had turned down a posting in Tharabruthnan because it would have parted him from his family for too long. The Imperial soldier could have been the ancestor of one of Arudal's own friends, perhaps even a kinsman, if he had chosen differently; and with that in mind, the Tharandrostan worked to allow him friendship, and to compel his obedience as little and as gently as possible.

Along the way, Arudal let Ostarak wander a little to sate his hunger for life-force with wild animals, for the Tharandrostan could not bear the knowledge of how dreadfully his prisoner was suffering from Shadow-hunger even at night, and certainly could not have forced him to ride unfed in the daylight. Full-fed, with the worst of his death-compulsion eased, and calmed by Arudal's gentle work in his mind, it was not long before the Imperial soldier had exhausted his knowledge of courtesies and relaxed into a rougher, more comfortable demeanour that reminded Arudal very much of Duke Azarlokan's guardsmen. He showed Arudal the trick he had used to disarm him and several others of the same sort, and one time, forgetting Arudal's station of birth altogether, Ostarak even reached out to pat him on the helm as if he would tousle his hair.

Rhys and Tirothar kept their distance from the Agathan, but Lostren often took a turn riding beside him, questioning Ostarak closely on the happenings of his living days, and though Lostren's face was covered by his helm and the scarves wrapped under it, the tautness of his posture and the occasional twitching of his fingers on the reins told Arudal that the Kantarean historian was suffering from an agony of academic frustration at not being able to take notes as he rode.

Two days from the edge of the Fallen Seat's territory, the messenger-signet on Arudal's finger began to tingle lightly and did not stop.

"It does not feel as it did before, sir," Arudal said. He chewed his lip, trying to think of how to explain the difference. "It is...less sharp, maybe. It seems to me now that before it was a warning, but now it is..." He glanced down at his hand. The silver design inlaid in the black stone flashed and glimmered in the broken sunlight through the snow-weighted branches above their heads, leaving a deep purple after-image behind Arudal's eyelids when he blinked. "It seems not as though there is power in it, but as if there were power gathering around it like sea-mist thickening in the evening. And...I do not think that it is a threat, sir."

"Hmm." Sir Salarond considered him for a moment, then turned to his other side where Lostren flanked him. "Lostren, should Ari take the ring off?"

"No," Lostren answered at once. Then, more thoughtfully, "...yes. I can't tell, sir. At first it seemed that it would save him from danger, then that it would put him into danger...It seems to me that there is a cloud over my sight, thickening as we near the Fallen Seat."

"Then, if you cannot use your Foresight, use your brains," Sir Salarond told him tartly. "You have gotten far too used to a certainty that you in all probability will not always have, if you do not mean to look like a Plainsman the rest of your life."

"I think that perhaps Ari should wear it until we have passed from the lands where the Elves will go, and take it off as soon as we reach those held by the Shadow-Emperor."

"My thoughts are the same. Ari, have Ostarak tell you the moment we cross the border, and remove the ring at once."

As they neared the edge of the lands around the Fallen Seat, Arudal found it harder and harder to keep his sight out of Shadow. It was snowing again, but the clouds brought his sight no easing. The Shadow-fog blinded him as if he were staring into the brightest sunlight, and Ostarak's sturdy little black-mailed figure was the only one in their party that he could recognise beyond four feet away. Arudal gave thanks to Amandeth that he was mounted on Inmanat, who could pick his own way through the stones and fallen branches and badger-holes without any guidance from his rider: if they had been walking, he would have had to ask someone to lead him, for unlike Ostarak, he could not simply pass through the trees' wide mossy trunks where they blocked his path.

"We will reach the border of the Emperor's Keeping in a few minutes," Ostarak said to Arudal at sunset of the second day. Arudal peered through the thick dark mist for Sir Salarond, but even in the dim faint light of evening through trees and clouds, he could see no more than the vaguest shapes of men on horses around him. Now? he thought. The Elves are hardly likely to ambush us so close. But an order was an order: a few minutes one way or another might make no difference here, but elsewhere, it could turn the course of a battle.

The tingling of the signet on Arudal's forefinger was growing stronger. It was a pleasant feeling, like a cat purring beneath his hand. When he looked down at it, he saw a faint purple-black corona of magic beginning to coruscate about his hand and arm.

"Now," Ostarak said softly. Arudal took the ring from his right hand, then stopped, frozen, holding it in the fingers of his left as though he were examining it in a jewelry shop. He could feel the Undead all about him, growing stronger as the last of the light faded, and reached out into the Shadow around without thought.

"Sir Salarond," Arudal murmured. "Do not be alarmed. There is no need to draw weapons. These are the true Emperor's men, who have come to greet us and to escort us in safety to the Imperial Seat."

As Arudal spoke, the Imperial troop rode out from the broad-trunked trees whose darkness had concealed them during the daylight hours. There were at least fifty of them, all armoured in heavy black plate. One, whose breastplate was enameled with the deep red field and black Sun of the late Empire, raised his visor and rose forward, reining his horse in before Arudal and bowing.

"Count Arudal Arumirun of Aglarek. The Emperor sends you his greetings, and requests and requires that you come with us. No harm shall be done to yourself or your companions: the Emperor holds you to be his honoured guests. I am Commander Sir Pharzehar Bardaratun of the House of Emelkhad, and my life shall answer for your safety and, so far as we are able to provide it, your comfort."

It was dark enough now for Arudal to recognise Sir Salarond by general outline. The Kantarean general bowed slightly in his saddle. "Sir, we appreciate the Emperor's courtesy and hospitality. However, you have erred slightly. It is I, rather than Count Arudal, who commands here - as surely your Emperor must know, since he seems well-acquainted with our names and styles."

Could Ostarak have told them? Arudal wondered. But Ostarak had never called him anything other than "Lord Arudal", and he had never bothered to correct the soldier with his precise title.

"Your Grace," Sir Pharzehar replied. "Our Imperial Master is aware of your respective ranks, both in your military and in your lands. Yet he commanded me most strictly to extend his invitation first to Count Arudal, and through him to the remainder of your party. As to why, I cannot speak, but I believe that no discourtesy is intended, and I apologize most sincerely if you have taken it as such. Now, I would ask that you ride with us until we are well away from the borders kept by the Accursed. Lodgings have been prepared for your comfort: we should reach them easily by dawn, but if you have need to stop and eat or otherwise refresh yourselves before then, please inform me. Ostarak, the Emperor is aware of the passing of Sir Darthumazad's troops and your personal state, and commands you to continue as Count Arudal's companion, orderly as appropriate, and personal guard until further notice."

Ostarak saluted - the raised-palm salute of Tharandrost, unchanged from Imperial days - and nudged his horse a little closer to Inmanat. The dark gelding tossed his head, eyes rolling and nostrils flaring as he tried to take the scent of the Shadow-steeds, and Arudal stroked his neck to calm him.

When the last dim light had faded through the snow, Lostren kindled a lantern to guide the other members of the White Company. The little flame hurt Arudal's eyes when he looked at it, blinding him for a few moments after he glanced away. Without his mind-work, he knew that Ostarak would have been grievously hard-put to bear their small campfires, he could feel the unease of the Agathim around him from the mere lamp-wick's flickering, like eddies in a dark pool.

Arudal's mind whirled with questions as they rode silently in the midst of the Undead soldiers. How did the Emperor know our titles? Could he have read my mind through the signet? Arudal did not think so. Not, at any rate, without alerting him: mind-magic and true magic were very different things, but where their effects were similar, someone who was skilled in one could often sense the workings of the other, especially someone whose shields were as well-trained as Arudal's own. Divination? But that would mean that true magic works in the Imperial Seat as it does in the Middle Land, unless the Emperor has a more gifted Mind-Seer than any we know. Again Arudal thought of his sense that the power to bring his sorceror-spells to life was still there, lacking only a single point of connection to link fuel and spark. Has the Emperor regained that link? Atharath and Gormok recognised the "tongue of sorcerors", and Berek spoke of the magic of the Mordhagoernim.

When they were two candlemarks from the border, Sir Pharzehar allowed them to stop for a meal of dried mutton and hardcakes. The White Company had come well-provisioned, not knowing what the Undead might be able to provide them with. Contemporary Imperial chronicles spoke of the amazing feasts served at the tables of the Emperors and their great lords - larks' tongues in aspic, enough to serve a thousand guests at once; swans with gilded feathers and fire breathing from their mouths; peacocks that, refeathered in their shimmering hides after roasting, strutted about the hall to music until the dance stopped, then collapsed into neatly carved heaps, their tough tasteless flesh transmuted into a tender delicacy of exquisite flavour by the alchemy of the Imperial kitchens...But ghosts did not eat; vampires fed only on the blood of the living; and the lesser Ukuthrim, the walking corpses of various types, preferred their meat alive or freshly dead. And what manner of lodgings can they have prepared for us?

No glimmer of dawn showed through the heavy clouds and thick trees; but Arudal's sight was so deep in Shadow by the time they stopped that Lostren had to take him by the hand and lead him into the house as if he were a child. The floor was stone-hard under his boots; he shuffled carefully behind his friend, for Lostren could easily step over something that would trip Arudal up. He could smell a faint lingering trace of rotten flesh in the cold air, like game frozen after it had hung too long.

"What does it look like?" Arudal asked.

"This building is made of stone. Elf-built, I think. The ceiling is set with windows, the buttresses carved in an Elven manner, with trailing tendrils and leaping stags. I think the roof was repaired recently: the lantern does not give enough light for me to see it well, but there are big dark patches up there, some covering the places where windows ought to be. Some of the mortar and plaster have crumbled away, but the floor is clean-swept, and there are streaks of clear ice on the walls, as though they were recently washed down. A fire is laid in the hearth beneath a spit, but not lit, and a young deer - this spring's birthing, if I do not miss my guess - is hanging, skinned and gutted, from a beam at the end of the room, with two plucked pheasants beside it. There is a table just in front of the game, laid with fine crystal and goldware, and several bottles upon it. There are three doors, one in each wall. I do not think this house could have been abandoned more than an hundred years, if that long. Probably more like twenty-five or fifty."

"You have keen eyes, Lord Lostren," Sir Pharzehar said. The Agathan had taken off his helm, his golden hair streaming over his black gorget and pauldrons. Even beneath the heavy plate, Arudal could see that the Imperial knight was slimly built, his narrow nose slightly arched and his blond eyebrows high-winged. The grey rims of his slanted eyes were almost silver-pale, the corona about their pupils lemon-amber. His finely chiseled lips curved in a faint smile. "We have been slowly pushing the Accursed back for some time. Yes, even with the aid of the Pretender: our Imperial Master made truce with him outside the city walls, for all of us must feed, and the best hunting is in the lands that the Accursed hold, or recently held."

And they have gained a full night's travel in fifty years or less, Arudal thought, a grim shiver tightening his jaw. What will the Emperor be able to do if we help him conquer his rival?

"Count Arudal, Sir Salarond, my lords," Sir Pharzehar went on. "I would ask you to not to leave this house during the hours of daylight unless you must, and not to go more than fifty feet from the door if you do. There will be lesser servants of our Imperial Master on guard outside, but they are somewhat distressing of aspect to those who are unaccustomed to them."

Walking corpses, perhaps ghouls, Arudal thought. Such creatures, protected by their decaying flesh, could abide the light of the Sun as the greater Undead could not.

"I fear that you must light your fires yourselves, but I believe that we have left you everything else you need. The door to the left leads to a bath; the doors to the centre and right to chambers with beds. If you have any other needs this day, please inform Ostarak of them."

"What if I need to take a dump?" Sir Thoron asked bluntly. "Have you forgotten that living Men do that? Or do we just crap in a corner and try not to step in it?"

Bloodless, the Agathim could not blush; but a faint memory of colour touched Sir Pharzehar's high-boned cheeks. "My pardon, sir. Ah...there is a privy outside, twenty yards from the right of the door, hidden by a clump of bushes. I will quickly see to it that it is made fit for you, and that your guards know to draw back when you would use it. Until then, if you can manage among the trees..."

And that explains the smell of walking corpses, Arudal thought. The Emperor must use the embodied Ukuthrim to do what his Agathim could not - to, for instance, carry water from a pool to sluice down the walls of an abandoned Elvish dwelling, gather wood to lay a fire, or cut pine-branches to sweep away years of dirt and birds' nests.

Although Arudal could not bear to look at the fires, their warmth seeped slowly through him. He had almost ceased to notice the aching chill in his bones; he was not sure that he was grateful for this reprieve from the cold, when they would have to ride on in the snow that night. Lostren went with him to help him bathe, describing the room to him. "The baths are made of wrought silver and carved white stone, shaped in the form of great nesting swans. The water flows in through pipes from raised silver tanks, some above fire-trenches and some not, so that you may choose hot and cold as you will - The Elves of this land did not neglect their crafts as they guarded it."

"I wonder what happened to them?" Arudal mused, pausing with a hand on the edge of the swan-tub. Even though he could not see it, he could feel the delicately wrought feathers, polished silver passing imperceptibly smooth into polished stone. "If they withdrew...or..."

After a moment, Lostren began to sing softly, as if to himself, the jingling rhymes of a simple Common ballad. Deep as the Telagon's speaking voice was, Arudal had expected him to be a low bass, but his singing range was surprisingly high. The faint ring of silver echoed his voice like far-off bells,

"The Stars shone bright on Galen Hill,
 But all their shafts were flown,
 The Dark Trolls yammering ringed them round,
 An hundred to each one.
'Wilt yield, wilt yield?' dark captain cried,
'Your kin lie in their blood,
 And if you yield me your swords,
 Your ransom I'll hold good...'"

Lostren's voice trailed off into silence. The Battle of Galen Hill had proven, as had many before and since, that Elves did not withdraw living from what they were sworn to hold. The crafters who had cut the stones of this house, whose long skilled fingers had shaped each feather of the swan-baths, were surely dead beneath the Shadow-swords of the Agathim, and Lostren's hands were cold as he helped Arudal into the bath.

Sir Shakhor and Rhys had done a splendid job of roasting the pheasants, and the bottles on the table proved to be berry-wine, sweet and exquisite even when watered to quarter-strength. "Of Elvish make, I think," Lostren commented. "I cannot imagine any wine surviving for seventeen hundred years without powerful spells of preservation, and this, though properly aged, still has a breath of freshness to it."

Ostarak looked wistfully at Arudal as the Tharandrostan felt for his goblet, lifted it, and sipped. "I wish I could taste wine again," he murmured. "So long in the dark, I have forgotten..."

When this is over, if all goes as I hope, then you shall, Arudal said silently to him. It only took a small spell, just enough magic infused into wine and cup that an Agathan could touch them, and Arudal had done a page's service in his grandmother's fortress even before he was sent to Duke Azarlokan.

I would thank you for that more than anything. I remember the words - sweet or dry, strong or smooth - I remember that I drank the soldier's ration and jested about its roughness, and that sometimes when I had carried a welcome message, a great lord would give me a cup of a fine vintage, but the tastes have all dried to cold ash in my memory.

To Arudal's Shadow-blind sight, the two of them might have been the only living men in the room, the rest of the party no more than foggy silhouettes. The Undead had other means than sight to sense, even to recognise the living; between the green earth and the Shadow-Realm, Arudal had only his eyes. He reached out to touch the Agathan's arm, the chain-mail icy under his fingertips.

You have a kind heart, Lord Arudal. If I can, I shall be pleased to serve you as long as you will have me.

Arudal did not know how much Ostarak's unspoken words sprang from the Agathan's own will and how much from his own work inside Ostarak's mind. Yet the offer still touched him, and he answered, So long as you may stay with me, I will be honoured to have you in my service..

Sir Salarond ordered that one man stay on watch inside the house while the rest of them slept. The corpse-stink was stronger in the bedrooms, as though it had soaked into the linens from rotting hands, but they were all too tired to mind much. Sir Shakhor and Rhys quickly jointed and packed the deer that had been roasting over the fire all day. The White Company party armoured up - though Arudal had to breathe through his mouth for the first few minutes until he got used to the stink of his gambeson again - and they were on their way once more.

Chapter 25: The Fallen Seat

"Walls shine white as Sun on snow
Glittering high to heavens' blue,
Ringing round the heart of all.
Birches green shade bright-paved streets,
Beneath the gleaming hooves' proud tread.
High-born ride in silk and steel,
Masters of the world's might.
Here the wisest wisdom gather,
Here the fairest, shimmering, drink
From bright gold, clear adamant..."
- "The Imperial Seat", unknown author, late Fifth Millennium

It took another night and a half of riding before they reached the Fallen Seat. The Undead had done nothing to keep up the old roads, for they had no need of them. Sir Eroth's horse had thrown the first shoe, and from the clattering clink of the others' hooves, Arudal thought it would not be long before more followed it; and Arudal's blindness to the green earth did not help speed them along either.

At last, near midnight of their third night in the territory of the Agathim, the party emerged from the woods. Arudal drew his breath in awe. There, untouched as if they had never fallen, towered the high white walls that ringed the Imperial Seat, gleaming stark as polished bone above the snow, with no crack or mortar to break their smoothness. It had taken fifty thousand slaves and the magic of the Old Empire to raise those walls. Only the Wrath had breached them - leaving them, according to Avalar, in heaps of shattered stone over the bodies of the dead and dying; but now they stood again as if they had never fallen. A blue glow played over them like the cold lightning flickering about tall sails in a storm: Arudal knew that no creature of Shadow could pass in or out of the Fallen Seat save by the appointed gates, and no living man could scale those ice-smooth heights.

Lostren nudged his horse close, reaching out for Arudal's reins. "I should lead you from here. The ground is treacherous, with fallen rocks everywhere from the ruins of the walls."

"Ruins? They stand unbroken."

"Not on the green earth," Lostren answered sadly. "...You see them?"

Arudal described what he saw to the other squire, and Lostren shook his head. "I almost wish that, at least for this moment, I could see as you do. The Wrath cast them down: jagged pieces stand here and there, like rotting teeth in a broken mouth, but for the most part, the city's walls lie shattered. Yet...as you speak of them I can almost see them, as if a touch of moonlight lay over the ruins."

Silently Arudal suffered Lostren to lead him along, Inmanat turning to follow the other squire's horse on his crooked path through the invisible heaps of fallen stone. The Imperial magics had been broken: was it the Emperor in Shadow who had set the wards about the City, raising the walls to the sight of the dead as he remembered them?

Sir Pharzehar led them along to a high-arched gate, its columns intricately carved with the battle-triumphs of Sagaron the Builder, who had ordered the new walls made to replace the plain stone of earlier days. The Imperial commander rode forward, but Lostren stopped, pulling Arudal's horse to a halt as well.

"We cannot enter here," Sir Salarond declared. "For you it may be a gate: for us it is a blockade of broken stone. We might climb it, if we had light and were not in full armour, but our horses cannot. There was a gap a short way back: may we pass through there?"

"As you must." Sir Pharzehar gestured gracefully. "Sir Aphanazor, Sir Dolnarak, Dame Garil: take four men each and accompany them, then ride quickly to catch up with us inside the walls."

The men dismounted; Arudal watched in fascination as the ghostly dark shapes of the White Company knights and their squires passed through the great wall like a scattering of mist. Then only he and Lostren were left.

"Come on, Ari," Lostren said. "I know what you see - but I promise you, it is not there. Close your eyes if you must so that I can guide you through."

"I...I don't think I can pass." Arudal gulped. He remembered how he had been unable to enter Sir Salarond's wards without the aid of their maker. The walls of the Fallen Seat might stand only in Shadow, but they would be as real to him as Ostarak's hand grasping his wrist.

"Shit."

Arudal raised an eyebrow: he had never heard Lostren swear before.

"Well, if you can't ride through, we'll have to climb. Give the horses to our guides, then I'll help you over as well as I can."

Arudal swallowed hard. He had done some rock-climbing in the mountains about the Hidden Estate, but never over the treacherous stones of a fallen ruin in the snow and ice - let alone feeling his way blindly along while seeing something wholly different. But there was no other choice, and so he handed over Inmanat's reins.

"Take your armour and cloak off as well. It'll be cold, but I think we'll warm up quickly enough."

Lostren had understated the case. Without his armour to block the wind and his cloak to keep the warmth in, Arudal was shivering violently in moments, hugging himself tightly and clenching his jaw to stop his teeth from chattering.

"Come on," Lostren said, taking his hand. "Follow me as closely as you can, and move carefully."

Even with Salarond's squire guiding him, the walk back to the gate was difficult enough. Lostren's lantern bobbed ahead to shoot painful flashes of light through the blackness of Arudal's sight. Several times Arudal lost his footing, and once he heard his gambeson rip on a rock. *I can't do this - Amandeth, I can't do this!* He shook his head. He would have to do it, or shame himself before the knights of the White Company. *And what will I tell Finvar when he is restored? He wouldn't balk, and Lostren is taking the risk of guiding me. And Sir Thoron has been a good knight to me: I cannot fail him now.*

When they came to the gate, Lostren set his lantern as high up as he could reach. Hands shaking in the cold, he crisscrossed one end of a coil of rope around his shoulders and beneath his armpits, then made a similar halter for Arudal with the other end. "There's ice on the stone, so we'll have to go very slowly. Can you do it?"

"I can," Arudal said through clenched teeth.

Even through his leather gloves, the cold of the frozen rocks stung Arudal's hands. He worked his fingers as he felt out for each handhold, trying to keep the blood flowing through them, but the numbness was seeping into his hands and feet like hemlock. They went in alternating steps, first Lostren moving, then, when he called, "Braced!", Arudal would go, calling up "Braced!" again when he had gotten a secure hold.

Grasping for a rock above his head, Arudal's fingers slipped on the ice and he slid until his full weight slammed into the rope halter, biting back a scream as his body cracked painfully into the broken stone. As he reached up again, gasping for breath, a slow hot worm of wetness trickled down his arm beneath the searing bite of cold air - his gambeson sleeve must have given way. He clenched and opened his fingers. *Only a scrape,* he told himself.

"Are you all right?" Lostren called.

"I'm fine," Arudal gritted, tightening his grip harder and boosting himself up over the next block. "There; I'm braced."

Lostren and Arudal did not dare to stand on the uncertain footing of the top. Crawling over the huge stones like ants on a gravel-heap, the two squires changed positions, Lostren starting down first.

"Braced!" Arudal called. He felt the tugging on the rope, heard the scraping in the blackness below as Lostren carefully felt his way down. Rock grated hard on rock; Arudal heard the sound of stone smashing beneath the other squire's cry just as Lostren's weight struck the end of the rope, nearly tearing him from his place. For a sickening instant, Arudal felt the stones sliding beneath his right glove as Lostren swung beneath him - *Amandeth, we're both going!* Then his numb hand caught on a jutting outcrop, and he clutched it as if it were a spar at the edge of a maelstrom.

"Can you reach anything?"

Lostren's deep voice came strained from the darkness, as though his throat had closed from terror...or pain. "No. Ari, I think...I think my arm's broken. I can't move it, anyway."

"I'm going to try to pull you up."

Carefully, ever so carefully, Arudal inched downward until he was able to wedge most of his body into a crack between two great blocks. *And all the gods help me if they shift!* He reached for the rope, slowly winding it in. He might not have been able to lift Thoron or Finvar in their plate harness with only the strength of his arms, but at least Lostren, even in full armour, was reasonably light. He heard the Telagon panting hard below - trying not to scream - and kept pulling until Lostren called, "That's enough, Ari. I'm on a ledge, not far below..." His hand patted Arudal's calf. "Right here."

Hanging on tightly to his lower hold with his right hand, Arudal curled his body around until he could grasp his toehold with his left. His arms were still trembling from the strain of lifting Lostren: he took a deep breath, forcing it out from his gut, and clung tightly, lowering himself one-handed into the darkness. Lostren steadied him with his good arm until they were both standing on the same ledge.

"You'll have to explore downward first, then see if you can come back and help me down," Lostren said tightly. "No, better: go down and tell the others what's happened. If I have some warm clothes, I'll be all right here until dawn, and then Shakhor and Rhys can help me down."

"I have a better answer than that. And I am a very great fool for not thinking of it before."

Arudal set his mind, concentrating on Sir Pharzehar's fair face, the precise accents of his voice...*Sir Pharzehar?*

Is all well? Where are you?

On the ruins of the wall halfway through the gate. Are there any vampires among those who serve His Imperial Majesty?

Of course...Count Arudal, why did you not mention your difficulty? The severe tone of the Imperial commander's mind reminded Arudal very much of Dr. Murakhon, the healer at his school. He forced his thoughts away from that with an effort.

Never mind. But be swift: Lord Telagon's arm may be broken, and we are both suffering grievously from the cold.

"What is it?" Lostren asked.

"Vampires," Arudal grated, "can fly. Unlike the Agathim, who, though only habit keeps their feet upon the earth, can seldom manage to bring themselves to go in manners other than they did when they were living...We could have been carried over in safety, had I not..." *Had I not come to think of our companions as if they were living men.*

Arudal saw the green magic-flicker about the dark shape first as it arrowed towards them, and readied himself to meet it. Most of the Agathim on the Hidden Estate came and went as they would, save when there were guests present, but the Ukuthrim, especially vampires, were a different matter. "The best of them," his grandmother had said, "are ravening animals: we may keep such monsters on harness and lead, but that makes them no less monsters. Keep your wits and strength about you when dealing with that breed, young Miru, and do so as little as you can help."

The vampire's face was long and pale as bone, its eyes icy red and a bit of blue-ice froth about the needle-tips of its fangs. Arudal touched its mind as carefully as he could, but its hunger almost staggered him, the all-consuming desire for the life-blood flowing through the hot veins of the two living Men before it. Yet he could also feel the spells that bound it in a tight-cutting net of adamant strands, so that it - he - could not even begin to struggle against the master's will.

"Lift us, then fly straight out until you are above the rest of our company, and bring us gently down to earth," Arudal commanded. He was close enough to Lostren to feel the other's shudder of repulsion as the vampire's bare thin arm tightened about his waist. Then the Ukuthran took hold of Arudal. The Tharandrostan could feel the cruel strength in the bony limb: the vampire could squeeze both of them in two within a heartbeat, and Arudal knew he longed to do just that, bathing his face in the steaming blood bursting out from their severed torsos and drinking himself bloated. The Ukuthran's lips pulled back from the long snake-teeth in a grimace of hatred, but he lifted them into the air, carrying them along the inner side of the gleaming wall. Below, Arudal saw the dark-gleaming helms and armour of their Imperial escort; the vampire floated down softly as a silk handkerchief on the breeze, setting the two squires on the ground and releasing them.

"Thank you," Arudal said. His grandmother had drilled that into him as well: Courtesy wasted is no harm done. The vampire did not reply, only rose into the air again and drifted off.

"Count Arudal, you should have explained the problem to me," Sir Pharzehar scolded as soon as they were down, a sharp edge of anger - or fear? - in his voice. "His Imperial Majesty forbade me most strictly to let any harm come to you, and how should I have explained it to him if you had been killed coming into the City?"

"Lostren Telagon," Sir Salarond snapped at the same time. "What in the Pits did you think you were playing at? Why didn't you tell me, and why, by Amanvon and Aviyani, did you not think about waiting until daylight when at least you could see what you were doing? And you, Arudal - I commanded you to keep yourself safe. Suppose you tell me how you thought that climbing an unstable rock-pile in the dark could possibly be construed as obeying that order?"

Arudal gulped, scrambling frantically for an answer. Before he could find one, Sir Thoron spoke up. "I see a pair of idiot squires who want a sound beating," the big knight rumbled. "But mine looks to be bleeding, so I'll let him off this time and hope the lesson's learned. How bad is your arm cut up, Ari? And why are you holding yours like that, Lostren?"

"Uh...it might be broken, sir," Lostren said, even as Arudal answered, "Just scraped, sir."

"Huh. Salarond, do you want to patch them up out here, or shall we get inside somewhere first?"

Sir Salarond probed at Arudal's forearm, his fingers biting into the wounded flesh like hot pokers. Arudal realized that the ripped sleeve was sodden with blood - No wonder I feel a little light-headed. "Stand still." The healer-knight reached into the pack of his horse, tying a bandage quickly about Arudal's injury. "That's quite deep, but I'll see to it properly as soon as we're in. Lostren, I'll have to take your gambeson off to look at you, and it's too cold to do that here. Rhys, Tirothar, fetch in their horses and armour, and we'll move along."

Arudal's arm was beginning to really hurt now, and he kept stumbling over rocks or bumping into them. He tried to be as silent as he could, but when he banged his shins into something large and sharp-edged, he could not suppress a soft hissing gasp.

"Are you all right there, squire?" Thoron asked.

"Yes, sir," Arudal forced out.

"He needs one of us to lead him, sir," Lostren supplied. "I was doing it outside, but..."

"To the Pits with it," Thoron muttered. "Here, Ari." He swept Arudal up in his arms as if the Tharandrostan weighed no more than a cat, carrying him easily through the darkness. Once in a while, Arudal saw a faint flare of witch-light glimmering in the distance. He could not make out the shapes of any of the buildings, but every so often they passed troops of ghostly sentries marching through the streets, their spectral armour silent in the night. There was something about the quiet unity of the soldiers that made Arudal think of paintings he had seen showing Tharabruthnan in its earliest days as a small military garrison and communications outpost, walled off against the hordes of wild Plainsmen outside, with only a few feet of stonework and the discipline of its men to keep it from being overrun and wiped out.

At last they came to a large mansion that glowed a faint blue in Arudal's Shadow-sight. He recognised the architecture of the Late Imperial days, the high sharp turrets and spiky stonework similar to that of his own family's mansion in Tharabruthnan. Does it look like that on the green earth? he wondered. Or is this, too, only a ghost's memory? The thought chilled him. It was too easy for him to see the roof's little spires caving in as the foundations shook, the elaborate stone lacing about the windows falling off to shatter on the streets below and black crevasses spiderwebbing through the white walls like the cracks in a piece of broken pottery. And I am not imagining it: this is home. The home of my race, at least; the West that I sought, that is still the dream of our hearts.

The entrance hall glowed more brightly, and in that light, Arudal could see the patterns of the serpentine moulding about the edges of the ceiling and the stern-faced marble statues to either side of the door. Sir Pharzehar led them to the right - Arudal noticed that the Agathan was able to open the doors himself: the whole building must be steeped in magic - into a great drawing room, its walls faced with black marble reliefs of battle and conquest. The carving was magnificently detailed and executed. Arudal could see the expressions on the soldiers' faces, agony and excitement and grim determination; the spittle on the mouth of a slave who writhed and cursed his captors, the sweat running down the backs of the chained men marching before the lord who rode triumphant with his falchion upraised - the first Duke Aglarek: Arudal knew his face and archaic armour, the square-topped greathelm beneath his arm that would go over the open-faced bascinet he wore and the strong-chinned conqueror's resolution, from the big painting over the mantlepiece in the drawing room of the Hidden Estate's small castle. I did not imagine it: this is truly my home. A black marble table stood at the far side of the hearth, bottles and crystal glasses gleaming upon it together with a gold tray of something Arudal could not see clearly. The ebony chairs around the table were carved with twining dragons, their teeth inlaid in ivory, and their eyes and wing-spines made of glittering gemstones.

"Be welcome, Lord Arudal of Aglarek, to the hall of your ancestors," Sir Pharzehar said. "It pleases His Imperial Majesty that you be lodged in your own house while you are in the City. All has been made ready for you. We regret that we could not have the fires burning to greet you, but His Imperial Majesty requests that you be the one to kindle the heart of the home, even as your living heartbeat brings your family's dwelling to life again."

Moving trancelike, Arudal took the tinderbox that Tirothar held out wordlessly to him, stepping forward over the soft rugs to the hearth in the centre of the room. That same phrase - the heart of the home - was used in Tharandrost as well for the fire that was never allowed to go out, even on Amandeth's Eve when all other flames were extinguished. Sparks showered bright from the flint in Arudal's hand, one catching on the charred cloth and glowing into an ember, flowering forth into flame beneath Arudal's breath as he fed it with the dry light moss and pine-slivers. The wood in the hearth had been well-laid, and Arudal caught the sweet scent of the oil that had soaked it as the fire licked up the smaller sticks, brightening until it ached at the back of his eyes and blinded him to what the faint magic-light had shown him.

"Rest and refresh yourselves," Sir Pharzehar told them. "I shall take you before His Imperial Majesty tomorrow evening. We have done our best to provide you with suitable clothing, but should it not be to your liking, you may wear your armour: the pride of soldiers is sufficient to do honour to His Imperial Majesty." The fair-haired Agathan bowed and withdrew.

"Morthugor take it all," Thoron muttered as Salarond gave Lostren a small cup of something from his pack and began to gently ease the squire's gambeson off. "They didn't clean this place up in any three days. Squire, do you have an explanation for this?"

"Sir, I think...I think magic must work here as it does in the Middle Land."

Lostren let out a small choked noise as his gambeson came free of his arm. The firelight had dimmed Arudal's vision to a play of shadows once more, but he could faintly see Sir Salarond's dark shape freezing into stillness.

"The gods withdrew their might from the West when they brought the Wrath down. All the gods who were wroth with the Empire," Salarond added in a prayerful whisper. "And if that is so, there may yet be one source of might for those to call upon who...will."

"Does that mean we have proper magic?" Sir Thoron demanded.

"Not through my hands."

"Nor mine," Sir Eroth whispered, his voice tightening with sudden realization, even as Arudal understood what their commander meant.

"Nor mine," said Arudal. Perhaps it was the pain in his arm beneath the bandage that impelled him to go on: "But surely healing could not stem from evil? If you tried, sir..?"

"The Twisted One can heal for his own purposes, or Martag would have far fewer soldiers," Sir Salarond said grimly. "I shall not risk it, least of all here. And speaking of risks, Squire Arudal Arumirun, I believe I asked you a question earlier. What in all the gods' names did you think you were doing, trying to scramble blind over the fallen gateway with only Lostren to help you?"

"Sir. I could think of no other way to get into the City, since I could not pass through the walls."

"It was my idea, sir," Lostren broke in. "I told him to do it, and I am senior to him."

"But hardly in command. Farther from it, in point of fact, than I had been thinking. I suppose you wanted to demonstrate how resourceful and quick-thinking you are when left on your own? You demonstrated it, all right. Do you - both of you - realize that on a regular army mission, that particular stupid stunt would have earned both of you something between twenty well-laid strokes and a court-martial?"

"Yes, sir," Lostren murmured in a subdued tone.

"Yes, sir," repeated Arudal.

"And do you think that, after that, I am still going to trust the two of you to go down into the Imperial Library by yourselves?"

Arudal looked at Lostren. The other squire's shape was as shadowy in the firelight as those of the rest of the living men in the room, but Arudal could just see the faint green-gold gleam of his eyes.

"As you command, sir," Lostren said at last.

Sir Salarond's head moved in a slight nod. "We shall see. You, at least, are about to pay in full for your stupidity. Sit down. Ari, Thoron, you two are the strongest here: I'll need you to hold him tight. This will probably hurt worse than a flogging, and he must stay still for it."

Lostren sat down in one of the ebony chairs. Sir Thoron took his feet, Arudal his good arm and his shoulder. Salarond gave his squire something that Arudal could not see clearly. "Bite on that."

Lostren put it into his mouth. Salarond took hold of the broken arm, bracing himself solidly against the heavy base of the chair. He nodded to his assistants, then yanked Lostren's arm straight in one swift jerk. Lostren made a muffled cry, and Arudal saw his eyes brighten as though a brief glimmer of lightning had flashed within his skull.

Rummaging through his pack, Salarond brought out what Arudal thought were probably the makings of a splint, then refilled the tiny cup he had given Lostren and handed it to Arudal. "Poppy syrup, not that either of you deserves it. Drink and then take your gambeson off. I'll have to sew your arm up, Ari, and you won't like that much better than Lostren liked having his pulled straight. The rest of you, go and light the fires throughout the house - Ostarak, you go with them to make sure nothing untowards happens," he added to the Agathan in Imperial. "Don't worry, I'll take care of Arudal."

The poppy syrup was already starting to take effect by the time Sir Salarond finished splinting Lostren's arm and turned to his second patient. Arudal's head felt cloudy, almost as dizzy and vague as he had been after being knocked unconscious, though without any pain, only a pleasant spreading warmth. He made no sound as Salarond unwrapped the blood-soaked bandage, but drew in his breath when he saw the injury. The rock had left a deep, jagged gash in his arm: he could see the thin layer of tattered white fat above the deep red muscle. The healer-knight shook his head. "Hold still. This will hurt."

Salarond poured something that felt like molten metal into Arudal's wound, swabbing it out expertly. In spite of the dose of painkiller he had just drunk, the Tharandrostan had to bite his lip to keep from crying out, but the pain faded swiftly beneath the dizzy poppy-warmth.

Arudal set his teeth as the healer-knight began to stitch his arm. The stabbing of the needle-point was not too bad, but the feeling of the thread actually drawing through his skin, even with the poppy deadening the pain and fuzzing his thoughts, was sickening. The blinding flames swayed wildly in front of his eyes, their shadows swirling over the faint blue gleam of the walls like a great fish's blood darkening sunlit water.

"All done," Salarond said, giving Arudal a light pat. "You'll have a bit of a scar to show from that, I think, but no real harm done. Now, let us see what our host has left us."

A deep bonging sound reverberated through the room. They all looked up in startlement.

"Someone is at the door," said Arudal.

Salarond spread out his shadowy hands. "This is your house."

By the time Arudal had reached the front door, Ostarak was already opening it. "Greetings, sir," the soldier said. "May I inform his Excellency who has come to see him?"

"I am Healer Laikhadal," a woman's clear voice came from outside. "His Imperial Majesty has sent me to see to the hurts of Count Arudal Aglarek and Lord Lostren Telagon."

"Show the Healer in, Ostarak," Arudal ordered.

The Agathi who stepped into his house was not what Arudal had expected. He had not been aware of it; but, perhaps from hearing too many songs of lovers longing from Shadow, somewhere in his mind Arudal was thinking that an ghostly woman met in the ruins of the Imperial Seat must be heartbreakingly beautiful. Instead, Healer Laikhadal was middle-aged, short and plump with a little snubby nose, her gray-streaked black hair cut bluntly about her face, and a brisk, no-nonsense way about her. Although in Shadow her robe looked gray, there was a faint hint of green about it - it would have been the colour of spring leaves, as healers' robes still were in both Tharandrost and Kantar. The right shoulder of her robe bore an Imperial shield with a doubled black sun: she must have been a military healer, and of high rank. She bowed to Arudal in the traditional Imperial fashion, palms pressed together before her face.

"You tore your arm on a rock, I am told. Let me see."

Arudal was already shivering hard in the icy air of the hallway, but obediently he held out his arm to her. Laikhadal clicked her tongue and shook her head. "Sewing! This is human flesh, not a piece of cloth." She took Arudal's arm firmly in her left hand, but the delicate tip of the small sharp knife in her right only passed straight through the stitches without cutting the thread. "A living man will have to take those out before I can heal you properly."

Arudal led the Agathi on to the drawing room, blinking against the burning light of the fire. Laikhadal's slanted amber-gray eyes squinted tight, then she turned her face away, but her voice was steady enough as she said, "Sit down, your Excellency. Whoever put those stitches in needs to take them out now."

She means to heal us - with the power of Morthugor? Arudal wondered. Can I refuse without offending the Emperor?..I doubt it.

Sir Salarond must have come to the same conclusion, for he said, "Healer, I am Sir Salarond, Earl dath Amerel. We thank you, and His Imperial Majesty, for your aid, as our magics do not work here as they did in our homeland."

"I can see that," Healer Laikhadal said sharply. "If you please, your Grace."

Arudal looked away as Salarond snipped down the line of little white stitches. They came out easily, each one only a faint slither of pain through his skin. Laikhadal put her hands on Arudal's wound, her icy touch numbing his torn flesh, and murmured something beneath her breath. At once, the lingering ache was gone, but a wave of dizziness rose through Arudal's head. "Stay there for a few minutes, your Excellency. Let me see the other one."

Lostren gasped sharply when her hand sank past his skin, and Arudal thought he saw the movement of the other squire flinching away from the Agathi. Shadow-Fear? he wondered. She is stronger than Ostarak: at least of the seventh rank, perhaps the eighth. If that is so, we have a problem. But then, it may only be that Lostren has never been touched by one of the Agathim before.

"That arm should stay immobilized for at least a day. Resplint it and bind it to his chest again - your Grace," Healer Laikhadal added belatedly, as if dragging from her Shadowed mind the faint new memory that Salarond was an Earl, not a medical orderly. "Are any more of your party in need of my services?"

"No, madam," Sir Salarond replied.

"Then I shall leave you now. A good evening to you."

Ostarak escorted the Healer awkwardly out - Arudal guessed that the messenger had been invited into great houses by servants before, but never served in one himself.

"Our host seems to think well of us," remarked Salarond. "I have seen Undead do many things before, but never heal."

"If they were Healers in life, their skills do not change in Shadow," Arudal said. "But it must have been long since she had a chance to practice her trade. There is no healing for the Agathim."

"And the healing I practice would, I think, serve the Undead ill, whatever they were in life," replied Sir Salarond. "Aviyani is the Lady of the green earth: even her might given in blessing would surely harm creatures of Shadow, if it could flow into them at all."

But Amandeth, too, has his healers, Arudal thought, though he did not say it aloud. And in the end, he is the Healer of all wounds.

Chapter 26

(The Last Emperor, bass) "Swords may conquer all that dies,
Magic conquer mind and soul -
Only Shadow conquers Death.
Friend of Men, and Shadow's Lord,
Free us from the Doom of Man!
Dark the Sun that each night dies,
Quench the Moon, grown but to shrink,
Only Shadow conquers Death.
One with everlasting Dark,
I shall take up Shadow's might,
I shall rule both Death and Fear,
And cast aside the paltry gods
Whose creations Death all dooms -
Only Shadow conquers Death.

- Aria: "Only Shadow Conquers Death" - Master Barakhel Lumithor, Prince
Avalar, Act III, scene iv

"The order of the day," Sir Salarond told his company the following evening, "is to co-operate with the Emperor so far as each of us may be able to the extent that his own conscience allows. If any of you must refuse a request, do so as politely as possible, keeping in mind that if we anger him, it is highly unlikely that we will survive to complete our mission - and that the risk to our own souls must be weighed against the evils that will arise if civil war breaks out in Kantar. We shall begin with showing our respect for our host by wearing the garb that he has provided."

Sir Thoron snorted. "Dear gods, Salarond! The Emperor's message was that armour was acceptable. I wouldn't show up in a Kantarean court in this condition, but, for the gods' sakes, he has walking corpses doing most of his labour. He's not going to notice the smell of a few unwashed gambesons, no matter how ripe they are. And what if something goes wrong?"

"If something goes wrong," Sir Eroth put in, "it will be us against a great number of extremely powerful Undead. I think it would be prudent to show our host as much courtesy as we can."

"Hmph. Well, squire, I hope you can figure that mess out."

As Arudal tried to arrange the folds of the heavy silken robe around his knight's body, he wondered, How did the Emperor manage to find an Imperial noble's clothes to fit a man Sir Thoron's size? Even if walking corpses had the wit to do fine tailoring, they could never have managed to hold something as delicate as a needle, not to mention the stains and stink their decaying flesh would leave on the cloth. Only if cloth and needle and thread were all enchanted...The fire warming the chamber he had shared with his knight made him all but blind, but when he looked closely, he could see the faint residual shimmer of magic, as if the thick nubbled silk had been dusted with fine flour, then shaken almost clean. How long did this take to prepare?And where did the cloth come from? The silky sable-fur on the wide collars and sleeves of the floor-length velvet overcoat - the Agathim might have hunted the animals, but how could they have tanned the hides?

Or was all of this kept from Imperial days by spells of preservation,the dead keeping every scrap of their living days that they could? It was possible, hoarding was almost an instinct with the Undead. Arudal wondered, as well, what colours the Emperor had ordered them dressed in. The colours of our own heraldries? He had never spent so long with his sight fully in Shadow before: among his companions, he was beginning to feel faintly disoriented, more and more conscious of the differences between what he could see and what they saw. The clothes the Emperor had given Arudal were magnificent: heavy dark silk shot through with metal threads for the robe, and to clasp it, a sword-belt adorned with elaborately filigreed roundels -gold, by the weight, probably matching the threading in the silk - set with thumb-sized black opals.

Did he choose them because they are a stone of Shadow, or because he knew I would like them? Was he watching us in Cirrod? Arudal's long overcoat was made of thick white fur mottled with faint gray spots - Ice-cat? - and lined with plush dark velvet. His gloves matched the robe, dark silk with metal threading, but they were lined with some thick sleek black fur that he did not recognise. The Emperor had also sent him a rolled cap of fur-edged velvet and a coronet of similar workmanship to the girdle. Arudal hesitated a moment before putting it on. Tharandrost had few sumptuary laws, but the gold coronet seemed, somehow, to claim a status beyond that of his birth. Except that Aglarek was a greater house in the Empire than Arudal in Tharandrost, he reminded himself. Does he mean to name me as Duke Aglarek? And if he does...what will I owe him in fealty?

Slowly Arudal set the heavy coronet on his head. I can always take it off, if I must.

"Put your fur hat over that, squire," Sir Thoron rumbled.

"Sir?"

"If you don't, you'll freeze the points off your little ears." The knight himself was wearing one of the sheepskin caps they had bought from Mikit's sister, laughably incongruous over his Imperial robes...but warm.

Although Arudal could not see his companions' faces when they gathered in the drawing room again, he could sense their unease in the way they stood and shifted about. Nervous at meeting the Emperor? Or... "Is all well?" he asked.

It was Tirothar who burst out, "Before Amanvon, Ari, have you no nerves at all? This place is...Haunted." He let out a little nervous laugh. "Beyond haunted. I don't know what to call it. For every ghost that shows itself to us, there must be a hundred lurking in the darkness. I'd rather be in the capital of Martag; at least Aramath is mostly peopled by living folk. I think I'd even kill to see the honest sight of a Dark Troll's warty face." He stopped breathlessly with a small embarassed sound.

"As he said," Rhys agreed quietly. "Look you, I do not fear this so greatly, for the wisewife I spoke to in the market at Felatar - do you remember her? - told me that I should see her again as a living man, and give her a treasure in thanks for her words. But every breath I take here seems to crawl cold through me. There is no place on the green earth, I'm thinking, that is so close to being the vestibule of Morthugor's Pits."

"What kind of shit is this?" Sir Thoron boomed. "Living or half-dead, warrior or mage - Men are Men, and there's damned few things beneath the dwellings of the gods that a sharp sword of Valderian steel won't deal with. At least Ari's keeping his head, even if he doesn't have half the sense the gods gave a butterfly sometimes. The rest of you, you'll be better off if you stop scaring yourselves and start thinking about the fighting to come."

Bravado and bluster, Arudal thought. He is as nervous as the rest of them. And this is something I was never taught: how it may be a squire's duty to voice misgivings that his knight cannot speak, so that the knight may reassure both of them with his brave words.

The deep boom of the doorbell sounded through the room. Arudal nodded to Ostarak, who glided silently to answer it.

Arudal had expected Sir Pharzehar, but the armoured Agathan who stepped into the drawing room was another man, black-haired and shorter than Arudal, with a white scar splitting one arched eyebrow into a fork. "Sir Sephabar, at your service, your Excellency. His Imperial Majesty requests and requires you and your companions to accompany me to his audience hall now."

"Where is Sir Pharzehar?" Arudal asked, a worm of fear beginning to gnaw in his heart. The fair Agathan had said that his life would answer for their safety. Had his foolish attempt to climb the broken gate doomed their courteous escort?

"He has been relieved of duty, your Excellency. If you will."

Sir Sephabar's carefully neutral phrase did nothing to relieve Arudal, but he followed the Undead knight out into the icy cold. Their mounts had been saddled for them, snorting and stamping restlessly where they were tethered outside. A courtesy to me, that I need not be led or carried? No: I am imagining too much.

The Imperial formal robes had always been designed so that their wearers might ride in processions. Arudal knew how to mount in such garb, but Sir Thoron muttered, "How in the Abyss am I supposed to get up in this, this dress?"

"Allow me, sir," Arudal said, bending to take up the long hems of his knight's robe and overcoat. "You hold them up like this..." He had to rearrange the robe's folding by touch once Sir Thoron was up, wishing that he could see well enough to know whether he had done it properly. Sir Salarond had no difficulty mounting, and the other knights and Tirothar managed well enough, but Lostren had to virtually lift Rhys floundering into the saddle.

Sir Sephabar leapt up on his own horse and they started off at a slow walk, ten of their escort riding before and ten behind. Arudal gave Inmanat his head, letting him follow the small burning brightness of Lostren's lantern around the invisible barriers of fallen stone and debris. As for himself, Arudal looked away from the flame, into the darkness where the Agathim still marched through the streets they remembered. Some, save for their paleness, looked just as they had in life: those who, like Ostarak, had clung to the realm bordering on the green earth out of duty or desperation or shock at their deaths.

Others, though their friends and kin would have known them, were clearly dead, their slanted eyes shining ghastly from graying skin in their own faint light: not true ghosts, but wights, bound to Shadow by spells that kept them from departing to whatever realms Men fared to when Amandeth brought their span to an end. Once in a while, Arudal caught sight of pale yellow-white figures scuttling over blackness, their clothes no more than tattered scraps of mist over their foxfire-streaked bodies - the Emperor's ghouls. And occasionally, among the pale faces of the dead soldiers, he saw the gleaming obsidian skin and glittering adamant eyes of a wraith, or the ice-mottled face and keen fang-tips of a vampire.

The ghosts, Arudal guessed, had mostly died in the Wrath or in the slave-revolt that followed, but he was less sure of the other Undead. Wights and wraiths were usually made by mighty spells, and vampires by deliberate enchantment or other vampires - but ghouls' bodies, however strongly charmed against decay, wore out in time: they would not have lasted seventeen hundred years. *And now we know what became of those who sought the Imperial Seat and never came out.* But there were more walking corpses in the City than Arudal would have guessed, knowing the fear in which the woods were held, especially since the Elves guarded it from without. *If the Emperor could watch us so closely in our travels, could he call others to him? Or has he others like Sir Darthumazad's troop, who must ride out, and who might be able to bring bodies back with them?*

The Imperial Palace rose high against the white glimmer of the walls. Arudal had expected a brilliant glow, but instead it shone with the blue-black sheen of polished onyx in the moonlight, as though the Shadow-light of its power had solidified into substance. Its stone spires and arching crenellations seemed as delicate as the strands of a spiderweb, as finely spiked as the legs of a butterfly, but at the same time, Arudal felt a great sense of weight, as though the least fragment of the delicate stone points, if it were to break and hurtle downwards, would crush the men and horses below it like snails smashed under a galloping steed's hooves.

The gates were wrought all of vorgath, the black metal gleaming greenish in Arudal's sight. They were solid, with the life-sized figures of two men on rearing horses facing each other in low relief, so perfectly modelled that Arudal could have made out a single eyelash or mane-hair, could almost hear the cries of salute that had come soundlessly from their crafted mouths for over two thousand years. Sir Sephabar spurred his horse forward, crying, "The Emperor's guests come! Give welcome to the Emperor's guests!"

The two black gates swung back with a tearing creak, and Arudal saw that their hinges had been grievously bent. Vorgath was used for crafting adamantine, for when an alchemist had finished shaping the black metal, nothing in the world could bend or break it. Yet at Avalar's touch, these gates had burst open: where they had twisted, they would never be straight again.

Arudal had seen paintings of the Imperial Palace's gardens in their sunlit splendour: slim ereth-trees blazing with red flowers like bright flames in the shadows of the great oaks, benches wrought all of silver and gold where the Emperors and their Empresses had sat to talk beside the leaping foam-plumes of fountains, lithe white leopards in jeweled collars stalking along marble pathways or sitting proudly in the shade of flowered arbours, their woven silk leads held in the gem-set gloves of high nobles. Now there was only blackness and empty silence, and the ice-pale faces of the ghostly guards standing before the tall arched doors.

Sir Sephabar dismounted, the rest of their escort doing likewise, and the living men followed their lead. The White Company horses stamped and tossed their manes as their riders gave the reins over to the Undead guardsmen, and Inmanat turned his head to nuzzle Arudal forlornly. Arudal stroked him, murmuring, "It's all right, my little horse. Nothing bad will happen to you, and I'll give you a treat when we get home tonight. Go on, and be good."

Their footsteps, the first living footfalls to sound through the halls of the Imperial Palace in many centuries, echoed hollowly from the inlaid marble walls and high ceilings, lonelier and more ghostly than the silent tread of the Agathan gliding before them, even as the single flame of Lostren's lamp blackened the dark hallway about its little circle of brightness. Arudal noticed that his companions were all crowding closer and closer to the light. He did not notice that he was drawing away from it until they turned a corner, leaving him momentarily alone with Ostarak. He wanted to wait a moment, to let his eyes cool until he could see in the dim Shadow-glow of the walls, and stare at the gemstone mosaics and carvings that had been the finest work of the greatest artists of millennia. But Ostarak whispered, "Lord, I think the Emperor will expect you to be at the fore," and they had to hasten to catch up, the sound of Arudal's footsteps pattering along the hall as though a lone pursuer hurried behind him.

The arched doors at the end of the hallway shone white, their adornment clear to Arudal's eyes. Hundreds of small panels of polished adamantine, set in a lacework of Valderian steel, glittered Shadow-rainbows over the hall. Each showed a minutely detailed scene from a different part of the Empire: flowering trees and strange beasts, bent-backed slaves lifting the Pillar of Dreams into place where it still stood in the city square of Fel's capital, fish leaping among graceful riverboats in little sprays of foam, a great long-furred cat slinking among the snow, its spots slightly faceted so that it seemed mottled with coloured light...Arudal's footsteps slowed without thought as he stared at it, searching. There, down near the bottom left corner of the left-hand door, was the harbour of Tharabruthnan with the soldiers marching along its walls, overlooked by a simple watch-tower upon a hill - the tower that shone black against the azure field of Tharandrost's arms, that had given the State its motto, "A Fortress Unyielding", and that still formed the heart of the Prince's palace, though the royal dwelling had grown about it through the years like a nautilus curling around and around its first pearly chamber.

A single silvery horn-note shivered through the icy air. The adamantine doors swung slowly open. A breath of frozen wind swept down the corridor, and Lostren's lantern sputtered and darkened, only the single glow of a red ember still burning down in the wick. In the same moment, an hundred empty wall-sconces burst into cold blue flame. Arudal could see more clearly by their light than he ever had in his life, on the green earth or in Shadow: Sir Thoron's eagle-nosed face, his scraggly brows lowered like a bull's at the charge, the elaborate fluting of Sir Sephabar's black backplate and elegantly spiked pauldrons, and the flickering, hypnotic glimmer of the enchanted light playing over the adamantine doors like the Northern corona over a field of sculptured ice.

"Come ye before His Imperial Majesty, twenty-seventh to sit upon the throne of his ancestors and bear the Empire's Crown," a woman's clear high voice sang. "Come ye in rejoicing, the Empire's sons returned home at last; come and be welcome at the Heart of the Earth, the seat of all might! The Friend of Men has kept his promise, as foretold after the gods of our slaves led the Last Revolt. Though long has His Imperial Majesty waited, it has not been in vain."

Sir Sephabar halted, gesturing them in through the shimmering doors. Sir Salarond nodded to Arudal, and the two of them doffed their hats, walking in together at the head of their party.

The blue flames burned along the seven hundred-foot length of the Imperial audience hall, reflected tiny in the countless gemstones of the precious mosaics lining the walls. The floor chimed softly beneath them, as though their boots barely caressed the rims of great silver bells with each step. Statues three times the height of a man, wrought in gold and silver, Valderian steel and ivory and vorgath, and slabs of precious and semi-precious stone, looked down dispassionately upon them from their pillars. Each wore a perfect replica of the Imperial Crown, a broad gold circlet set with rubies carved into the shape of sunbursts, and Arudal recognised the images of past Emperors and Empresses. There was Darzlarak, the Fourteenth Emperor, with a jessed and hooded falcon perched upon his wrist: it was he who had declared that the foes of the Empire should no longer be slain, but shackled, that through humility they might learn the ways of civilization, and their labour go to rebuilding the destruction their hosts had wrought.

Sagaron the Builder held a mason's chisel and hammer; beyond him, the gray sapphires of her eyes glinting around their gold pupil-rims like the eyes of a living woman, was the Sixteenth Empress Aphanakanil the Lawmaker, holding an adamant-lettered scroll of translucent silvery steel-glass in her hand. The Twelfth Emperor, Ramuraph, bore a compass and sextant; his malachite pillar rose and curled like the crest of a great wave, edged with a pearly foam of opals, for it was he who had first sent the Empire's ships to seek out the Middle Land again.

Closest to the throne rose the image of Kathabar himself, the First Emperor. He alone was mounted: his horse was wrought from the pearly-shimmering ivory of a great dragon's tooth, so perfectly carved that, staring at it, it seemed that time had stopped in that single moment when the magnificent stallion lifted his front hoof, his thick tail caught in mid-swish. Adamant-dust rainbows glittered from the steel of Kathabar's armour; his face gleamed with the same dragon-ivory brightness as the sleek flanks of his steed, framed by the silver-streaked vorgath of his streaming hair...

The later statues, closer to the doors, were cracked and broken: Tirikhizador was missing his left arm, great chunks of Darzlir's carnelian gown had fallen away, leaving her tarnished silver legs and body to gleam through the holes in the translucent red veil like the smudged flesh of a tavern wench in a tattered shift, and the harp she had held was a mess of loose gold wires, holes gaping dully from the twisted frame where once gems or pieces of inlay had been set. Indizer's pillar had broken to pieces; he stood propped slightly askew upon the floor, and Arudal could see the dark jagged crack in the ivory where his head had been set back upon his shoulders. If there had ever been a statue of the Last Emperor, it had fallen altogether to pieces or been taken away.

Yet all that splendour paled before the one who sat enthroned at the end of the hall, watching as the White Company party made its small way across the great room's floor. Once the wall behind the throne had been covered all in rubies, the Imperial Sun upon it wrought in burning topaz. But that had burst beneath the Wrath, its very stones exploding when Avalar lifted his hand. Now the Emperor sat before a veil of deep red light, like a shining curtain of blood falling from the great heart-veins; and behind his head, black and pitiless as a shark's eye, glimmered the darkened Sun of the Fallen. The Ruby Throne no longer gleamed clear red, but opaque, shadowed within by a thick mist of countless tiny fissures.

Avalar had written that he had ordered the old Imperial Regalia destroyed. Still, the Emperor wore the same crown whose image shone on the heads of his predecessors along the hall - a ghostly manifestation, real only in the Undead ruler's memory? Or had Avalar's order, in those last tumultuous days of the Fall, been secretly circumvented by those whose hearts were still loyal to their black god? The Emperor's robes were of a velvet so dark that it seemed black until he moved, shimmering red from the folds of his sleeve as he lifted his arm, pointing down at his guests with a gold sceptre tipped by a fist-sized ruby carved into the shape of a crowned horse's head - pointing straight at Arudal. The weight of his power crashed around them like the mast-high waves of a storm-tossed sea: Arudal heard a faint whimper behind him, and thought he smelled a taint of feces in the frozen air.

Yet, though every muscle in his body shook, and it seemed to him that he could feel his skull beginning to crack within from the effort, he looked up to meet the Emperor's gaze. Then darkness shimmered over Arudal's sight, and he had to lock his knees to keep from falling. The Emperor's eyes, Imperial steel-and-amber, burned like tiny lightless suns, boring into Arudal like adamant drills. But it was the sight of his face that sent the shivers rippling outward through the Tharandrostan's body: the slightly pointed nose and small firm chin, the delicate angle of jaw and high-set cheekbones, the sharp arch of his black eyebrows, and most of all, the expression of his slanted eyes - remote, but at the same time intensely probing, as though he were examining Arudal carefully through a telescope from a distance. Arudal had played beneath that gaze as a child, though the portrait that had hung in the drawing room of his House's city mansion since the building was first raised had only captured a little of that unnerving intent calmness.

"My son," said the Fallen Emperor - once Duke Arurak Aglarek, father of Arudal Agathusaftan who had founded the House of Arudal. "We have waited for you a very long time."

How should I salute an Emperor? Arudal gibbered to himself. He knew how to bow to a Duke, how to kneel to a prince, to a ruling prince, to the King of Kantar - but though Kantar was an empire in all but name, no living man still bore the title of Emperor. As best I can.

Arudal went down upon his knees, bowing his head as the Emperor's words sank in. Even to that shocking address, there was a touch of familiarity; and that gave him the bravery to say, as he would have to a Shadowed kinsman at the Hidden Estate, "Your Imperial Majesty, I am Arudal Arumirun, the fifth to bear that name in direct line of descent from your son Arudal, who founded his House in Tharandrost. Some fifteen hundred years have passed since his death, Sire."

"Ah." The Emperor's breath hissed out in a faint sigh, hardly more than the last breath sighing from dead lungs. "The blood runs strong. Are you the last of Our line?"

"Your line has thrived, Sire: I have a younger brother, and many cousins of our founder's descent and powers. But I am the heir to the House of Arudal."

"It is well. Rise, and come forward."

Arudal forced his shaky legs - dear Amandeth, do not let me fall! to carry him forward to the broken carnelian steps leading up to the Ruby Throne. This close, Emperor Arurak's power felt like a physical weight, crushing him so that it was a struggle to draw each breath.

Can he read the thoughts of the living? Arudal wondered in horror. If so, the Emperor made no sign of it. He halted Arudal one step below the top of the dais with a gesture, reaching out to touch him. Arudal saw their twinned shadows on the steps, wavery and faint in the red witchlight glowing behind the Ruby Throne, but the Agathan's as solid as that of Arudal himself. As he had thought, the Emperor was an arch-lich, with the power to shape for himself a body that did not bleed nor feel pain, and might pass through walls unharmed, but was real enough on the green earth to do all that a living man might. Save kindle fire: true flame is the bane of Shadow-flesh.

Emperor Arurak lifted Arudal's chin with one icy finger, turning his descendant's head first to one side, then the other, in the familiar gesture of examining a child's facial configuration. Arudal shivered at the burning-cold touch, but bore it patiently, knowing that the Emperor had no cause for disappointment with him.

"The blood runs strong," the Undead ruler said again. "Stronger than We could have hoped. We had feared that the gift We bought with such pain and effort might have died in the seed of Our sons, but instead it has thrived beyond Our dreams."

What does he mean? Arudal wondered.

"It is not fitting," the Emperor breathed, so softly that even standing less than a foot from the throne, Arudal could barely hear him, "for Our son to be squire to a man of lesser blood. And We know how bravely you have borne yourself upon this journey. Kneel, Arudal."

Bewildered, Arudal knelt before him. Emperor Arurak's hand closed upon the pearly shimmer of his sword's polished dragon-tooth hilt, drawing the weapon forth from its black-gemmed sheath. The blade seemed to ripple beneath the shifting red brightness, thin lightning-flashes of sinking greenish-black and rainbow-shot white light running up and down its length in a wavering pattern. Arudal realized that it was pattern-welded of vorgath and Valderian steel, a greater triumph of the alchemist's art than any weapon he had heard of among Men, save, perhaps, the King's Sword of Kantar.

"Arudal of Aglarek, you have proven yourself worthy of your blood upon the battlefield, daring death and hardship unflinchingly to return from afar to your home. Hereby do We, Emperor Arurak, twenty-seventh of the line of First Emperor Kathabar to sit upon the Ruby Throne, dub you knight."

Arudal had to clench his fists and bite his lip to keep from crying out as the searing of the Emperor's sword burned cold through his flesh - right shoulder, left shoulder, top of the head. Had he not been kneeling already, he might have fallen, even at that slightest touch of the weapon's flat, even given in honour and peace; he knew that so much as the brush of the sword's edge could kill him. The cold-flaming patterns along the blade still flashed behind Arudal's eyelids when his Undead ancestor had sheathed the sword.

The blow of Emperor Arurak's fist snapped Arudal's head back, shocking his whole face numb. "Let this be the last blow you receive without answer. Rise, Sir Arudal of Aglarek, Knight of the Empire, in the name of the Friend of Men, whose gift is the blessing of Our line. Our knight, may your faithfulness endure as long as that of your blood, undiluted through all the centuries of Our rule."

Arudal let the Agathan take his hands, raising him to his feet. His face felt like shattered ice from the blow: even had he known what to say, he could not have moved his jaw to speak.

Bring forth the emblems of knighthood, the Emperor called silently. Two of his knights glided out of the shadows. One bore a silk cushion on which rested a gold fealty-chain and gold spurs inset with star rubies; the other carried a white belt from which dangled a sword, likewise sheathed and fitted with gold and star rubies, its hilt of the same opalescent dragon-tooth as the Emperor's. Arudal could see the faint blue-purple glow of magic about them as one of the knights fixed the spurs to his heels and the other girded the sword-belt about his waist.

There was nothing else he could do: he bowed his head to the Emperor, letting the Undead ruler set the chain of fealty about his neck.

Emperor Arurak arose, his deep velvet robes brushing silently across the Ruby Throne. "We have much to discuss. All of you shall accompany Us now."

He turned, lifting his hand, and a doorway darkened in the veil of red light behind the throne. The footsteps of the White Company party whispered muffled up the stairs around the throne-dais. Still shocky from what he had just undergone, Arudal fell into place beside Sir Thoron, his new spurs clinking softly as he walked. He was grateful that he could not see the expression on his knight-father's face.

This is not real, Arudal said to himself. The Undead cannot be knighted or make knights; the chivalry of Martag is acknowledged only when we cannot afford to offend by denying it. As soon as we are out of here, I shall be Thoron's squire again. And even were the Fallen Emperor not Undead, Tharandrostans were never knighted by foreign powers: when a Tharandrostan earned his spurs as a squire in Kantar, the accolade was not given by the White Crown, but passed along as a recommendation to the Prince. This is but a play of shadows.

The Emperor led them into a smaller room. The same cold blue flames flared from the empty wall-sconces that had burned in the hallway and the throne room - Arudal assumed that his companions could see in their light. With only the witchlight-fire burning in the hearth, the tapestries that hung on the wall did nothing to muffle the icy cold of the Imperial Palace. Arudal could see the slight glow of magic about the tapestries: a spell of preservation, he thought, for otherwise they could not have lasted so long.

But they had clearly been mended in a hurry once, with thread that was an imperfect match for the original. Emperor Daladan's white armour was scored through with cream-coloured streaks; the faint dark splotches mottling the coat of his roan horse were too large and irregular for a steed's natural dappling; and an incongruous helm had been hastily stitched in to cover a hole where the head of the half-naked barbarian charging the Emperor with upraised sword had been. A black scattering of indelible scorch-marks marred the delicate colours of the tapestry which showed one of the plumper Empresses seated by a fountain, stroking the huge red Western Tree-Cat in her lap, and a large patch of green-marbled wall gleamed bare where one hanging had been taken down altogether.

Arurak's repairs? Arudal wondered. Or Avalar's? The same faint smell of rot that Arudal had noticed in other rooms that had been cleaned by walking corpses hung in the air here, and there were enough chairs for all of them around the long ebony table with its inlaid eagles of silver, malachite, and ivory. A large map of the City lay on the table, with a slim gold pointing-rod beside it.

Emperor Arurak settled himself at the head of the table. "Be seated. We know already what you want. If it were in Our power, We should give it freely to you for Our son's sake, but We do not hold the Imperial Libraries. However, since Our intrusion into the zone of truce will mean fighting in any case, you will have the chance to earn your boon fairly." He picked up the gold pointing-rod, his delicate fingers turning it thoughtfully. "You shall tell Us your capabilities in full detail, and then We shall tell you the situation, and we may see what we can do. Your Grace." He raised a slanted black eyebrow at Sir Salarond.

Arudal noticed that the White Company's commander delicately skirted around mentioning his priestly functions, and said nothing of magical healing. The Emperor looked at Sir Salarond in surprise when he started to describe the Kantarean warhorses in combat.

"We had wondered why you brought - forgive me - what appeared to be plough-horses on such a journey, and why you should use saddles that hampered your mobility so greatly. Even with only a few of you mounted, this may prove a great advantage. The Pretender is not so...flexible of mind as We Ourselves, and may find it difficult to recognise what is happening to his troops."

Flexible of mind, indeed, Arudal thought, a cold chill running down his spine. The White Company did not, could not, realize how remarkable Emperor Arurak was for an Agathan: except for addressing Arudal as his son, which might indeed have been a deliberate convenience to avoid the ungainly list of generations between them, the Undead ruler had shown no sign of the usual confusion of the Agathim when faced with changes in the living world. The only other Undead of whom Arudal had ever heard that said was the Lord of Martag himself. But if the Pretender has managed to keep the stalemate going this long, his power cannot be too much less - and we are to face him in battle? Arudal took a deep breath, trying to keep his ramrod-straight posture from freezing into locked immobility. However it might be on the green earth outside, here in this Shadow-realm he was a knight: he would not disgrace his ancestor's accolade, unrecognisable elsewhere though it might be.

When Sir Salarond, Sir Thoron, Sir Eroth, and Sir Shakhor had spoken - Sir Salarond translating for Thoron, who spoke no Imperial, and Shakhor, who did not speak it well - Arudal waited for Lostren, the most senior of the squires, to say something, but Lostren sat quiet.

"Sir Arudal?" Salarond prompted.

Arudal was too well-trained to show his start, but he swallowed hard to clear his throat before he spoke. "Ah...I fight with sword and buckler, though not as well as the...the other knights of our company. I do not know how to fight from a warhorse. You know of my gifts of the mind. I am Shadow-sighted, and will need aid to keep me from being harmed by physical obstacles that I cannot see. I am also the most qualified of this party to seek through the older genealogical documents in the Imperial Library."

After hearing their accounts of themselves, the Emperor sat silent for a moment. Arudal could sense that his mind was reaching out, but, without forcibly prying into his thoughts, could not tell what he was saying.

"We have summoned Our two chief commanders, Sir Edrakhor and Sir Garnamel. They shall be here shortly."

Although Arudal feared it might be dangerous for him to speak up, a sense of guilty responsibility impelled him to say, "Sire, may I ask what has become of Sir Pharzehar?"

His Undead ancestor regarded him cooly, his eyes gleaming like clear ice over steel-set topaz. "That is hardly your concern, Sir Arudal."

"Sire, the attempt to climb the gate was my own foolish error. If it has led to the harm of a good soldier, it should be my punishment to know of it."

"In our living days, he would have atoned for Our kinsman's shed blood with every drop of his own. You may set your mind at ease, however. We have not so many men that We can waste a competent commander. Sir Pharzehar shall be allowed to atone for his disgrace in the thickest of battle, and, should he acquit himself well enough and survive, he shall be reinstated."

"Thank you, Sire."

The Emperor gestured negligently with the golden rod. "Ask Us no more questions of that sort, Sir Arudal. Your namesake was ever a little too soft-hearted. We sent him to Tharabruthnan to serve against the rebels in order to cure him of that fault; We shall be disappointed if We find that you have inherited it along with his looks."

Sir Edrakhor and Sir Garnamel entered together. Sir Garnamel was huge for a pureblooded Imperial, nearly four inches taller than Arudal and broad in proportion. He wore full plate armour, carrying a helm underneath his arm - by old habit; the gear of the Undead existed only in their thoughts. A thin puckering seamed the flesh from his left cheekbone down to his jaw: the original wound must have smashed his face in completely, to leave a mark even under magical healing. Next to his massive companion, Sir Edrakhor looked delicate, almost childlike, in his pale robes, though he was of much the same size and build as Arudal. Is that how I look among the Kantareans? Arudal wondered. In spite of his size, Sir Garnamel moved as smoothly and gracefully as if his joints had been made of well-oiled and polished metal, and Arudal thought his tread would have been silent even in life. Sir Edrakhor's salute to his Emperor was the quick neat gesture of a mage accustomed to perfect precision in every pass of his hands.

"How may we serve you, Your Imperial Majesty?" the mage-knight asked.

"We believe that We have, at last, the means to break our stalemate with the Pretender. Attend to Us carefully."

Both Agathim straightened slightly, their eyes widening. Arudal recognised the look on their faces. The Emperor was holding them with the power of his mind, forcing a shaft of awareness past the barriers of the death-bonds on their thoughts, just as Arudal's cousins in the Spectral Service would do with ghosts that had to be sent out to accomplish some task without living direction.

Briefly - and, Arudal was sure, for the benefit of the living men there, for the Emperor could have passed his information silently to his subordinates' minds - the Undead ruler described the White Company's resources. "The talents of Sir Arudal and Lord Lostren are to be used sparingly, if at all. While the fighting is going on, they, together with a chosen squad, are to descend into the Imperial Library and seek out certain documents which they require."

Arudal blinked. He had not expected the Emperor to go along with the White Company's plan so easily. And he knew what we wanted: he must have ways of listening to us even within my house. He would have to find some way to tell the Kantareans, if they didn't know already: in many ways, they seemed to be a people obsessed with privacy. Of course, they don't grow up with their relatives reading their minds - nor expect that the House of Procreation will help them breed.

The Emperor turned back to his map. "The Pretender's chief forces are usually stationed here, here, and here..."

The two knights were - thanks to their ruler's work in their minds, Arudal suspected - more readily able to adapt to the Kantareans than Arudal had thought they would be: which was to say, vague enough even through his and Salarond's efforts at translation to make Sir Thoron start barking at them. They knew the City well, but asking them to shift their strategy from the long defense to a renewed attack was almost more than they could manage. Almost: but with frequent reminders to keep them on track, and constant questioning as to what their suggestions were intended to do, it slowly became clear even to Thoron that here, even in their Shadow-ruin, were two of the greatest military minds of the Fallen Empire's last days.

It was nearly dawn by the time the initial battle-plans were finalized. Arudal's feet and hands were numb inside his sealskin boots and fur-lined gloves, and his face felt like a mask of ice that would crack and shatter if he moved it enough to speak. The Emperor had provided his living guests with food, but it was all cold: a fine-chopped venison tartare, strips of trout pickled in wine and herbs, and hard ration-bread that must have lain under a spell of preservation since Avalar's day - preserved from habit, when a supply officer forgot that dead soldiers would no longer need their daily issue?

The thought of food also brought a darker suspicion to Arudal's mind. Save for the vampire who had rescued himself and Lostren at the gate, none of the Agathim he had seen closely in the City were suffering noticeably from Shadow-hunger. The Emperor and his officers could not be ranging out to hunt beasts every few days: truce or no truce, the Pretender would surely not have missed such opportune chances to rid himself of his rival as such a habit would offer. Skilled hands had stitched Imperial formal robes to the measures at least of Sir Thoron and Rhys, if not all of the party: only Arudal, Lostren, and Salarond were close enough to the Imperial type that preserved garments might have been found to fit them.

Arudal thought of the slow-moving, pale Plainsman slaves at the Hidden Estate, their life-strength deliberately kept drained so that they might not even dream of running to betray what they saw of their masters' work. After his ancestor's rebuke, he knew better than to ask; but he could not help wondering if, in the dungeons below the City, there might be Elvish captives who had not seen the light of the Sun for years, only the faint Shadow-glimmer of their captors coming to feed. Elves, surely, for without fire, Men could not live through a winter here. And Elvish life-strength was far more warming to the Undead...*I think it is very well that Dame Karsil is not with us.*

Arudal clung gratefully to Inmanat's warmth on his way back. *If it gets much colder,* he thought, *maybe I should suggest that we bring our horses into the house with us. The halls are high and wide enough, and Imperial nobles of the late days did far wilder things than stabling their horses in their chambers.*

Suddenly there was a rustling and commotion, then Sir Eroth saying sharply, "Keep those on, squire - that's an order!"

"Don't need them, sir," Tirothar's slurred voice mumbled. "Too hot...too close here. Have to breathe. Fugoff. Sir."

Arudal looked back, but saw only the play of shadows in the darkness. "Grab him!" Sir Salarond shouted. There was a brief ringing flurry of hooves, then nothing but the sound of Tirothar's hoarse breathing and swearing so muffled that Arudal could not make it out. "Quickly as we can, now. Gods grant we left enough wood on the fires!"

The streets were too treacherous to trot down - how in Amandeth's name will they ever be able to charge? Arudal thought - but they walked as swiftly as they could, Inmanat breaking into a smooth four-beat rack to keep up with the bigger horses. Have our spells failed? Arudal did not dare to say it aloud, but Lostren looked back at him as if he had heard the thought.

"Are you all right? Shivering?"

"I stopped shivering a while ago. I'm just cold now."

"Oh, dear."

"What's the matter?"

"It's too cold."

"No colder than it's been, surely?"

"Yes, but this is the first time we've gone so long without moving hard. Tirothar is the worst off right now, but if we don't get inside and warmed up soon..."

"But he wanted to take his clothes off," Arudal protested. If Lostren was in a bad enough state of mind to deny the obvious so firmly...Shadow-Fear was not usually subtle, but what could it do to ordinary Men, to be so close to a power like the Emperor, accompanied by the strongest Agathim of his realm? Tirothar had been the weakest of them when Sir Darthumazad's troop attacked. Of course he would give way first, but could Lostren and Rhys be far behind? Even the knights, hardened by decades of fighting Undead as they were, would not be immune forever: in time, the stones of the strongest citadel must fall under ceaseless bombardment.

And then what would I do? Ask the Emperor for an escort of Agathim, perhaps: it might be safer for him than relying on Dame Karsil to bring him alive back to the eastern shore. By the time they reached the gates around Arudal's mansion, the Tharandrostan was shivering again, so hard that he could not stop his teeth from chattering.

Sir Eroth carried Tirothar in swiftly, laying him down by the fire. The lanky squire had stopped struggling: now his eyes were closed, his face peaceful and his breathing slow and deep.

"Build up the fire as quickly as you can!" Thoron said to Arudal.

Arudal moved to obey, but Sir Salarond raised a hand to stop him. "You do it, Rhys. Eroth, take your clothes and your squire's off and lie directly atop him beneath your cloaks. I assure you that none of us will think anything untoward of it, and body heat, flesh to flesh, is the best and safest way to warm one who is suffering from the cold. Lostren, start water boiling, then fetch more blankets and cloaks for everyone. Sir Arudal may assist if he chooses, but I doubt that the Emperor wishes to hear his new-knighted kinsman being ordered about as if he were a squire."

Arudal almost wished he could see the look on Sir Thoron's face as the big Kantarean stopped, stunned. The misty dark outlines of his hands twitched as though he were unsure as to whether he should cuff Arudal's ear or embrace him. "You mean…" Thoron whispered as if the Emperor might be close enough to physically overhear him, and Salarond made a gesture that Arudal could not see clearly.

Sir Thoron stepped forward to clasp Arudal's wrists. "Congratulations…Sir Arudal," Thoron said, a strange note of uncertainty in his rough voice.

"Thank you, sir."

Each of the knights, then the squires, congratulated Arudal in turn. Even Sir Salarond lifted a hand from his patient to clasp Arudal's right wrist briefly. Arudal could hear the strain in their voices, and did not blame them. By the time Rhys had offered his congratulations, only the control learned as a page was keeping Arudal from squirming in embarassment as well as shivering from the bone-deep cold. But *my knighthood is real so long as we are in the Fallen Seat, or might as well be.*

By the time Tirothar awoke, Arudal's teeth had stopped chattering - from true warmth this time. So that the whole party could watch each other for the signs of dangerous chilling, Sir Salarond had carefully described the symptoms of cold-sickness, including the paradoxical ones of ceasing to shiver and, as with Tirothar, the disordered mind and urge to disrobe. *If Finvar were alive here, he would have recognised those signs at once,* Arudal thought. *But…he is brave enough to bear it, surely, but this is no place for warm hands and a warm heart.*

Sir Shakhor and Rhys, who had had the wit to dress in several layers of wool beneath the Imperial garb, were in the best state, but they were all suffering from the cold to some degree, and Sir Salarond had refused to give vargwe to anyone except Tirothar. "We are likely to need it worse before this is over," the healer said grimly, and no one could argue.

"Where 'm I?" Tirothar mumbled vaguely from beneath Eroth. "Wha' happen'?" He squirmed weakly as though to free himself from his knight's weight, but Sir Eroth held him pinned.

"Can you feel this?" asked Salarond.

"Feel wha'?"

"Severe frostbite," Salarond said at last, straightening up and rubbing his lower back. "I cannot do more here. Arudal, I fear you must summon the healer who aided you and Lostren last night."

Arudal looked at Ostarak, waiting patiently beside his chair. The easiest, and perhaps the most proper, thing would be for him to send his guardsman in search of Healer Laikhadal. But there was another way to do it…

He breathed deeply, remembering the path his thoughts had travelled the night before, the sound of Sir Pharzehar's clear precise voice in his mind…*Sir Pharzehar?*

Your Majesty! Oh...you. Even in thought, the Agathan's voice sounded tired, pained, the echo of Shadow-hunger resonating between them like the tingling aftermath of a heavy blow. Last night Sir Pharzehar had been full-fed; as far as Arudal knew, he could not be in this condition now unless he had been compelled into sunlight for a full day, the scorching brightness quickly eating away his borrowed strength and leaving him naked to the agony of the burning daylight and the racking pain of his own hunger. It was cruelly easy to torture the Undead: the effort lay in preventing their pain, or easing it.

Sir Pharzehar - I am sorry.

It seemed to Arudal that he could almost see the golden-haired knight, his chiseled features taut and drawn with pain, turning his head away. *I earned this by my carelessness. Do not interfere, or it will be the worse for both of us.*

I am sorry. But we need aid, and you are the only man here I know well enough to call unseen.

What manner of aid?

One of our company is badly frostbitten. Healer Laikhadal was sent to us last night: can you send her again?

I shall see that it is done. The Undead knight did not have the strength left to make more than the most feeble effort at shutting Arudal out of his mind, but Arudal respectfully withdrew, though he could have torn his own flesh from guilt. Technically Sir Pharzehar had earned his punishment - if anything, the Emperor had been merciful - but that did nothing to assuage Arudal's knowledge that the Agathan was suffering because of Arudal's stupidity. Because I could not bear to stress further how I differ from my companions.

When Healer Laikhadal arrived, she saw to Tirothar with barely a word to the rest of them, save for a bow to Arudal and a curt nod to Salarond. But as she was leaving, she said, "You may be pleased to know that Sir Pharzehar has been unbound from the day-stake and allowed to feed." She bowed briefly to Arudal again and departed.

"Opinions on our proposed course of action?" Sir Salarond asked when the healer was gone.

"I'd be happier if it didn't involve having at least one of us to nursemaid each of those ghostly loonies through the battle," grumbled Sir Thoron. "I don't care how great they were in their day, they won't do us any good if they can't remember where and when they're supposed to be fighting. The Emperor seems sharp enough; you'd think he could have come up with someone more, more..."

"Coherent?" supplied Eroth.

"That would be the word."

"The Agathim are inclined to cling to old habits of mind," said Arudal. "It would be better if the Emperor himself were directing them, but I think he is correct in saying that he will need all his own power to keep the Pretender himself engaged. If the Emperor's foe were not close to being his equal, the City would no longer be divided in two."

"Sir Arudal, can you give me your appraisal of the Emperor's personal strength?"

"As you know, sir, there are several different schools of thought in classifying the Undead above the ninth rank. Most Kantareans who study this matter allow the twelfth rank to be the highest. We divide the classifications of the most powerful Agathim more specifically, up to a fifteenth rank, but it is generally agreed by all that the Lord of Martag represents the top of the scale."

Salarond waved a shadowy hand. "Yes, Ari, I know all that. I asked for your opinion, not a beginner's lecture in necromantic theory."

Arudal blinked the water from his eyes at the Kantarean's offhand address. He knew what it meant; and after he had been hailed as the Fallen Emperor's son by direct descent, and accepted knighthood from the Agathan's hands...he was not sure that he would have trusted himself so easily. "I have never myself encountered an Agathan above what we would call the eleventh rank before, so I cannot be as specific as I would like. But...if the Emperor is not a match for the Lord of Martag, though I would not rule that out, he cannot be far beneath him, both in terms of direct power and of the - the will, the mind-strength, that allows him to hold to his current knowledge of where he is and what is happening. The ability to come into full physical manifestation on the green earth aids in that, but most liches are only a little more - coherent, if you will - than other Agathim. You saw as much this past night, for both Sir Edrakhor and Sir Garnamel are solid enough to cast shadows."

The plan was simple enough: Arudal had learned in school that the best tactics usually were. It was based on two abilities the living had that the dead did not - the ability to pass wards against Shadow and the ability to bear the nearness of fire - and one of the few inventions of the Middle Land that the West had never known: the violent explosive nitre. Though he had known better than to say anything when they mentioned it to the Emperor, Arudal had been shocked and terrified to realize that between their vials and glass-bulbed arrow-tips, the four White Company knights had close to a pound of the stuff: far more than enough to leave a great smoking crater in the ground in place of the Aglarek mansion, if it all went off at once. Nitre exploded on impact: Arudal thought of the battering their ship had taken on the crossing, and was deeply grateful that he had not known about the knights' dangerous hoard at the time, or he might never have stopped shaking.

"We ride up, we throw it at the Pretender's palace or where-ever he's hiding when the magical duel starts, it goes boom," Thoron had succinctly put it. "We kill three hundred Undead on the way. No problem, if our support troops are up to the job and Sirs Spook and Spookier there can remember for a quarter-candlemark that we're on their side." Sir Salarond had translated that as, "Assuming that we have sufficient support to fight through the Pretender's troops, the nitre is more than powerful enough to destroy his Pretender's palace and everything within it." Still, from the cold-eyed sideways look Sir Edrakhor had given Thoron, Arudal suspected that the mage was also a Mind-Reader powerful enough to take the meaning of what the blunt knight had said, even if he could not understand the words in Common.

In addition to the nitre, the Emperor had assured the White Company that he could supply them with a quantity of Imperial clingfire to use along their way. The ancient compound was not explosive, and required considerably more impact to take flame than nitre needed to burst; but unlike nitre, it would keep burning, even under water or in deep snow, until extinguished by suffocation or lack of fuel, and could, if enough were employed, even eat through stone. Fortunately, Avalar had managed to clear out the major streets in his brief time as ruler of the West, so that the Kantarean knights would be able to fight from horseback.

They would be accompanied by mounted archers and mages to deal with the inevitable archery and magical attacks from the upper stories of the houses, and by such infantry as the Emperor could spare from among those who were powerful enough themselves to bear the near presence of flames - though, by laying down a trail of clingfire, the White Company knights would be able to clear out most of their foes. Meanwhile, the Emperor would himself engage the Pretender directly in a duel of magic, so that he would be forced to his destruction one way or another: either physical annihilation beneath the flame-blast of nitre, as fatal to the Undead as to the living, or magical annihilation at the hands of his rival if his concentration failed and he tried to flee.

"Sir...it almost seems too easy," Lostren said when Sir Salarond had summarized their battle plan once more. "For a few men to end a seventeen hundred year-old stalemate...I cannot see any faults in the plan, but I must confess that it bothers me."

"Perhaps Sir Arudal can explain it to you better than I. Ari?"

"The chief difference we make by entering onto the board is based on the importance of wards against Shadow-wights on both sides. I think I mentioned to you that it takes more strength to break a ward than to set it? Neither the Emperor nor the Pretender, and certainly none of their subordinates, could cross each other's wards. Hence almost all their skirmishes took place in the no-man's land between, with occasional concessions of territory. But also, neither of them could afford to lose many of their followers, since there would be no replacing them after a point. Yes, the Emperor, and likely the Pretender, can call Ukuthrim from Shadow - have done: thus the vampires and so forth. But there is a limit to how many such beings even the strongest may hold in his power, either by true magic or by mind-magic. In any case, we can reach the Pretender's palace because we are able to pass freely where they are walled off. Further, our fires - especially the clingfire, which will eat quickly through sigils on stones - may break his wards down altogether, or at least weaken them. Then, the Emperor's troops got little use out of such tactics before because, even if he could have broken through - say, by tossing jars of clingfire from a safe distance and pushing past before the wards could be repaired - he did not have enough freely-moving men to do better than an evenly-matched battle, and the Empire did not reach its size by engaging in one-on-one combat with equally trained and disciplined opponents. He would not, I think, be willing to take this risk if he were not certain of destroying his foe, and without us, there was no way to achieve that certainty."

"What of the Pretender's response to us? The Emperor seemed confident that he had shielded us from his foe's divinations while watching us himself. While I am less than experienced in such things, and perhaps not qualified to speak..." Arudal saw the flickering glimmer of Lostren's green-gold eyes, as though Salarond's squire were glancing about for an unseen listener. There would have been nothing strange in a Tharandrostan speaking so, but it was unlike Lostren to be so - so exaggeratedly - humble... "Is there any chance that this may be, ah, overconfidence?"

Arrogance, to be precise, Arudal thought. But now it was his turn to restrain his words for the unseen listener. "As you should know by now, divinations can be unpredictable. Particularly mind-magic: if the Pretender, or any of his followers, have the gift of Foresight - which is highly likely, it was always strong in our race - even if he has been unable to follow us magically, he is probably preparing for something. Our advantage is that his preparations are likely to be incompletely performed, hence incompletely effective."

"As are ours, ultimately," Sir Salarond cut in. "But we have been over the most possible of the Pretender's responses, and made our plans accordingly. Unless you have something specific in mind...or a premonition?"

"No, sir. I would have spoken if I did."

"We can safely assume only that our part in this will not be as easy as it sounds. It never is. The question is, can we make it work even when things start going wrong? Unless we are taken completely by surprise in some way - and believe me, I want all of you to think about how that could happen - I think we can. In any event," Salarond added quietly, "to the best of the Emperor's knowledge, you and Arudal have only your task to worry about, and, barring any surprises that are beyond his capability to predict, that ought to go smoothly. It should be clear enough which of you has the command, both there, and, if it comes to it, upon your return." Mindful of their position, he did not say, Succeed or fail, we are only a diversion: the mission is in your hands now - and forever, if we do not survive. Still, Arudal heard the words in his commander's quietly strained voice, and was not sure whether that calmed him, or terrified him beyond recognition of fear. "Now, this house is well-guarded. No one will sit watch today: I want you all to be well-rested and in good fighting condition tomorrow. Anyone who finds that he has difficulty sleeping should let me know."

Chapter 27: Shadows and Swords

As planned, Arudal's guards came for him an hour before sunset - early enough that the Pretender's sentries were unlikely to be able to keep much of a watch on the no-man's-land, late enough that, if they were unexpectedly forced to retreat from the Imperial Libraries, the Agathim would only have had to be out in daylight for a little time. They were all full-fed - on whom? - and their helms hid their faces, but their stances trembled with the tension of men strained almost beyond what they could bear.

To Arudal's relieved surprise, it was Sir Pharzehar who raised his visor, shakily saluting him with a dark-gauntleted hand. "Sir Arudal. I have been charged with your safety once more. I shall not fail you, or my Emperor, again. Let us go."

The Agathim fell into step around Arudal and Lostren, shields up and swords out. The other White Company members were armouring themselves: there was no time for the farewells that Arudal had expected, only, as they marched out, Sir Thoron calling, "Best of luck, you two."

"And to you, sir," Arudal called back, Lostren murmuring assent. Their gauntlets clinked as Lostren took Arudal by the hand to lead him through the treacherous streets. The daytime City in Shadow was black as a wood at night to Arudal, save for the occasional glimmer of magic. Without the Agathim patrolling the streets, it felt more deserted to Arudal than it had in the full of night's haunting. Once or twice a tallow-white gleam caught the corner of his eye - a ghoul or walking corpse scuttling out of sight. Otherwise, there were only the armoured men marching silently about him, and the half-seen shadow of Lostren walking ahead beneath the golden tracery of glitter on his helm. A sudden pain cramped up from his left hand, and Arudal realized that he was clutching his buckler so hard that his forearm was already sore. Even the deep breaths of meditation could not force his tight belly to relax; but at the same time, he wanted to weep for joy. Soon he would be in the Imperial Library - the repository of the greatest lore of the Empire: even the great Royal Library in Var Ineth held only a few texts from the Imperial Library, the tiny fraction that Avalar had been able to steal in his flight.

Arudal saw the deep violet shimmer of the Emperor's border ward from several streets away, the jagged outlines of ruined houses standing up black against its lightless sheen. They were almost to the ward when the rotting green phosphorescence began to crawl just at the edge of what he could make out to the sides through the eyeslits of his helm, and he scented a whiff of decomposing flesh on the icy air. Avalar wrote of whole wings of the Imperial Library sealed off by collapsed walls. *We may need the strength of the ghouls to dig our passage through swiftly and with little risk: they are but the instruments of achieving our will...And you were dealing with ghouls on the Hidden Estate since you first came back from Duke Azarlokan's household,* Arudal scolded himself. *You could control all of them at once with only a little effort of your mind: what are you afraid of?*

But Grandmother Zinadir, Arudal realized as the ghouls crept into view, had always insisted that walking corpses, if they weren't mummified, be disposed of in good order. Though the shell-fragment of soul within the ghouls kept their muscles from decaying quite too far to move their bones, these were far past the state Zinadir considered intolerable. "Rot shows over the stomach first," she had always said. "When their bellies start swelling and going green, it's time to get rid of them: they're about to become unhygenic."

Unhygenic, Grandmother! Arudal thought, staring at their fleshly companions. The Ukuthrim's abdomens had split open, scraps of rot-black intestines dangling from the gaping wounds - scraps seething with little white maggots: flies could feed and breed endlessly in the half-preserved flesh of the walking dead, dungheap-warmed even in this winter by their ceaseless decay. Above the gaping wounds, the ghouls' greenish-black skin was sunken between their ribs, bits of pale bone showing through the rotting tatters. Fangs showed through the holes decomposition had eaten in their cheeks; their hair was sloughing off in patches with the melting skin of their scalps, and their long black nails had thickened into claws.

One might have lain long in the water: a layer of what looked like yellow-white tallow coated his body, thicker about his cheeks and the hanging sides of his open belly. *Partial saponification,* Arudal told himself, the gruesome details that Uridar had tried to frighten his younger cousin with now a peculiar source of comfort. Arudal's helm-padding was not thick enough to block out the wet sucking sound of the ghouls' glazed eyeballs moving in rotting sockets, and he swallowed hard, suddenly hot and nauseated as though a high fever burned in his body.

"Amandeth's chosen ones must not fear the signs of his passing," Uridar had said in a more serious mood once, when Arudal balked at looking at engravings showing the stages of decomposition. "Save for the bodies of Elves which fade into earth when their spirits are gone, all flesh comes to this in time." Arudal would not look away; but he thought of Finvar's corpse in its packing of snow, and his friend's gruesome advice on dealing with his own innards. If it had not been winter...

"Ari," Lostren said in a soft undertone, "you're bending my gauntlet-plates. If you squeeze any tighter, you're going to break my bones."

Arudal loosened his grip, moving his fingers on the buckler's handle to work some blood back into them. He felt ashamed of himself. Lostren had probably seen bodies as bad, or worse, after real battles. Yet Arudal wore the knight's belt and spurs - and granted by an Emperor of Shadow, at that.

They stepped through the Emperor's ward. It felt like stepping through an icy waterfall, the chill tingling all through Arudal's body - not painful, but so strong that he could not have borne it for more than a heartbeat. He staggered, but Lostren held him upright until he had gotten his balance again. They went on through the eerie stillness of the abandoned streets, Arudal's heart pounding as he strained about for the slightest hint of the presence of Undead beyond his guards and tatter-fleshed workers.

The Imperial Library glimmered with the same faint magic that shone in the walls of the Imperial Palace and Arudal's own mansion. A spell of preservation over the whole? Arudal devoutly hoped so: he was a philologist, not a paleographer trained to handle crumbling manuscripts. And what time and insects might have wrought after flames and collapse...The books will be whole enough. They must be.

The Library's doors were glittering bronze, wrought with the images of great scholars and poets. Arudal recognised a few of them: broad-browed Master Darnalokan, author of The Virtues of Herbs; the long bony face of Mistress Dalkinir, the finest poet of the Fourth Millennium, wreathed with the word-smith's crown of three-petaled silver ristuzimar flowers; the birdlike tilt of Magister Rakhazer's head above the hammer and phial that symbolized his work as an alchemist unsurpassed among Men...

Lostren walked straight through the door as if it were not there. Arudal let go of the squire's hand as the edge of his buckler struck the bronze, the Elf-made shield resounding off the door like the clapper of a great bell. Its echoes trembled away under Arudal's feet as Sir Pharzehar yanked the door open and shoved his charge in so hard that Arudal almost fell, snapping, "Inside, quick!" The Agathim crowded through in the space of a heartbeat; the door boomed shut. Red light flashed from something in Sir Pharzehar's gauntlet as he touched it, and a moment later, worms of red brightness were crawling up and down over the metal so swiftly that it almost made Arudal dizzy to look at it. Something was hissing and crackling nastily; Arudal glanced around, but though the guards stood at attention with their swords drawn, they were not moving as if to face a danger.

"What was that?" Arudal asked. Lostren was still staring out, his green-gold eyes gleaming wide from his helm-bars.

"Black rain," the Kantarean said. "It's still coming down outside, eating through the stones..."

"It is well that we came in daylight," added Sir Pharzehar. "They were quick enough to respond to the sound there as it was. Unless we are sure that the Emperor has secured his triumph when we come out, we shall wait until dawn and leave by a different exit."

Can you manage that? Arudal wanted to ask. He could already feel the first little rats of Shadow-hunger beginning to gnaw at a few of the Agathim around him. Shielded inside, or in darkness, they could last another night or two easily, but even a few minutes of daylight would drain the last of their strength. Yet he knew that it would shame Sir Pharzehar for him to ask that question.

The Undead knight reached into a small pouch hanging from his white leather belt. He brought out two stones that glowed with a cool blue radiance. "The Emperor instructs me to tell you that these will make it possible for you, Lord Lostren, to see in here without kindling fire, for all of us to see such dangers as may exist outside the Shadow-realm - and for you, Lord Arudal, to read with ease."

"Thank you," Arudal said, taking his stone. He had not thought of how his Shadow-sight would affect his ability to read books that had no more enchantment than a spell of preservation upon them. It would have made their task greatly harder, if Lostren had been forced to stumble through reading the Middle and Old Imperial of the older documents aloud for him to translate.

The stones' light and the background shimmer of the Library itself showed Arudal a strange double image. In the slight Shadow-brightness of the walls, they stood in an edifice raised in the flower of Middle Imperial style: pillars of white stone soared up to peaked stone-lace arches far, far above Arudal's head; the faintest patterns of colour gleamed from the dark glass of the high windows, and tables of swirling-mottled agate rose seamlessly from the agate floor. Yet, at the same time, an ugly piece of oilcloth sagged about ten feet above their heads, resting on heaps of rubble shored up by timbers, and broken tiles and bare dirt showed through the translucent Shadow-ripples of coloured stone. A blue-lit shower of snow fell outside, hissing horribly into the black pools eating through the scattered rocks and broken stone pathway behind the ghostly bronze door. Two of the ghouls had not made it inside in time: one writhed in two halves, its fanged mouth opening and closing silently and its legs drumming a furious tattoo as the dark splashes sank in through its rotting flesh, while the other, its head and shoulders already gone, lay quietly dissolving in one of the black puddles.

The dark beak of Sir Pharzehar's visor turned away, as though he could not bear to look at what the Library had become on the green earth. Arudal could see him clearly in both lights, for he was in full manifestation; but for a moment, his daylight image half-wavered into mist.

"I could have dwelt here for another eternity, and my sorrow would have been less for not seeing this," the Agathan murmured. "Nor do I know whether you are the better for seeing the Library in our memories as well as looking upon its sundered corpse. It is kinder not to have known the slain."

Arudal could not help glancing at the huddled ghouls, as though he might see the ruins of features he knew on their rotting skulls. Their stink was stronger in here, and he could hear the faint dull splashing of one's decaying flesh dripping nameless fluid onto the broken floor. A terrifying thought crossed his mind: what if the woods were not safe even outside the Elves' watch? If Finvar's body were taken...

With an effort of will, Arudal turned his mind back to the prizes waiting for him further inside the Library, even as Ostarak said stolidly, "Best not to think about that, sir. Do you know where we're supposed to go?"

"Oh, yes," Sir Pharzehar sighed. He straightened, looking about. "Shield the stones a moment."

In the dim witchlight, Arudal saw the knight striding towards a bronze door wrought with the image of a tree that bore flowers and fruit and leaves at once. Even without Sir Pharzehar's guidance, he would have recognised it: the same image marked the House of Procreation in Tharabruthnan.

Arudal and Lostren uncovered their stones just in time to see the dark-armoured Agathan coming out of a heap of rubble against the wall. Sir Pharzehar nodded to the ghouls, which began to tear at the jagged chunks of stone with the unnatural strength of the walking dead, tossing away boulders their own size as if they were pebbles. Arudal wanted to cry out to them to be careful...but there was nothing here to be careful of, save himself and Lostren, and the ghouls were assiduously avoiding throwing the broken pieces of wall and ceiling anywhere near them.

Even with the tireless power of the ghouls chewing rapidly through the rubble, their progress down the caved-in hallway seemed maddeningly slow when set against the Shadow-vision of the shining corridor with its rows of brightly polished doors to either side.

"Do you notice something odd about this?" Lostren whispered.

"What?"

"No rats, no spiders, no bats. You and I are the only living things here."

"It's a good sign," Arudal whispered hopefully back. "Surely the spells of preservation would have kept vermin out."

Lostren said nothing, and the ghouls kept digging. Eventually they unearthed the first door. In the light of the blue stones, it sagged pitifully to one side, hinges mostly broken and beautiful mouldings battered into shapeless lumps. Still, the huge room beyond was in surprisingly good condition. The blue-marbled tiles on the floor were cracked, shards of stone crunching beneath the two living men's boots as they walked in. The slim stone legs of the tables had also given way when the earth shook, their slabs fallen and cracked, and several of the shelves had collapsed, spilling their precious cargo on the floor, but other than that, the room had taken little damage.

Arudal drew a deep breath, letting it out slowly. Stale as it was, the air seemed to thrill through his lungs with promise. Had he been alone, he might have gone down on his knees; as it was, he took off his gauntlets, tucking them under his belt, and gave Ostarak his buckler, walking over to carefully lift one of the books from the floor. The embossed leather binding was still smooth, and though the pages were crumpled where the book had lain open on them for seventeen hundred years, the parchment was still supple, the black letters sharp-edged against the bleached hide and the red and gold and green of the marginal illumination bright and clear even in the enchanted light.

For a brief moment, Arudal envisioned himself returning home with a load of texts from the Imperial Library. A public ceremony of donation to the Prince's Library - Prince Norombar was something of an historian himself: there would be the Prince's personal thanks, a medal, perhaps...or even a knighthood, a dubbing performed in the light of day, with his father smiling with pride and tears of joy in his mother's eyes? Even young as Arudal was, it was not impossible...But the daydream misted swiftly away: Arudal had the book now, and all the others that had waited through the centuries. He brushed the crumpled pages as straight as he could, closing the book carefully and looking at the name and dates on the cover. Adarluz, Fourth Millennium 200-400: not a familiar House, and so late, it was almost certainly not one of those that was relevant to the pedigrees of either Duke Garthin or Duke Helak. Reluctantly Arudal put it down, following Lostren to the shelves.

I wonder if the Sun has set yet. Or the battle begun? Arudal thought. He forced it from his mind: there was nothing he could do to help his companions now, except complete his part of the mission as well and swiftly as possible.

"I could almost regret that no librarians...survived?...until now," Lostren murmured drily, echoing Arudal's thoughts. Still, the Imperial Library was arranged neatly. It took little time to determine that the volumes in this room went back no further than the genealogies surviving in Kantar. What they sought would be further down the hall, probably in the late Second or early First Millennium.

Past the collapsed entryway, the corridor was largely clear, but Sir Pharzehar insisted that the ghouls go first. "The whole structure has been weakened, and spells of preservation cannot repair damage already done. If their footsteps do not bring the ceiling down, you may go carefully. But do not resist if I pick you up and throw you out of harm's way! I might be able to explain broken bones: there is no excuse I can offer for your death under my protection."

Although the rooms beyond were in better state, their doors intact and fewer shelves collapsed, the books themselves - carefully preserved, but ancient by the time of the Fall - were far more fragile. Arudal held his breath each time he picked one up, terrified at what his touch would do to it. Though Lostren was not actually treating the manuscripts carelessly, he seemed to be handling them with far less concern, and finally Arudal's nerves broke and he snapped, "For Amandeth's sake, please be more careful with those!"

Lostren sighed. "Ari, I know how to handle old manuscripts. Do you see me smudging my fingers across the letters? Parchment in good condition is a lot more durable than you think. Here, this may be one of Garthin's."

At last Arudal had several of the heavy genealogical documents laid out on one of the surviving tables, and was ready to begin work in earnest. Lostren had been able to recognise the names, but the rest of the details were written in Old Imperial: now it was up to Arudal alone.

"This will take you some time, won't it?" Lostren asked. Although his helmet hid his expression, Arudal could recognise the eagerness sparking in his voice, like the barking of a scent-hound lunging against its leash.

"Yes."

"If you don't mind, I'll take a couple of your guards and look around for a few minutes. I won't go far, but I don't think I can be much help to you now, and..."

I am supposed to be in command, Arudal thought. He knew perfectly well that the safety here was an illusion, that splitting their forces was a bad idea. On the other hand, they should set a guard anyway, lest a foe trap them in this room. And the gods forbid that we should fight where there was a risk of harming the books here!

"Sir Pharzehar, would you set a guard and a ghoul at each entrance?"

"The entrances are already guarded by our men," the Undead knight replied. "I set those with the skill of Mind-Speaking to watch, so that they can alert you immediately if they see any danger approaching."

"Do you see any objection to Lord Lostren exploring elsewhere?"

"Not for the moment. Lieutenant Gathukali, Lieutenant Minliphalaz, go with him. Take two of the ghouls to test for stability in front of Lord Lostren. Migathi, report back to Sir Arudal at once if there is any danger."

Arudal blinked: the first name was a woman's. Gathukali was a couple of inches shorter than the men around her, and her armour was made for a full-breasted figure - how had he not noticed? Because I didn't think of it? Anyway, it doesn't matter now. Even if Sir Pharzehar had addressed her by the affectionate diminutive, strange in the mouth of the formal soldier...had they been, once?

"Be very careful, and don't take long," Arudal told Lostren.

"Yes, sir."

Arudal stood dazed for a moment as Lostren and his guards left the room. He would have expected the phrase to be sarcastic. But Lostren had spoken naturally, easily, as to a superior - as to a real knight, genuinely set in command over him.

Later for that, as well. Arudal turned back to his books, taking off his gloves to turn the pages as carefully as he could. Spelling had not been standardized in the Old Imperial period: just as Sir Shakhor had proved his full worth in the woods, so, Arudal realized, only someone with his own training in language and philology could have made sense of these manuscripts, lacking as they did all the later glosses and translations which graced the few Old Imperial manuscripts surviving in the West. If only I had dared to bring ink in here! But we shall be taking these books back with us, he reminded himself, forcibly dragging his thoughts away from the pure philological treasure before him and back to his duty of unraveling the two rival genealogies.

It was not, as Arudal had suspected, a question of one simple point of seniority, or at least not one that could be easily found. The bloodlines of the Imperial noble houses, if not as inbred as those of Tharandrost, nevertheless crossed and recrossed each other for millennia, and each branch of descent required him to seek out at least two other books for corroboration. And whenever he straightened from stooping over the table to rub his aching lower back for a moment, or passed his hand over his eyes to stop the clumsy archaic letters from crawling in his vision, Arudal found himself thinking of the fighting that must, surely, be going on outside now. He had wanted to say a few last words to each of his companions before they went into battle - to tell Sir Thoron how good it was to be his squire, to thank Sir Salarond for bringing him, encourage Tirothar...

If they came into the Library now, alive and victorious, Arudal thought that he would even embrace Rhys. *My wits are melting. Back to work.* Intent on a discrepancy in what seemed to be the final twist of Helak's intricate pedigree, Arudal did not notice when Lostren and his guards came back. It was not until he straightened his back again, rolling his neck to hear the little bones crackling back into place, that Lostren coughed uncomfortably and said, "Ari, can you leave that for a moment?"

Arudal started as if pricked by a dagger. "Is there news of the battle yet?"

"No. Nothing like that." Muffled by his helm, Lostren's voice seemed oddly toneless. "I have found something I think you should see. We got through to the late history section, and the ghouls broke into a sealed chamber for me..."

"Can it wait?"

"I really think you should read it now."

Reluctantly Arudal went over to take the heavy book from Lostren's hands. Lostren had marked his place with a fingertip; Arudal carried it open to the table, gently nudging aside two genealogical texts to make room for it.

The book was written in a modern Imperial almost identical to that still spoken in Tharandrost, but the scribe's handwriting was particularly spiky and elaborate, so that it took longer for Arudal to decipher it than he should have. It seemed to be a journal of some sort; at least, the entries were dated. Year-Turn 15, Fourth Millennium 864 - near the beginning of the Last Emperor's reign.

Our dear cousin Arurak, Duke Aglarek, asked Our permission for an experiment. With the aid of High Priest Agathaman, he wishes to try to shift Our royal bloodline's gift of the Mindspeaking powers entirely into Shadow, so that he may be able to control and commune with the Ukuthrim as he is now able to do the living. We are of divided mind, as there is some risk of his death, and considerable risk that he will be transferred entirely into the Shadow-realm as a result of the rite..

Arudal turned the page, not thinking, only scanning down through the entries until he saw his ancestor's name again..

Year-Turn 17, Fourth Millennium 864. We have given Our cousin Arurak Our permission to attempt his experiment, on the condition that he allow High Priest Agathaman to set a spell on him which, should he be translated fully into the Shadow-Realm, will bind him to continue in the service of the Imperial Crown, even unto departing beyond the worlds' rings should We so will it. Our cousin accepted this upon the reciprocal condition that, should his translation take place, We will permit him to continue unimpeded in the holding and rule of his lands both inherited and awarded. Being apprised of the advantages to the enhancement of his necromantic skills which would accrue with the success of his experiment, We agreed to grant this concession, and to provide such materials as High Priest Agathaman agrees are necessary for the ritual. The experiment will take place on Sundark Eve.

Year-Turn 22, Fourth Millennium 864. Our cousin Arurak reported his success! At the cost of approximately eighty thousand crowns' worth of powdered vorgath and various precious stones (full details in Seneschal's records) and six of the Accursed given by slow means to the Friend of Men, he managed to completely translate Kathabar's line-gift to the Shadow-Realm while remaining alive upon the green earth, performing a demonstration of same for me. The Lord of Shadows blessed him greatly, conferring upon him also the gift of mediumship, which had not previously been known in any branch of Emperor Kathabar's line.

We enquired as to whether this ritual might be repeated for others, but, the limitations of expense aside, High Priest Agathaman counsels me that a second success could not be expected: the Lord of Shadows is not a tame spirit to call. Nevertheless, this is to be counted as a great triumph, and both his Grace and his Blessedness shall receive a full Imperial Commendation for their achievement. But the final test shall come when We see if Our cousin is able to pass his altered gift on to his children. We have ordered him to marry Dolgubel Mistress Agathudalil forthwith, in hopes that her powerful mediumistic talent will further enhance his and increase the chances of carrying the blessing of the Friend of Men on to future generations...

Arudal looked up. The room spun around him; bright things flashed in the corner of his vision. He could feel his gorget pressing hard against his voice-box, and a bitter trickle of bile seared the back of his throat. Amandeth, Amandeth. Friend of Men...At that, he bent over, his stomach twisting in painful spasms as he tried to choke back his retching.

"Call them off me, Ari," Lostren said evenly. Eyes watering, Arudal coughed hard and swallowed several times to clear the burning foulness from his throat. Sir Pharzehar stood with the point of his sword resting lightly on the joint between Lostren's gorget and his breastplate, and the tip of Ostarak's black blade hovered just before the squire's eye-slit.

"We await your command, Sir Arudal," Sir Pharzehar stated.

"He...He has not harmed me. I was taken by a brief fit, only. Please stand down."

The two Agathim sheathed their weapons and stepped away from Lostren. The Kantarean remained where he was, without the slightest change in his stance. Arudal met his eyes, but could not speak. The only words that came to him seemed banal, idiotic: Why did you have to show me this?

The implications tumbled through Arudal's mind like boulders down the side of a cliff, each knocking three others free. A full Imperial Commendation - publicly recognised. Prince Khatirost must have known - not only condoned, but supported this: even in the earliest days, before close breeding became common for our race, our House was urged to breed within itself for the sake of our line-gift..

And now I know why we stand so low in Tharandrost's roll of precedence. Just as the Hidden Estate was a State secret altogether so long, and even now is not spoken of outside our House... Avalar would just have come to manhood when Duke Arurak received the public blessing for his deed; he would have remembered - did remember. Avalar had written of "the Emperor's blessing given to a deed foul enough to be the direct handiwork of the Twisted One, the deliberate corruption of Amanvon's gift to our race", as the first point in his life when he had wondered if the Empire was beyond the most virtuous Emperor's power to rescue. Arudal had always thought that to refer to the use of tortured sacrifices to extend the lifespans of the Last Emperor and his favourite councilors beyond the gift of longevity granted to the Imperial lines; he had never imagined that what Avalar called 'Amanvon's gift' was actually one of the Mind-gifts usually attributed to the god. Though they did not know it, everything that the Kantareans and Dame Karsil said about Tharandrost - and about me, Amandeth help me! - must, after all, be true.

Lostren, why did you have to show me this?

"I didn't know," Arudal said.

How, knowing this, can I ever go back home?

The stones' glow shone blue from Lostren's darkening pupils, overlaying the brightening green-gold of his eyes in Shadow. Although Lostren's helm hid his expression, as Arudal knew his own must do for him, the Tharandrostan heard the sharp intake of the other's breath.

"We still have Finvar to think of," Lostren said, as though he had heard the words in Arudal's head.

Arudal's mind seized up like a rusty spyglass locking on a single distance. His ears rang faintly, as though he had been standing in the bell of one of the great foghorns that sang out the nearness of Tharandrost's rocky coast in the mist. Since there was nothing else Arudal could say, or think, he turned around and went back to the genealogies.

Arudal did not know how much time had passed, but he was on the last set of books when he heard a strange voice in his mind, sharp and cold as breaking ice. Sir Arudal, His Imperial Majesty requires your presence now. Your guards are to escort you. You shall leave by the secondary exit at the end of the Hall of Ancestry, but there are no immediate dangers threatening your departure.

"We have to go now," Arudal said numbly. "The Emperor would see me."

Without speaking, Lostren helped him gather the precious books into the padded bags they had brought. Their guards took up their positions again, Sir Pharzehar on Arudal's right and Ostarak on Arudal's left. At the end of the hallway, Sir Pharzehar went forward and touched his gauntlet to the heavy bronze door. Something clicked within, and it swung open.

As Arudal and Lostren stepped outside the Imperial Library, their stones' blue glow died, leaving Arudal's sight in Shadow. He stopped still, listening to the rustle of Lostren shifting the heavy bags about on his shoulders. Even through their ice-chill gauntlets and heavy gloves, it seemed to Arudal that he could feel the warmth of the other's hand, like a fire on the far side of a thick door.

Arudal strained his ears for the sounds of fighting as they walked swiftly back towards the Emperor's wards, but he heard nothing. There would be noise only where the living fought - if any of the White Company had survived - and he could not bring himself to reach for the minds of the dead.

Two of the Emperor's guards strode forward from the gates of the Imperial Palace as Arudal, Lostren, and their escort approached, saluting sharply. "Sir Arudal," said the one on the right. "You are to come with us. Lord Lostren, you have His Imperial Majesty's permission to return to Sir Arudal's house. Sir Pharzehar, you and your men may escort Lord Lostren."

Arudal passed his two bags over to Lostren. The Kantarean grunted as he took their weight, shrugging his shoulders to settle them on it. "Can you manage?" Arudal asked.

"I shall have to. Don't worry."

The guards led Arudal through the darkness where the gardens had been and into the Palace, past the magnificent gemmed mosaics of the hall and through the adamantine doors. They turned sharply in unison and left Arudal alone by the empty space where the Last Emperor's statue might have stood.

As before, Emperor Arurak sat on the Ruby Throne, his white skin and black hair standing out sharply against the deep red of throne and robes and the curtain of ruddy witch-fire behind him. The Agathim did not tire as living men did, but there was something about the Undead ruler's posture and expression - the least slump to his shoulders, the shadow of his eyelids weighting his tilted gray eyes - that seemed to echo a ghost's long-faded memory of his lost flesh's bone-deep exhaustion. Yet he was smiling just as Arudal's father had smiled when he had beaten Sir Adarthan of the Tower's Guard in the Sunheight Tourney three years ago. Arudal felt a sudden urge to run to him, put his head in the Agathan's lap, and weep like a child. But the realization of what he had read in the Imperial Library - six of the Accursed given by slow means to the Friend of Men - still knotted his entrails tight and spun dizzily in his head, and he was afraid that if he moved too fast he would either faint or spew.

"Approach, Our son," the Emperor said. "We have the victory."

Though his awareness torn was between suppressing the desire to hasten towards his ancestor and controlling the trembling of his gut, Arudal's legs bore him down the hall with the graceful dignity that his five years of training as a page had ingrained in his muscles. He mounted the dais and went to both knees before the clouded Ruby Throne, his own heartbeat thudding sickeningly in his ears. There was no other sound in the hall, and Arudal knew it was his turn to speak.

"You...you overcame the Pretender, Your Majesty?"

"By strength of will, at last. For your return proved Our triumph, and thus made it sure, while he had no vision of what should happen were he to conquer Us, save his desire for the Ruby Throne. That desire held him to Shadow from life, and gave him the strength to withstand Us all this while. But at the end, it was not enough."

"What of my companions, Your Majesty?"

"They fight still, if they are not slain. In a little while, you shall aid Us to set Our armour on, and We shall go to the battlefield. But now there is a more important matter before Us."

"Your Majesty?"

Emperor Arurak reached forward, taking Arudal by the hand. Solid though his grip was, it still shocked icy through the bones of Arudal's arm as the Emperor raised him up. "You are the heir of Our line, the living proof of Our triumph. But more than that: you shall be the means by which We turn outwards from Our long silence, to regain Our rightful place and bring the Empire back from the realm of memory to the green earth. As We spoke of before, there are many things that living men can do that the Ukuthrim cannot."

Ukuthrim, not Agathim, Arudal thought, dazed and retreating to what he knew best. The term Agathan must have been constructed in Tharandrost after the Wrath, then…Perhaps when one of my forebears could not bear to call his kin monsters, though they had passed into Shadow…

"We are your liege lord and you are Our knight, born of the last folk in the Middle Land who still keep the Empire's true ways. Though you yet live on the green earth, you are closer to your kin in Shadow than to your warm companions, but they cannot deny your worth. Now that you have come home at last, it is Our will that you shall sit with Us on the Ruby Throne: at the roots of your soul, by the very blood in your veins, you were bred and born for this."

In Tharandrost, I would have served in secrecy, becoming Master of the Hidden Estate when Grandmother Zinadir passes into Shadow. I would have been known only to my family and those whom the Prince sets to deal with us. In Kantar, knowing what I am, even my dearest friends were quick to mistrust me. Here - and reaching elsewhere from here - I could have all the honour my line was denied at the State's founding, not in spite of what I am, but because of it.

"Yes," Emperor Arurak said softly. Again it struck Arudal how much his liege - for I accepted the strokes of knighthood from his hand, whatever was in my thoughts then - looked like his father: the same straight thought-line between his slanted black eyebrows, the deep-graven marks of sternness about his mouth softened by the gentle curve of his lips as he gazed at his son. "Yes, you would."

The Emperor stood, lifting the ruby-set Imperial Crown from his head. "Sir Arudal, your duty to your companions is done, your oaths wholly fulfilled and your purpose with them accomplished. Now set your hands between Ours on this emblem of Our rule, worn by every holder of the Ruby Throne from the First Emperor Kathabar onwards, and we shall swear our oaths. Our son, you shall be co-Emperor and one with Us, and together we shall restore the lost glories of our people."

Arudal took off his gauntlets and reached up, grasping the thick gold circlet. The cold nubbles of the rubies tingled against his palms; he felt the metal freezing to his skin. I shall never be able to release it.

Arudal did not know what he was going to do until he did it. Without thought, he flung himself completely open, taking the last step up to the throne so that his breastplate and Emperor Arurak's velvet-clad chest both pressed hard against the Imperial Crown. The Emperor surged into him, immense, unbelievable, rending his mind raggedly like a sword tearing through sheer silk. White starbursts of pain exploded through Arudal's eyes; he could not feel his body any longer, only the endless depth of cold. Yet he tore himself further and further open, straining through as if he would rip his flesh away from the inside out like pulling off a rabbit's pelt with one fierce yank. His mouth opened to scream as he fell, but he did not hear his own cry: he heard nothing, saw nothing, except for the blackness devouring the last spark of light in his eyes.

Chapter 28: Awakening

"The heart's healing is slow: tears water the seed.
Thread-thin, bone-white roots creep first in hiding
Beneath earth that seems scorched and barren forever.
But by the time the first bud pricks out green,
Life's web spreads already deep through the heart,
Drawing from sorrow strength needed to rise -
Proof that joy must flower again, in time."

- "After the War of Ruin", Perelan Haregift

Arudal drifted, the sea rocking peacefully beneath him. He saw nothing but gray fog around him; he was not sure whether his eyes were open or closed, nor did he particularly care. He thought he could hear the far-off strains of a sweet, haunting melody, but he was not sure about that either.

Then it seemed to him that someone was calling his name. Still, Arudal did not bother to answer. He was content enough where he was, the movement of the water and the softness of the mist soothing him into stillness. He had a vague feeling that something had happened, but it was over now: no one could ask anything more of him for a while.

"Ari," the voice - a man's voice, familiar, though he could not place it - called insistently. "Ari, wake up. Ari! Damn it, squire, I know you're in there! If you don't answer me, you'll spend the rest of this voyage running the decks!"

"Jus' a quarter-candlemark longer," Arudal mumbled sleepily. He didn't need to be woken up; his eyes were open, and school was out anyway.

"Quarter-candlemark, my big hairy...Ari!"

Arudal grunted in surprise as the powerful embrace drove the air from his lungs. He blinked hard, and after a moment, he could make out vague features through the fog. A big, broad-shouldered man, with a keen eagle-beak of a nose and long scraggly dark hair... "Sir Thoron?"

"Praised be all the gods!" Thoron said, letting go of Arudal at last. "You have a lot of training to catch up on, squire. Do you know how long you've been - asleep?"

"Sir?" Arudal's memory was coming back slowly now. His palms stung painfully where he had grasped the Imperial Crown, as though he held a double fistfull of nettles. And...

Finvar! If he had lost his friend's soul, after all that had passed...

I'm here, Ari. You weren't, not for a while. Or at least I couldn't find you, though I couldn't get out, either. It seemed to Arudal that he could see the inside of his own mind: a window with the glass blown out by a high wind, only a few jagged diamond-shards still glittering like shattered teeth about the edges of the frame, and Finvar's solid figure standing in the middle of it. Arudal had not even thought of his squire-brother in his moment of choice, and the burst of his shame brought a little warmth to his chilled face.

You made the right choice, Finvar assured him. *If you'd stopped to worry, or held back to protect me, for a sliver of a heartbeat - your body might be here now, but it wouldn't be either of us in it.*

Arudal realized that his shields were almost completely destroyed. He knew he should be alarmed; but Finvar's warmth in his mind felt like a fur coat wrapping him about inside, and now...Well, his part of the mission was done, and it should be possible to restore the Artegalian to his own flesh soon anyway.

"I'll give you a hint," Thoron continued, oblivious to Arudal's internal dialogue. "We're a month into the voyage home."

"What happened? I mean..."

"Maybe you can tell us that when Salarond says you're up to it. Wait a moment. Salarond!" he bellowed. "Ari's awake!"

Arudal heard the sound of footsteps running over the deck, then the door opening, and he saw the shadows moving through the mist, Karsil shining Elf-bright behind them. Sir Salarond's wiry shape coalesced from the fog as the healer moved closer. His gray hair was dripping with sweat, a large patch of wetness sticking his plain tunic to his chest; he must have just come from strenuous training.

"Ari! Thank Aviyani! How long have you been awake?" As he spoke, the healer-knight tucked a couple of pillows under Arudal's back to support him.

"About two or three mumbles worth," Thoron answered for him. "You think I'd let the Mountain Sleeper wake up and not call you?"

"What happened?" Arudal asked again. "Is everyone...did everyone survive the battle?"

The corners of Salarond's mouth tightened, and although no tears fell from his slanted eyes, Arudal could see the water-brightness shining over their steel-and-amber like an unrippled pond. "Sir Shakhor and Tirothar didn't make it. The gods receive them both. Tirothar got an arrow right through an eye-slit - that would have been fatal even in the Middle Land; it pierced his brain beyond any hope of repair. And Shakhor - his horse stumbled on something and went down, and the ghouls got him even before we had a chance to wheel round."

Arudal drew in a deep breath of grief, almost wishing that he could have stayed in his silent peace. But the feeling of it had almost faded already from his mind: he remembered only that he remembered it, not what it had been like. He still felt weak, and terribly tired, but his head was clearing quickly, even with Finvar's sorrow echoing his own so closely that they might have been a harpstring ringing unplucked to the note of a tuning fork.

We never got a chance to go hunting together with those damned lions Tirothar was always on about, Finvar said, his mind-voice choked as if he were fighting back tears. *Stupid southerner never learned to drink ale properly, either. I had so much yet to show him, but we could never get him out of the habit of tilting his shield at that odd slant so he could see clearly. That must have been what killed him, tilting it at the wrong second...And Sir Shakhor was one of the best men in the White Company. I never enjoyed myself more with the Company than that one time he and Sir Thoron went up to the woods of Carlin together...*

"After the battle, they brought the bodies back to the house," Lostren went on. "I told them where you were, and we were just about to go to the Palace when Sir Pharzehar and Ostarak knocked on the door. Ostarak was carrying you, and I would have sworn he was trying not to cry - if the, uh, Agathim can cry."

"They can cry," Arudal answered softly. "Sometimes forever... So what happened?"

"Sir Pharzehar told us that the Emperor was gone, and that, since Sir Edrakhor and Sir Garnamel had gone down in the fighting, he was now in command of what was left of the Imperial Army, on both sides. He thought you were dead, but he said that we could stay as long as we liked and take what we pleased from the City itself. He was a great deal less happy than the Emperor was about letting us go away with the documents from the Library, and he made us swear an oath that any books we took, we would send back someday."

Arudal thought of the Library as it still existed in Shadow - in Sir Pharzehar's memory - and smiled. The Imperial knight had been faithful to his oaths long past his death; but with the Emperor gone and the long struggle for the City over, he would be free of all compulsions save his own soul's deepest will. Though Arudal lacked the gift of Foresight, he thought that the next time wanderers from the Middle Land dared the Imperial Seat - bearing four heavy sacks of genealogical compilations, perhaps - there might be more truth than jest to Lostren's ironic observation about an Undead keeper of the Library.

Just what the world needs, Finvar muttered in his mind, and Arudal had to stifle a laugh. Yet he could not forget that the Imperial Seat was not the Hidden Estate, where the Undead had their lawful prey: Sir Pharzehar might gain his heart's desire in Shadow, but he would still have to feed on the living - however the Agathim of the Imperial Seat managed it.

"Did you think I was dead?" Arudal asked.

Lostren looked uncomfortably at Sir Salarond; Salarond looked Arudal straight in the eye. "By any standards you care to name, you were. We laid you out on a great pyre beside Tirothar and Sir Shakhor with your armour on, still holding the Imperial Crown - there was no way to get it away from you without hacking your hands apart, and we thought that you had earned the right to bear the sign of your triumph to the gods. When we kindled the flame, Ostarak began to fade. I believe he had chosen to go on: he was gone before the fire reached your body."

Farewell, Ostarak, Arudal prayed silently. I wish I had taken the chance to enchant wine for you to taste one last time. May you have the best vintages where-ever you have gone. Like all the Fallen, the Imperial soldier had prayed to Morthugor - but Arudal could not bring himself to believe that Amandeth had doomed him to the Pits: however he prayed, Ostarak had been too good a man for that. I turned his mind towards trust and friendship for me, yes, but not so strongly that he should have sought to follow me beyond the worlds' rings: though I helped raise the sail, the wind that blew him there sprang from his own heart.

And next year, Arudal thought, I will not be able to stand silent when the names of the beloved dead are spoken at the Feast of Amandeth. Sir Shakhor, Tirothar, Ostarak...Have I grown stronger, or only hardened, that, though I mourn, the weight of these three deaths is not enough to crack my heart across?

"And then," Rhys said, his voice lilting like grass rippling beneath the wind, "we were amazed, for look you, the flames were rising all about you. They fastened on the flesh of Tirothar, and on the torn remains of my dear knight-father - the best man that ever Gwydydd shaped to walk the woods, or Ymwra to ride the green fields - but scorching not so much as a single hair upon you, nor even singeing your clothes or the sheaths of the swords laid over you. Whatever touched you was as well-warded from the fire as if it had lain at the bottom of a great snow-drift. We did not know whether it was a god or spirit that held its hand over you, or whether it had something to do with the Imperial Crown, or Berek's spells of protection, or all of them - Sir Eroth is after thinking that perhaps the Crown magnified the spells in some way - but at any rate, we took you out of the flames before matters could change, and hastened back."

But the Imperial Crown never preserved its wearer in death. Yet as I am almost certain to pass into Shadow when I die - did my own gift turn inwards on itself, as so often happens with agathurokim so that they become ghosts, but trapping me instead in Shadow within the enchantment warding my body, or even within the Crown, so that when we came close enough to the Middle Land's magic, I could be restored? Instead of speaking -or thinking - further on that, Arudal said, "And what about Finvar? I still have him."

"His body is healed and breathing," Sir Salarond assured him. "He wants only his soul. Which, I suspect, you are in no state to give him yet; but so far as he is concerned, there is no problem."

If I am ever able to bring myself to use my talents again, Arudal thought.

Finvar replied, Better do it at least once. I love you, but I'm not sure I want to marry you quite yet.

"And what of Berek and Malni?"

"I'm here," Malni said from further back in the room. When Arudal squinted, he could just make out her tall figure next to Dame Karsil. "We left Berek with a caravan of his father's men going into Hatin's City from Cirrod. I'd say there were plenty of wagers lost and won when he showed up, all right." Her Common was almost perfect now, Arudal noticed absently.

I never got to say goodbye to Berek properly, Arudal thought. There were things I wanted to talk to him about.

The Tharandrostan looked up at Karsil. He barely dared speak to her: to her, there had never been any question about the nature of Arudal's heritage. But he thought the others there would speak up for him if she grew angry, and no one else would even know what his question meant. "Had Berek learned...?"

"Loyalty, certainly," Karsil answered. "Chivalry - perhaps. Compassion - who can tell? And as for Hatin's City in times to come...?" She looked straight into Arudal's eyes, and Arudal knew they were both remembering children trapped in worse than slavery, and healing's cost to the poor: a slower death from starvation than illness, but death nevertheless. "Perhaps one of us shall come back when Berek is lord, or some time after, and find out which of our seeds sprouted and which rotted in fallow earth. But let my squire tell you the rest of what befell."

"We made all haste down to the coast to meet the ship," Malni went on. "You missed some excitement then, too. One of the crew-members tried to kill Verhin the cook and take his place so he could poison the lot of us. But Verhin's like you, or at least he sees ghosts. He says he was warned that something was amiss by the cat that haunts the ship and - well, he was in the gallery with a lot of sharp knives around and on-guard when the attack came."

"Did the traitor confess to you for whom he was working? Or get a chance to?" Arudal added, thinking of how deftly the cook's knife had flickered when he was gutting fish.

"Verhin bled him until he passed out," Lostren supplied. "As we suspected, he was an agent of Martag. He was meant to make sure that we never returned to Kantar - for himself, he had an amulet which would summon a lesser daemon to bear him, and whatever we had gotten as well, safely back. Interestingly, the daemon in your stone was no part of his plan, nor did he know anything about the scrying-stones: the first truly seems to have been random sabotage of Secret Service supplies, and the second..." Lostren shrugged. "We may never know."

So the daemon outwitted us. The agent of Martag had indeed been loyal to his service, nor had his amulet been meant directly to either harm the White Company party or reveal it to its seekers, and there had not been another creature of Shadow actually on board the ship. The information they had gotten had been true, but meaningless within its context.

Arudal's blanket had slipped down from his chest. He tried to pull it up, but the stinging pain in his hands kept him from getting a grip on it. Looking at his injuries, he saw that the palms and the undersides of his fingers were skinned where he had held the Imperial Crown, red and shiny-dry under a greasy film, like blisters with the loose skin cut off too early. "What happened to my hands?" he asked Sir Salarond.

"You held the Imperial Crown for, literally, months. Then, a couple of days ago, you started breathing again and your grip relaxed. When the Crown came away, your skin came with it. I tried to heal your hands, but they wouldn't respond: you will have to heal naturally, and may always need to wear gloves for swordwork. I salved them, but since you weren't moving, there seemed no point in bandaging them. I wondered if you would sleep until you were completely healed. But the Crown itself is with the rest of your things, as is the sword the Emperor gave you and a few other small items. I would advise you to have it carefully examined before you touch it again."

"Speaking of finds from the City, I almost forgot, Ari," Lostren said. "When we discovered that you weren't, um, completely dead, I brought a couple of books from the Imperial Library in the hopes that you would be able to read them. You should feel very privileged: I doubt there is anyone else on the green earth - or in Shadow - that Sir Pharzehar would consider lending his treasures to for their personal pleasure. In fact, he helped me find them. Just a moment."

Lostren tiptoed out of the cabin, coming back with three gold-embossed volumes. "Here. An etymological dictionary of Middle High Imperial, written in Third Millennium 549; a copy of what Sir Pharzehar told me is the first dictionary of Old High Imperial, First Millennium 877; and a collection of prayers and songs in Proto-Imperial, compiled in First Millennium 20."

Arudal gasped. None of the books were known in the Middle Land, and only two short poems in Proto-Imperial had been preserved there. Each of them was more than enough material for a thesis - enough material to fill the three hundred years or so remaining of his lifetime: the hope that had borne him on this journey had found its fulfillment's harbour at last.

"I don't know how to thank you. This is..."

"You killed the Fallen Emperor. And died doing it, or near enough. And...I think I did you a bad turn, there in the Library."

"I don't know." If Lostren had not shown him the Last Emperor's journal - would Arudal have been able to do what he had done? Or would he even have been tempted not to do it? But I think the Emperor was reading my mind, there at the last: I was deeply enough in Shadow that it might have been possible. And if I had not believed that I could take his offer, would he have believed it?

Lostren coughed, looking down awkwardly. "Well, anyway. These should keep you busy while you're recovering."

Arudal laughed, then began to cough himself, spitting up a bit of something nasty-tasting.

"Fluid pooling in your lungs," Sir Salarond diagnosed. "I can do something about that, at least." He put his hands on Arudal's chest, murmuring. A soothing warmth spread out from his hands, and Arudal's cough was gone, but he found himself yawning hugely instead. "My patient is tired," said the healer-knight. "Out: you'll all see plenty of him later."

Karsil and Malni lingered as Sir Salarond rearranged Arudal's pillows so that he could lie down comfortably. Arudal thought the White Company commander was about to say something to them, but as he turned towards the Elf and her squire, Karsil began to sing.

"Black sky nestles the stars' fair lights,
 Trees murmur their soft leaf-tongue,
 Reaching up from their earth-bound roots..."
Malni's voice, low and slighly sandy, but true, came in under Karsil's as both support and contrast, like dark earth at the roots of a pale-barked ereth tree, the simple, beautiful harmony sinking into Arudal's ears like a dollop of honey sinking slowly into wine,
"Spring from silent echoes of song,
 Sing in silent echoes of spring."
Karsil's high soprano rose unfettered again.
"From my eyes glint the stars all mute,
 Sap rises quiet in heart-veins,
 Rushing, the river gleams without sate,
 Again Malni picked up the last two lines beneath Karsil,
 Runs echoing over bright stones,
 Shines echoes of stars as it runs.

Arudal lay lulled halfway to sleep, thinking as the Elf's voice soared, Karsil never sang for me before. She sang where I could hear her, but not for me.

Blossoms glimmer in shadow-dark grass,
White candle-flames in soft airs,
Swaying cool beneath wind's caress -
'Stars' bright breath over them pours,
 Pour blooms' sweet breath to the stars.'

This time Malni went on, repeating the first verse, "Black sky nestles the stars' fair lights..." Then Arudal's eyes sprang open, for he could hear the pure lilting song of a dethil rising and falling above the squire's husky voice. Karsil stood with her eyes half-closed. Her mouth was open, but her lips did not move, and the high bright sound purled ceaselessly from her throat over the words Malni sang, so that it seemed to Arudal almost as if he were transported back to the garden where the little night-bird had voiced its heart-wringingly fair music to Karsil and himself. He closed his eyes, letting the two women's voices waft him gently to sleep.

Arudal gained strength quickly over the next weeks. The deep Shadow-mist that had lain over his sight when he awoke cleared a little; he would never again see even as well as he had before in daylight, but in the familiar confines of the ship, he was able to get about without difficulty, so that none of his companions could tell the new extent of his daytime blindness. He spent a great deal of time in meditation, painstakingly rebuilding his shattered mind-shields. Somewhere beneath his waking thoughts, Arudal found as he searched deeper into himself, he had hoped that sending his forebear beyond the worlds' rings would, if he survived, have cleansed his line-gift of the Shadow-taint: instead, it seemed to have strengthened it.

Did Arurak have the agathurok talent? he wondered, more than once. Did he even know about it? Surely such a thing would have been mentioned in the Last Emperor's journal, or else Arudal's forebear would have said something. Emperor Arurak had wanted to possess his descendant, there at the last. Otherwise, even weakened as the Agathan had been by his struggle with his rival, Arudal would never have been able to pull him in and through. It seemed, thinking on it, that what he had done was something like the movements of mithlapar by which a small woman could guide the strength of a larger attacker into a headlong fall; but such techniques very seldom worked when the aggressor was aware of what would happen if she or he rushed to overpower the victim by sheer brute force. And if he did not know - Did Amandeth, after all, work to reshape what was twisted into a thing of good, as a skilled crafter shapes beauty from sea-gnawed driftwood?

That, perhaps, Arudal would never know until his god called him beyond the worlds, but the possibility was enough to calm his heart whenever he looked into the mirror and saw Emperor Arurak's features reflected in his own Shadow-darkened eyes. As before, the one consistent annoyance of Arudal's recovery was Malni. Far from being angry at his deception, she seemed more infatuated with him than ever; and it helped matters little that, as soon as Sir Salarond cleared him to start light sword-training again, Dame Karsil asked him to help her squire with learning the Elven style.

"You are a hero," Malni said to him at last, as Arudal leaned panting on the ship's rail with his helm off, letting the wind cool his sweat-soaked hair. He still tired easily, as though he had drained his own store of life-strength down to the mud and rocks at the bottom of the well, with only the thin trickle of a stream left to refill it. "Why should I not love you?"

"I do not sharen thy feeling," Arudal answered stiffly, his old clumsiness with the Common tongue creeping back for the first time in a long while. "I am betrothed at home, and thou art not of my kith. Go to Rhys. The two of you mighten be shaped for each other; and he is still deep in grief for Sir Shakhor: it might be that thou couldst aid in healing his heart."

"Rhys said that your race despises his more than anything that lives, and that you hated him when you first met. How is it that you have come to care for him so? Or are you only trying to get rid of me into the nearest arms?" A glint of anger steeled Malni's blue eyes - or it might have been the first shining of tears; Arudal could not tell.

"I served for a little time as finavi's squire. I would not dishonour her, or my... squire-sister, by counselling you towards an unworthy man."

Malni swallowed hard. When she could speak again, she said, "Maybe I will think about it. Have you got your breath back?"

At last Arudal felt strong enough, and sure enough of his control, that he was ready to dare the difficult task of setting Finvar's soul back into his living flesh. One of the ship's cabins was cleared out except for the bed on which Finvar's naked body lay. The Artegalian's eyes were closed as if in sleep, thick ash-blond hair fanning out over his pillow and his broad bare chest rising and falling slowly. The warm light of the white candles wavered softly over Finvar's pale skin with the gentle rise and fall of the ship. Sir Salarond stood by the door, in case Finvar's heart should stop with the shock, and Sir Thoron had insisted on being present as well: he watched, his eagle-nosed face grave, as Arudal slipped off his tunic and breeches and lay full-length atop Finvar's body.

Arudal could feel himself blushing hotly under their knight's gaze, uncomfortably aware of the warmth of Finvar's skin against his own, the firm power of the Artegalian's muscles under the velvety padding of his healthy plumpness and the scent of his clean thick hair tickling Arudal's nose. But someday Arudal would have to perform with Arothir under the eyes of a mage and a psychic healer from the House of Procreation: he breathed deeply, forcing his embarassment back until he could feel nothing but Finvar's chest lifting and sinking in perfect unison with him, Arudal's own pulse gradually slowing until it seemed that a single heart beat between them.

Arudal took a last breath and lowered his face until his lips touched Finvar's, closing his eyes, breathing slowly out into his friend's mouth, and pressing his awareness inwards with careful inexorability. For a moment, it seemed to Arudal that he was in two places at once: feeling Finvar's solid flesh beneath him as though he lay along the warm back of a powerful horse, and, at the same time, lying on his back beneath Arudal's own surprising lightness and tight-muscled strength, tasting the slight sweetness of cinnamon on his breath...Just in time, Arudal stopped himself from sinking too deeply.

Twice, now, he had untangled their minds; he knew how to ease away the skeins of Finvar's thoughts without breaking them, gently disengaging the other squire from himself as though he were soothing a hound's paw out of a wire snare.

Arudal opened his eyes. The Artegalian's were still closed, and Arudal's heart jolted: had Finvar slipped all the way from both bodies, Arudal easing him, not into his own flesh, but beyond the worlds' rings? Involuntarily, his hands tightened on Finvar's heavy shoulders.

Finvar's pale eyelashes fluttered. Arudal's strength all flowed out of his limbs in a warm tide of relief, leaving him slumped bonelessly on top of his squire-brother. Finvar looked up into his eyes, then, as if realizing where he was, glanced quickly about the room. Arudal's face was so close to Finvar's that he could feel the blush warming the other youth's cheeks when he saw the two knights watching them. Finvar did not actually jerk away, but Arudal could feel the Artegalian's muscles tightening beneath him, and self-consciously pushed himself up with his arms so that their chests no longer touched.

Finvar averted his eyes from Sir Thoron's uncomfortably. Suddenly, he muttered, "Ah, sod it. You saved my life...Come here, Ari." He reached up to drag Arudal back against his chest and kissed him soundly, then looked up at Sir Thoron, a defiant flush reddening his rounded cheeks. "And I don't want to hear anything about it. Sir."

Thoron grinned. "It's good to have you both back, squires. Better get well fast: I'm going to get as much work as I can out of the two of you while I still have your service."

"Get off my patient now, Ari," Sir Salarond ordered. "I want to have a look at him."

Arudal had not blushed when Finvar kissed him, but he could feel his cheeks flaming now as he rolled away, quickly getting into his clothes again. Still, his embarassment was nothing to the flood of happiness and relief that filled him as he looked at Finvar sitting up on the bed, fair hair disheveled about his thick shoulders and tilted gray-amber eyes bright with life.

The last task left to Arudal before they neared home waters was to restore the natural appearances of himself and his companions. Sir Salarond, however, only waved him away.

"Amanvon and Aviyani know I went through enough on this mission to gray my hair altogether," the healer-knight said ruefully. "It was happening naturally, in any case. Don't waste your effort."

"I was light-haired as a small child, and I like it well enough this way," Finvar added.

That left only Lostren and Arudal himself. Arudal had expected Lostren to be eager to get rid of the proof of his family's drop of Plainsman blood, but the Kantarean noble bit his lip, worrying at it thoughtfully before he spoke. "I don't know. If I were Lord Dan Iragal - the eldest son of my House - then there would be no choice. Even if I were second-born, it would make a difference. But there are three brothers between me and politics; that is why I was looking for an academic career. And what manner of fool would I be if I threw away the gift of Foresight because I could not bear to admit to its source, like a clumsy jeweler chipping a large gem to pieces because he had made its setting too small? No: however uncomfortable it may be sometimes, I shall not barter my own substance for a false claim about my distant ancestors, however deeply I might once have believed in it."

Is that meant to counsel me, as well? Arudal wondered. In truth, he had been tempted to leave his own hair golden, as if, he realized, to proclaim that he was closer to the Elves than to Arurak Aglarek who had bought the twisting of their line-gift with six Elvish lives, their expense to be accounted along with the prices of gems and vorgath by the Last Emperor's seneschal. Yet he remembered his Mind-Healer telling him when he had wept over the humiliation of being sent to the school library while the other students his age were learning archery, "If part of you, knowing or not, seeks to deny the burdens that your ability brings, then you will build yourself a wall in secret, to block your talent when you need it most."

When Arudal had finished his spell, he sat still for a few moments to shake off the slight dizziness, then reached for his mirror.

"I will get used to it," he told himself firmly, wrenching his gaze back to his black-haired reflection. "How will my father feel if I flinch away when he comes to welcome me home?" He put the mirror down and opened his chest, lifting out the neatly-folded clothes and stacking them on his narrow bed. The Imperial Crown lay at the bottom, its gold and rubies glowing dully against the cream-streaked red wood. Within its ring were the ruby-set spurs and chain Emperor Arurak had given him; beside it rested the sword, the opalescent gleam of its dragon-tooth hilt shining inside the neat white coil of the Imperial knight's belt. Arudal unhooked the sheath from the belt, lifting the sword out. It was the best weapon he had ever held, or was ever likely to: King Edril's blade, though passed down from Avalar through the generations of Kantarean rulers, was no finer. Tomorrow he would start practicing with it.

Chapter 29: The Prince's Judgement

"Full-awesome and royal, a storm is his ire,
His mind shines in darkness to kindle our fire,
Shaped forth by the gods as our ruler and hope,
Gift beyond all that we understand.
In battle and bloodshed, upon wind-tossed wave,
We give our lives to him, to spend or to save,
And trust in his wisdom to judge and command
For the life of his folk and his land."
- "Hymn to the Prince," Tharandrostan anthem

They were two weeks' sailing from the Middle Land when, at sword-training one morning, Dame Karsil backed up and touched the point of her blunted practice blade to the deck. She did not shade her brow against the light with her hand as a Man would; the Sun's brightness dazzled through her green eyes as though it struck through shallow water. "Is that not a greatship of Tharandrost?"

Arudal had no hope of seeing the ship, but the others lowered their weapons as well, taking their helms off and squinting eastward against the sunlight.

"Helmsman, about course," Sir Salarond ordered. "Evasive maneuvers as necessary."

The dromon spun nimbly over the low swells as Miraran barked orders to the sailors hauling on their ropes. Wind freshened the sails as they turned, lifting the ship more swiftly.

"She's gaining fast," Sir Eroth reported. "No doubt that she's following us."

Sir Salarond stared over the rear starboard rail, weighing their choices. He straightened abruptly. "Put about. We'll go to meet her. That is the Pride of Tharabruthnan."

Arudal drew in his breath. The Pride of Tharabruthnan was Prince Norombar's flagship. "Is the Prince on board, sir?"

"I cannot see the flags clearly enough yet..." Sir Salarond watched until another light gust of wind skipped over the waves, tugging at their sails. "Yes."

Belatedly by some ten months, it came to Arudal that he had defied the Prince's personal decree by going with the expedition to the West. Being squire to a Kantarean knight was acceptable enough - but what would be said about him using his oath to Sir Thoron as a means to dodge a ranking diplomatic officer's enquiries and break a law of the State?

Finvar clapped Arudal on the shoulder, gauntlet ringing off his squire-brother's pauldron. "Don't look so scared, Ari. We'll protect you." Arudal managed a sickly smile.

"Armour down, scrub off, into dress uniforms or formal equivalent, weapons by your own choice," Salarond ordered. "Estimated time of rendevous?"

Miraran spared a glance to starboard. "Perhaps half a candlemark, sir."

"Just enough time. Get to it."

Fortunately, the White Company's dress uniform was simple enough to get into that Sir Thoron needed no help changing clothes: his squires had only to give his formal knee-length boots a swift polish to get the dust off and brush the wet tangle of his dark hair into some semblance of order. The tunic was deep azure velvet with the eight-pointed star of Kantar embroidered in gold thread upon the chest. The right shoulder bore the emblem of the White Company, an argent lancer upon a light azure field; the left showed Sir Thoron's own heraldry, a greathelm gules on a field or. Although the velvet was neatly creased along the lines where it had lain folded for close to a year, the dust had shaken out of it easily, and the deep azure silk of his trousers might have been freshly washed that morning. Thoron's heavy chain of fealty was plain gold, his spurs gold set with Kantar's eight-pointed star of topaz; he wore a short cape of deep azure velvet trimmed with cloth-of-gold. The only incongruous detail was the scuffed and stained white leather of his sword-belt - shabby against the fine cloths and gold of the uniform, though it matched his craggy features and rough calloused hands better than the silk and velvet did.

Finvar had a simpler version of the dress uniform, lacking the cape, made in heavy blue linen instead of velvet and silk, and displaying Thoron's arms in place of those of the White Company on his right shoulder. He passed his sleeve quickly over his coronet and set it on his head, looking up to catch Arudal staring.

"Ugly, isn't it?" Finvar said, smiling brightly.

Dear as the Artegalian was to him, Arudal had to admit that ugly was the only word for the coronet of the heir to Helludal. The upper part was shaped roughly like a castle's battlements, but each crenellation bore a Stone Troll's severed head rendered in full gruesome detail, with lolling tongues, wide staring eyes, and even tiny teardrop-shaped emeralds dribbling down unevenly from each tattered gold neck. Arudal had to look a little closer to see the details on the lower part of the ring, which was just as well: the gold's molding showed the dismembered bodies of the Stone Trolls with stalks of ripe wheat shooting up between the corpses.

"It grieves me to say this," Arudal answered soberly, "but one of your forebears had all the taste and elegance of a drunken Dwarf."

"My father's coronet is even bigger and uglier. As is he." Finvar grinned. "Do you need some help with your dress?"

It was as well that the Kantarean uniforms were relatively simple, because Arudal did need a little assistance to get dressed in time. He wore the same blue-back silk robe with white seed-pearl embroidery he had worn in Lord Hatneth's hall, with the Count-heir's circlet of silver set with black star sapphires holding his damp hair back. Though he girded his waist with the battered squire's belt Sir Thoron had given him, draping the silver chain of fealty to his knight about his neck. Arudal knew that his belt - so worn and scraped now that the red dye was hardly visible - must look even more out of place on his clothes than his knight's did, especially with the magnificent ruby-set sheath and opalescent hilt of the Imperial sword glittering and shimmering against it, but he wore it proudly.

If his squiring to Sir Thoron had started out as a legal trick - even, as Arudal had suspected sometimes, as halfway a practical joke on Dr. Grímhjálm's part - it had become as true as anyone's.

Arudal was just giving the silver-filigreed toe-points of Valderian steel on his good shoes a final polish when he felt the dromon glide to a halt. "Up to the deck, squires," Sir Thoron boomed, striding out of the cabin with Arudal and Finvar trailing obediently behind him.

Even through the day-mist, Arudal could see that the Pride of Tharabruthnan towered over the Kantarean dromon like an ancient oak-tree over a small bush. The Tharandrostan greatship's sides were painted a gleaming pale blue, with the two words of her name - Khatir Tharabruthnu - standing out in stark black strokes. A shield had been outlined on her bow, showing the arms of Tharandrost, the single vorgath tower on the light azure field, with the State's motto, A Fortress Unyielding, scribed in delicate black lines below. Arudal felt the cold creeping into his bowels, like dark seawater seeping into a ship's hold through an unseen crack in the planking. *They wouldn't have sent a greatship, let alone the Prince's flagship, just for me - would they? Unless the Prince had decreed his crime hideous enough for a formal trial of treason...But surely he would have ordered me brought back to Tharabruthnan for that, not come to me himself?*

Of the Kantarean knights and their squires, only Arudal and Malni were not in uniform. Malni wore a plain blue gown girdled with her red squire's belt, her silver chain of fealty dangling between her firm little breasts. Her female presence made Arudal feel more out of place in his long silk robe, especially when he saw how little even Rhys' ruddy close-cropped beard and gangly Plainsman build distracted from the uniform that marked him as part of the White Company unit - though Rhys' squire-belt was looped about his shoulder rather than his waist, as was the custom when a squire's knight was slain and he still wished to mark his station and loyalty.

Dear Amandeth, how can we take a free Plainsman to greet the Prince? But Arudal would not be the one to speak against it: he knew that, at need, his comrades would defend him just as fiercely as they would stand up for Rhys - as he himself would, if it came down to that.

The Pride of Tharabruthnan lowered a rope ladder, its strands looking ridiculously small and fragile against the greatship's side. In order of rank, each of the White Company members climbed down the dromon's side to the Kantarean ship's small landing-boat. Malni, coming last, had a great deal of difficulty holding her skirt about her legs and her grip on the ladder at the same time. Arudal had seen on shipboard that climbing did not come easy to her: she outweighed him by at least a stone, and though her arms were quite strong for a Common woman's, she had never climbed so much as a tree in her village. And even Arudal, hampered as much by his robes as Karsil's squire by her gown, found himself wishing more and more profusely that Sir Thoron had thought to get him a squire's uniform when his knight had requisitioned the plate armour.

The boat crossed the short reach between the two ships. "Permission to come aboard?" Sir Salarond shouted up to the deck in his flawless Imperial.

"Permission granted," the crisp reply came down.

Going up the rope ladder in his formal garb would have been easier than coming down, if Arudal had not been uncomfortably conscious that there was a female just below him. *She won't look; I'm sure she's having enough trouble pulling herself up as it is.*

Thoughts of Malni and the mechanics of climbing a rope ladder in his long robes distracted Arudal until he reached the deck, but when he climbed over the railing, his knees were trembling so hard that he had to steady himself with a hand on the silken wood for a moment. The knight who stood watching them was not dressed in the blue uniform of the Tharandrostan navy: his adamantine breastplate glittered clear over the black tunic and deep red trousers of the Silent Guard. The insignia-chain around his neck bore a single medal, a black sea-eagle enamelled upon a blue field inside two gold rings: a lieutenant-commander.

"Welcome aboard, your Grace, my lords and ladies, your Excellency," he said. "Refreshments are served in the Prince's Hall. If you will follow me…"

Arudal felt as though a fist had unclenched from around his heart. He did not know what the protocol for crimes against the State was - none had happened in his lifetime, to his knowledge - but he was sure that if he were to be tried, he would have been arrested at once, not cordially greeted by an officer of the Silent Guard and invited for refreshments.

As they followed the lieutenant-commander along the deck, Arudal was conscious of a strange feeling. The small muscles of his face and body were relaxing as they had hardly ever done since he had left Tharandrost for Var Perenil, as if, somewhere deep below his awareness, he knew he was home. But he could also sense his sight trying to slip into Shadow as he caught the precise day-misted movements of the sailors and soldiers along the deck in the edges of his vision, and could not shake the nagging feeling that, if he let his eyes darken, he would be able to see them clearly…*as if I were back in the Fallen Seat.*

The Prince's Hall of the *Pride of Tharabruthnan* was all that Arudal could have expected. Though he could not see well enough to make out the details of the murals on the walls, their jewel-like greens and blues, opalescent whites and shining blacks, nevertheless filled him with a sense of great beauty. The floor was planked with exotic hardwoods from the far South, deep rich purple and red with streaks of cream swirling through the grain. In the calm spring weather, no waves reached high enough to stain the sparkling windows with white patches of salt.

A huge crystal candelabra hung from the ceiling, though there were no candles in it. The long oval table in the middle of the room was made of ivory inlaid with malachite and lapis. Crystal decanters of deep red and pale golden wine, interspersed with clear water and gently steaming carafes of black-roast tea, glittered along its length between plates of elaborately beautiful small food: flowers whose white and pink petals were parchment-thin slices of smoked fish, centred with black heaps of caviare and surrounded by feathery fronds of chervil; sculptures in ruddy-brown pate and tartare, tiny peeled songbird-eggs piled in the huge creamy shells of ostrich eggs…

A broad-shouldered man in a light azure silken tabard embroidered with the Vorgath Tower - one of the Prince's own servants - gave Arudal a plate of delicacies and asked what he would have to drink. His perfectly polished manners reminded Arudal, with a sudden pang, of Ostarak's unschooled efforts to act as his orderly, and Arudal had to swallow down a lump in his throat before he said, "Dry white wine, half-watered, please."

"Very good, sir."

Arudal dipped his tiny silver spoon into the caviare, letting a few eggs roll about on his tongue for a moment before they burst with the familiar salty-musky flavour. There were a surprising number of people in the room, as though the Prince had brought half his court with him. Arudal wished that he could see their faces: it had become easy for him to identify his White Company companions by size and stance, as long as he could make their shapes out at all, but it had been too long since he had been in any sizable gathering.

"Miru!" a cracked female voice said by his shoulder. Arudal looked around in surprise. It was his grandmother Zinadir, swathed in deep red silk and a silvery sealskin cape. Zinadir was leaning on her sharp-tipped stave of polished red yew bound with patterned Valderian steel - the stave of the ruler of the Hidden Estate; thirty years ago, she had used it only for magic and ceremonial occasions, but now, two decades past her three hundredth year, it was support as well as weapon and emblem of office. From her girdle hung a dagger with a gleaming vorgath hilt and sheath, the pommel set with small adamants in the shape of a tower - the ceremonial weapon honouring her two hundred years in the Spectral Service; other commemorative knives identified their bearers' posts more clearly, but the vorgath was given to all those who had done their military service to the State in a classified posting. Zinadir looked up at him, then approvingly down at the sword at his side. "That's Imperial work, isn't it?"

"Yes, Grandmother." Arudal might have been taken aback at her brusque greeting - after all, he had been missing for nearly a year. But his father's mother had never been one for voicing her affections: it told him more that she had left the Hidden Estate for the first time in fifteen years. He bent to brush his lips against her soft withered cheek, inhaling the faint scent of myrrh and spices that always hung about Zinadir from her work.

"You'll tell me after your debriefing, if you can. Arukhat! Where's that boy gotten to?"

"Here, Grandmother," Arudal's brother said, appearing out of the thronging mist and offering Zinadir his arm. He had grown a little even in the last year: ten years younger, he was already as tall as his elder sibling, though still sharp-boned and awkward in the folds of his black silken robe. The tilted corners of his gray-golden eyes crinkled with delight. "Praise Amandeth, you're back. We were told..."

Their grandmother raised a finger. "Ts ts. Everything in due time, Little Miru, and no information until after the debriefing, if you please."

Arudal knew that being called "Little Miru" annoyed his brother even more than being addressed by the diminutive irritated him, but Arukhat hardly seemed to notice this time. "Come on, the parents and Miri - "Arothir - "and Uridar are over this way."

Since Arukhat's gifts of Mindspeaking were for the living, not the dead, he did not suffer from the Shadow-blindness of their line-talent. With the smoothness of long practice, he guided Zinadir and Arudal through the crowd, until Arudal stood before his parents at last.

Count Arumir and Countess Minlulin were dressed in their finest court garb, black silks and velvets with silver trimming and gray-pearl embroidery, wearing coronets which matched Arudal's except for the addition of large black pearls tipping each of the points. Arudal's father also wore his full knightly regalia: gleaming white belt, fealty-chain and adamant-set spurs of adamantine-dusted Valderian steel, and his great-great-grandfather's sword with the sheath of green-black sea-dragon's hide. A few more strands of silver than Arudal had remembered streaked Minlulin's coiled black braids; otherwise, they had not changed in the slightest.

Though Arudal's smile was unfeigned, his back tightened as Count Arumir scolded gently, "My son, you have been gone a very long time." Almost the same words...almost the same face! But Arudal's father was grinning at him with a look of heartfelt joy that was nothing like the cold pride of the Fallen Emperor, and when the Count reached out to clasp his son's wrist, his hand was warm with life. "We look forward to hearing everything you are allowed to tell us when the time comes." Then, though Tharandrostans seldom displayed their feelings so openly in public, Arumir pulled his son into a tight embrace. When his father let go of him, Arudal turned to kiss his mother on the cheek, and he could see that her long black eyelashes were spiked with wetness.

"We are so glad to have you home," Countess Minlulin murmured. "Poor Arothir was nearly mad with worry."

Arudal glanced over her shoulder to his golden-haired cousin. Arothir smiled and shrugged slightly, as if they didn't both know for whom Minlulin was really speaking.

"I'm glad to be home, Mother," he said. At the moment, at least, it was true, although he could feel a faint stirring of dread beneath his happiness, like a trail of ants marching under a ripe sweet peach, at the thought of the debriefing to come. *For to say it, I must think it...*

Arothir and Uridar came forward to trade wrist-clasps with Arudal. Uridar, the son of Arudal's mother's brother, wore the black robes and black star sapphire medallion of his office as a priest of Amandeth. On him, the family features were exaggerated to homeliness, all points and angles, but enlivened by a sense of humour that, like a strong wine, had grown dry and mellow with maturity. He greeted Arudal cheerfully, but with a disconcerting intentness in his gold-centred eyes, as though his growing experience in the temple of the Judge of Souls had taught him how to discern the smallest signs of a troubled heart.

Looking at Arothir, Arudal caught his breath: he might have been gazing at a female twin of himself as he had been in the West. Arothir had the same peak-tipped ears, sharp-arched golden eyebrows, and delicate moulding of cheekbones and jawline that had let Arudal pass for Elvish kin - she could almost have been Karsil's half-sister. Her tilted leaf-shaped eyes, clear ice-gray about the amber corona ringing their pupils, stared up into his with the wide, half-startled look of the Shadow-misted. Arothir's rich golden hair hung straight to her waist, held back from her face by her ruby-set silver coronet.

Although she was entitled to the dress uniform of a Communications lieutenant, today she wore the deep gules and argent of the Ramozapar House, her father's line. The cut of her dark red velvet gown with its white fur trim at neck, wrists, and hem, though modest, was still close enough to show her excellent configuration, draping softly over her full breasts and broad swimmer's shoulders. A girdle of ruby-set silver plates gathered the rich material in at Arothir's waist, its deep folds flaring slightly over her trim little hips and falling straight to her matching velvet shoes. After looking up at Malni and Karsil for so long, it was a relief for Arudal to see a woman an inch shorter than himself.

"Do you know yet if you will be staying in Tharabruthnan for some time?" his cousin asked after they had exchanged greetings. Her voice was light and even, as if the question were no more than a pleasantry, but Arudal knew what she meant: Shall we be wedded soon?

"I won't know until later." And much as I worried about my homecoming, now that I am here, I do not know if I can bring myself to go back to a student's life in Var Perenil. Yet Arudal could not imagine himself married, either...

Arothir seemed about to say something else, but she stopped, her eyes widening.

Turn around and make your respect, she said sharply into his mind - it occurred to Arudal then that he had forgotten just how bossy Arothir could be. The Prince is behind you.

Startled as he was, Arudal turned with reasonable grace, bowing with his palms pressed together before his face, as was appropriate for greeting Tharandrost's ruler at an informal occasion. Straightening, he needed a moment to take in what he saw. He recognised the ruling Prince's crown of ice-clear adamantine sculpted with a ring of towers - the same heraldic principle, in truth, as the coronet of Helludal, but crafted with exquisite delicacy and subtlety - and the pale azure robes trimmed with sable and set with tiny adamants. But Prince Norombar had been some sixty years older than Arudal's father: past two hundred, solid and graying, with the first wrinkles showing on his forehead and in the corners of his eyes. The man who stood before Arudal in the regalia of Tharandrost's ruler was close to Arudal's own age, lithely muscled and clear-skinned, though there was something in the set of his chiseled young face and the depth of his steel-and-amber eyes that suggested wisdom beyond his years. Taught from childhood how disconcerting his own agathurok's stare could be, Arudal was not accustomed to being daunted by anyone else's gaze, but more than his usual politeness made him drop his eyes.

Prince Dolkhat? he thought. Ruling Prince now; but that would mean that Prince Norombar is dead. Or abdicated...No; he was far too young to give over the Adamantine Crown, unless some sudden ill struck him, and I cannot think of any infirmity save age that our healers could not have dealt with...

"Greetings, Count Arudal," said Prince Dolkhat. "We are glad to see you here, as the question of your safe return was a matter of some concern to Us. We look forward to hearing the account of your adventure very shortly."

"Yes, Your Highness...Thank you, Your Highness," Arudal stammered.

"I trust you found your travels as a squire with the White Company as illuminating as I did myself when I served under Sir Salarond."

"Your Highness, it was..." Arudal stopped, trying to think of how he could possibly describe their mission. The only thing that came to his mind was the phrase Sir Thoron had used on the journey towards the West: Half-planned, half-legal, mostly half-arsed, and altogether successful.

Prince Dolkhat's laugh was soft, with an edge of ruefulness in it like a single leaf of wormwood in a sweet cordial. "Indeed." The Prince nodded to Arudal's family. "Lady Zinadir, your Excellencies, Lady Arothir, Lord Uridar. If you will excuse Us, We require Count Arudal's presence."

Prince Dolkhat strode quickly through the hall. Twice he stopped, raising an eyebrow, and someone broke from conversation, joining them. Arudal recognised Sir Daurar as soon as the diplomat came close enough. Prince Dolkhat's other choice was a slender older woman in the light azure and silver robes of the Dalapar - seven of the most powerfully gifted minds in the State, the Prince's personal guard who also served as his most trusted counsellors.

"Sir Daurar, Count Arudal, I believe you have already met. Lady Eplateril, Count Arudal." Arudal bowed to Eplateril, and she returned him a polite nod.

Eight members of the Silent Guard stood outside the stateroom to which the Prince led them. The knights came to attention at once, saluting sharply in unison. "Your orders, Your Highness?" asked the unit's commander, a heavy-featured soldier with a braid of waist-length black hair.

"Continue on guard, Dame Gathukhizir. We are not to be disturbed."

Arudal blinked at the title. The Silent Guard's gravelly voice had not given her sex away; she was as tall as most men, five foot six or so, and there was nothing feminine about either her face or her stockily muscled shape. Sterile from birth - yet Arudal could not help his pang of envy, sharp as the familiar shock of biting down on copper: but for his ancestor's taint, he, too, could have been a member of the elite fighting unit from which the handicaps of his talent had barred him.

The stateroom was luxuriously appointed, its velvet-cushioned chairs deep and comfortable. Surprisingly so; granting his lack of experience with the military, Arudal still thought they were more suitable to sitting about after dinner with sweet wine than to an official debriefing.

The Prince sat up straight, fixing his gaze on Arudal. "We hardly need to say that this discussion is classified at the highest levels. Arudal, when we are through, you will be told what is acceptable for general repetition."

"Yes, Your Highness."

"Our father was informed of your mysterious disappearance with the White Company, but, in accordance with his general policy of inactivity in regards to the world outside Tharandrost's borders, did not choose to follow it up. With the growing instability of the Kantarean political climate, We saw that such a policy was no longer to Our benefit, and Challenged him for the sake of the realm. Upon Our victory, We devoted considerable resources to the attempt to locate you, both for the sake of your own value to the State, and from concern as to the activities for which you had been recruited by Kantar. However, your distance and the protections against scrying, both with magic and mind-magic, that were upon you, meant that We could not keep a full watch - even though," the Prince added with the slightest smile of satisfaction, "the wards on your vessel were not enough to keep Our diviners from tracing it as you got closer, since they had your person to fix upon. We know that you were on the Western continent, moving towards the area of the Imperial Seat, and that your soul was concealed in Shadow and wrapped about in remarkably powerful magic for a time, but returned to the green earth some weeks ago. Now We require a complete account from the time when you were first approached by the White Company."

Arudal had to use all his self-control not to physically squirm. As a Tharandrostan, he had his duty to his Prince - but he was sworn to Sir Thoron, and, at least in theory, the personal oath of fealty was supposed to override the normal ties of citizenship.

"Your Highness," Arudal said painfully. "I may not speak of this without Sir Thoron's permission."

Prince Dolkhat only looked at Arudal. Arudal dug his nails into his palms, his bowels twisting with guilt. A squire who betrayed his country under orders of his knight could still be hanged for treason, even though the bond of chivalric fealty was a legal tie as well as a moral one. *But this secret will do no harm to the State*, Arudal thought desperately. *It is a matter for Kantar, not for us.*

The Prince's eyes narrowed, his nostrils flaring. "The affairs of Kantar are Our affairs as well. We have been allied with the White Crown for nearly seventeen hundred years, and cannot turn our backs at such a time as this, when King Edril's realm threatens to break asunder. Tell Us."

Arudal shook his head desperately, like a horse trapped in a tiny stable during a thunderstorm; he would have reared and plunged if he could have. "Your Highness, do you command me to break my squire's oath?"

If Prince Dolkhat recognised Arudal's panic - and Tharandrost's royal line had been bred for mind-magic more carefully than any other, so that, to Dolkhat's empathic sense, Arudal's frantic fear must feel like a thousand tiny birds breaking their wings against a window in frenzied terror - his calm face showed no sign of it. "Your loyalty to your knight, and to your oath, does you credit," he mused. The Prince's steady gaze shifted away into empty space, and the gold ring around his pupils seemed to flare more brightly, even as his eyes glazed over. Arudal recognised Prince Dolkhat's absent stare of concentration at once: it was the look of a Mind-Speaker touching another's thoughts.

The Prince blinked, his eyes focusing on Arudal once more. "If you were no longer bound by a squire's vows, would you then be willing to do as We require?"

"Sir Arudal, your duty to your companions is done, your oaths wholly fulfilled and your purpose with them accomplished..." But that had not been so: there was more to Arudal's oath, or his duty, than the letter of a contract. Yet by the same token, I have my duty to the State - yet I would not betray the friends who trust me. And the Prince can command me to request release from my vow, but he cannot command Sir Thoron to release me; though, if I ask it now... A sharp spasm of pain ripped through Arudal's chest at the thought of what he would have to do. But surely I knew all along that I could not continue as Thoron's squire past this mission?

"Your Highness," Arudal said at last, "will you allow me converse alone with Sir Salarond before I must answer that question?"

"Not Sir Thoron?" A smile flickered at the corners of Prince Dolkhat's lips, so quickly that it was gone before Arudal was sure he had seen it. "For the sake of your honour - and make no mistake, Our subjects' honour is Our own, for which reason We have not yet simply commanded you to speak - We shall grant your request. Inform Dame Gathukhizir when you have reached a decision."

"You know that I am under direct orders from the White Crown to preserve the confidentiality of this mission," Salarond told Arudal severely. The healer-knight sat straight-backed on the edge of one of the too-comfortable chairs, and Arudal felt like a clumsy schoolchild who had been called up for spattering ink with his quill once too often.

"Yes, sir. I am asking for your counsel as judge and as priest, not for your orders as commander."

"I see. An hypothetical situation, then."

"If you will, sir."

"In that case, I shall ask you an hypothetical question. Can you think of any effect that the Prince's knowledge of the purpose of our mission would have upon Kantar?"

Arudal thought about it. The genealogies would take time yet to untangle: their purpose had been to find the information that would make a decision between the rival claimants possible, not to make the decision themselves. The Prince's knowledge that a legitimate resolution was possible...could only aid that resolution. Unless it was his purpose to destabilize Kantar, that Tharandrost might profit from its chaos: the Empire might have done that in its latter millennia. In which case, the Pride of Tharabruthnan, with its large troop of Silent Guardsmen and the Dalapar aboard, could, no matter what skills or talents the Secret Service crew had, easily annihilate the Kantarean dromon and the documents that Tirothar and Sir Shakhor - not to mention Finvar, but for Arudal's mind-gifts - had died for. But if he would do that, then I can no longer be a Tharandrostan. No more than I could have aided Emperor Arurak, when it came to the moment of choice.

"Only to its good," Arudal said firmly.

Salarond smiled, the look on his lean face - satisfied? Does he want me to tell Prince Dolkhat what he cannot, to enlist his former squire's aid?

"Then, if you were no longer bound by your oath and through that fealty obliged to obey the commands of the White Crown, and if you were to report all our actions to your Prince, whom would you be betraying?"

"No one."

"Have you found the answer to your question then, Ari?"

"Yes, sir. Thank you."

Arudal stood up to tell Dame Gathukhizir that he was ready to answer the Prince's last question, but Salarond stopped him with a wave of his hand as the Tharandrostan turned towards the door. "Ask them to let his Highness know that I would speak to him myself before he proceeds with you, if he finds that acceptable."

Arudal repeated Sir Salarond's request to the muscular female knight. Her heavy black brows drew together in concentration as she looked off into empty air. "His Highness gives you permission to return to the Prince's Hall. Sir Bagnugar, be so good as to accompany his Excellency."

Arudal peered about in search of his family, wanting the reassurance of their presence more than anything. A hand touched his arm, and he started violently. "It's all right, Ari. Just me," Finvar said. Arudal looked at him gratefully, glad for the distraction - although he could not bear to think of telling Finvar that he would soon no longer be the Artegalian's squire-brother. "Are you looking for that blond girl? - Is she the cousin you're betrothed to, by the way?"

"Yes."

"Amanvon, if I had a cousin who looked like that, I wouldn't mind being told to marry her," Finvar said fervently. "I was hoping she wasn't taken, but at least she's going to a good home."

Even tense and frightened as he was, Arudal almost laughed at that.

"What's funny?"

"You sound as though you're talking about one of your wolfhounds."

Finvar thought about it a moment, then laughed himself. "That's a compliment, if you like. Will you introduce me to her? I promise I'll behave...There she is."

Finvar guided Arudal through the crowd. The Artegalian's heavy build and ash-blond hair were conspicuous enough to draw attention, and at five foot eight, he was taller than most of the Tharandrostan men. Though Finvar seemed at ease with the quick furtive glances as they walked through the hall, he hung onto his squire-brother even after they had reached Arudal's family as though Arudal were an amulet of safe passage. Count Arumir quirked a slanted eyebrow. "Back so soon? Who is your companion?" He did not ask, Is all well? but Arudal could see the worried question in his bright amber-gray eyes - Arumir was not an agathudal, but an empath; if they had been alone, he would have had as much of his son's fears out as Arudal was permitted to tell.

"He doesn't speak Imperial very well, Father." Arudal switched over to Common. "Father, this is my squire-brother, Lord Finvar dath Helludal. Finvar, my father, Count Arumir."

"A pleasure to meet you, Lord Finvar," Arudal's father said, clasping Finvar's wrist heartily. He glanced at Finvar's other hand, still on Arudal's arm, and smiled. "You are my son's beloved friend?"

"Uh?" Finvar said, wrinkling his nose in puzzlement.

"Not exactly," Arudal said in Imperial. "And the expression doesn't exist in Common, Father." Before his father could say anything else embarassing, Arudal hastened through the rest of the introductions. Finvar clasped wrists with Arukhat and Uridar, bowed formally to Zinadir and Minlulin; but he stepped forward to lift Arothir's hand in his, brushing his lips against the back of her palm. Arothir jerked back in shock as Arukhat and Uridar took reflexive half-steps forward to defend her. Finvar's head snapped back beneath an invisible blow.

Dear gods, thought Arudal, have I gotten so used to foreigners that I didn't notice that in time to stop him?

"I'm sorry," Finvar said, bewildered. "What did I do?" The white mark on his right cheek was slowly reddening; Arothir had slapped him hard with her mind.

"That's a Kantarean custom, Miri," Zinadir told Arothir tartly. "Stop gaping, the boy didn't mean anything by it. Lord Finvar, here it is not acceptable for a man to make intimate contact with a fertile woman, especially one who is unmarried."

"Oh. I...I'm sorry. I really didn't mean to offend, Lady Arothir. Please forgive me?"

Arothir's delicate nostrils narrowed, and she shifted her stance, settling her weight a little. Finvar would not recognise the threat, but Arudal did, reflecting ruefully that he had also forgotten his cousin's bad temper. He knew that Arothir would never disgrace her family by doing physical violence in public, especially not to a foreign guest and most especially not on the Prince's flagship. Still, the suggestion that she might like to was extraordinarily rude.

Arudal leaned forward. "If you don't stop it right now, I'm going to throw all your dolls overboard," he whispered in Imperial: his direst threat from their childhood. Arothir glared at him, but could not sustain it, her mouth twitching into a reluctant smile. We are splashing each other in sunlit water; but soon the ebb tide will suck back into a maelstrom.

"Of course, Lord Finvar," Arothir told the Artegalian sweetly.

Finvar suddenly started, his hand tightening reflexively on Arudal's arm, but he recovered quickly, bowing to Arothir with a courtly smile. "As is your pleasure, my lady."

It was Arothir's turn to look at Finvar in confusion. Arudal knew she had just spoken in his mind; probably something like, But if you touch me again, I'll kill you.

"Well-said, Finvar," Arudal murmured. "Welcome to the family."

"Lord Finvar, Arudal, will you be introducing us to your knight today?" Arudal's mother asked swiftly before any of them could make matters worse.

Arudal was about to answer when the deep ringing call of a bass horn echoed through the Prince's Hall. His bickering with Arothir had loosened some of his tension; now it sprang back like the stave of a snapped bow, catching him in the gut, and for a horrible moment Arudal was afraid that he might lose control of his bowels. Glancing about nervously, he saw now that high-backed benches carved from the same deep purple and red woods as the hall's planking had been laid out on either side of the long table. At the end of the hall, the glitter of Prince Dolkhat's throne shone clear even through the thick day-mist on Arudal's sight.

Though wrought in adamantine, it was no more than a low chair, starkly plain except for the two horses' heads on the back corners - the style of the old Imperial officer's chairs, a reminder, like the formal wearing of weapons, of the State's origins as a military colony.

"You should sit beside your knight," Count Arumir said quietly to his son. "Go on, now."

The White Company knights and their squires were seated in a row right at the front. Rhys was holding up well, although his green eyes showed more white than usual. Malni simply looked stunned; Karsil sat rigidly silent; but Sir Eroth and Lostren both seemed comfortable enough, though they were sitting forward as though they expected something to happen. Sir Thoron grinned fearsomely at Arudal as he slid into his place, which made Arudal feel even worse. Amandeth, how can I tell him that I have to withdraw my squire's oath?

The bass horn sounded again, three lengthy deep blasts shivering through the floor-planks, followed by the drumbeat of boot-steps. Nine of the Silent Guard knights marched down the hall in a square, three by three; behind them, around Prince Dolkhat, walked the five men and two women in the pale blue and white robes of the Dalapar, followed by another square of nine Silent Guards.

Prince Dolkhat seated himself on his glittering throne as his guards arranged themselves about him. When they were all in position, he lifted his hand. Hovering flames sprang forth above the crystal branches of the ceiling candelabra, moving gently as the candelabra swung with the slow roll of the greatship. A herald in the Prince's livery stepped forward.

HEAR AND HEARKEN, YE NOBLE ONES! As was customary in Tharandrost, the herald spoke only in a mind-voice, though one so powerful only the completely insenate could fail to hear it. The more sensitive would have to put up their shields; it came muted, although clear, to Arudal's half-Shadowed mind. THE COURT OF PRINCE DOLKHAT NOROMBARUN, RULER OF THARANDROST, NOW BEGINS. ATTEND YE TO THE WORDS OF THE FLOWER OF OUR RACE; ATTEND YE TO THE WISDOM OF THE HIGHEST OF OUR BLOOD; ATTEND YE TO THE WILL OF THE PRINCE. The bass horn blew once more, pure and deep in the silence of the ship-hall, as the herald withdrew.

Prince Dolkhat spoke both aloud - the Prince's courtesy to his Kantarean guests, Arudal knew - and in the minds of his court. "Ye nobles of Tharandrost, We call ye to witness Our words this day. Of all the honours of Our realm, there is one that may never be conferred by birth or preference, but only won by painful struggle of body or mind, by the nobility of soul shown forth in deeds of valour and chivalry: that is the honour of knighthood."

Arudal froze in his place. It had not shocked him half so much when the Fallen Emperor granted him the knightly accolade to loose him from his squire's vow - granted in Shadow and a ghost's mind, it had been no more real on the green earth than the remembered outer doors of the Imperial Library. But Dolkhat was Tharandrost's Prince, and a knight himself: how could he even think of creating another knight for the sake of the legal technicality which would free Arudal from his oath? It had been one thing for a scholar to be temporarily squired to a foreigner under such a pretense, but...

The Prince continued, his mind-voice beating away the midges of Arudal's thoughts. "We bear this burden, as did Our father Norombar before us: that it is the most able of Our men, the most valued seed of Our race, whom We must risk in the greatest dangers, and place as a sea-break between Tharandrost and her foes. They go willingly at Our command, upholding that discipline which has preserved Our people and the ways of our forebears from the earliest days. Yet there are some who set forth unasked when they see peril or hope, to offer their lives without stint for the sake of those who wait behind: by this is the flower of chivalry known. As Prince of Tharandrost, and Ourself a knight, it is Our honour and duty to recognise those who have thus shown forth the heart of knighthood. Count Arudal Arumirun, come forth!"

Arudal had not lost his footing in a mild sea since he was old enough to toddle, but he was shaking so hard that he almost stumbled when the gentle rise of the ship over a swell caught him by surprise. He made his way forward, kneeling before the Adamantine Throne.

"Although Count Arudal's deeds themselves must be clothed in silence for the sake of the State, I would call those who know them to speak for him. Sir Thoron of the White Company, come forth!" The Prince paused, and Arudal guessed that he was repeating his words in Common within Sir Thoron's mind.

Arudal heard his knight's heavy tread on the hardwood planks, then Thoron's rough voice. "Your Highness, you know I am a man for fighting rather than speaking. Ari - Count Arudal - didn't become my squire because he wanted to, but because he had to. But he grew into one of the best I've had. Even when he was afraid, he never let it stop him from doing the right thing, and for..." For a Tharandrostan, Arudal thought, smiling in spite of himself... "Um, anyway, he was always pretty well-behaved. He was a good squire; I'm proud to have had the training of him, and he'll make a good knight for you."

"Thank you, Sir Thoron. Sir Salarond, Earl dath Amerel, come forward."

Though Sir Salarond did not seem to speak loudly, his voice filled the great hall. "Count Arudal came to us as a gently raised child, whose soul longed for learning rather than for war. Yet he stood without flinching even in his very first fight, though we faced dark and powerful foes. As Sir Thoron's squire, he bore himself bravely and courteously, ever willing to risk his life in order to save those of his comrades. Arudal is true to his friends, staunch against his foes in battle, and merciful to them in victory. He is kind to those below him; obedient to those set above him; towards the gods, devout; and chivalrous towards all. Ultimately, Arudal stood by himself against an evil unexpected and far beyond his strength. He triumphed by bravery, by the power of his mind-gifts, and by his heart's choice of what was right in the crucial moment, giving himself over to death without thought. I do not know how it came about that Arudal was preserved, nor what it was that restored him to us: I can only call it the blessing of the gods, and be thankful. However it was that the life Arudal gave was given back to him, his presence in the ranks of your chivalry will be an ornament to the realm."

Is he truly talking about me? Arudal wondered. I was so close to taking the Fallen Emperor's offer, though he cannot know it...

"Thank you, Sir Salarond. Count Arudal Arumirun, by the gifts Amandeth has given you, it is yours to do battle in Shadow and in secret. Your bloodline is a treasure of the State; now you have proven yourself truly worthy of it."

Looking up into Prince Dolkhat's face as he spoke, Arudal felt his stomach twist. Only the Mistress or Master of the Hidden Estate - and the Prince - were allowed to read the hidden archives of the House of Arudal. Though Prince Dolkhat's thoughts were shielded by adamant, he could not conceal the knowledge shadowing his eyes, no more than Arudal could hide the Shadow-chill of his own stare. His gaze fixed on the Prince's, Arudal was suddenly certain, without any phantom-gleam of doubt, that Dolkhat knew the same thing he had discovered in the darkness of the Imperial Library. The foul rite by which Duke Arurak had twisted the god-spark of Amanvon into Shadow and set his corruption of the Imperial line's mind-gift into the seed of his sons, and following on that, the choice of Prince Khatirost to protect and nurture Morthugor's touch...He knows.

"Arudal Arumirun, will you swear the oath of knighthood now?"

"I will," Arudal answered numbly, for he did not know what else to say. The Prince took Arudal's hands between his, speaking the words of the oath, and Arudal repeated them.

"I, Count Arudal Arumirun, now swear this oath. I shall uphold the realm of Tharandrost, its ruler and its laws and its folk, with sword and mind, ever faithful to my Prince and to my folk. I shall use all my power, fighting in such manner as is meetest for me, to defend women and children and all the weak; when need be, to strike down those who would harm them; to do justice and never injustice all the days of my life, and to strive for what is right, in the manner laid down for the order of chivalry in its earliest days. I shall never swear falsely, nor serve madness or vanity or a twisted will, but shall ride in the ways of honour, loyalty, and truth, whatever betide."

Prince Dolkhat held Arudal's hands tightly in his, his gaze never leaving Arudal's for a second. As sure as Arudal was of the Prince's knowledge, now he understood this: the Prince knew from whence the House's gift had sprung, but he also knew all of what Arudal had done with it, whether Sir Salarond had told him or he had found out by other means. That bright awareness flickered inside Arudal's mind - the brush of Dolkhat's thoughts, leaving Arudal with the sense of what the Prince would not say, neither openly nor between them in the privacy of their touch. Arudal's heart tightened with emotion as he spoke the final sentences of the vow, as if to press the last drop of his blood out in the words.

"Here I give my fealty and obedience to my Prince, to serve him in word and deed and will till the gods call me beyond the worlds' rings. So I, Count Arudal Arumirun, swear to you, Prince Dolkhat Norombarun, before Amanvon, Lord of Starlight, and Amandeth, Lord of Judgement."

"And for Our part, Count Arudal, We swear this to you. We shall defend you and that which is yours with all Our might of mind and sword; We shall uphold your honour as Our own, for the honour of Our subjects is the honour of Our realm. We shall return oath for oath, faith for faith, truth for truth, and while you are true to Us, We shall never fail you. So We, Prince Dolkhat Norombarun, swear this to you, Count Arudal Arumirun, in the sight of Amanvon, Lord of Starlight, and Amandeth, Lord of Judgement. Arudal, give Us your sword."

Arudal drew the Imperial blade slowly from his waist. The reflections of the Prince's flames above rippled down the patterns of black light-drinking vorgath and flashing silver Valderian steel. Careful as he was, as he handed the weapon hilt-first to Prince Dolkhat, its keen edges split the red brand-scars of the Imperial Crown on his palms, a thin trickle of bright red blood crawling down his upraised arms.

The Prince lifted the blade, his gaze running along its mingled light and darkness. "We give this sword, now to be the sword of your knighthood, into your hands again. Bear it well and carefully, holding in mind that it has not one edge, but two: let these be the edges of your discernment, severing good from evil, wisdom from folly, honour from dishonour." And the green earth from Shadow, the Prince said silently to Arudal, holding out the blade for him.

Arudal closed his hand on the hilt of his sword again, his blood reddening its opalescent smoothness. This matchless weapon, too, had been his ancestor's gift, and in the flame-brightened patterns on its blade, he read another thing. The knowledge of his mind-strength's source was a daemon's information: true in itself, but, nevertheless, meaningless within the fullness of the truth. It would be Arudal's duty as a knight, with mind and two-edged sword, to seek out that full truth by which his inheritance became a blessing, serving, rather than thwarting, the gods.

Prince Dolkhat drew his sword as Arudal sheathed his. He tapped Arudal with the flat, both shoulders, then the top of his head. "Arudal Arumirun, I dub thee once - I dub thee twice - I dub thee knight."

Though the Prince did not lift his hand, his mind-power struck Arudal's face like a clenched fist, snapping his head back and bringing a drop of blood to his lip. "May you receive no other blow without giving answer." Prince Dolkhat sheathed his sword, taking Arudal's blood-smeared hands to lift him up. "Arise, Sir Arudal, Knight of the Adamant."

BIOGRAPHY

K.Gundarsson: June 28, 1967 - Sept 29, 2021

From his humble beginnings, Gundarsson would make his mark on the world by writing on the most rare and obscure myths breathing new life into them, for a new generation of readers. His fictional works written under Stephan Grundy focused on mythology and history and were met with international success. Along with his fictional works, Gundarsson made a name for himself writing books on Germanic Paganism (also known as heathenry) and Germanic Culture. He is an Elder in the organization The Troth where he has dedicated a majority of his life influencing major changes in the organization, including the development of anti-racist and anti-sexist ideals. He has fought for equality in trans-gendered communities, as well as fighting for the acceptance of Loki. Gundarsson has shaped heathenry through his numerous academic and fictional works as well as his extensive articles, thesis papers and his creation and sustainment of the lore program within The Troth. His hobbies included wood-working, jewelry making and gardening as well as historical re-enactment.

The Three Little Sisters

The Three Little Sisters is an indie publisher that puts authors first. We specalize in the strange and unusual. From titles about pagan and heathen spirituality to traditional fiction we bring books to life.

https://the3littlesisters.com